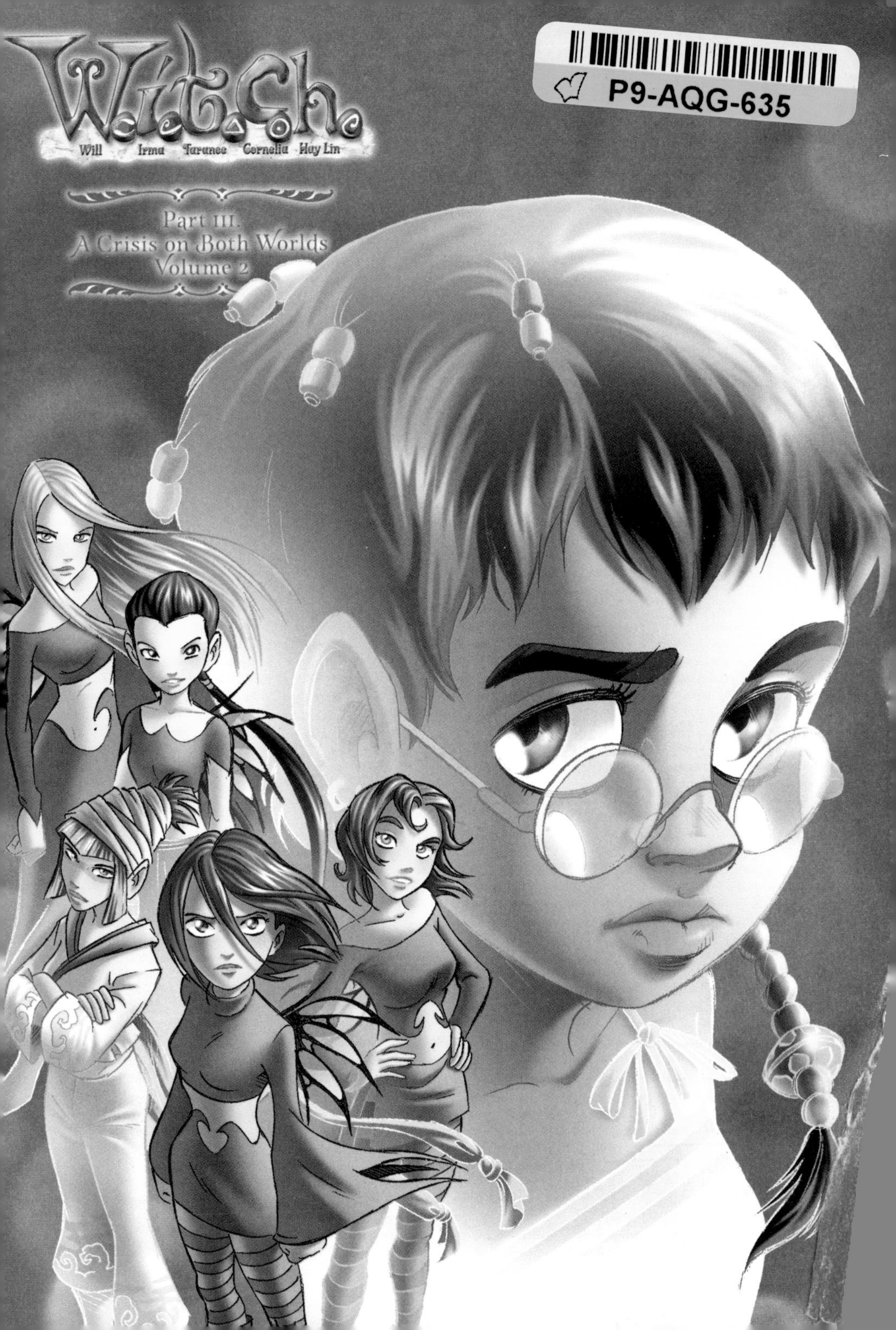
W.i.t.c.h.
Will Irma Taranee Cornelia Hay Lin
Part III.
A Crisis on Both Worlds
Volume 2

W.i.t.c.h.

Will   Irma   Taranee   Cornelia   Hay Lin

Part III.
A Crisis on Both Worlds
Volume 2

CONTENTS

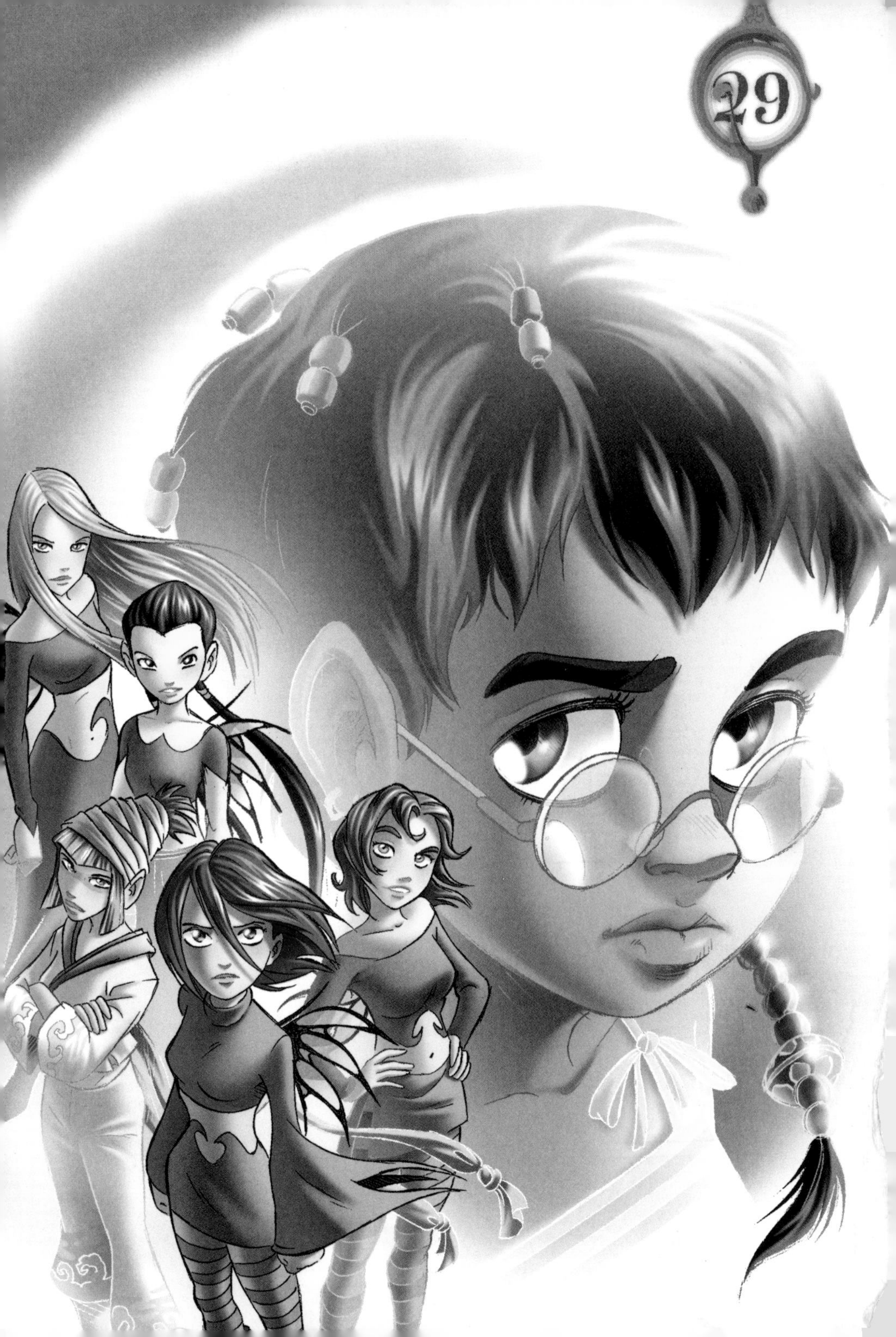
29

The Lesser Evil

"Why? Why am I not in Meridian with him?"

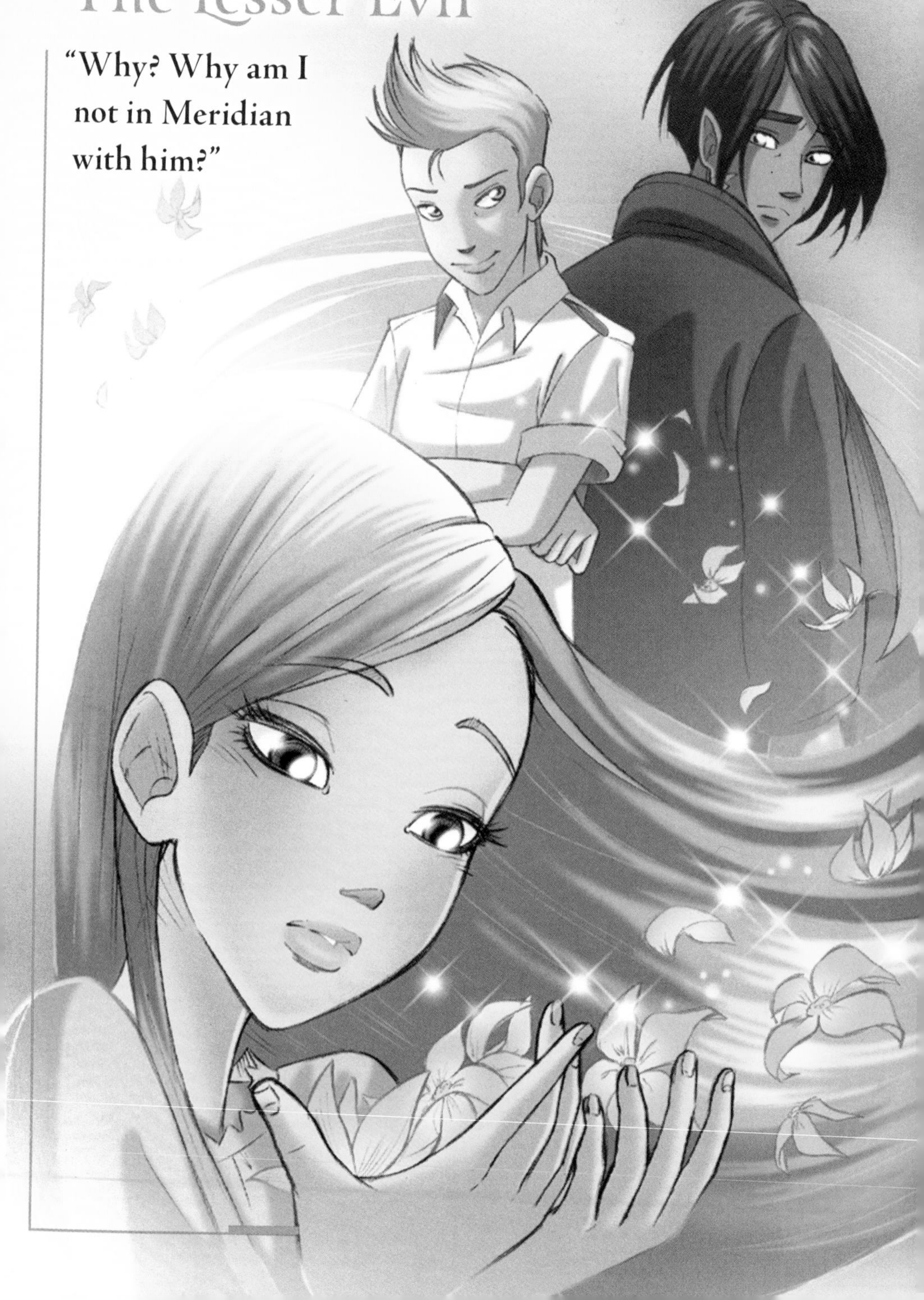

FLUT

DRIP...DRIP...

DRIP...DRIP...

...INTONES YUA, COMMENTING ON THE MAGIC BREWING IN HER PRISON...

DRIP...DRIP...

...THE BANSHEE RECITES, AS THE DROPS TRICKLE UPWARD...

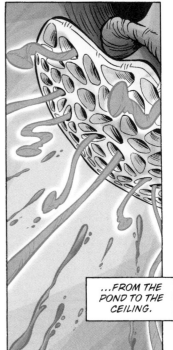

...FROM THE POND TO THE CEILING.

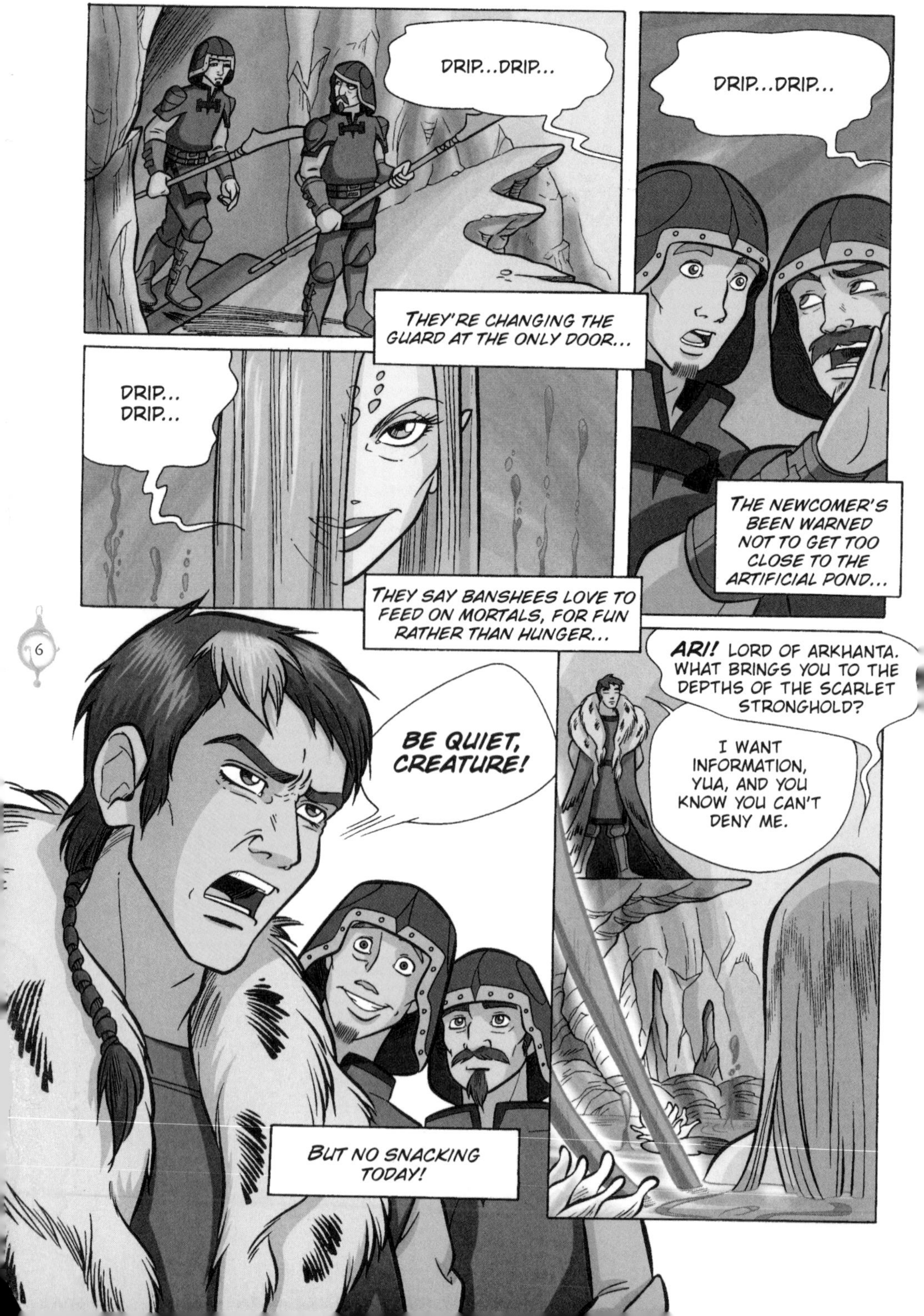
DRIP...DRIP...
DRIP...DRIP...
THEY'RE CHANGING THE GUARD AT THE ONLY DOOR...
DRIP... DRIP...
THE NEWCOMER'S BEEN WARNED NOT TO GET TOO CLOSE TO THE ARTIFICIAL POND...
THEY SAY BANSHEES LOVE TO FEED ON MORTALS, FOR FUN RATHER THAN HUNGER...
ARI! LORD OF ARKHANTA. WHAT BRINGS YOU TO THE DEPTHS OF THE SCARLET STRONGHOLD?
I WANT INFORMATION, YUA, AND YOU KNOW YOU CAN'T DENY ME.
BE QUIET, CREATURE!
BUT NO SNACKING TODAY!

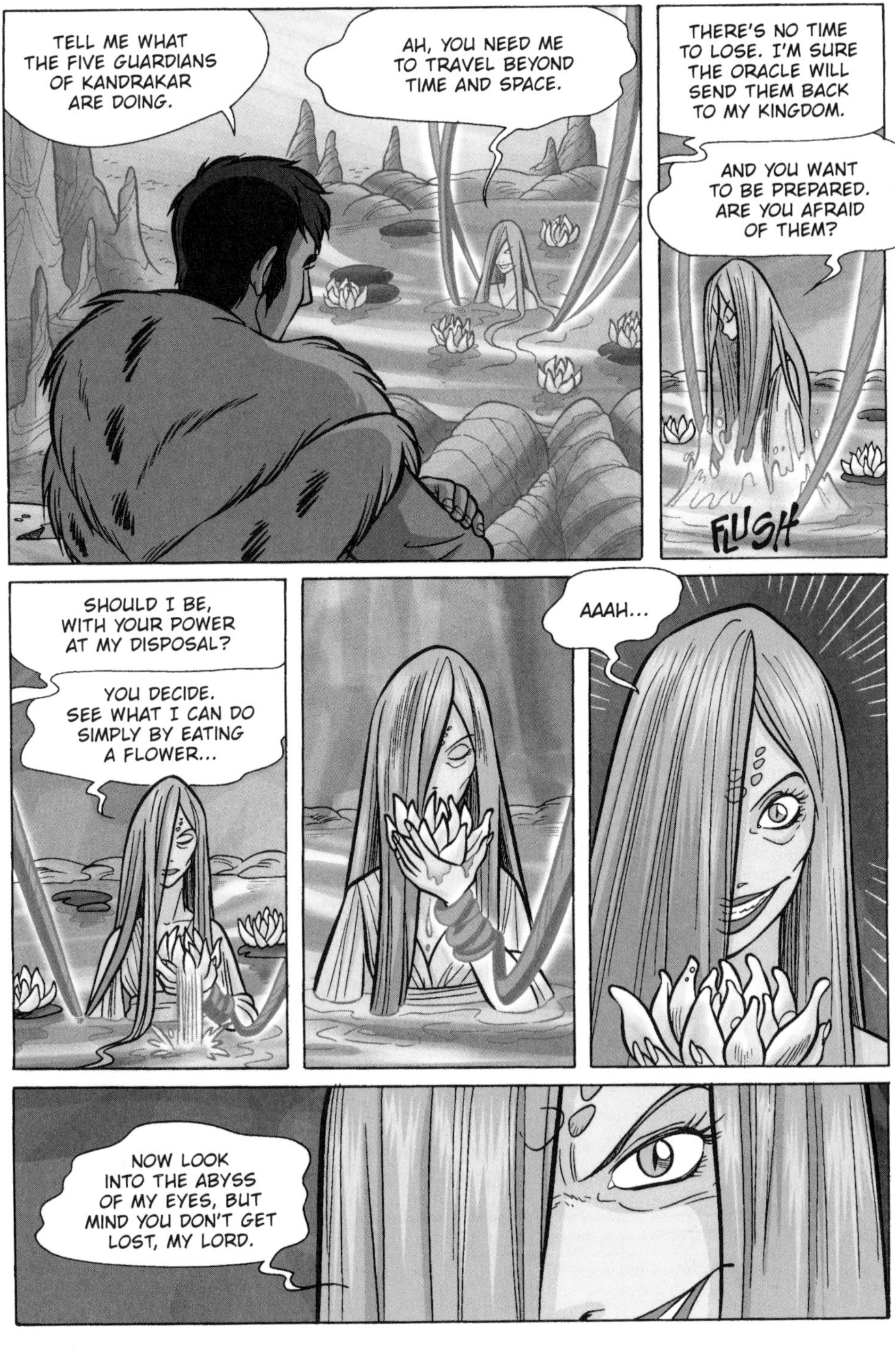
TELL ME WHAT THE FIVE GUARDIANS OF KANDRAKAR ARE DOING.
AH, YOU NEED ME TO TRAVEL BEYOND TIME AND SPACE.
THERE'S NO TIME TO LOSE. I'M SURE THE ORACLE WILL SEND THEM BACK TO MY KINGDOM.
AND YOU WANT TO BE PREPARED. ARE YOU AFRAID OF THEM?
FLUSH
SHOULD I BE, WITH YOUR POWER AT MY DISPOSAL?
YOU DECIDE. SEE WHAT I CAN DO SIMPLY BY EATING A FLOWER...
AAAH...
NOW LOOK INTO THE ABYSS OF MY EYES, BUT MIND YOU DON'T GET LOST, MY LORD.

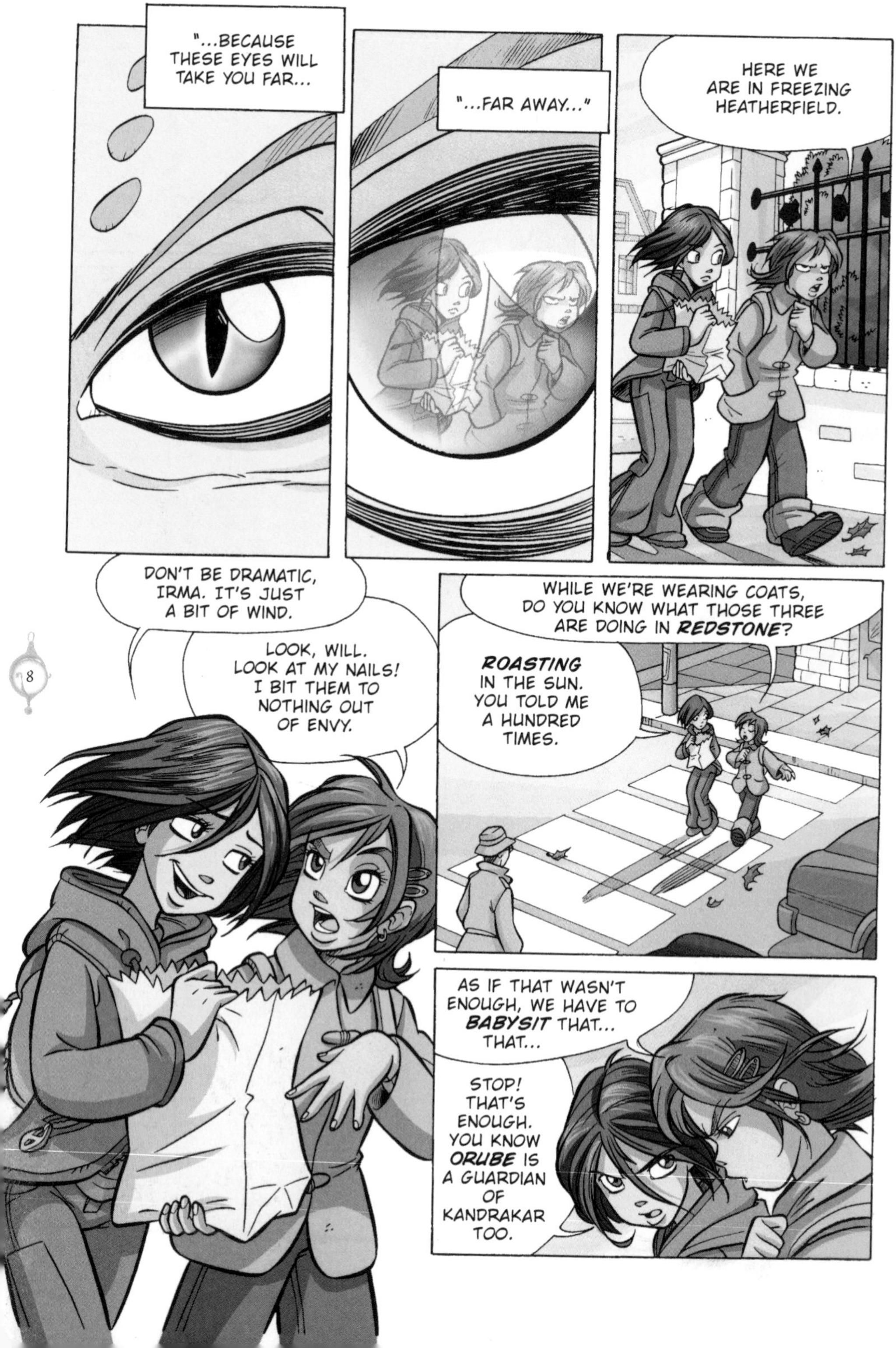
"...BECAUSE THESE EYES WILL TAKE YOU FAR...
"...FAR AWAY..."
HERE WE ARE IN FREEZING HEATHERFIELD.
DON'T BE DRAMATIC, IRMA. IT'S JUST A BIT OF WIND.
LOOK, WILL. LOOK AT MY NAILS! I BIT THEM TO NOTHING OUT OF ENVY.
WHILE WE'RE WEARING COATS, DO YOU KNOW WHAT THOSE THREE ARE DOING IN REDSTONE?
ROASTING IN THE SUN. YOU TOLD ME A HUNDRED TIMES.
AS IF THAT WASN'T ENOUGH, WE HAVE TO BABYSIT THAT... THAT...
STOP! THAT'S ENOUGH. YOU KNOW ORUBE IS A GUARDIAN OF KANDRAKAR TOO.

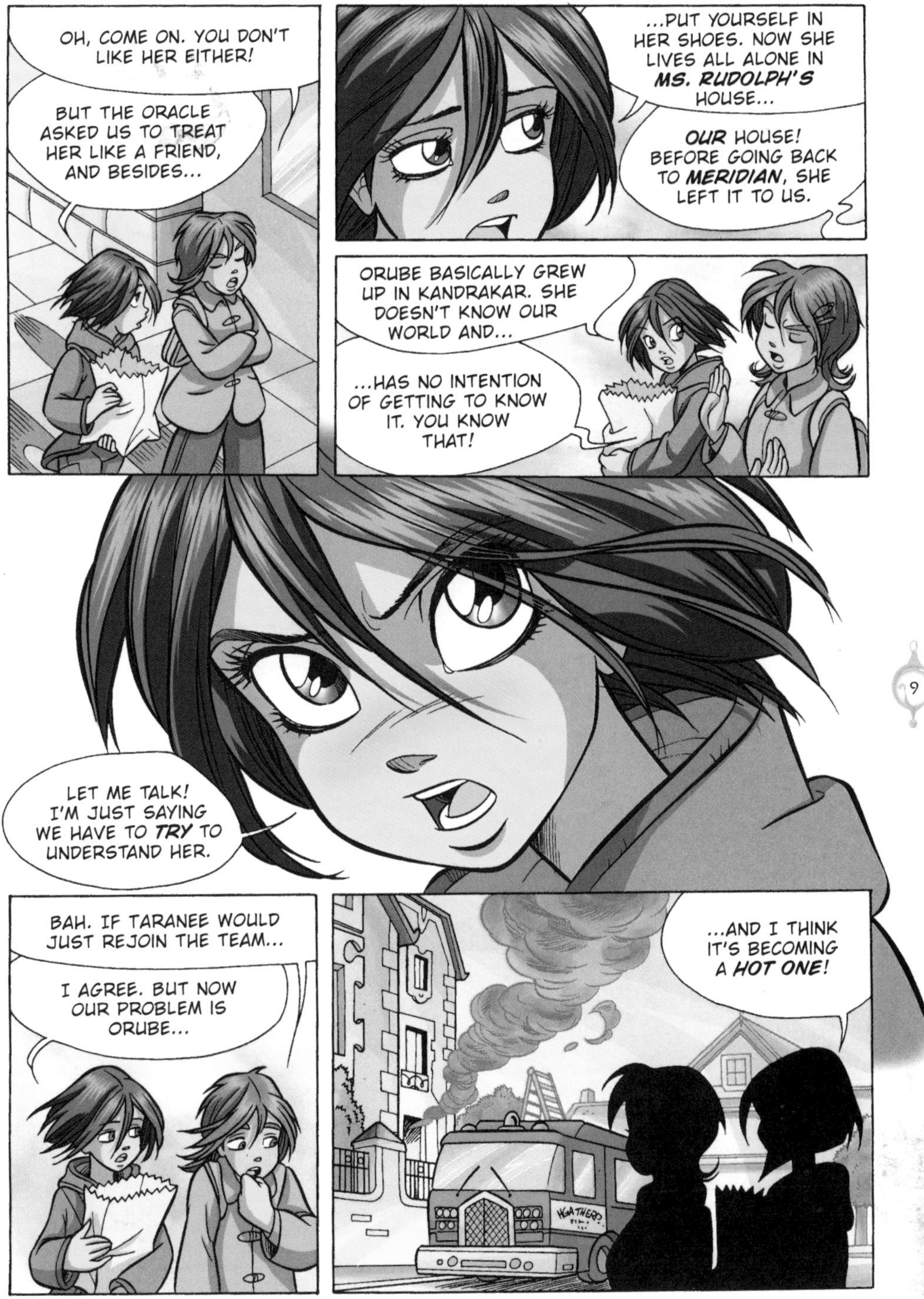
OH, COME ON. YOU DON'T LIKE HER EITHER!
BUT THE ORACLE ASKED US TO TREAT HER LIKE A FRIEND, AND BESIDES...
...PUT YOURSELF IN HER SHOES. NOW SHE LIVES ALL ALONE IN MS. RUDOLPH'S HOUSE...
OUR HOUSE! BEFORE GOING BACK TO MERIDIAN, SHE LEFT IT TO US.
ORUBE BASICALLY GREW UP IN KANDRAKAR. SHE DOESN'T KNOW OUR WORLD AND...
...HAS NO INTENTION OF GETTING TO KNOW IT. YOU KNOW THAT!
LET ME TALK! I'M JUST SAYING WE HAVE TO TRY TO UNDERSTAND HER.
BAH. IF TARANEE WOULD JUST REJOIN THE TEAM...
I AGREE. BUT NOW OUR PROBLEM IS ORUBE...
...AND I THINK IT'S BECOMING A HOT ONE!

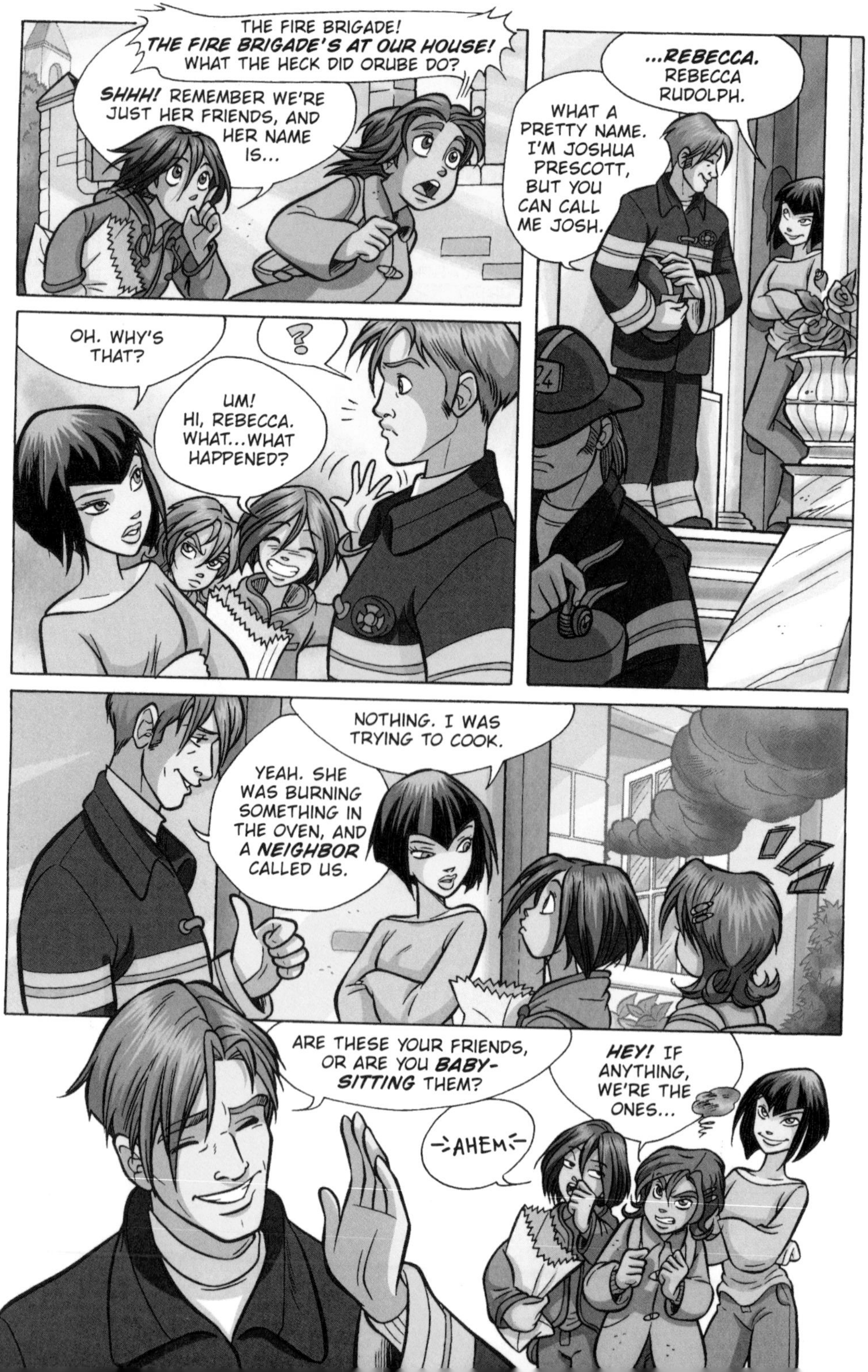
THE FIRE BRIGADE! THE FIRE BRIGADE'S AT OUR HOUSE! WHAT THE HECK DID ORUBE DO?
SHHH! REMEMBER WE'RE JUST HER FRIENDS, AND HER NAME IS...
...REBECCA. REBECCA RUDOLPH.
WHAT A PRETTY NAME. I'M JOSHUA PRESCOTT, BUT YOU CAN CALL ME JOSH.
OH. WHY'S THAT?
?
UM! HI, REBECCA. WHAT...WHAT HAPPENED?
NOTHING. I WAS TRYING TO COOK.
YEAH. SHE WAS BURNING SOMETHING IN THE OVEN, AND A NEIGHBOR CALLED US.
ARE THESE YOUR FRIENDS, OR ARE YOU BABY-SITTING THEM?
HEY! IF ANYTHING, WE'RE THE ONES...
AHEM

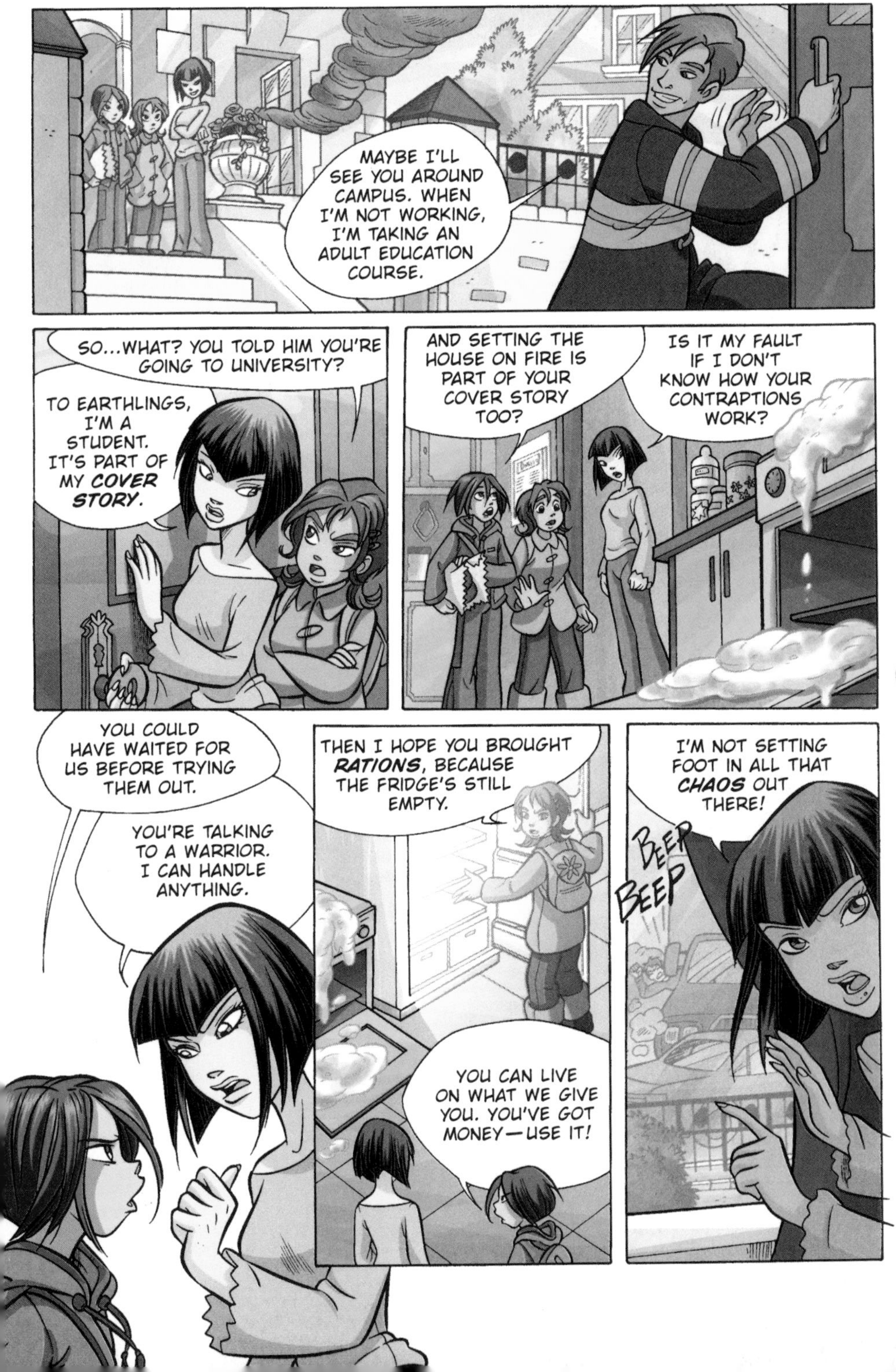
MAYBE I'LL SEE YOU AROUND CAMPUS. WHEN I'M NOT WORKING, I'M TAKING AN ADULT EDUCATION COURSE.
SO...WHAT? YOU TOLD HIM YOU'RE GOING TO UNIVERSITY?
TO EARTHLINGS, I'M A STUDENT. IT'S PART OF MY *COVER STORY*.
AND SETTING THE HOUSE ON FIRE IS PART OF YOUR COVER STORY TOO?
IS IT MY FAULT IF I DON'T KNOW HOW YOUR CONTRAPTIONS WORK?
YOU COULD HAVE WAITED FOR US BEFORE TRYING THEM OUT.
YOU'RE TALKING TO A WARRIOR. I CAN HANDLE ANYTHING.
THEN I HOPE YOU BROUGHT *RATIONS*, BECAUSE THE FRIDGE'S STILL EMPTY.
YOU CAN LIVE ON WHAT WE GIVE YOU. YOU'VE GOT MONEY—USE IT!
BEEP BEEP
I'M NOT SETTING FOOT IN ALL THAT *CHAOS* OUT THERE!

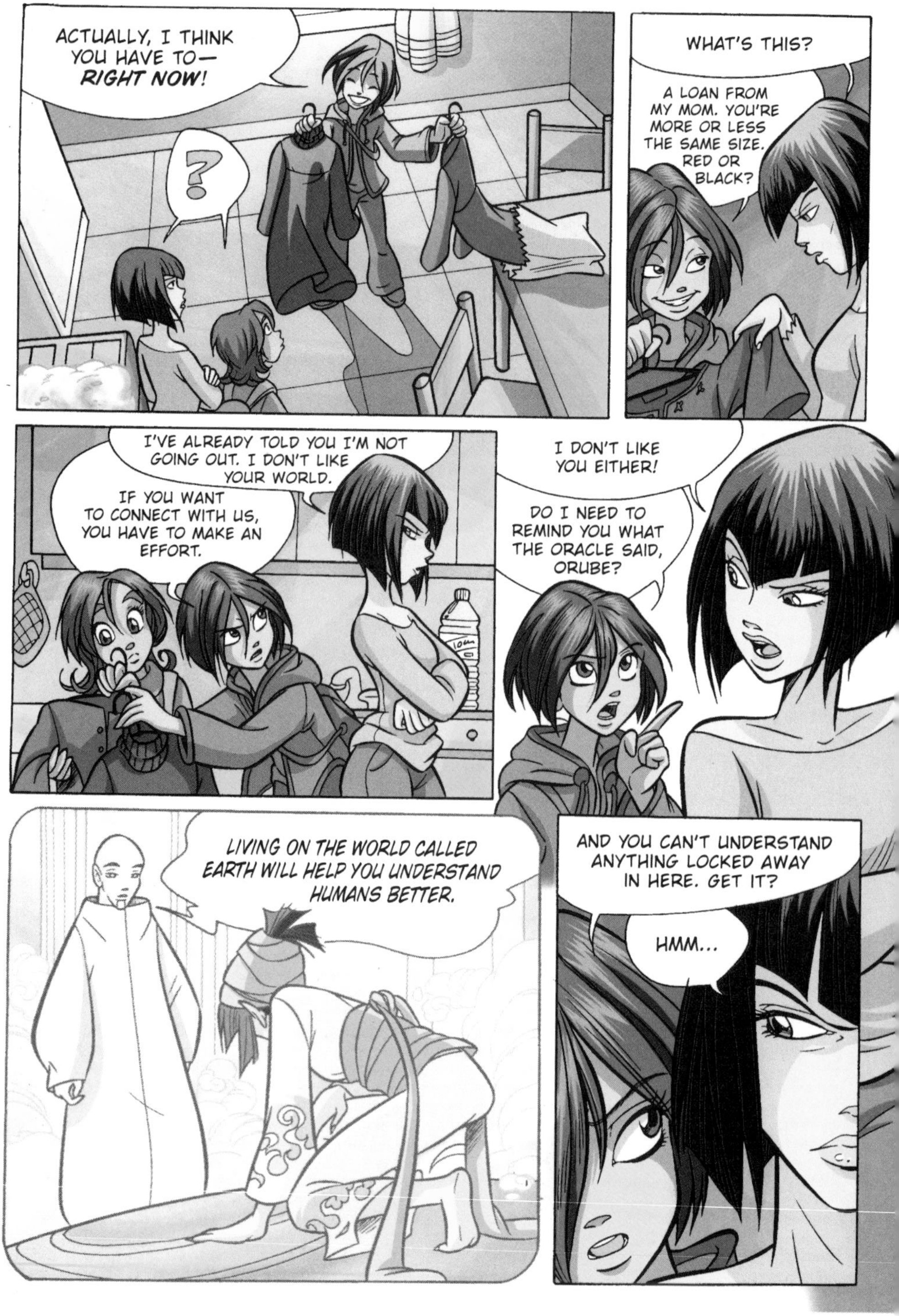
ACTUALLY, I THINK YOU HAVE TO— RIGHT NOW!
?
WHAT'S THIS?
A LOAN FROM MY MOM. YOU'RE MORE OR LESS THE SAME SIZE. RED OR BLACK?
I'VE ALREADY TOLD YOU I'M NOT GOING OUT. I DON'T LIKE YOUR WORLD.
IF YOU WANT TO CONNECT WITH US, YOU HAVE TO MAKE AN EFFORT.
I DON'T LIKE YOU EITHER!
DO I NEED TO REMIND YOU WHAT THE ORACLE SAID, ORUBE?
LIVING ON THE WORLD CALLED EARTH WILL HELP YOU UNDERSTAND HUMANS BETTER.
AND YOU CAN'T UNDERSTAND ANYTHING LOCKED AWAY IN HERE. GET IT?
HMM...

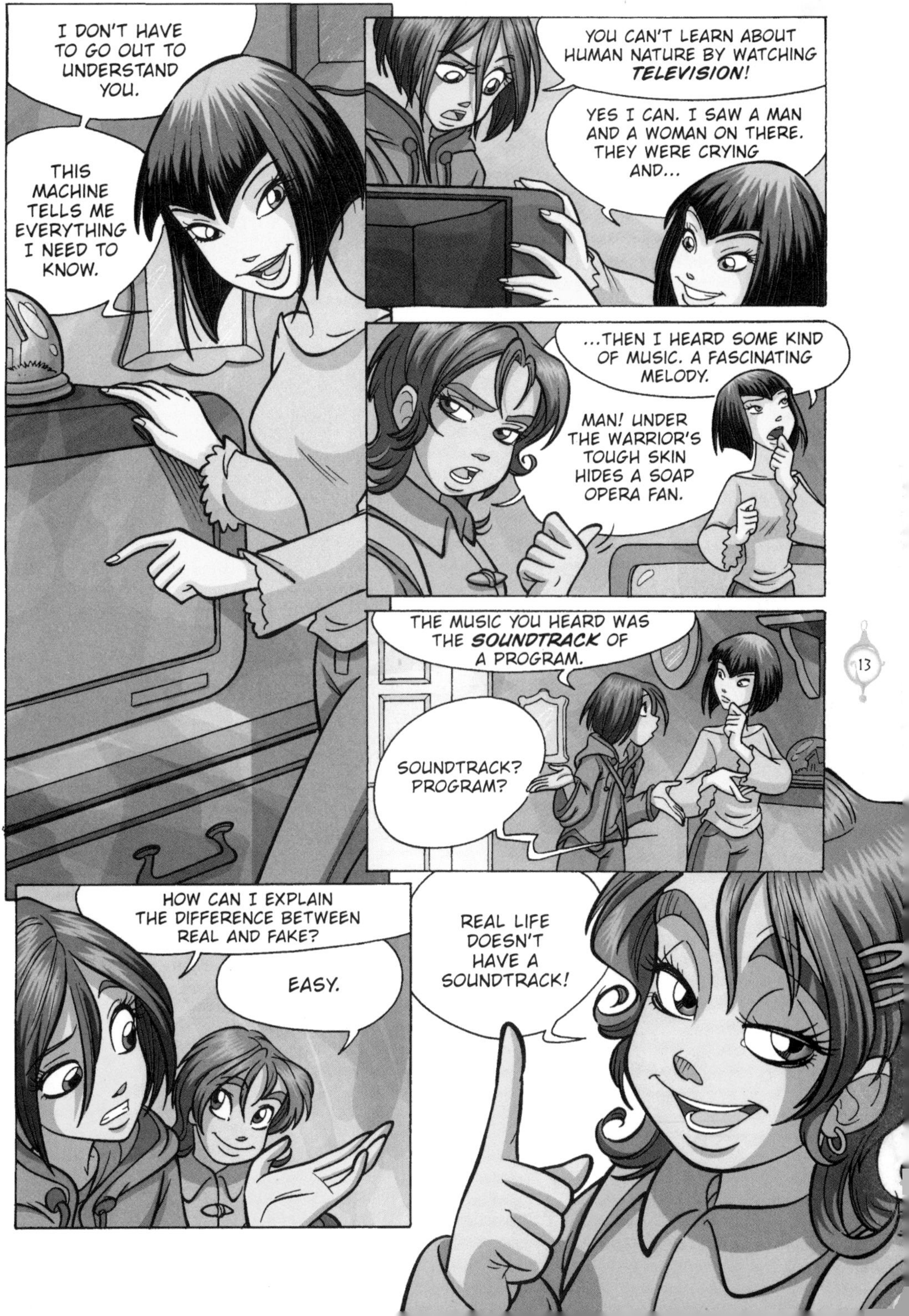
I DON'T HAVE TO GO OUT TO UNDERSTAND YOU.
THIS MACHINE TELLS ME EVERYTHING I NEED TO KNOW.
YOU CAN'T LEARN ABOUT HUMAN NATURE BY WATCHING *TELEVISION*!
YES I CAN. I SAW A MAN AND A WOMAN ON THERE. THEY WERE CRYING AND...
...THEN I HEARD SOME KIND OF MUSIC. A FASCINATING MELODY.
MAN! UNDER THE WARRIOR'S TOUGH SKIN HIDES A SOAP OPERA FAN.
THE MUSIC YOU HEARD WAS THE *SOUNDTRACK* OF A PROGRAM.
SOUNDTRACK? PROGRAM?
HOW CAN I EXPLAIN THE DIFFERENCE BETWEEN REAL AND FAKE?
EASY.
REAL LIFE DOESN'T HAVE A SOUNDTRACK!

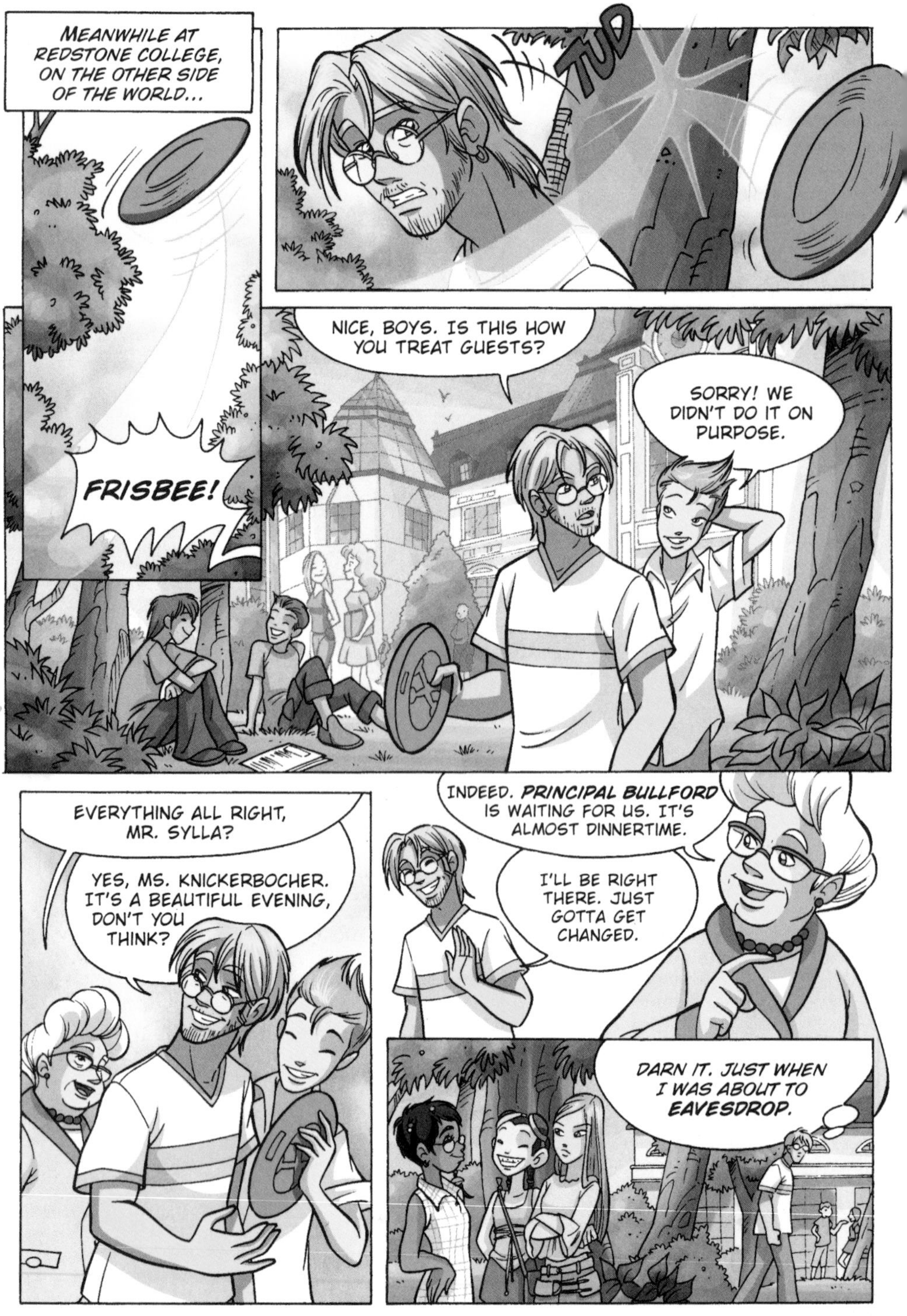

MEANWHILE AT REDSTONE COLLEGE, ON THE OTHER SIDE OF THE WORLD...
FRISBEE!
TUD
NICE, BOYS. IS THIS HOW YOU TREAT GUESTS?
SORRY! WE DIDN'T DO IT ON PURPOSE.
EVERYTHING ALL RIGHT, MR. SYLLA?
YES, MS. KNICKERBOCHER. IT'S A BEAUTIFUL EVENING, DON'T YOU THINK?
INDEED. PRINCIPAL BULLFORD IS WAITING FOR US. IT'S ALMOST DINNERTIME.
I'LL BE RIGHT THERE. JUST GOTTA GET CHANGED.
DARN IT. JUST WHEN I WAS ABOUT TO EAVESDROP.

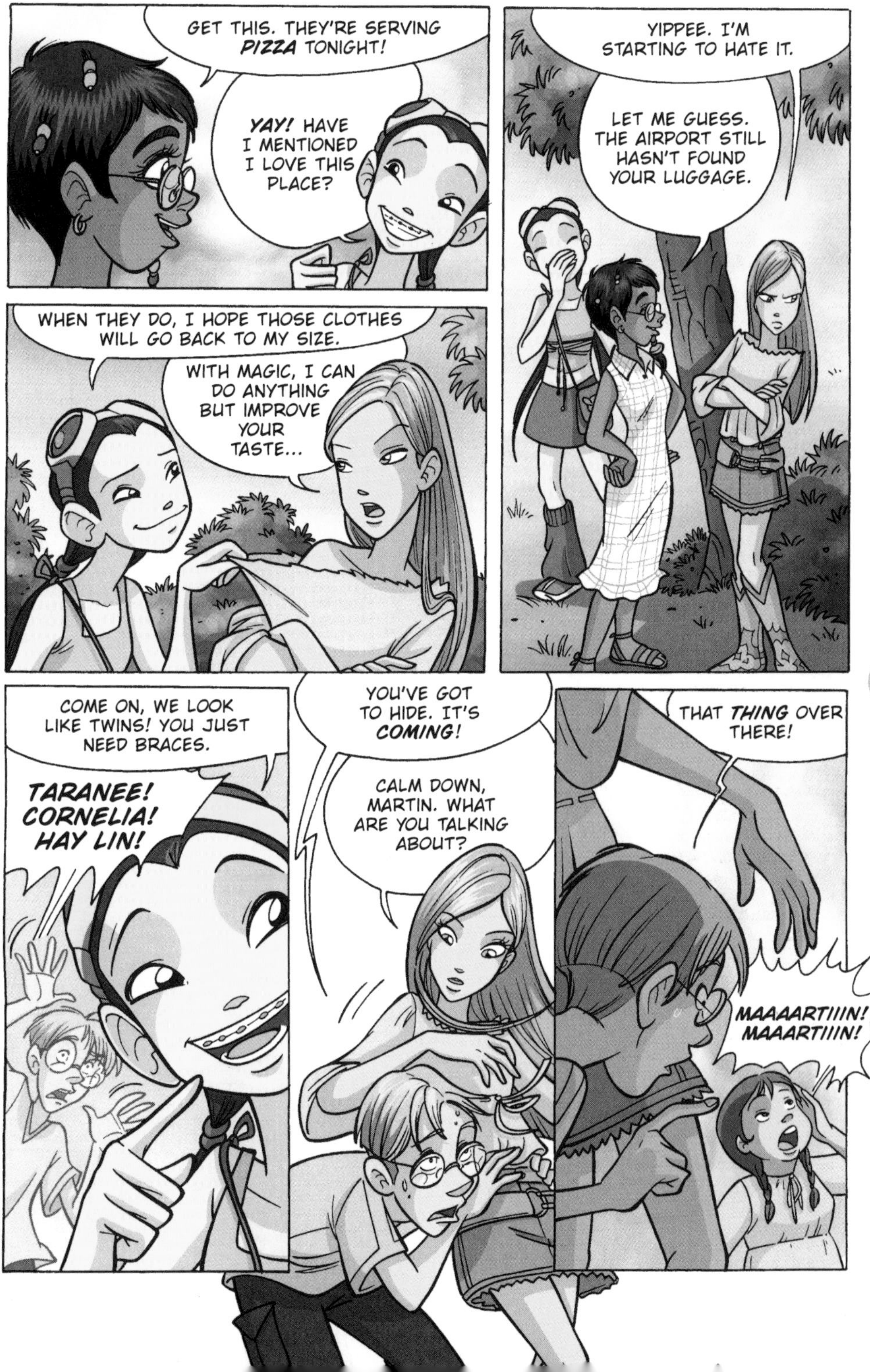
GET THIS. THEY'RE SERVING PIZZA TONIGHT!
YAY! HAVE I MENTIONED I LOVE THIS PLACE?
YIPPEE. I'M STARTING TO HATE IT.
LET ME GUESS. THE AIRPORT STILL HASN'T FOUND YOUR LUGGAGE.
WHEN THEY DO, I HOPE THOSE CLOTHES WILL GO BACK TO MY SIZE.
WITH MAGIC, I CAN DO ANYTHING BUT IMPROVE YOUR TASTE...
COME ON, WE LOOK LIKE TWINS! YOU JUST NEED BRACES.
TARANEE! CORNELIA! HAY LIN!
YOU'VE GOT TO HIDE. IT'S COMING!
CALM DOWN, MARTIN. WHAT ARE YOU TALKING ABOUT?
THAT THING OVER THERE!
MAAAARTIIIN! MAAARTIIIN!

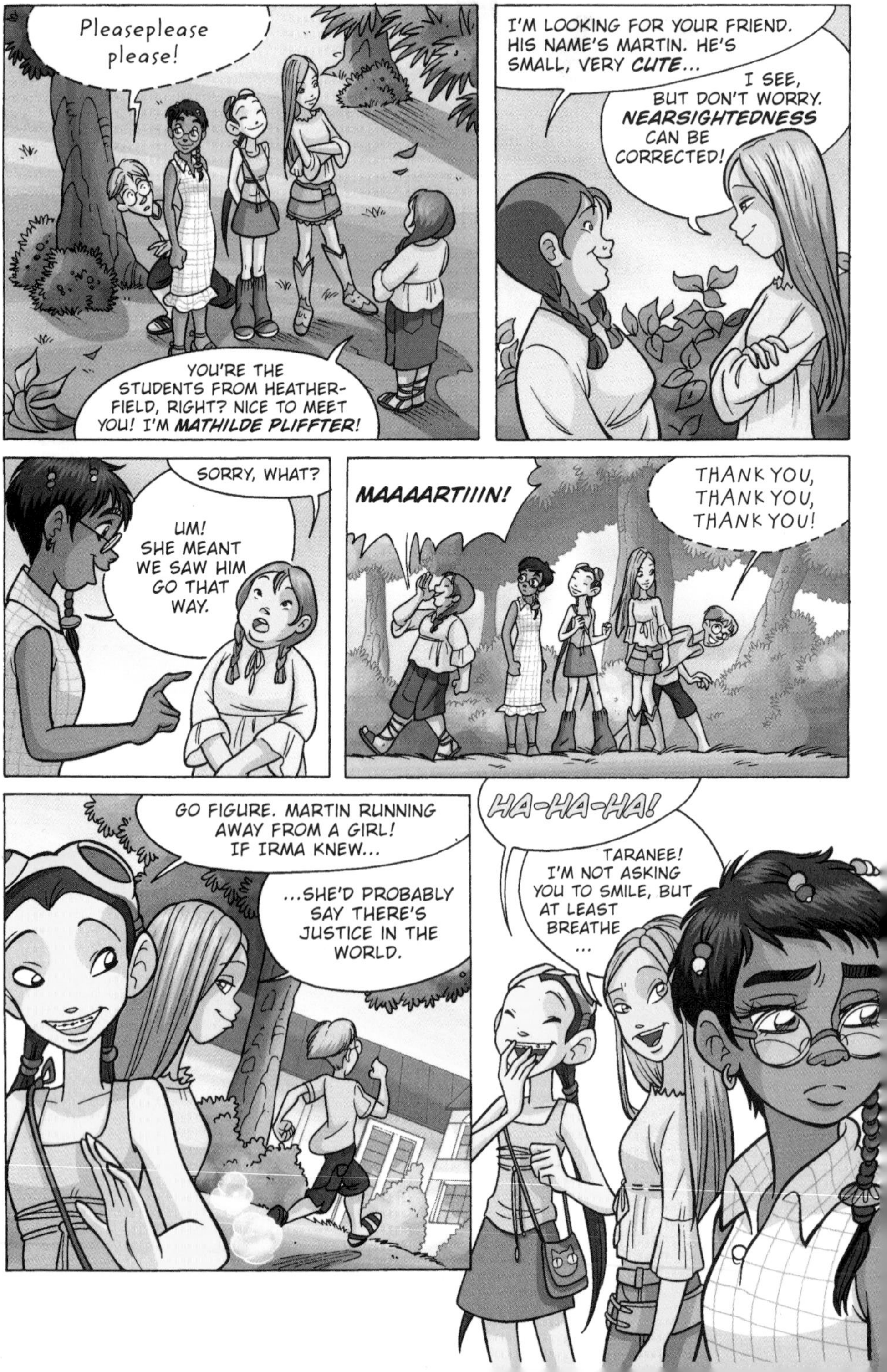
Pleaseplease please!
YOU'RE THE STUDENTS FROM HEATHER-FIELD, RIGHT? NICE TO MEET YOU! I'M MATHILDE PLIFFTER!
I'M LOOKING FOR YOUR FRIEND. HIS NAME'S MARTIN. HE'S SMALL, VERY CUTE...
I SEE, BUT DON'T WORRY. NEARSIGHTEDNESS CAN BE CORRECTED!
SORRY, WHAT?
UM! SHE MEANT WE SAW HIM GO THAT WAY.
MAAAARTIIIN!
THANK YOU, THANK YOU, THANK YOU!
GO FIGURE. MARTIN RUNNING AWAY FROM A GIRL! IF IRMA KNEW...
...SHE'D PROBABLY SAY THERE'S JUSTICE IN THE WORLD.
HA-HA-HA!
TARANEE! I'M NOT ASKING YOU TO SMILE, BUT AT LEAST BREATHE ...

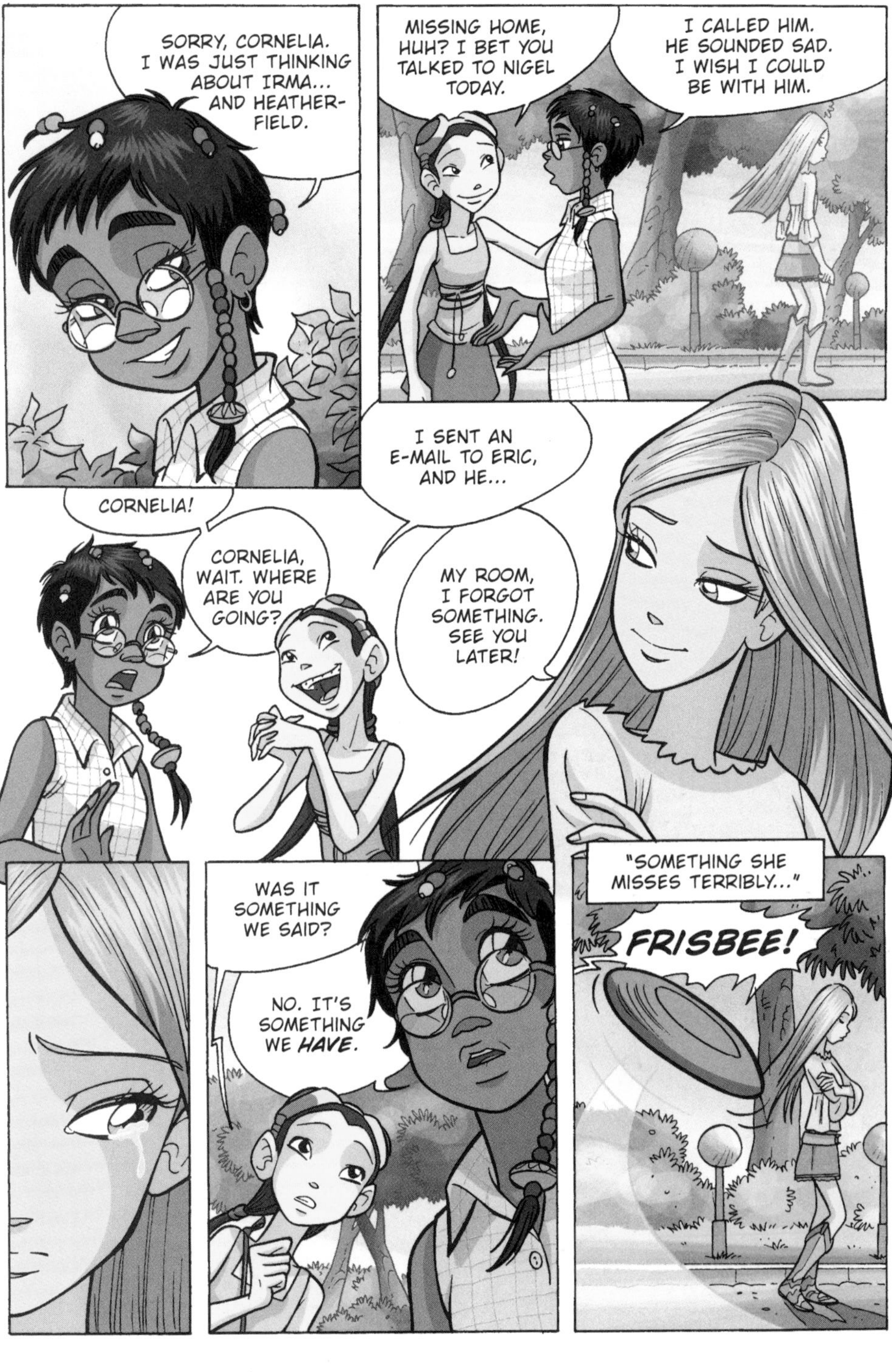
SORRY, CORNELIA. I WAS JUST THINKING ABOUT IRMA... AND HEATHER-FIELD.
MISSING HOME, HUH? I BET YOU TALKED TO NIGEL TODAY.
I CALLED HIM. HE SOUNDED SAD. I WISH I COULD BE WITH HIM.
I SENT AN E-MAIL TO ERIC, AND HE...
CORNELIA!
CORNELIA, WAIT. WHERE ARE YOU GOING?
MY ROOM, I FORGOT SOMETHING. SEE YOU LATER!
WAS IT SOMETHING WE SAID?
NO. IT'S SOMETHING WE *HAVE*.
"SOMETHING SHE MISSES TERRIBLY..."
FRISBEE!

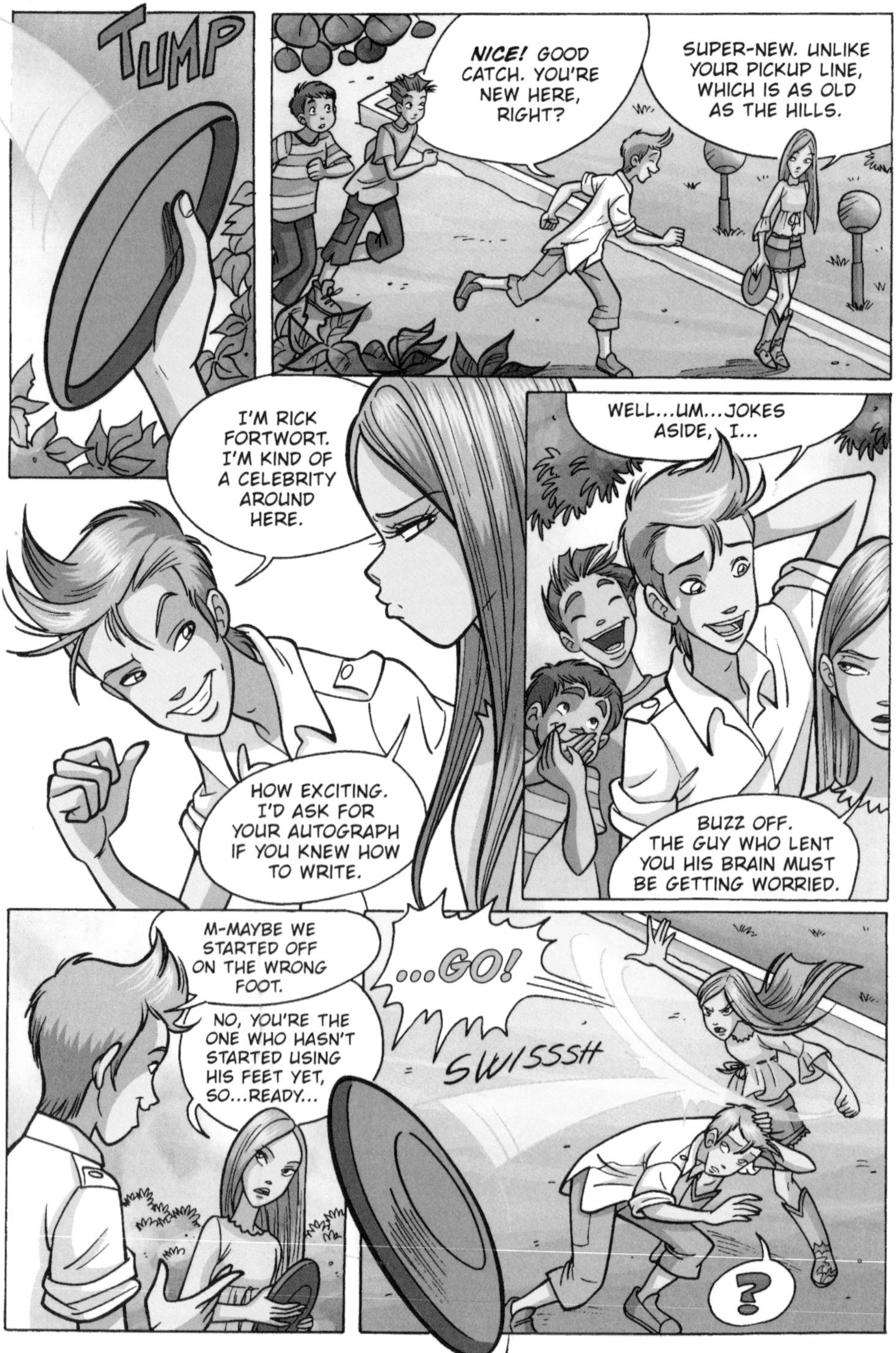

TUMP
NICE! GOOD CATCH. YOU'RE NEW HERE, RIGHT?
SUPER-NEW. UNLIKE YOUR PICKUP LINE, WHICH IS AS OLD AS THE HILLS.
I'M RICK FORTWORT. I'M KIND OF A CELEBRITY AROUND HERE.
HOW EXCITING. I'D ASK FOR YOUR AUTOGRAPH IF YOU KNEW HOW TO WRITE.
WELL...UM...JOKES ASIDE, I...
BUZZ OFF. THE GUY WHO LENT YOU HIS BRAIN MUST BE GETTING WORRIED.
M-MAYBE WE STARTED OFF ON THE WRONG FOOT.
NO, YOU'RE THE ONE WHO HASN'T STARTED USING HIS FEET YET, SO...READY...
...GO!
SWISSSH
?

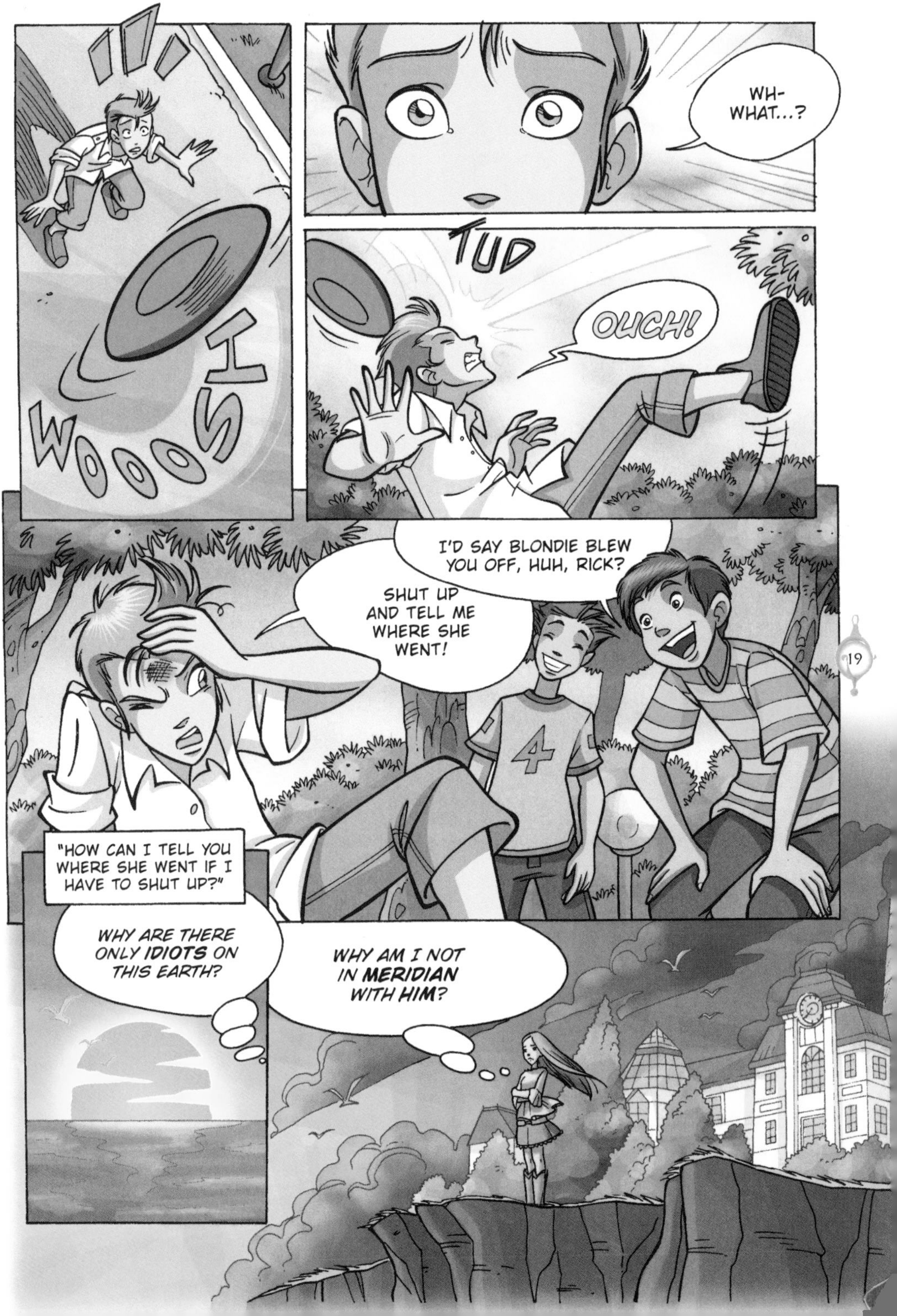
WOOOSH
WH-
WHAT...?
TUD
OUCH!
I'D SAY BLONDIE BLEW YOU OFF, HUH, RICK?
SHUT UP AND TELL ME WHERE SHE WENT!
"HOW CAN I TELL YOU WHERE SHE WENT IF I HAVE TO SHUT UP?"
WHY ARE THERE ONLY ***IDIOTS*** *ON THIS EARTH?*
WHY AM I NOT IN ***MERIDIAN*** *WITH* ***HIM****?*

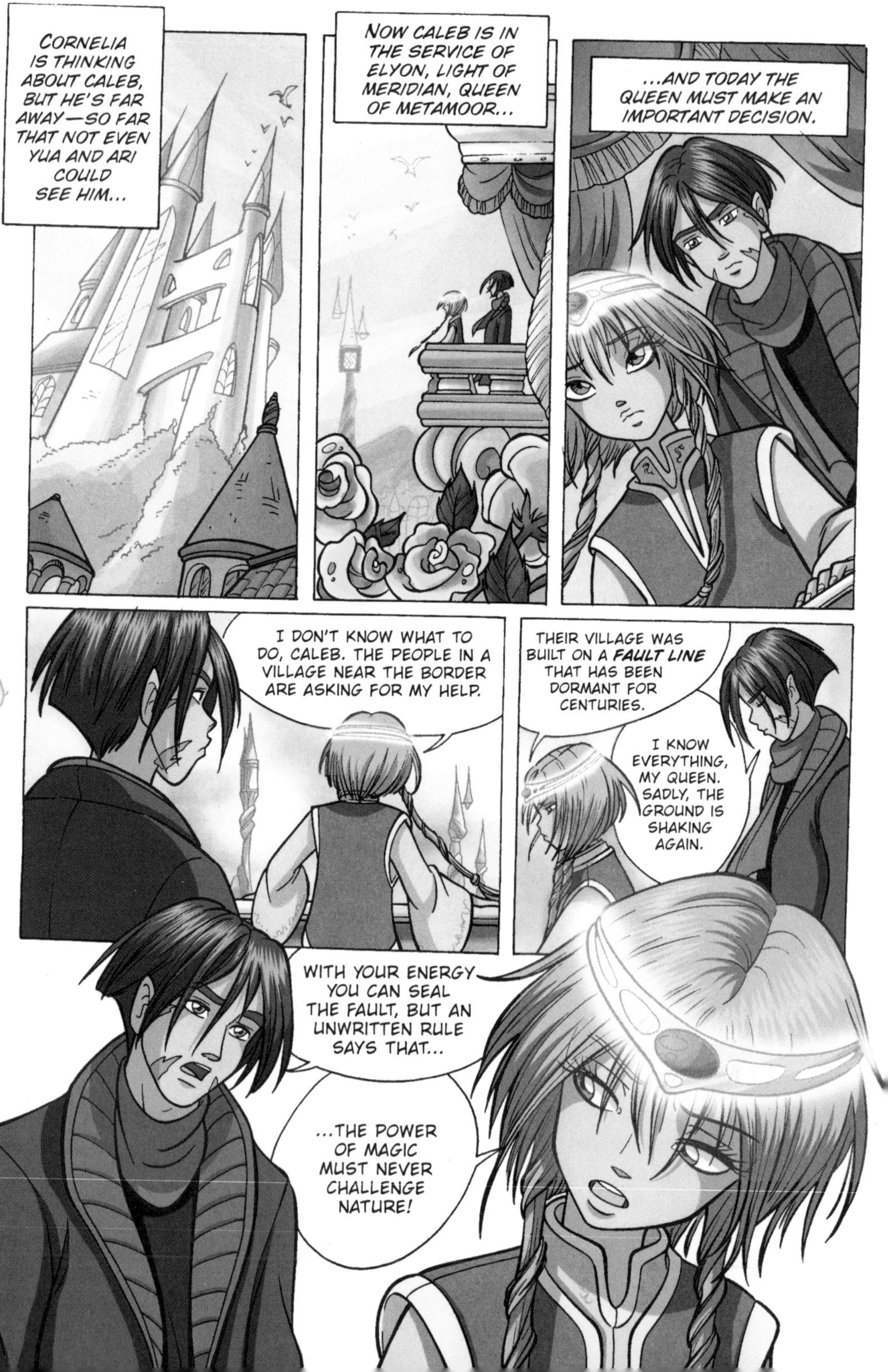

CORNELIA IS THINKING ABOUT CALEB, BUT HE'S FAR AWAY—SO FAR THAT NOT EVEN YUA AND ARI COULD SEE HIM...
NOW CALEB IS IN THE SERVICE OF ELYON, LIGHT OF MERIDIAN, QUEEN OF METAMOOR...
...AND TODAY THE QUEEN MUST MAKE AN IMPORTANT DECISION.
I DON'T KNOW WHAT TO DO, CALEB. THE PEOPLE IN A VILLAGE NEAR THE BORDER ARE ASKING FOR MY HELP.
THEIR VILLAGE WAS BUILT ON A ***FAULT LINE*** THAT HAS BEEN DORMANT FOR CENTURIES.
I KNOW EVERYTHING, MY QUEEN. SADLY, THE GROUND IS SHAKING AGAIN.
WITH YOUR ENERGY YOU CAN SEAL THE FAULT, BUT AN UNWRITTEN RULE SAYS THAT...
...THE POWER OF MAGIC MUST NEVER CHALLENGE NATURE!

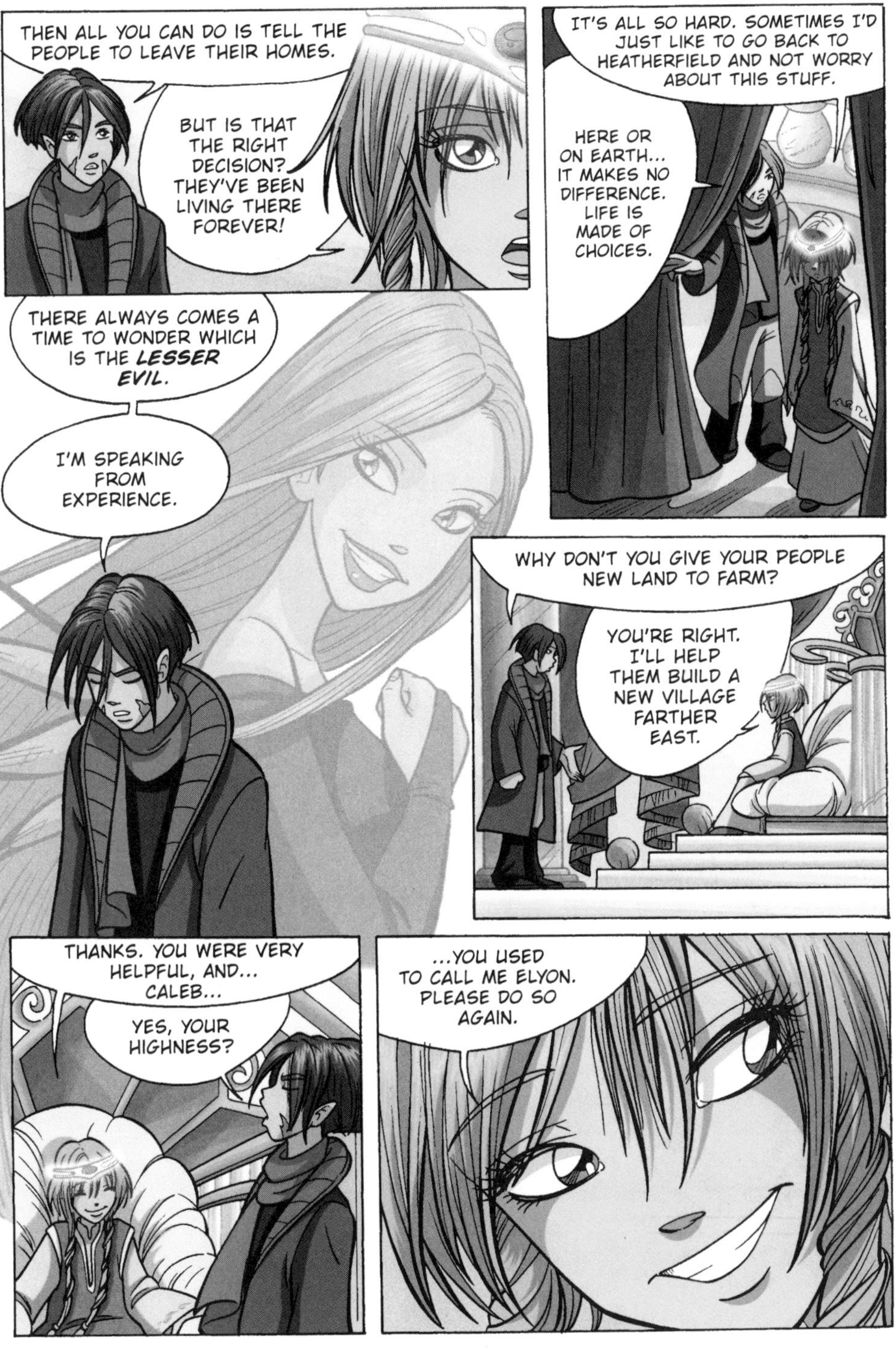

THEN ALL YOU CAN DO IS TELL THE PEOPLE TO LEAVE THEIR HOMES.
BUT IS THAT THE RIGHT DECISION? THEY'VE BEEN LIVING THERE FOREVER!
IT'S ALL SO HARD. SOMETIMES I'D JUST LIKE TO GO BACK TO HEATHERFIELD AND NOT WORRY ABOUT THIS STUFF.
HERE OR ON EARTH... IT MAKES NO DIFFERENCE. LIFE IS MADE OF CHOICES.
THERE ALWAYS COMES A TIME TO WONDER WHICH IS THE **LESSER EVIL**.
I'M SPEAKING FROM EXPERIENCE.
WHY DON'T YOU GIVE YOUR PEOPLE NEW LAND TO FARM?
YOU'RE RIGHT. I'LL HELP THEM BUILD A NEW VILLAGE FARTHER EAST.
THANKS. YOU WERE VERY HELPFUL, AND... CALEB...
YES, YOUR HIGHNESS?
...YOU USED TO CALL ME ELYON. PLEASE DO SO AGAIN.

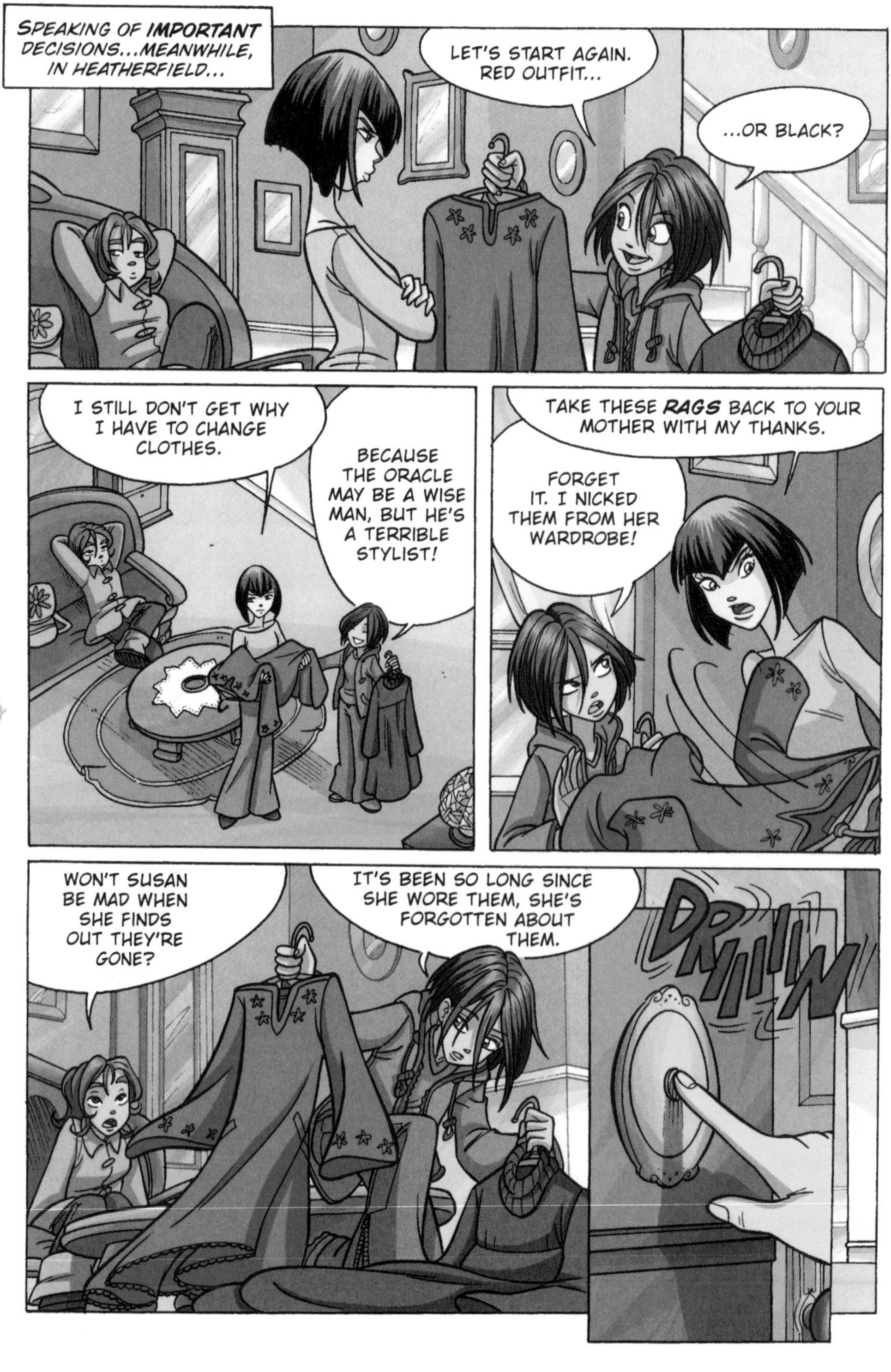
SPEAKING OF **IMPORTANT** DECISIONS... MEANWHILE, IN HEATHERFIELD...
LET'S START AGAIN. RED OUTFIT...
...OR BLACK?
I STILL DON'T GET WHY I HAVE TO CHANGE CLOTHES.
BECAUSE THE ORACLE MAY BE A WISE MAN, BUT HE'S A TERRIBLE STYLIST!
TAKE THESE ***RAGS*** BACK TO YOUR MOTHER WITH MY THANKS.
FORGET IT. I NICKED THEM FROM HER WARDROBE!
WON'T SUSAN BE MAD WHEN SHE FINDS OUT THEY'RE GONE?
IT'S BEEN SO LONG SINCE SHE WORE THEM, SHE'S FORGOTTEN ABOUT THEM.
DRIIIIN

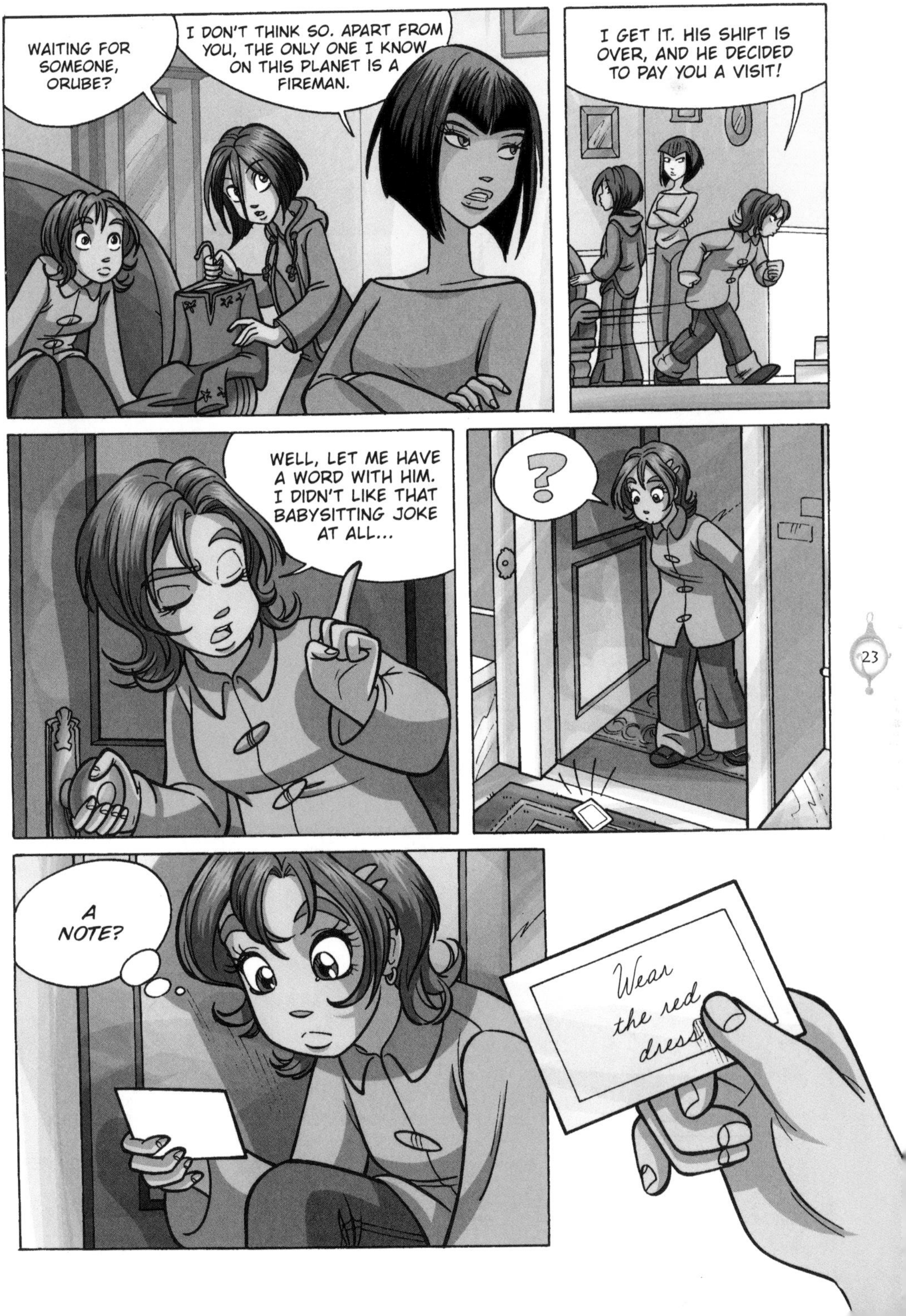
WAITING FOR SOMEONE, ORUBE?
I DON'T THINK SO. APART FROM YOU, THE ONLY ONE I KNOW ON THIS PLANET IS A FIREMAN.
I GET IT. HIS SHIFT IS OVER, AND HE DECIDED TO PAY YOU A VISIT!
WELL, LET ME HAVE A WORD WITH HIM. I DIDN'T LIKE THAT BABYSITTING JOKE AT ALL...
?
A NOTE?
Wear the red dress

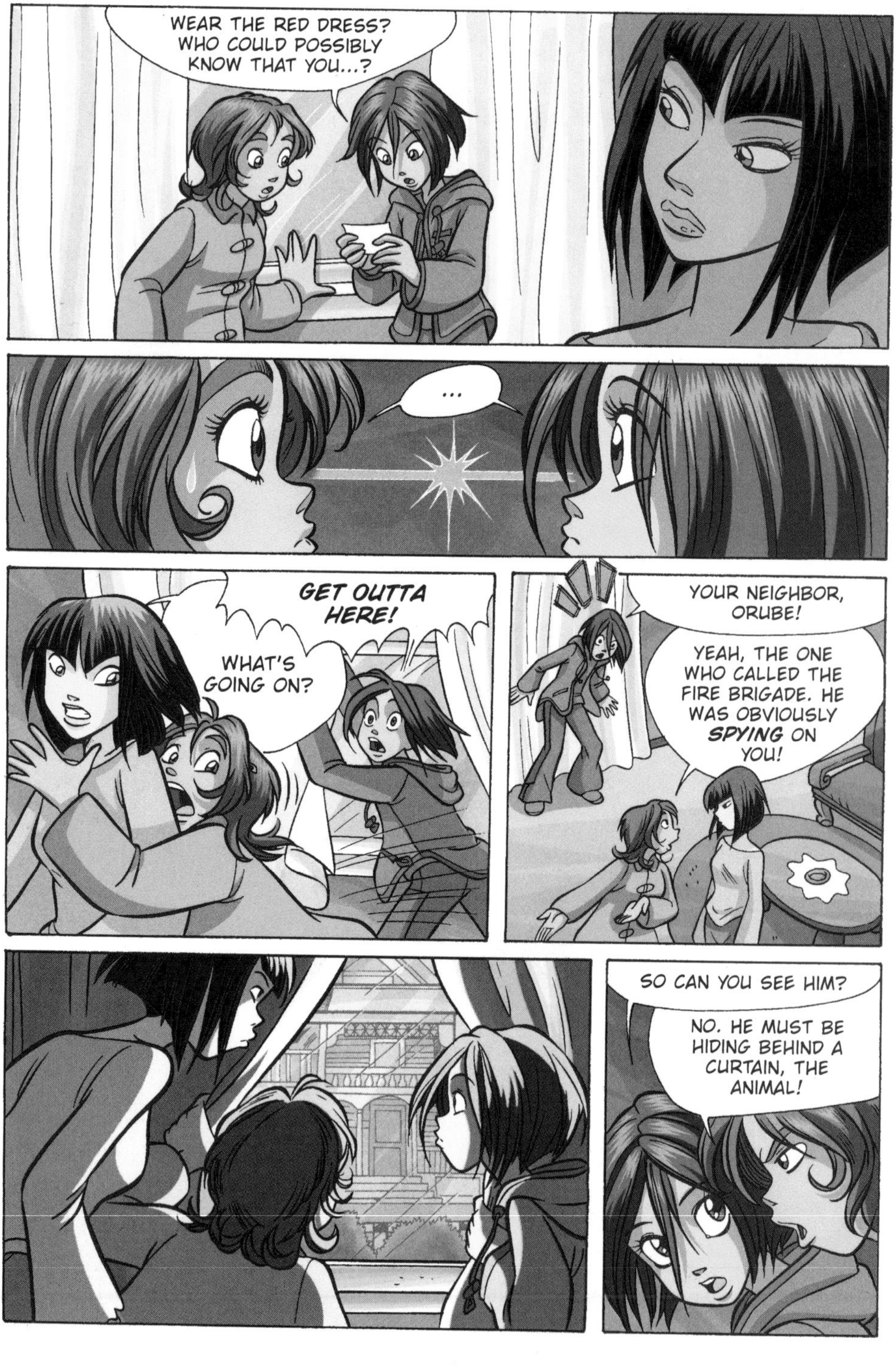
WEAR THE RED DRESS? WHO COULD POSSIBLY KNOW THAT YOU...?
...
GET OUTTA HERE!
WHAT'S GOING ON?
YOUR NEIGHBOR, ORUBE!
YEAH, THE ONE WHO CALLED THE FIRE BRIGADE. HE WAS OBVIOUSLY SPYING ON YOU!
SO CAN YOU SEE HIM?
NO. HE MUST BE HIDING BEHIND A CURTAIN, THE ANIMAL!

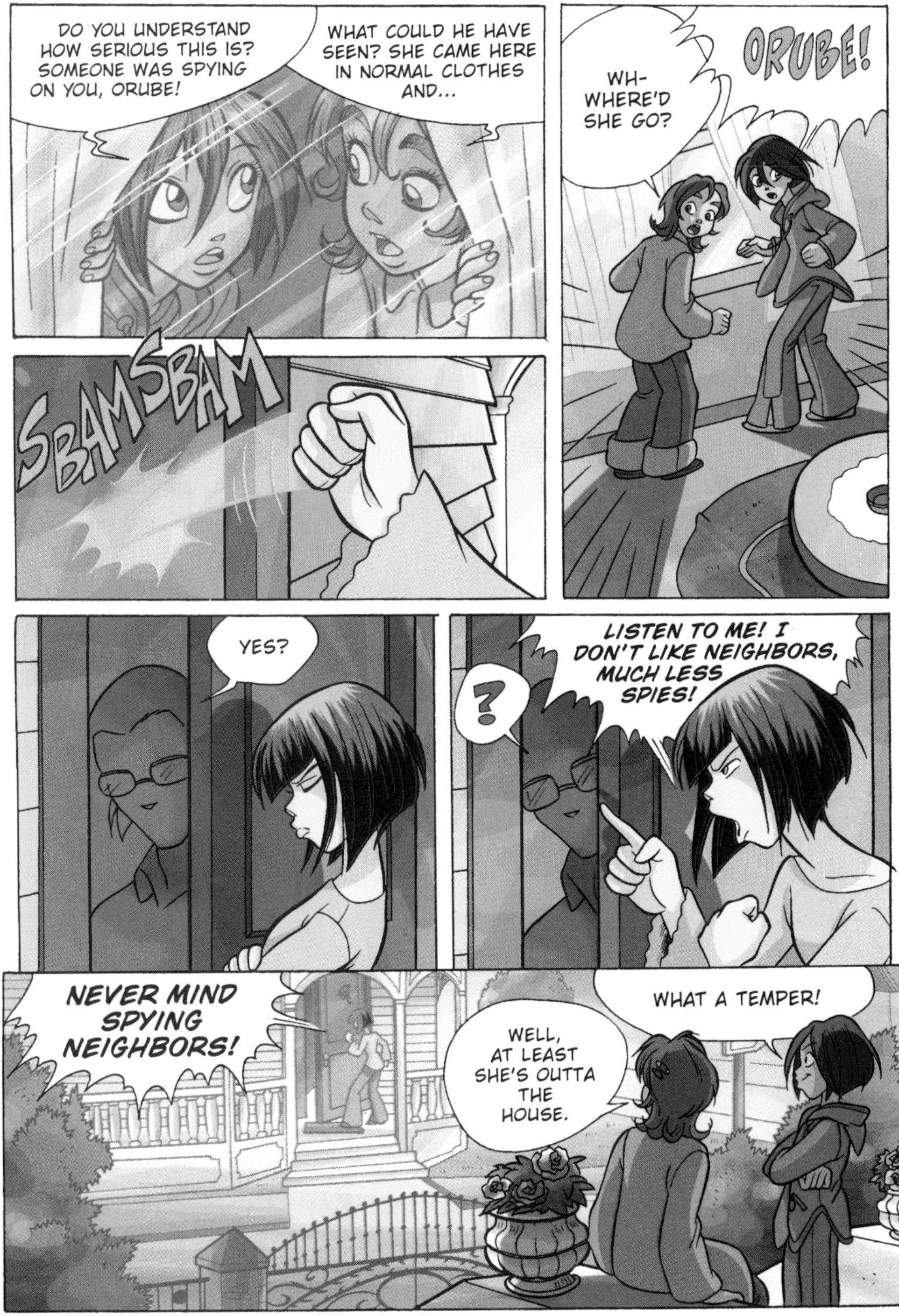
DO YOU UNDERSTAND HOW SERIOUS THIS IS? SOMEONE WAS SPYING ON YOU, ORUBE!
WHAT COULD HE HAVE SEEN? SHE CAME HERE IN NORMAL CLOTHES AND...
ORUBE!
WH- WHERE'D SHE GO?
SBAMSBAM
YES?
?
LISTEN TO ME! I DON'T LIKE NEIGHBORS, MUCH LESS SPIES!
NEVER MIND SPYING NEIGHBORS!
WHAT A TEMPER!
WELL, AT LEAST SHE'S OUTTA THE HOUSE.

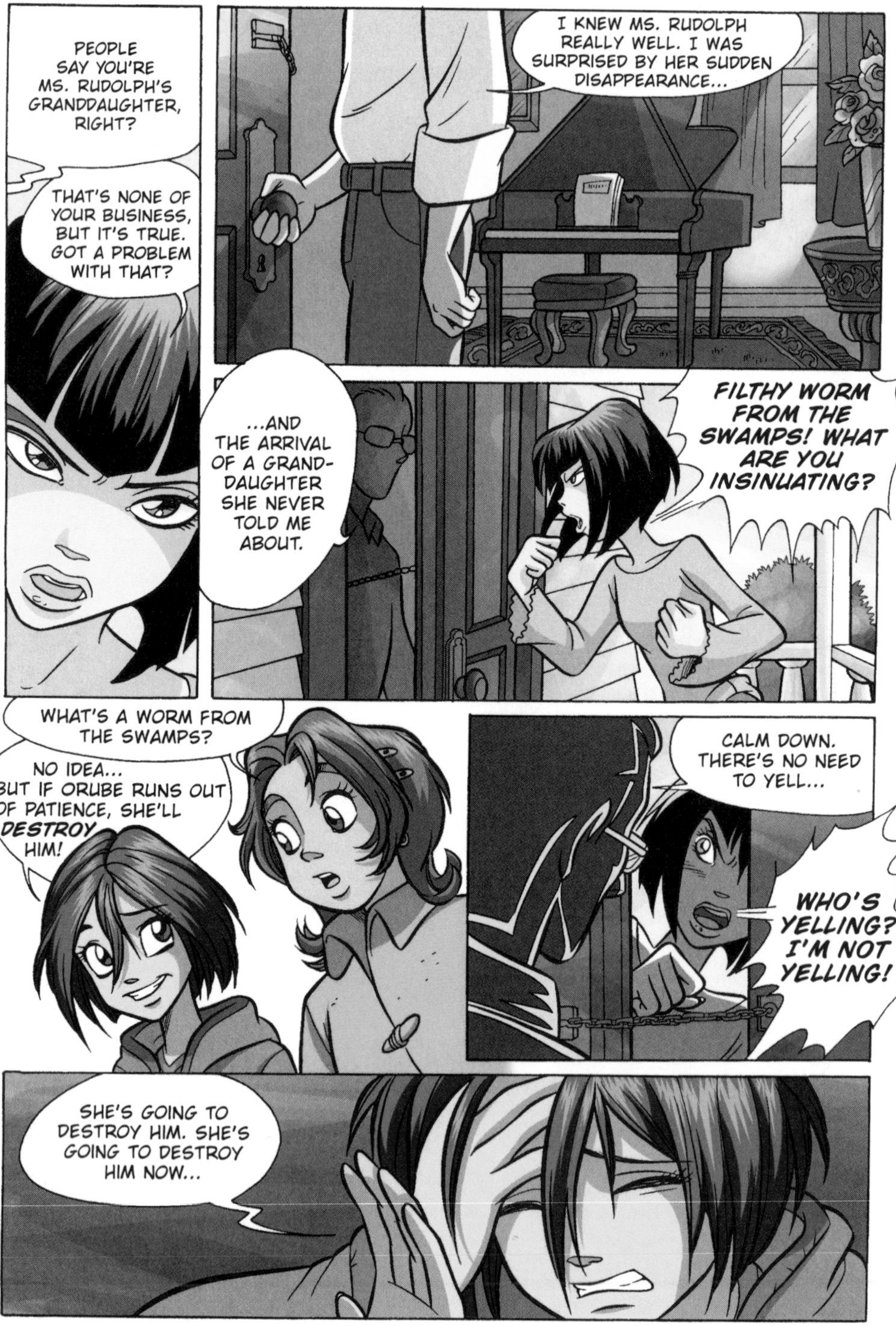

PEOPLE SAY YOU'RE MS. RUDOLPH'S GRANDDAUGHTER, RIGHT?
THAT'S NONE OF YOUR BUSINESS, BUT IT'S TRUE. GOT A PROBLEM WITH THAT?
I KNEW MS. RUDOLPH REALLY WELL. I WAS SURPRISED BY HER SUDDEN DISAPPEARANCE...
...AND THE ARRIVAL OF A GRAND-DAUGHTER SHE NEVER TOLD ME ABOUT.
FILTHY WORM FROM THE SWAMPS! WHAT ARE YOU INSINUATING?
WHAT'S A WORM FROM THE SWAMPS?
NO IDEA... BUT IF ORUBE RUNS OUT OF PATIENCE, SHE'LL DESTROY HIM!
CALM DOWN. THERE'S NO NEED TO YELL...
WHO'S YELLING? I'M NOT YELLING!
SHE'S GOING TO DESTROY HIM. SHE'S GOING TO DESTROY HIM NOW...

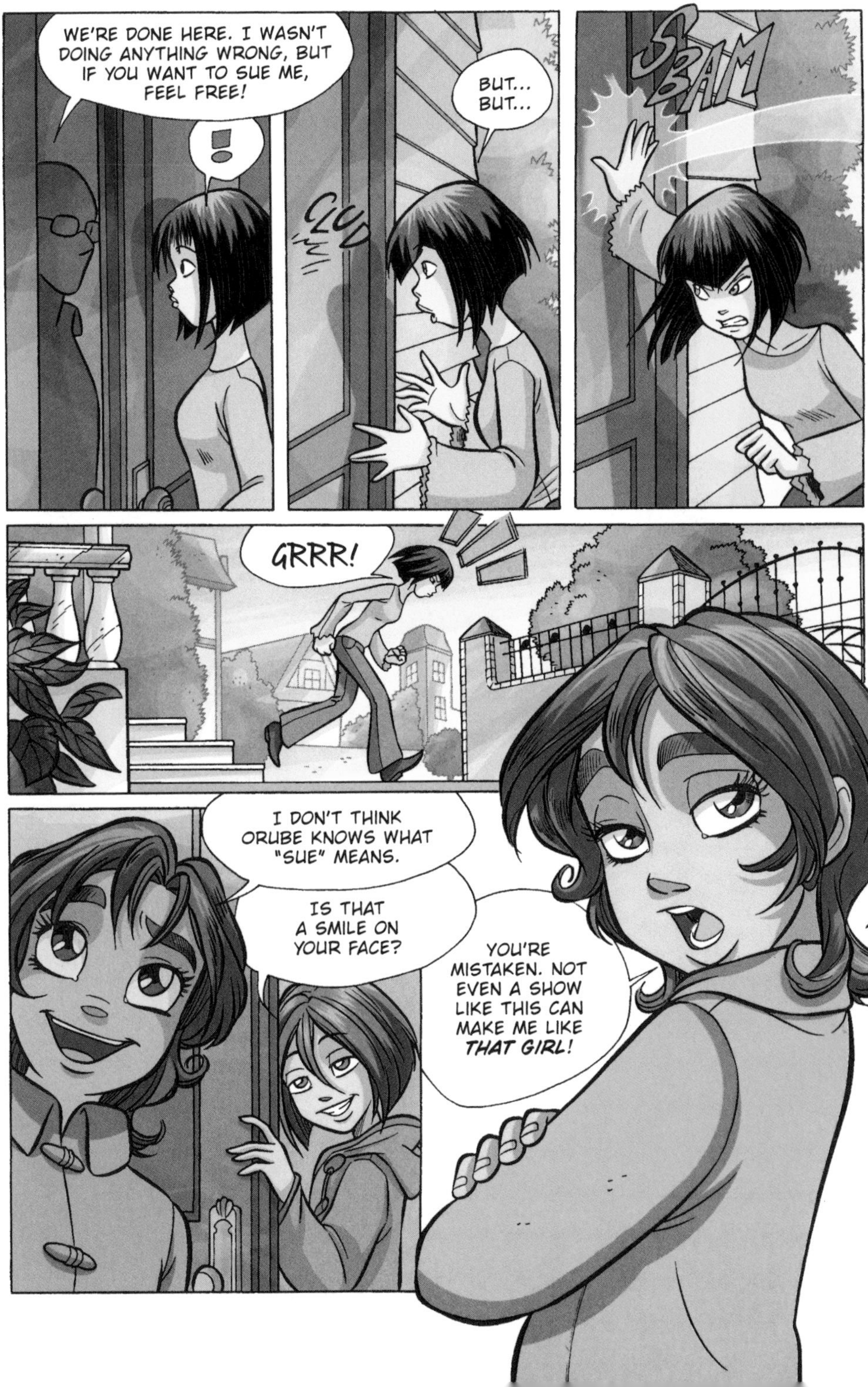
WE'RE DONE HERE. I WASN'T DOING ANYTHING WRONG, BUT IF YOU WANT TO SUE ME, FEEL FREE!
!
BUT... BUT...
CLUD
SBAM
GRRR!
I DON'T THINK ORUBE KNOWS WHAT "SUE" MEANS.
IS THAT A SMILE ON YOUR FACE?
YOU'RE MISTAKEN. NOT EVEN A SHOW LIKE THIS CAN MAKE ME LIKE ***THAT GIRL***!

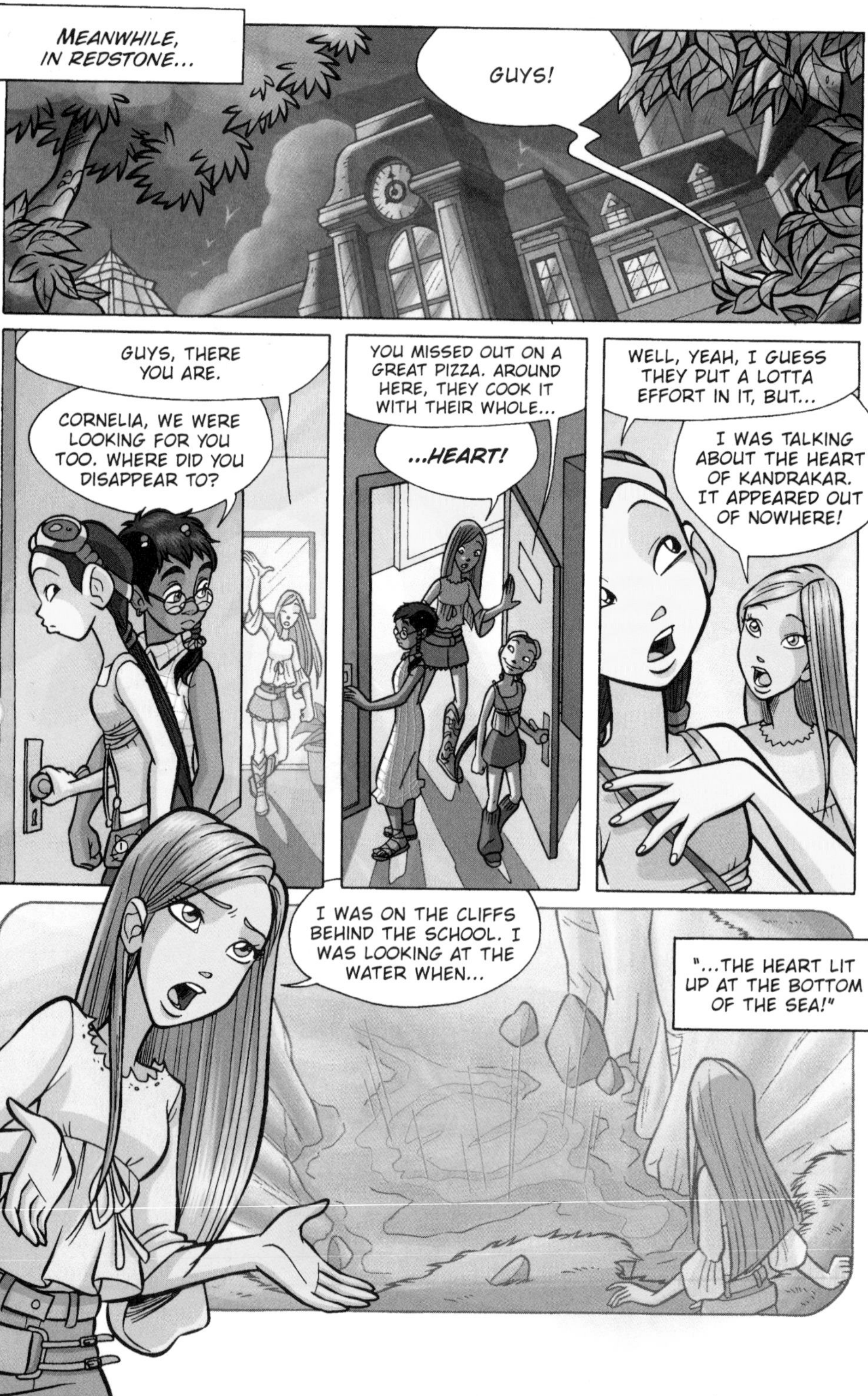
MEANWHILE, IN REDSTONE...
GUYS!
GUYS, THERE YOU ARE.
CORNELIA, WE WERE LOOKING FOR YOU TOO. WHERE DID YOU DISAPPEAR TO?
YOU MISSED OUT ON A GREAT PIZZA. AROUND HERE, THEY COOK IT WITH THEIR WHOLE...
...HEART!
WELL, YEAH, I GUESS THEY PUT A LOTTA EFFORT IN IT, BUT...
I WAS TALKING ABOUT THE HEART OF KANDRAKAR. IT APPEARED OUT OF NOWHERE!
I WAS ON THE CLIFFS BEHIND THE SCHOOL. I WAS LOOKING AT THE WATER WHEN...
"...THE HEART LIT UP AT THE BOTTOM OF THE SEA!"

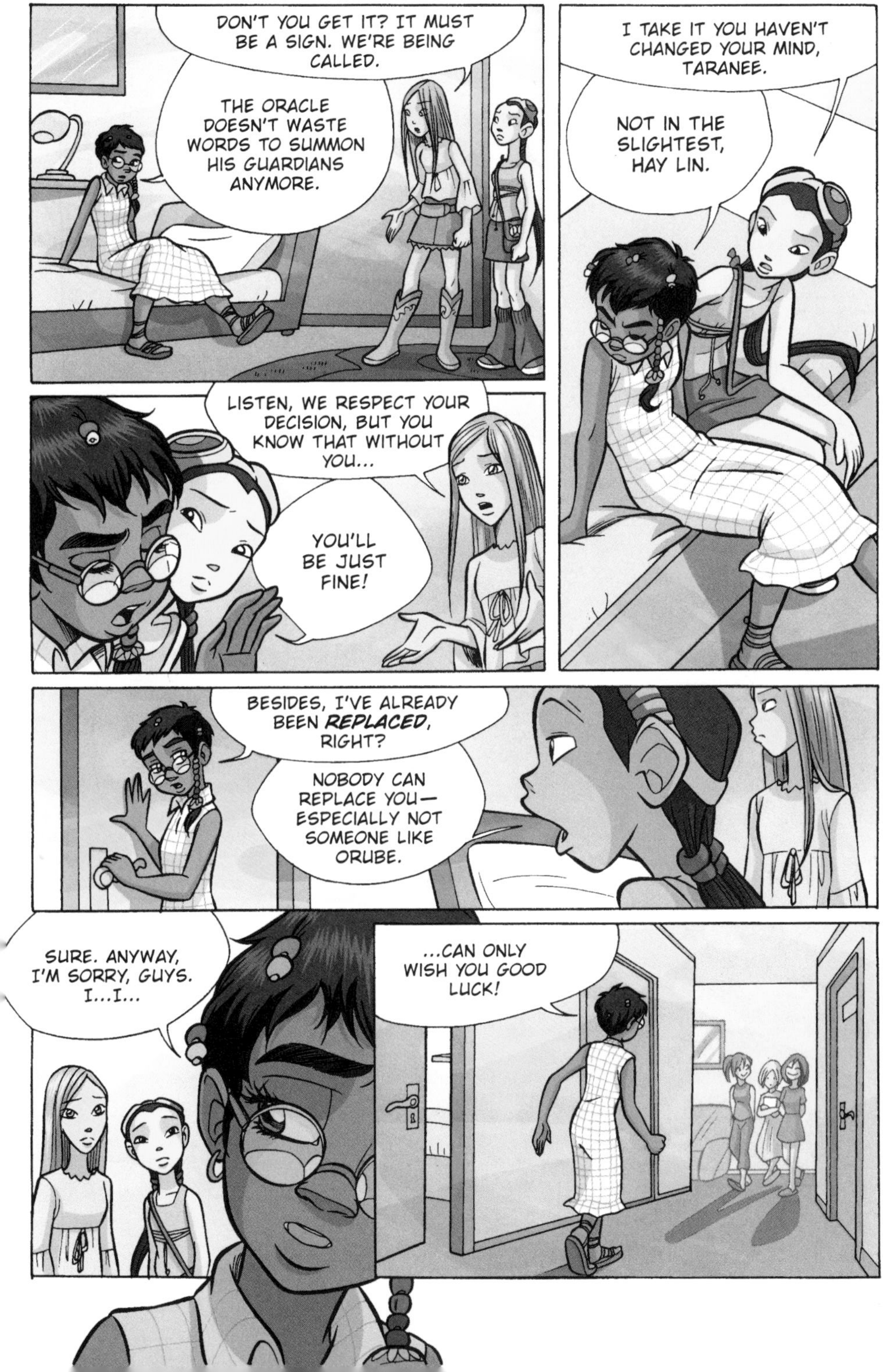
DON'T YOU GET IT? IT MUST BE A SIGN. WE'RE BEING CALLED.
THE ORACLE DOESN'T WASTE WORDS TO SUMMON HIS GUARDIANS ANYMORE.
I TAKE IT YOU HAVEN'T CHANGED YOUR MIND, TARANEE.
NOT IN THE SLIGHTEST, HAY LIN.
LISTEN, WE RESPECT YOUR DECISION, BUT YOU KNOW THAT WITHOUT YOU...
YOU'LL BE JUST FINE!
BESIDES, I'VE ALREADY BEEN *REPLACED*, RIGHT?
NOBODY CAN REPLACE YOU— ESPECIALLY NOT SOMEONE LIKE ORUBE.
SURE. ANYWAY, I'M SORRY, GUYS. I...I...
...CAN ONLY WISH YOU GOOD LUCK!

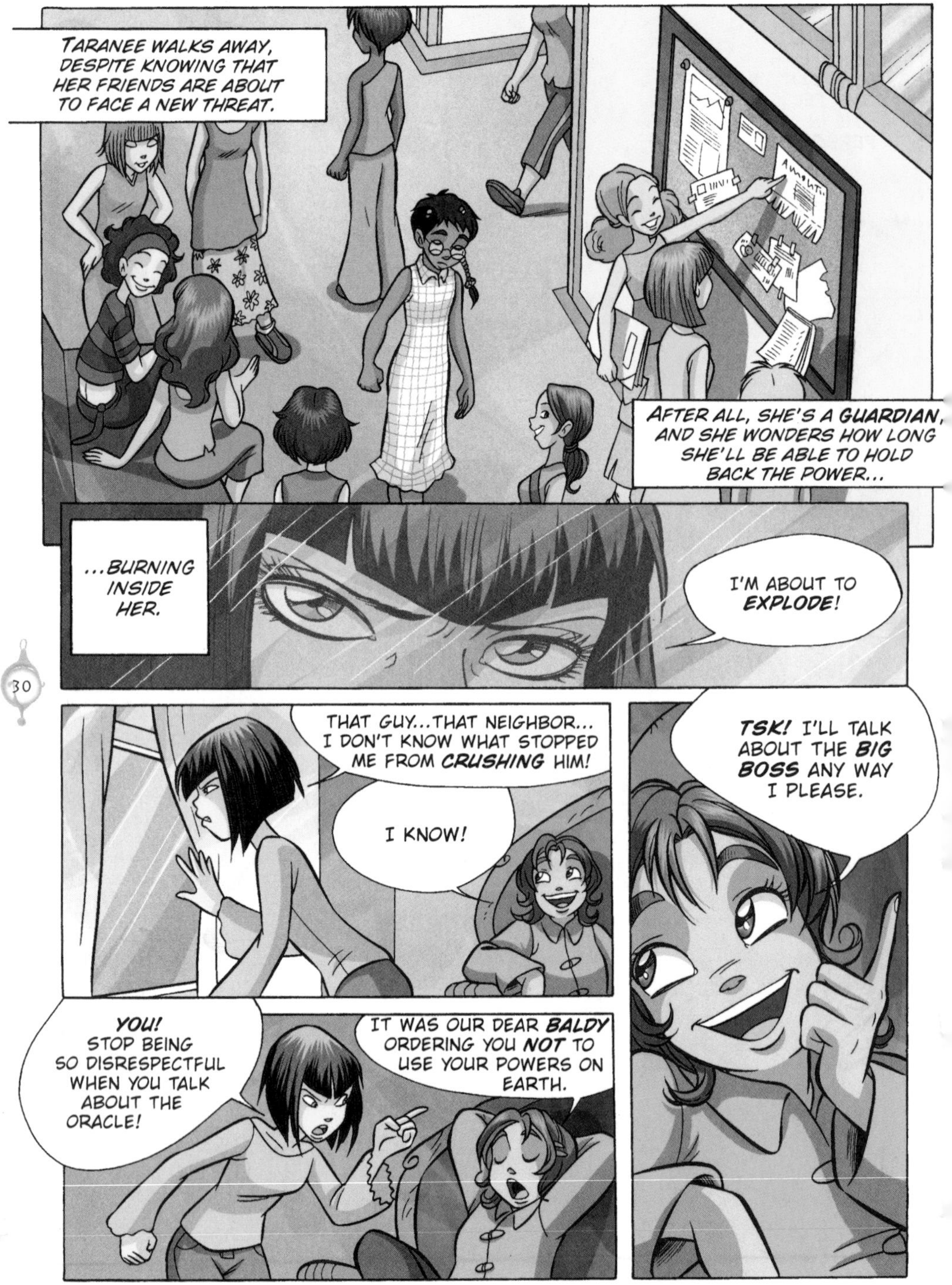

TARANEE WALKS AWAY, DESPITE KNOWING THAT HER FRIENDS ARE ABOUT TO FACE A NEW THREAT.
AFTER ALL, SHE'S A GUARDIAN, AND SHE WONDERS HOW LONG SHE'LL BE ABLE TO HOLD BACK THE POWER...
...BURNING INSIDE HER.
I'M ABOUT TO EXPLODE!
THAT GUY...THAT NEIGHBOR... I DON'T KNOW WHAT STOPPED ME FROM CRUSHING HIM!
I KNOW!
IT WAS OUR DEAR BALDY ORDERING YOU NOT TO USE YOUR POWERS ON EARTH.
YOU! STOP BEING SO DISRESPECTFUL WHEN YOU TALK ABOUT THE ORACLE!
TSK! I'LL TALK ABOUT THE BIG BOSS ANY WAY I PLEASE.

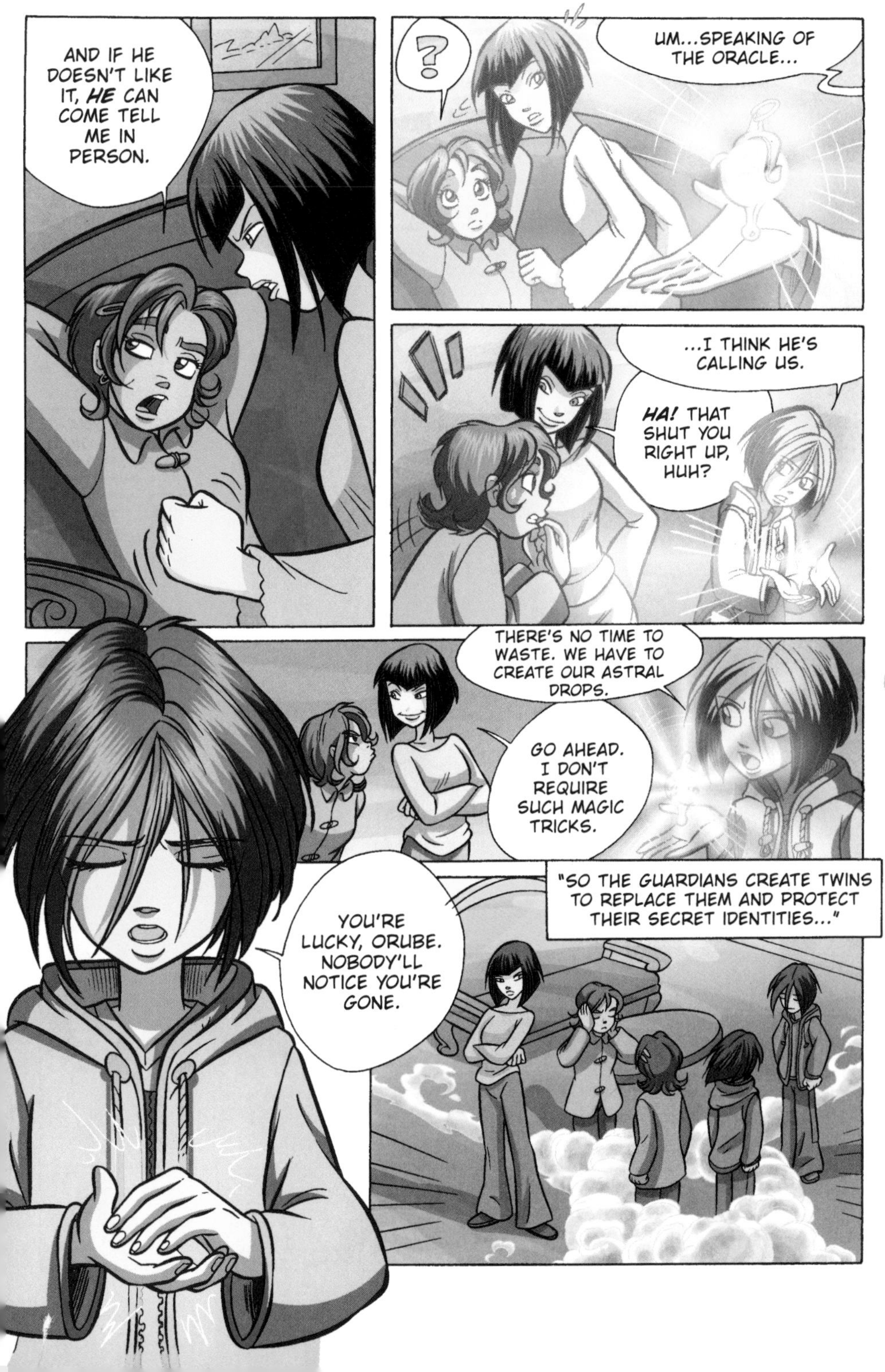

AND IF HE DOESN'T LIKE IT, HE CAN COME TELL ME IN PERSON.
?
UM...SPEAKING OF THE ORACLE...
...I THINK HE'S CALLING US.
HA! THAT SHUT YOU RIGHT UP, HUH?
THERE'S NO TIME TO WASTE. WE HAVE TO CREATE OUR ASTRAL DROPS.
GO AHEAD. I DON'T REQUIRE SUCH MAGIC TRICKS.
YOU'RE LUCKY, ORUBE. NOBODY'LL NOTICE YOU'RE GONE.
"SO THE GUARDIANS CREATE TWINS TO REPLACE THEM AND PROTECT THEIR SECRET IDENTITIES..."

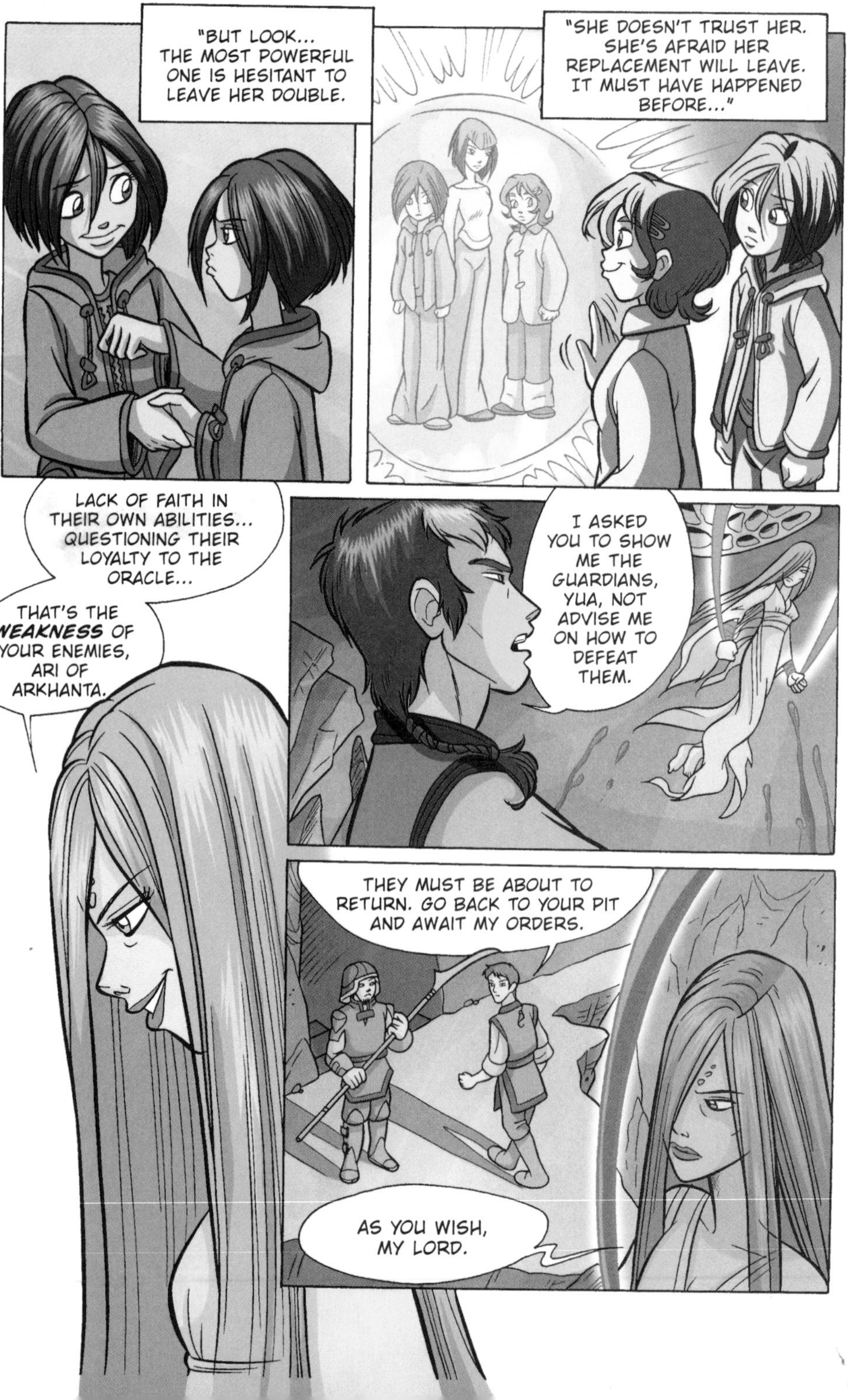
"BUT LOOK... THE MOST POWERFUL ONE IS HESITANT TO LEAVE HER DOUBLE.
"SHE DOESN'T TRUST HER. SHE'S AFRAID HER REPLACEMENT WILL LEAVE. IT MUST HAVE HAPPENED BEFORE..."
LACK OF FAITH IN THEIR OWN ABILITIES... QUESTIONING THEIR LOYALTY TO THE ORACLE...
THAT'S THE WEAKNESS OF YOUR ENEMIES, ARI OF ARKHANTA.
I ASKED YOU TO SHOW ME THE GUARDIANS, YUA, NOT ADVISE ME ON HOW TO DEFEAT THEM.
THEY MUST BE ABOUT TO RETURN. GO BACK TO YOUR PIT AND AWAIT MY ORDERS.
AS YOU WISH, MY LORD.

SURE. GO. I'LL BE HERE WAITING. I'LL COUNT THE DROPS OF WATER TO PASS THE TIME.

OR...HMM... MAYBE I COULD COUNT THE DROPS OF *SWEAT* ON THIS FRIGHTENED CREATURE.

DRIP...

DRIP...

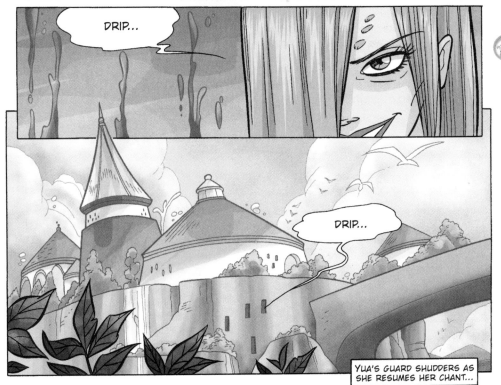

DRIP...

YUA'S GUARD SHUDDERS AS SHE RESUMES HER CHANT...

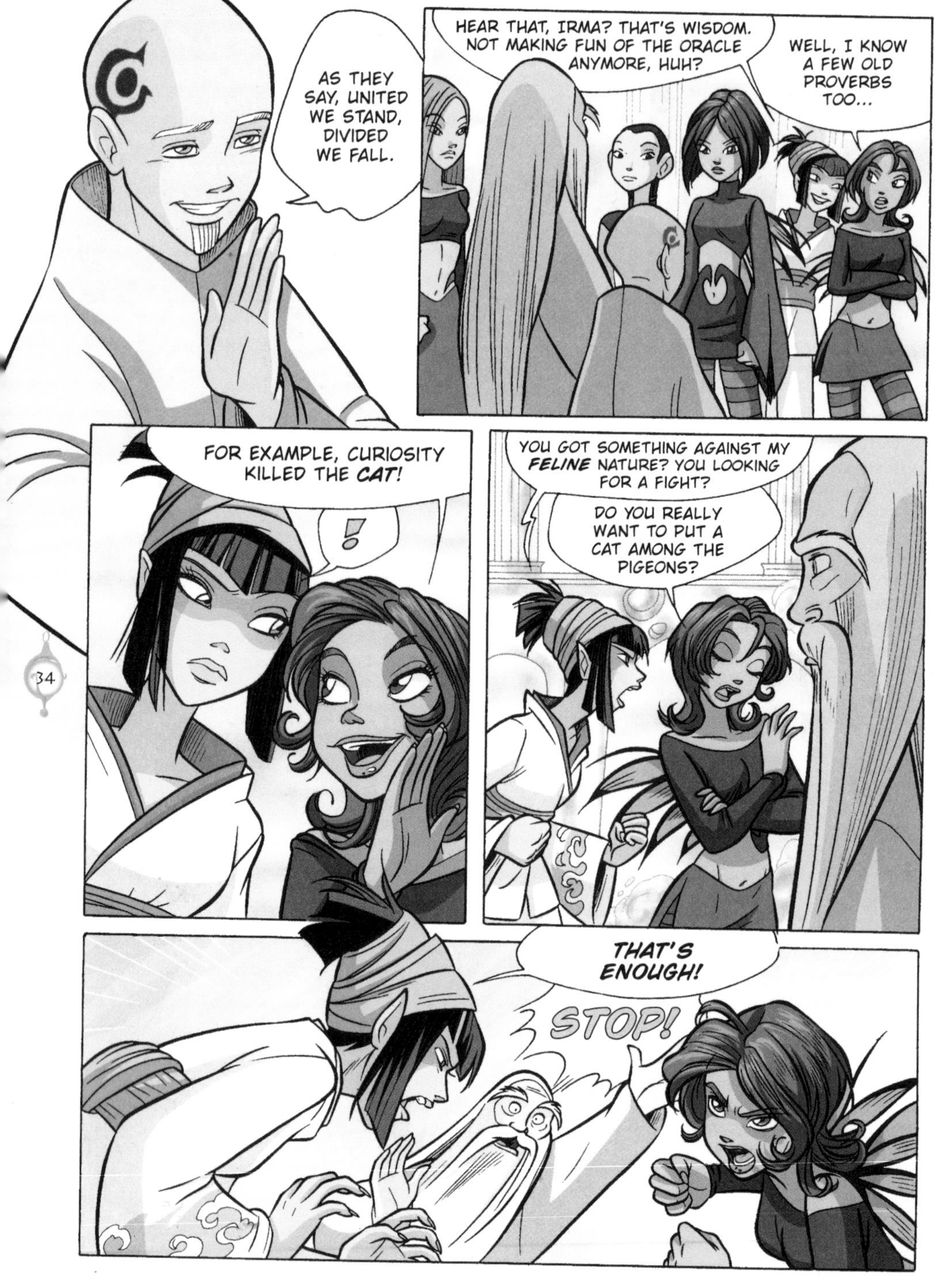
AS THEY SAY, UNITED WE STAND, DIVIDED WE FALL.
HEAR THAT, IRMA? THAT'S WISDOM. NOT MAKING FUN OF THE ORACLE ANYMORE, HUH?
WELL, I KNOW A FEW OLD PROVERBS TOO...
FOR EXAMPLE, CURIOSITY KILLED THE *CAT*!
!
YOU GOT SOMETHING AGAINST MY *FELINE* NATURE? YOU LOOKING FOR A FIGHT?
DO YOU REALLY WANT TO PUT A CAT AMONG THE PIGEONS?
THAT'S ENOUGH!
STOP!

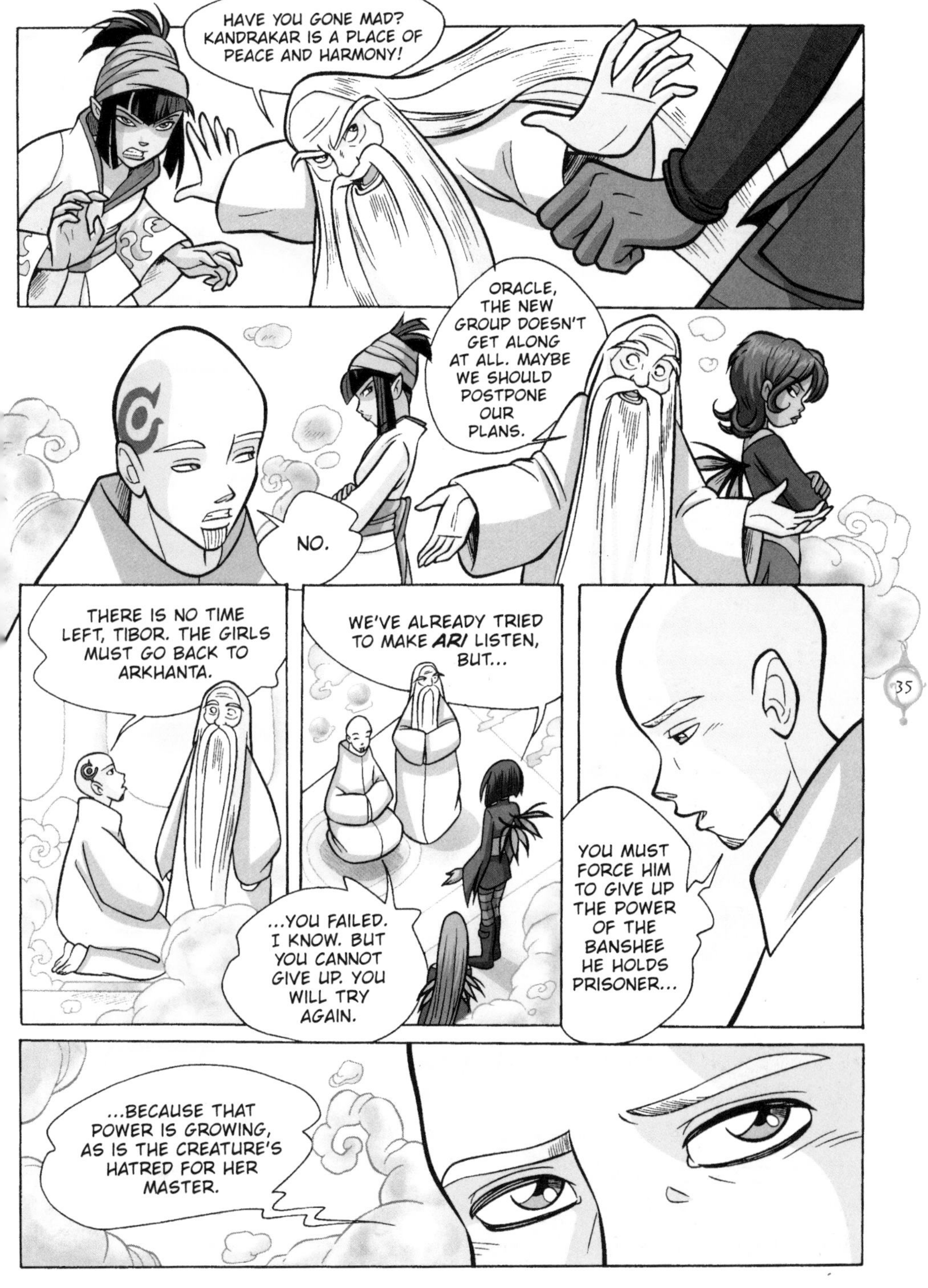
HAVE YOU GONE MAD? KANDRAKAR IS A PLACE OF PEACE AND HARMONY!
ORACLE, THE NEW GROUP DOESN'T GET ALONG AT ALL. MAYBE WE SHOULD POSTPONE OUR PLANS.
NO.
THERE IS NO TIME LEFT, TIBOR. THE GIRLS MUST GO BACK TO ARKHANTA.
WE'VE ALREADY TRIED TO MAKE ARI LISTEN, BUT...
...YOU FAILED. I KNOW. BUT YOU CANNOT GIVE UP. YOU WILL TRY AGAIN.
YOU MUST FORCE HIM TO GIVE UP THE POWER OF THE BANSHEE HE HOLDS PRISONER...
...BECAUSE THAT POWER IS GROWING, AS IS THE CREATURE'S HATRED FOR HER MASTER.

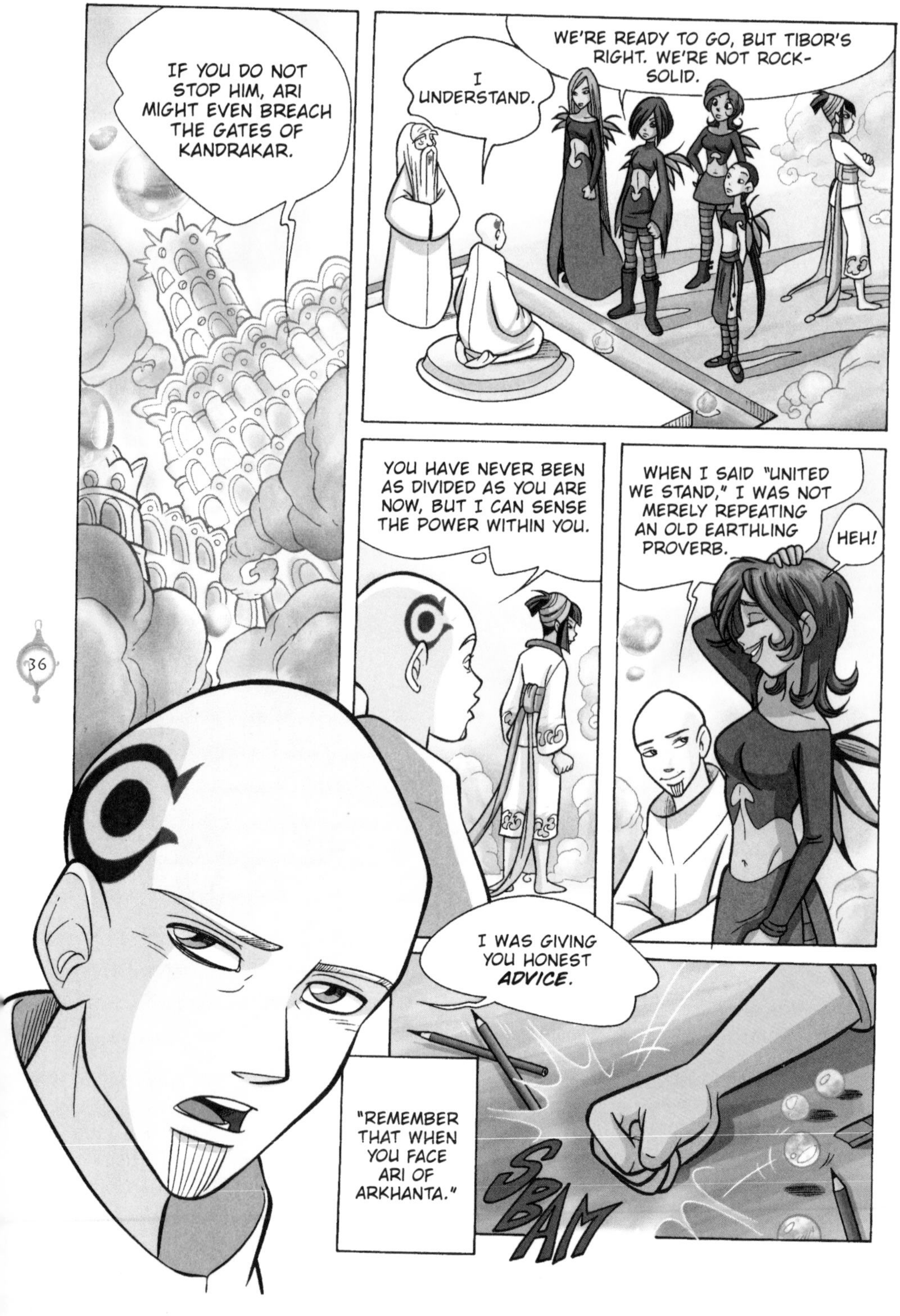

IF YOU DO NOT STOP HIM, ARI MIGHT EVEN BREACH THE GATES OF KANDRAKAR.
I UNDERSTAND.
WE'RE READY TO GO, BUT TIBOR'S RIGHT. WE'RE NOT ROCK-SOLID.
YOU HAVE NEVER BEEN AS DIVIDED AS YOU ARE NOW, BUT I CAN SENSE THE POWER WITHIN YOU.
WHEN I SAID "UNITED WE STAND," I WAS NOT MERELY REPEATING AN OLD EARTHLING PROVERB.
HEH!
I WAS GIVING YOU HONEST ADVICE.
"REMEMBER THAT WHEN YOU FACE ARI OF ARKHANTA."
SBAM

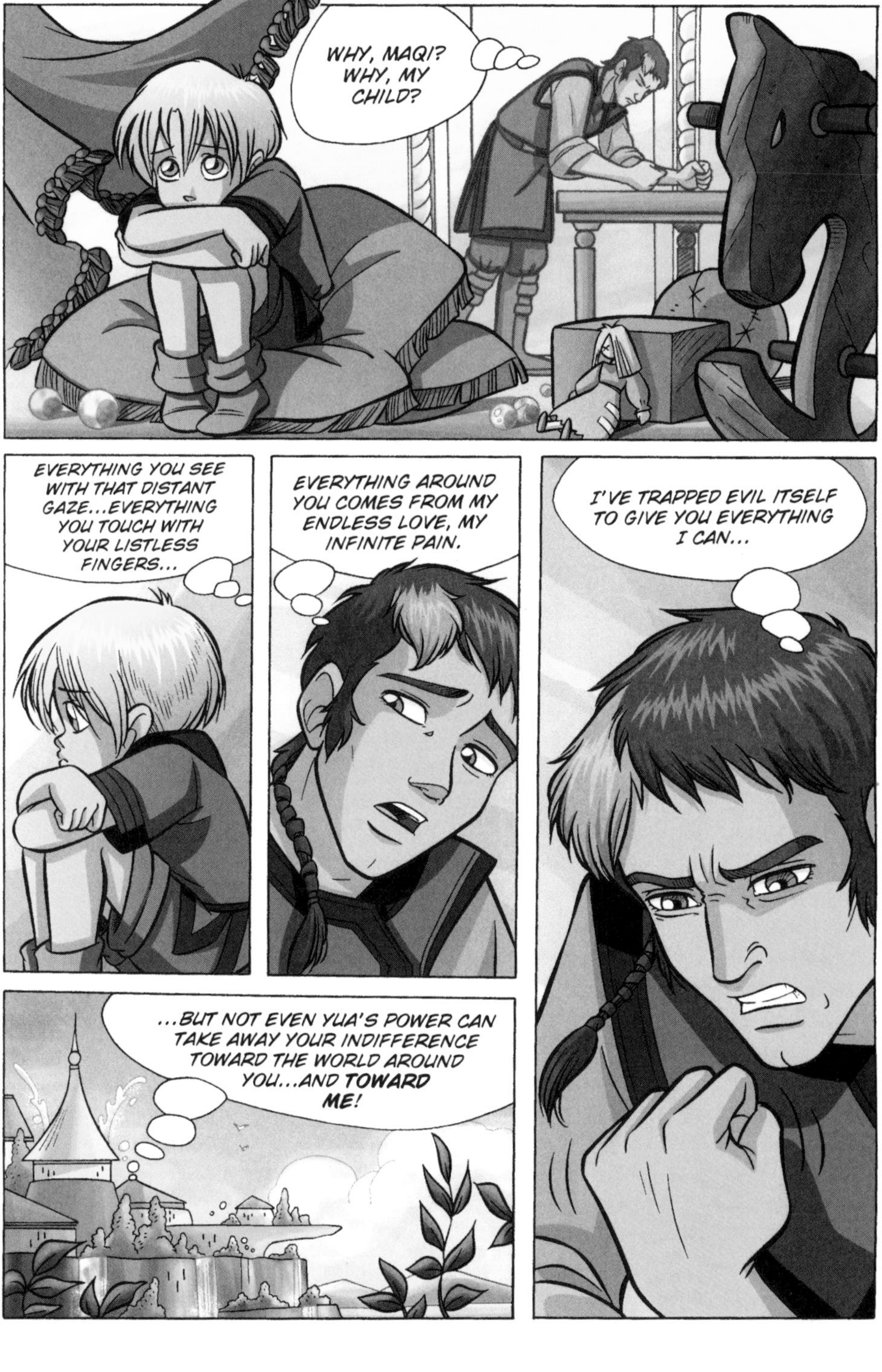
WHY, MAQI? WHY, MY CHILD?
EVERYTHING YOU SEE WITH THAT DISTANT GAZE...EVERYTHING YOU TOUCH WITH YOUR LISTLESS FINGERS...
EVERYTHING AROUND YOU COMES FROM MY ENDLESS LOVE, MY INFINITE PAIN.
I'VE TRAPPED EVIL ITSELF TO GIVE YOU EVERYTHING I CAN...
...BUT NOT EVEN YUA'S POWER CAN TAKE AWAY YOUR INDIFFERENCE TOWARD THE WORLD AROUND YOU...AND **TOWARD ME!**

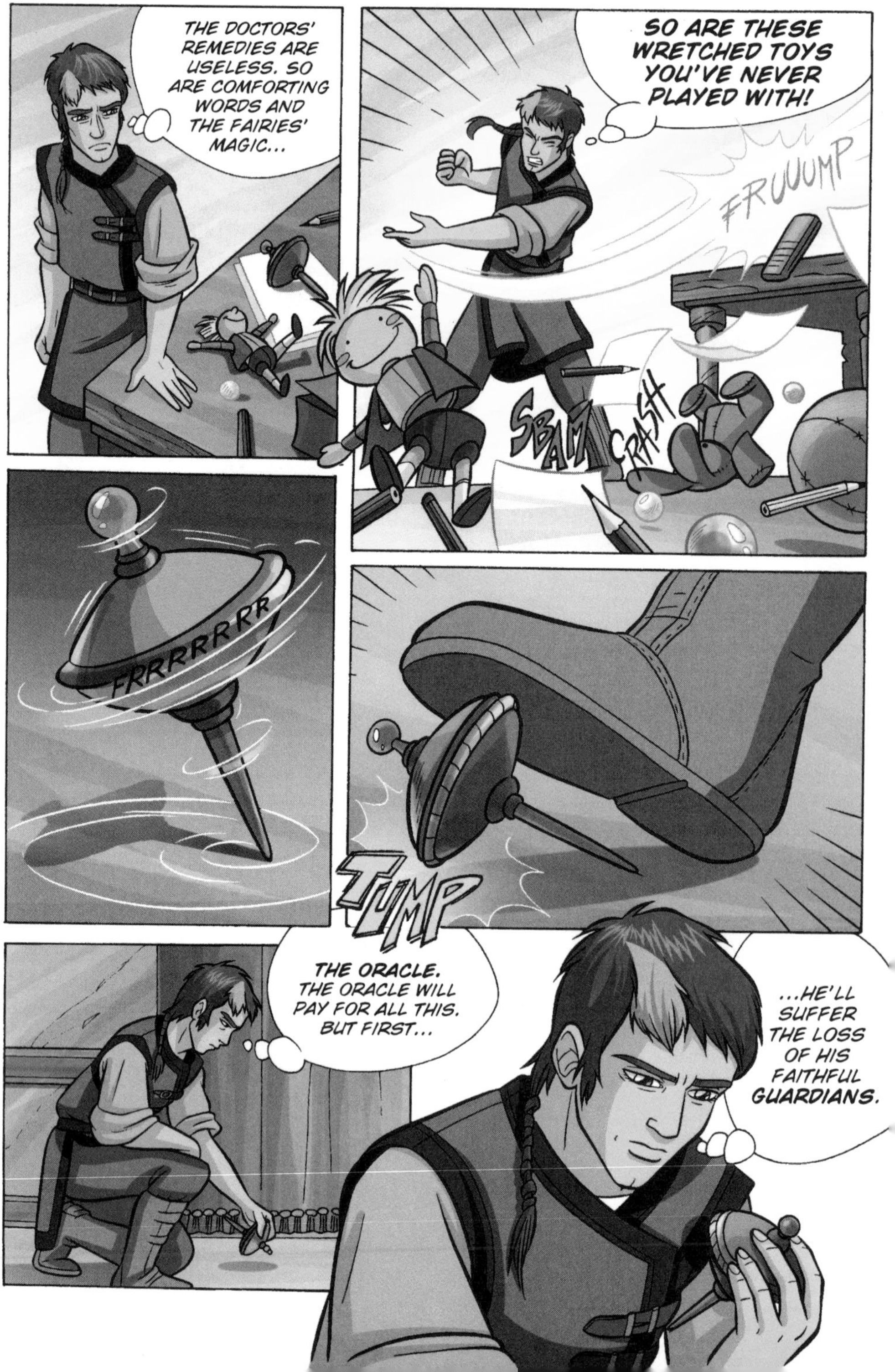
THE DOCTORS' REMEDIES ARE USELESS. SO ARE COMFORTING WORDS AND THE FAIRIES' MAGIC...
SO ARE THESE WRETCHED TOYS YOU'VE NEVER PLAYED WITH!
FRUUUMP
SBAM
CRASH
FRRRRRRRR
TUMP
THE ORACLE. THE ORACLE WILL PAY FOR ALL THIS. BUT FIRST...
...HE'LL SUFFER THE LOSS OF HIS FAITHFUL GUARDIANS.

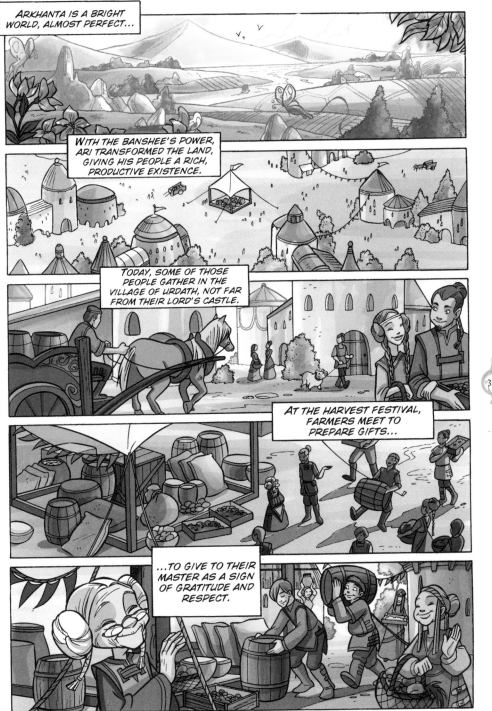

ARKHANTA IS A BRIGHT WORLD, ALMOST PERFECT...

WITH THE BANSHEE'S POWER, ARI TRANSFORMED THE LAND, GIVING HIS PEOPLE A RICH, PRODUCTIVE EXISTENCE.

TODAY, SOME OF THOSE PEOPLE GATHER IN THE VILLAGE OF URDATH, NOT FAR FROM THEIR LORD'S CASTLE.

AT THE HARVEST FESTIVAL, FARMERS MEET TO PREPARE GIFTS...

...TO GIVE TO THEIR MASTER AS A SIGN OF GRATITUDE AND RESPECT.

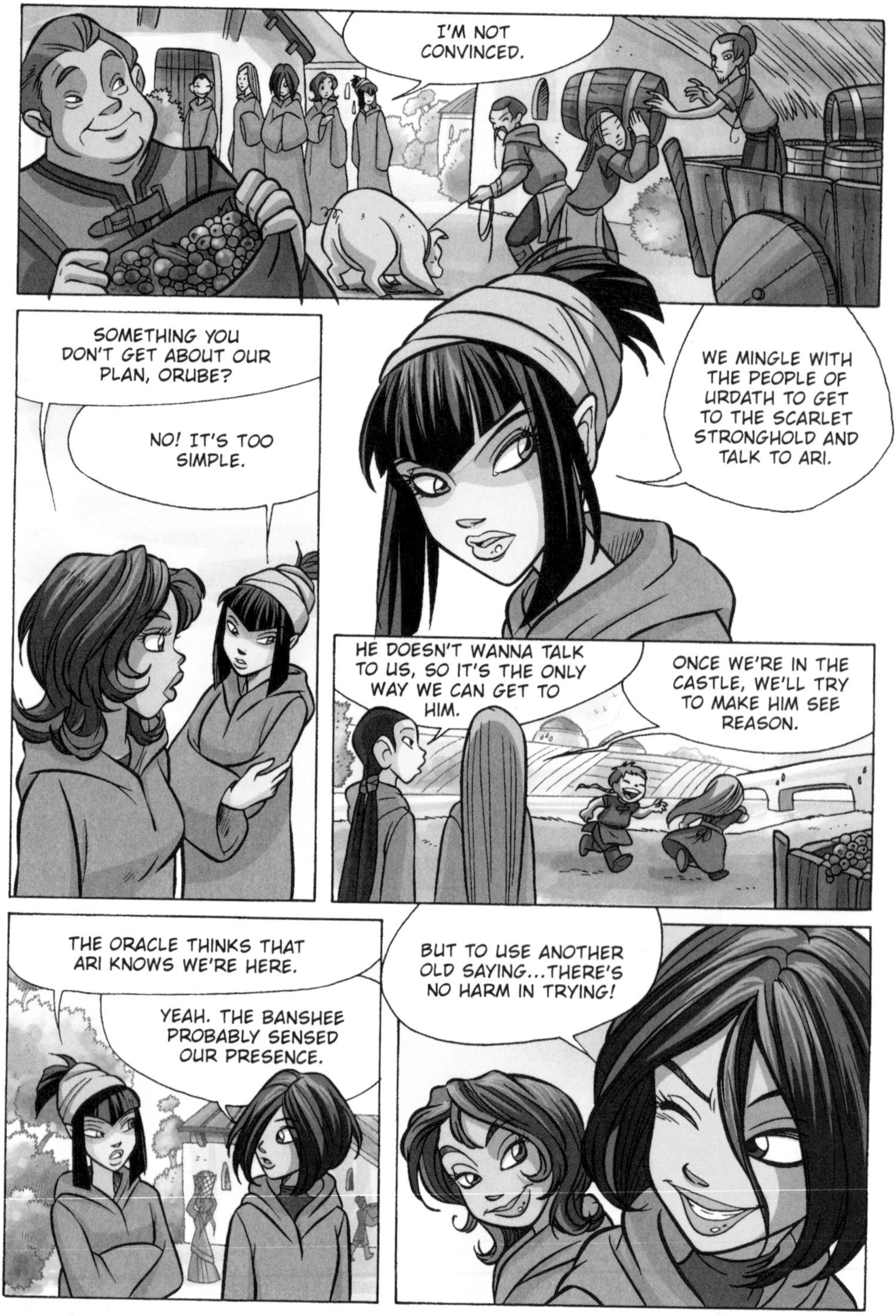
I'M NOT CONVINCED.
SOMETHING YOU DON'T GET ABOUT OUR PLAN, ORUBE?
NO! IT'S TOO SIMPLE.
WE MINGLE WITH THE PEOPLE OF URDATH TO GET TO THE SCARLET STRONGHOLD AND TALK TO ARI.
HE DOESN'T WANNA TALK TO US, SO IT'S THE ONLY WAY WE CAN GET TO HIM.
ONCE WE'RE IN THE CASTLE, WE'LL TRY TO MAKE HIM SEE REASON.
THE ORACLE THINKS THAT ARI KNOWS WE'RE HERE.
YEAH. THE BANSHEE PROBABLY SENSED OUR PRESENCE.
BUT TO USE ANOTHER OLD SAYING...THERE'S NO HARM IN TRYING!

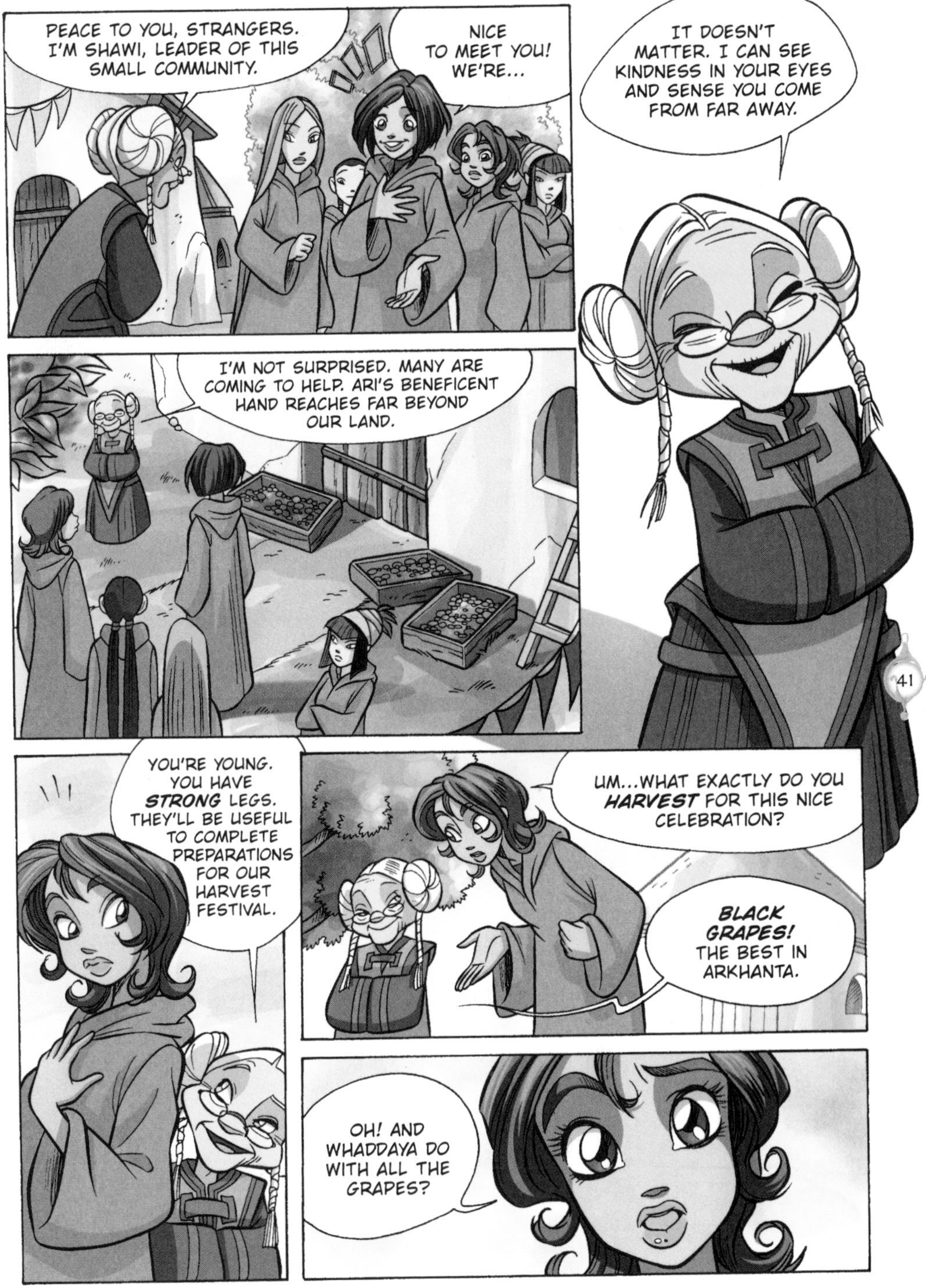
PEACE TO YOU, STRANGERS. I'M SHAWI, LEADER OF THIS SMALL COMMUNITY.
NICE TO MEET YOU! WE'RE...
IT DOESN'T MATTER. I CAN SEE KINDNESS IN YOUR EYES AND SENSE YOU COME FROM FAR AWAY.
I'M NOT SURPRISED. MANY ARE COMING TO HELP. ARI'S BENEFICENT HAND REACHES FAR BEYOND OUR LAND.
YOU'RE YOUNG. YOU HAVE ***STRONG*** LEGS. THEY'LL BE USEFUL TO COMPLETE PREPARATIONS FOR OUR HARVEST FESTIVAL.
UM...WHAT EXACTLY DO YOU ***HARVEST*** FOR THIS NICE CELEBRATION?
BLACK GRAPES! THE BEST IN ARKHANTA.
OH! AND WHADDAYA DO WITH ALL THE GRAPES?

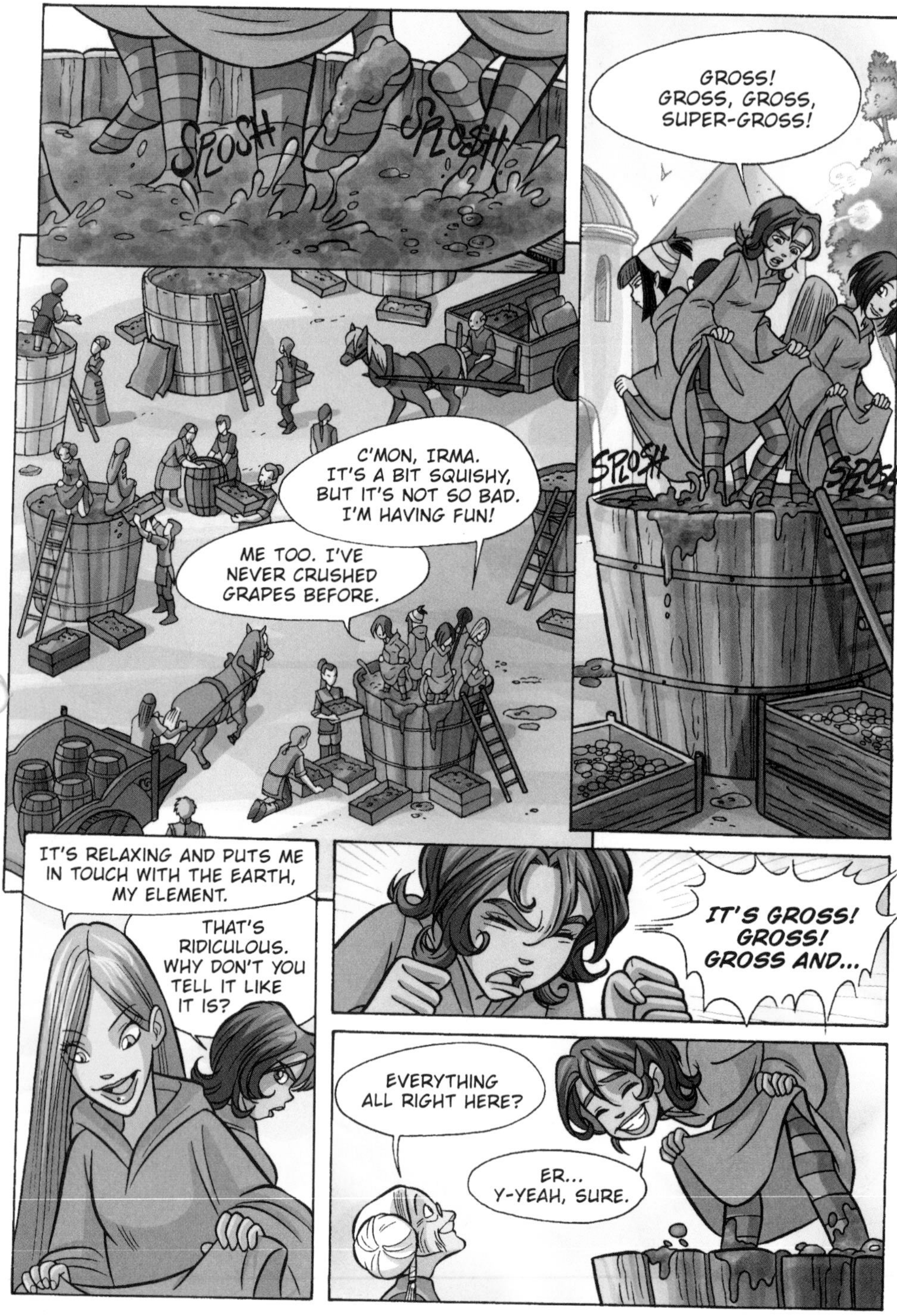
SPLOSH
SPLOSH
GROSS! GROSS, GROSS, SUPER-GROSS!
SPLOSH
SPLOSH
C'MON, IRMA. IT'S A BIT SQUISHY, BUT IT'S NOT SO BAD. I'M HAVING FUN!
ME TOO. I'VE NEVER CRUSHED GRAPES BEFORE.
IT'S RELAXING AND PUTS ME IN TOUCH WITH THE EARTH, MY ELEMENT.
THAT'S RIDICULOUS. WHY DON'T YOU TELL IT LIKE IT IS?
IT'S GROSS! GROSS! GROSS AND...
EVERYTHING ALL RIGHT HERE?
ER... Y-YEAH, SURE.

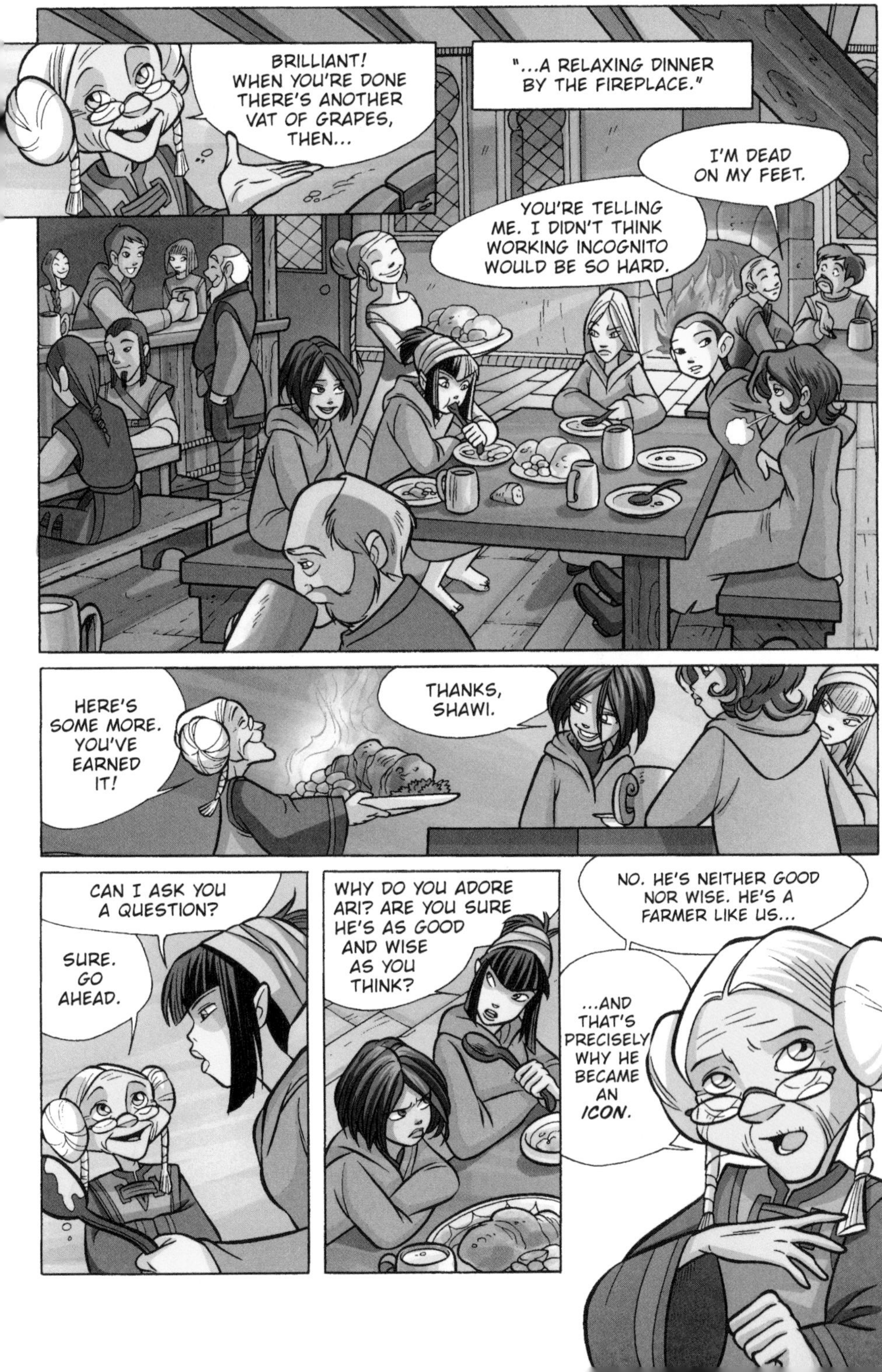
BRILLIANT! WHEN YOU'RE DONE THERE'S ANOTHER VAT OF GRAPES, THEN...
"...A RELAXING DINNER BY THE FIREPLACE."
I'M DEAD ON MY FEET.
YOU'RE TELLING ME. I DIDN'T THINK WORKING INCOGNITO WOULD BE SO HARD.
HERE'S SOME MORE. YOU'VE EARNED IT!
THANKS, SHAWI.
CAN I ASK YOU A QUESTION?
SURE. GO AHEAD.
WHY DO YOU ADORE ARI? ARE YOU SURE HE'S AS GOOD AND WISE AS YOU THINK?
NO. HE'S NEITHER GOOD NOR WISE. HE'S A FARMER LIKE US...
...AND THAT'S PRECISELY WHY HE BECAME AN *ICON*.

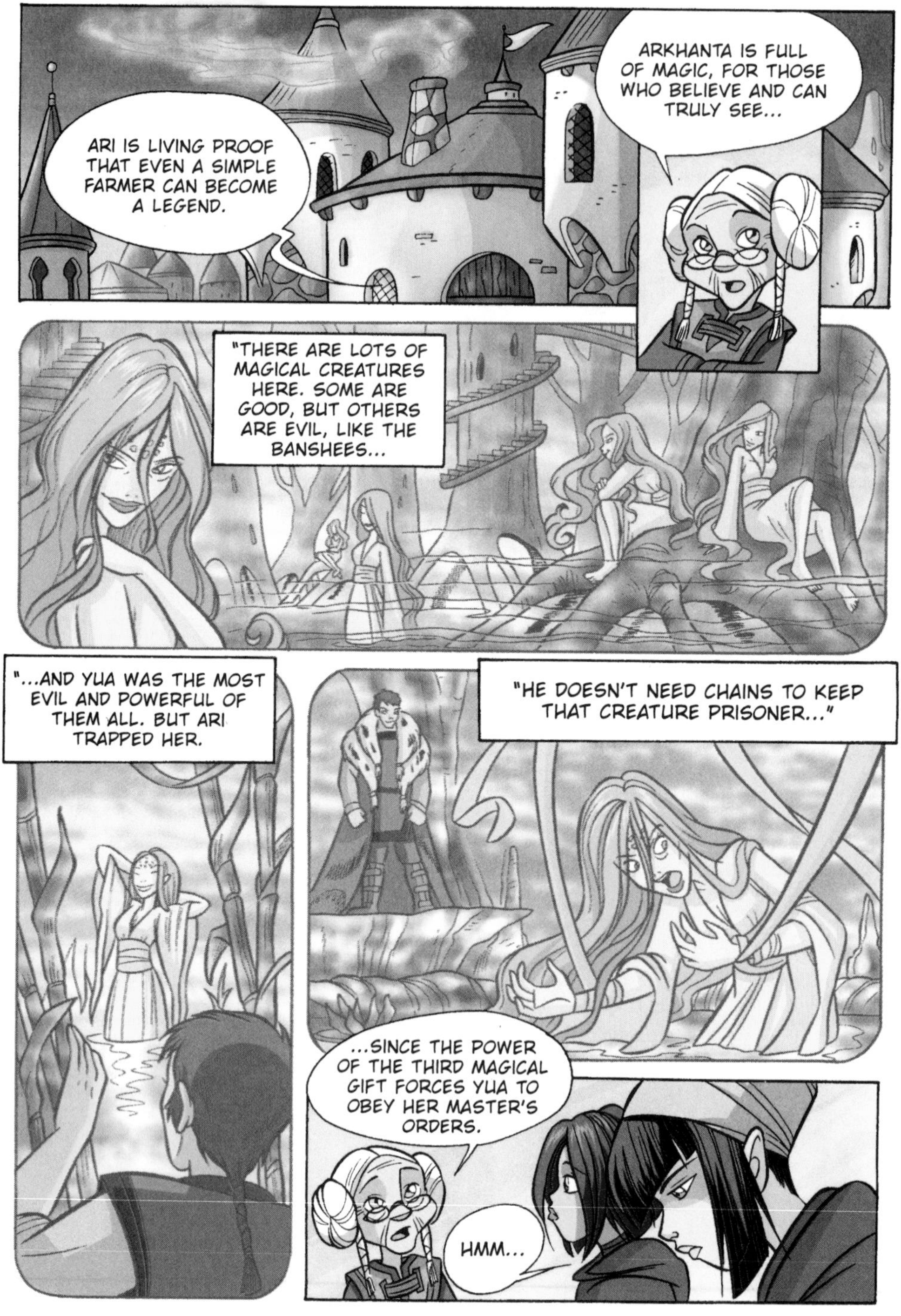
ARI IS LIVING PROOF THAT EVEN A SIMPLE FARMER CAN BECOME A LEGEND.
ARKHANTA IS FULL OF MAGIC, FOR THOSE WHO BELIEVE AND CAN TRULY SEE...
"THERE ARE LOTS OF MAGICAL CREATURES HERE. SOME ARE GOOD, BUT OTHERS ARE EVIL, LIKE THE BANSHEES...
"...AND YUA WAS THE MOST EVIL AND POWERFUL OF THEM ALL. BUT ARI TRAPPED HER.
"HE DOESN'T NEED CHAINS TO KEEP THAT CREATURE PRISONER..."
...SINCE THE POWER OF THE THIRD MAGICAL GIFT FORCES YUA TO OBEY HER MASTER'S ORDERS.
HMM...

WHAT IF SOMEONE FREED THE BANSHEE?

NO! HOW CAN YOU SPEAK SUCH MADNESS? IT WOULD BE A *CATASTROPHE.*

THE BANSHEE MUST REMAIN IMPRISONED BECAUSE, ONCE FREED, SHE'D UNLEASH HER *WRATH.*

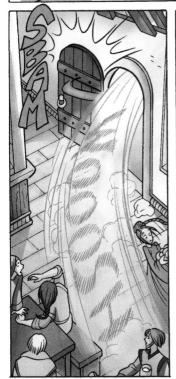

HAY LIN! WHAT'S GOING ON?

DON'T ASK ME! I'M NOT DOING IT!

BY THE CLOUDS OF KANDRAKAR! LOOK OVER THERE. WHAT'S THAT?

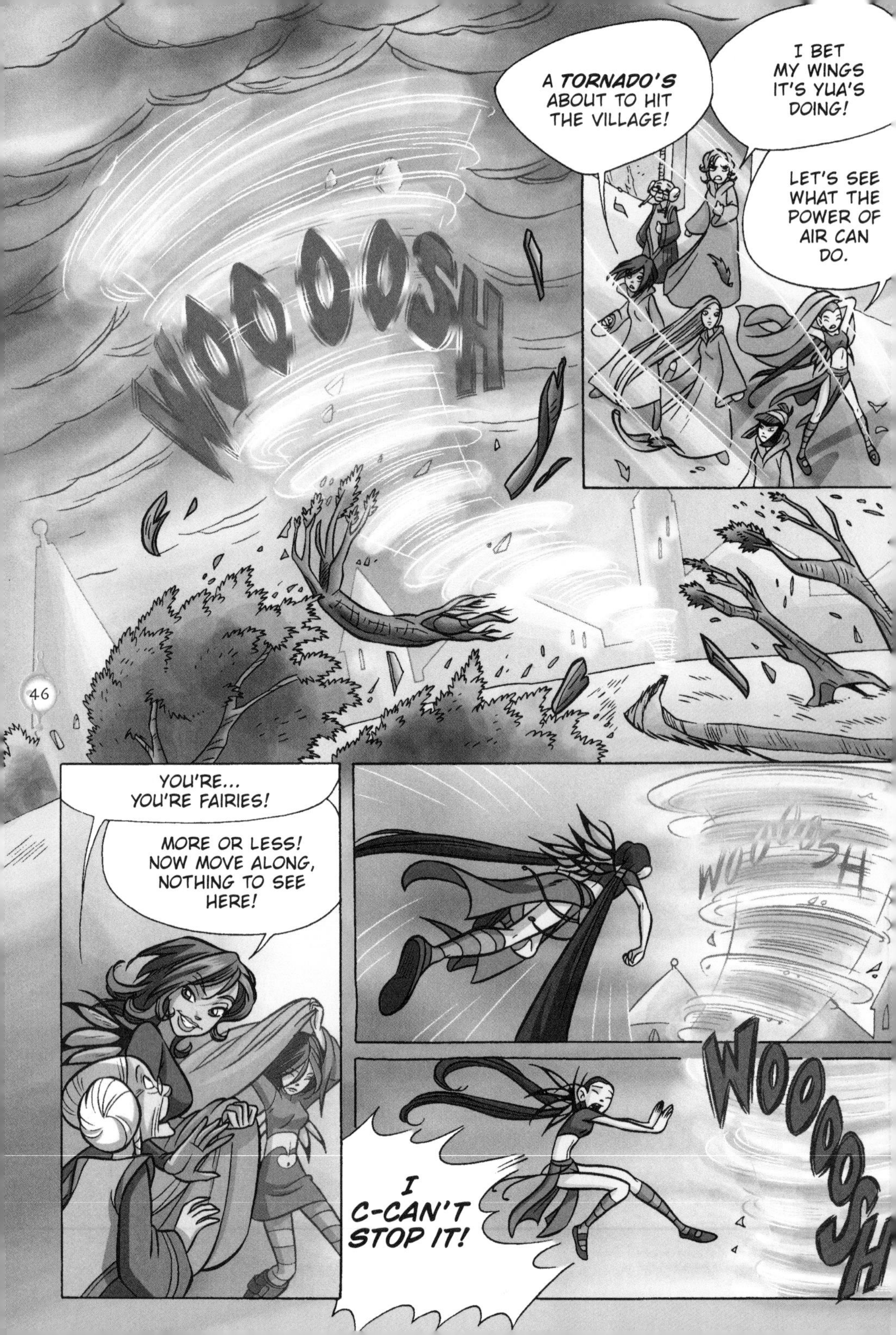
A *TORNADO'S* ABOUT TO HIT THE VILLAGE!
I BET MY WINGS IT'S YUA'S DOING!
LET'S SEE WHAT THE POWER OF AIR CAN DO.
WOOOOSH
YOU'RE... YOU'RE FAIRIES!
MORE OR LESS! NOW MOVE ALONG, NOTHING TO SEE HERE!
WOOOOSH
I C-CAN'T STOP IT!
WOOOOSH

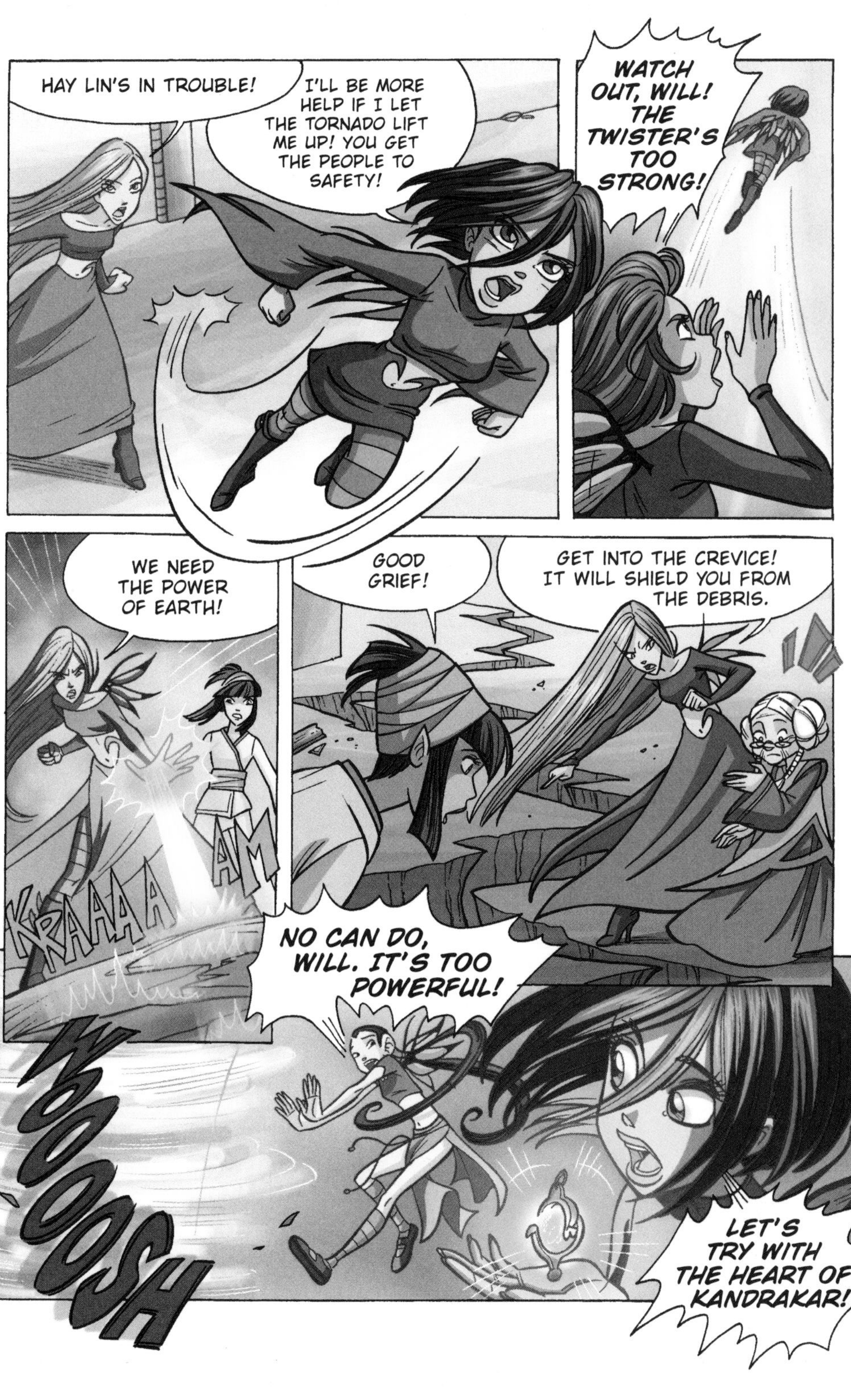
HAY LIN'S IN TROUBLE!
I'LL BE MORE HELP IF I LET THE TORNADO LIFT ME UP! YOU GET THE PEOPLE TO SAFETY!
WATCH OUT, WILL! THE TWISTER'S TOO STRONG!
WE NEED THE POWER OF EARTH!
KRAAAAAM
GOOD GRIEF!
GET INTO THE CREVICE! IT WILL SHIELD YOU FROM THE DEBRIS.
NO CAN DO, WILL. IT'S TOO POWERFUL!
WOOOOSH
LET'S TRY WITH THE HEART OF KANDRAKAR!

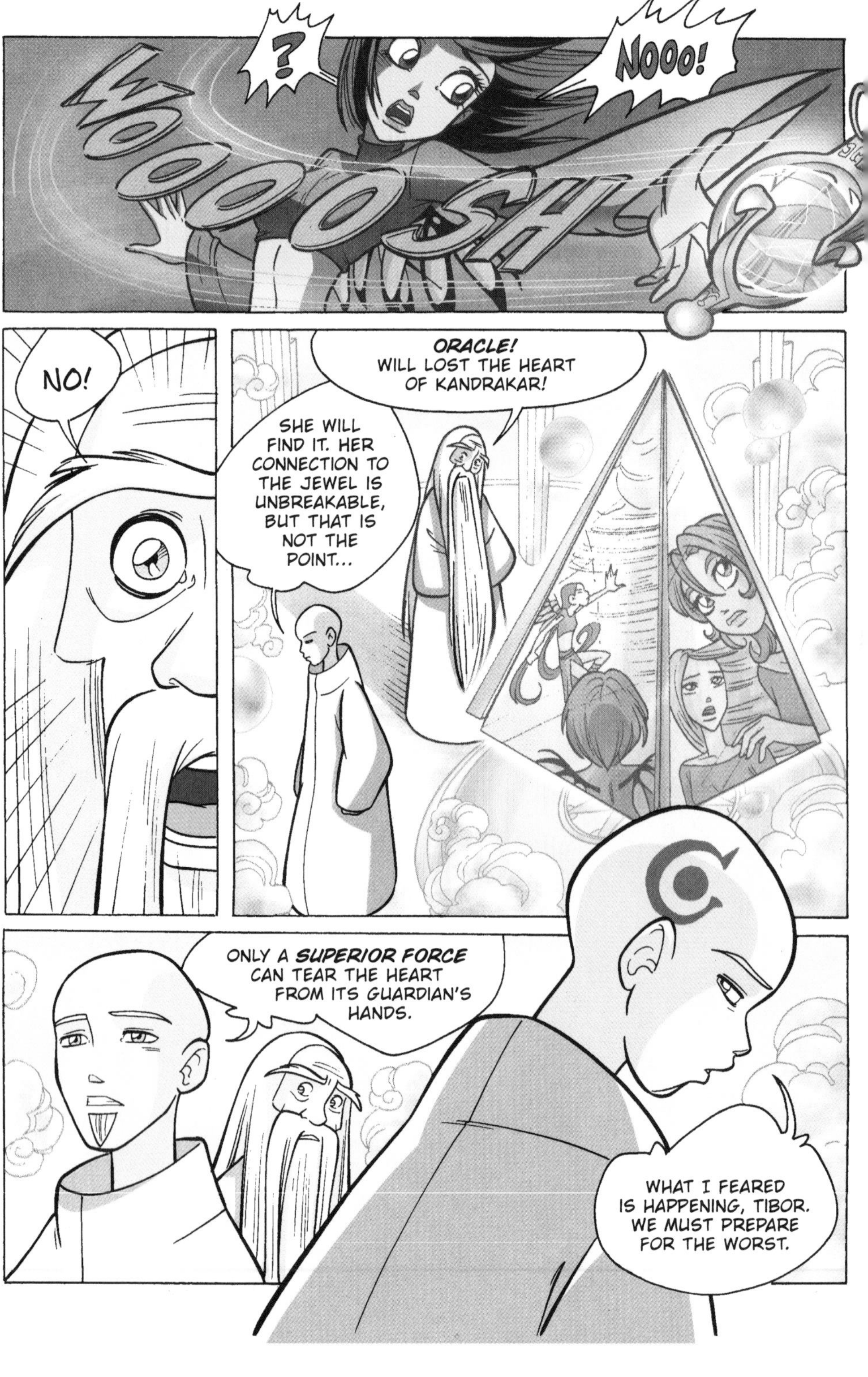
?
NOOO!
WOOOOOSH
NO!
ORACLE! WILL LOST THE HEART OF KANDRAKAR!
SHE WILL FIND IT. HER CONNECTION TO THE JEWEL IS UNBREAKABLE, BUT THAT IS NOT THE POINT...
ONLY A SUPERIOR FORCE CAN TEAR THE HEART FROM ITS GUARDIAN'S HANDS.
WHAT I FEARED IS HAPPENING, TIBOR. WE MUST PREPARE FOR THE WORST.

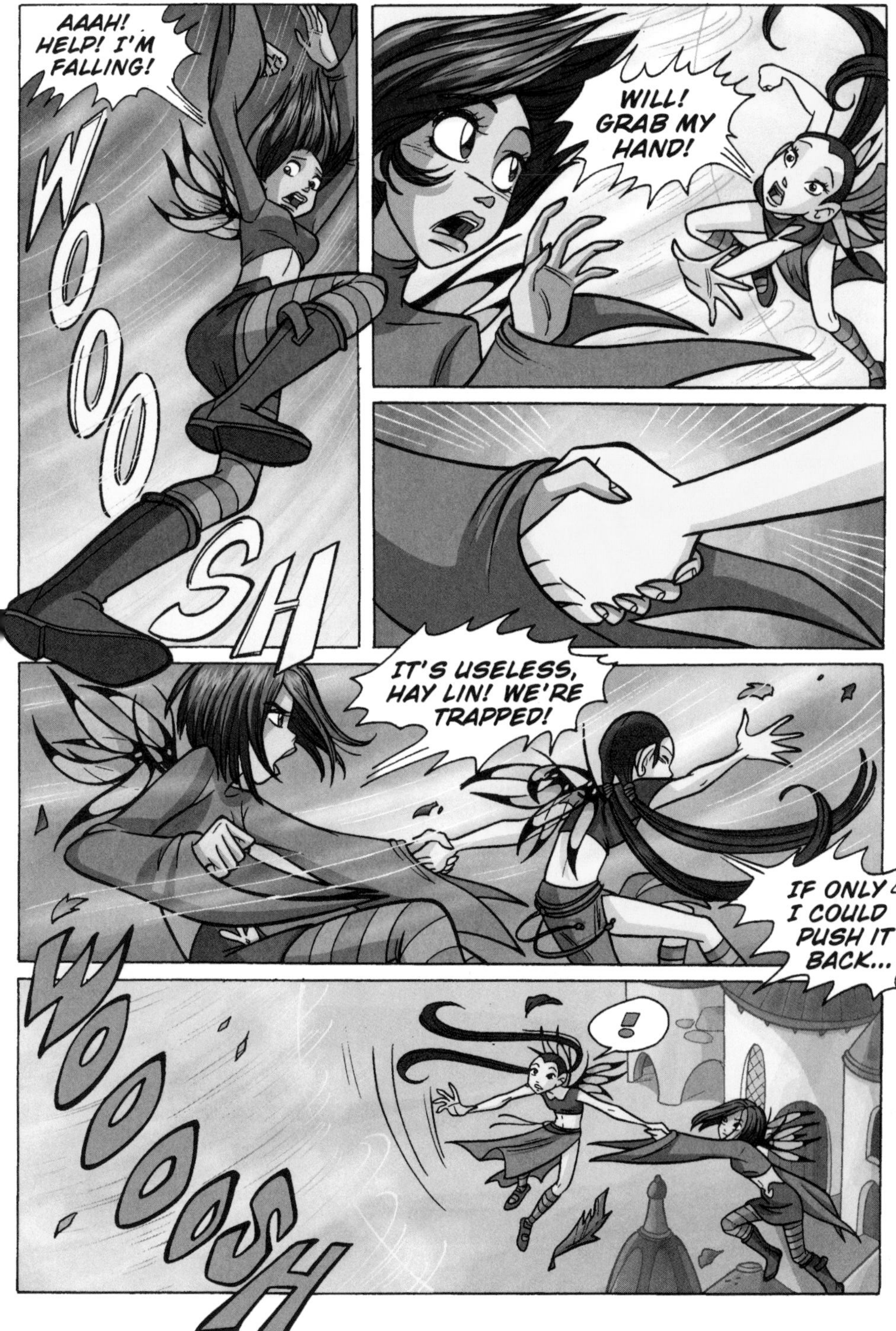
AAAH! HELP! I'M FALLING!
WOOOOSH
WILL! GRAB MY HAND!
IT'S USELESS, HAY LIN! WE'RE TRAPPED!
IF ONLY I COULD PUSH IT BACK...
!
WOOOOOSH

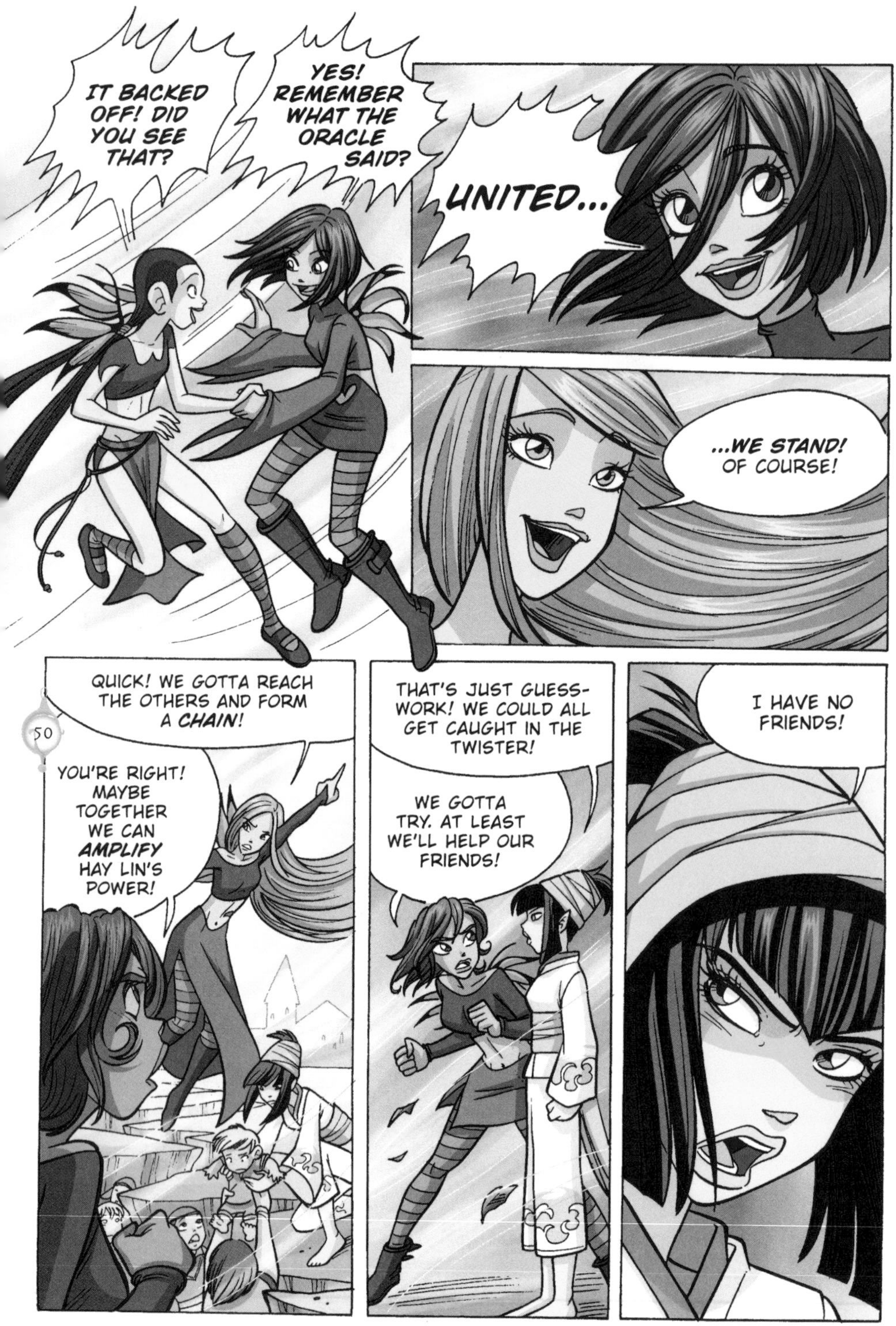
IT BACKED OFF! DID YOU SEE THAT?
YES! REMEMBER WHAT THE ORACLE SAID?
UNITED...
...WE STAND! OF COURSE!
QUICK! WE GOTTA REACH THE OTHERS AND FORM A CHAIN!
YOU'RE RIGHT! MAYBE TOGETHER WE CAN AMPLIFY HAY LIN'S POWER!
THAT'S JUST GUESS-WORK! WE COULD ALL GET CAUGHT IN THE TWISTER!
WE GOTTA TRY. AT LEAST WE'LL HELP OUR FRIENDS!
I HAVE NO FRIENDS!

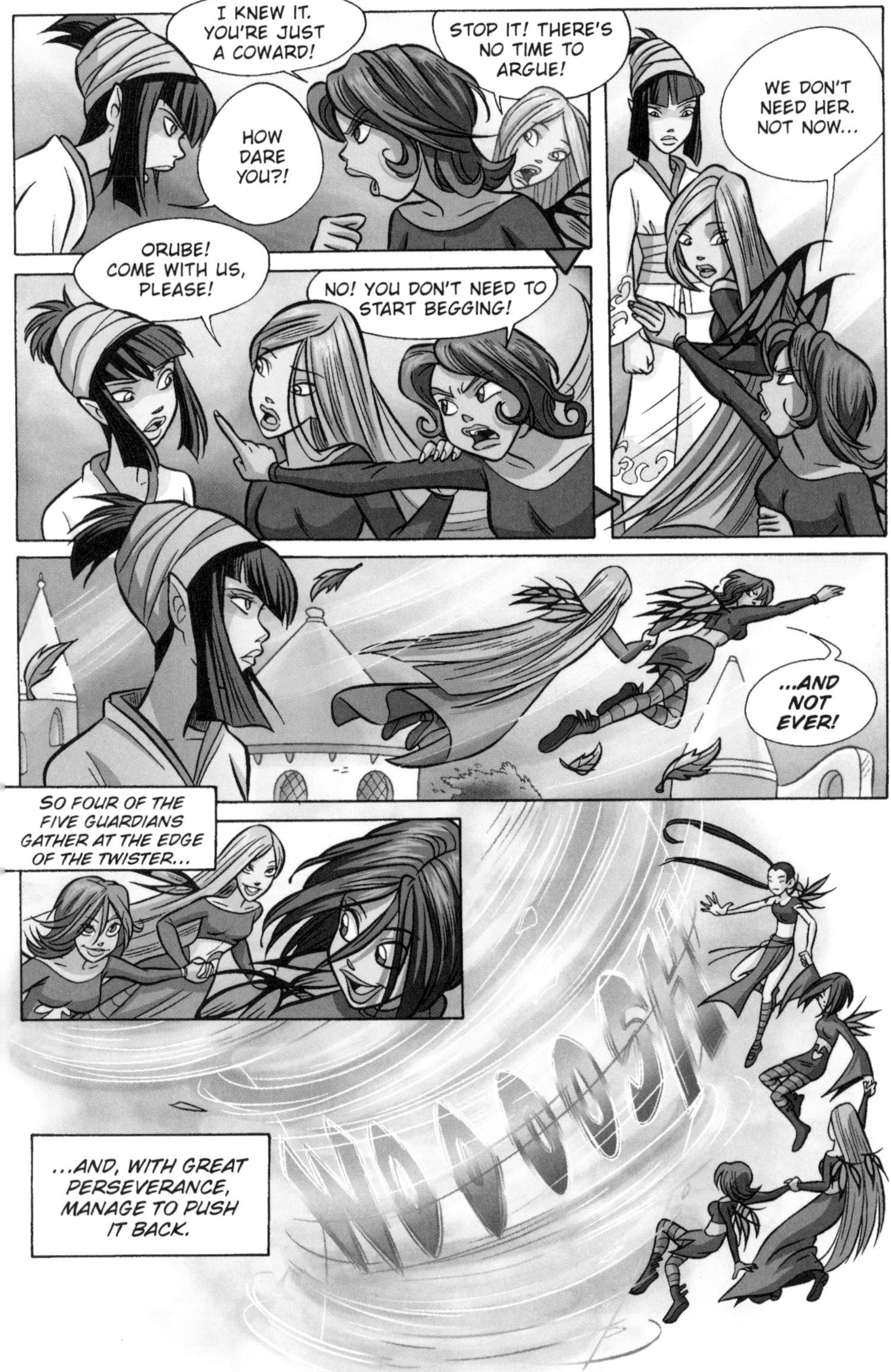
I KNEW IT. YOU'RE JUST A COWARD!
HOW DARE YOU?!
STOP IT! THERE'S NO TIME TO ARGUE!
WE DON'T NEED HER. NOT NOW...
ORUBE! COME WITH US, PLEASE!
NO! YOU DON'T NEED TO START BEGGING!
...AND NOT EVER!
SO FOUR OF THE FIVE GUARDIANS GATHER AT THE EDGE OF THE TWISTER...
WHOOOOSH
...AND, WITH GREAT PERSEVERANCE, MANAGE TO PUSH IT BACK.

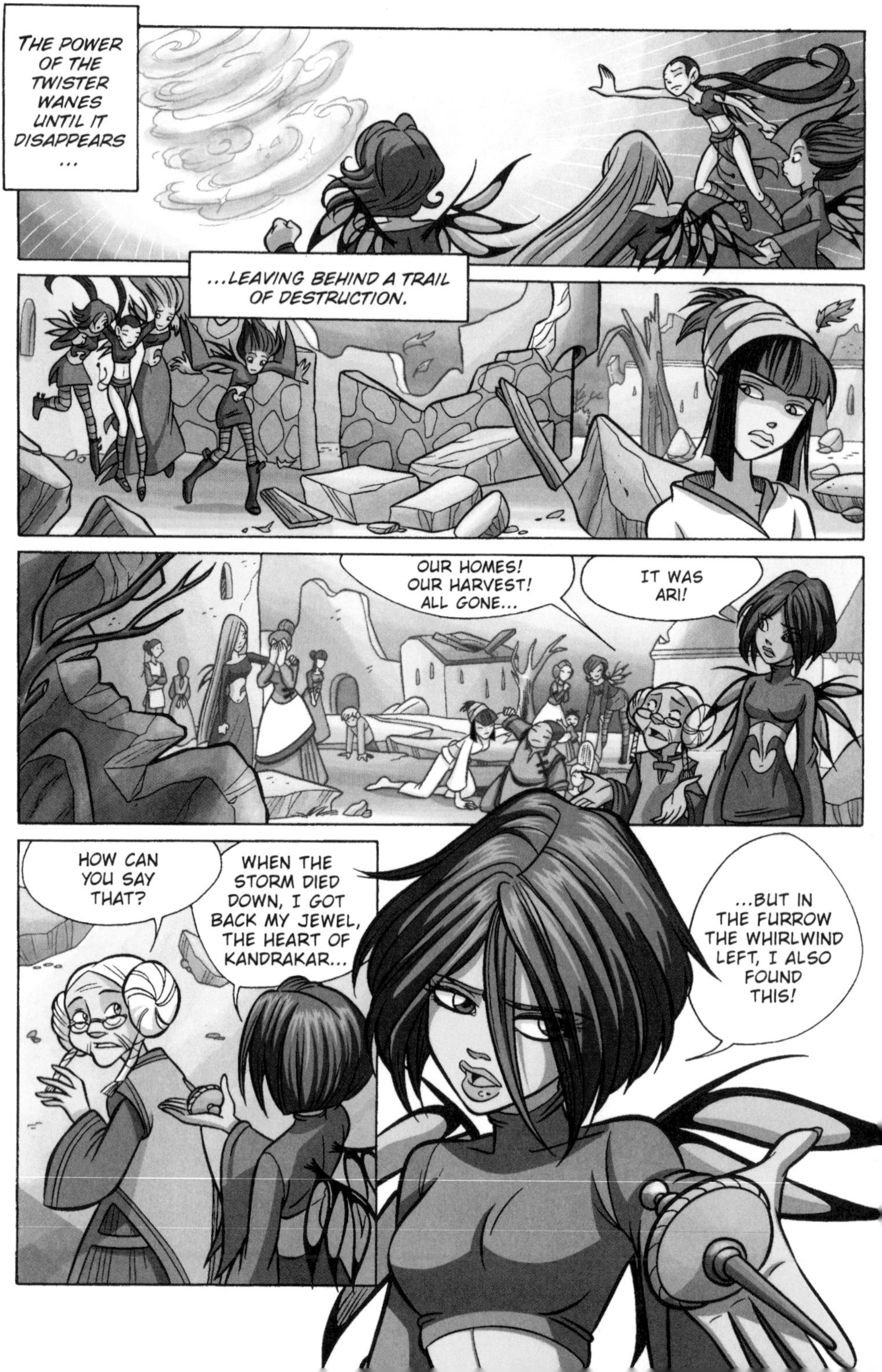
THE POWER OF THE TWISTER WANES UNTIL IT DISAPPEARS ...
...LEAVING BEHIND A TRAIL OF DESTRUCTION.
OUR HOMES! OUR HARVEST! ALL GONE...
IT WAS ARI!
HOW CAN YOU SAY THAT?
WHEN THE STORM DIED DOWN, I GOT BACK MY JEWEL, THE HEART OF KANDRAKAR...
...BUT IN THE FURROW THE WHIRLWIND LEFT, I ALSO FOUND THIS!

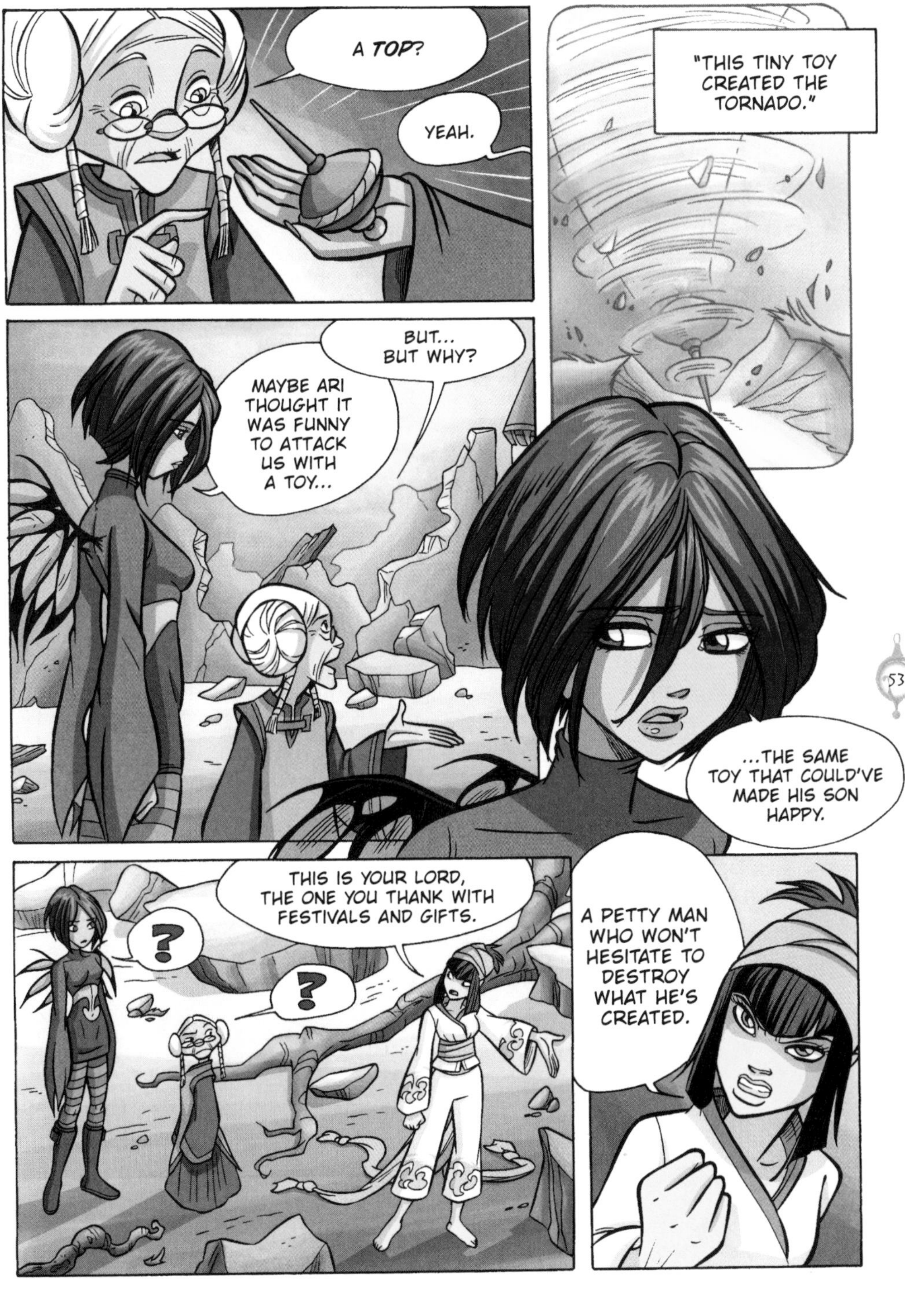
A TOP?
YEAH.
"THIS TINY TOY CREATED THE TORNADO."
BUT... BUT WHY?
MAYBE ARI THOUGHT IT WAS FUNNY TO ATTACK US WITH A TOY...
...THE SAME TOY THAT COULD'VE MADE HIS SON HAPPY.
?
?
THIS IS YOUR LORD, THE ONE YOU THANK WITH FESTIVALS AND GIFTS.
A PETTY MAN WHO WON'T HESITATE TO DESTROY WHAT HE'S CREATED.

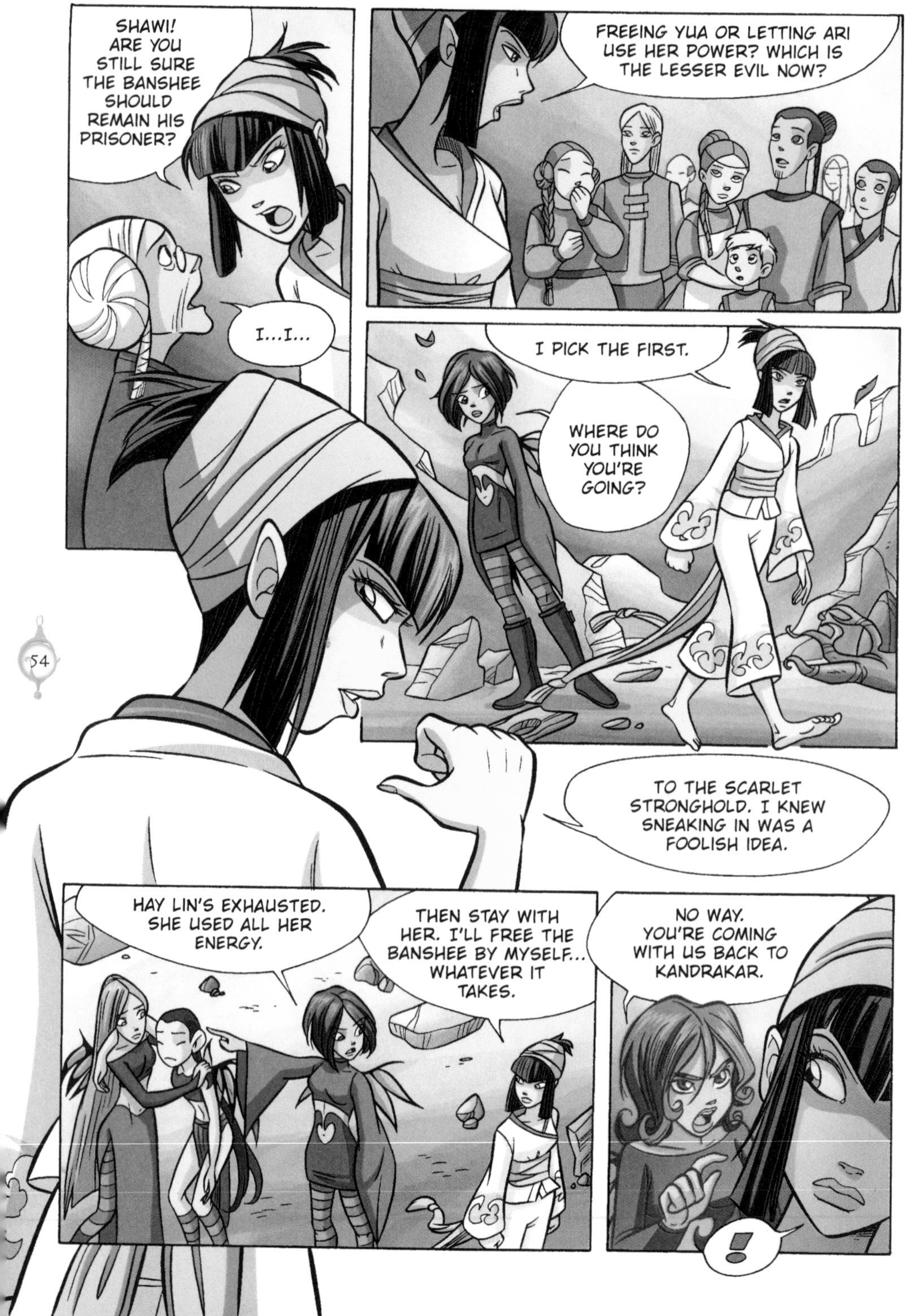
SHAWI! ARE YOU STILL SURE THE BANSHEE SHOULD REMAIN HIS PRISONER?
FREEING YUA OR LETTING ARI USE HER POWER? WHICH IS THE LESSER EVIL NOW?
I...I...
I PICK THE FIRST.
WHERE DO YOU THINK YOU'RE GOING?
TO THE SCARLET STRONGHOLD. I KNEW SNEAKING IN WAS A FOOLISH IDEA.
HAY LIN'S EXHAUSTED. SHE USED ALL HER ENERGY.
THEN STAY WITH HER. I'LL FREE THE BANSHEE BY MYSELF... WHATEVER IT TAKES.
NO WAY. YOU'RE COMING WITH US BACK TO KANDRAKAR.
!

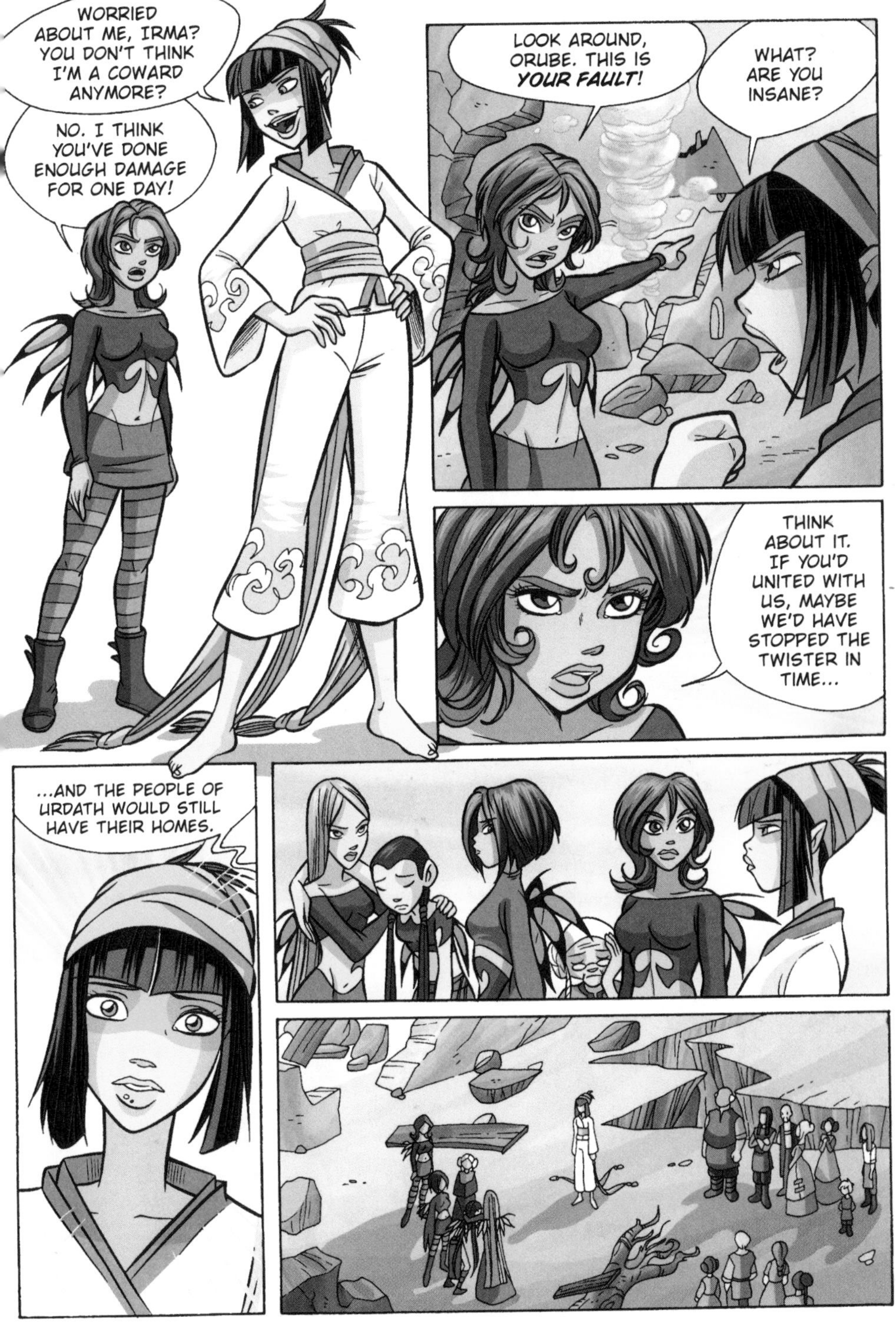
WORRIED ABOUT ME, IRMA? YOU DON'T THINK I'M A COWARD ANYMORE?
NO. I THINK YOU'VE DONE ENOUGH DAMAGE FOR ONE DAY!
LOOK AROUND, ORUBE. THIS IS ***YOUR FAULT***!
WHAT? ARE YOU INSANE?
THINK ABOUT IT. IF YOU'D UNITED WITH US, MAYBE WE'D HAVE STOPPED THE TWISTER IN TIME...
...AND THE PEOPLE OF URDATH WOULD STILL HAVE THEIR HOMES.

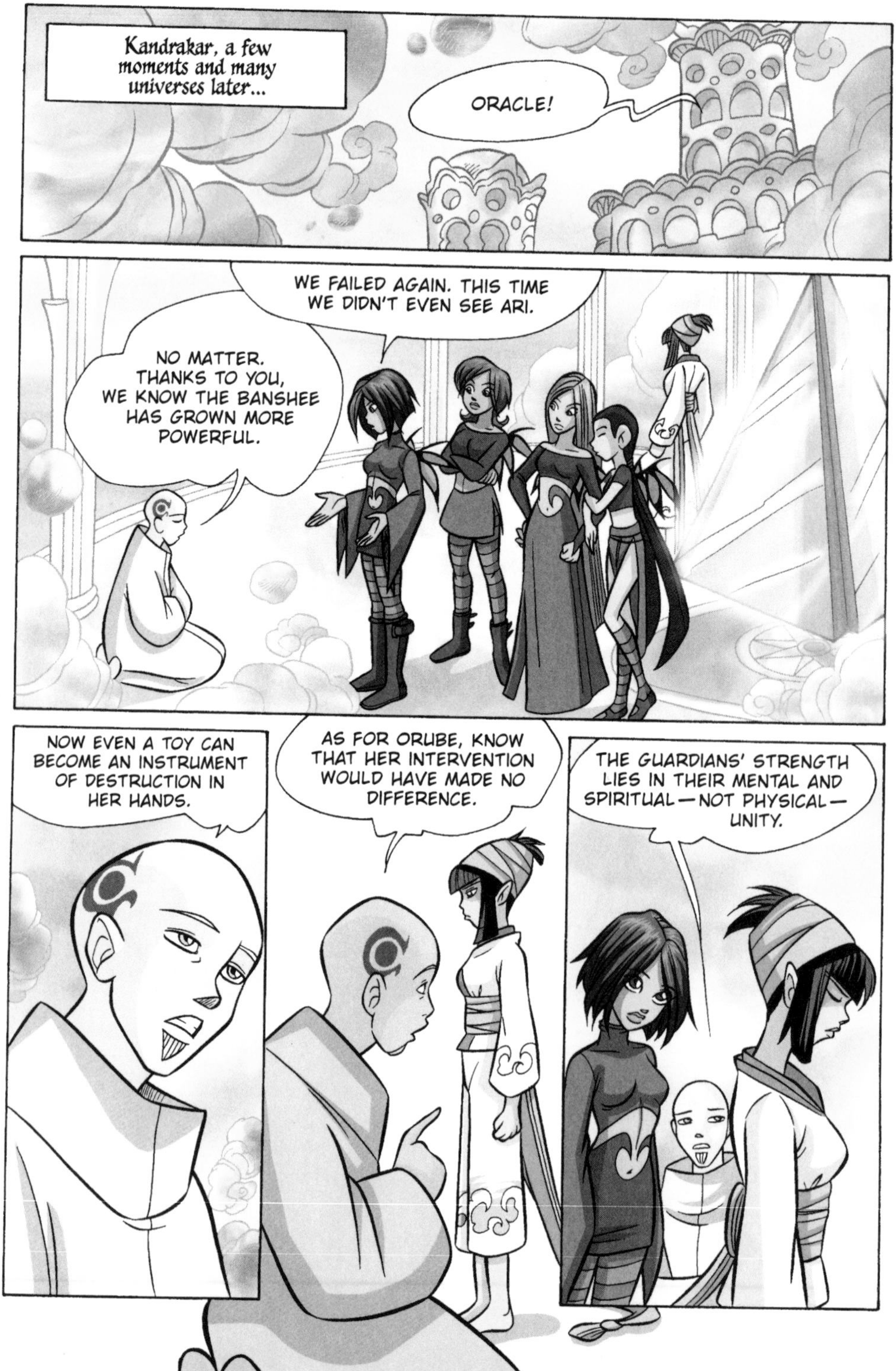
Kandrakar, a few moments and many universes later...
ORACLE!
WE FAILED AGAIN. THIS TIME WE DIDN'T EVEN SEE ARI.
NO MATTER. THANKS TO YOU, WE KNOW THE BANSHEE HAS GROWN MORE POWERFUL.
NOW EVEN A TOY CAN BECOME AN INSTRUMENT OF DESTRUCTION IN HER HANDS.
AS FOR ORUBE, KNOW THAT HER INTERVENTION WOULD HAVE MADE NO DIFFERENCE.
THE GUARDIANS' STRENGTH LIES IN THEIR MENTAL AND SPIRITUAL—NOT PHYSICAL—UNITY.

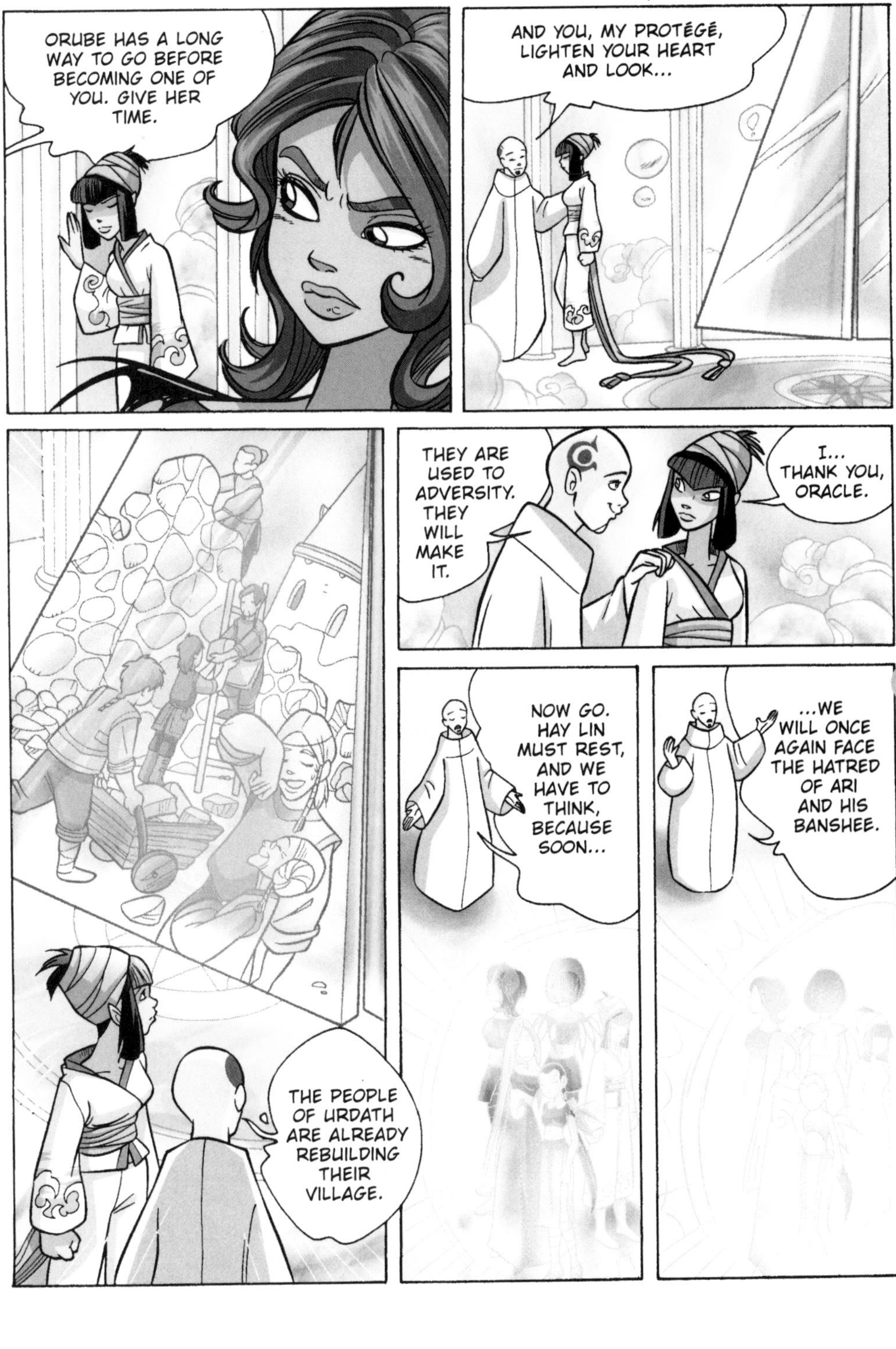

ORUBE HAS A LONG WAY TO GO BEFORE BECOMING ONE OF YOU. GIVE HER TIME.
AND YOU, MY PROTÉGÉ, LIGHTEN YOUR HEART AND LOOK...
THE PEOPLE OF URDATH ARE ALREADY REBUILDING THEIR VILLAGE.
THEY ARE USED TO ADVERSITY. THEY WILL MAKE IT.
I... THANK YOU, ORACLE.
NOW GO. HAY LIN MUST REST, AND WE HAVE TO THINK, BECAUSE SOON...
...WE WILL ONCE AGAIN FACE THE HATRED OF ARI AND HIS BANSHEE.

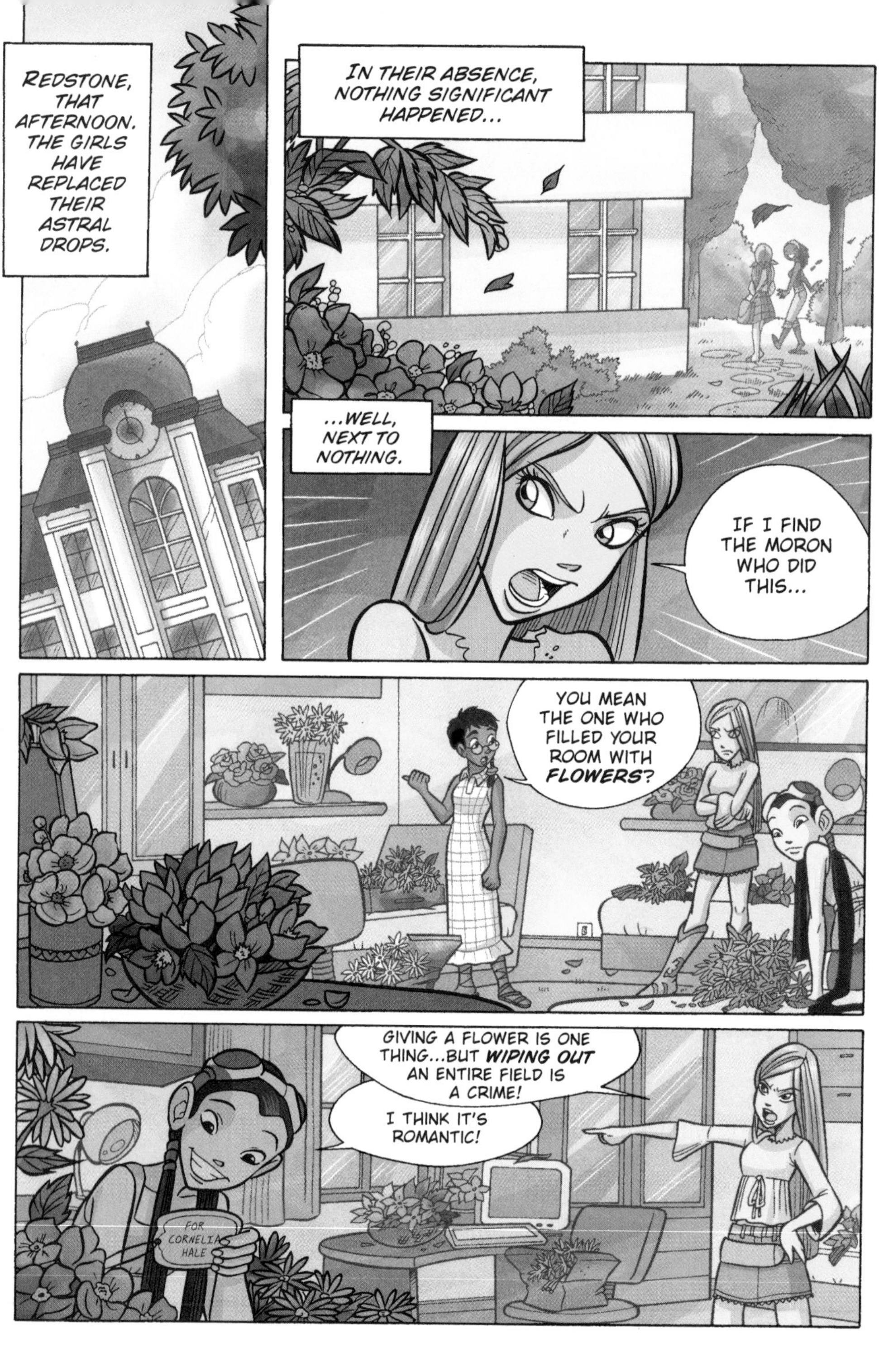

REDSTONE, THAT AFTERNOON. THE GIRLS HAVE REPLACED THEIR ASTRAL DROPS.
IN THEIR ABSENCE, NOTHING SIGNIFICANT HAPPENED...
...WELL, NEXT TO NOTHING.
IF I FIND THE MORON WHO DID THIS...
YOU MEAN THE ONE WHO FILLED YOUR ROOM WITH **FLOWERS**?
GIVING A FLOWER IS ONE THING...BUT **WIPING OUT** AN ENTIRE FIELD IS A CRIME!
I THINK IT'S ROMANTIC!
FOR CORNELIA HALE

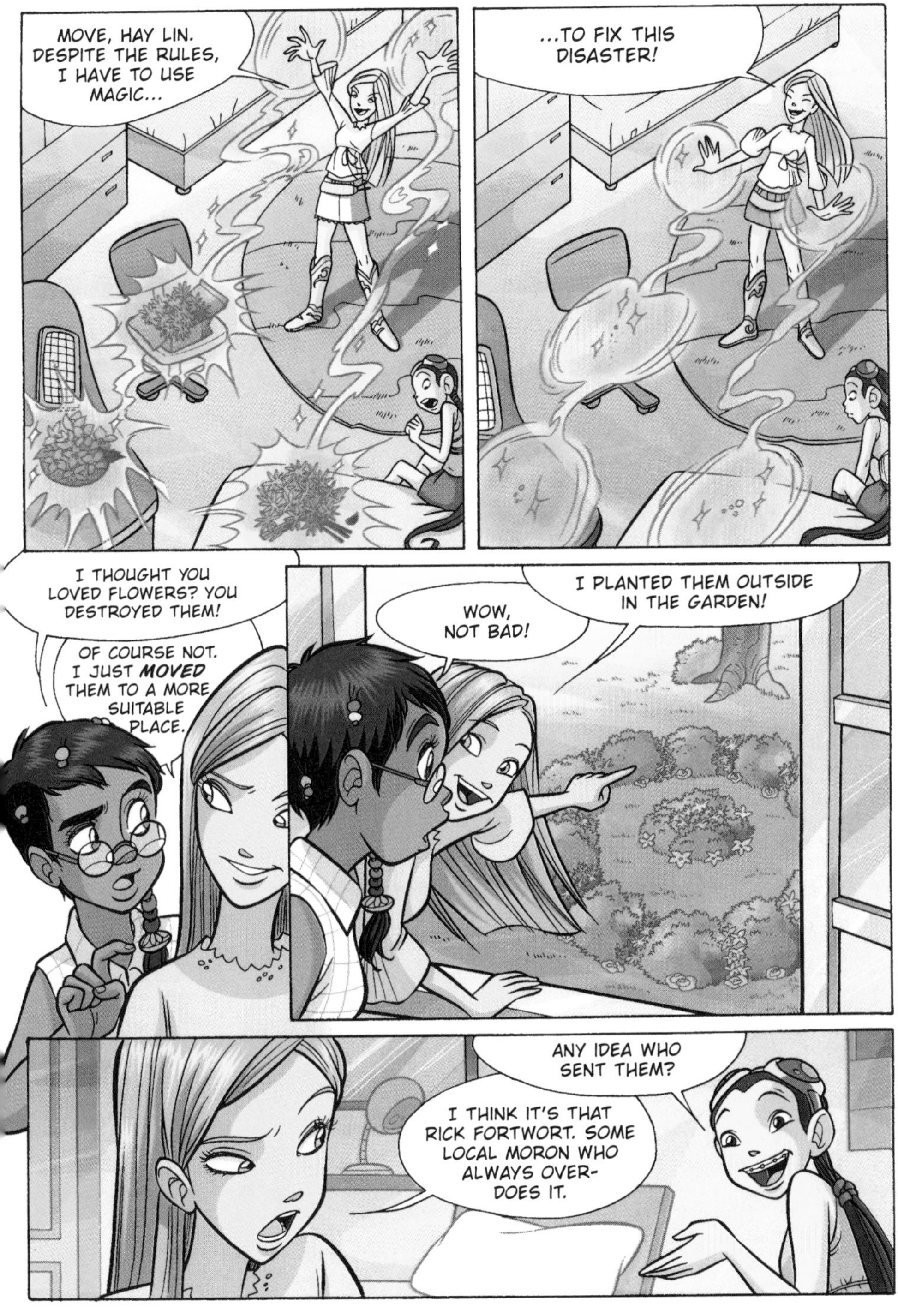

MOVE, HAY LIN. DESPITE THE RULES, I HAVE TO USE MAGIC...
...TO FIX THIS DISASTER!
I THOUGHT YOU LOVED FLOWERS? YOU DESTROYED THEM!
OF COURSE NOT. I JUST *MOVED* THEM TO A MORE SUITABLE PLACE.
WOW, NOT BAD!
I PLANTED THEM OUTSIDE IN THE GARDEN!
ANY IDEA WHO SENT THEM?
I THINK IT'S THAT RICK FORTWORT. SOME LOCAL MORON WHO ALWAYS OVER-DOES IT.

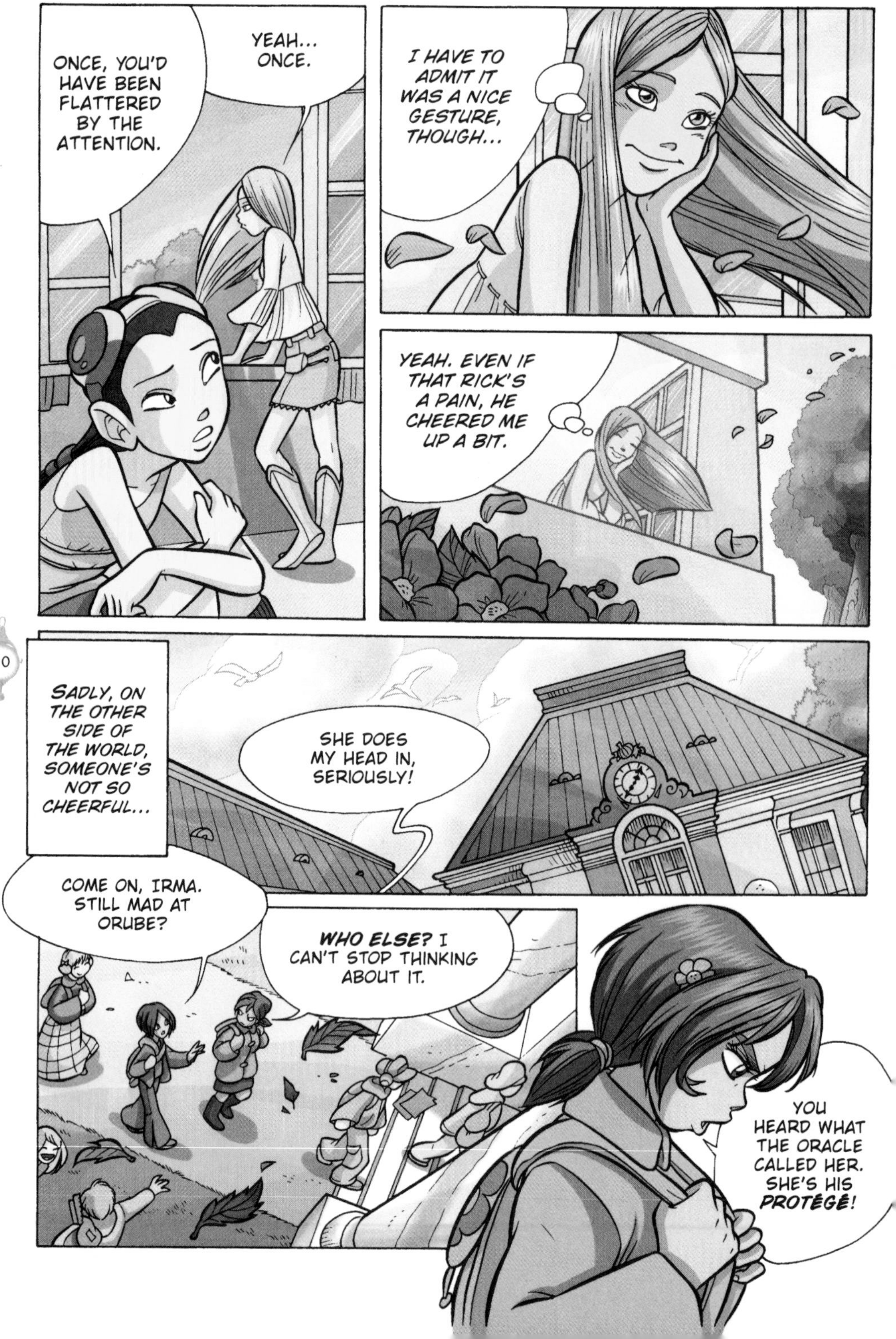
ONCE, YOU'D HAVE BEEN FLATTERED BY THE ATTENTION.
YEAH... ONCE.
I HAVE TO ADMIT IT WAS A NICE GESTURE, THOUGH...
YEAH. EVEN IF THAT RICK'S A PAIN, HE CHEERED ME UP A BIT.
SADLY, ON THE OTHER SIDE OF THE WORLD, SOMEONE'S NOT SO CHEERFUL...
SHE DOES MY HEAD IN, SERIOUSLY!
COME ON, IRMA. STILL MAD AT ORUBE?
WHO ELSE? I CAN'T STOP THINKING ABOUT IT.
YOU HEARD WHAT THE ORACLE CALLED HER. SHE'S HIS PROTÉGÉ!

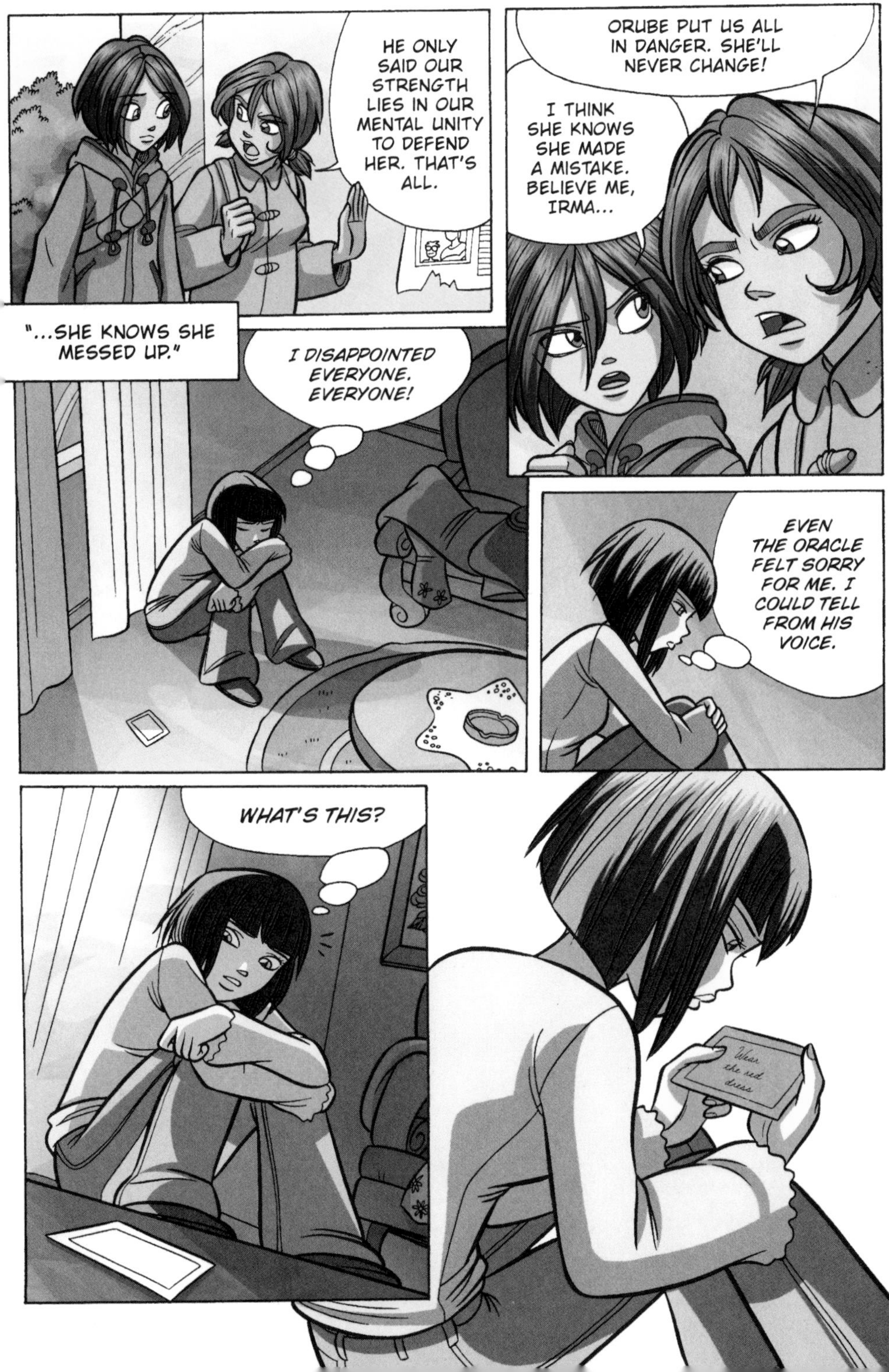

HE ONLY SAID OUR STRENGTH LIES IN OUR MENTAL UNITY TO DEFEND HER. THAT'S ALL.
ORUBE PUT US ALL IN DANGER. SHE'LL NEVER CHANGE!
I THINK SHE KNOWS SHE MADE A MISTAKE. BELIEVE ME, IRMA...
"...SHE KNOWS SHE MESSED UP."
I DISAPPOINTED EVERYONE. EVERYONE!
EVEN THE ORACLE FELT SORRY FOR ME. I COULD TELL FROM HIS VOICE.
WHAT'S THIS?
Wear the red dress

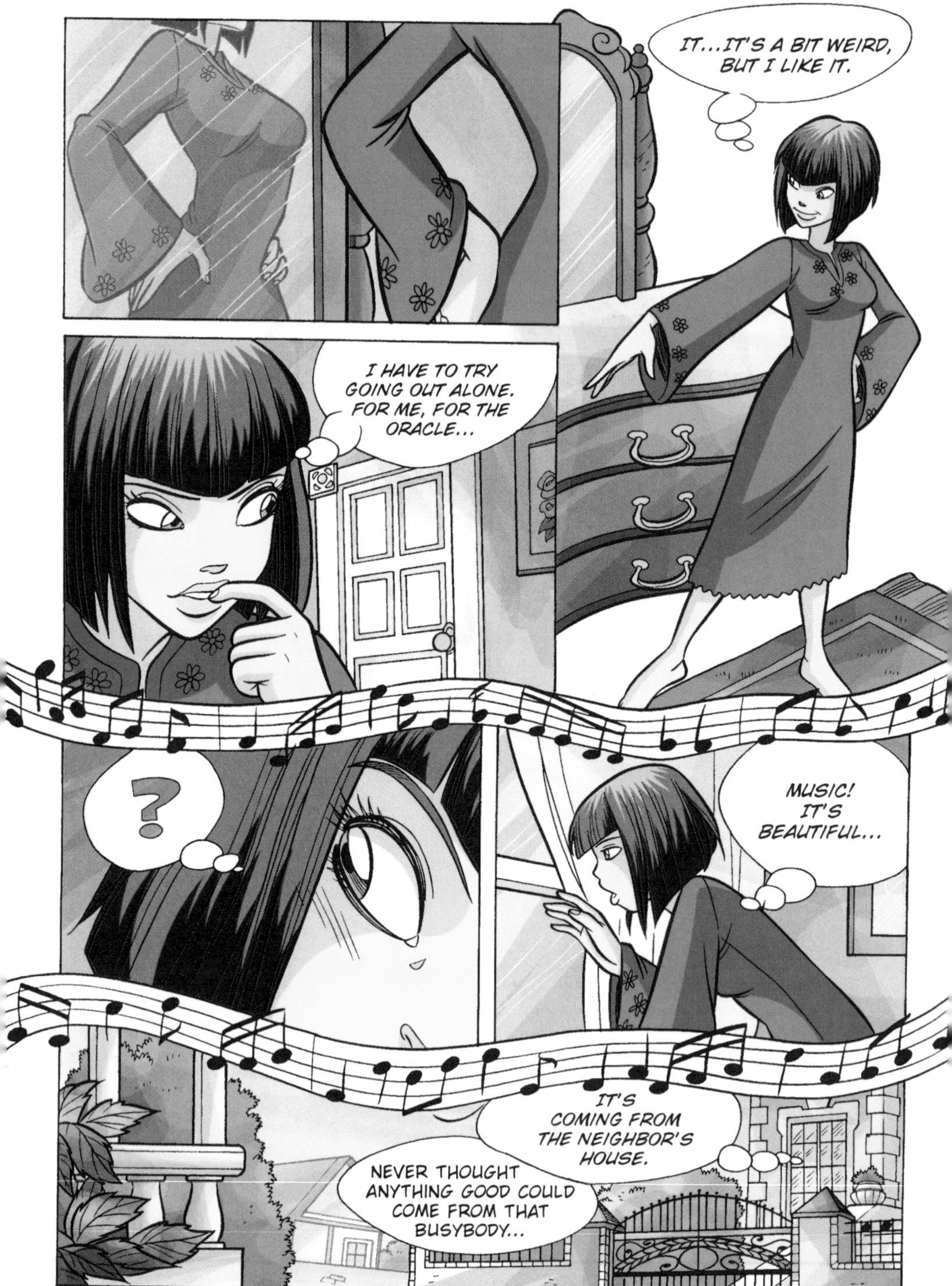
IT...IT'S A BIT WEIRD, BUT I LIKE IT.
I HAVE TO TRY GOING OUT ALONE. FOR ME, FOR THE ORACLE...
?
MUSIC! IT'S BEAUTIFUL...
IT'S COMING FROM THE NEIGHBOR'S HOUSE.
NEVER THOUGHT ANYTHING GOOD COULD COME FROM THAT BUSYBODY...

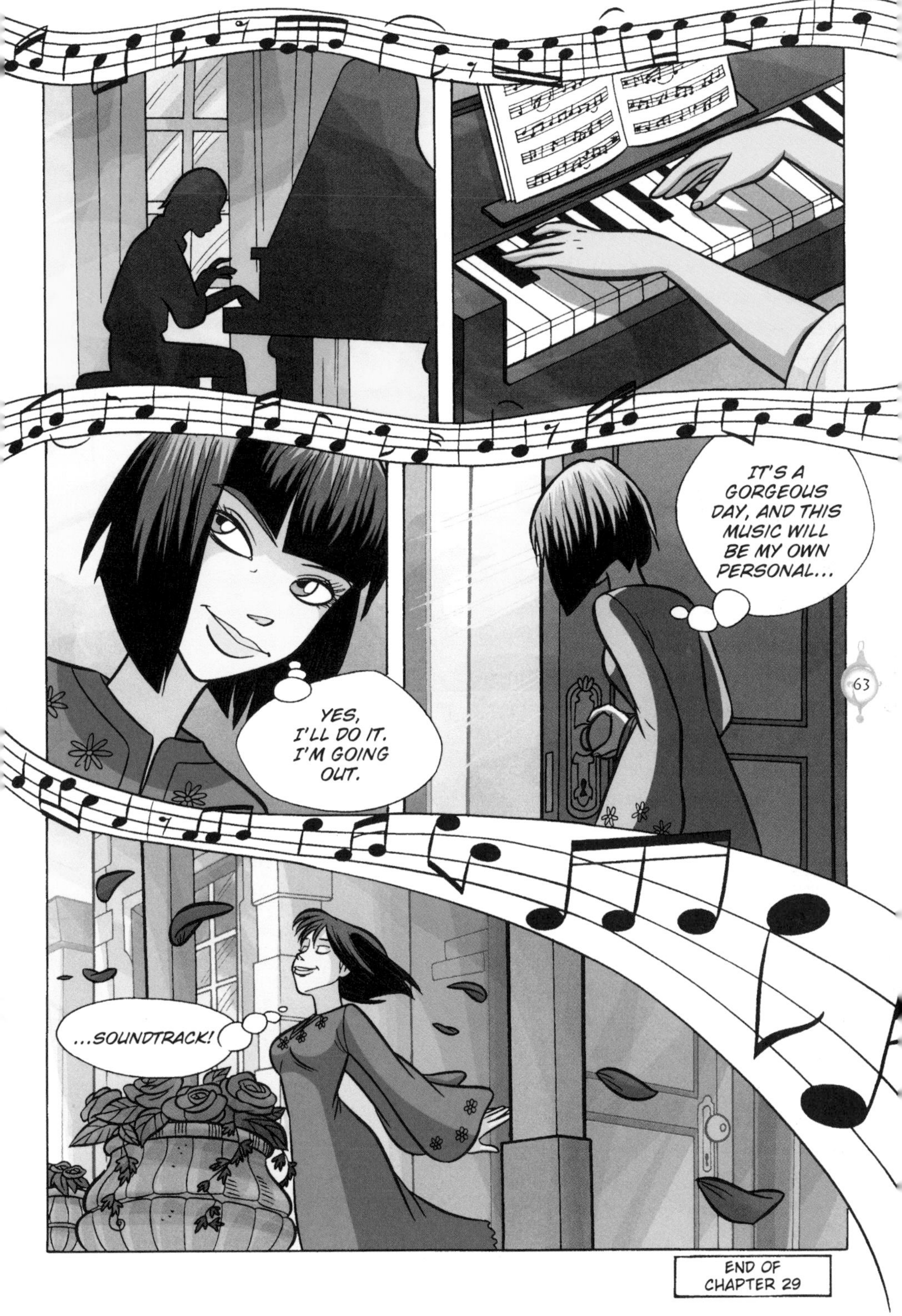
IT'S A GORGEOUS DAY, AND THIS MUSIC WILL BE MY OWN PERSONAL...
YES, I'LL DO IT. I'M GOING OUT.
...SOUNDTRACK!

END OF CHAPTER 29

W.i.t.c.h.

Will   Irma   Taranee   Cornelia   Hay Lin

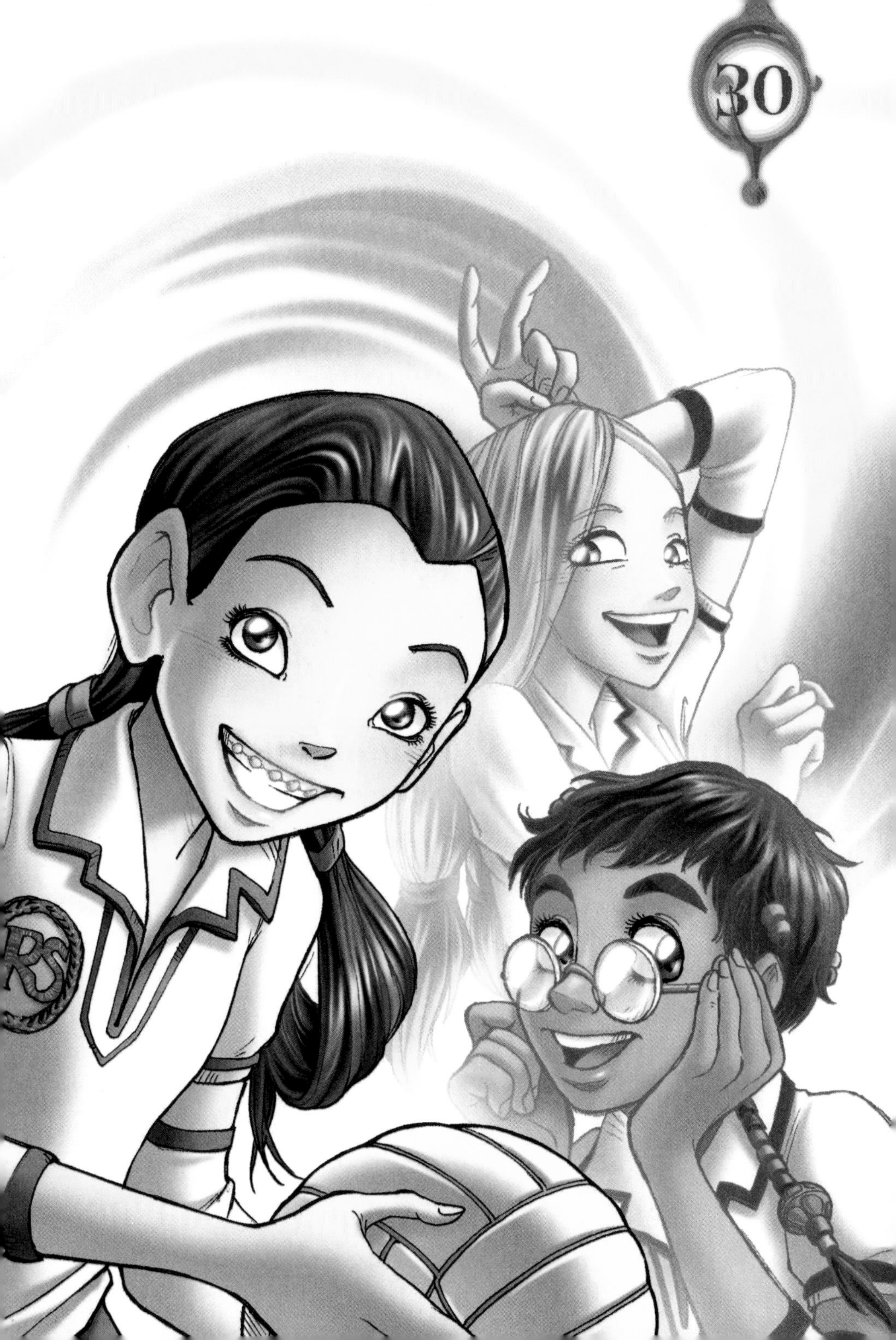

30

The Path of the Wind

"We're people with feelings! That means something!"

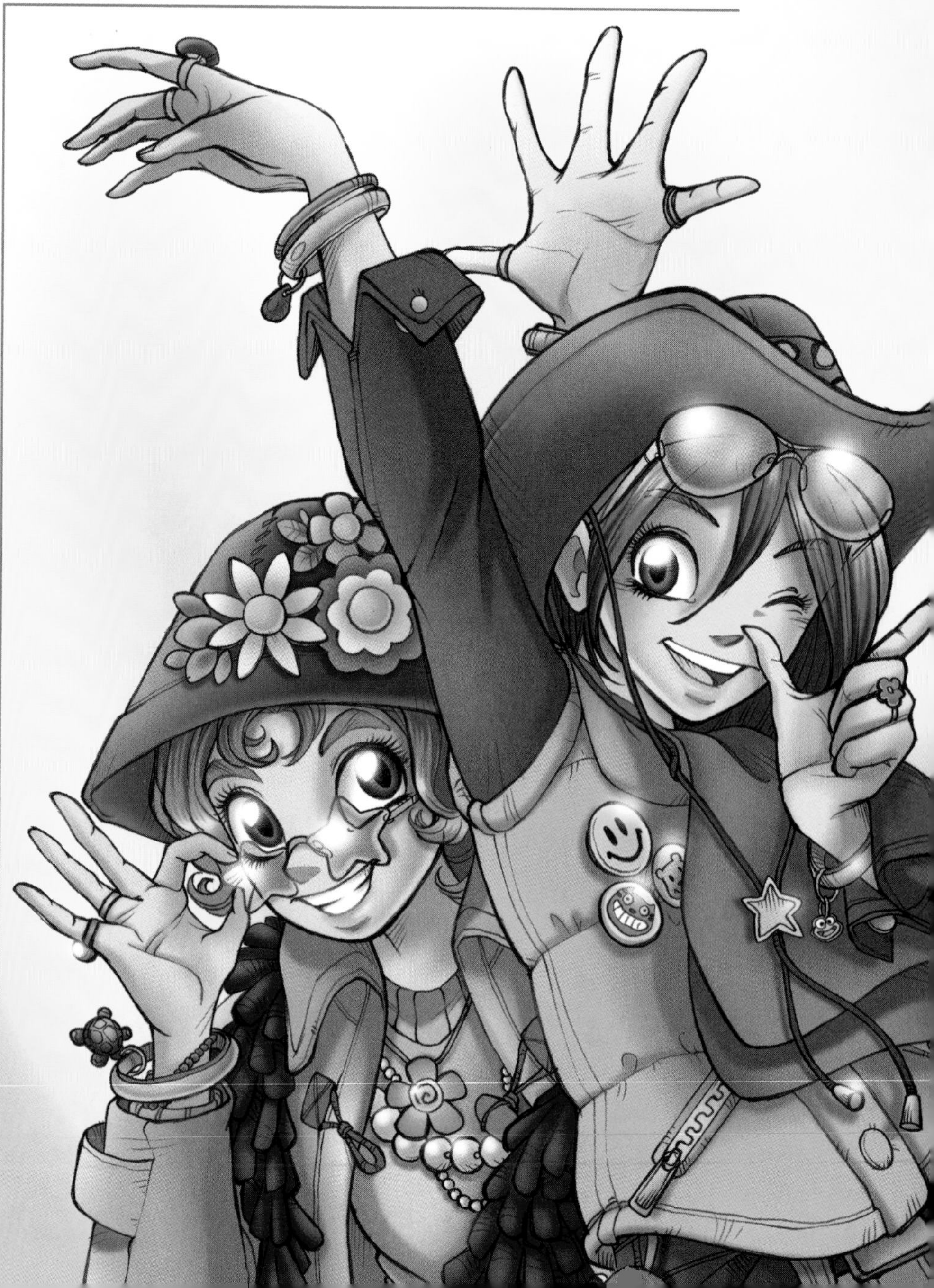

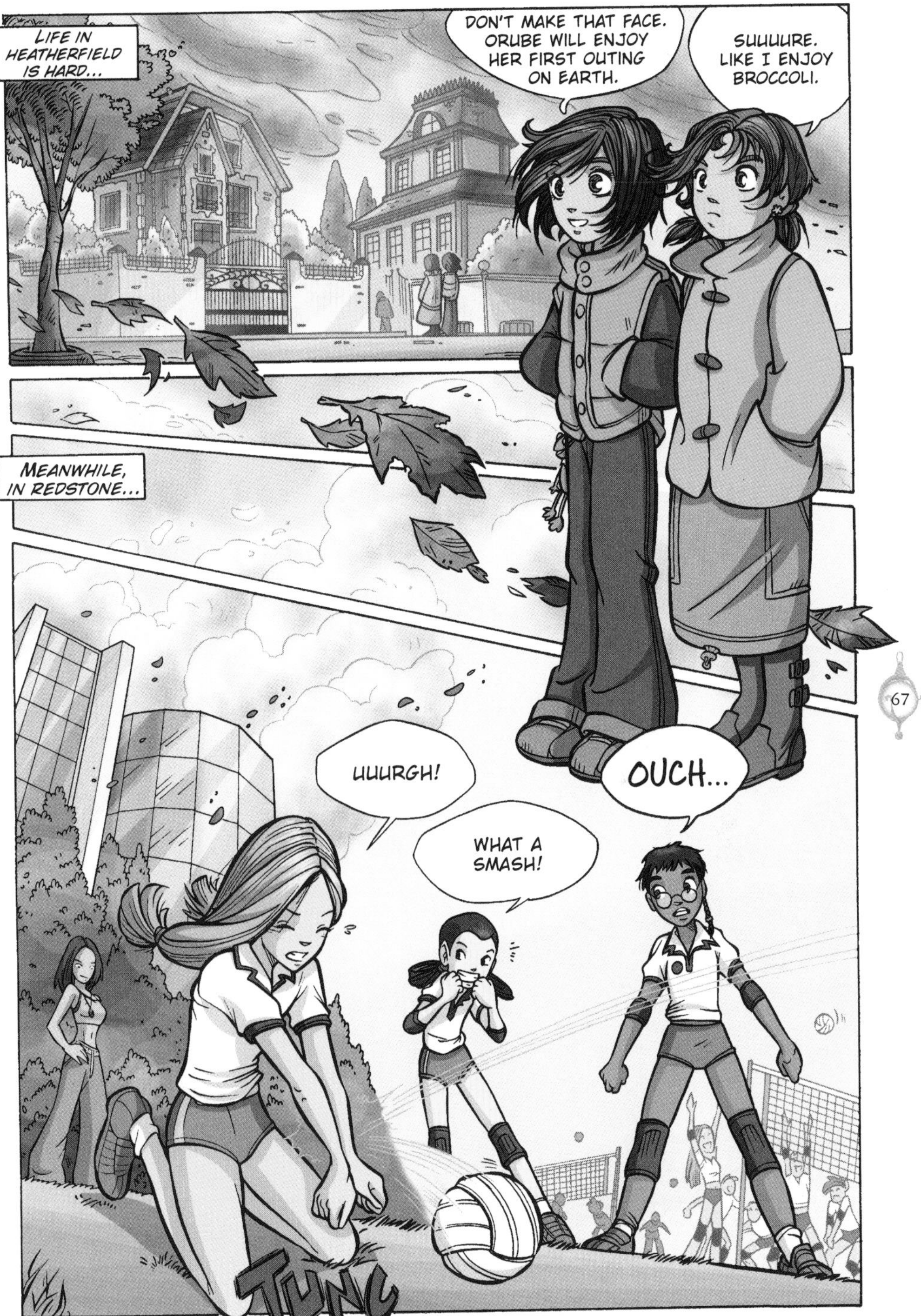

LIFE IN HEATHERFIELD IS HARD...
DON'T MAKE THAT FACE. ORUBE WILL ENJOY HER FIRST OUTING ON EARTH.
SUUUURE. LIKE I ENJOY BROCCOLI.
MEANWHILE, IN REDSTONE...
UUURGH!
OUCH...
WHAT A SMASH!
TUNC

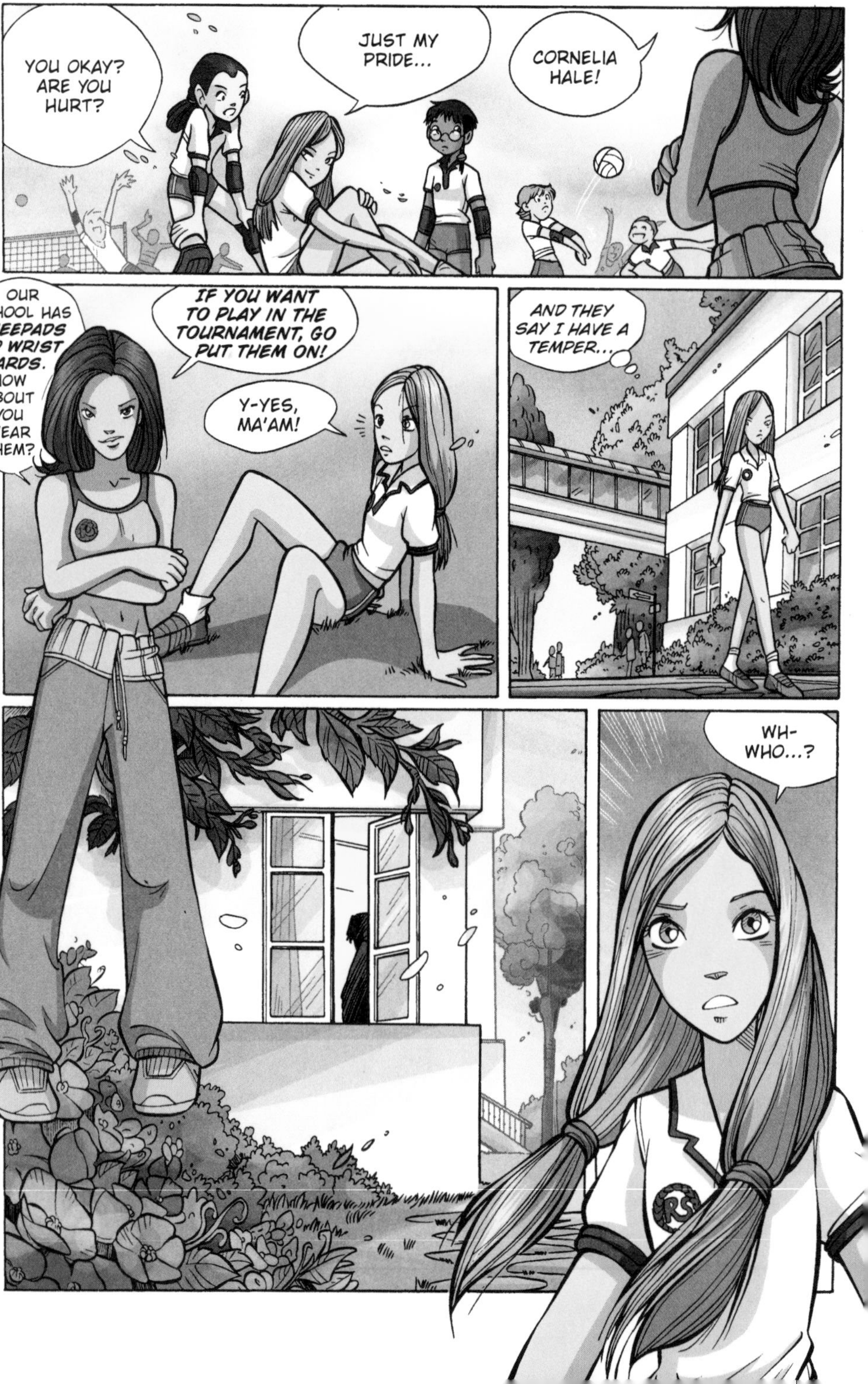
YOU OKAY? ARE YOU HURT?
JUST MY PRIDE...
CORNELIA HALE!
OUR SCHOOL HAS **KNEEPADS AND WRIST GUARDS**. HOW ABOUT YOU WEAR THEM?
IF YOU WANT TO PLAY IN THE TOURNAMENT, GO PUT THEM ON!
Y-YES, MA'AM!
AND THEY SAY I HAVE A TEMPER...
WH- WHO...?

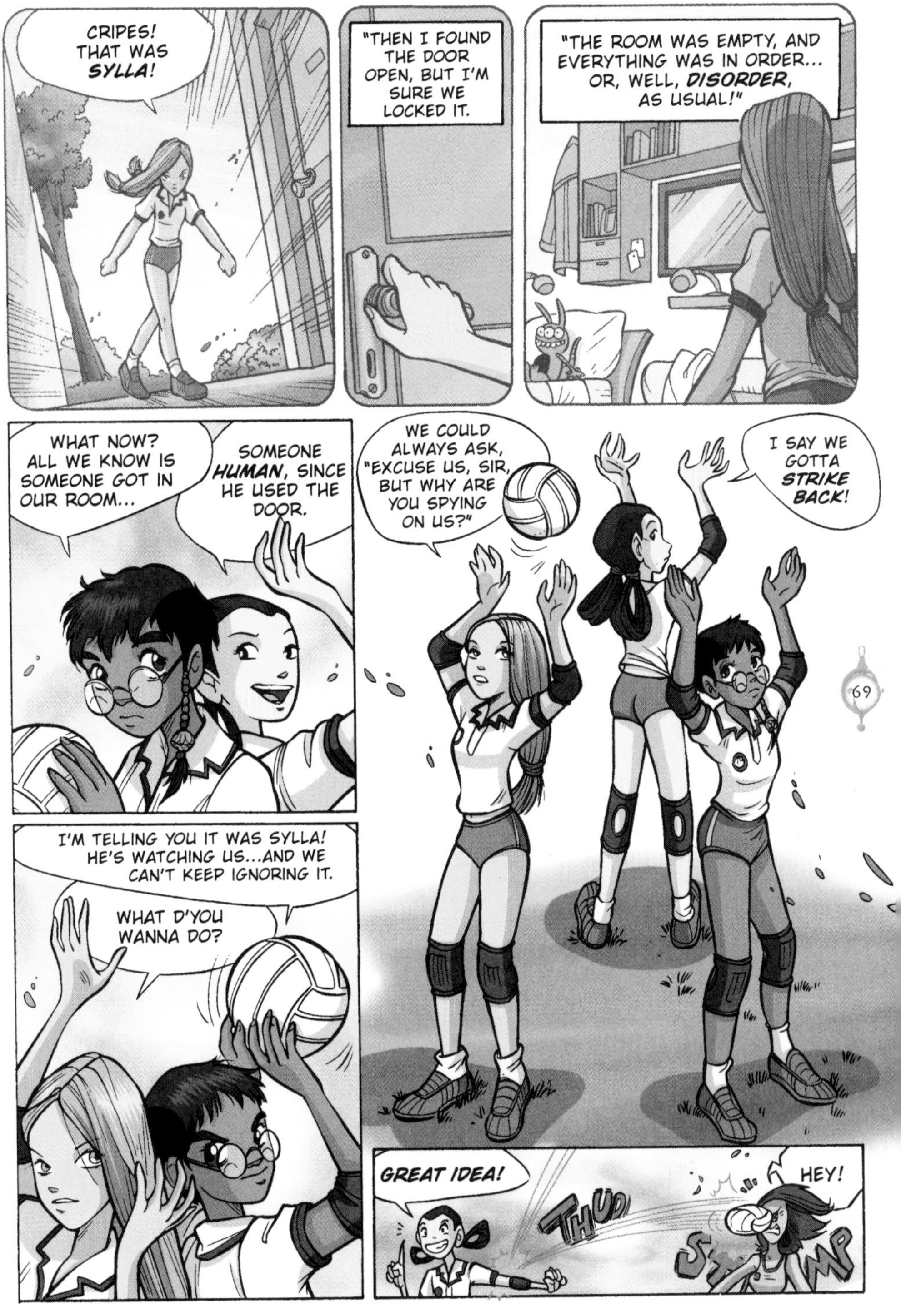

CRIPES! THAT WAS SYLLA!
"THEN I FOUND THE DOOR OPEN, BUT I'M SURE WE LOCKED IT.
"THE ROOM WAS EMPTY, AND EVERYTHING WAS IN ORDER... OR, WELL, DISORDER, AS USUAL!"
WHAT NOW? ALL WE KNOW IS SOMEONE GOT IN OUR ROOM...
SOMEONE HUMAN, SINCE HE USED THE DOOR.
WE COULD ALWAYS ASK, "EXCUSE US, SIR, BUT WHY ARE YOU SPYING ON US?"
I SAY WE GOTTA STRIKE BACK!
I'M TELLING YOU IT WAS SYLLA! HE'S WATCHING US...AND WE CAN'T KEEP IGNORING IT.
WHAT D'YOU WANNA DO?
GREAT IDEA!
THUD
SMP
HEY!

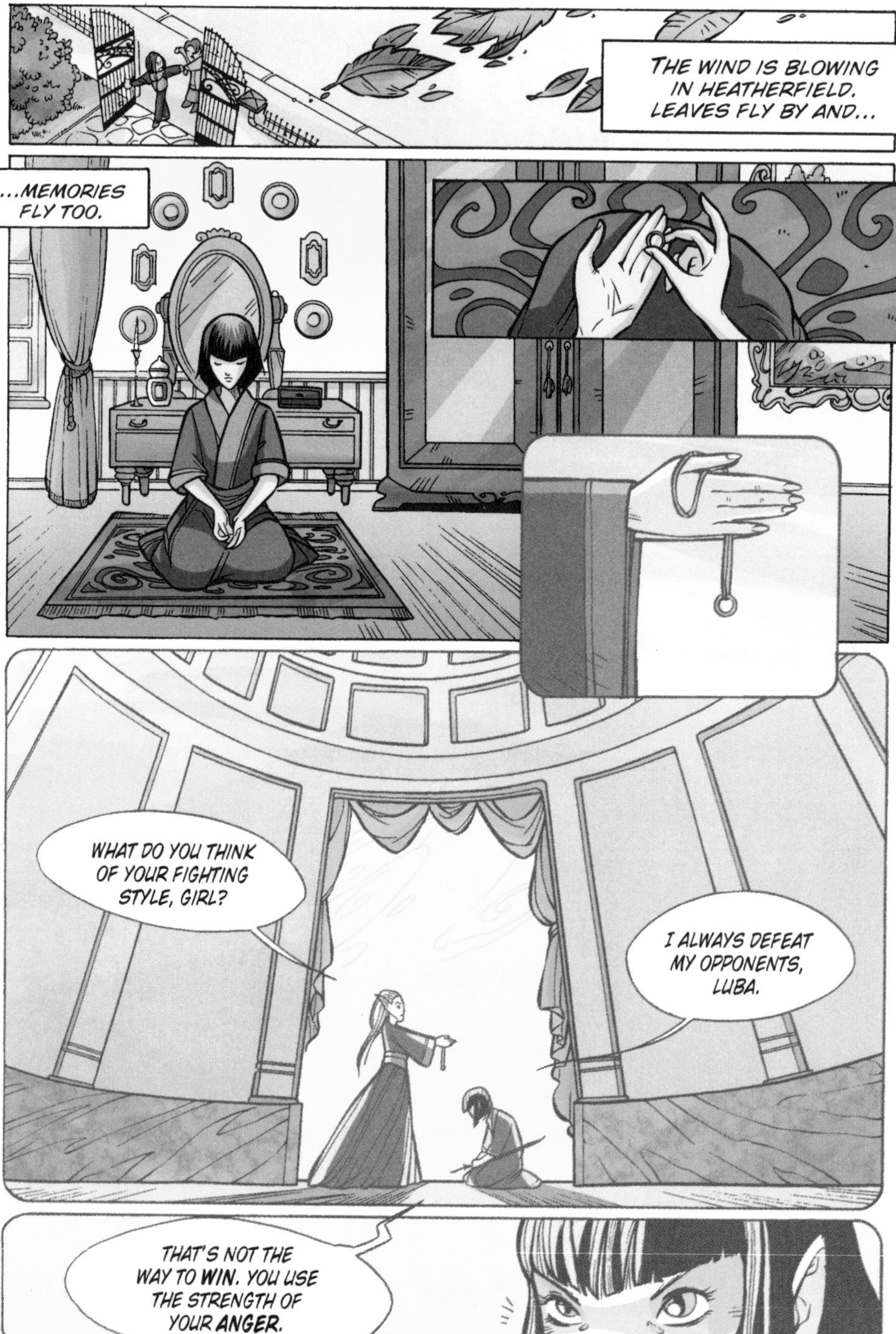
THE WIND IS BLOWING IN HEATHERFIELD. LEAVES FLY BY AND...
...MEMORIES FLY TOO.
WHAT DO YOU THINK OF YOUR FIGHTING STYLE, GIRL?
I ALWAYS DEFEAT MY OPPONENTS, LUBA.
THAT'S NOT THE WAY TO WIN. YOU USE THE STRENGTH OF YOUR ANGER.

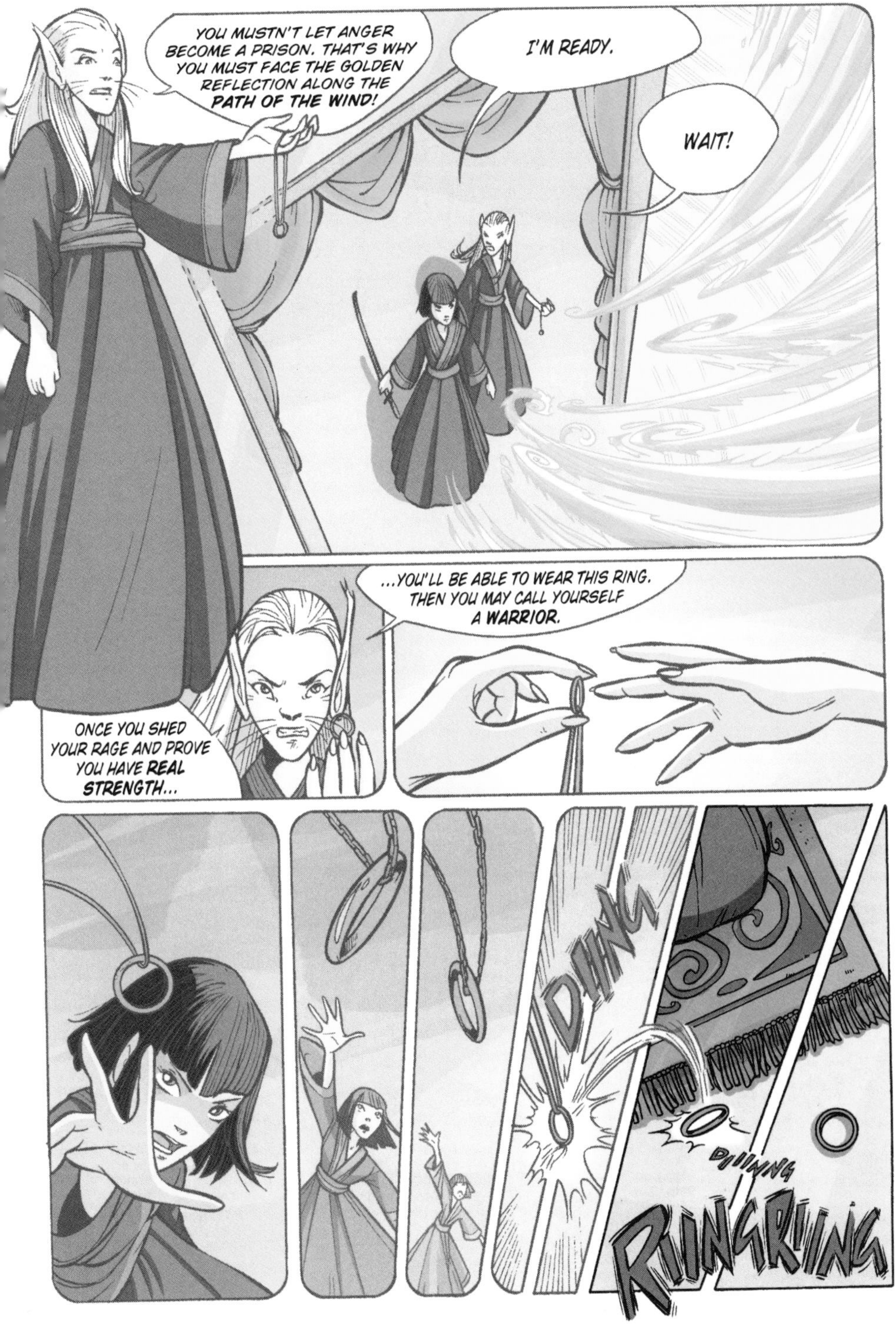
YOU MUSTN'T LET ANGER BECOME A PRISON. THAT'S WHY YOU MUST FACE THE GOLDEN REFLECTION ALONG THE PATH OF THE WIND!
I'M READY.
WAIT!
ONCE YOU SHED YOUR RAGE AND PROVE YOU HAVE REAL STRENGTH...
...YOU'LL BE ABLE TO WEAR THIS RING. THEN YOU MAY CALL YOURSELF A WARRIOR.
DIING
DIIING
RIINGRIING

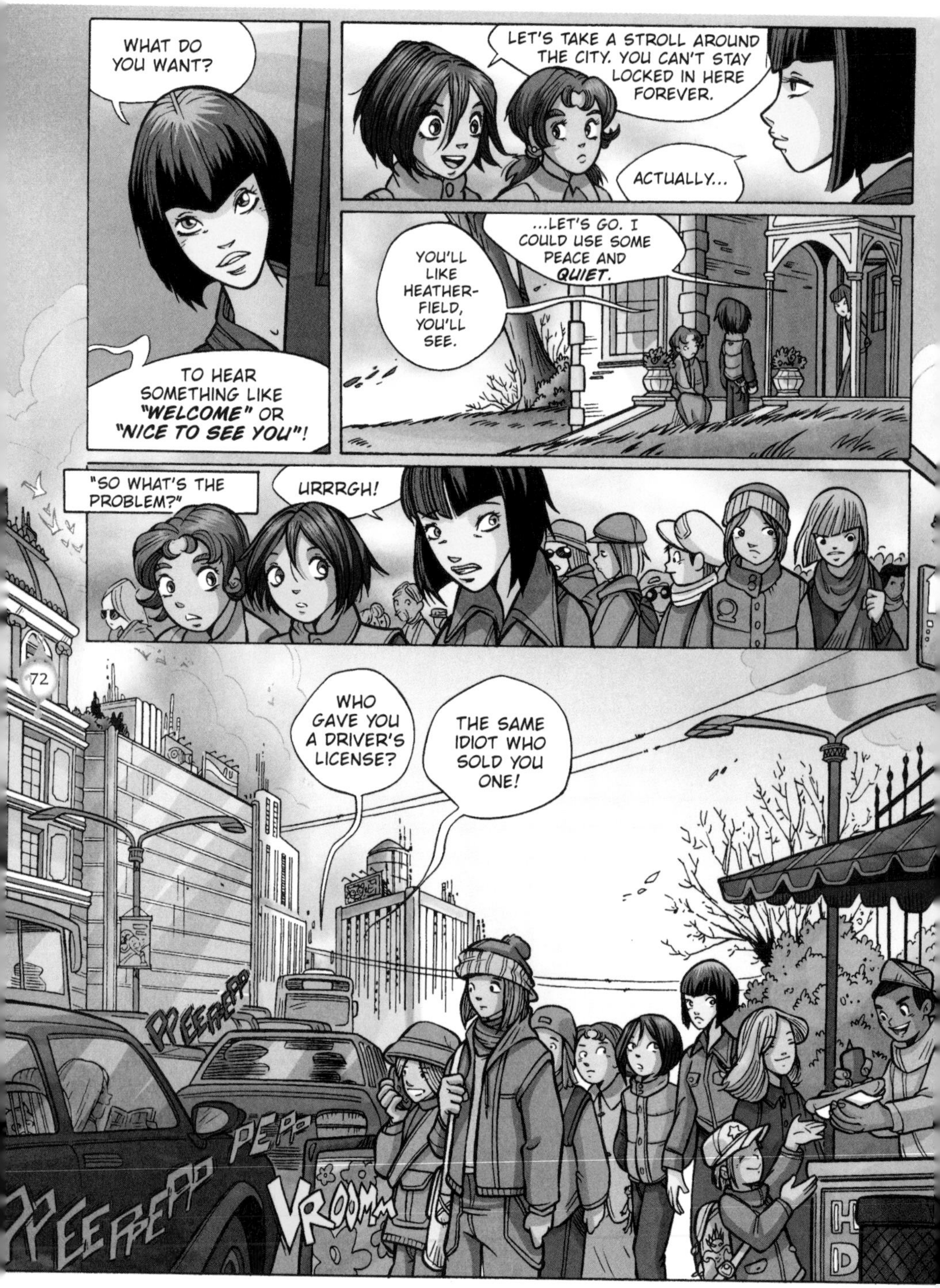
WHAT DO YOU WANT?
TO HEAR SOMETHING LIKE "WELCOME" OR "NICE TO SEE YOU"!
LET'S TAKE A STROLL AROUND THE CITY. YOU CAN'T STAY LOCKED IN HERE FOREVER.
ACTUALLY...
...LET'S GO. I COULD USE SOME PEACE AND QUIET.
YOU'LL LIKE HEATHER-FIELD, YOU'LL SEE.
"SO WHAT'S THE PROBLEM?"
URRRGH!
WHO GAVE YOU A DRIVER'S LICENSE?
THE SAME IDIOT WHO SOLD YOU ONE!
PPEEPEEP
PEEP
PPEEPEEP
VROOMM

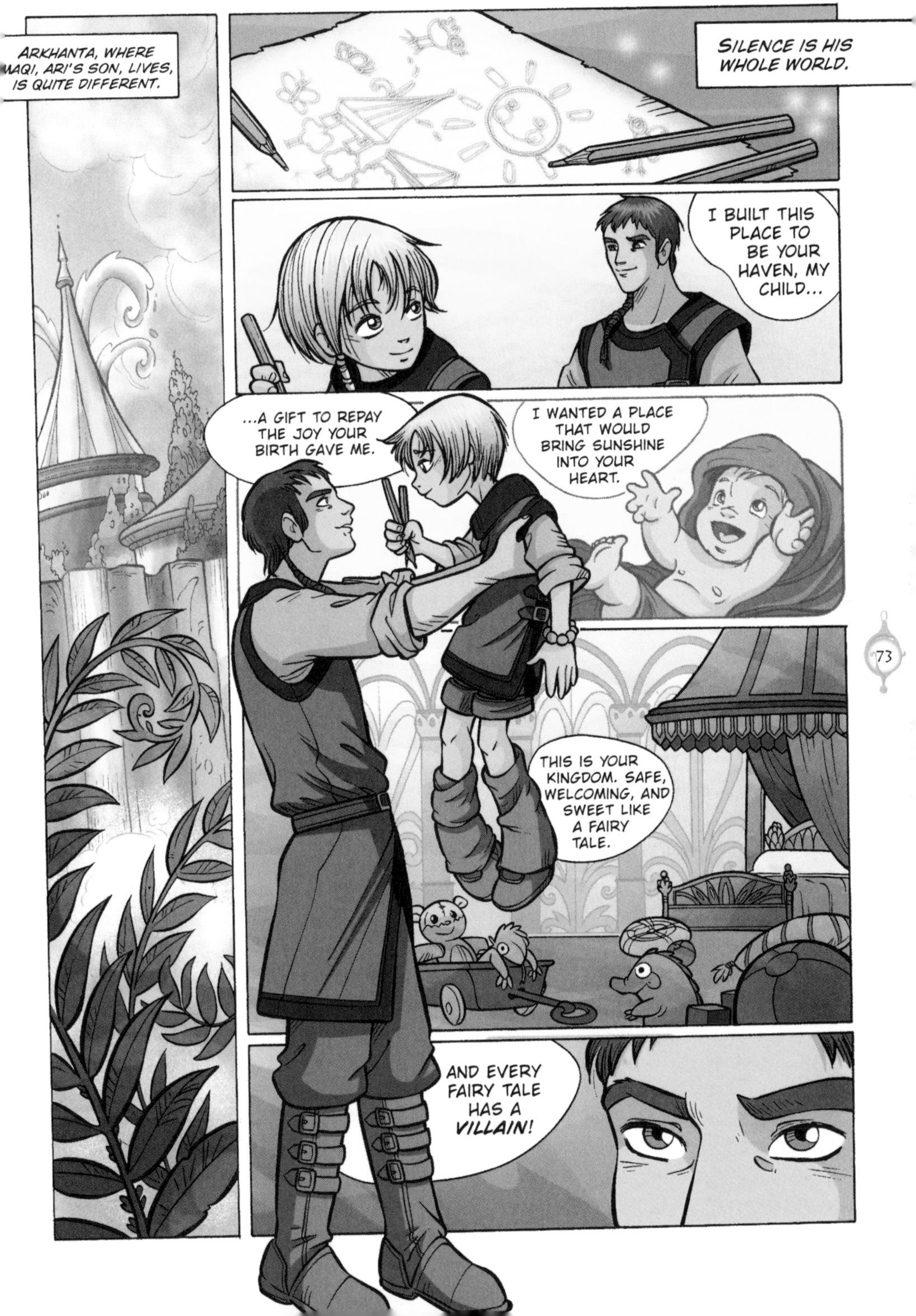
ARKHANTA, WHERE
MAQI, ARI'S SON, LIVES,
IS QUITE DIFFERENT.
SILENCE IS HIS
WHOLE WORLD.
I BUILT THIS PLACE TO BE YOUR HAVEN, MY CHILD...
...A GIFT TO REPAY THE JOY YOUR BIRTH GAVE ME.
I WANTED A PLACE THAT WOULD BRING SUNSHINE INTO YOUR HEART.
THIS IS YOUR KINGDOM. SAFE, WELCOMING, AND SWEET LIKE A FAIRY TALE.
AND EVERY FAIRY TALE HAS A *VILLAIN*!

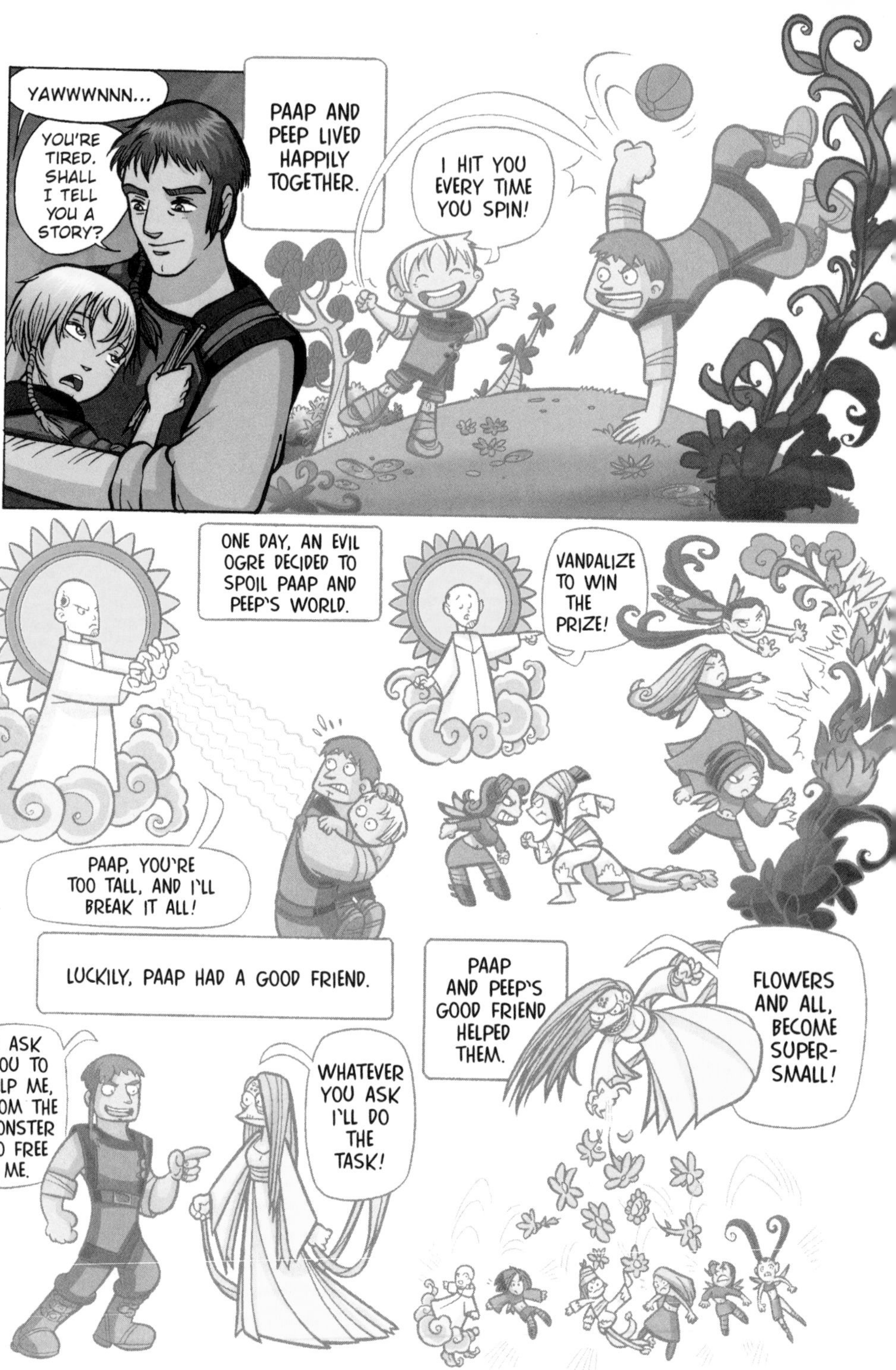

YAWWWNNN...
YOU'RE TIRED. SHALL I TELL YOU A STORY?
PAAP AND PEEP LIVED HAPPILY TOGETHER.
I HIT YOU EVERY TIME YOU SPIN!
ONE DAY, AN EVIL OGRE DECIDED TO SPOIL PAAP AND PEEP'S WORLD.
VANDALIZE TO WIN THE PRIZE!
PAAP, YOU'RE TOO TALL, AND I'LL BREAK IT ALL!
LUCKILY, PAAP HAD A GOOD FRIEND.
PAAP AND PEEP'S GOOD FRIEND HELPED THEM.
FLOWERS AND ALL, BECOME SUPER-SMALL!
I ASK YOU TO HELP ME, FROM THE MONSTER TO FREE ME.
WHATEVER YOU ASK I'LL DO THE TASK!

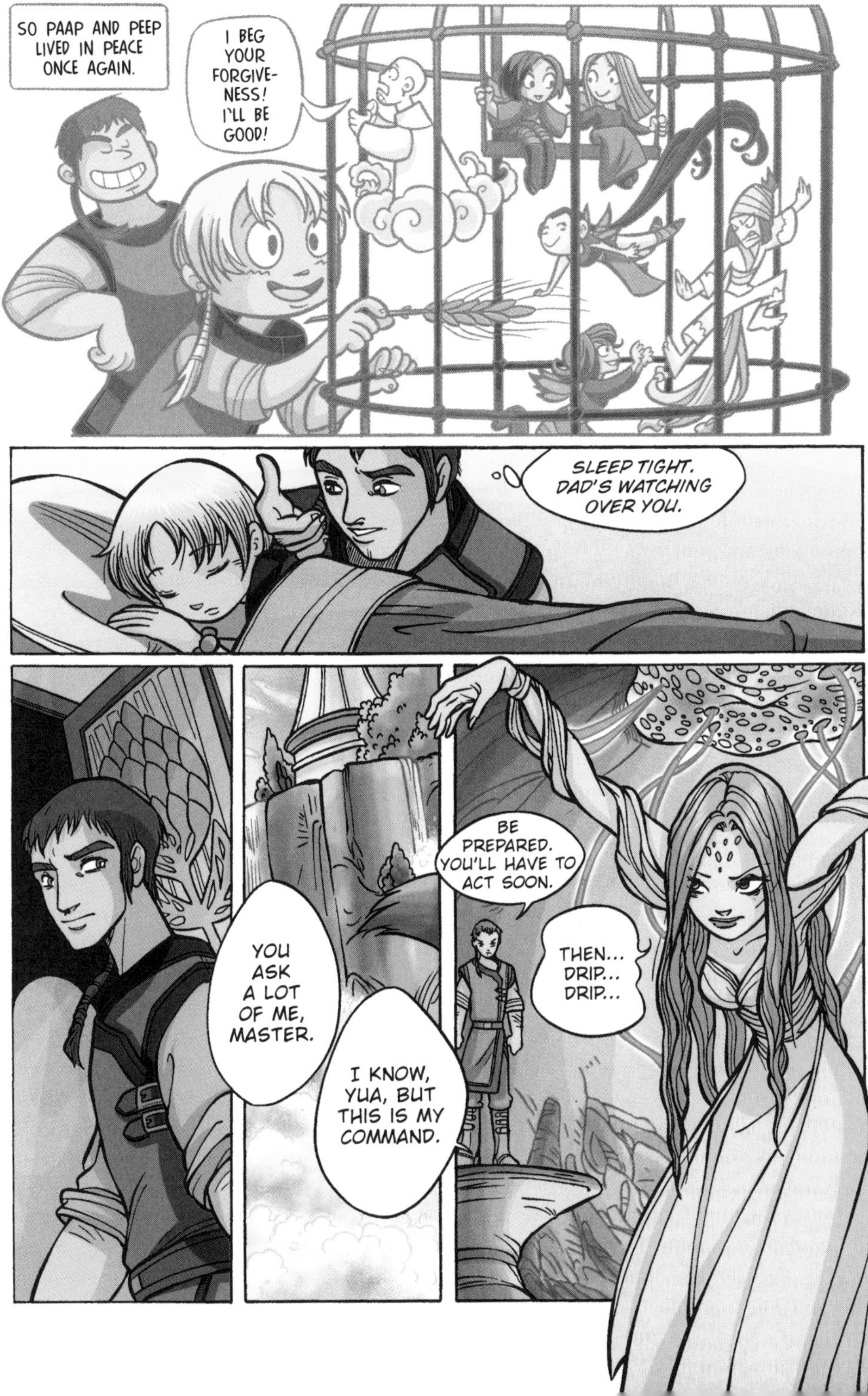
SO PAAP AND PEEP LIVED IN PEACE ONCE AGAIN.
I BEG YOUR FORGIVE-NESS! I'LL BE GOOD!
SLEEP TIGHT. DAD'S WATCHING OVER YOU.
YOU ASK A LOT OF ME, MASTER.
I KNOW, YUA, BUT THIS IS MY COMMAND.
BE PREPARED. YOU'LL HAVE TO ACT SOON.
THEN... DRIP... DRIP...

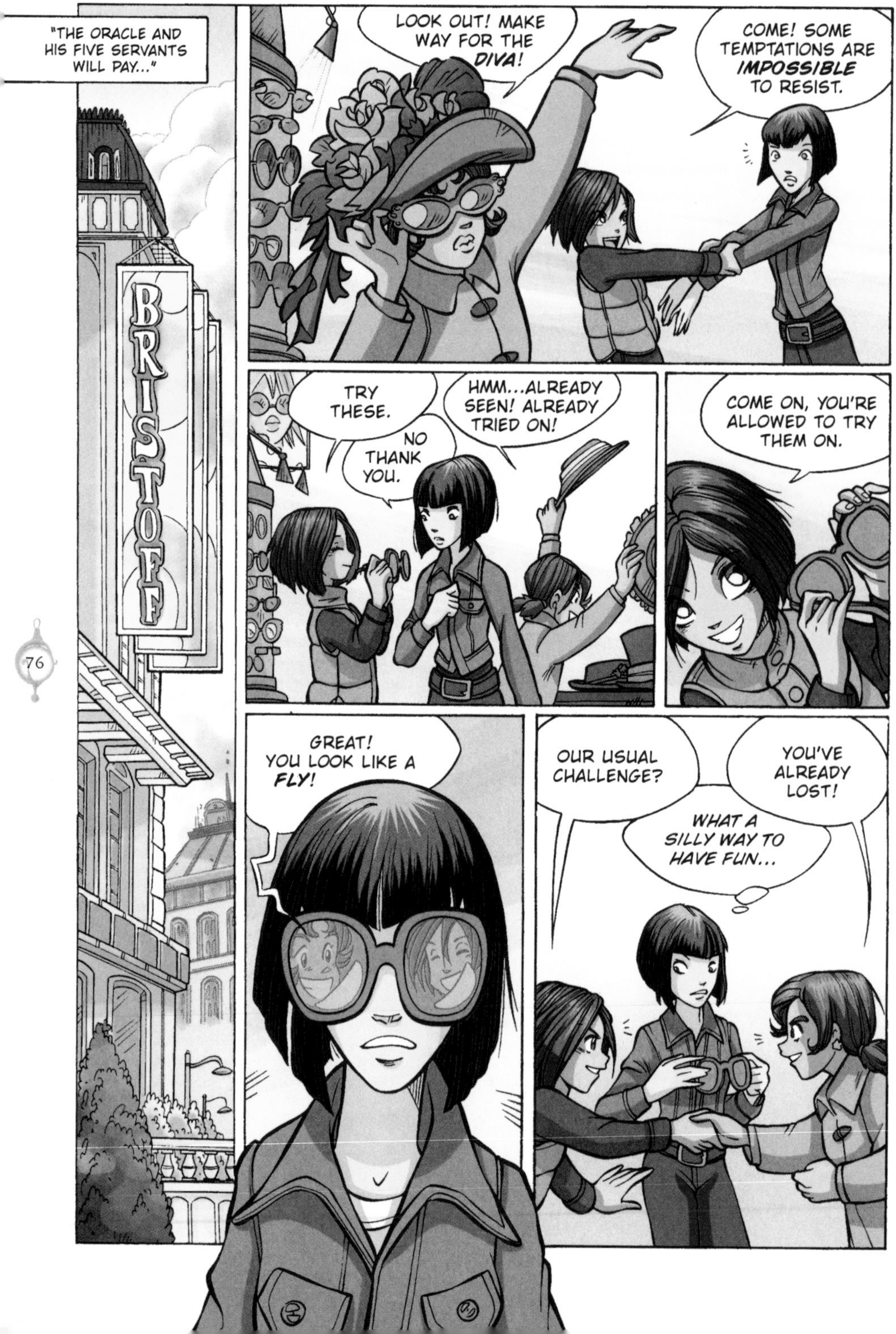
"THE ORACLE AND HIS FIVE SERVANTS WILL PAY..."
BRISTOFF
LOOK OUT! MAKE WAY FOR THE *DIVA*!
COME! SOME TEMPTATIONS ARE *IMPOSSIBLE* TO RESIST.
TRY THESE.
NO THANK YOU.
HMM...ALREADY SEEN! ALREADY TRIED ON!
COME ON, YOU'RE ALLOWED TO TRY THEM ON.
GREAT! YOU LOOK LIKE A *FLY*!
OUR USUAL CHALLENGE?
YOU'VE ALREADY LOST!
WHAT A SILLY WAY TO HAVE FUN...

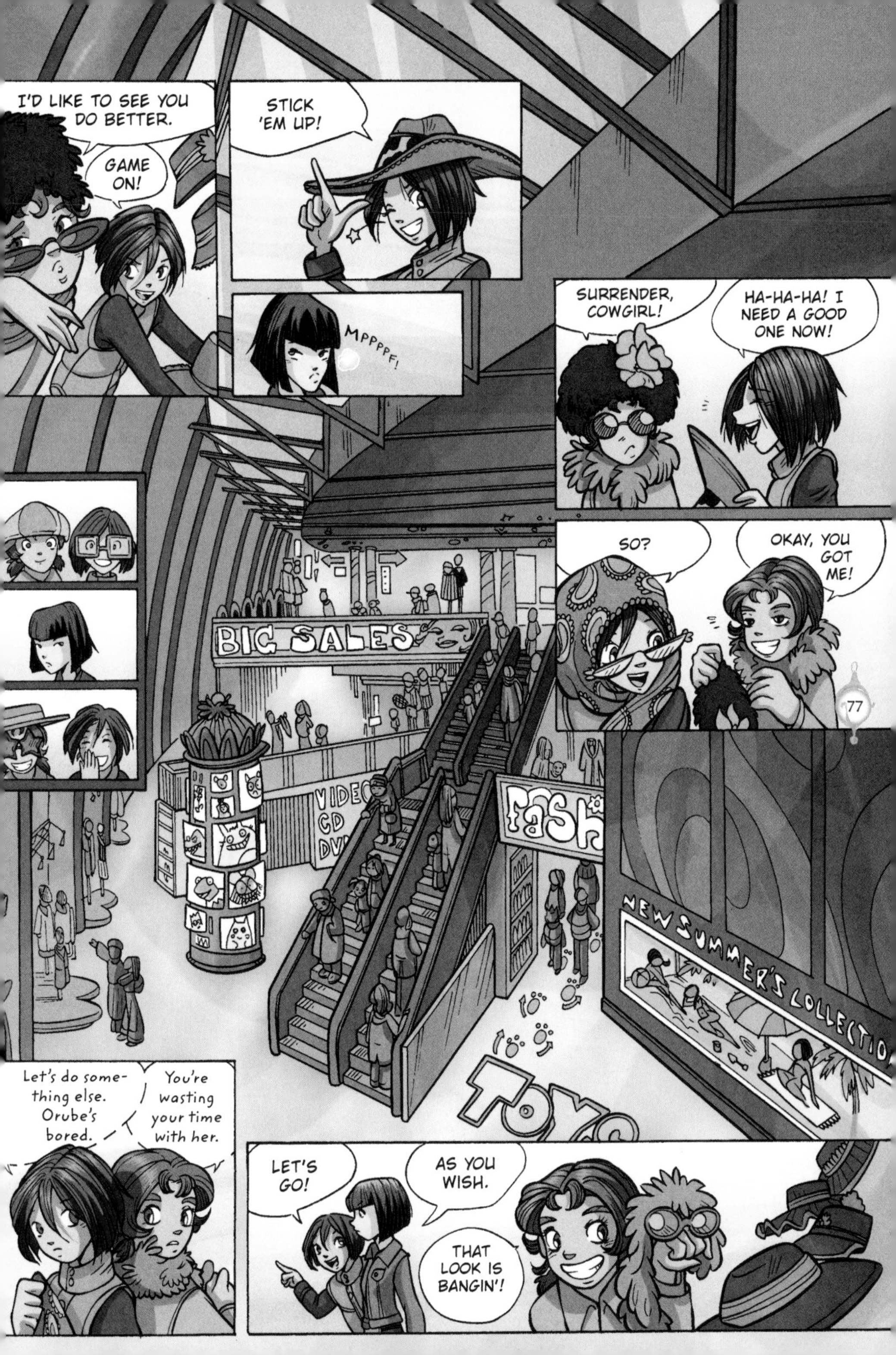

I'D LIKE TO SEE YOU DO BETTER.
GAME ON!
STICK 'EM UP!
MPPPPF!
SURRENDER, COWGIRL!
HA-HA-HA! I NEED A GOOD ONE NOW!
SO?
OKAY, YOU GOT ME!
BIG SALES
VIDEO
CD
DVD
NEW SUMMER'S COLLECTION
Let's do something else. Orube's bored.
You're wasting your time with her.
LET'S GO!
AS YOU WISH.
THAT LOOK IS BANGIN'!

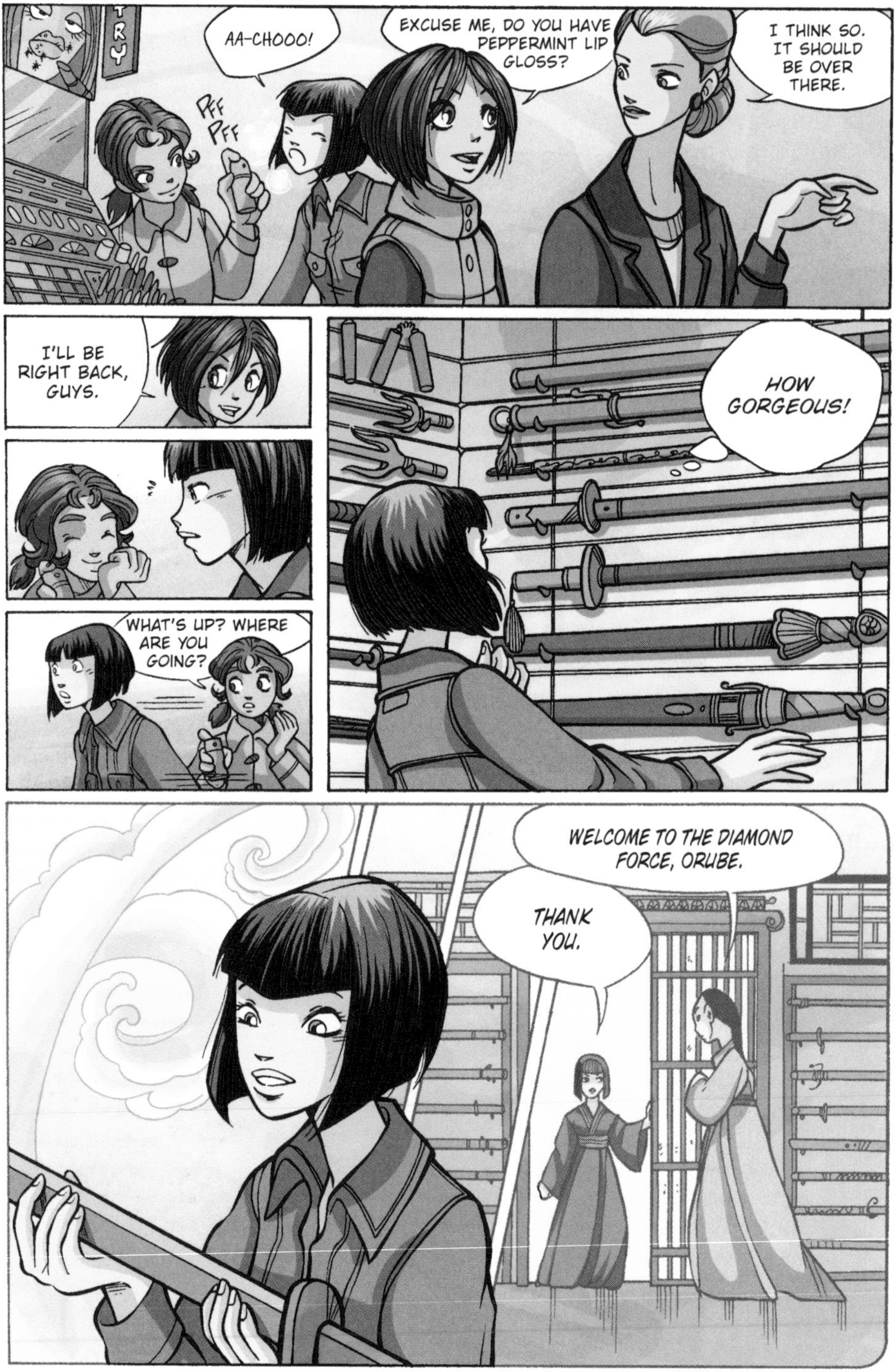
TRY
AA-CHOOO!
PFF PFF
EXCUSE ME, DO YOU HAVE PEPPERMINT LIP GLOSS?
I THINK SO. IT SHOULD BE OVER THERE.
I'LL BE RIGHT BACK, GUYS.
WHAT'S UP? WHERE ARE YOU GOING?
HOW GORGEOUS!
WELCOME TO THE DIAMOND FORCE, ORUBE.
THANK YOU.

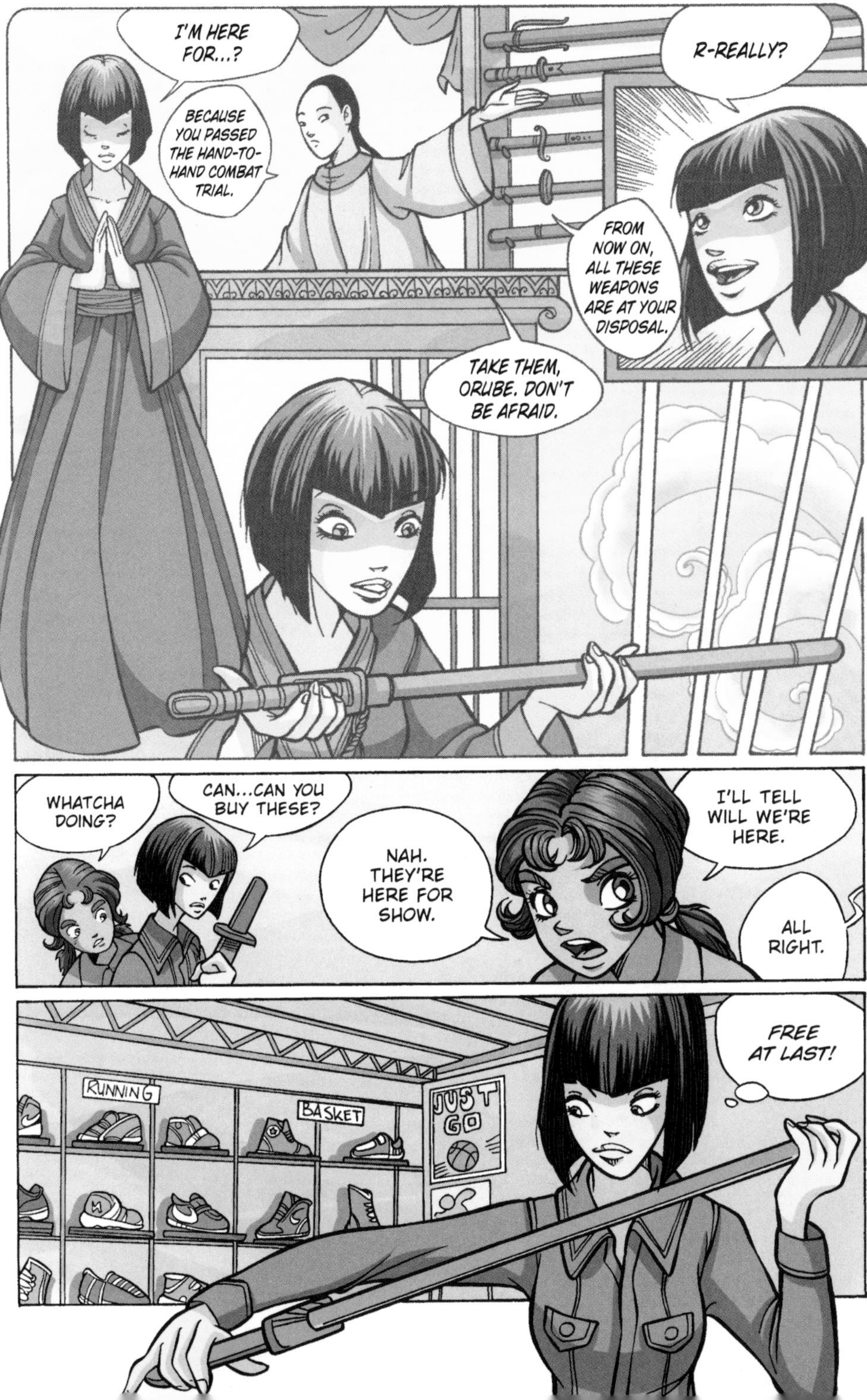
I'M HERE FOR...?
BECAUSE YOU PASSED THE HAND-TO-HAND COMBAT TRIAL.
R-REALLY?
FROM NOW ON, ALL THESE WEAPONS ARE AT YOUR DISPOSAL.
TAKE THEM, ORUBE. DON'T BE AFRAID.
WHATCHA DOING?
CAN...CAN YOU BUY THESE?
NAH. THEY'RE HERE FOR SHOW.
I'LL TELL WILL WE'RE HERE.
ALL RIGHT.
FREE AT LAST!
RUNNING
BASKET
JUST GO

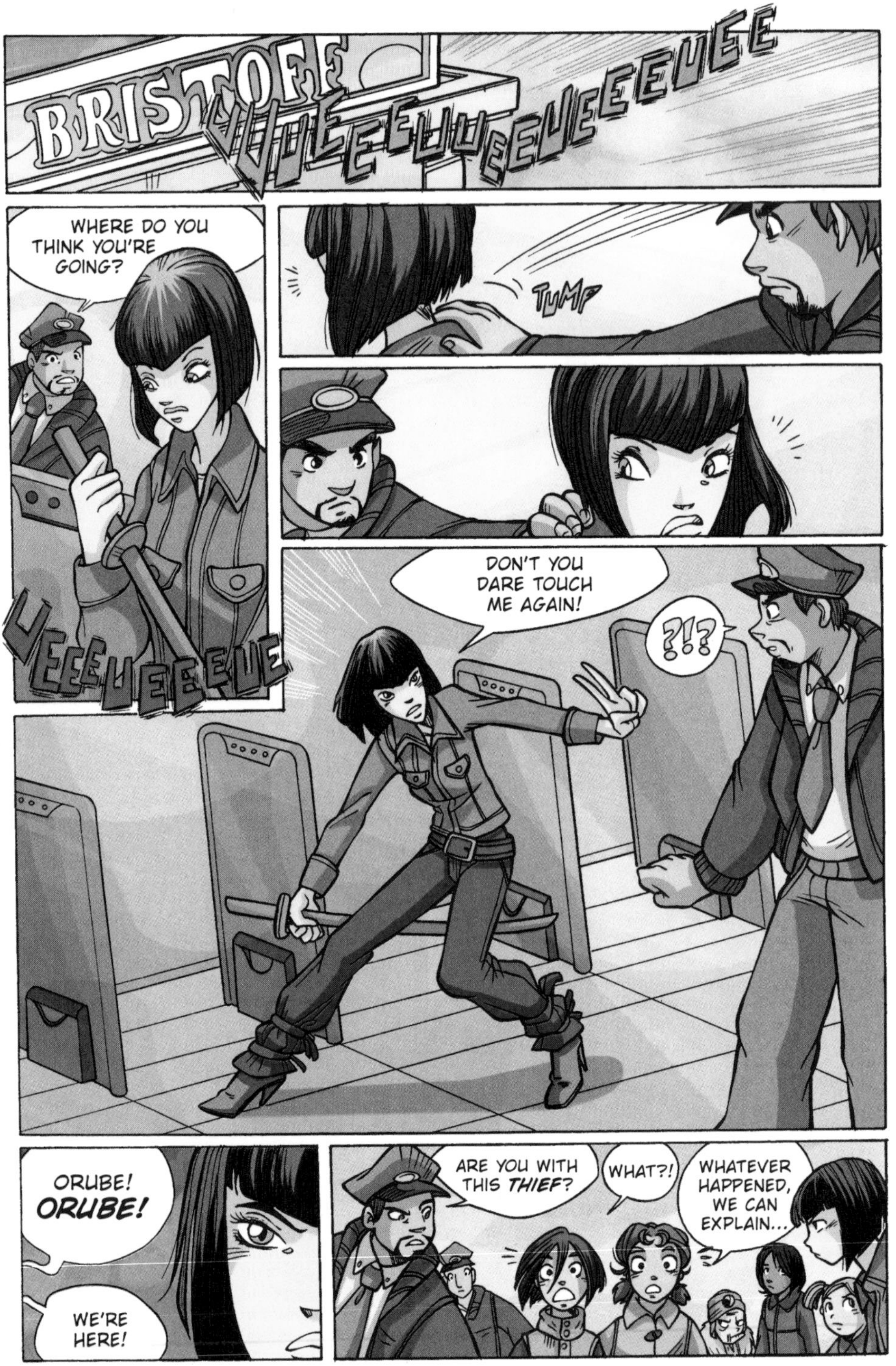
BRISTOFF
VUUEEEUUUEEEUEEEUEE
WHERE DO YOU THINK YOU'RE GOING?
TUMP
UEEEUEEEUE
DON'T YOU DARE TOUCH ME AGAIN!
?!?
ORUBE! ORUBE!
WE'RE HERE!
ARE YOU WITH THIS THIEF?
WHAT?!
WHATEVER HAPPENED, WE CAN EXPLAIN...

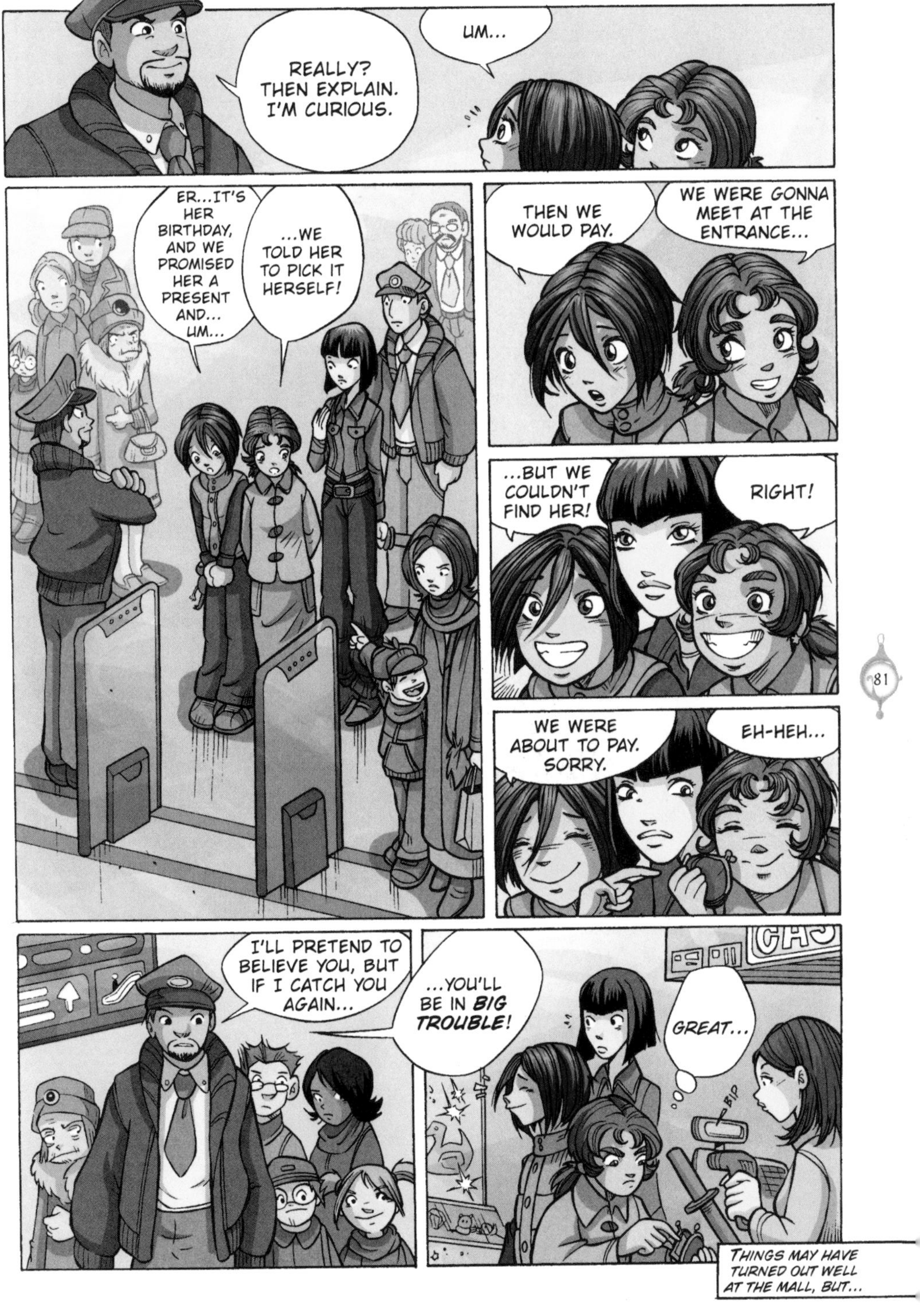
REALLY? THEN EXPLAIN. I'M CURIOUS.
UM...
ER...IT'S HER BIRTHDAY, AND WE PROMISED HER A PRESENT AND... UM...
...WE TOLD HER TO PICK IT HERSELF!
WE WERE GONNA MEET AT THE ENTRANCE...
THEN WE WOULD PAY.
...BUT WE COULDN'T FIND HER!
RIGHT!
WE WERE ABOUT TO PAY. SORRY.
EH-HEH...
I'LL PRETEND TO BELIEVE YOU, BUT IF I CATCH YOU AGAIN...
...YOU'LL BE IN BIG TROUBLE!
GREAT...
BIP
THINGS MAY HAVE TURNED OUT WELL AT THE MALL, BUT...

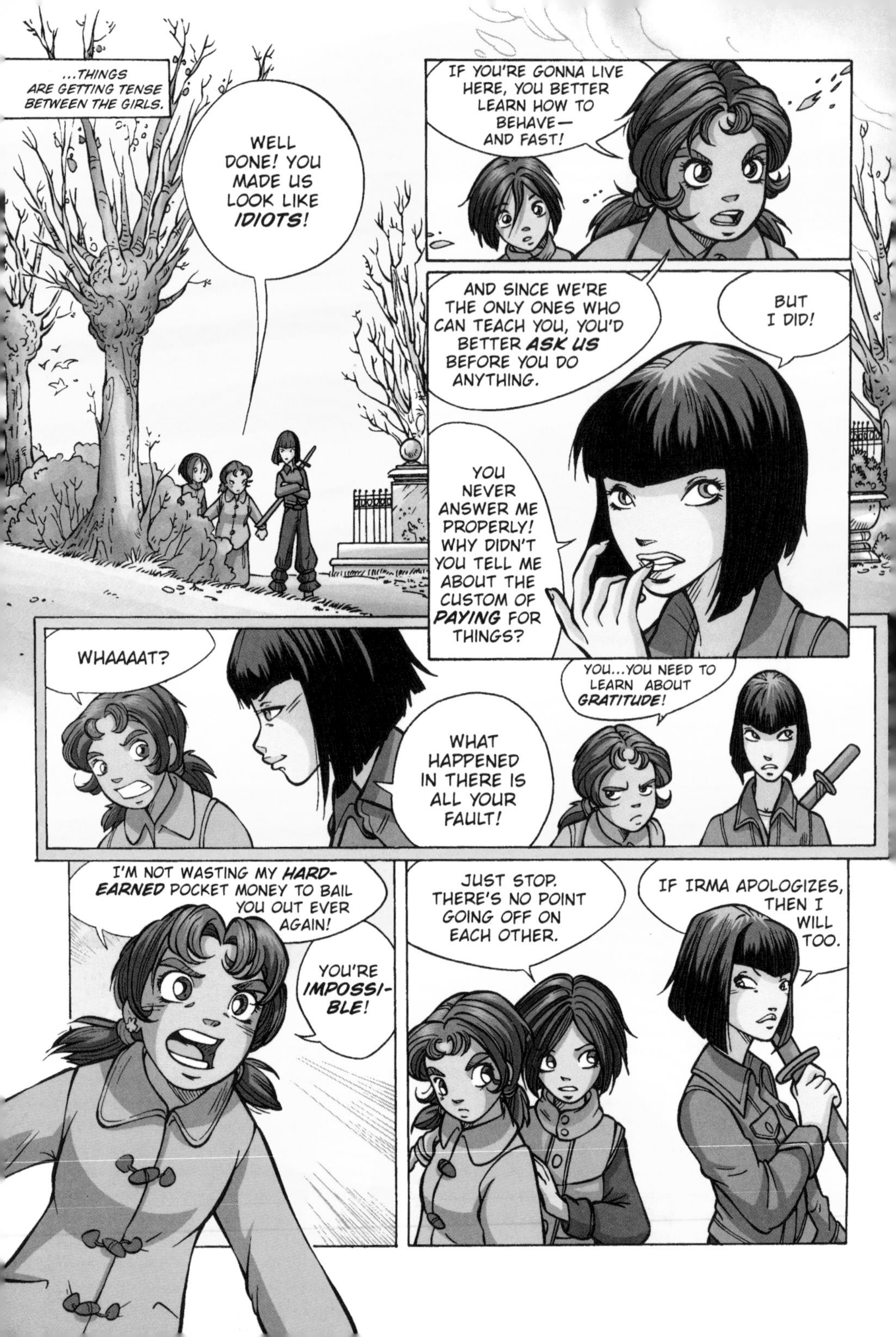
...THINGS ARE GETTING TENSE BETWEEN THE GIRLS.
WELL DONE! YOU MADE US LOOK LIKE IDIOTS!
IF YOU'RE GONNA LIVE HERE, YOU BETTER LEARN HOW TO BEHAVE—AND FAST!
AND SINCE WE'RE THE ONLY ONES WHO CAN TEACH YOU, YOU'D BETTER ASK US BEFORE YOU DO ANYTHING.
BUT I DID!
YOU NEVER ANSWER ME PROPERLY! WHY DIDN'T YOU TELL ME ABOUT THE CUSTOM OF PAYING FOR THINGS?
WHAAAAT?
YOU...YOU NEED TO LEARN ABOUT GRATITUDE!
WHAT HAPPENED IN THERE IS ALL YOUR FAULT!
I'M NOT WASTING MY HARD-EARNED POCKET MONEY TO BAIL YOU OUT EVER AGAIN!
YOU'RE IMPOSSIBLE!
JUST STOP. THERE'S NO POINT GOING OFF ON EACH OTHER.
IF IRMA APOLOGIZES, THEN I WILL TOO.

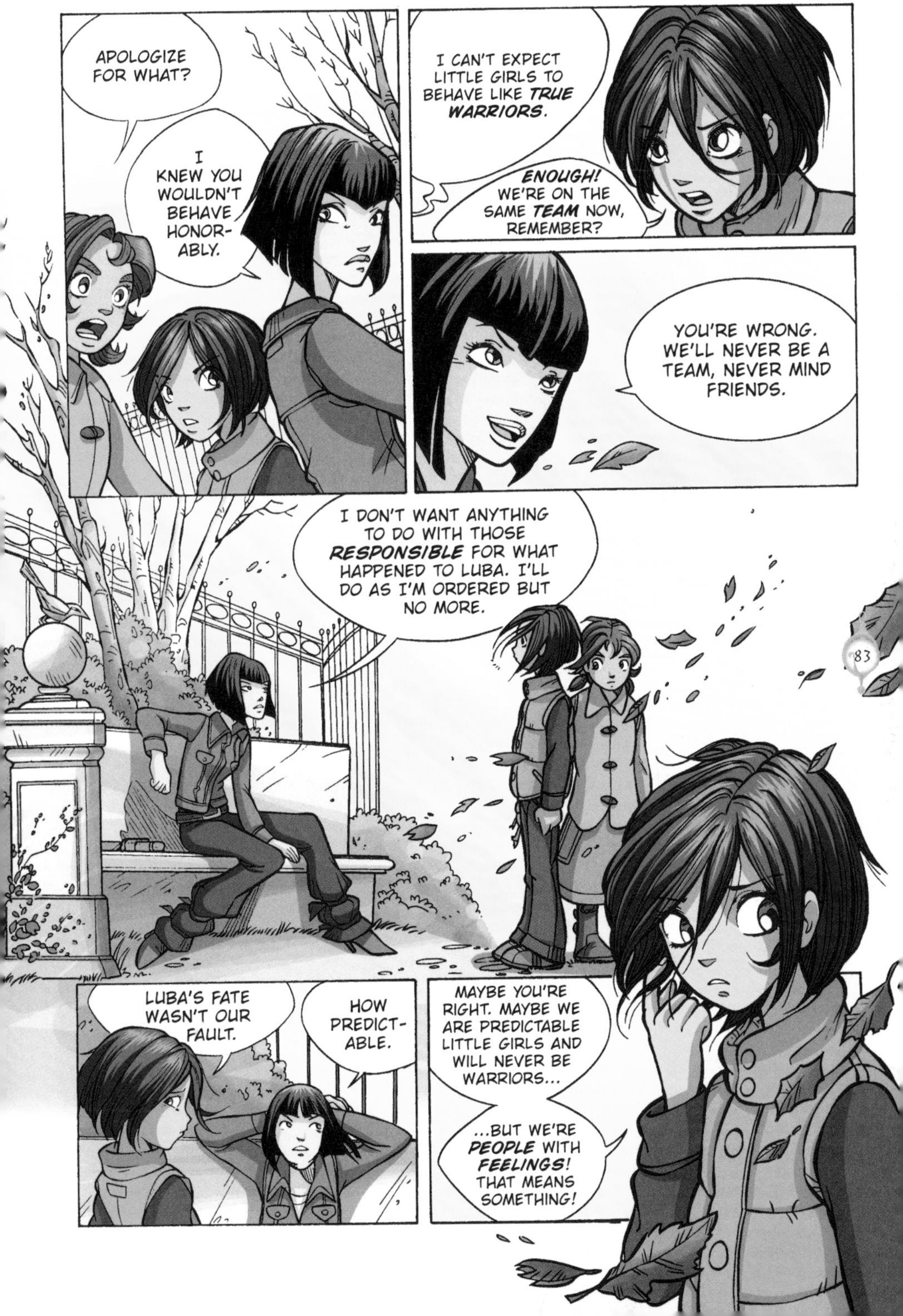
APOLOGIZE FOR WHAT?
I KNEW YOU WOULDN'T BEHAVE HONOR-ABLY.
I CAN'T EXPECT LITTLE GIRLS TO BEHAVE LIKE TRUE WARRIORS.
ENOUGH! WE'RE ON THE SAME TEAM NOW, REMEMBER?
YOU'RE WRONG. WE'LL NEVER BE A TEAM, NEVER MIND FRIENDS.
I DON'T WANT ANYTHING TO DO WITH THOSE RESPONSIBLE FOR WHAT HAPPENED TO LUBA. I'LL DO AS I'M ORDERED BUT NO MORE.
LUBA'S FATE WASN'T OUR FAULT.
HOW PREDICT-ABLE.
MAYBE YOU'RE RIGHT. MAYBE WE ARE PREDICTABLE LITTLE GIRLS AND WILL NEVER BE WARRIORS...
...BUT WE'RE PEOPLE WITH FEELINGS! THAT MEANS SOMETHING!

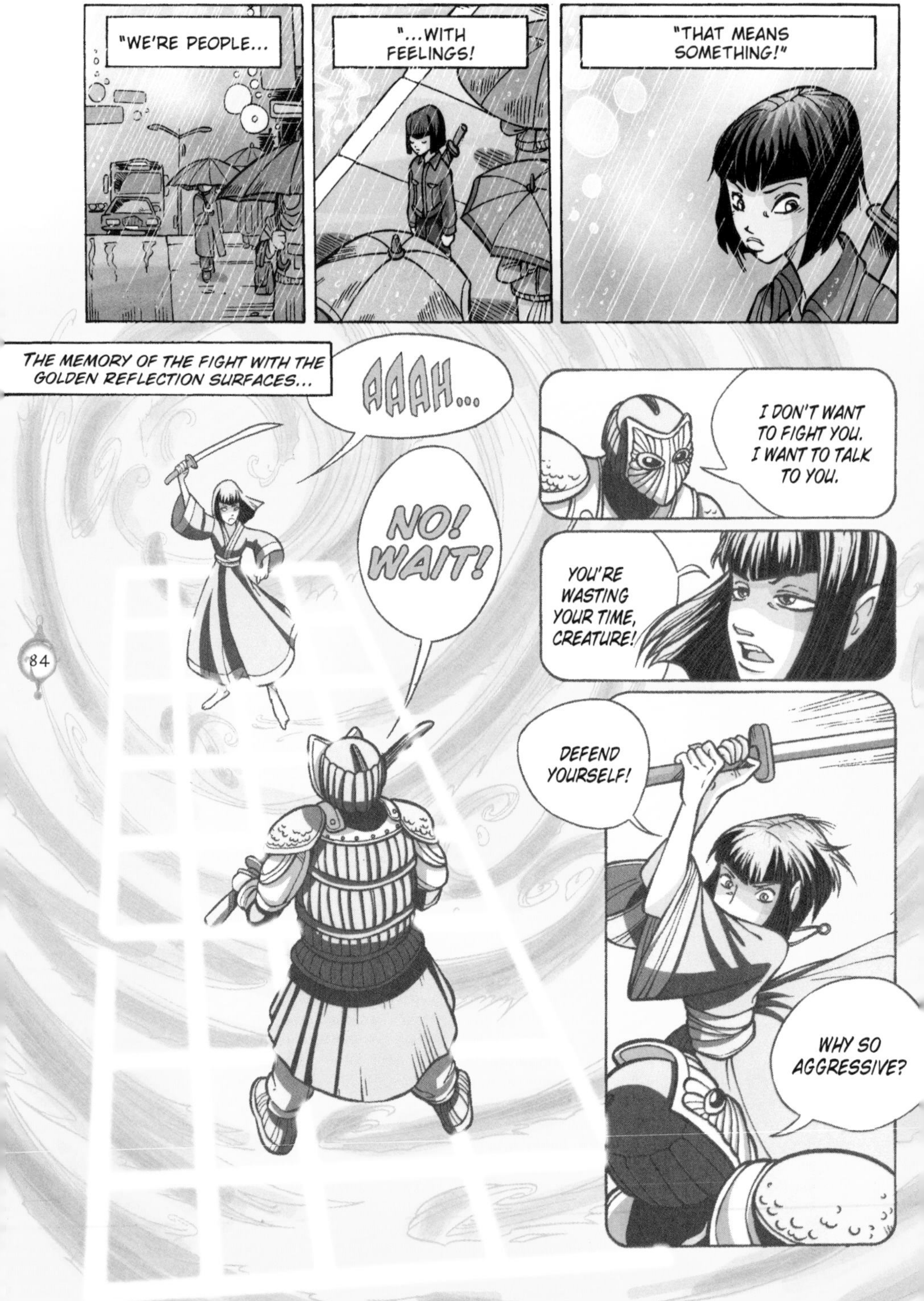
"WE'RE PEOPLE...
"...WITH FEELINGS!
"THAT MEANS SOMETHING!"
THE MEMORY OF THE FIGHT WITH THE GOLDEN REFLECTION SURFACES...
AAAH...
NO! WAIT!
I DON'T WANT TO FIGHT YOU. I WANT TO TALK TO YOU.
YOU'RE WASTING YOUR TIME, CREATURE!
DEFEND YOURSELF!
WHY SO AGGRESSIVE?

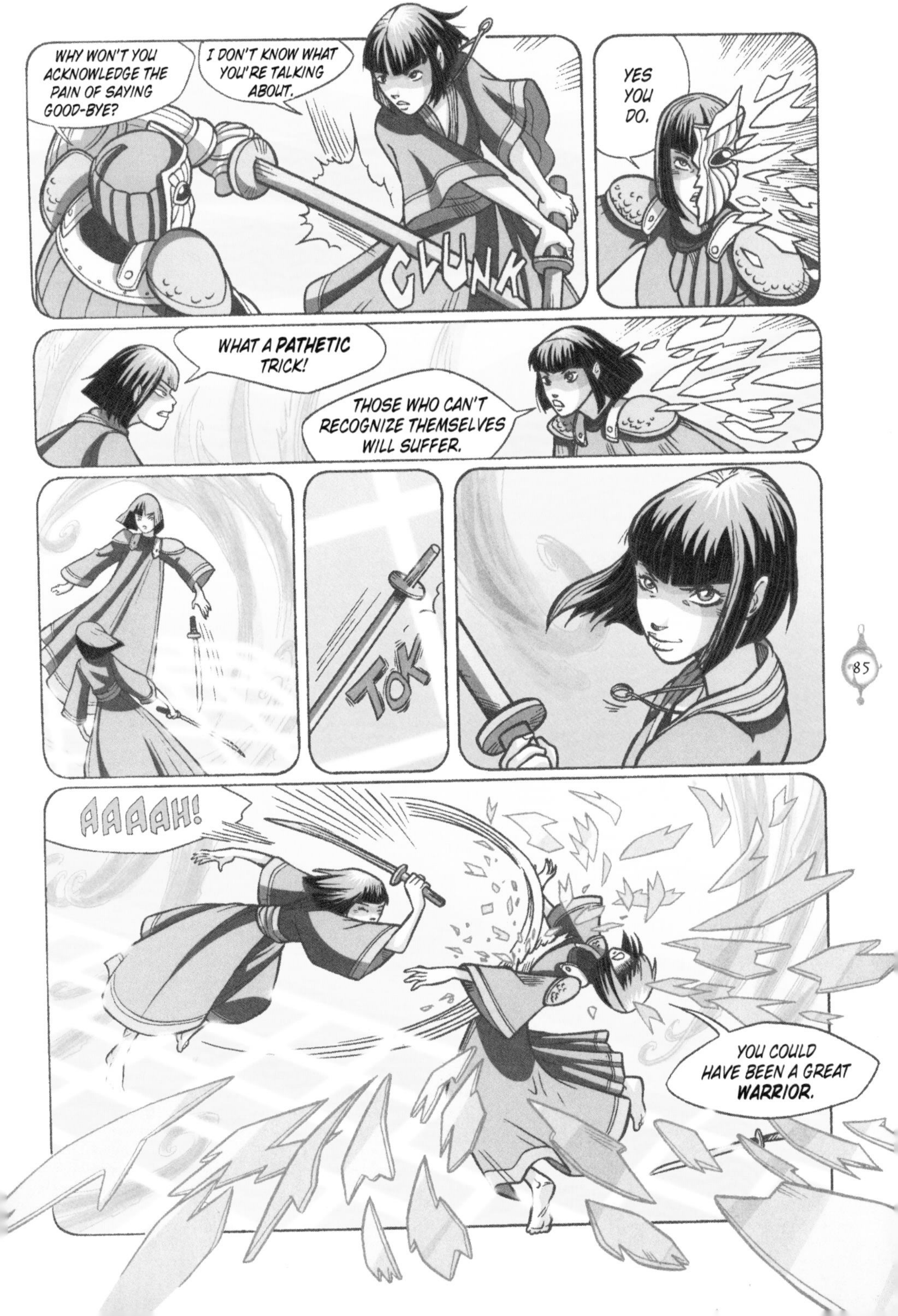

WHY WON'T YOU ACKNOWLEDGE THE PAIN OF SAYING GOOD-BYE?
I DON'T KNOW WHAT YOU'RE TALKING ABOUT.
CLUNK
YES YOU DO.
WHAT A PATHETIC TRICK!
THOSE WHO CAN'T RECOGNIZE THEMSELVES WILL SUFFER.
TOK
AAAAH!
YOU COULD HAVE BEEN A GREAT WARRIOR.

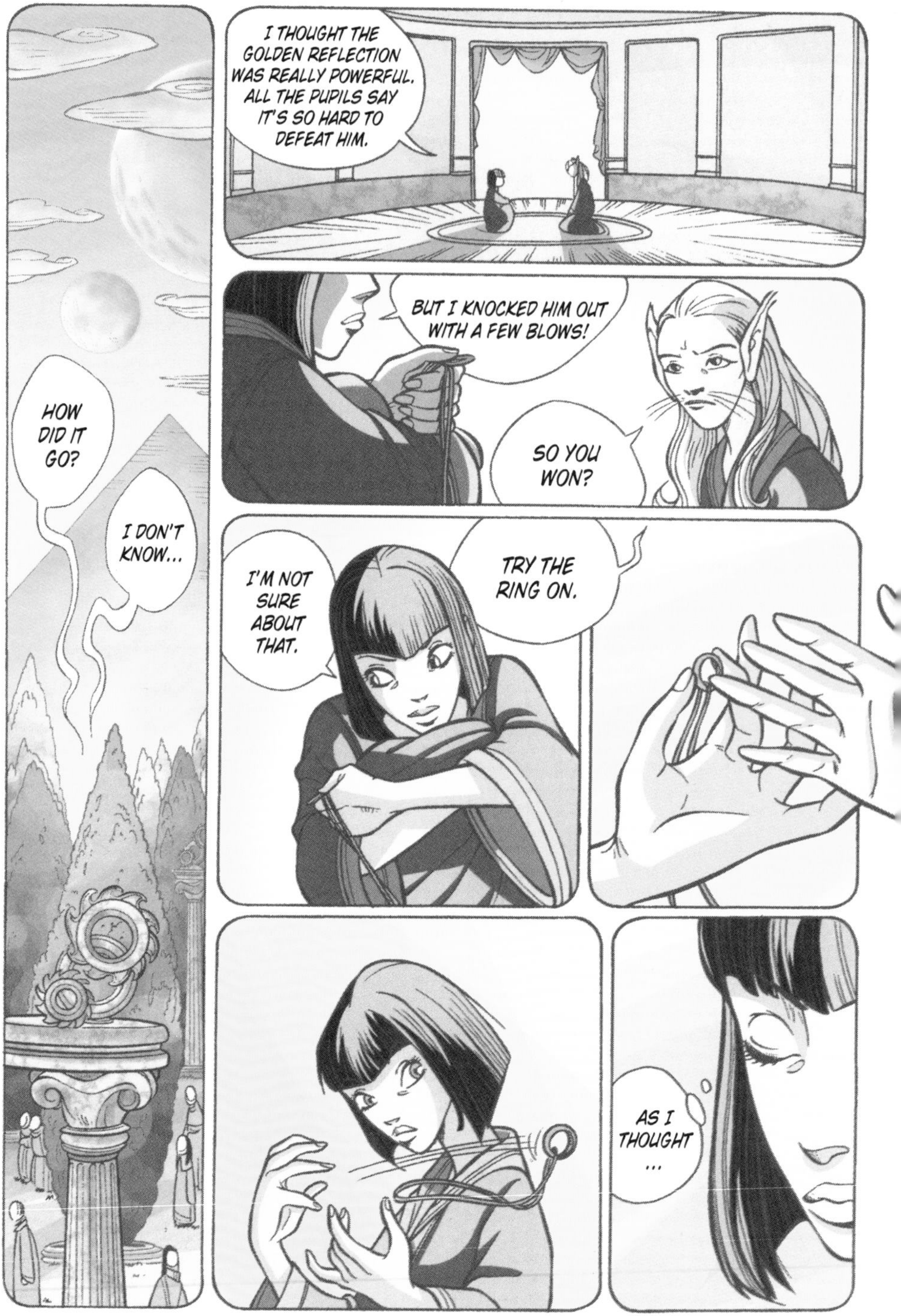
HOW DID IT GO?
I DON'T KNOW...
I THOUGHT THE GOLDEN REFLECTION WAS REALLY POWERFUL. ALL THE PUPILS SAY IT'S SO HARD TO DEFEAT HIM.
BUT I KNOCKED HIM OUT WITH A FEW BLOWS!
SO YOU WON?
I'M NOT SURE ABOUT THAT.
TRY THE RING ON.
AS I THOUGHT ...

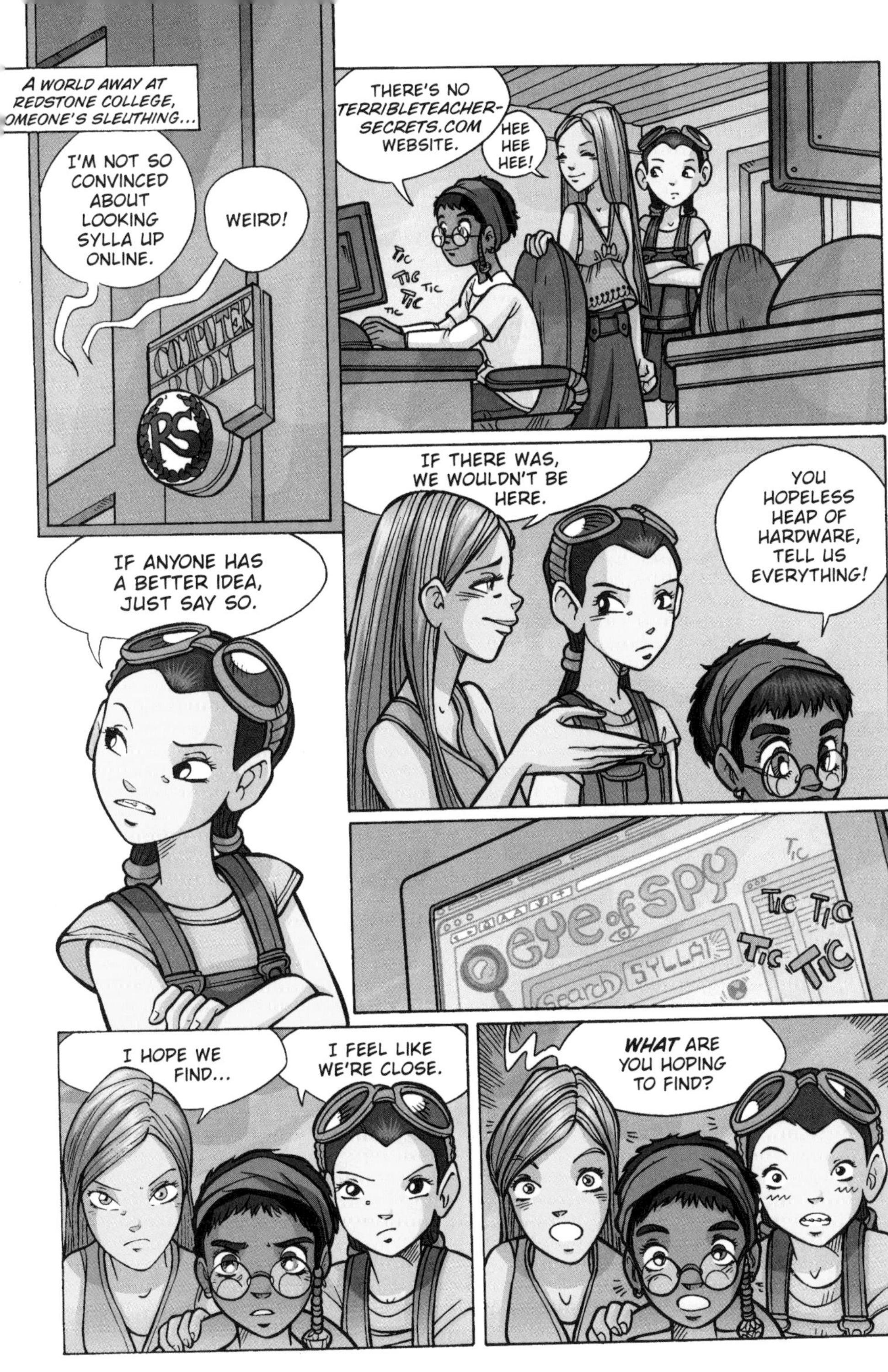

A WORLD AWAY AT REDSTONE COLLEGE, OMEONE'S SLEUTHING...
I'M NOT SO CONVINCED ABOUT LOOKING SYLLA UP ONLINE.
WEIRD!
COMPUTER ROOM
RS
THERE'S NO TERRIBLETEACHER-SECRETS.COM WEBSITE.
HEE HEE HEE!
TIC TIC TIC TIC TIC
IF THERE WAS, WE WOULDN'T BE HERE.
YOU HOPELESS HEAP OF HARDWARE, TELL US EVERYTHING!
IF ANYONE HAS A BETTER IDEA, JUST SAY SO.
eye of spy
SYLLA|
Search
TIC TIC TIC TIC TIC
I HOPE WE FIND...
I FEEL LIKE WE'RE CLOSE.
WHAT ARE YOU HOPING TO FIND?

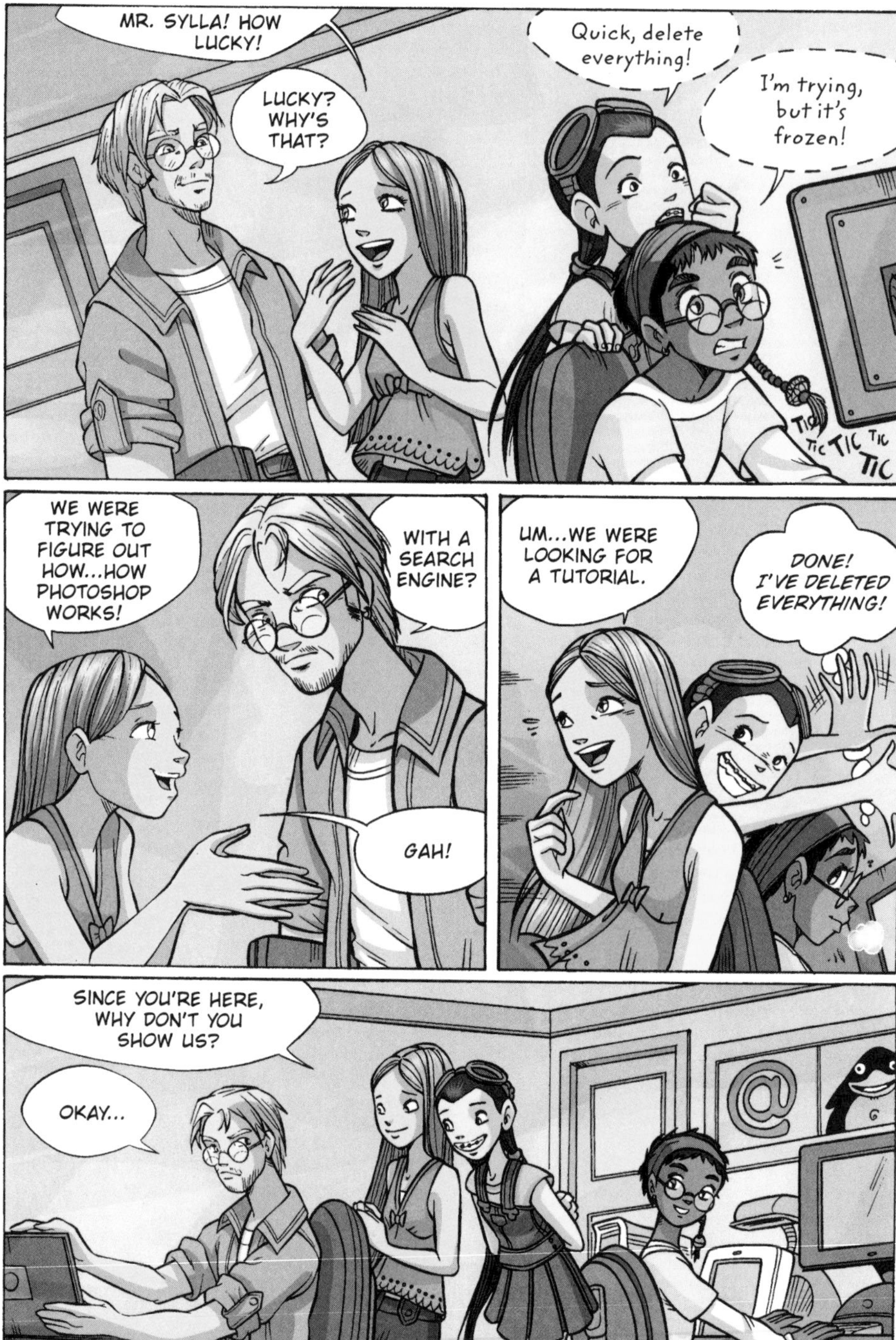
MR. SYLLA! HOW LUCKY!
LUCKY? WHY'S THAT?
Quick, delete everything!
I'm trying, but it's frozen!
TIC TIC TIC TIC TIC
WE WERE TRYING TO FIGURE OUT HOW...HOW PHOTOSHOP WORKS!
WITH A SEARCH ENGINE?
GAH!
UM...WE WERE LOOKING FOR A TUTORIAL.
DONE! I'VE DELETED EVERYTHING!
SINCE YOU'RE HERE, WHY DON'T YOU SHOW US?
OKAY...

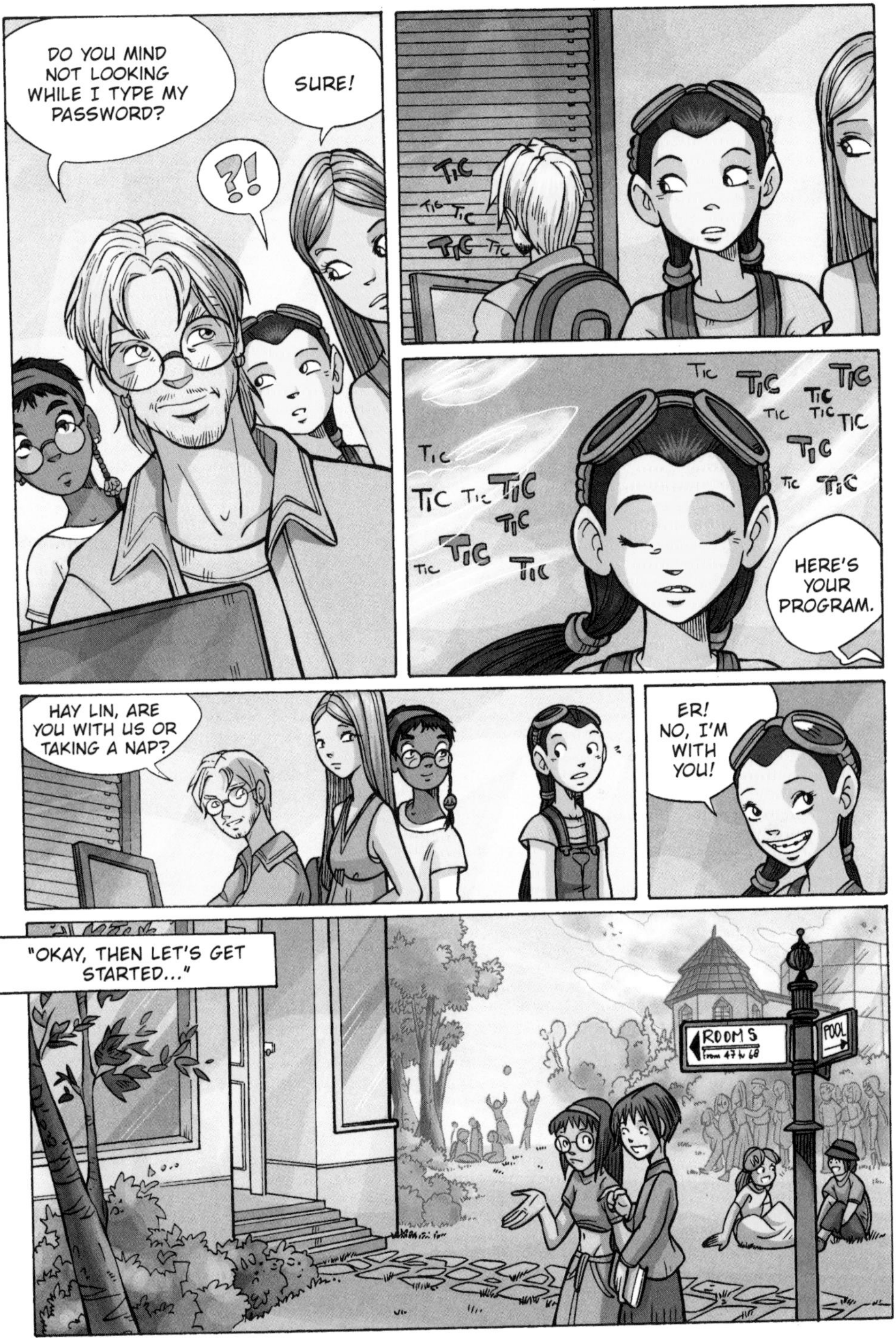
DO YOU MIND NOT LOOKING WHILE I TYPE MY PASSWORD?
SURE!
?!
TIC TIC TIC TIC TIC
TIC TIC TIC TIC TIC TIC TIC TIC TIC TIC TIC TIC TIC TIC TIC TIC TIC TIC
HERE'S YOUR PROGRAM.
HAY LIN, ARE YOU WITH US OR TAKING A NAP?
ER! NO, I'M WITH YOU!
"OKAY, THEN LET'S GET STARTED..."
ROOMS
from 47 to 68
POOL

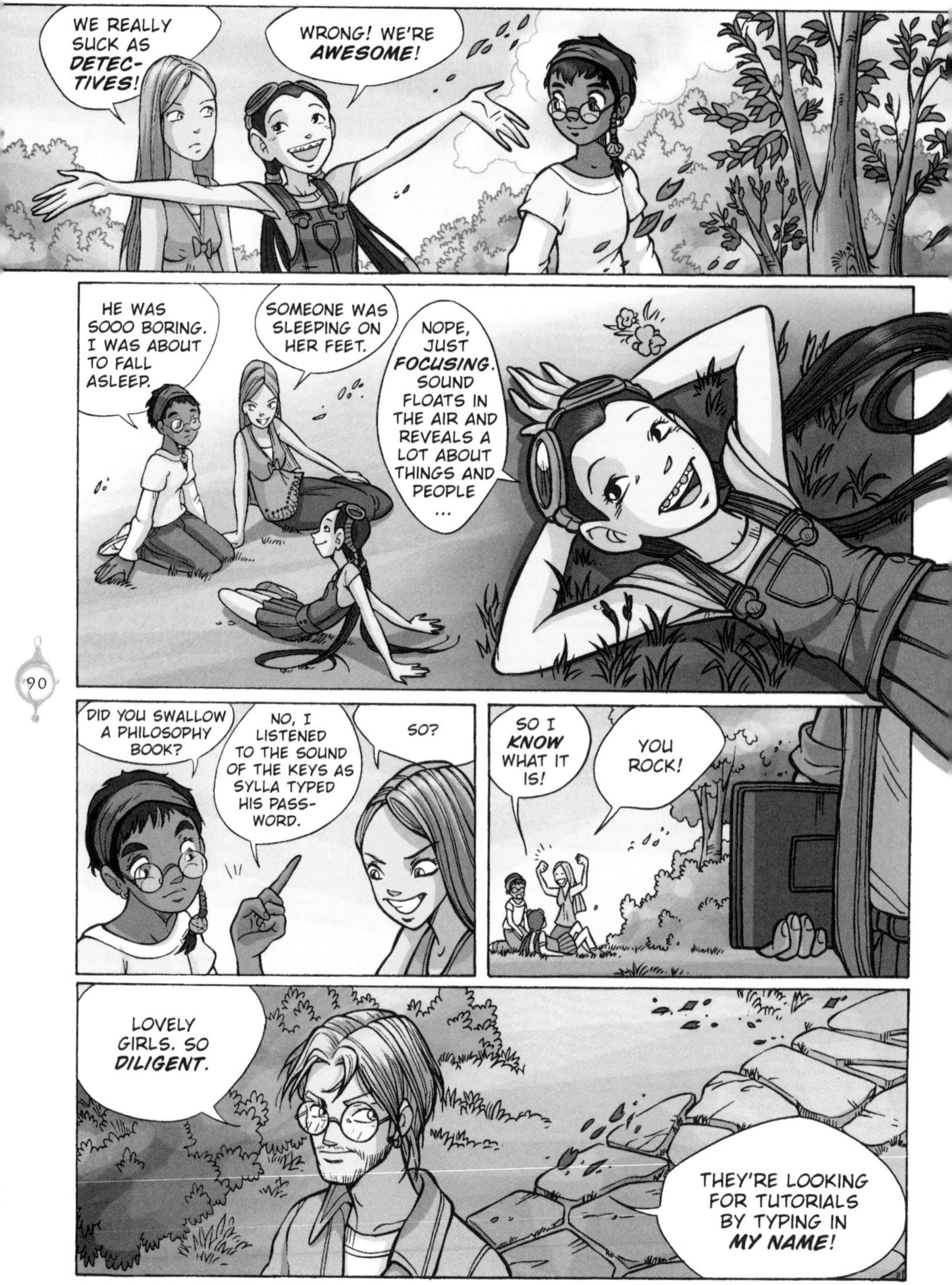
WE REALLY SUCK AS DETECTIVES!
WRONG! WE'RE AWESOME!
HE WAS SOOO BORING. I WAS ABOUT TO FALL ASLEEP.
SOMEONE WAS SLEEPING ON HER FEET.
NOPE, JUST FOCUSING. SOUND FLOATS IN THE AIR AND REVEALS A LOT ABOUT THINGS AND PEOPLE ...
DID YOU SWALLOW A PHILOSOPHY BOOK?
NO, I LISTENED TO THE SOUND OF THE KEYS AS SYLLA TYPED HIS PASSWORD.
SO?
SO I KNOW WHAT IT IS!
YOU ROCK!
LOVELY GIRLS. SO DILIGENT.
THEY'RE LOOKING FOR TUTORIALS BY TYPING IN MY NAME!

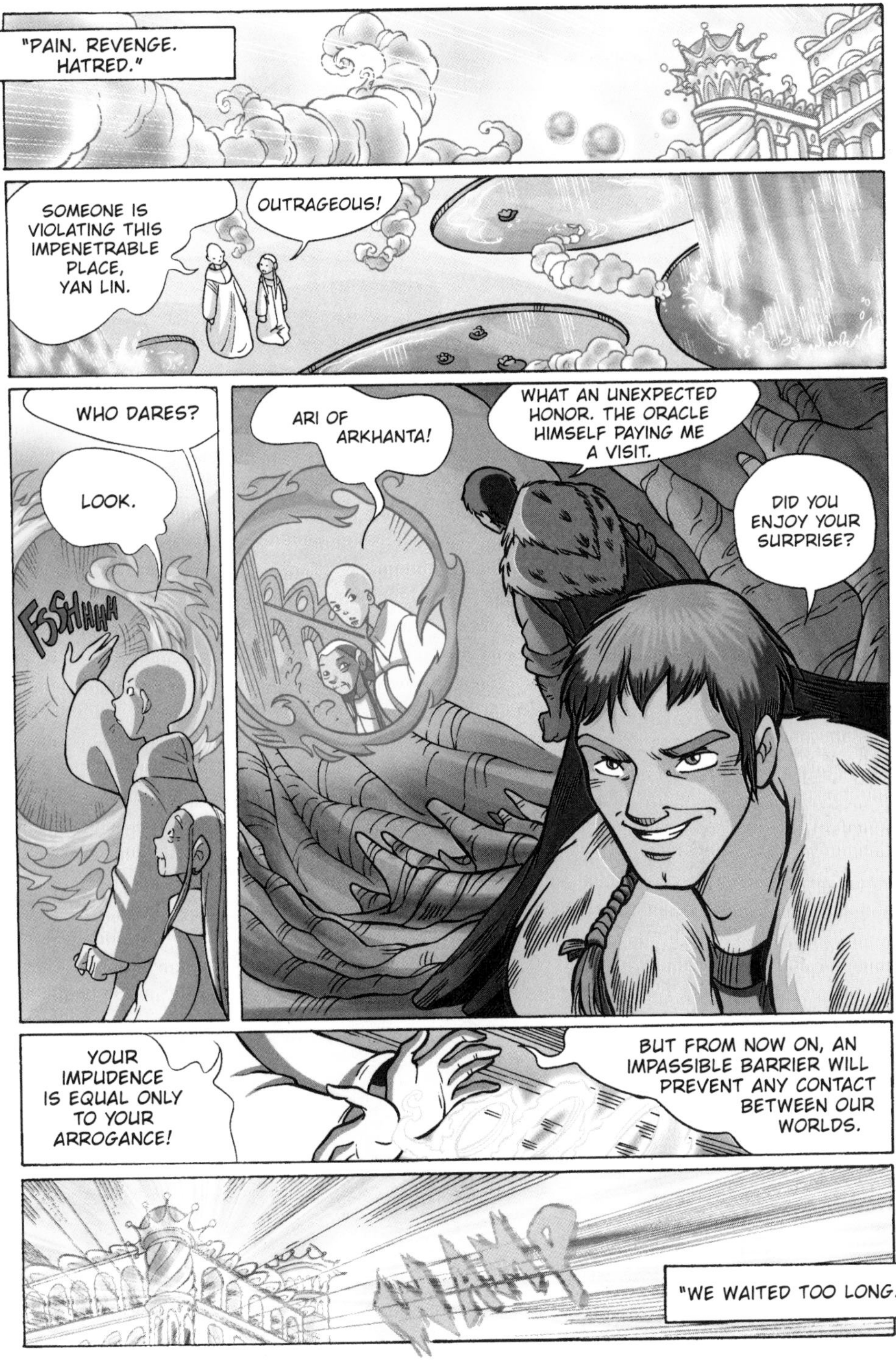
"PAIN. REVENGE. HATRED."
SOMEONE IS VIOLATING THIS IMPENETRABLE PLACE, YAN LIN.
OUTRAGEOUS!
WHO DARES?
LOOK.
FSSHHHH
ARI OF ARKHANTA!
WHAT AN UNEXPECTED HONOR. THE ORACLE HIMSELF PAYING ME A VISIT.
DID YOU ENJOY YOUR SURPRISE?
YOUR IMPUDENCE IS EQUAL ONLY TO YOUR ARROGANCE!
BUT FROM NOW ON, AN IMPASSIBLE BARRIER WILL PREVENT ANY CONTACT BETWEEN OUR WORLDS.
"WE WAITED TOO LONG."

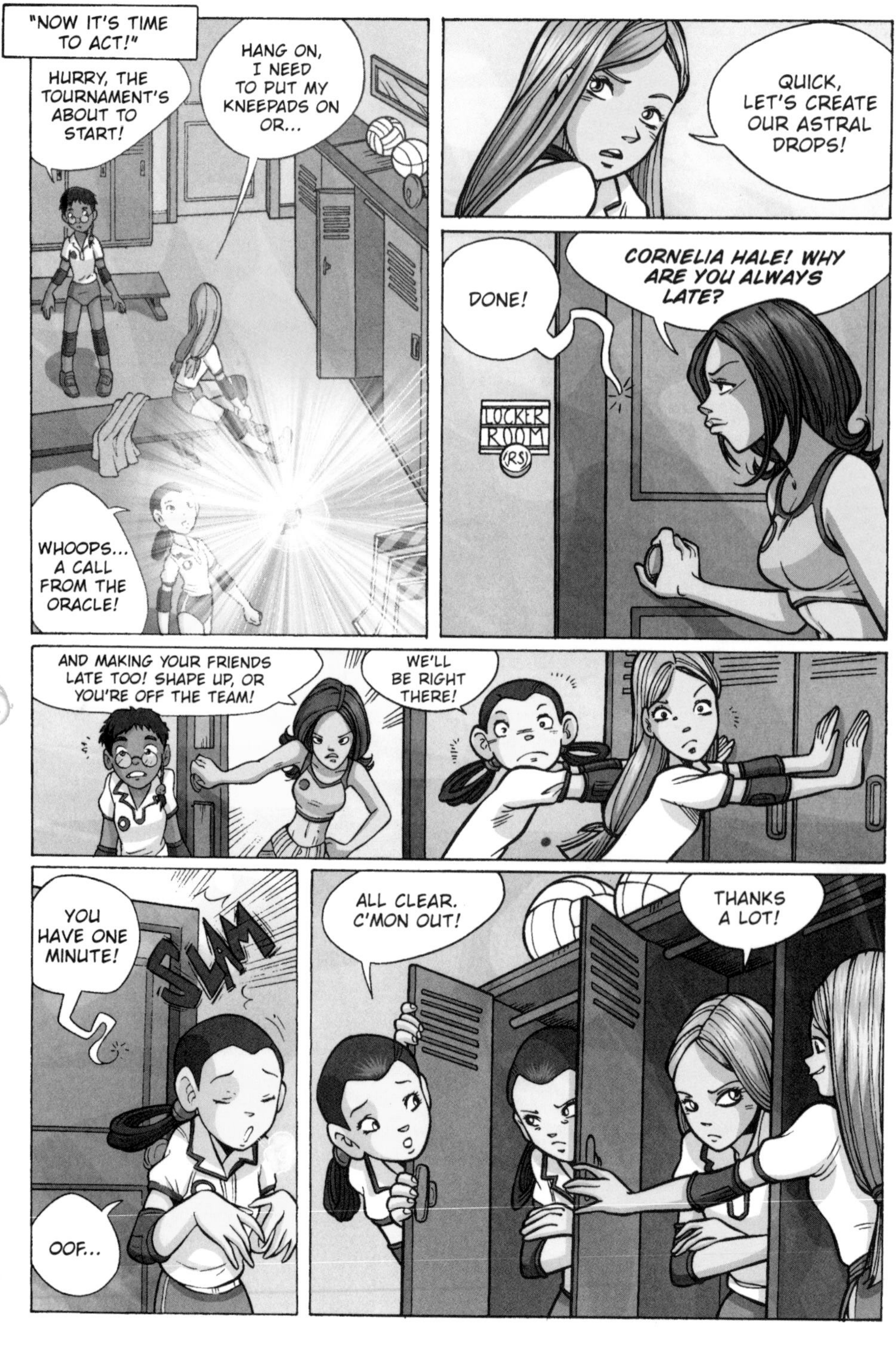
"NOW IT'S TIME TO ACT!"
HURRY, THE TOURNAMENT'S ABOUT TO START!
HANG ON, I NEED TO PUT MY KNEEPADS ON OR...
WHOOPS... A CALL FROM THE ORACLE!
QUICK, LET'S CREATE OUR ASTRAL DROPS!
DONE!
CORNELIA HALE! WHY ARE YOU ALWAYS LATE?
LOCKER ROOM
RS
AND MAKING YOUR FRIENDS LATE TOO! SHAPE UP, OR YOU'RE OFF THE TEAM!
WE'LL BE RIGHT THERE!
YOU HAVE ONE MINUTE!
SLAM
OOF...
ALL CLEAR. C'MON OUT!
THANKS A LOT!

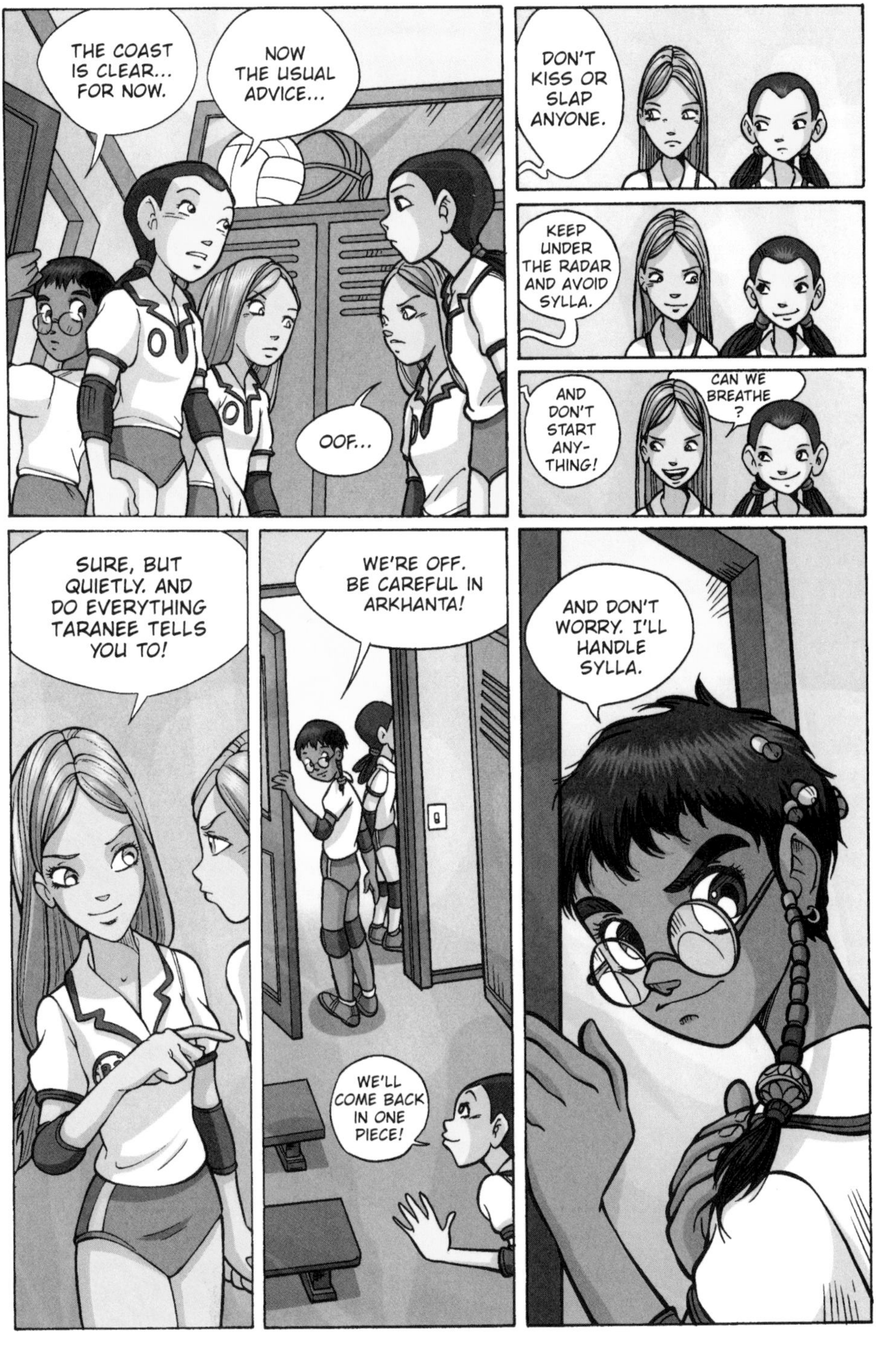
THE COAST IS CLEAR... FOR NOW.
NOW THE USUAL ADVICE...
OOF...
DON'T KISS OR SLAP ANYONE.
KEEP UNDER THE RADAR AND AVOID SYLLA.
AND DON'T START ANY-THING!
CAN WE BREATHE?
SURE, BUT QUIETLY. AND DO EVERYTHING TARANEE TELLS YOU TO!
WE'RE OFF. BE CAREFUL IN ARKHANTA!
WE'LL COME BACK IN ONE PIECE!
AND DON'T WORRY. I'LL HANDLE SYLLA.

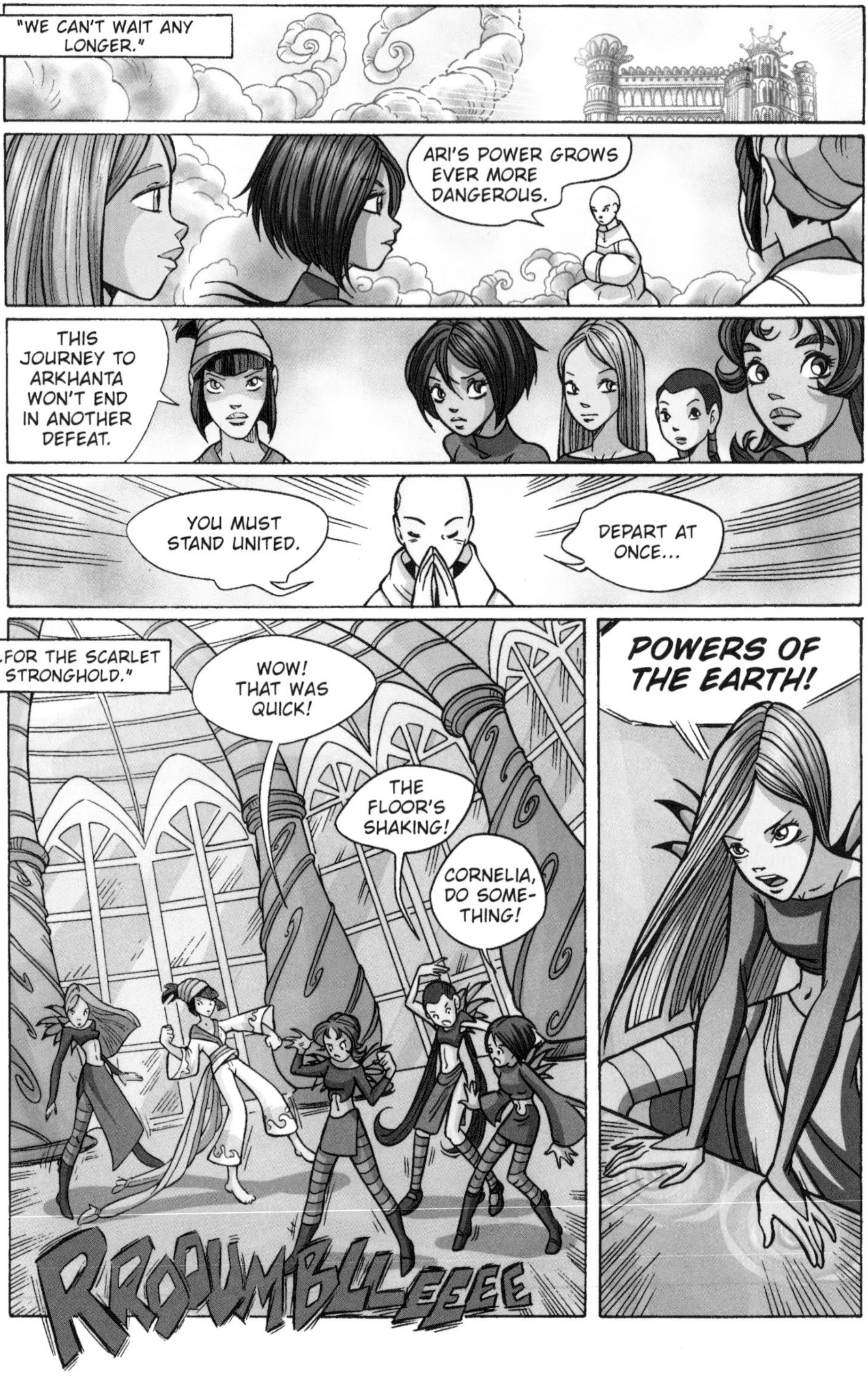
"WE CAN'T WAIT ANY LONGER."
ARI'S POWER GROWS EVER MORE DANGEROUS.
THIS JOURNEY TO ARKHANTA WON'T END IN ANOTHER DEFEAT.
YOU MUST STAND UNITED.
DEPART AT ONCE...
"...FOR THE SCARLET STRONGHOLD."
WOW! THAT WAS QUICK!
THE FLOOR'S SHAKING!
CORNELIA, DO SOME-THING!
RROOUMBLLEEEE
POWERS OF THE EARTH!

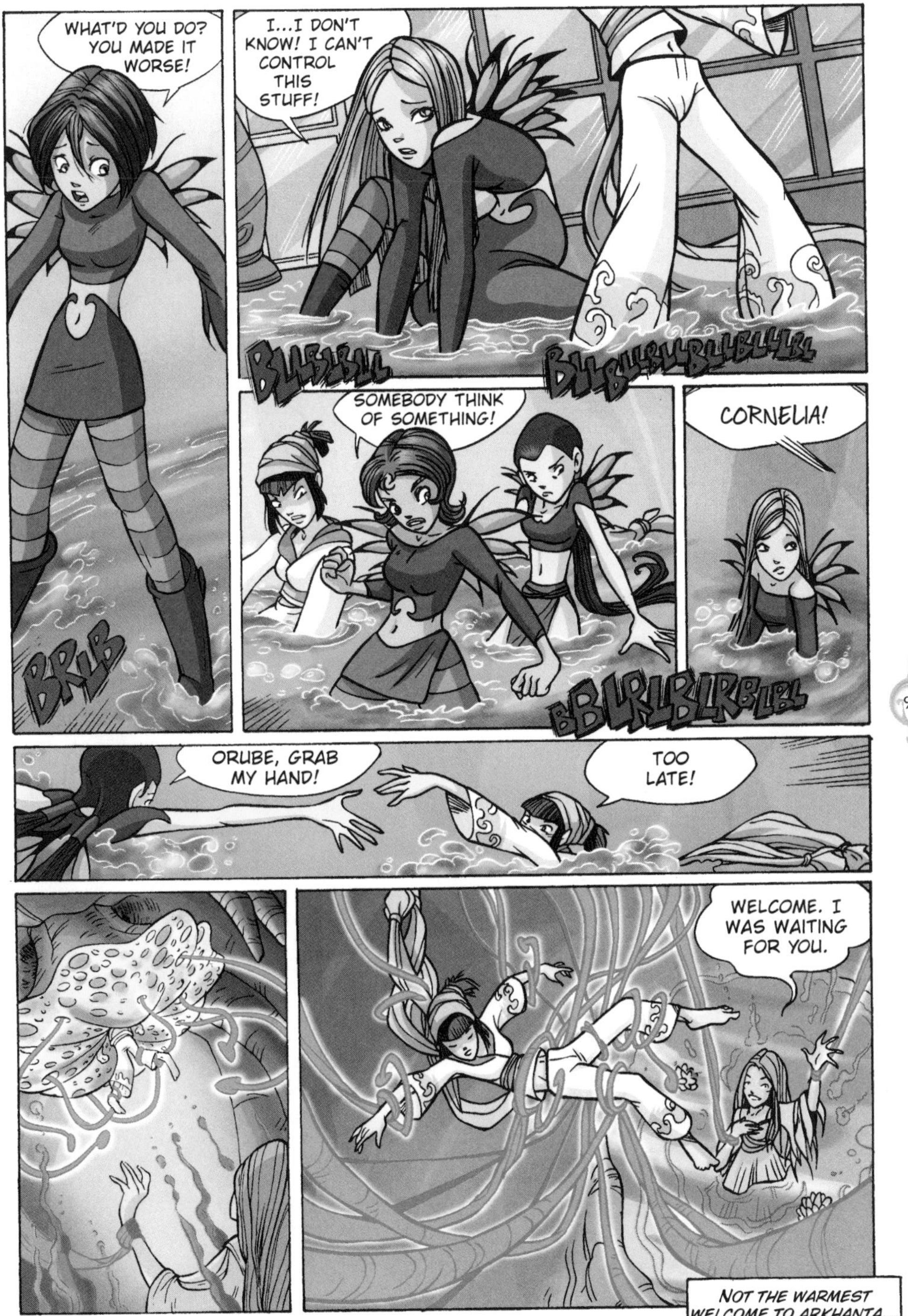
WHAT'D YOU DO? YOU MADE IT WORSE!
I...I DON'T KNOW! I CAN'T CONTROL THIS STUFF!
SOMEBODY THINK OF SOMETHING!
CORNELIA!
ORUBE, GRAB MY HAND!
TOO LATE!
WELCOME. I WAS WAITING FOR YOU.
NOT THE WARMEST WELCOME TO ARKHANTA...

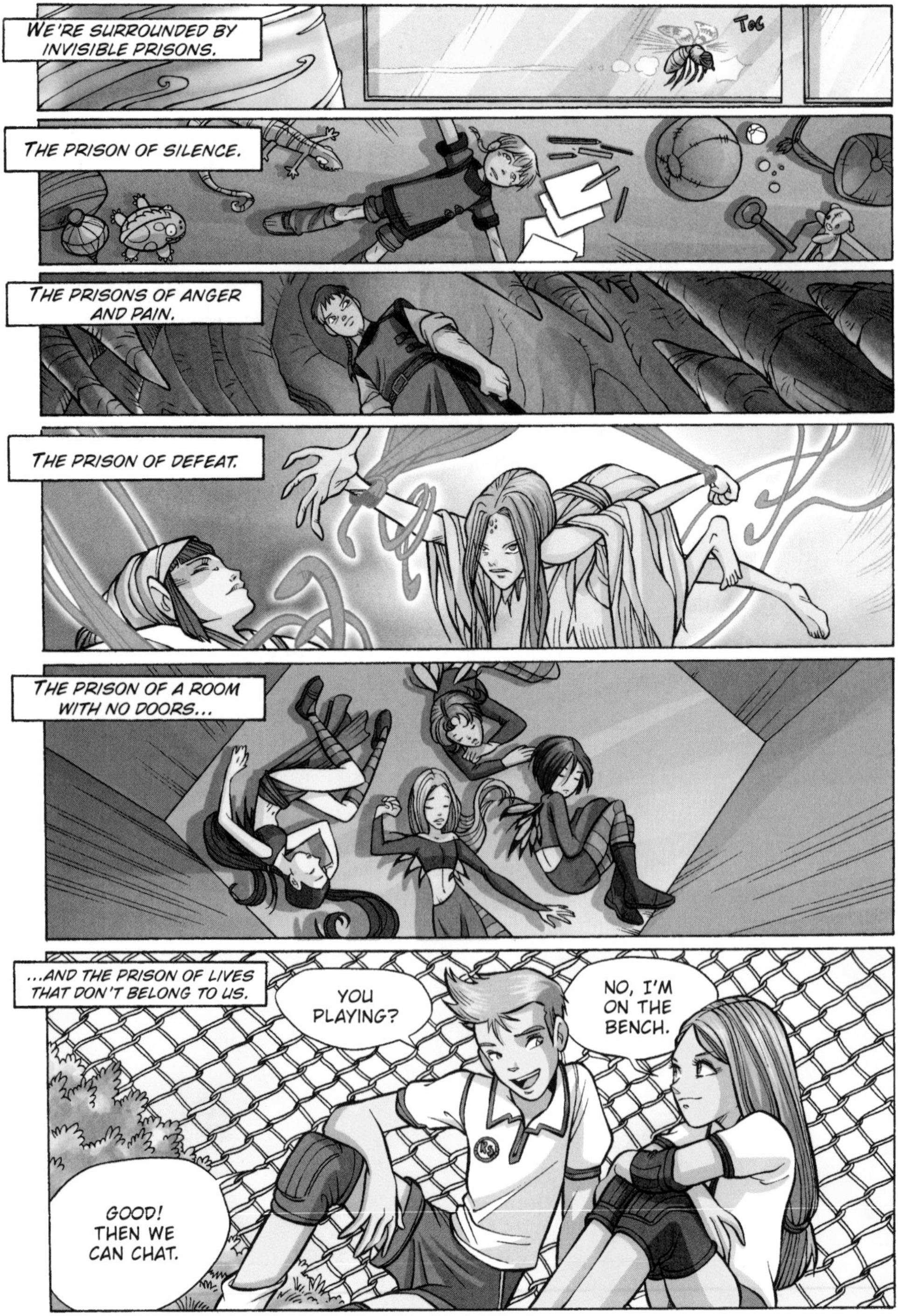
WE'RE SURROUNDED BY INVISIBLE PRISONS.
TOC
THE PRISON OF SILENCE.
THE PRISONS OF ANGER AND PAIN.
THE PRISON OF DEFEAT.
THE PRISON OF A ROOM WITH NO DOORS...
...AND THE PRISON OF LIVES THAT DON'T BELONG TO US.
YOU PLAYING?
NO, I'M ON THE BENCH.
GOOD! THEN WE CAN CHAT.

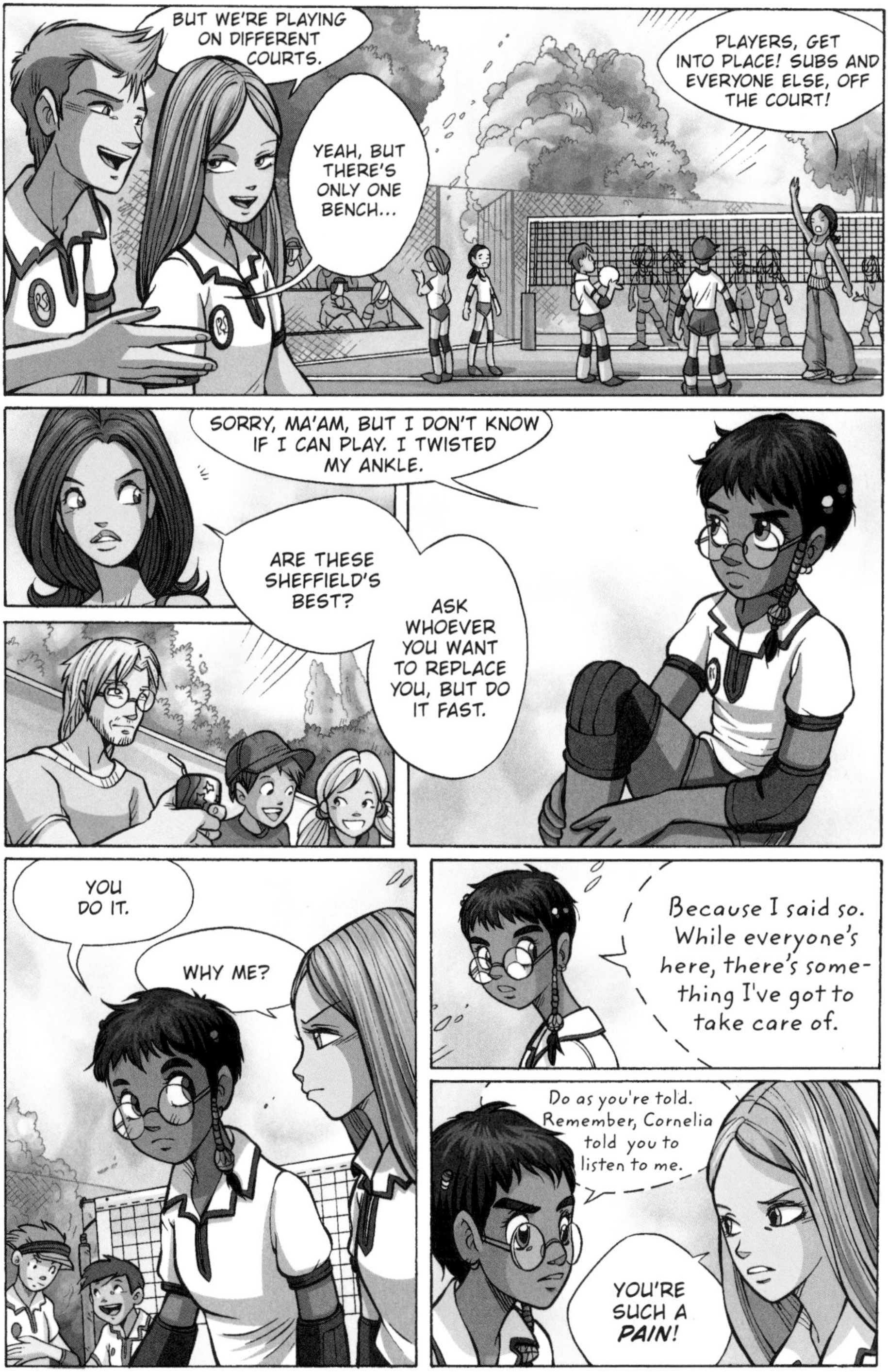
BUT WE'RE PLAYING ON DIFFERENT COURTS.
YEAH, BUT THERE'S ONLY ONE BENCH...
PLAYERS, GET INTO PLACE! SUBS AND EVERYONE ELSE, OFF THE COURT!
SORRY, MA'AM, BUT I DON'T KNOW IF I CAN PLAY. I TWISTED MY ANKLE.
ARE THESE SHEFFIELD'S BEST?
ASK WHOEVER YOU WANT TO REPLACE YOU, BUT DO IT FAST.
YOU DO IT.
WHY ME?
Because I said so. While everyone's here, there's something I've got to take care of.
Do as you're told. Remember, Cornelia told you to listen to me.
YOU'RE SUCH A PAIN!

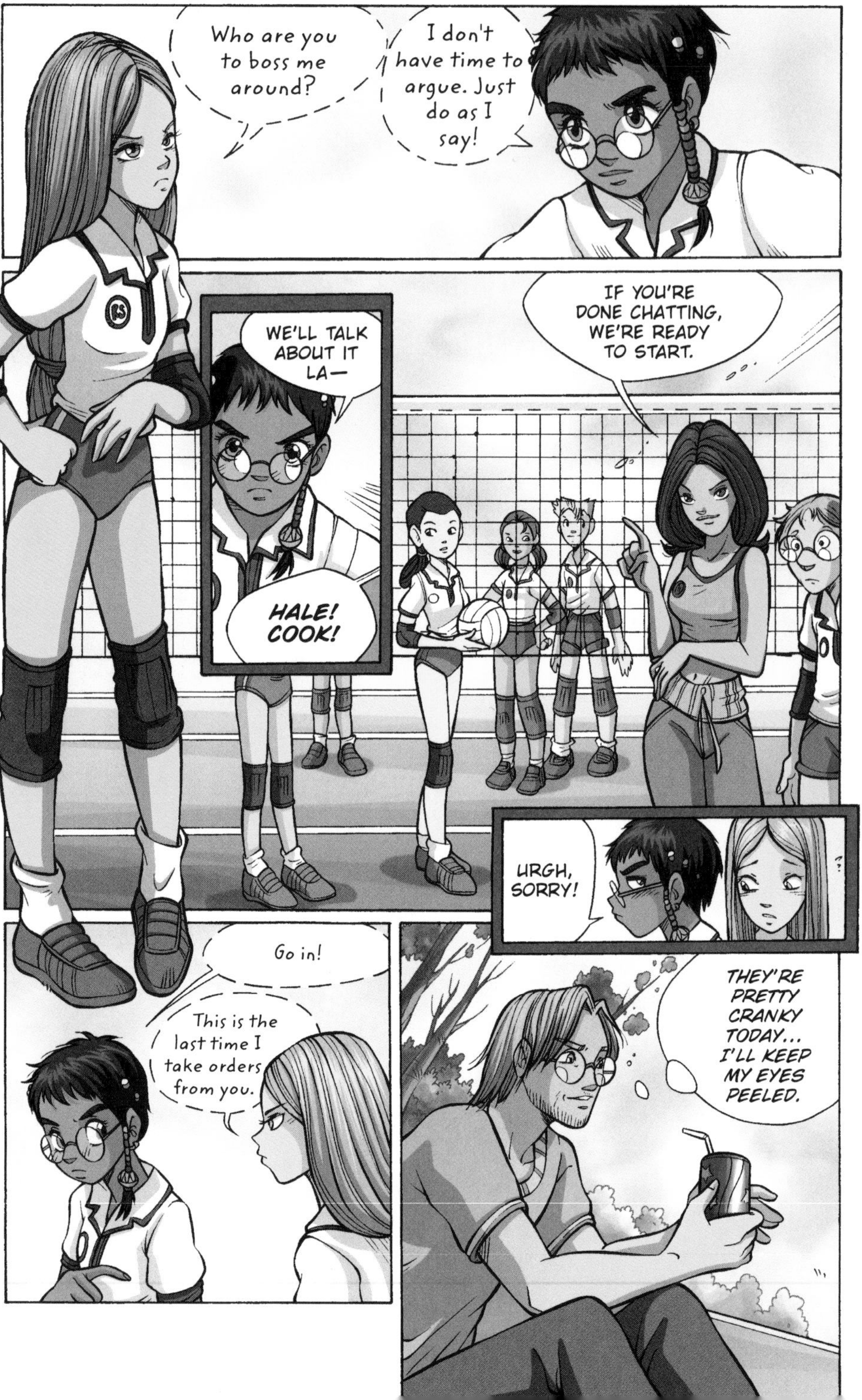
Who are you to boss me around?
I don't have time to argue. Just do as I say!
WE'LL TALK ABOUT IT LA—
HALE! COOK!
IF YOU'RE DONE CHATTING, WE'RE READY TO START.
URGH, SORRY!
Go in!
This is the last time I take orders from you.
THEY'RE PRETTY CRANKY TODAY... I'LL KEEP MY EYES PEELED.

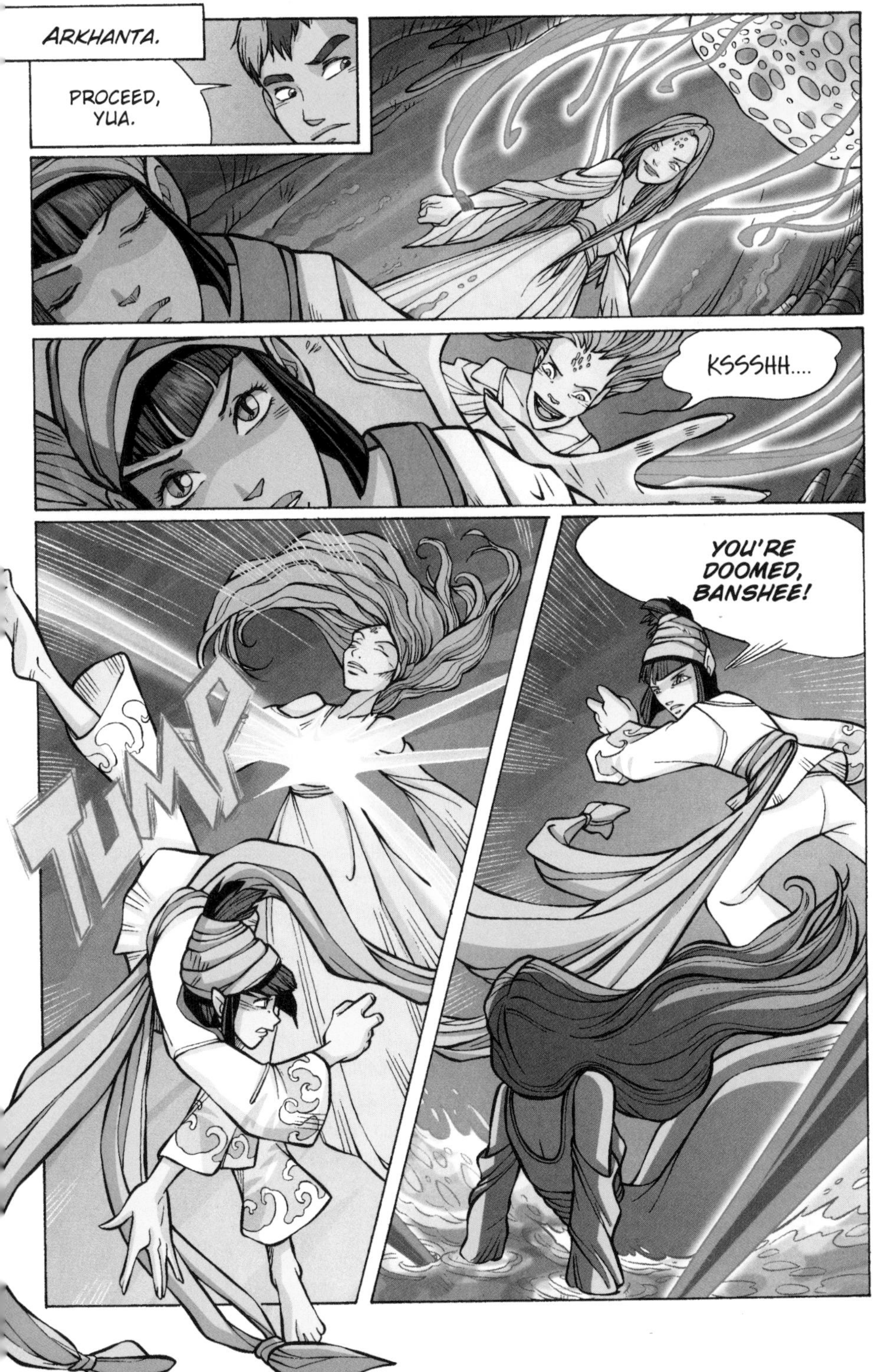
ARKHANTA.
PROCEED, YUA.
KSSSHH....
TUMP
YOU'RE DOOMED, BANSHEE!

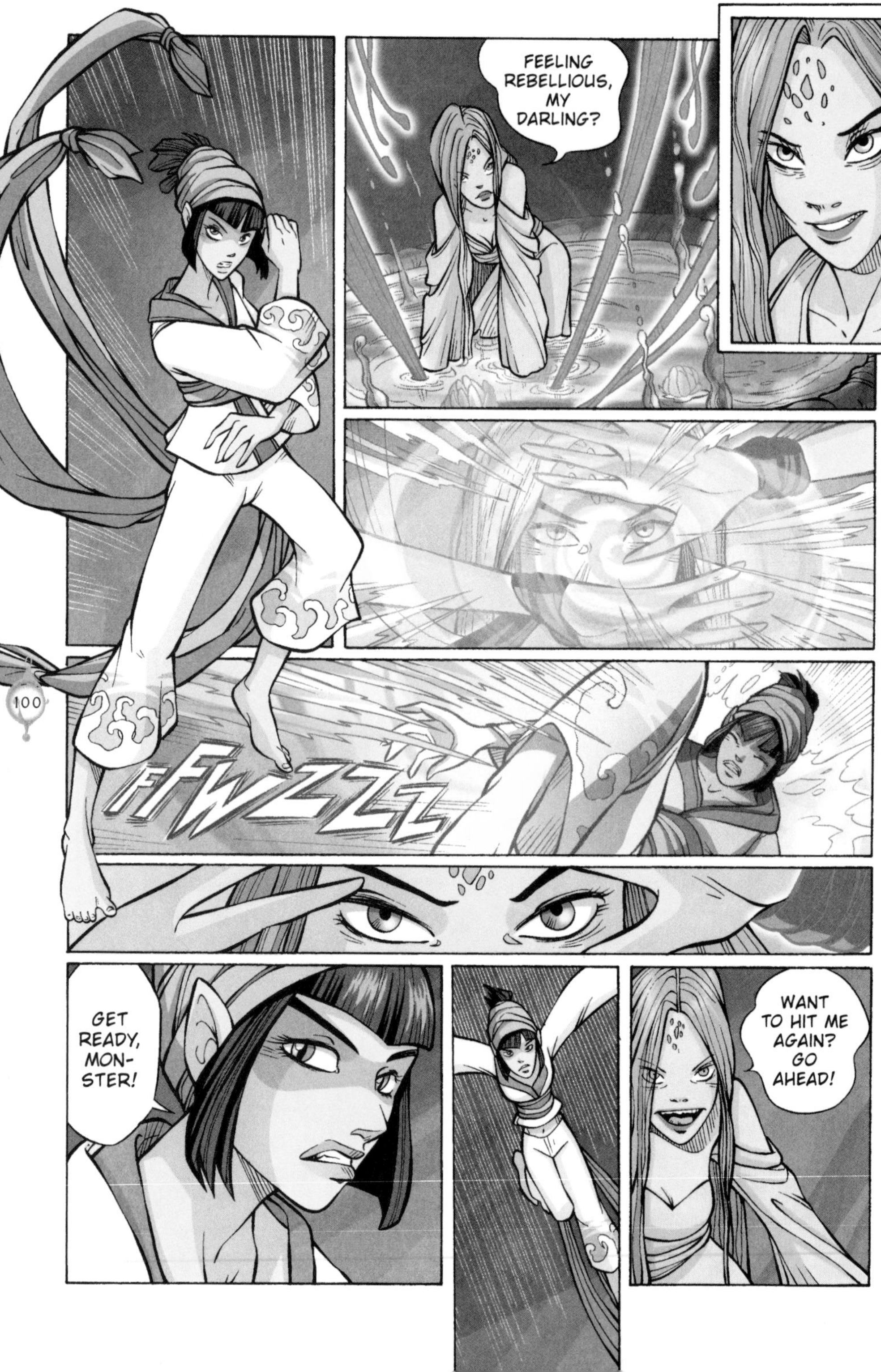
FEELING REBELLIOUS, MY DARLING?
FFWZZZZ
GET READY, MON-STER!
WANT TO HIT ME AGAIN? GO AHEAD!

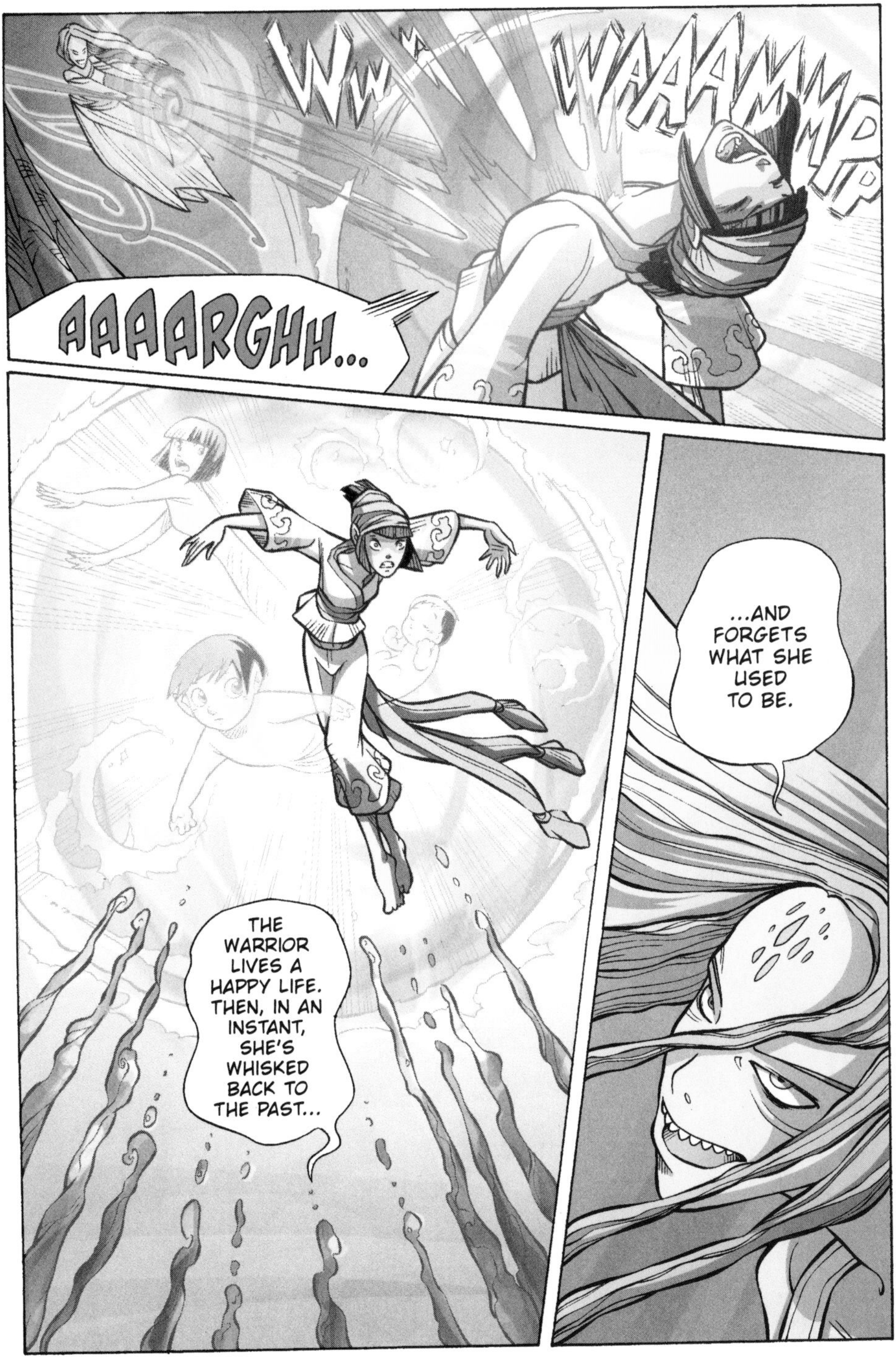
WWA WAAAMMMP
AAAARGHH...
THE WARRIOR LIVES A HAPPY LIFE. THEN, IN AN INSTANT, SHE'S WHISKED BACK TO THE PAST...
...AND FORGETS WHAT SHE USED TO BE.

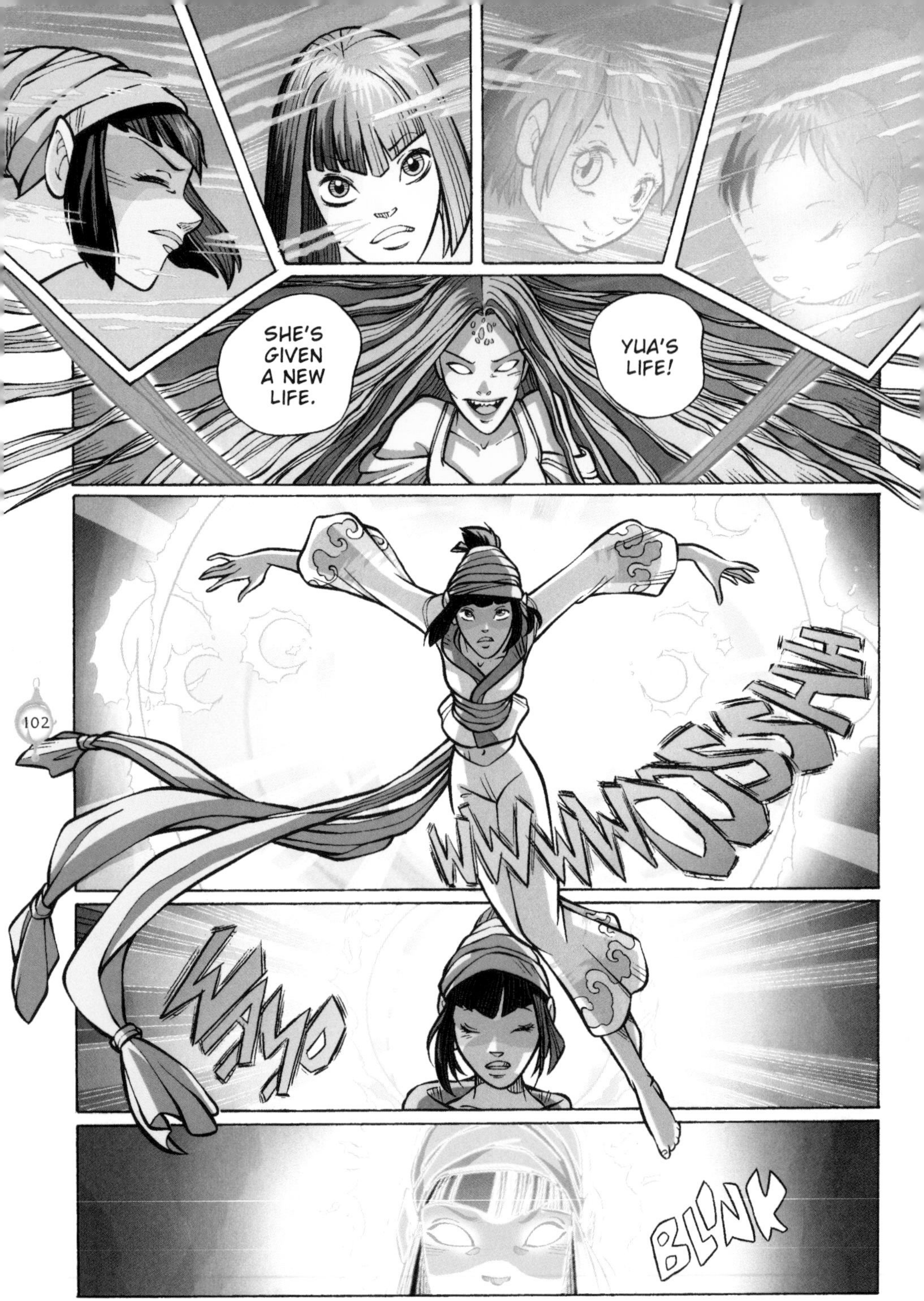
SHE'S GIVEN A NEW LIFE.
YUA'S LIFE!
WWWWOOSHAH
WAMO
BLINK

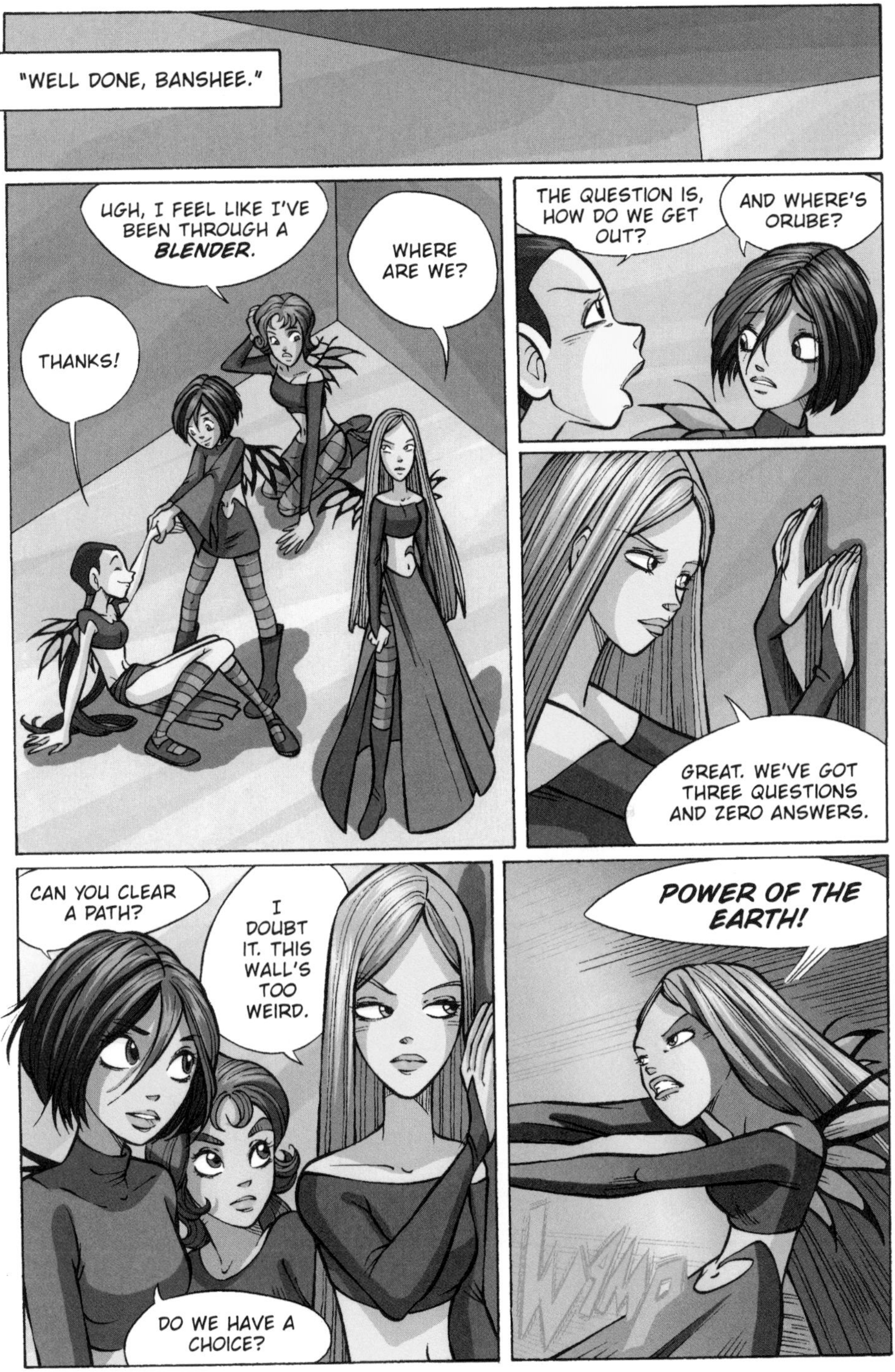
"WELL DONE, BANSHEE."
UGH, I FEEL LIKE I'VE BEEN THROUGH A **BLENDER**.
WHERE ARE WE?
THANKS!
THE QUESTION IS, HOW DO WE GET OUT?
AND WHERE'S ORUBE?
GREAT. WE'VE GOT THREE QUESTIONS AND ZERO ANSWERS.
CAN YOU CLEAR A PATH?
I DOUBT IT. THIS WALL'S TOO WEIRD.
DO WE HAVE A CHOICE?
POWER OF THE EARTH!

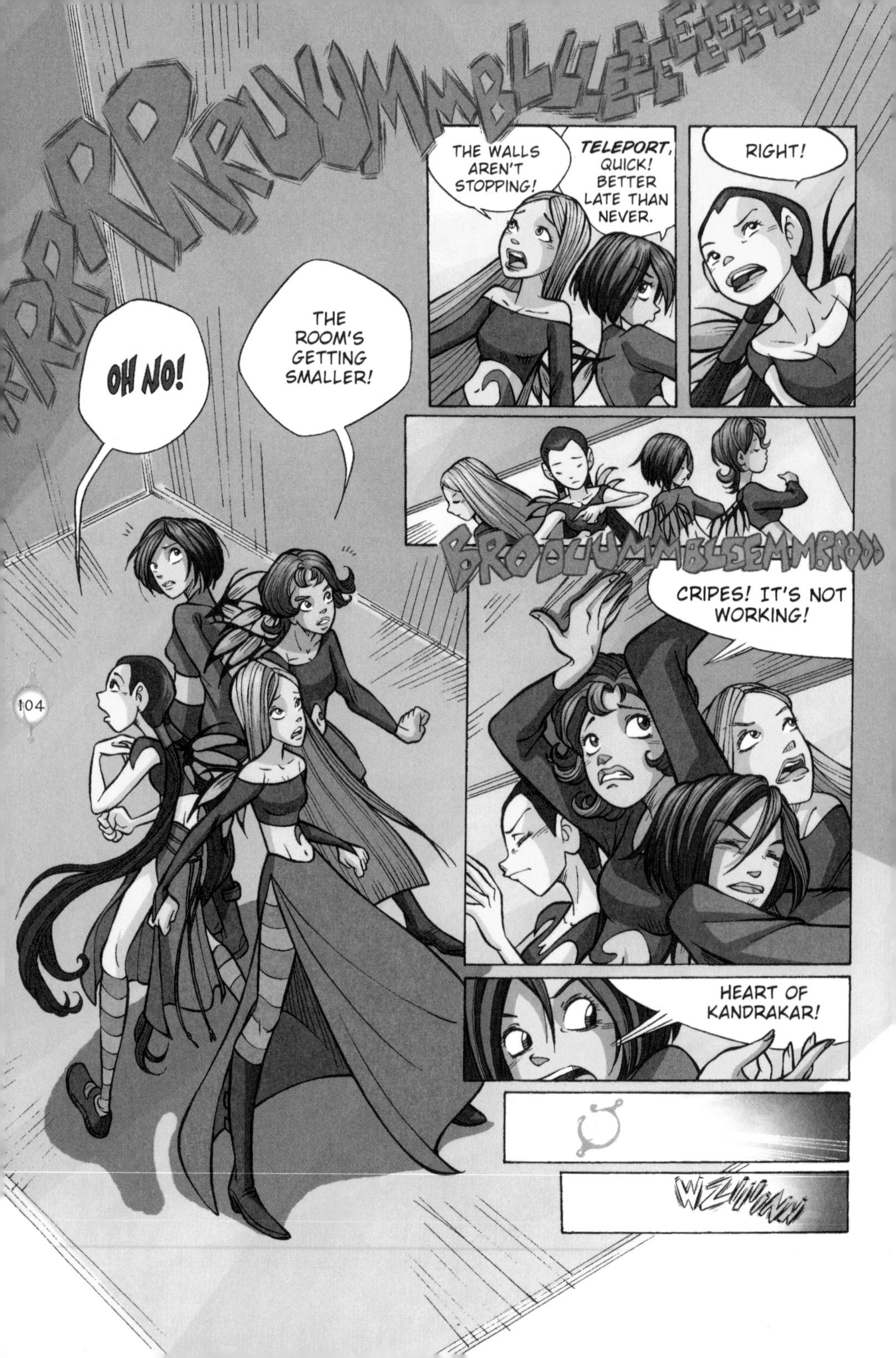
OH NO!
THE ROOM'S GETTING SMALLER!
THE WALLS AREN'T STOPPING!
TELEPORT, QUICK! BETTER LATE THAN NEVER.
RIGHT!
CRIPES! IT'S NOT WORKING!
HEART OF KANDRAKAR!

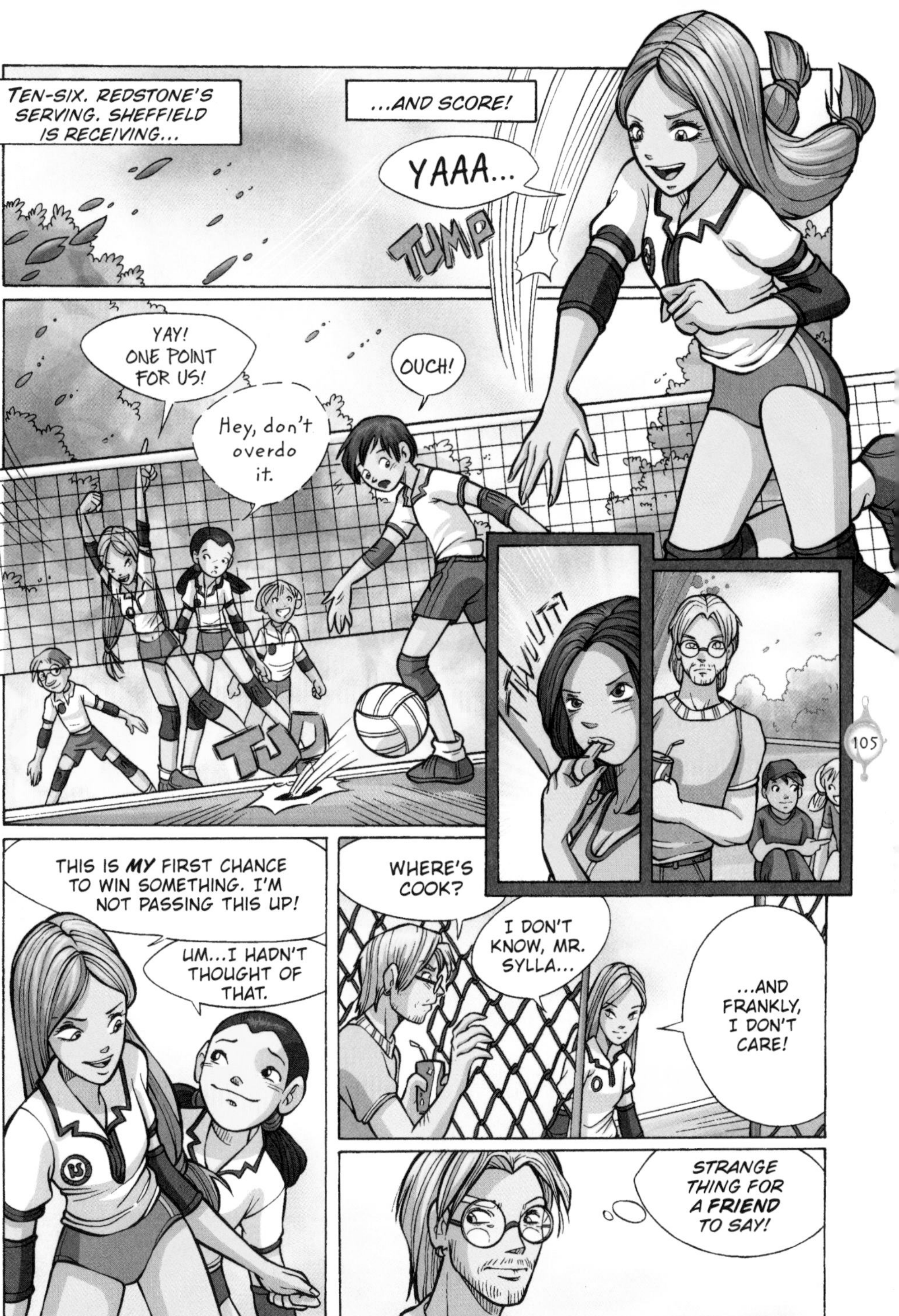
TEN-SIX. REDSTONE'S SERVING. SHEFFIELD IS RECEIVING...
...AND SCORE!
YAAA...
TUMP
YAY! ONE POINT FOR US!
Hey, don't overdo it.
OUCH!
TUD
TWUUT!
THIS IS MY FIRST CHANCE TO WIN SOMETHING. I'M NOT PASSING THIS UP!
UM...I HADN'T THOUGHT OF THAT.
WHERE'S COOK?
I DON'T KNOW, MR. SYLLA...
...AND FRANKLY, I DON'T CARE!
STRANGE THING FOR A FRIEND TO SAY!

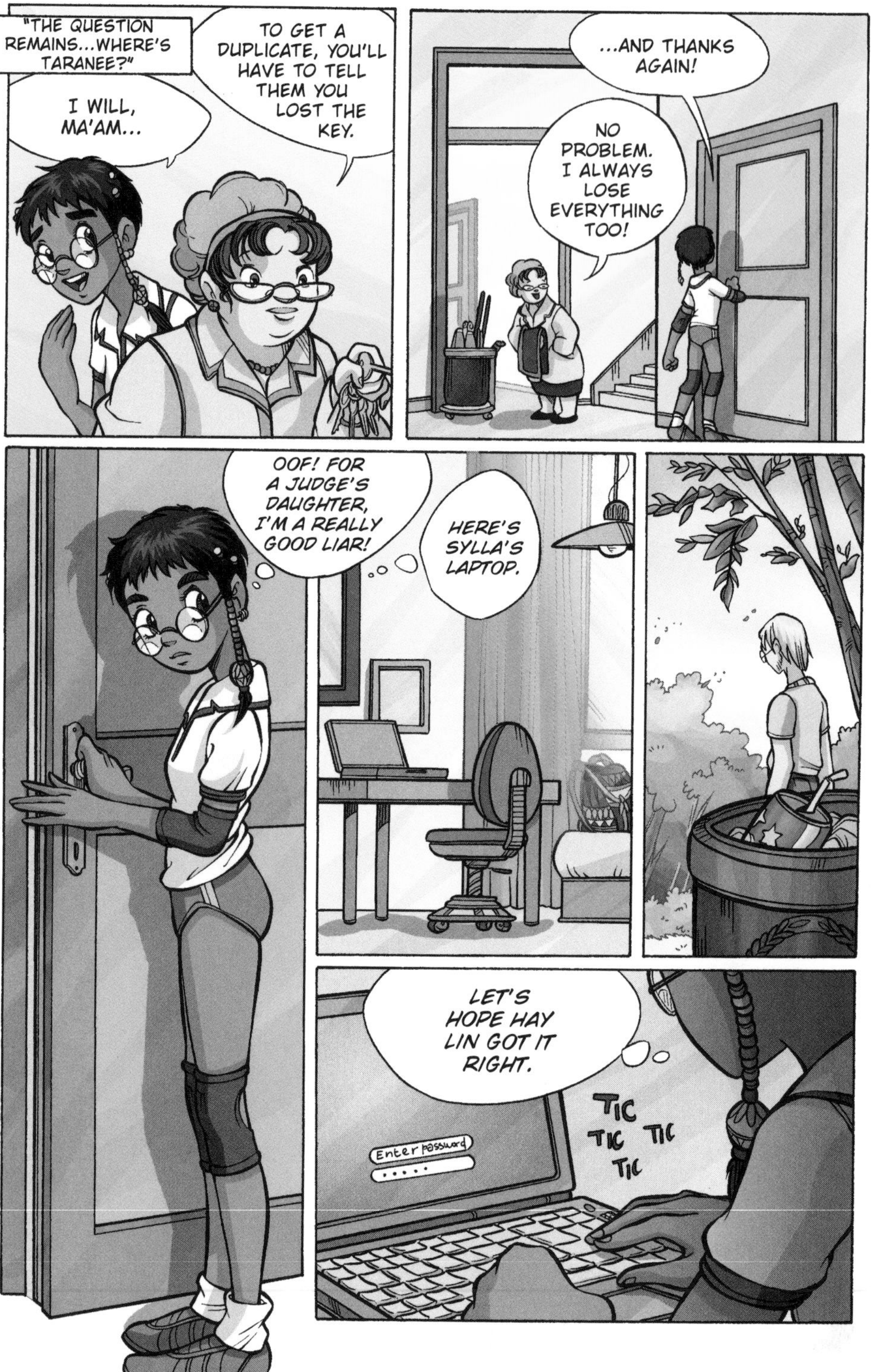
"THE QUESTION REMAINS...WHERE'S TARANEE?"
TO GET A DUPLICATE, YOU'LL HAVE TO TELL THEM YOU LOST THE KEY.
I WILL, MA'AM...
...AND THANKS AGAIN!
NO PROBLEM. I ALWAYS LOSE EVERYTHING TOO!
OOF! FOR A JUDGE'S DAUGHTER, I'M A REALLY GOOD LIAR!
HERE'S SYLLA'S LAPTOP.
LET'S HOPE HAY LIN GOT IT RIGHT.
Enter password
TIC TIC TIC TIC

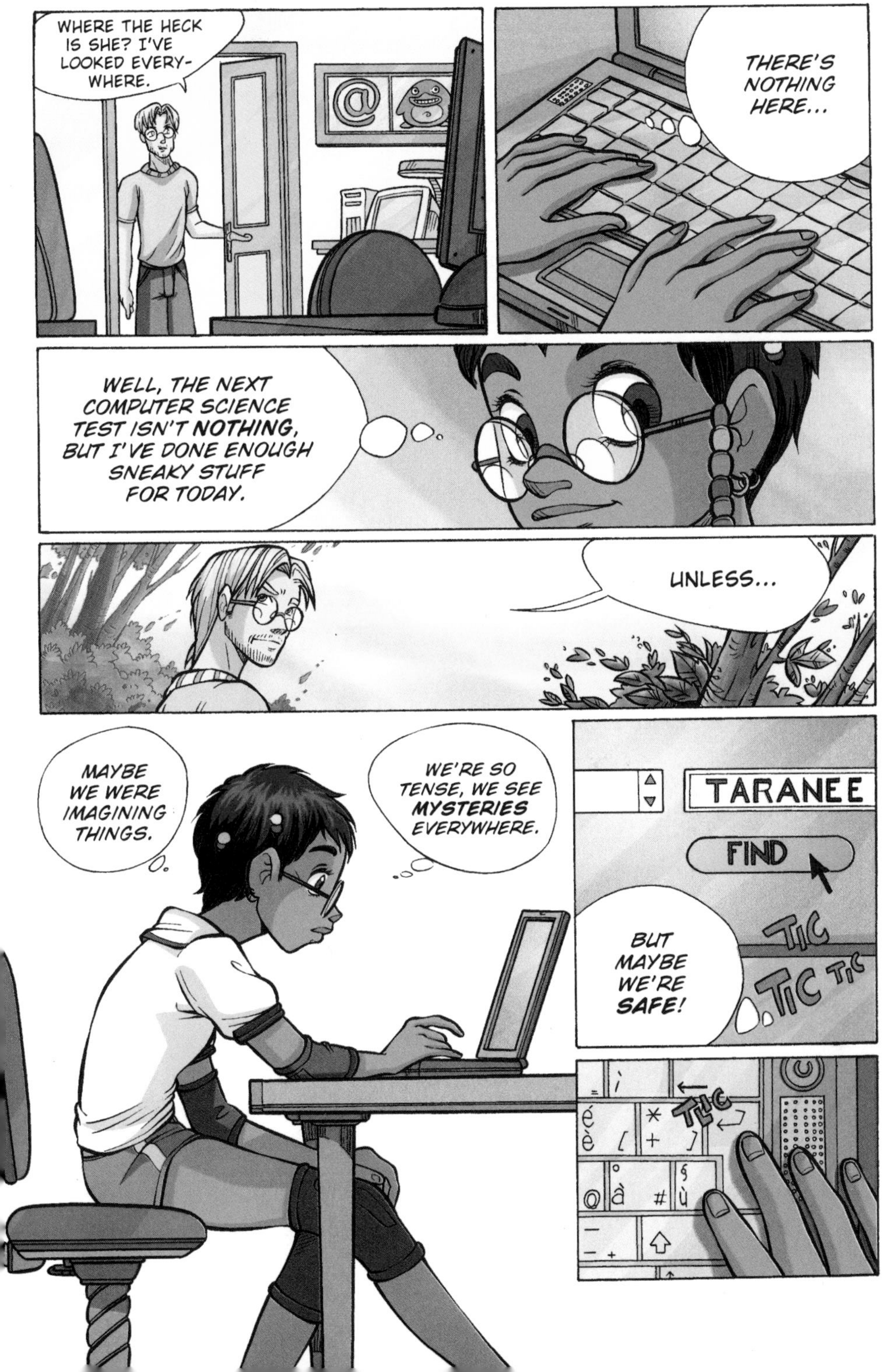
WHERE THE HECK IS SHE? I'VE LOOKED EVERY-WHERE.
THERE'S NOTHING HERE...
WELL, THE NEXT COMPUTER SCIENCE TEST ISN'T **NOTHING**, BUT I'VE DONE ENOUGH SNEAKY STUFF FOR TODAY.
UNLESS...
MAYBE WE WERE IMAGINING THINGS.
WE'RE SO TENSE, WE SEE **MYSTERIES** EVERYWHERE.
TARANEE
FIND
BUT MAYBE WE'RE **SAFE**!
TIC
TIC TIC
TIC

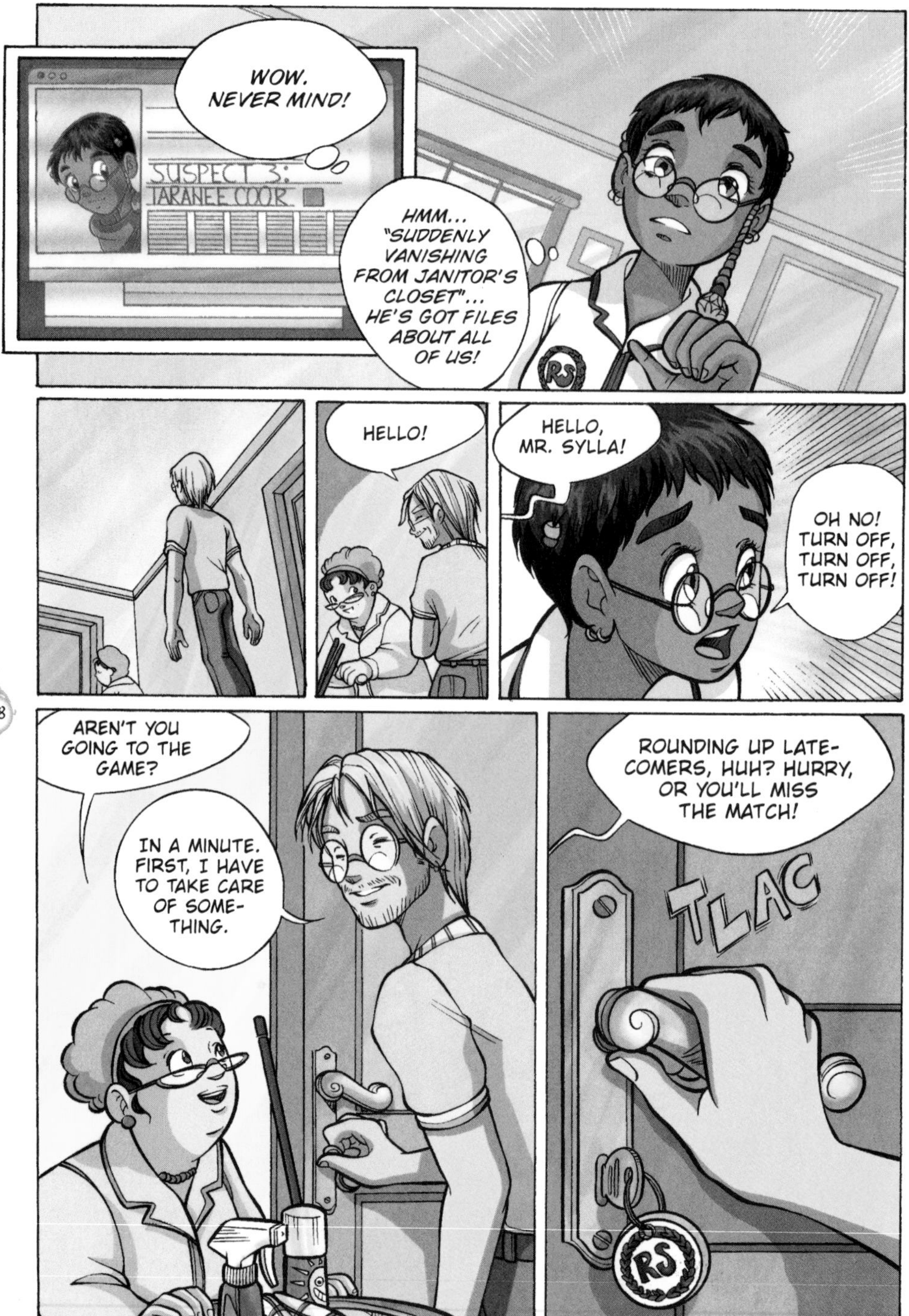
SUSPECT 3:
TARANEE COOR
WOW. NEVER MIND!
HMM... "SUDDENLY VANISHING FROM JANITOR'S CLOSET"... HE'S GOT FILES ABOUT ALL OF US!
HELLO!
HELLO, MR. SYLLA!
OH NO! TURN OFF, TURN OFF, TURN OFF!
AREN'T YOU GOING TO THE GAME?
IN A MINUTE. FIRST, I HAVE TO TAKE CARE OF SOME-THING.
ROUNDING UP LATE-COMERS, HUH? HURRY, OR YOU'LL MISS THE MATCH!
TLAC

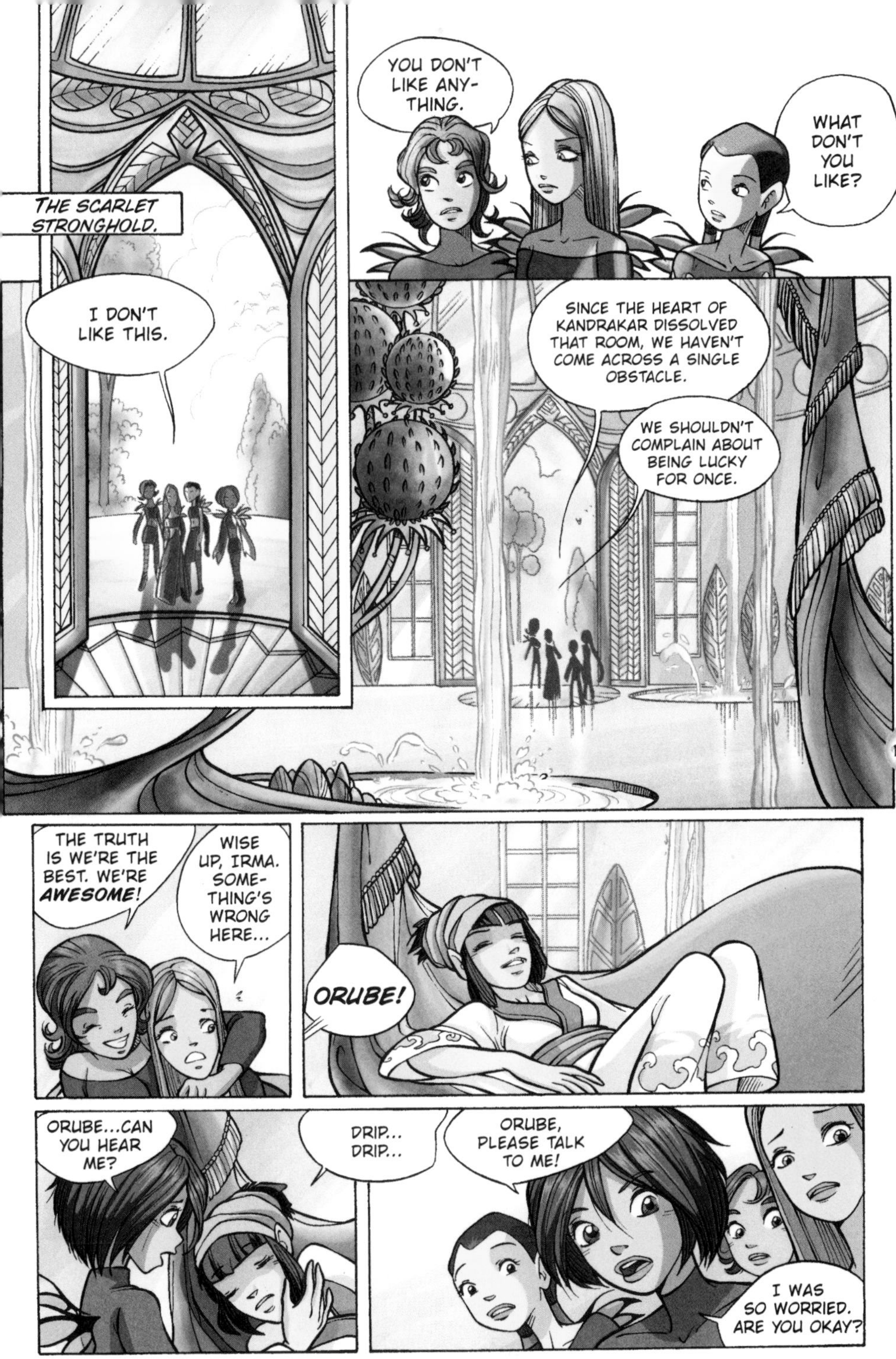
THE SCARLET STRONGHOLD.
I DON'T LIKE THIS.
YOU DON'T LIKE ANY-THING.
WHAT DON'T YOU LIKE?
SINCE THE HEART OF KANDRAKAR DISSOLVED THAT ROOM, WE HAVEN'T COME ACROSS A SINGLE OBSTACLE.
WE SHOULDN'T COMPLAIN ABOUT BEING LUCKY FOR ONCE.
THE TRUTH IS WE'RE THE BEST. WE'RE ***AWESOME***!
WISE UP, IRMA. SOME-THING'S WRONG HERE...
ORUBE!
ORUBE...CAN YOU HEAR ME?
DRIP... DRIP...
ORUBE, PLEASE TALK TO ME!
I WAS SO WORRIED. ARE YOU OKAY?

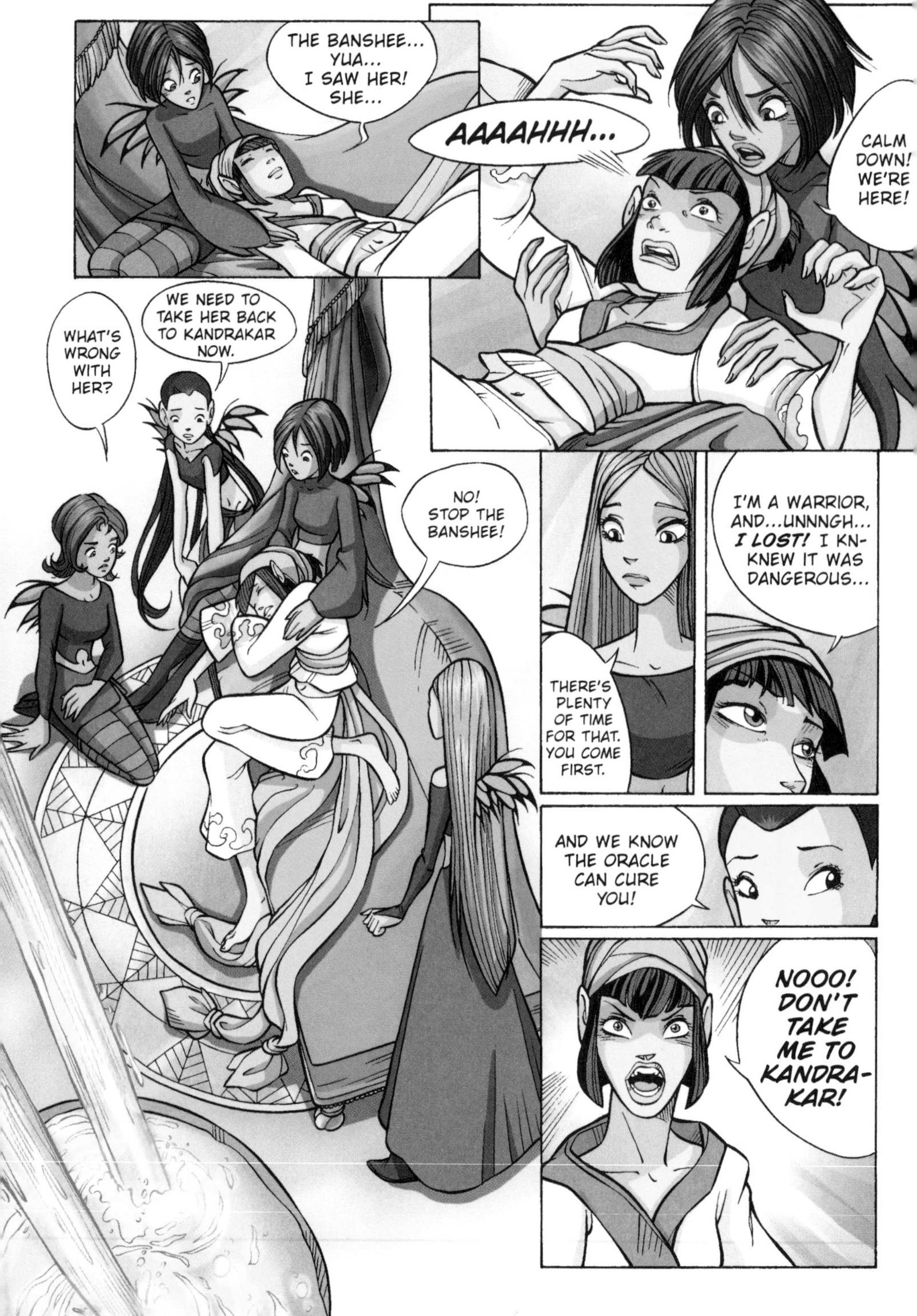
THE BANSHEE... YUA... I SAW HER! SHE...
AAAAHHH...
CALM DOWN! WE'RE HERE!
WHAT'S WRONG WITH HER?
WE NEED TO TAKE HER BACK TO KANDRAKAR NOW.
NO! STOP THE BANSHEE!
I'M A WARRIOR, AND...UNNNGH... I LOST! I KN-KNEW IT WAS DANGEROUS...
THERE'S PLENTY OF TIME FOR THAT. YOU COME FIRST.
AND WE KNOW THE ORACLE CAN CURE YOU!
NOOO! DON'T TAKE ME TO KANDRA-KAR!

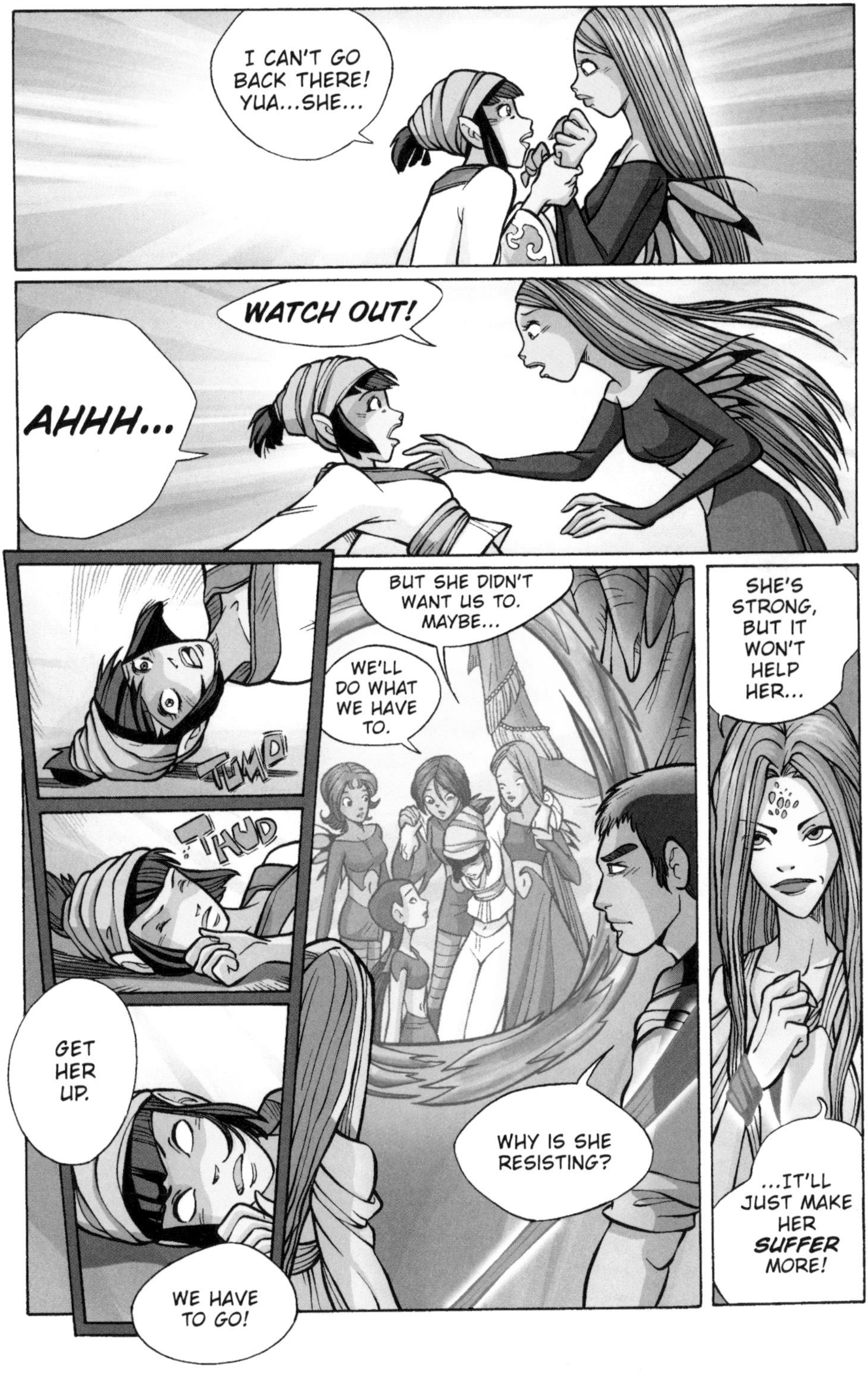
I CAN'T GO BACK THERE! YUA...SHE...
WATCH OUT!
AHHH...
THUMP
THUD
GET HER UP.
WE HAVE TO GO!
BUT SHE DIDN'T WANT US TO. MAYBE...
WE'LL DO WHAT WE HAVE TO.
WHY IS SHE RESISTING?
SHE'S STRONG, BUT IT WON'T HELP HER...
...IT'LL JUST MAKE HER SUFFER MORE!

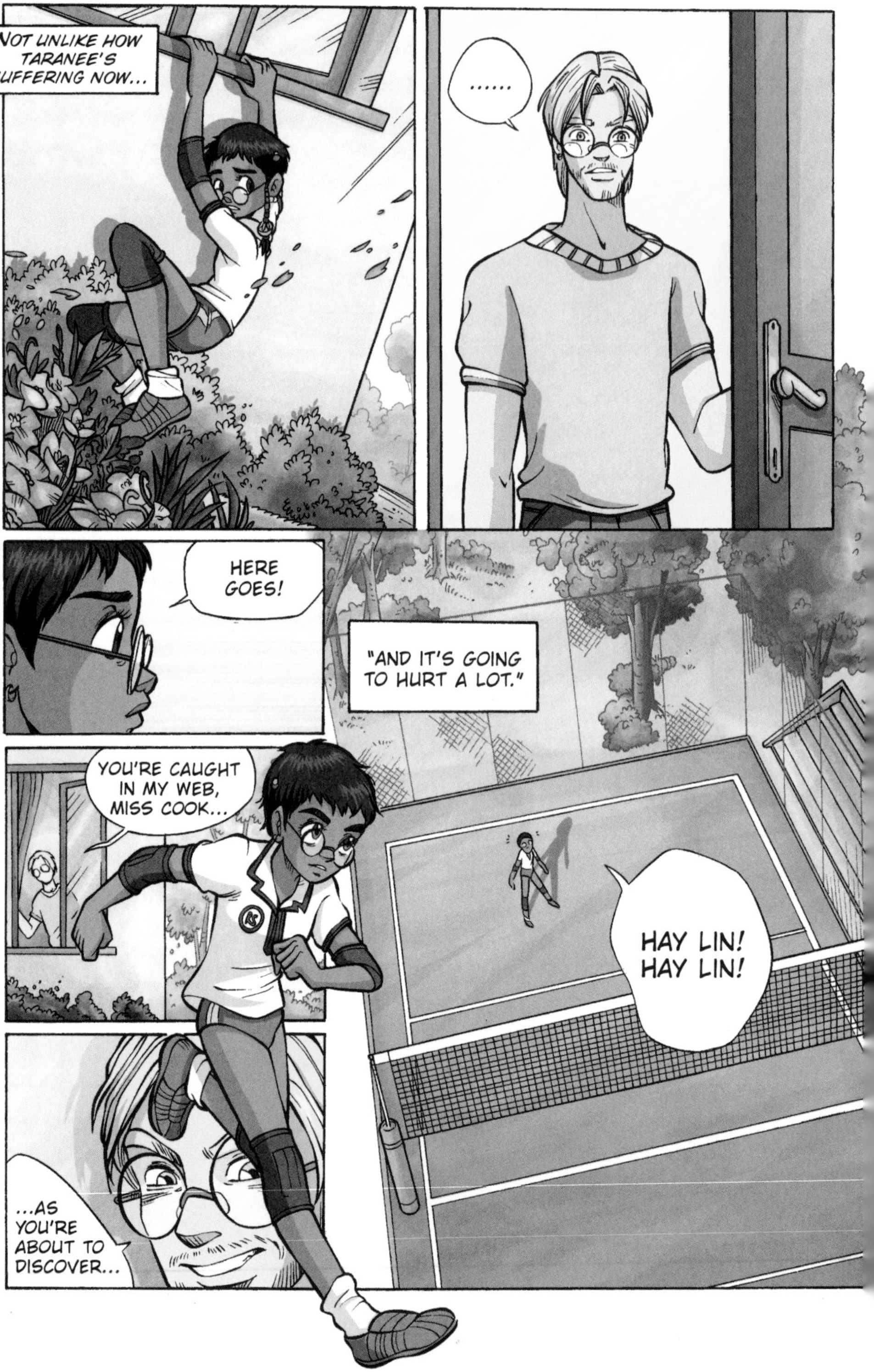
NOT UNLIKE HOW TARANEE'S SUFFERING NOW...
......
HERE GOES!
"AND IT'S GOING TO HURT A LOT."
YOU'RE CAUGHT IN MY WEB, MISS COOK...
HAY LIN! HAY LIN!
...AS YOU'RE ABOUT TO DISCOVER...

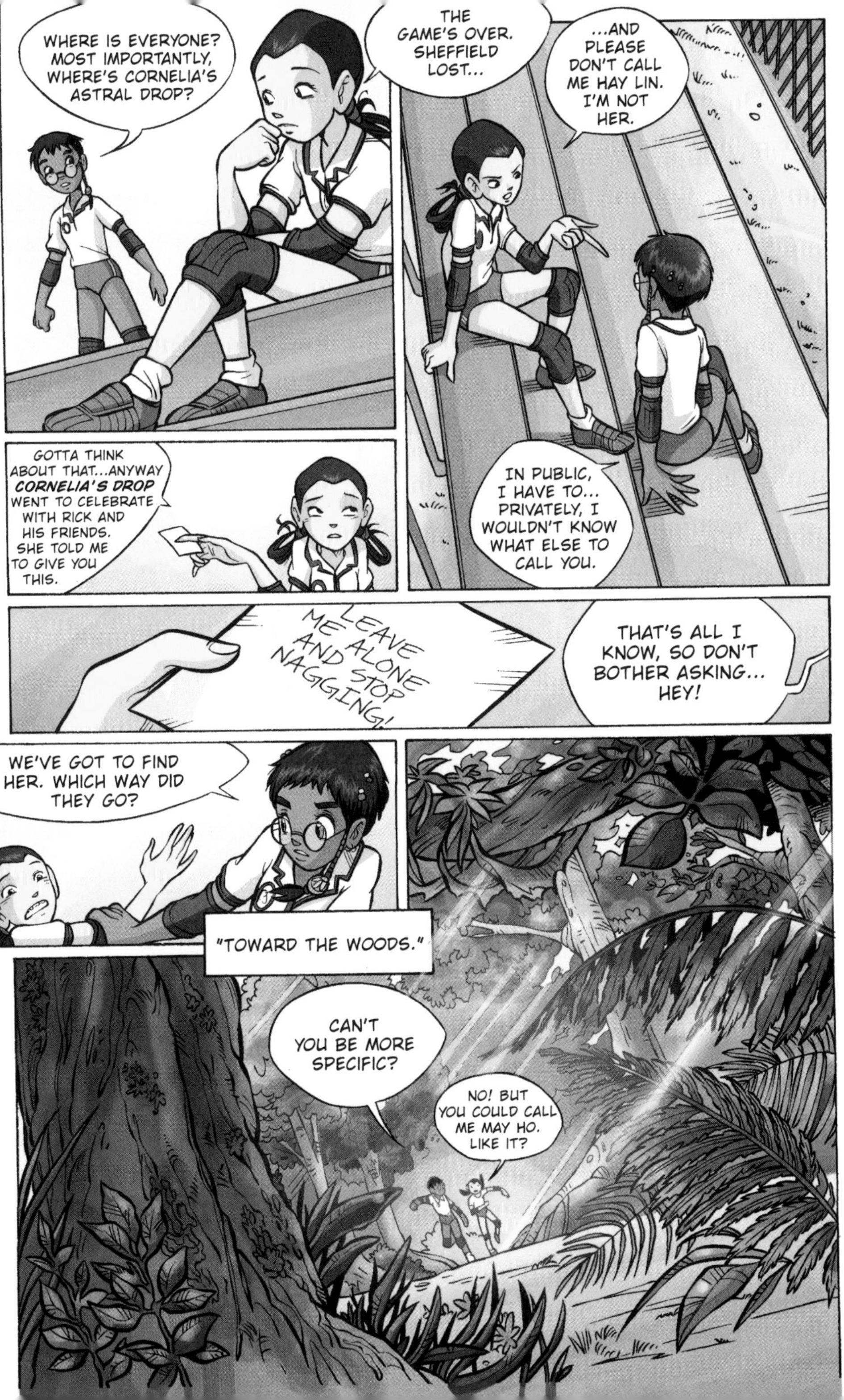

WHERE IS EVERYONE? MOST IMPORTANTLY, WHERE'S CORNELIA'S ASTRAL DROP?
THE GAME'S OVER. SHEFFIELD LOST...
...AND PLEASE DON'T CALL ME HAY LIN. I'M NOT HER.
GOTTA THINK ABOUT THAT...ANYWAY **CORNELIA'S DROP** WENT TO CELEBRATE WITH RICK AND HIS FRIENDS. SHE TOLD ME TO GIVE YOU THIS.
IN PUBLIC, I HAVE TO... PRIVATELY, I WOULDN'T KNOW WHAT ELSE TO CALL YOU.
LEAVE ME ALONE AND STOP NAGGING!
THAT'S ALL I KNOW, SO DON'T BOTHER ASKING... HEY!
WE'VE GOT TO FIND HER. WHICH WAY DID THEY GO?
"TOWARD THE WOODS."
CAN'T YOU BE MORE SPECIFIC?
NO! BUT YOU COULD CALL ME MAY HO. LIKE IT?

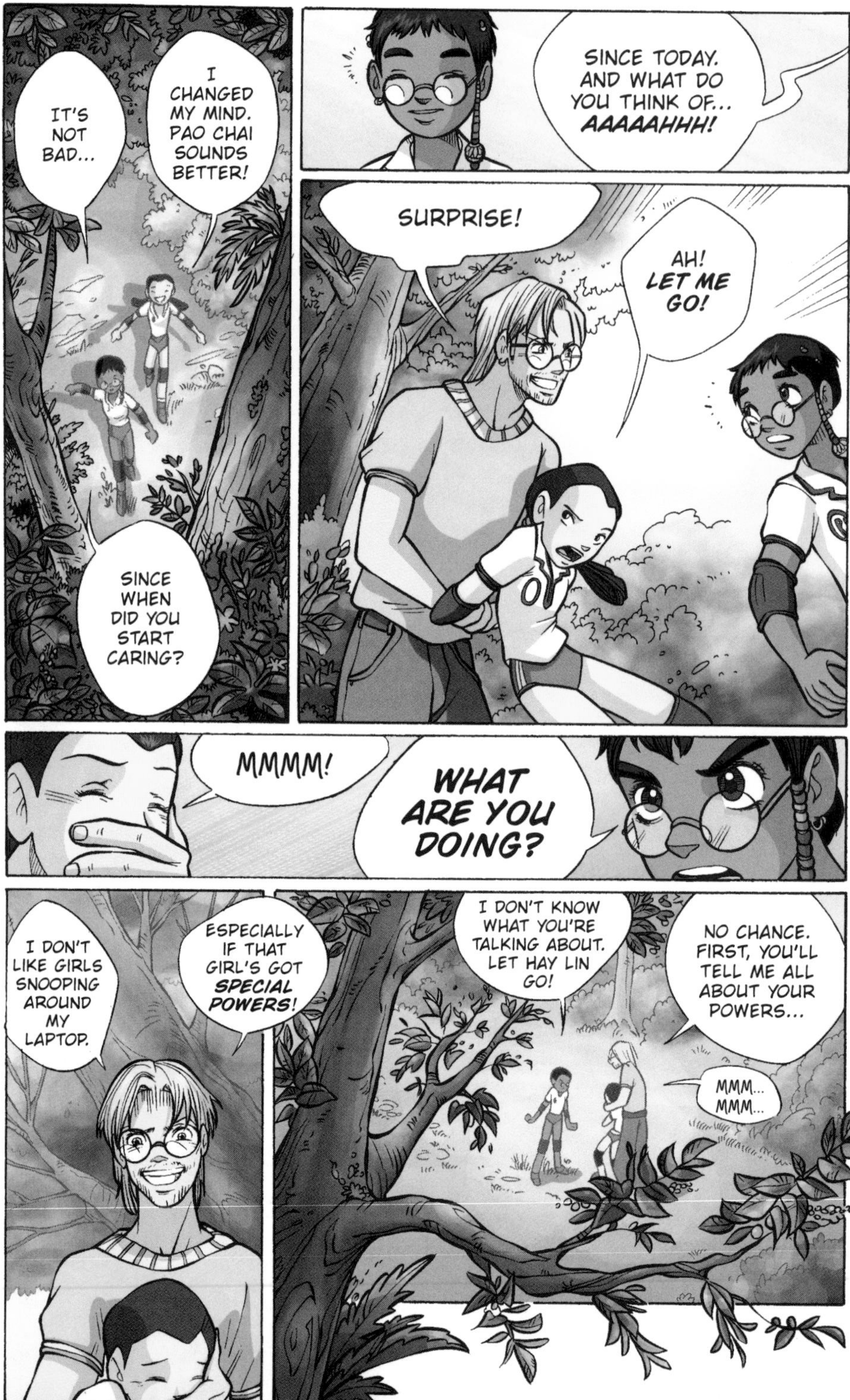
I CHANGED MY MIND. PAO CHAI SOUNDS BETTER!
IT'S NOT BAD...
SINCE WHEN DID YOU START CARING?
SINCE TODAY. AND WHAT DO YOU THINK OF... AAAAAHHH!
SURPRISE!
AH! LET ME GO!
MMMM!
WHAT ARE YOU DOING?
I DON'T LIKE GIRLS SNOOPING AROUND MY LAPTOP.
ESPECIALLY IF THAT GIRL'S GOT SPECIAL POWERS!
I DON'T KNOW WHAT YOU'RE TALKING ABOUT. LET HAY LIN GO!
NO CHANCE. FIRST, YOU'LL TELL ME ALL ABOUT YOUR POWERS...
MMM... MMM...

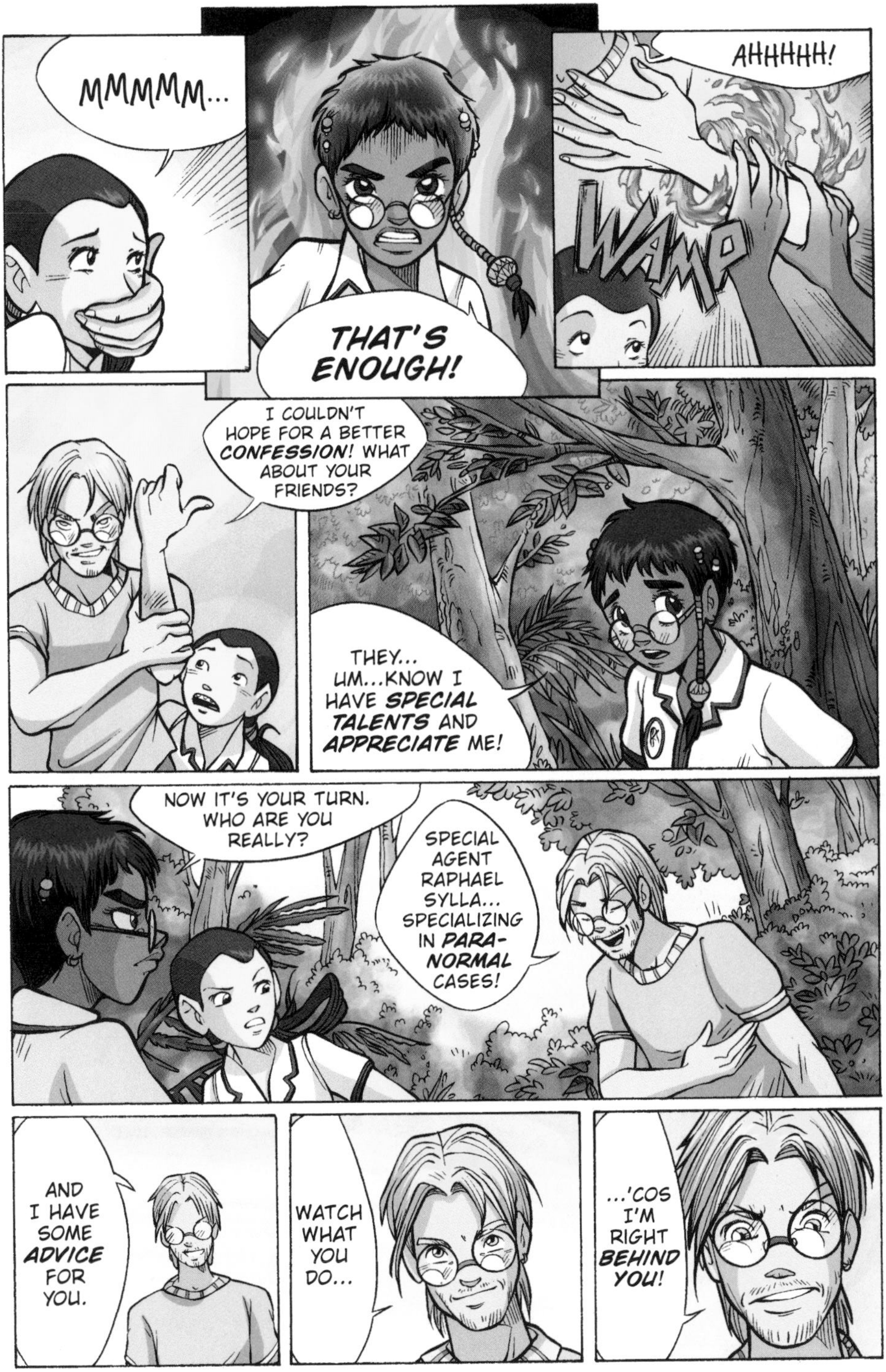
MMMMM...
THAT'S ENOUGH!
AHHHHH!
WAMP
I COULDN'T HOPE FOR A BETTER CONFESSION! WHAT ABOUT YOUR FRIENDS?
THEY... UM...KNOW I HAVE SPECIAL TALENTS AND APPRECIATE ME!
NOW IT'S YOUR TURN. WHO ARE YOU REALLY?
SPECIAL AGENT RAPHAEL SYLLA... SPECIALIZING IN PARA-NORMAL CASES!
AND I HAVE SOME ADVICE FOR YOU.
WATCH WHAT YOU DO...
...'COS I'M RIGHT BEHIND YOU!

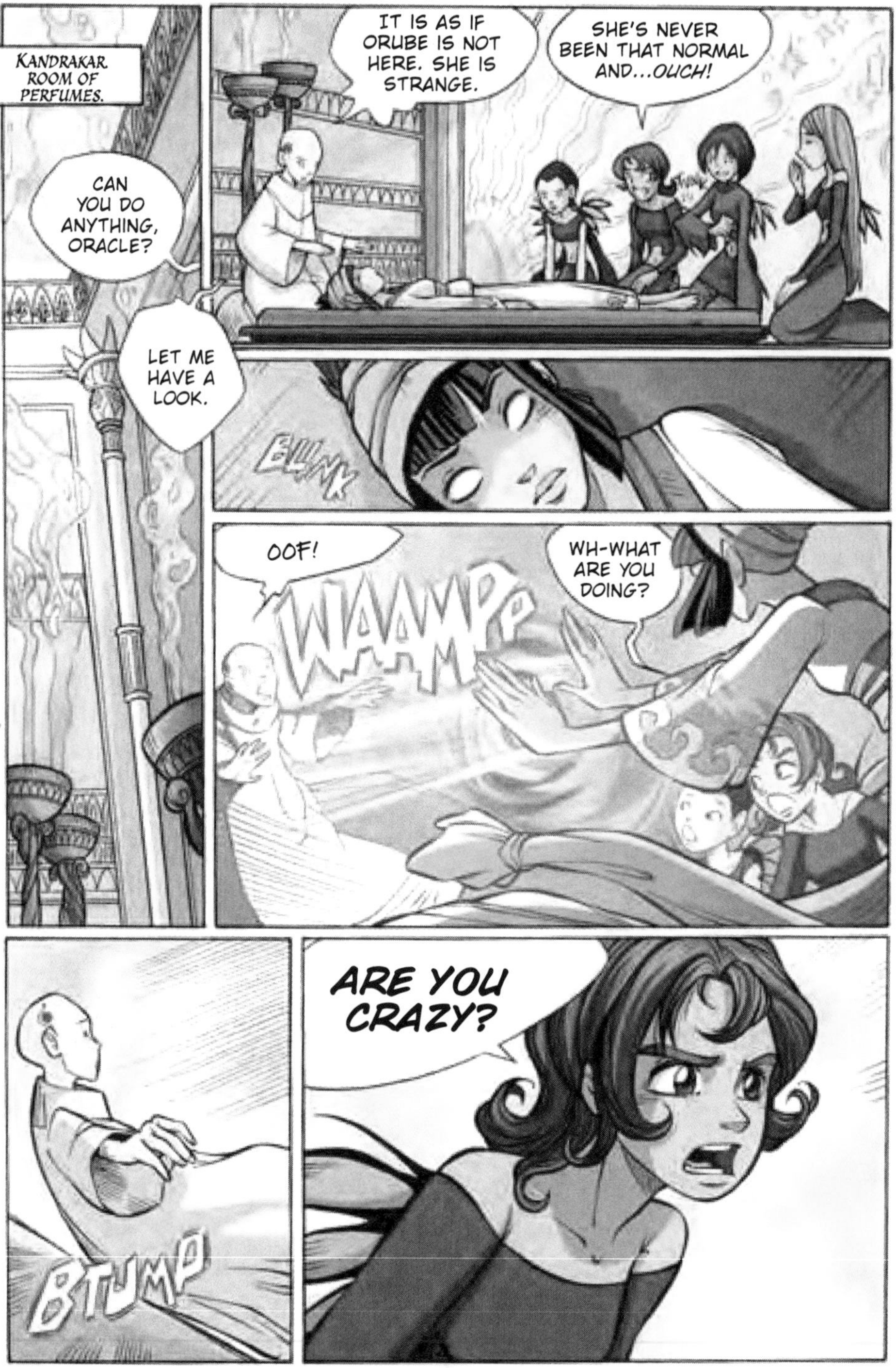
KANDRAKAR. ROOM OF PERFUMES.
IT IS AS IF ORUBE IS NOT HERE. SHE IS STRANGE.
SHE'S NEVER BEEN THAT NORMAL AND...OUCH!
CAN YOU DO ANYTHING, ORACLE?
LET ME HAVE A LOOK.
BLINK
OOF!
WH-WHAT ARE YOU DOING?
WAAMP
BTUMP
ARE YOU CRAZY?

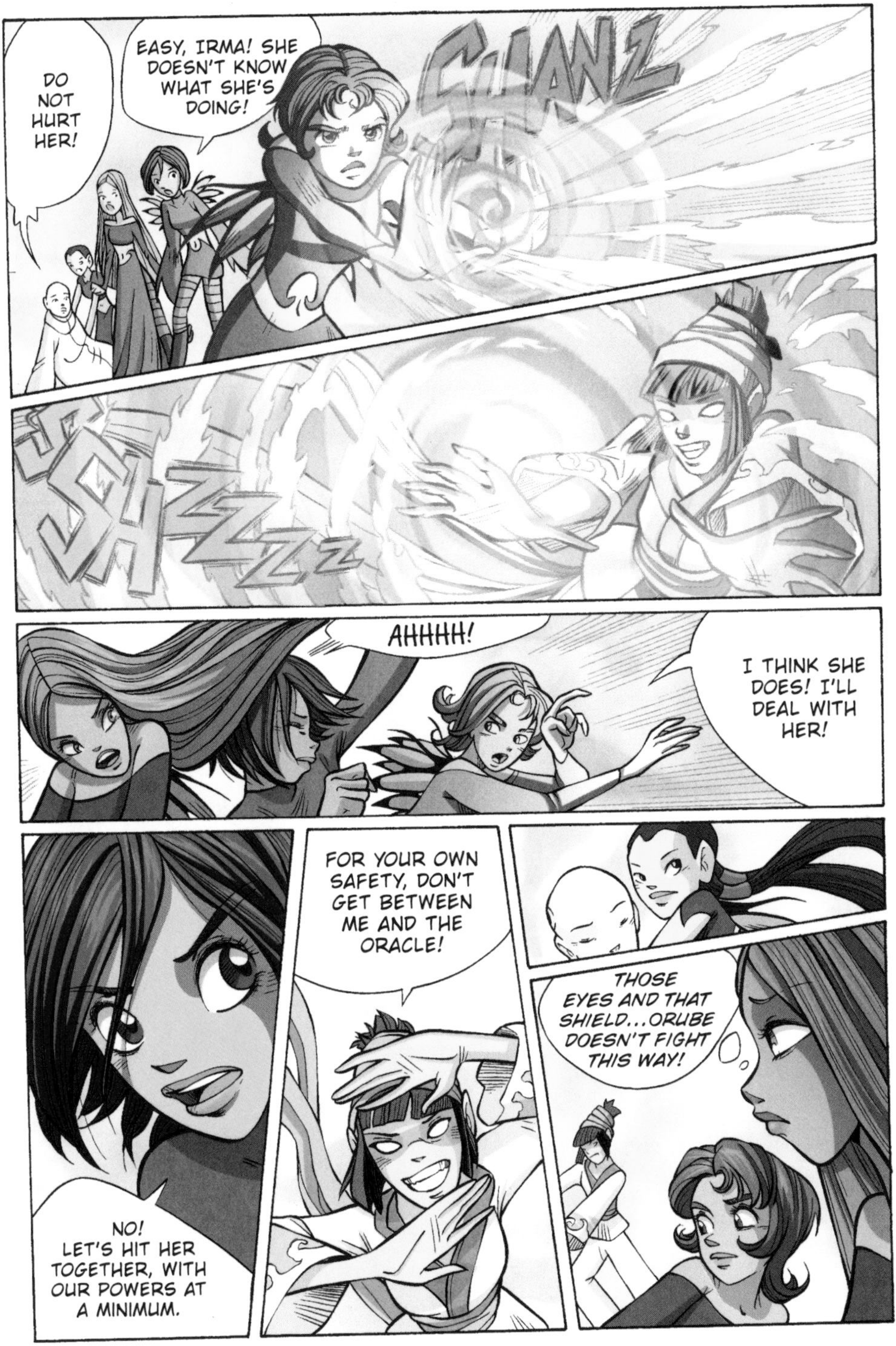
DO NOT HURT HER!
EASY, IRMA! SHE DOESN'T KNOW WHAT SHE'S DOING!
AHHHH!
I THINK SHE DOES! I'LL DEAL WITH HER!
NO! LET'S HIT HER TOGETHER, WITH OUR POWERS AT A MINIMUM.
FOR YOUR OWN SAFETY, DON'T GET BETWEEN ME AND THE ORACLE!
THOSE EYES AND THAT SHIELD...ORUBE DOESN'T FIGHT THIS WAY!

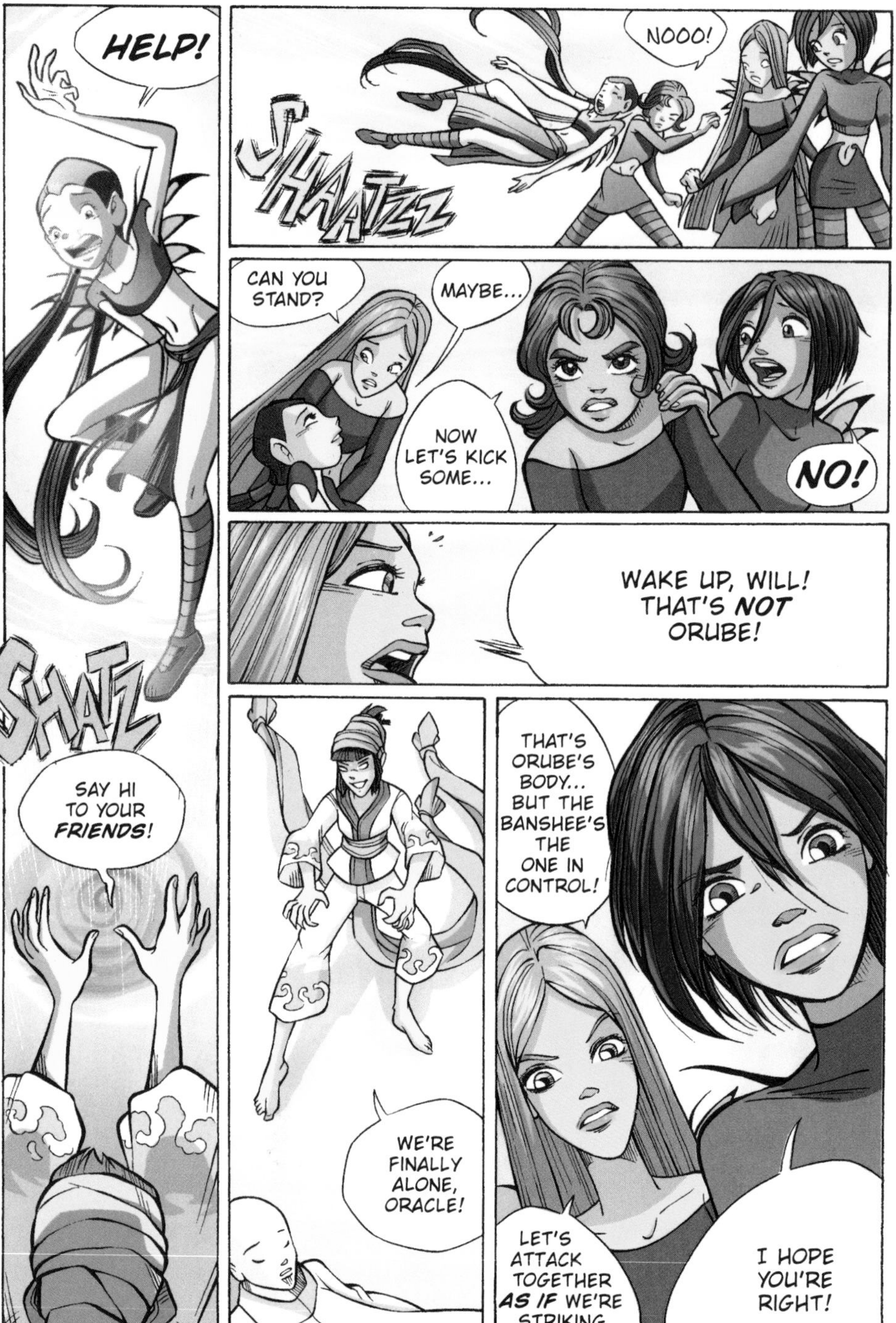
HELP!
SHATZ
SAY HI TO YOUR FRIENDS!
NOOO!
SHHAATZZZ
CAN YOU STAND?
MAYBE...
NOW LET'S KICK SOME...
NO!
WAKE UP, WILL! THAT'S NOT ORUBE!
WE'RE FINALLY ALONE, ORACLE!
THAT'S ORUBE'S BODY... BUT THE BANSHEE'S THE ONE IN CONTROL!
LET'S ATTACK TOGETHER AS IF WE'RE STRIKING YUA!
I HOPE YOU'RE RIGHT!

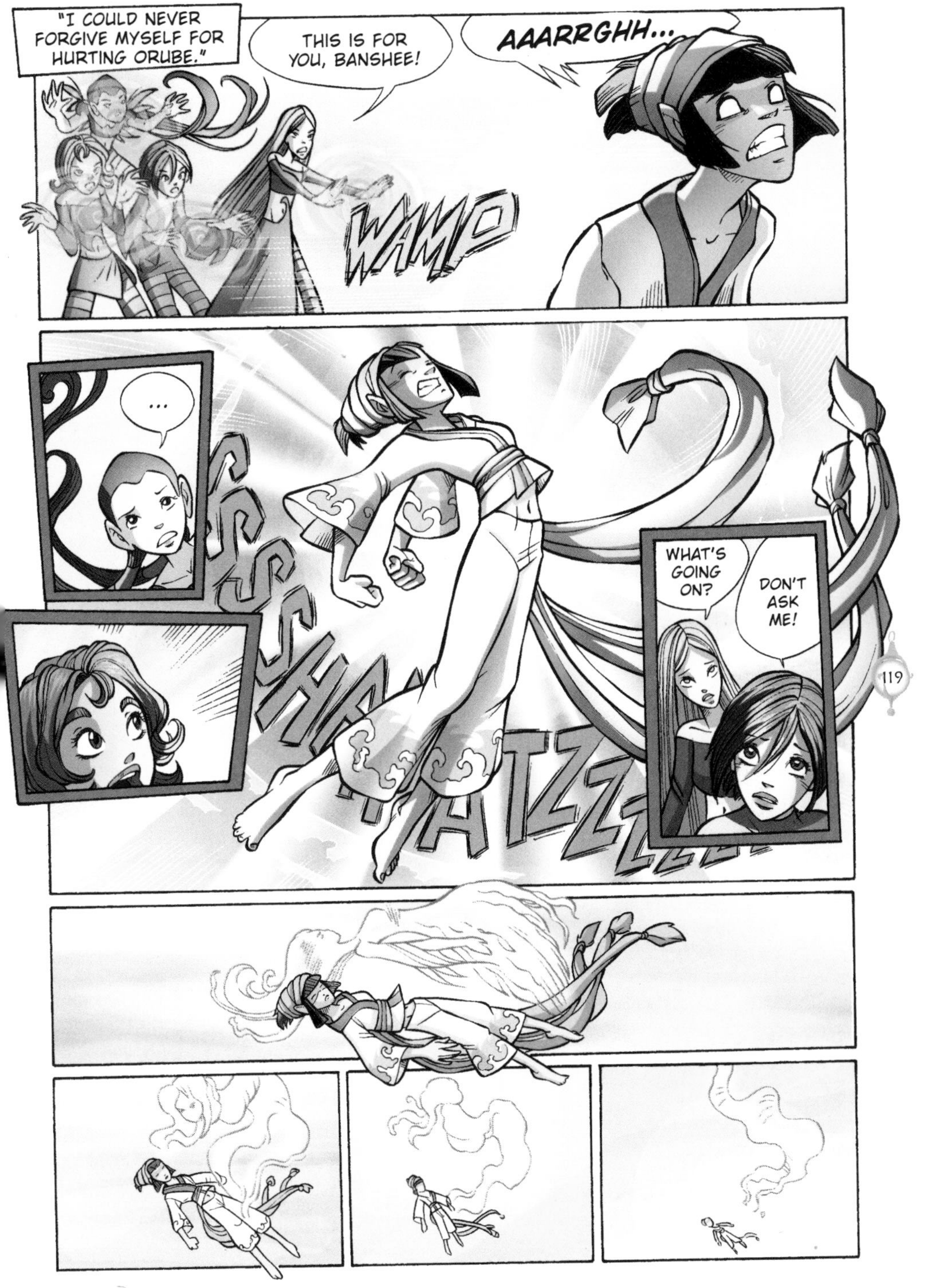
"I COULD NEVER FORGIVE MYSELF FOR HURTING ORUBE."
THIS IS FOR YOU, BANSHEE!
AAARRGHH...
WAMP
...
SSSHHHHATZZZZ
WHAT'S GOING ON?
DON'T ASK ME!

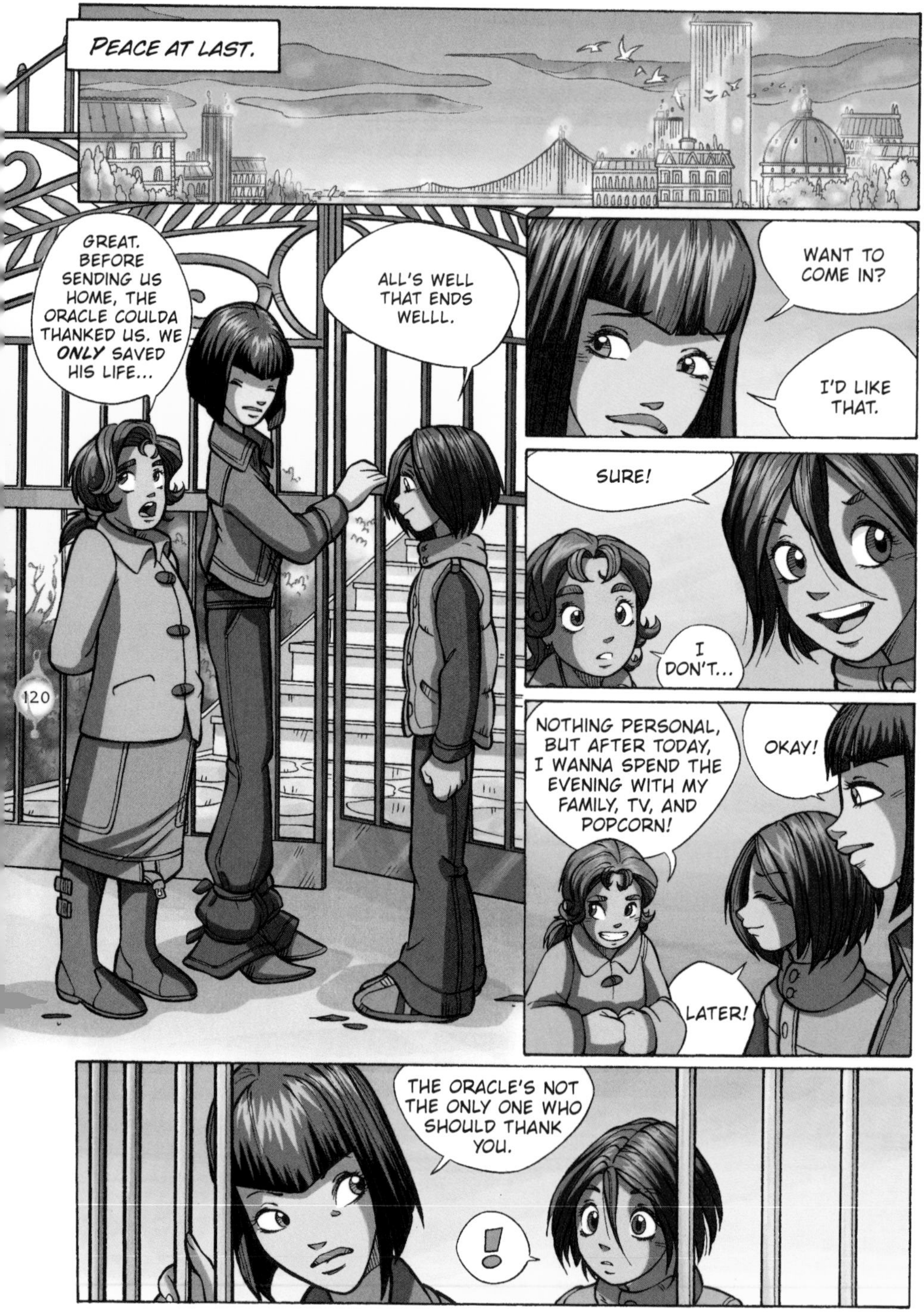
PEACE AT LAST.
GREAT. BEFORE SENDING US HOME, THE ORACLE COULDA THANKED US. WE ONLY SAVED HIS LIFE...
ALL'S WELL THAT ENDS WELLL.
WANT TO COME IN?
I'D LIKE THAT.
SURE!
I DON'T...
NOTHING PERSONAL, BUT AFTER TODAY, I WANNA SPEND THE EVENING WITH MY FAMILY, TV, AND POPCORN!
OKAY!
LATER!
THE ORACLE'S NOT THE ONLY ONE WHO SHOULD THANK YOU.
!

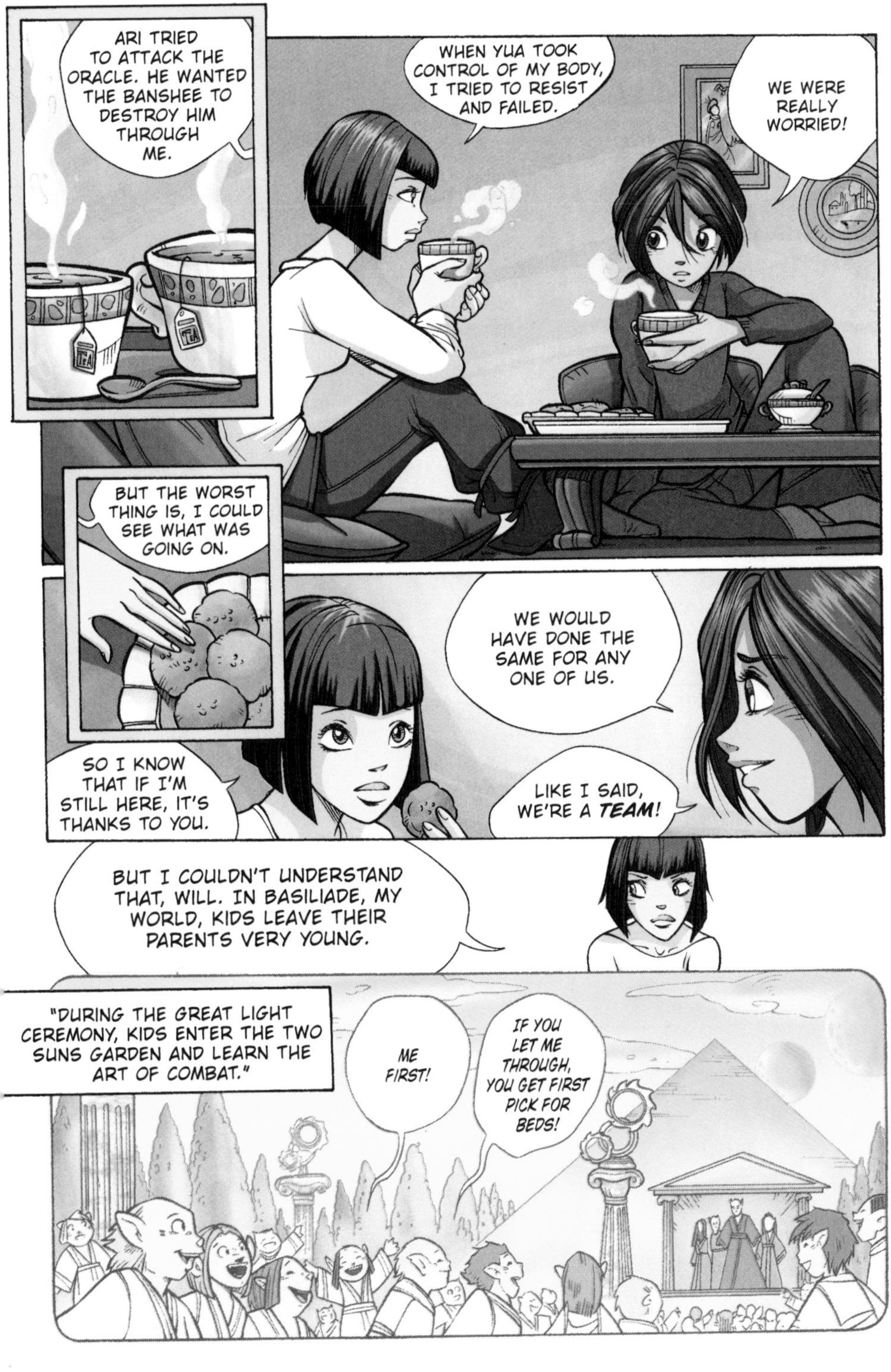
ARI TRIED TO ATTACK THE ORACLE. HE WANTED THE BANSHEE TO DESTROY HIM THROUGH ME.
WHEN YUA TOOK CONTROL OF MY BODY, I TRIED TO RESIST AND FAILED.
WE WERE REALLY WORRIED!
BUT THE WORST THING IS, I COULD SEE WHAT WAS GOING ON.
WE WOULD HAVE DONE THE SAME FOR ANY ONE OF US.
SO I KNOW THAT IF I'M STILL HERE, IT'S THANKS TO YOU.
LIKE I SAID, WE'RE A TEAM!
BUT I COULDN'T UNDERSTAND THAT, WILL. IN BASILIADE, MY WORLD, KIDS LEAVE THEIR PARENTS VERY YOUNG.
"DURING THE GREAT LIGHT CEREMONY, KIDS ENTER THE TWO SUNS GARDEN AND LEARN THE ART OF COMBAT."
ME FIRST!
IF YOU LET ME THROUGH, YOU GET FIRST PICK FOR BEDS!

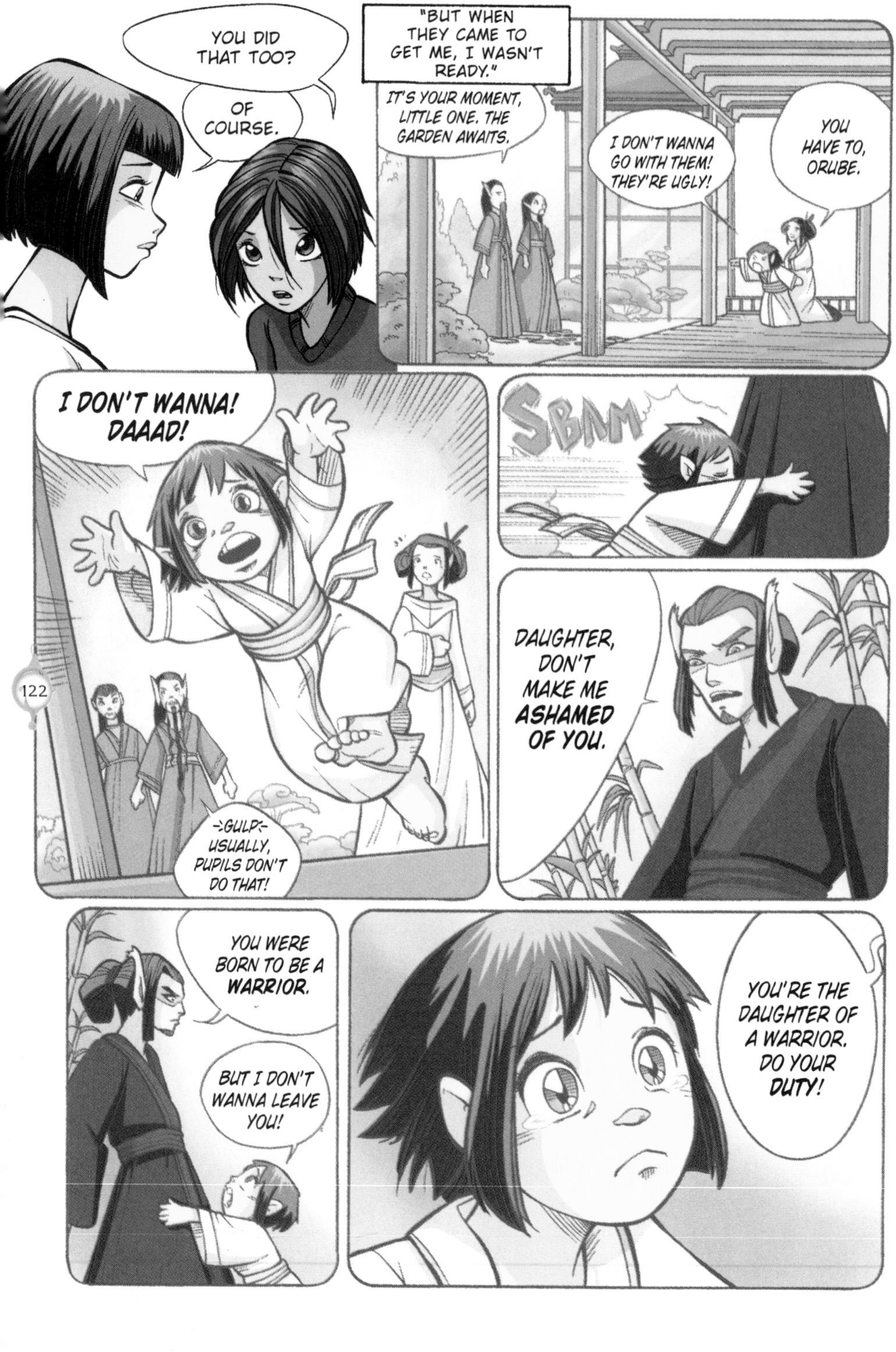

YOU DID THAT TOO?
OF COURSE.
"BUT WHEN THEY CAME TO GET ME, I WASN'T READY."
IT'S YOUR MOMENT, LITTLE ONE. THE GARDEN AWAITS.
I DON'T WANNA GO WITH THEM! THEY'RE UGLY!
YOU HAVE TO, ORUBE.
I DON'T WANNA! DAAAD!
GULP USUALLY, PUPILS DON'T DO THAT!
SBAM
DAUGHTER, DON'T MAKE ME ASHAMED OF YOU.
YOU WERE BORN TO BE A WARRIOR.
BUT I DON'T WANNA LEAVE YOU!
YOU'RE THE DAUGHTER OF A WARRIOR. DO YOUR DUTY!

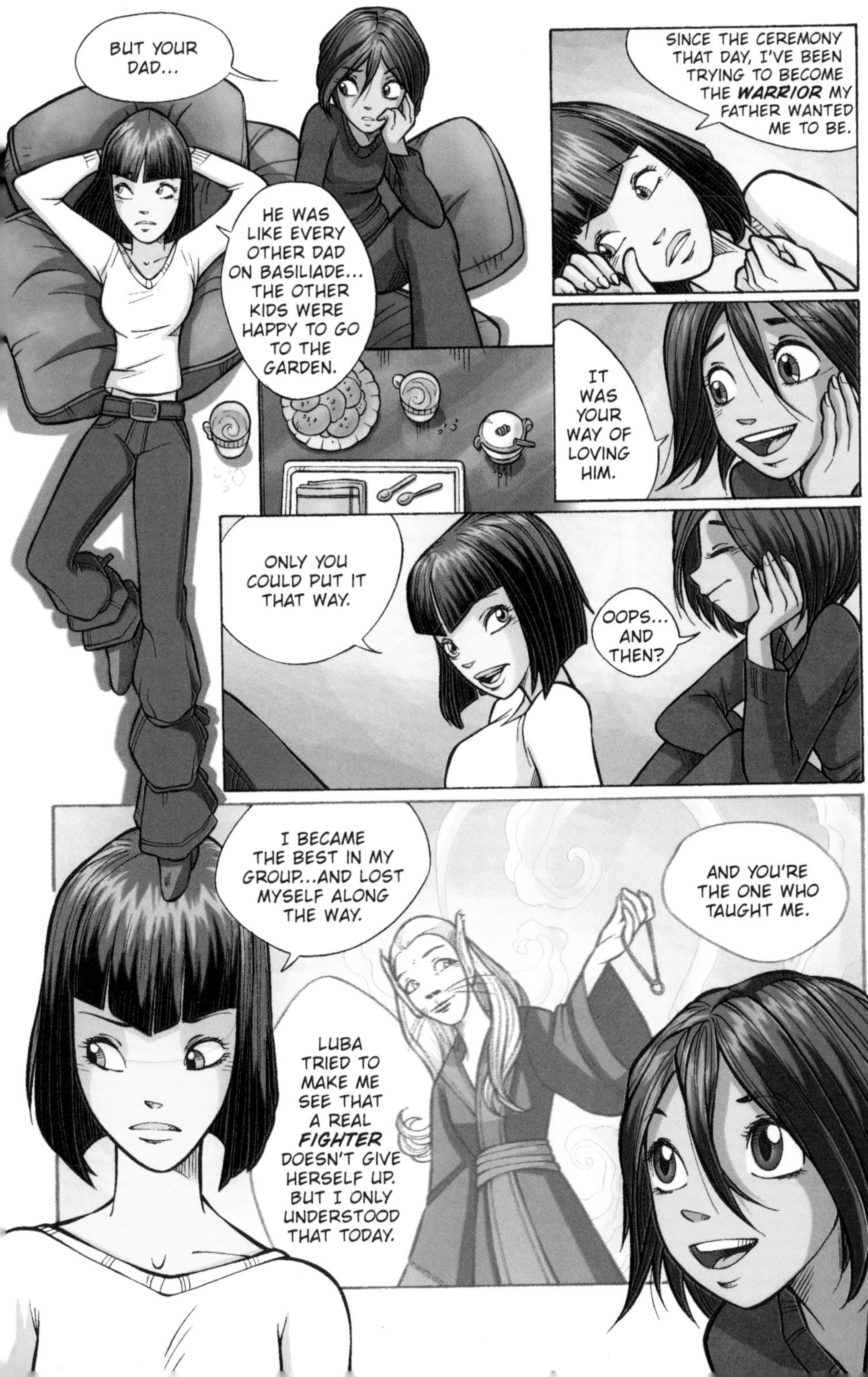
BUT YOUR DAD...
HE WAS LIKE EVERY OTHER DAD ON BASILIADE... THE OTHER KIDS WERE HAPPY TO GO TO THE GARDEN.
SINCE THE CEREMONY THAT DAY, I'VE BEEN TRYING TO BECOME THE **WARRIOR** MY FATHER WANTED ME TO BE.
IT WAS YOUR WAY OF LOVING HIM.
ONLY YOU COULD PUT IT THAT WAY.
OOPS... AND THEN?
I BECAME THE BEST IN MY GROUP...AND LOST MYSELF ALONG THE WAY.
AND YOU'RE THE ONE WHO TAUGHT ME.
LUBA TRIED TO MAKE ME SEE THAT A REAL **FIGHTER** DOESN'T GIVE HERSELF UP. BUT I ONLY UNDERSTOOD THAT TODAY.

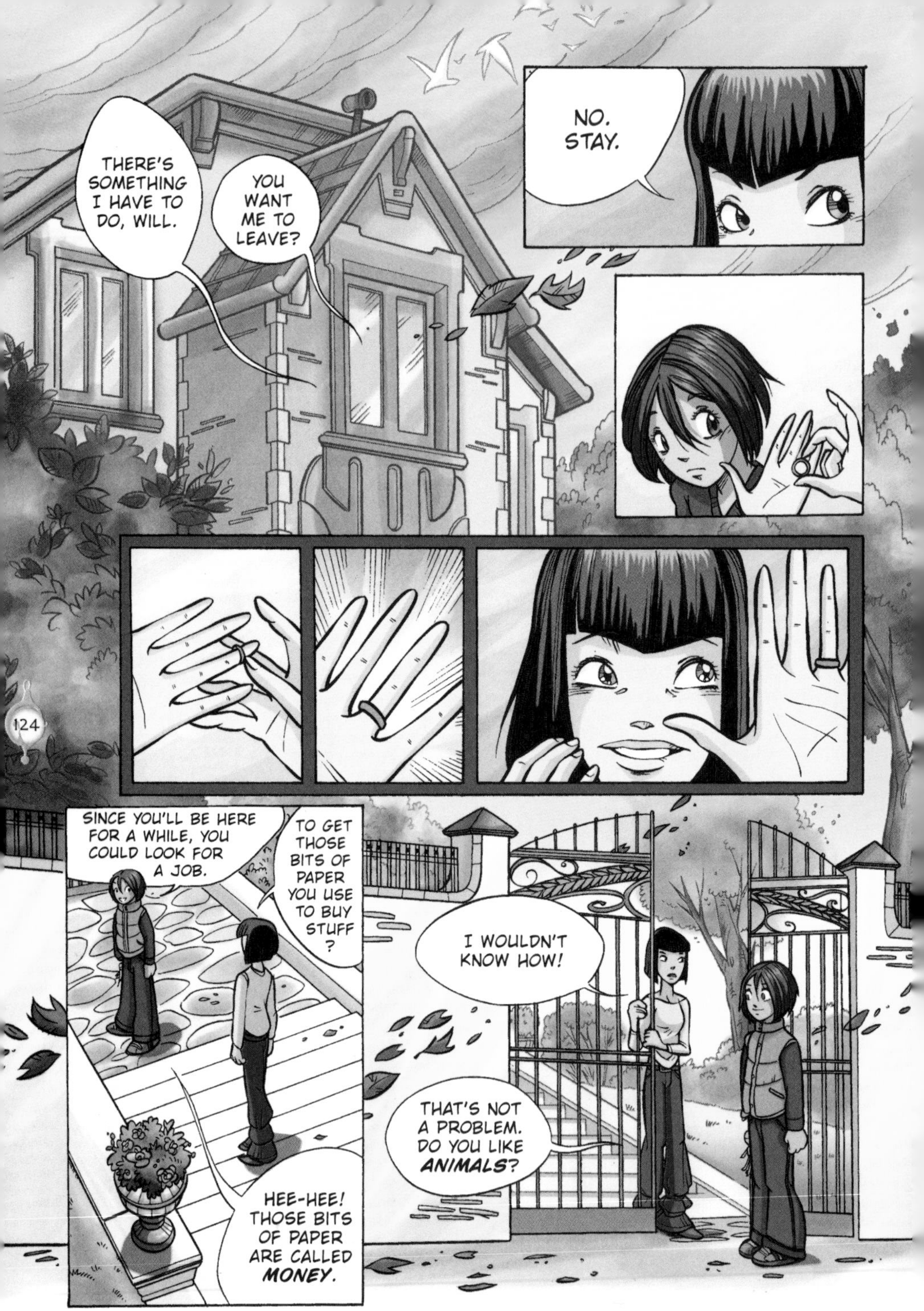
THERE'S SOMETHING I HAVE TO DO, WILL.
YOU WANT ME TO LEAVE?
NO. STAY.
SINCE YOU'LL BE HERE FOR A WHILE, YOU COULD LOOK FOR A JOB.
TO GET THOSE BITS OF PAPER YOU USE TO BUY STUFF?
HEE-HEE! THOSE BITS OF PAPER ARE CALLED **MONEY**.
I WOULDN'T KNOW HOW!
THAT'S NOT A PROBLEM. DO YOU LIKE **ANIMALS**?

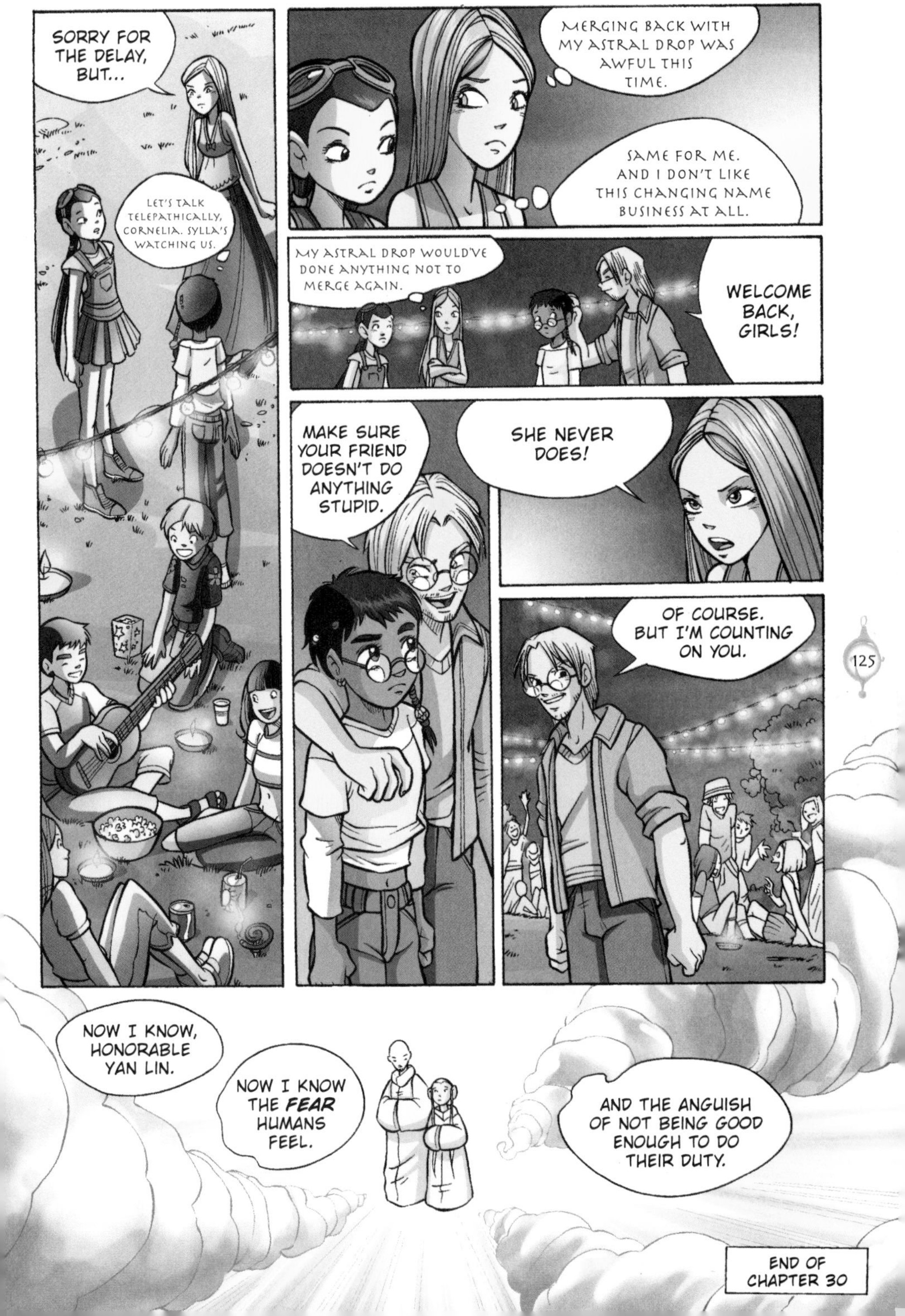

SORRY FOR THE DELAY, BUT...
LET'S TALK TELEPATHICALLY, CORNELIA. SYLLA'S WATCHING US.
MERGING BACK WITH MY ASTRAL DROP WAS AWFUL THIS TIME.
SAME FOR ME. AND I DON'T LIKE THIS CHANGING NAME BUSINESS AT ALL.
MY ASTRAL DROP WOULD'VE DONE ANYTHING NOT TO MERGE AGAIN.
WELCOME BACK, GIRLS!
MAKE SURE YOUR FRIEND DOESN'T DO ANYTHING STUPID.
SHE NEVER DOES!
OF COURSE. BUT I'M COUNTING ON YOU.
NOW I KNOW, HONORABLE YAN LIN.
NOW I KNOW THE FEAR HUMANS FEEL.
AND THE ANGUISH OF NOT BEING GOOD ENOUGH TO DO THEIR DUTY.
END OF CHAPTER 30

W.i.t.c.h.

Will Irma Taranee Cornelia Hay Lin

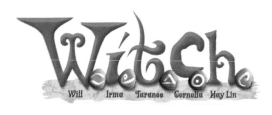

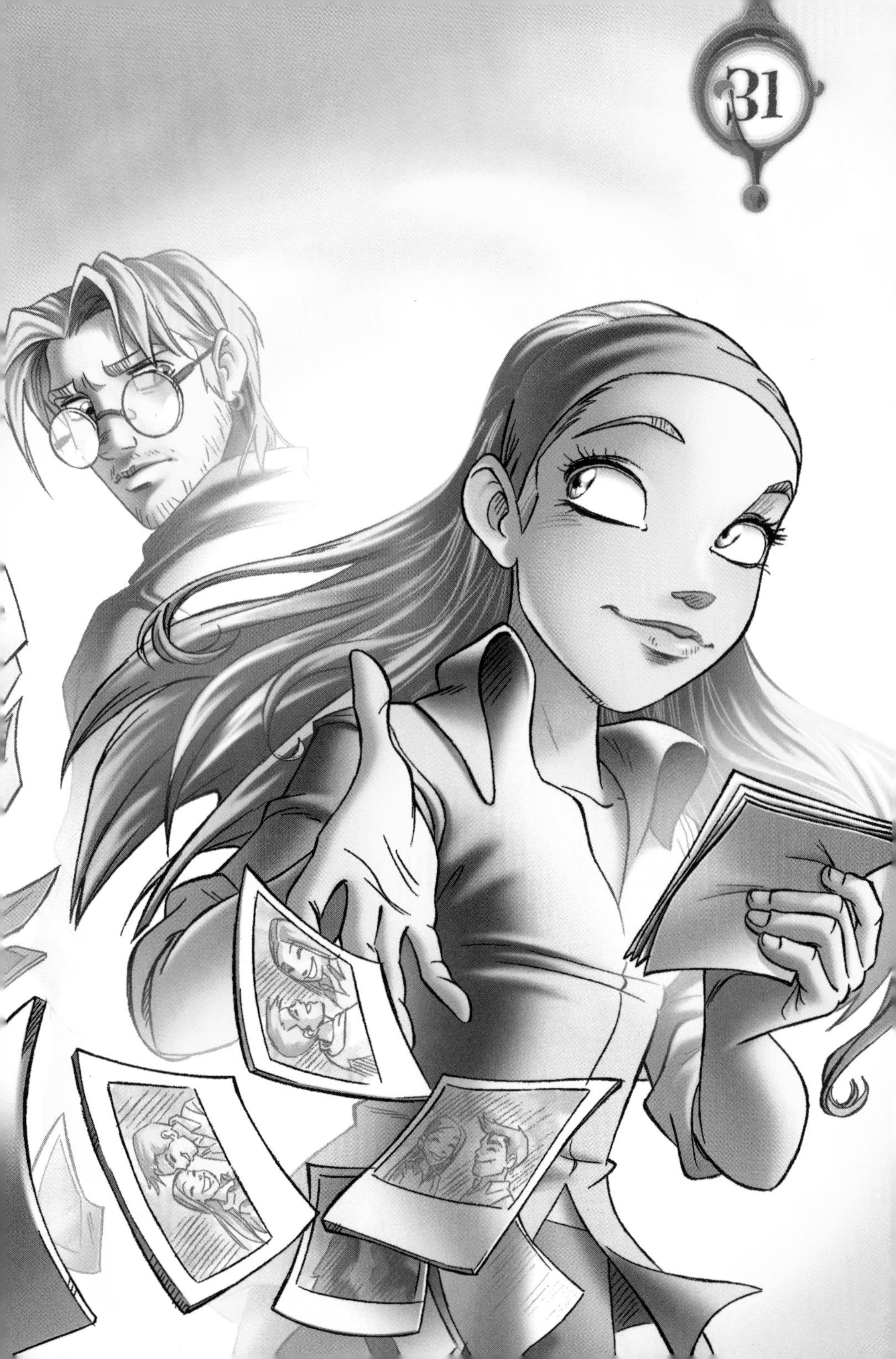
31

The Voice of Silence

"Her warrior mask hides a generous soul."

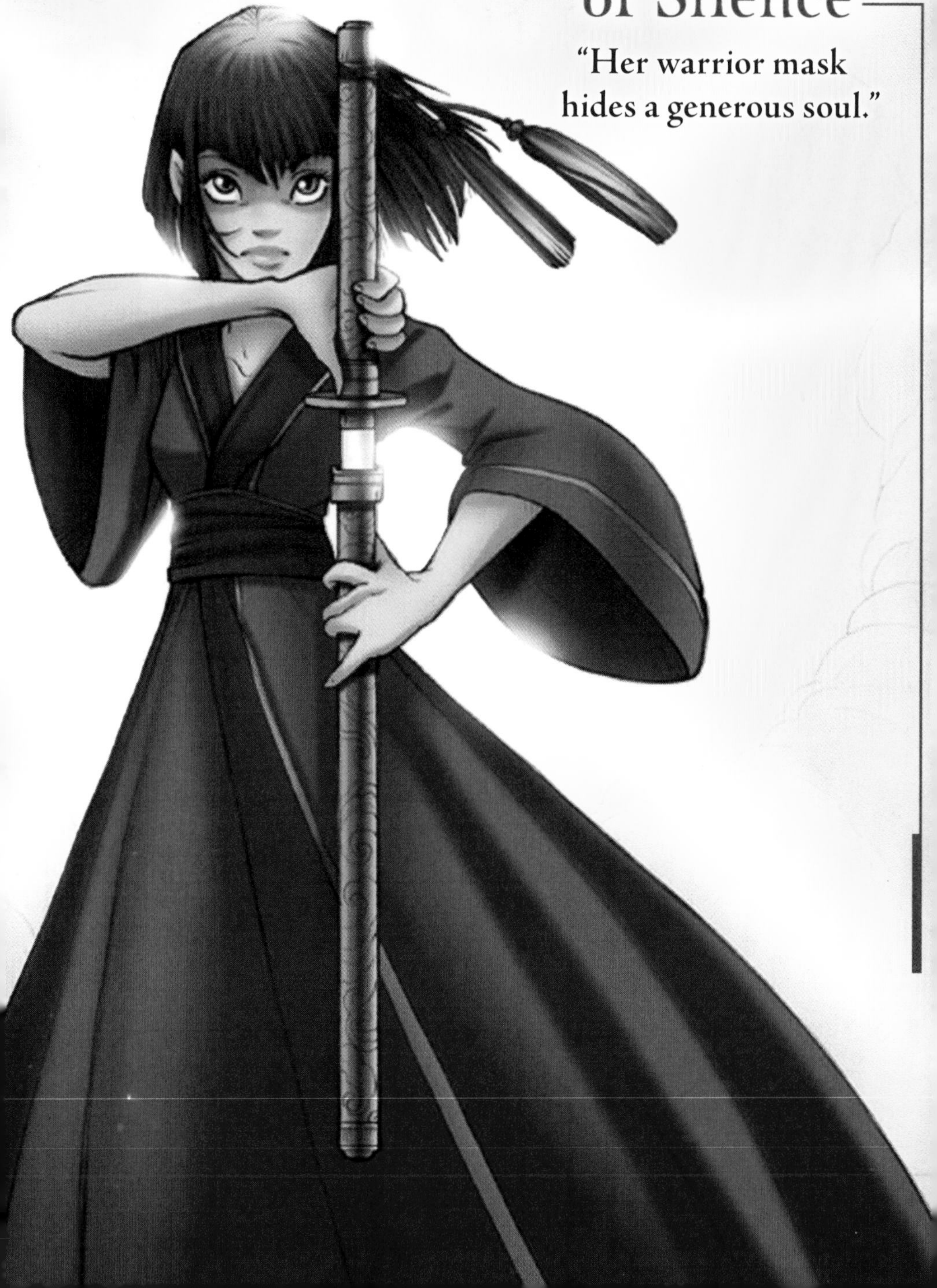

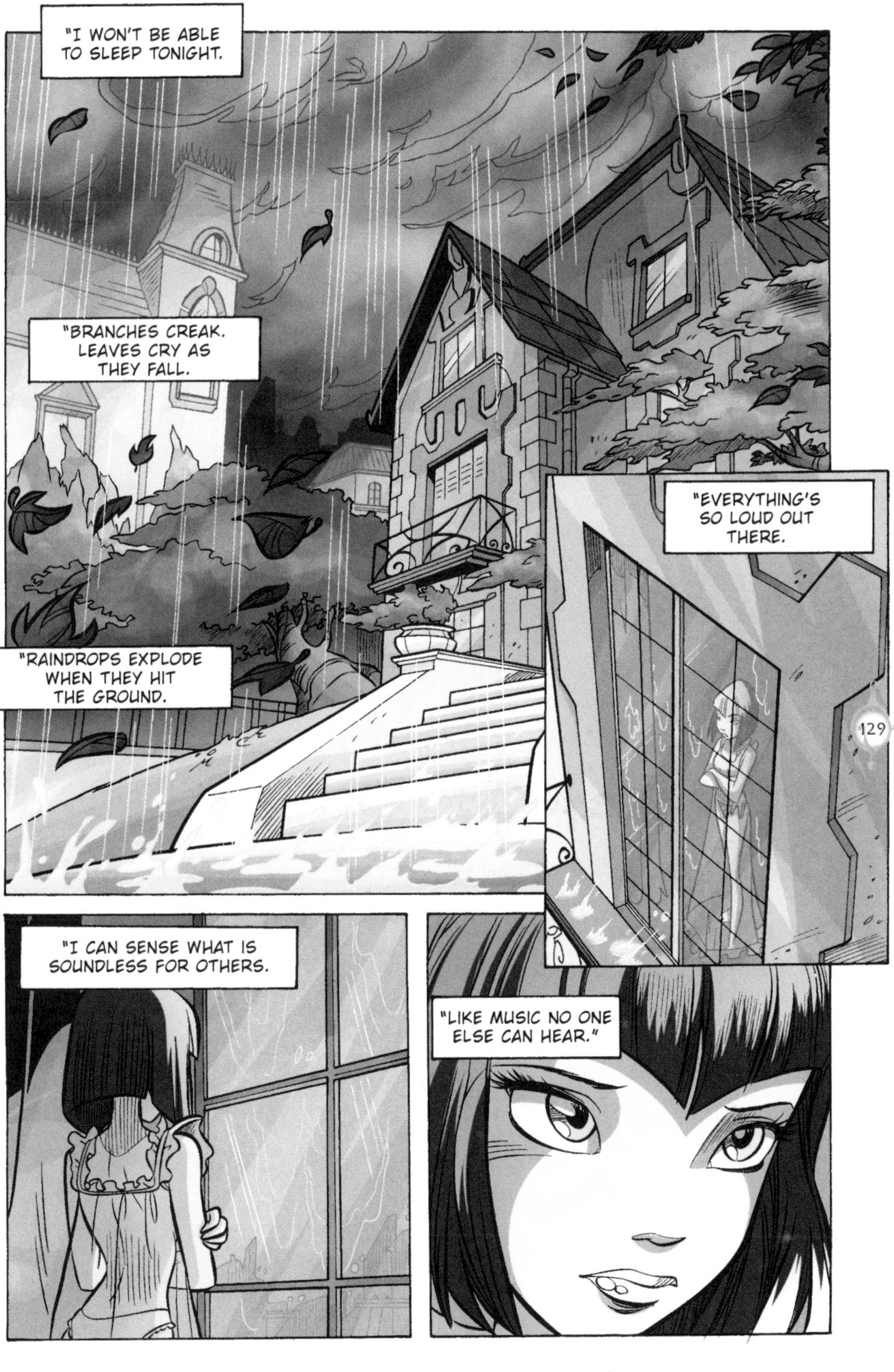
"I WON'T BE ABLE TO SLEEP TONIGHT.
"BRANCHES CREAK. LEAVES CRY AS THEY FALL.
"RAINDROPS EXPLODE WHEN THEY HIT THE GROUND.
"EVERYTHING'S SO LOUD OUT THERE.
"I CAN SENSE WHAT IS SOUNDLESS FOR OTHERS.
"LIKE MUSIC NO ONE ELSE CAN HEAR."

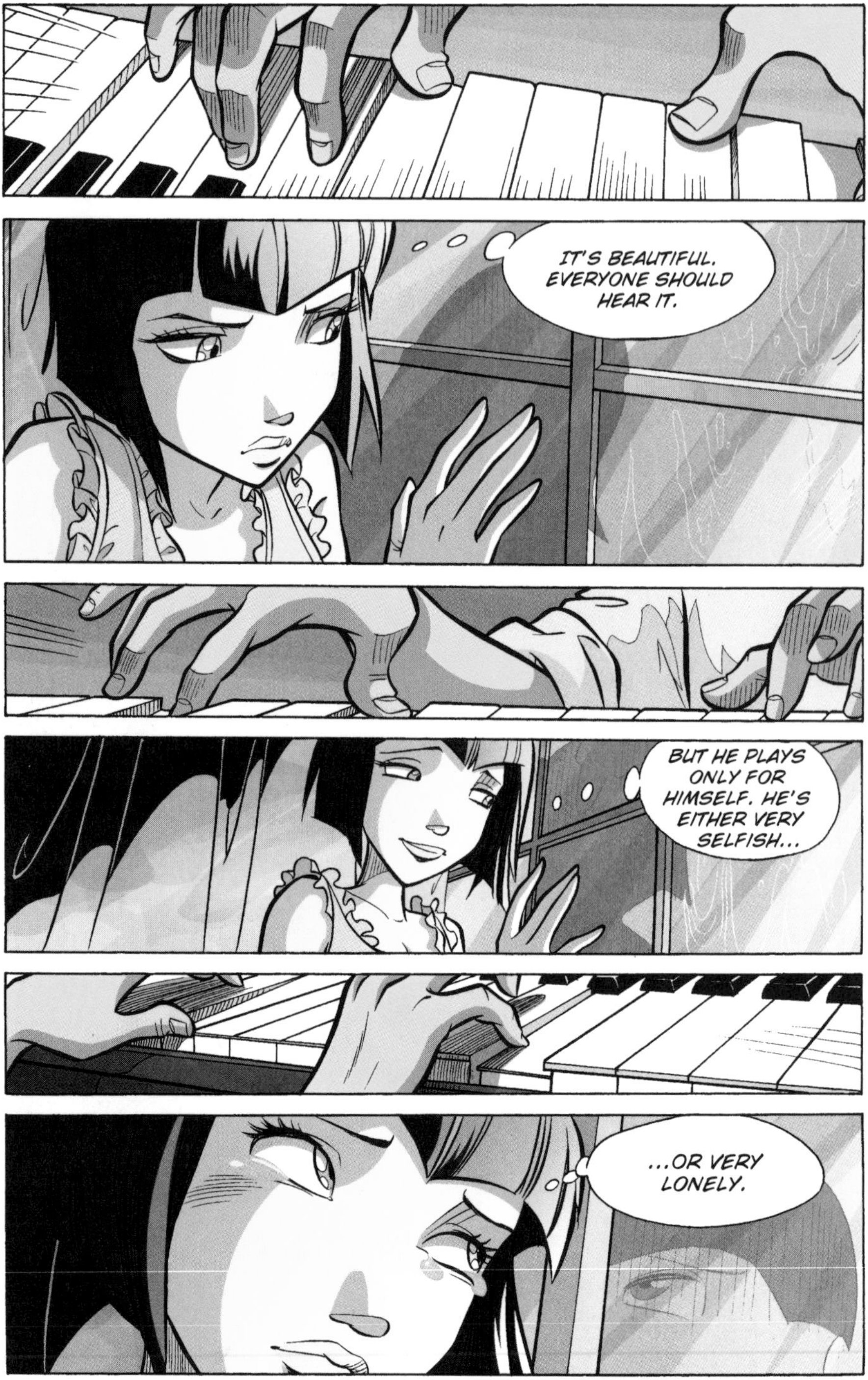
IT'S BEAUTIFUL. EVERYONE SHOULD HEAR IT.
BUT HE PLAYS ONLY FOR HIMSELF. HE'S EITHER VERY SELFISH...
...OR VERY LONELY.

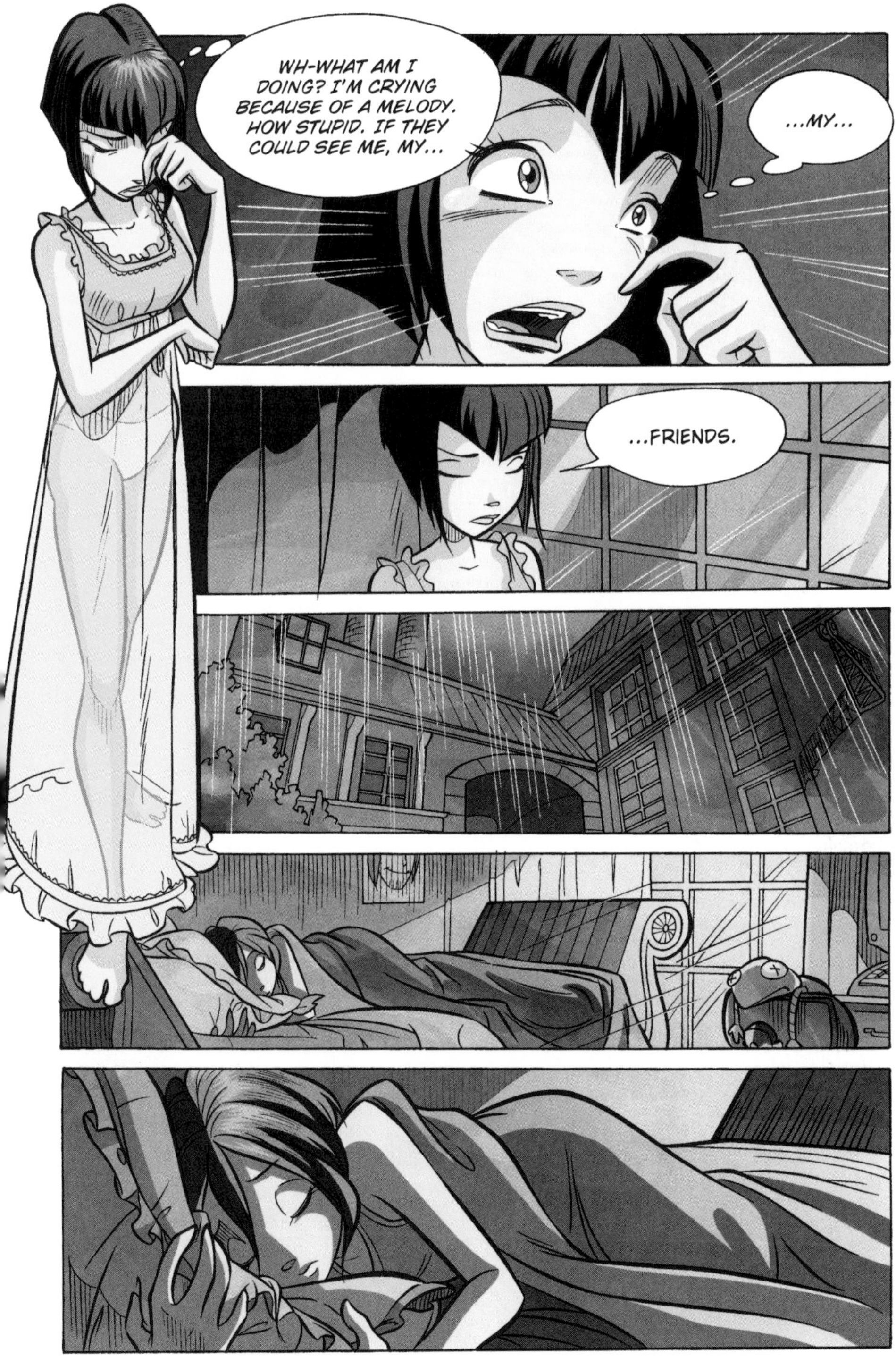
WH-WHAT AM I DOING? I'M CRYING BECAUSE OF A MELODY. HOW STUPID. IF THEY COULD SEE ME, MY...
...MY...
...FRIENDS.

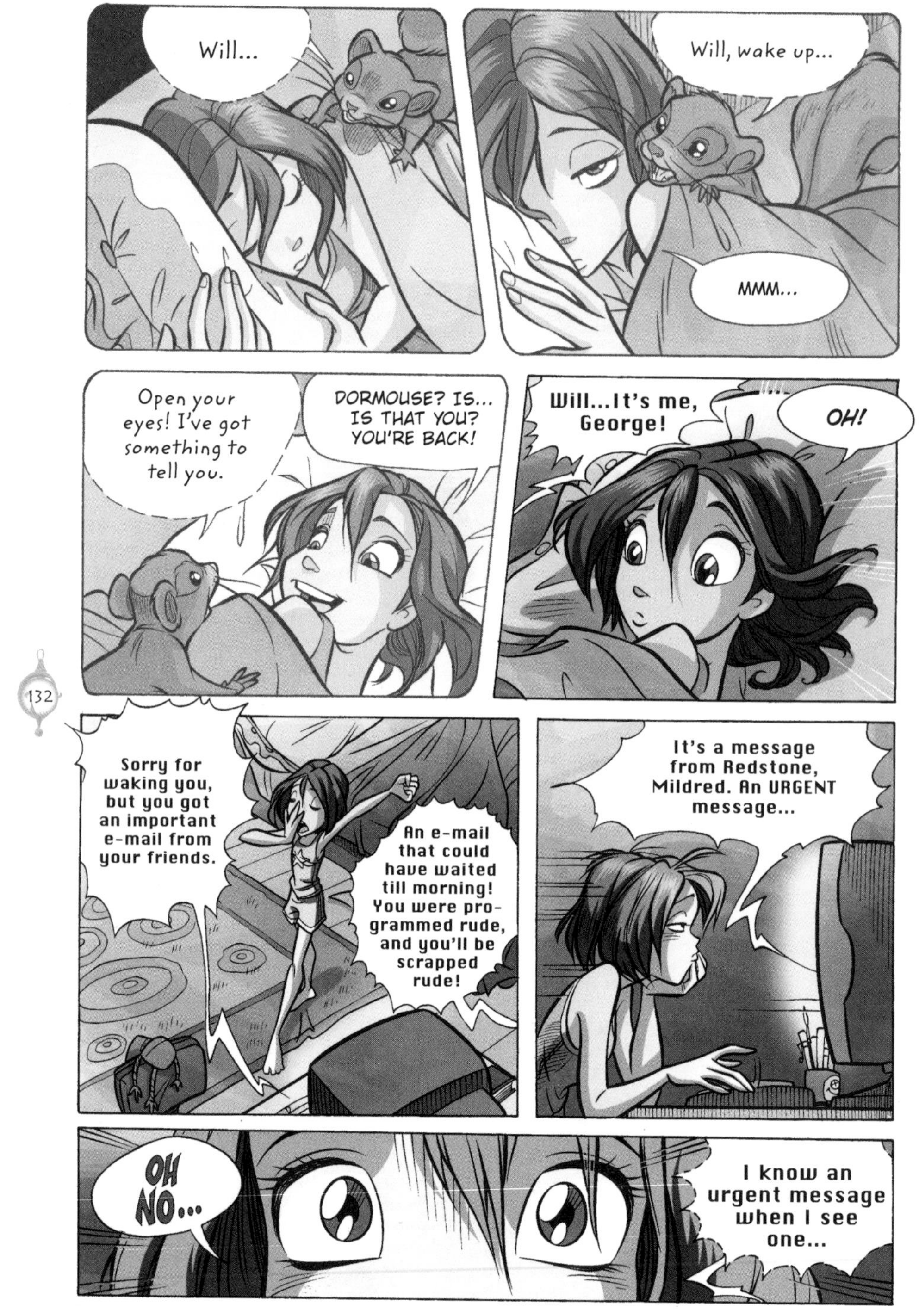
Will...
Will, wake up...
MMM...
Open your eyes! I've got something to tell you.
DORMOUSE? IS... IS THAT YOU? YOU'RE BACK!
Will...It's me, George!
OH!
Sorry for waking you, but you got an important e-mail from your friends.
An e-mail that could have waited till morning! You were programmed rude, and you'll be scrapped rude!
It's a message from Redstone, Mildred. An URGENT message...
OH NO...
I know an urgent message when I see one...

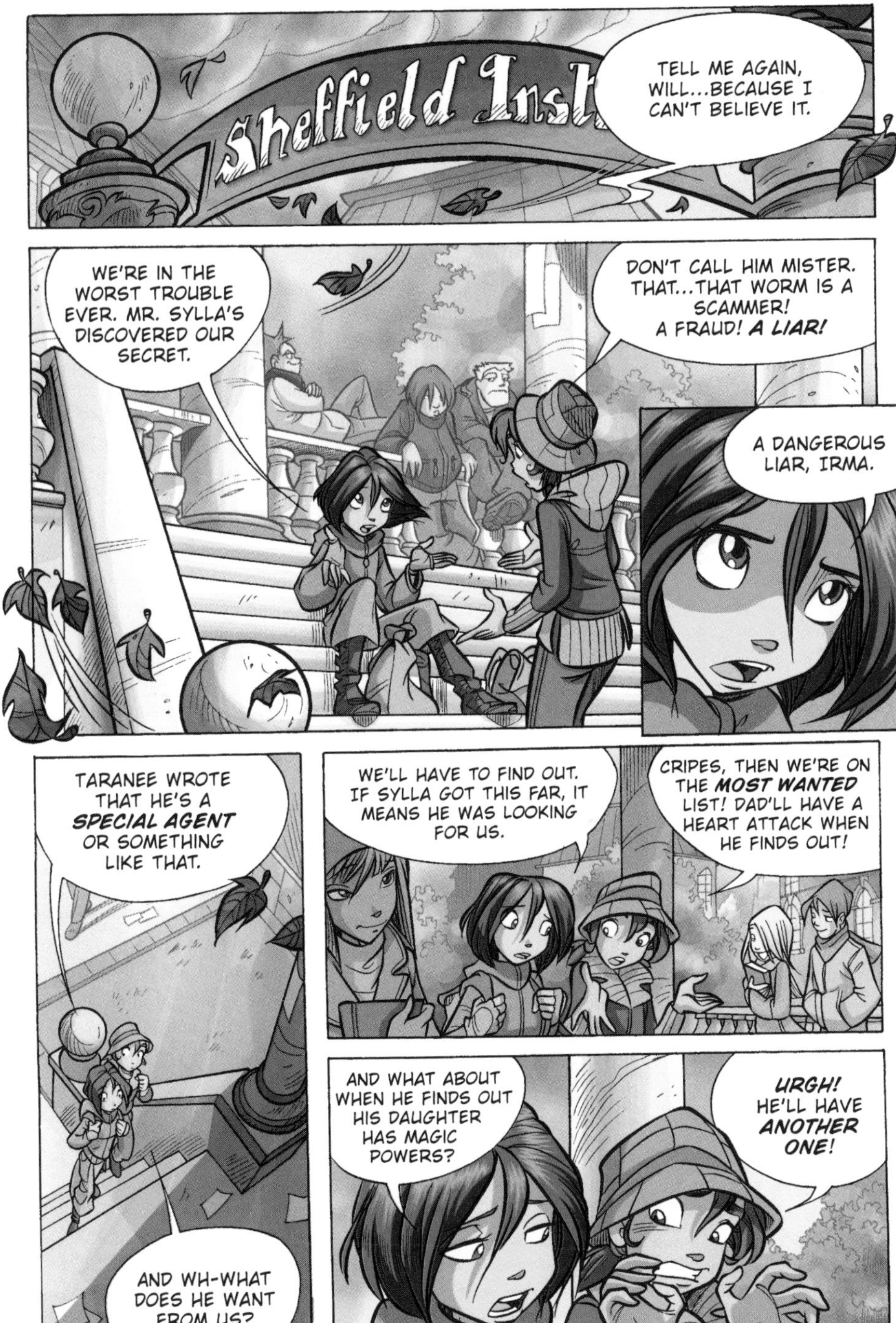
Sheffield Inst
TELL ME AGAIN, WILL...BECAUSE I CAN'T BELIEVE IT.
WE'RE IN THE WORST TROUBLE EVER. MR. SYLLA'S DISCOVERED OUR SECRET.
DON'T CALL HIM MISTER. THAT...THAT WORM IS A SCAMMER! A FRAUD! ***A LIAR!***
A DANGEROUS LIAR, IRMA.
TARANEE WROTE THAT HE'S A ***SPECIAL AGENT*** OR SOMETHING LIKE THAT.
AND WH-WHAT DOES HE WANT FROM US?
WE'LL HAVE TO FIND OUT. IF SYLLA GOT THIS FAR, IT MEANS HE WAS LOOKING FOR US.
CRIPES, THEN WE'RE ON THE ***MOST WANTED*** LIST! DAD'LL HAVE A HEART ATTACK WHEN HE FINDS OUT!
AND WHAT ABOUT WHEN HE FINDS OUT HIS DAUGHTER HAS MAGIC POWERS?
URGH! HE'LL HAVE ***ANOTHER ONE!***

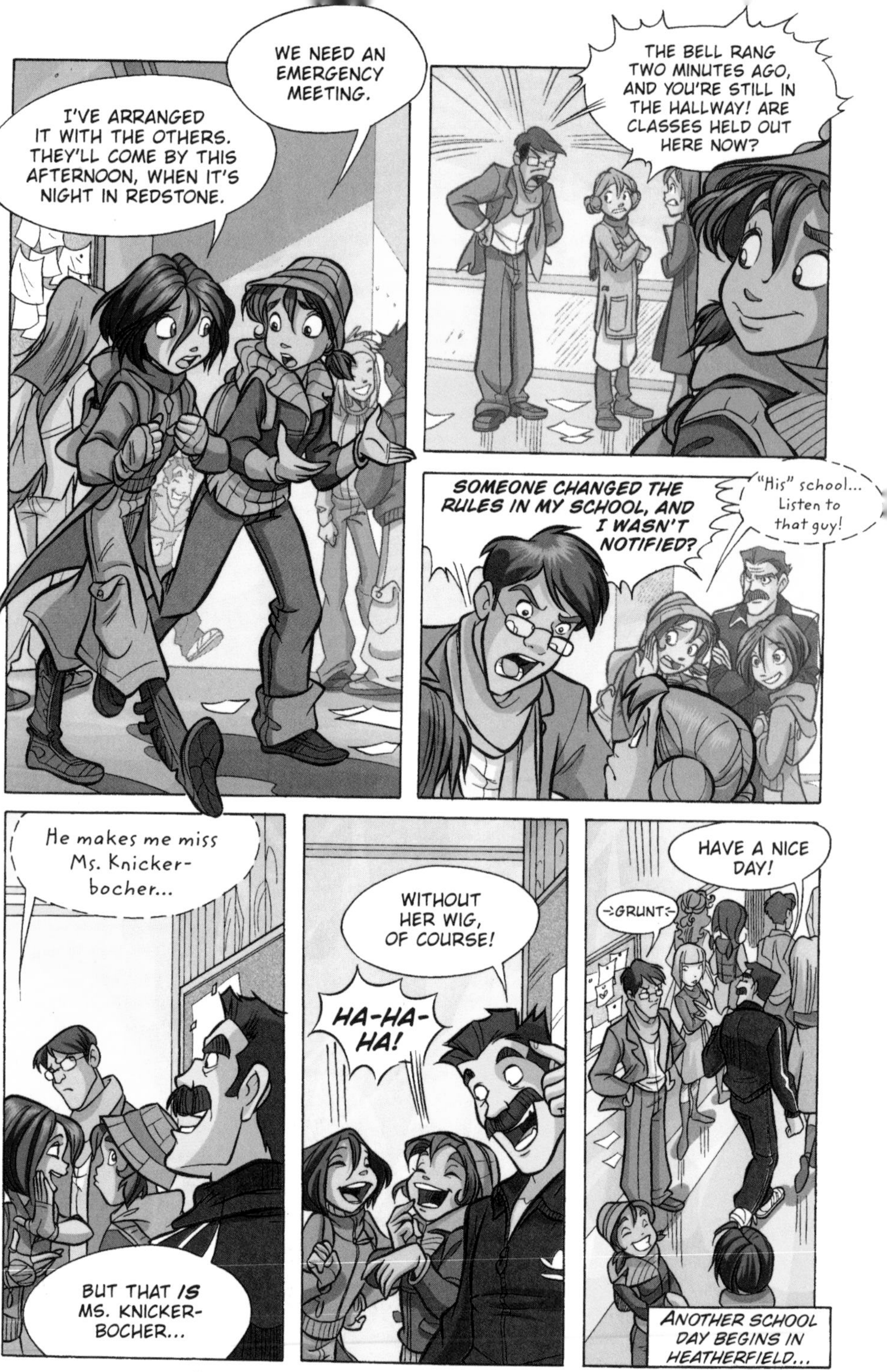
WE NEED AN EMERGENCY MEETING.
I'VE ARRANGED IT WITH THE OTHERS. THEY'LL COME BY THIS AFTERNOON, WHEN IT'S NIGHT IN REDSTONE.
THE BELL RANG TWO MINUTES AGO, AND YOU'RE STILL IN THE HALLWAY! ARE CLASSES HELD OUT HERE NOW?
SOMEONE CHANGED THE RULES IN MY SCHOOL, AND I WASN'T NOTIFIED?
"His" school... Listen to that guy!
He makes me miss Ms. Knicker-bocher...
BUT THAT IS MS. KNICKER-BOCHER...
WITHOUT HER WIG, OF COURSE!
HA-HA-HA!
HAVE A NICE DAY!
GRUNT
ANOTHER SCHOOL DAY BEGINS IN HEATHERFIELD...

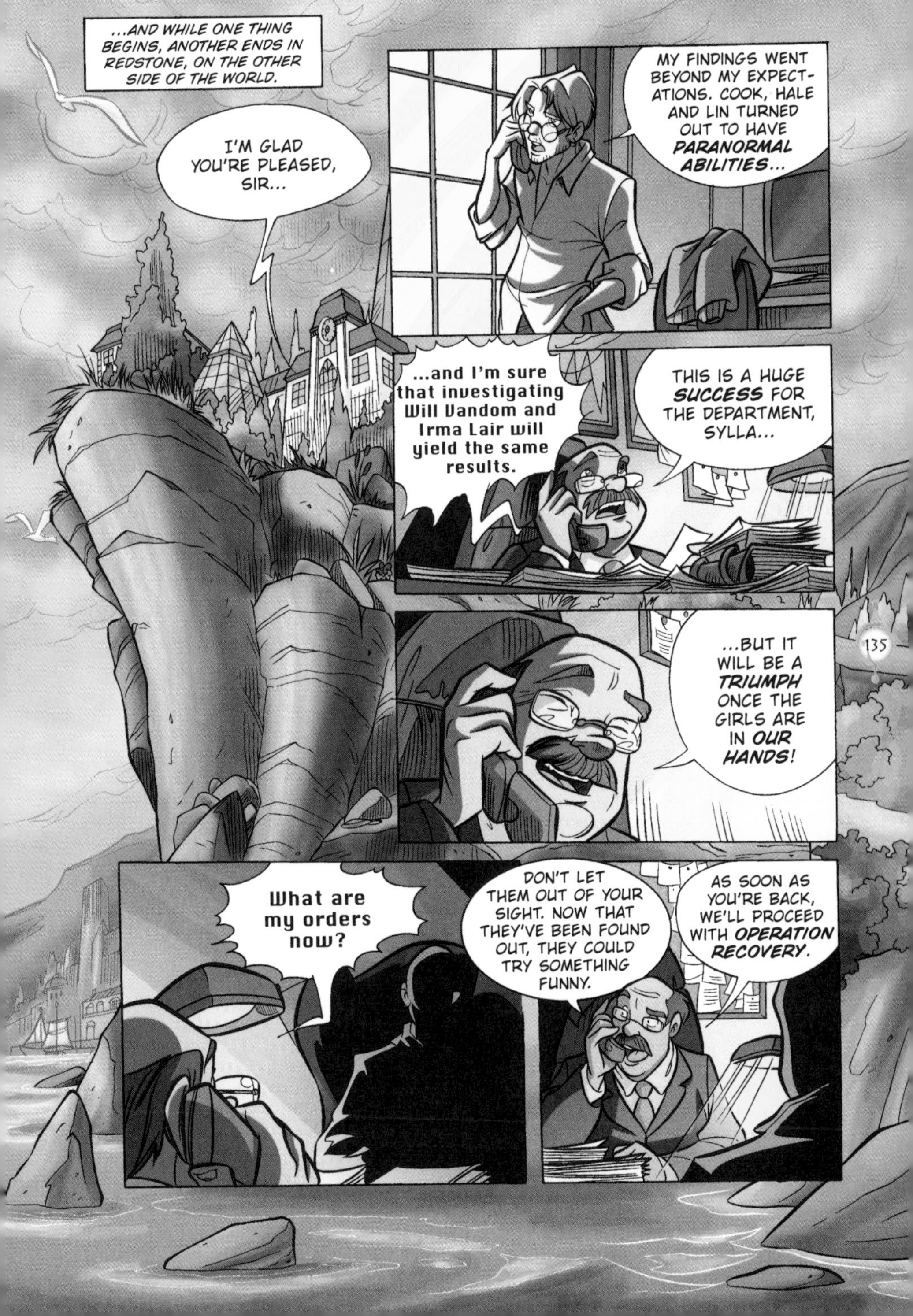
...AND WHILE ONE THING BEGINS, ANOTHER ENDS IN REDSTONE, ON THE OTHER SIDE OF THE WORLD.
MY FINDINGS WENT BEYOND MY EXPECTATIONS. COOK, HALE AND LIN TURNED OUT TO HAVE PARANORMAL ABILITIES...
I'M GLAD YOU'RE PLEASED, SIR...
...and I'm sure that investigating Will Vandom and Irma Lair will yield the same results.
THIS IS A HUGE SUCCESS FOR THE DEPARTMENT, SYLLA...
...BUT IT WILL BE A TRIUMPH ONCE THE GIRLS ARE IN OUR HANDS!
What are my orders now?
DON'T LET THEM OUT OF YOUR SIGHT. NOW THAT THEY'VE BEEN FOUND OUT, THEY COULD TRY SOMETHING FUNNY.
AS SOON AS YOU'RE BACK, WE'LL PROCEED WITH OPERATION RECOVERY.

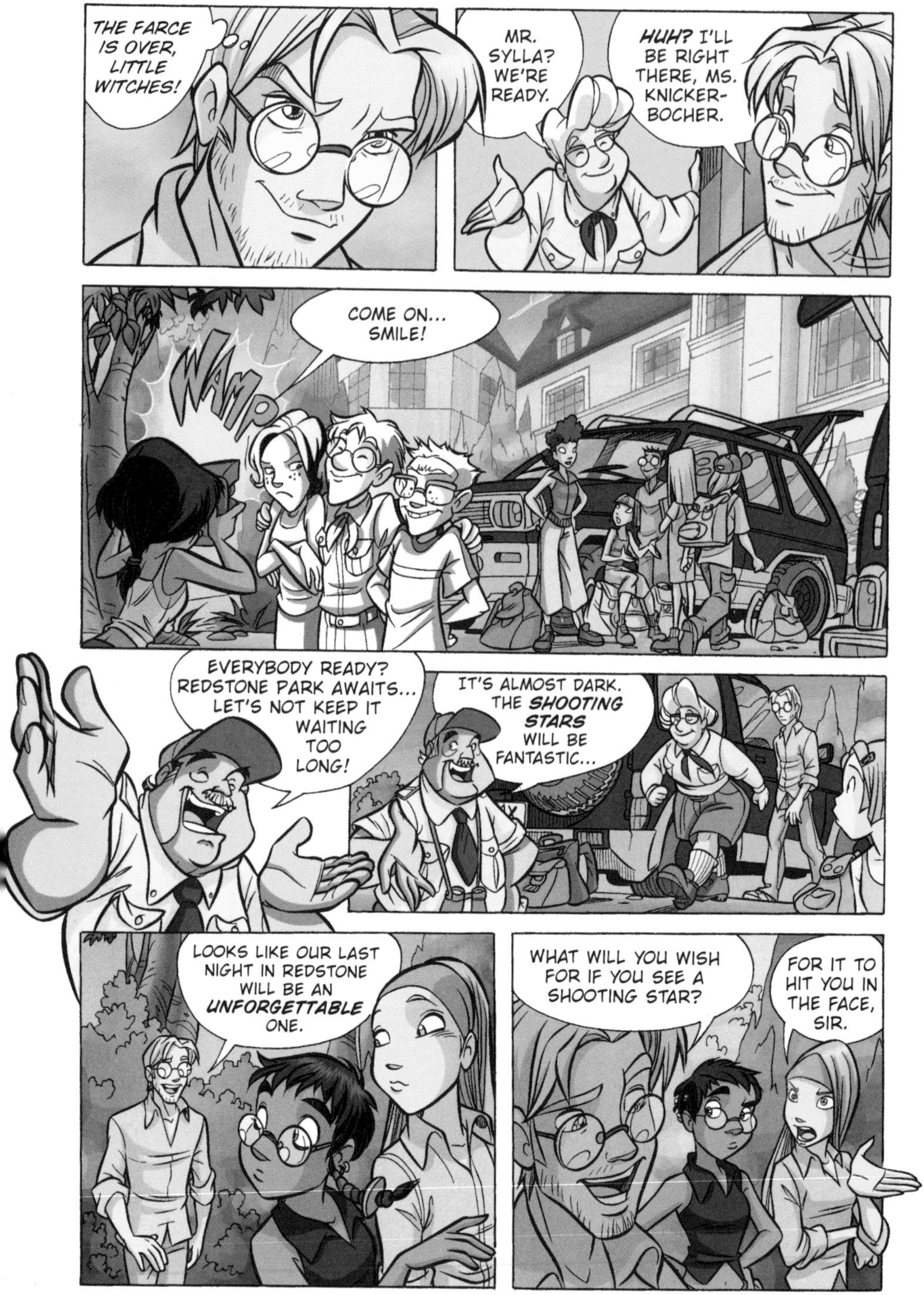
THE FARCE IS OVER, LITTLE WITCHES!
MR. SYLLA? WE'RE READY.
HUH? I'LL BE RIGHT THERE, MS. KNICKER-BOCHER.
COME ON... SMILE!
WAMP
EVERYBODY READY? REDSTONE PARK AWAITS... LET'S NOT KEEP IT WAITING TOO LONG!
IT'S ALMOST DARK. THE SHOOTING STARS WILL BE FANTASTIC...
LOOKS LIKE OUR LAST NIGHT IN REDSTONE WILL BE AN UNFORGETTABLE ONE.
WHAT WILL YOU WISH FOR IF YOU SEE A SHOOTING STAR?
FOR IT TO HIT YOU IN THE FACE, SIR.

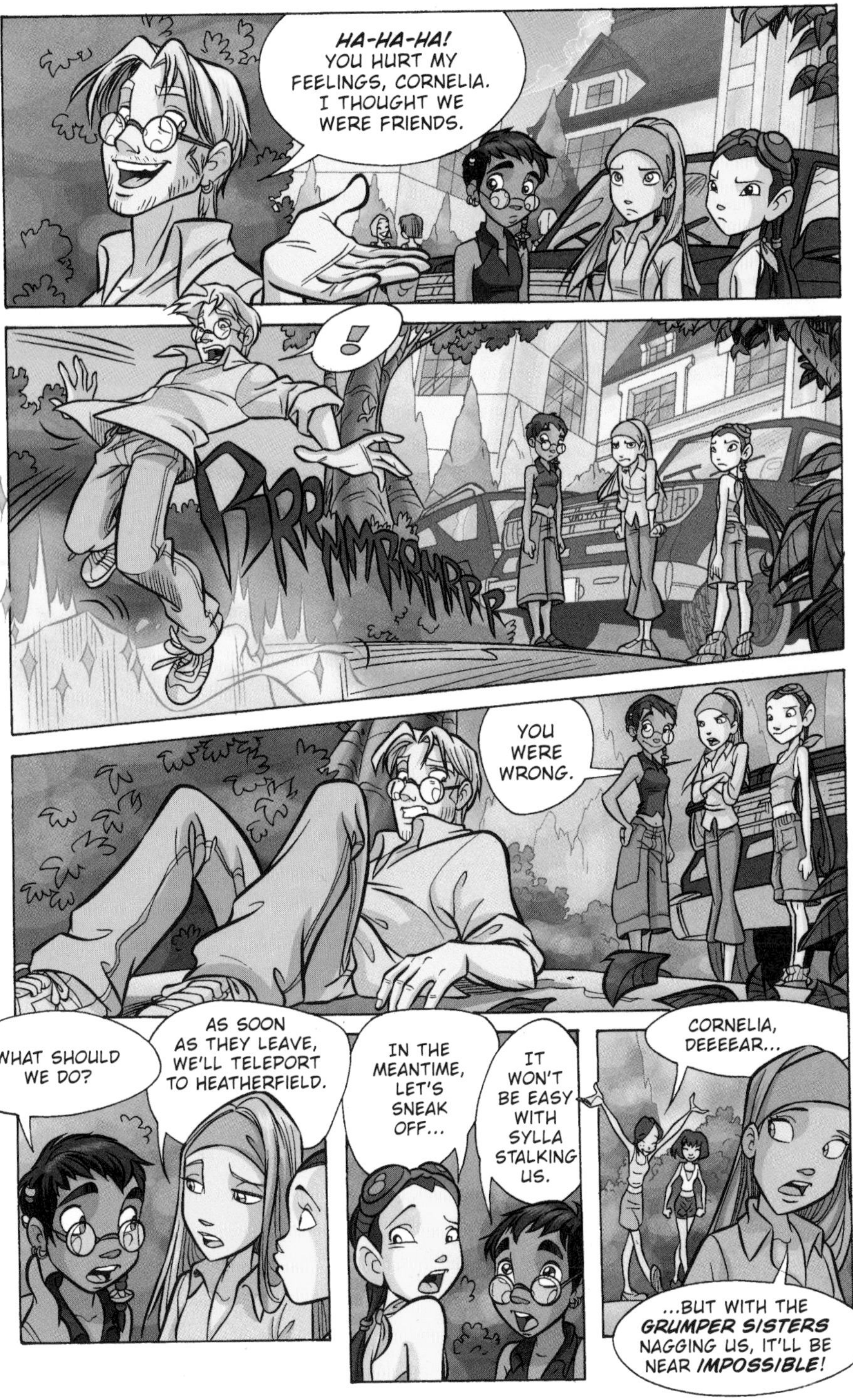

HA-HA-HA! YOU HURT MY FEELINGS, CORNELIA. I THOUGHT WE WERE FRIENDS.
!
BRRRMMRRMRRR
YOU WERE WRONG.
WHAT SHOULD WE DO?
AS SOON AS THEY LEAVE, WE'LL TELEPORT TO HEATHERFIELD.
IN THE MEANTIME, LET'S SNEAK OFF...
IT WON'T BE EASY WITH SYLLA STALKING US.
CORNELIA, DEEEEAR...
...BUT WITH THE GRUMPER SISTERS NAGGING US, IT'LL BE NEAR IMPOSSIBLE!

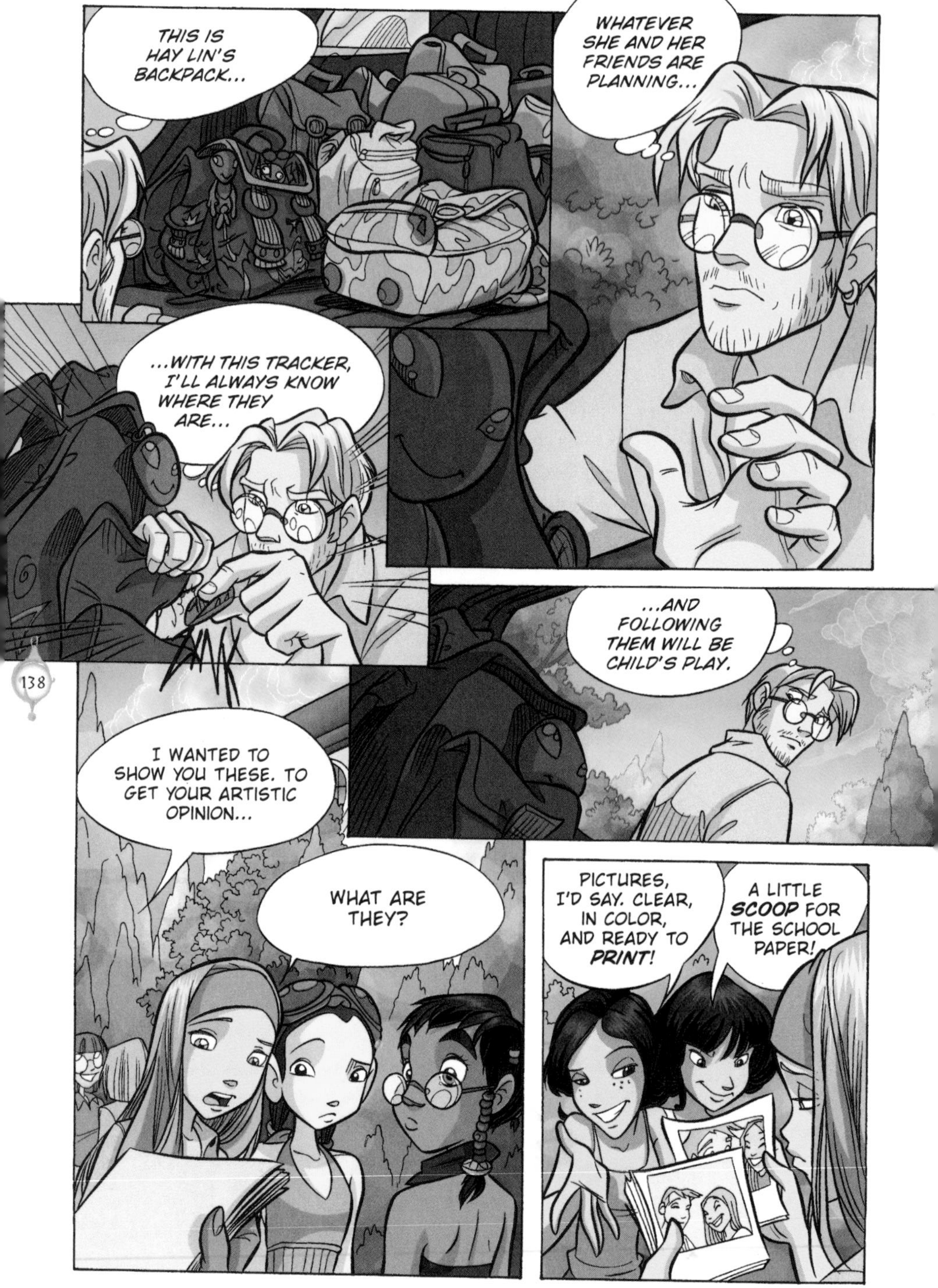
THIS IS HAY LIN'S BACKPACK...
WHATEVER SHE AND HER FRIENDS ARE PLANNING...
...WITH THIS TRACKER, I'LL ALWAYS KNOW WHERE THEY ARE...
...AND FOLLOWING THEM WILL BE CHILD'S PLAY.
I WANTED TO SHOW YOU THESE. TO GET YOUR ARTISTIC OPINION...
WHAT ARE THEY?
PICTURES, I'D SAY. CLEAR, IN COLOR, AND READY TO PRINT!
A LITTLE SCOOP FOR THE SCHOOL PAPER!

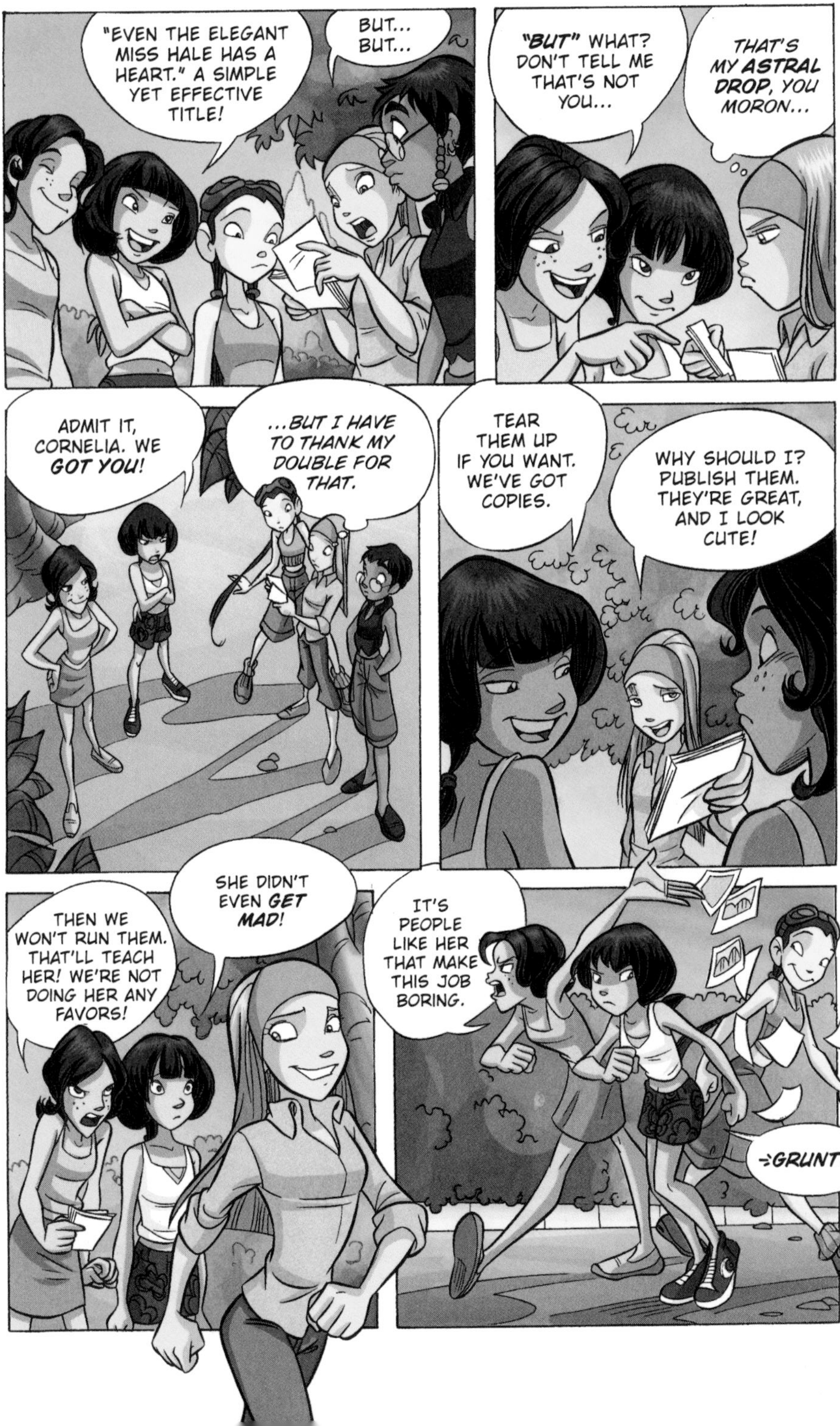
"EVEN THE ELEGANT MISS HALE HAS A HEART." A SIMPLE YET EFFECTIVE TITLE!
BUT... BUT...
"BUT" WHAT? DON'T TELL ME THAT'S NOT YOU...
THAT'S MY ASTRAL DROP, YOU MORON...
ADMIT IT, CORNELIA. WE GOT YOU!
...BUT I HAVE TO THANK MY DOUBLE FOR THAT.
TEAR THEM UP IF YOU WANT. WE'VE GOT COPIES.
WHY SHOULD I? PUBLISH THEM. THEY'RE GREAT, AND I LOOK CUTE!
THEN WE WON'T RUN THEM. THAT'LL TEACH HER! WE'RE NOT DOING HER ANY FAVORS!
SHE DIDN'T EVEN GET MAD!
IT'S PEOPLE LIKE HER THAT MAKE THIS JOB BORING.
GRUNT

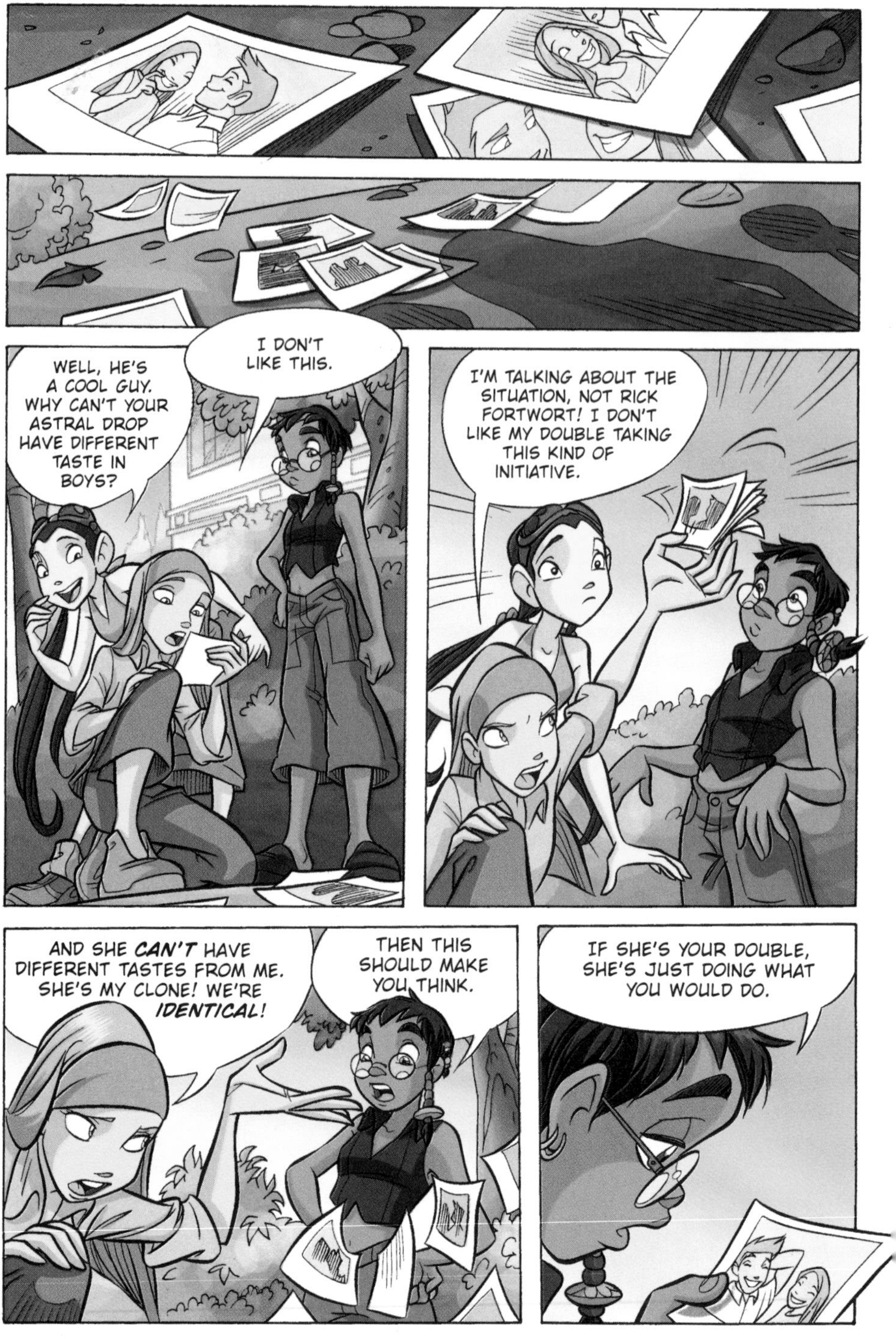
WELL, HE'S A COOL GUY. WHY CAN'T YOUR ASTRAL DROP HAVE DIFFERENT TASTE IN BOYS?
I DON'T LIKE THIS.
I'M TALKING ABOUT THE SITUATION, NOT RICK FORTWORT! I DON'T LIKE MY DOUBLE TAKING THIS KIND OF INITIATIVE.
AND SHE *CAN'T* HAVE DIFFERENT TASTES FROM ME. SHE'S MY CLONE! WE'RE *IDENTICAL*!
THEN THIS SHOULD MAKE YOU THINK.
IF SHE'S YOUR DOUBLE, SHE'S JUST DOING WHAT YOU WOULD DO.

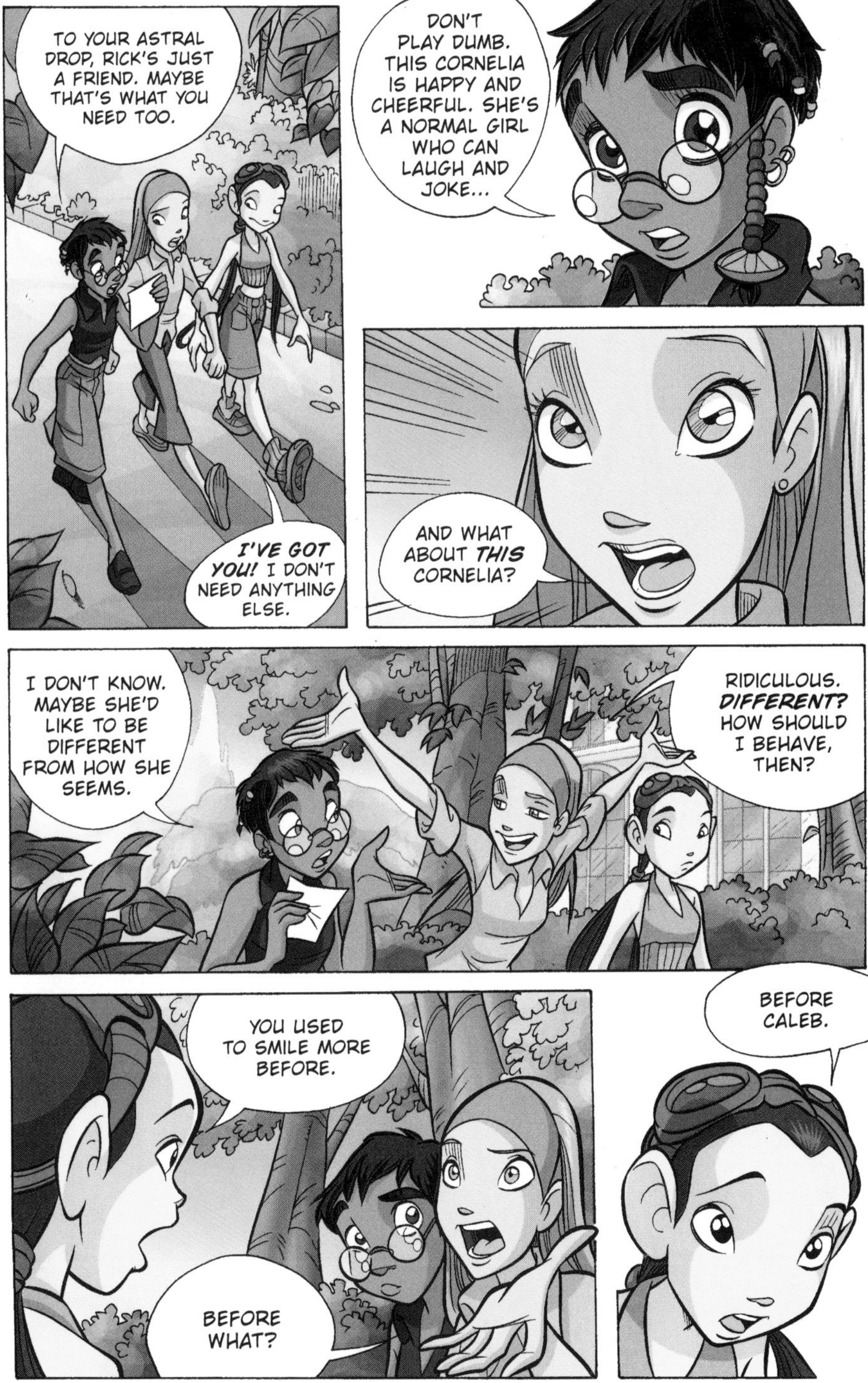
TO YOUR ASTRAL DROP, RICK'S JUST A FRIEND. MAYBE THAT'S WHAT YOU NEED TOO.
I'VE GOT YOU! I DON'T NEED ANYTHING ELSE.
DON'T PLAY DUMB. THIS CORNELIA IS HAPPY AND CHEERFUL. SHE'S A NORMAL GIRL WHO CAN LAUGH AND JOKE...
AND WHAT ABOUT THIS CORNELIA?
I DON'T KNOW. MAYBE SHE'D LIKE TO BE DIFFERENT FROM HOW SHE SEEMS.
RIDICULOUS. DIFFERENT? HOW SHOULD I BEHAVE, THEN?
YOU USED TO SMILE MORE BEFORE.
BEFORE WHAT?
BEFORE CALEB.

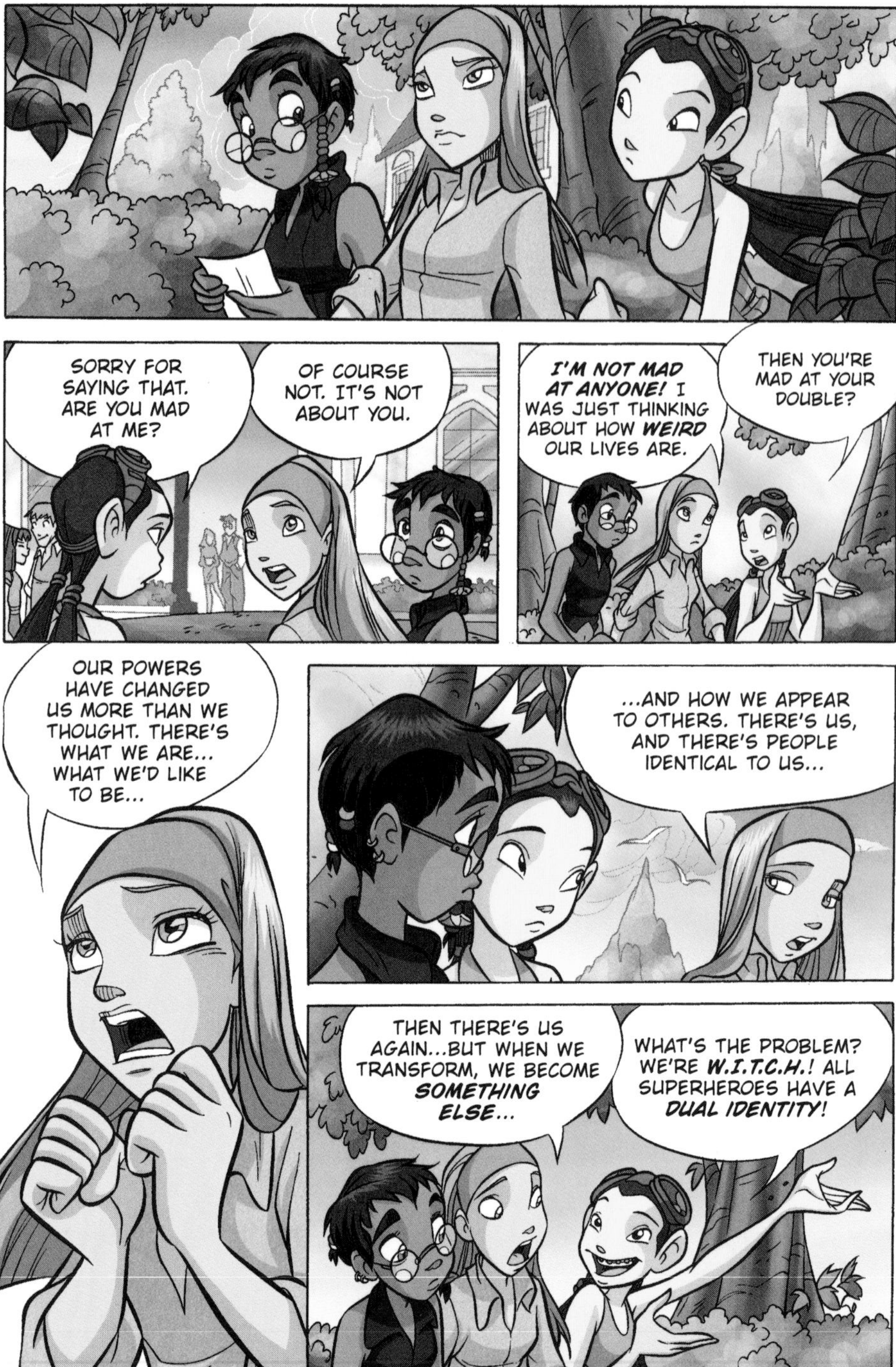

SORRY FOR SAYING THAT. ARE YOU MAD AT ME?

OF COURSE NOT. IT'S NOT ABOUT YOU.

I'M NOT MAD AT ANYONE! I WAS JUST THINKING ABOUT HOW *WEIRD* OUR LIVES ARE.

THEN YOU'RE MAD AT YOUR DOUBLE?

OUR POWERS HAVE CHANGED US MORE THAN WE THOUGHT. THERE'S WHAT WE ARE... WHAT WE'D LIKE TO BE...

...AND HOW WE APPEAR TO OTHERS. THERE'S US, AND THERE'S PEOPLE IDENTICAL TO US...

THEN THERE'S US AGAIN...BUT WHEN WE TRANSFORM, WE BECOME *SOMETHING ELSE*...

WHAT'S THE PROBLEM? WE'RE *W.I.T.C.H.!* ALL SUPERHEROES HAVE A *DUAL IDENTITY!*

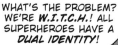

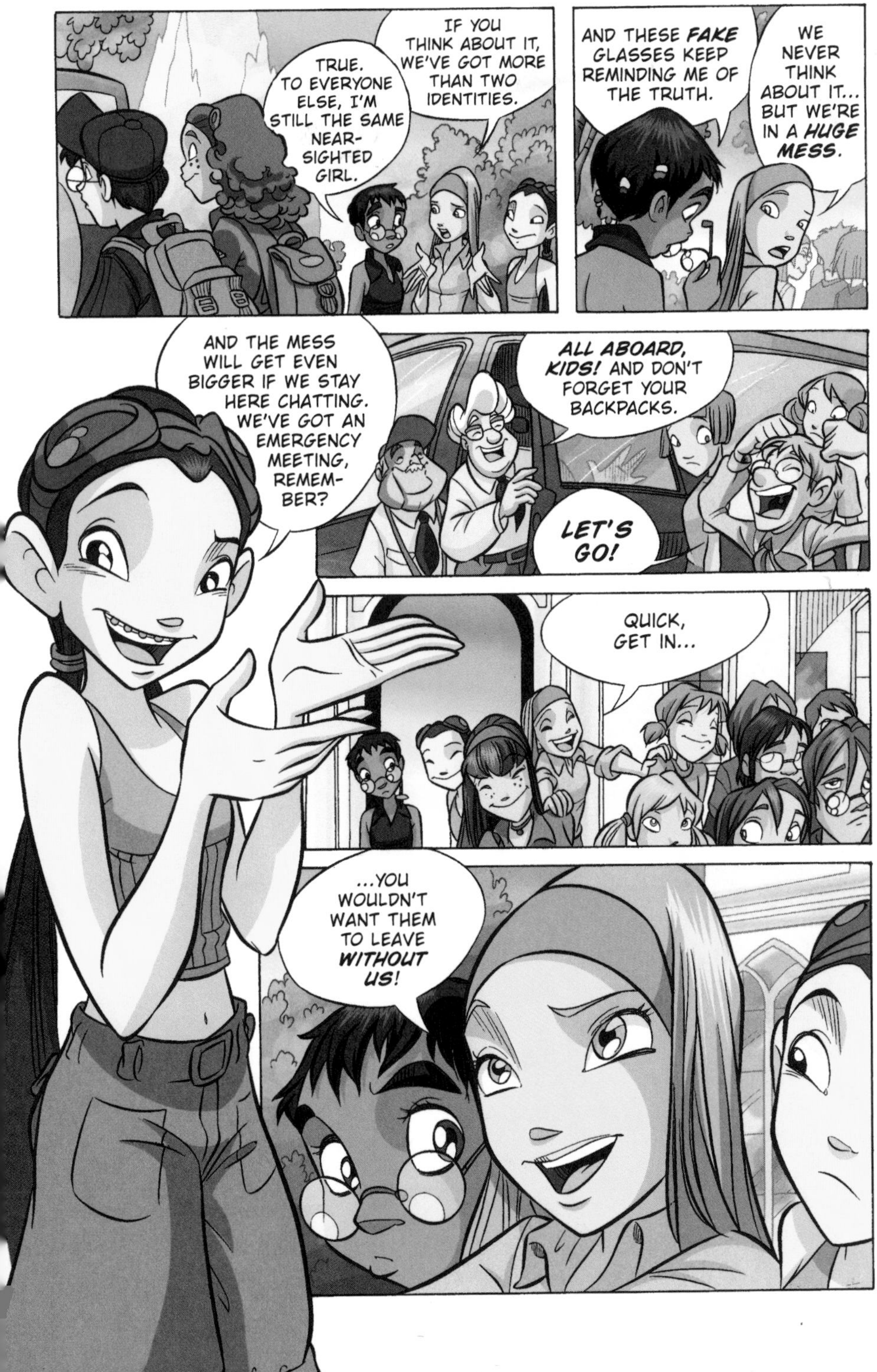
TRUE. TO EVERYONE ELSE, I'M STILL THE SAME NEAR-SIGHTED GIRL.
IF YOU THINK ABOUT IT, WE'VE GOT MORE THAN TWO IDENTITIES.
AND THESE FAKE GLASSES KEEP REMINDING ME OF THE TRUTH.
WE NEVER THINK ABOUT IT... BUT WE'RE IN A HUGE MESS.
AND THE MESS WILL GET EVEN BIGGER IF WE STAY HERE CHATTING. WE'VE GOT AN EMERGENCY MEETING, REMEMBER?
ALL ABOARD, KIDS! AND DON'T FORGET YOUR BACKPACKS.
LET'S GO!
QUICK, GET IN...
...YOU WOULDN'T WANT THEM TO LEAVE WITHOUT US!

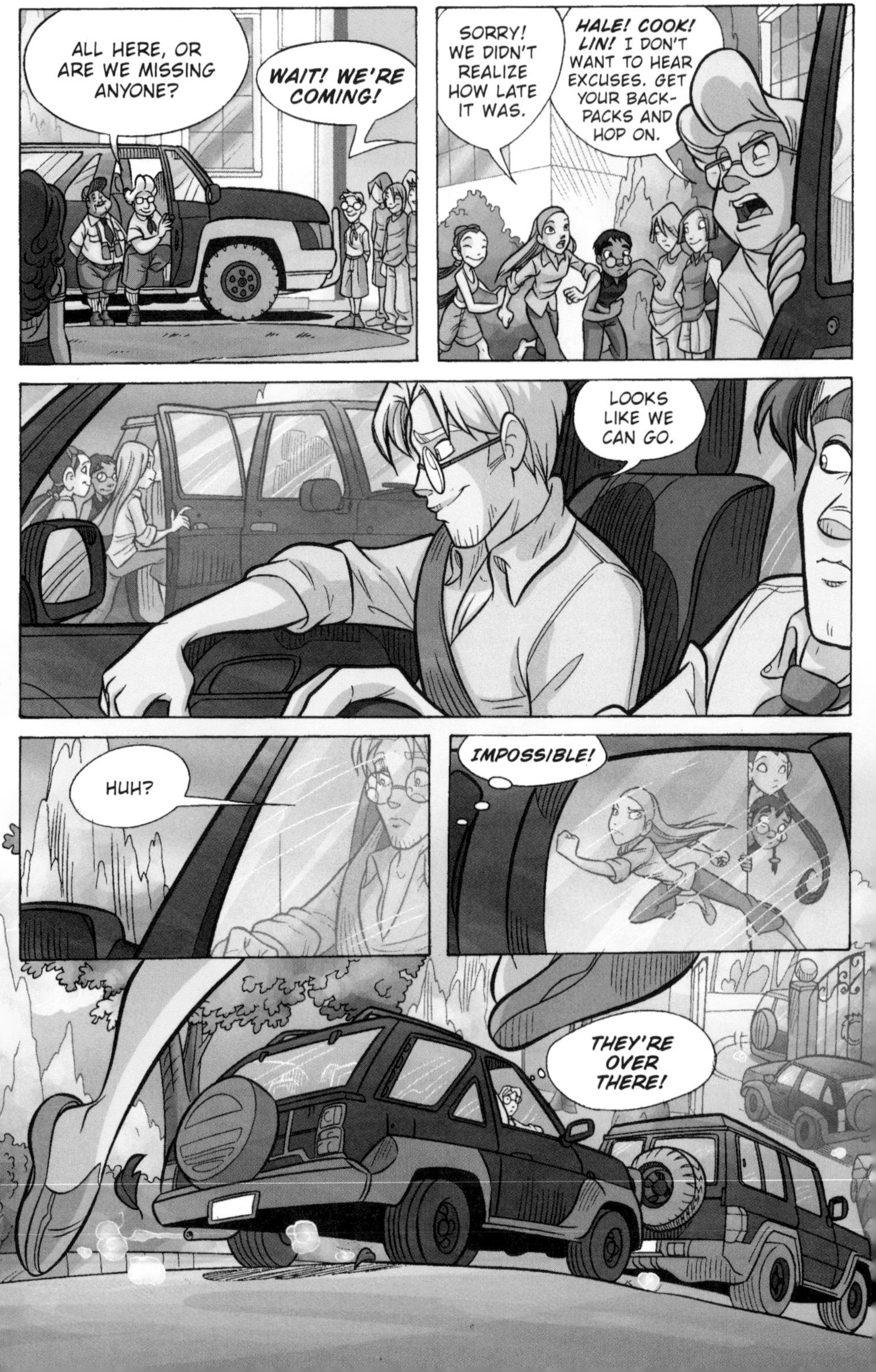
ALL HERE, OR ARE WE MISSING ANYONE?
WAIT! WE'RE COMING!
SORRY! WE DIDN'T REALIZE HOW LATE IT WAS.
HALE! COOK! LIN! I DON'T WANT TO HEAR EXCUSES. GET YOUR BACK-PACKS AND HOP ON.
LOOKS LIKE WE CAN GO.
HUH?
IMPOSSIBLE!
THEY'RE OVER THERE!

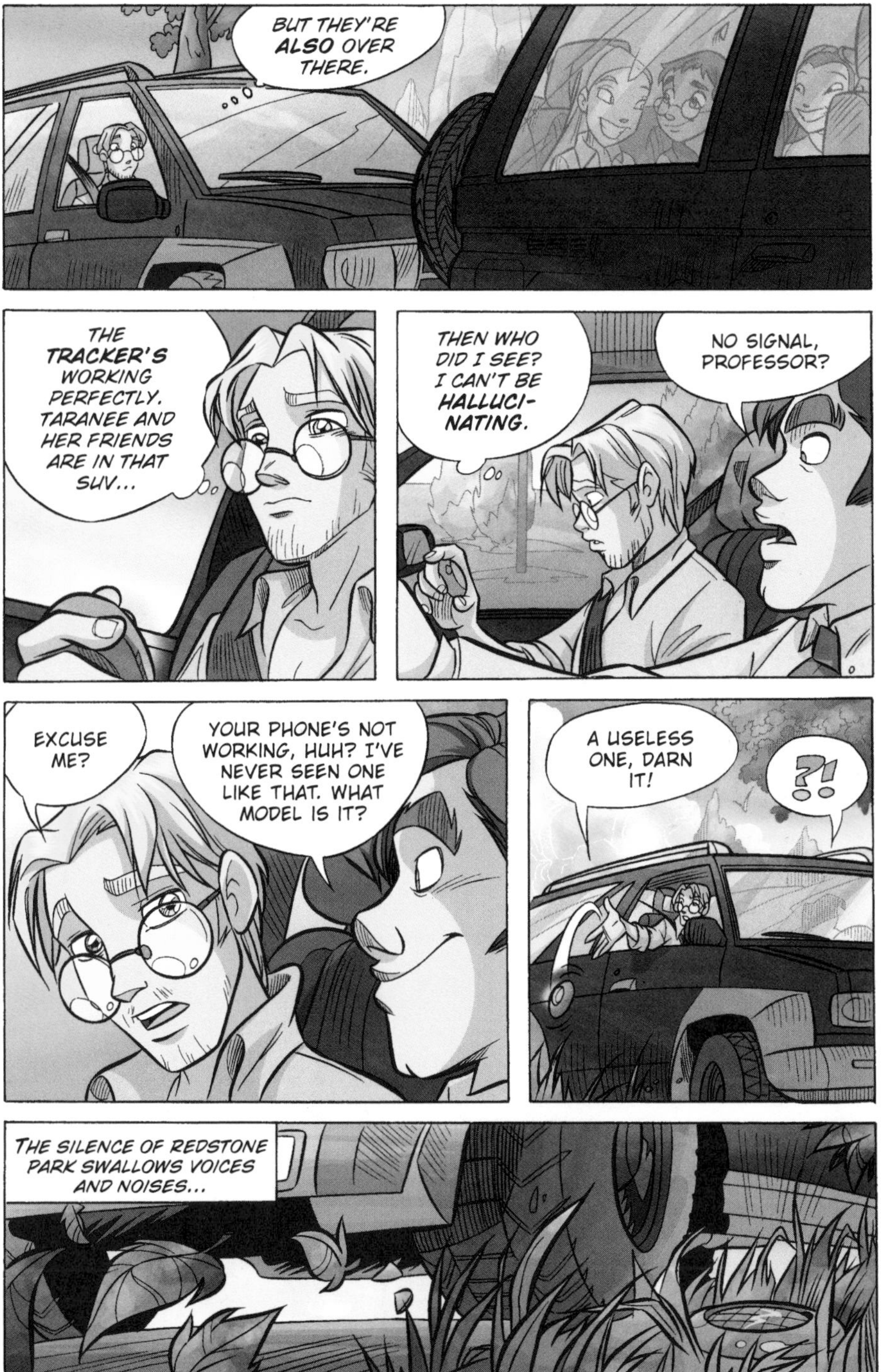
BUT THEY'RE **ALSO** OVER THERE.
THE **TRACKER'S** WORKING PERFECTLY. TARANEE AND HER FRIENDS ARE IN THAT SUV...
THEN WHO DID I SEE? I CAN'T BE **HALLUCINATING**.
NO SIGNAL, PROFESSOR?
EXCUSE ME?
YOUR PHONE'S NOT WORKING, HUH? I'VE NEVER SEEN ONE LIKE THAT. WHAT MODEL IS IT?
A USELESS ONE, DARN IT!
?!
THE SILENCE OF REDSTONE PARK SWALLOWS VOICES AND NOISES...

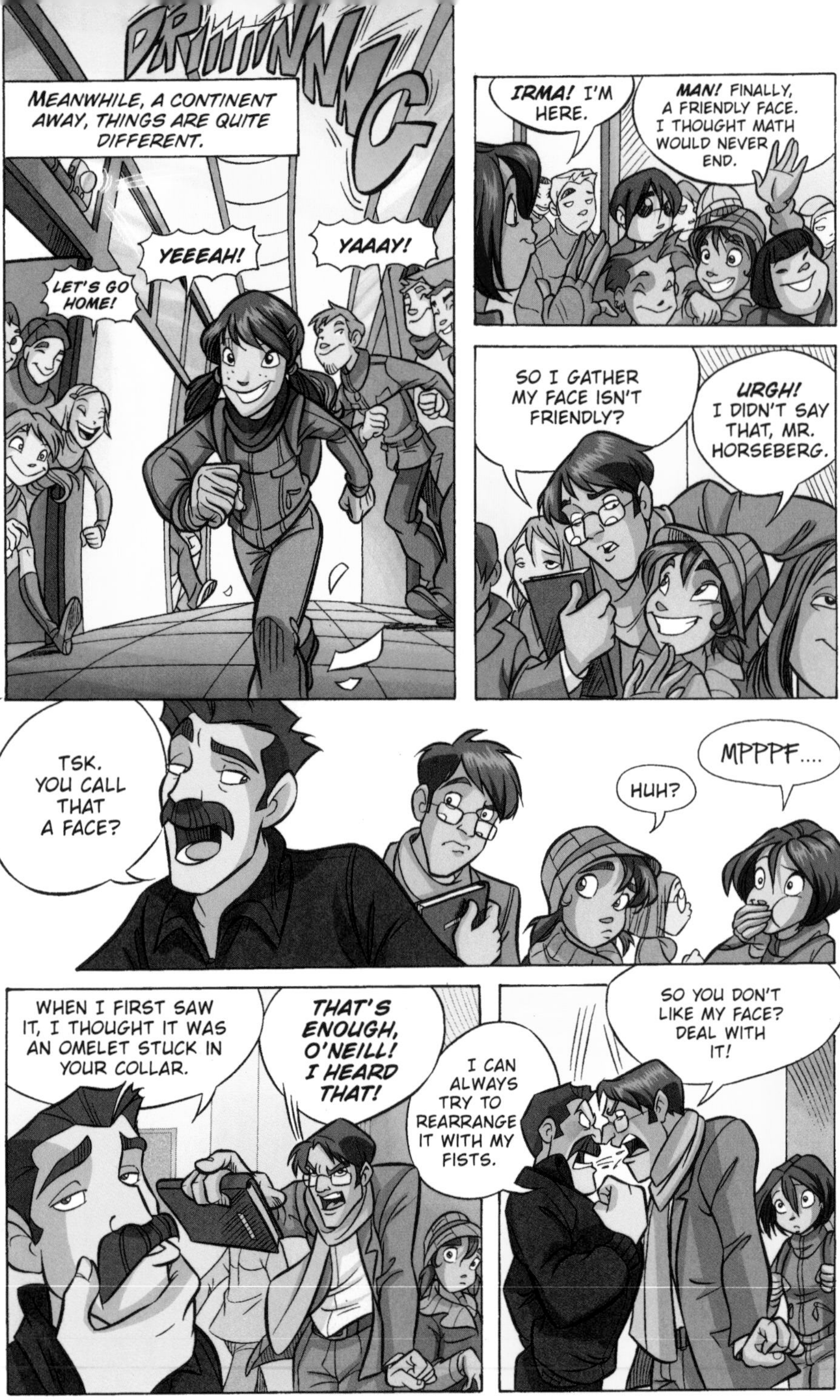
DRIIIINNNG
MEANWHILE, A CONTINENT AWAY, THINGS ARE QUITE DIFFERENT.
LET'S GO HOME!
YEEEAH!
YAAAY!
IRMA! I'M HERE.
MAN! FINALLY, A FRIENDLY FACE. I THOUGHT MATH WOULD NEVER END.
SO I GATHER MY FACE ISN'T FRIENDLY?
URGH! I DIDN'T SAY THAT, MR. HORSEBERG.
TSK. YOU CALL THAT A FACE?
HUH?
MPPPF....
WHEN I FIRST SAW IT, I THOUGHT IT WAS AN OMELET STUCK IN YOUR COLLAR.
THAT'S ENOUGH, O'NEILL! I HEARD THAT!
SO YOU DON'T LIKE MY FACE? DEAL WITH IT!
I CAN ALWAYS TRY TO REARRANGE IT WITH MY FISTS.

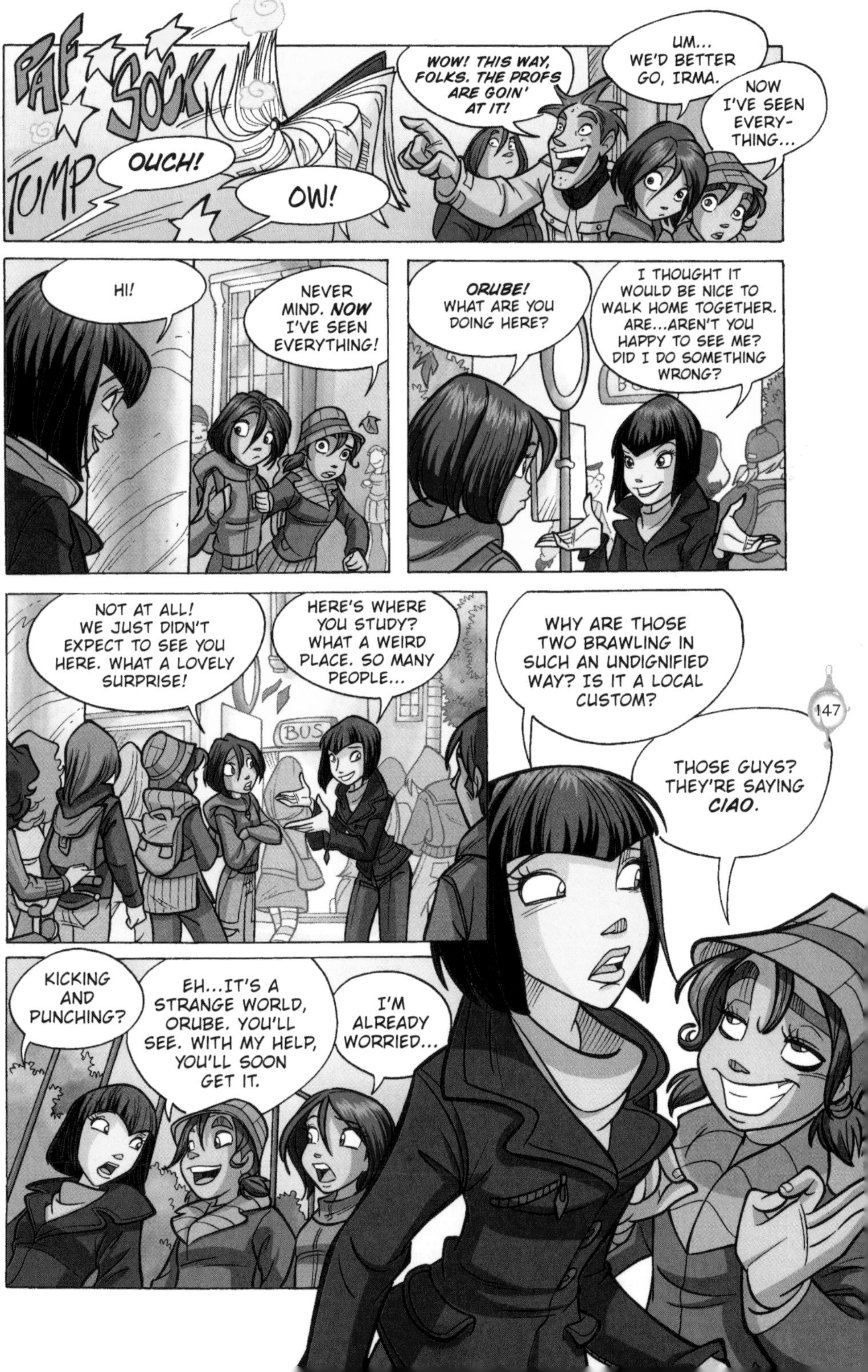
PAF
SOCK
TUMP
OUCH!
OW!
WOW! THIS WAY, FOLKS. THE PROFS ARE GOIN' AT IT!
UM... WE'D BETTER GO, IRMA.
NOW I'VE SEEN EVERY-THING...
HI!
NEVER MIND. NOW I'VE SEEN EVERYTHING!
ORUBE! WHAT ARE YOU DOING HERE?
I THOUGHT IT WOULD BE NICE TO WALK HOME TOGETHER. ARE...AREN'T YOU HAPPY TO SEE ME? DID I DO SOMETHING WRONG?
NOT AT ALL! WE JUST DIDN'T EXPECT TO SEE YOU HERE. WHAT A LOVELY SURPRISE!
HERE'S WHERE YOU STUDY? WHAT A WEIRD PLACE. SO MANY PEOPLE...
BUS
WHY ARE THOSE TWO BRAWLING IN SUCH AN UNDIGNIFIED WAY? IS IT A LOCAL CUSTOM?
THOSE GUYS? THEY'RE SAYING CIAO.
KICKING AND PUNCHING?
EH...IT'S A STRANGE WORLD, ORUBE. YOU'LL SEE. WITH MY HELP, YOU'LL SOON GET IT.
I'M ALREADY WORRIED...

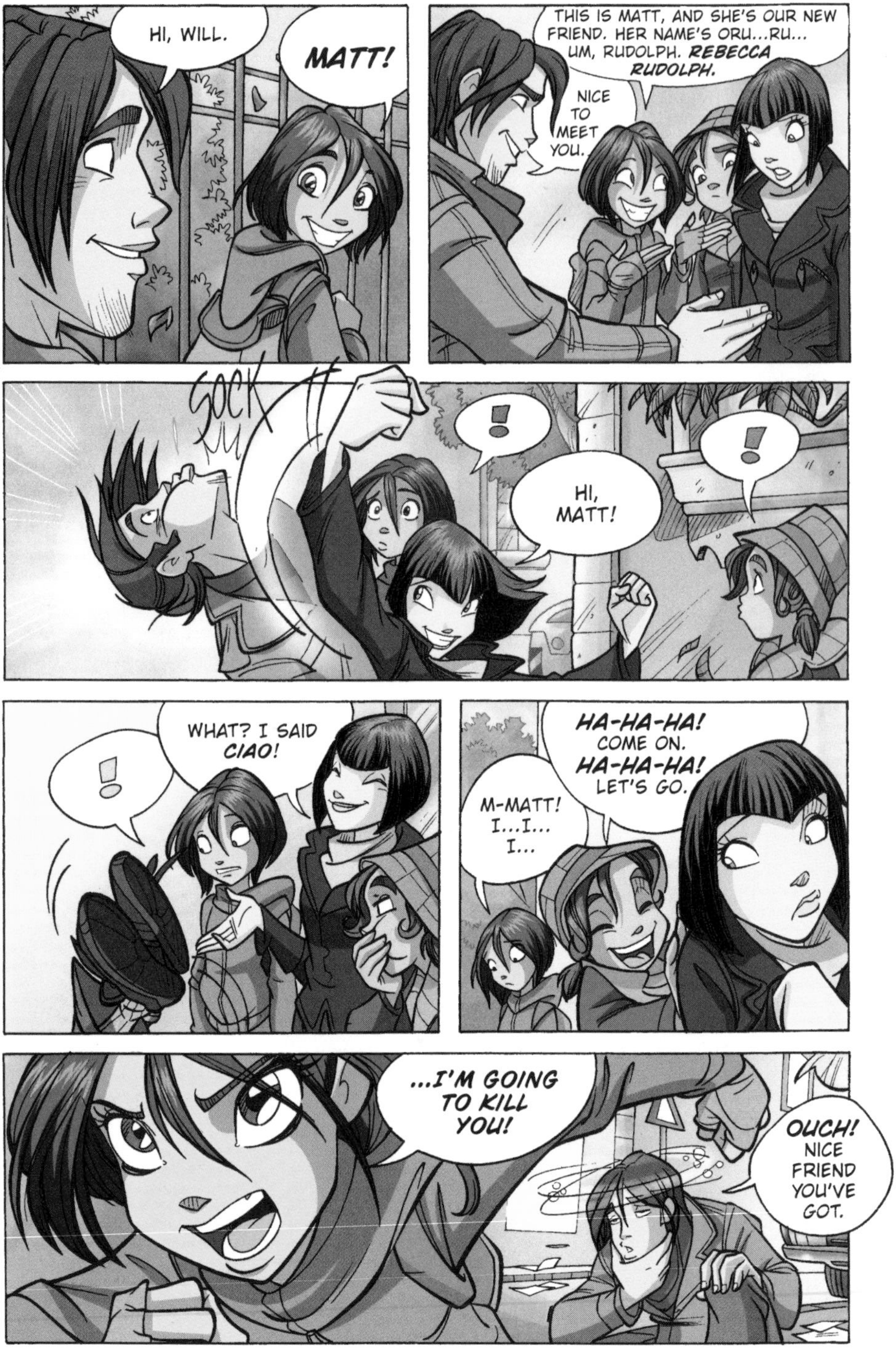
HI, WILL.
MATT!
THIS IS MATT, AND SHE'S OUR NEW FRIEND. HER NAME'S ORU...RU... UM, RUDOLPH. REBECCA RUDOLPH.
NICE TO MEET YOU.
SOCK
!
HI, MATT!
!
!
WHAT? I SAID CIAO!
HA-HA-HA! COME ON. HA-HA-HA! LET'S GO.
M-MATT! I...I... I...
...I'M GOING TO KILL YOU!
OUCH! NICE FRIEND YOU'VE GOT.

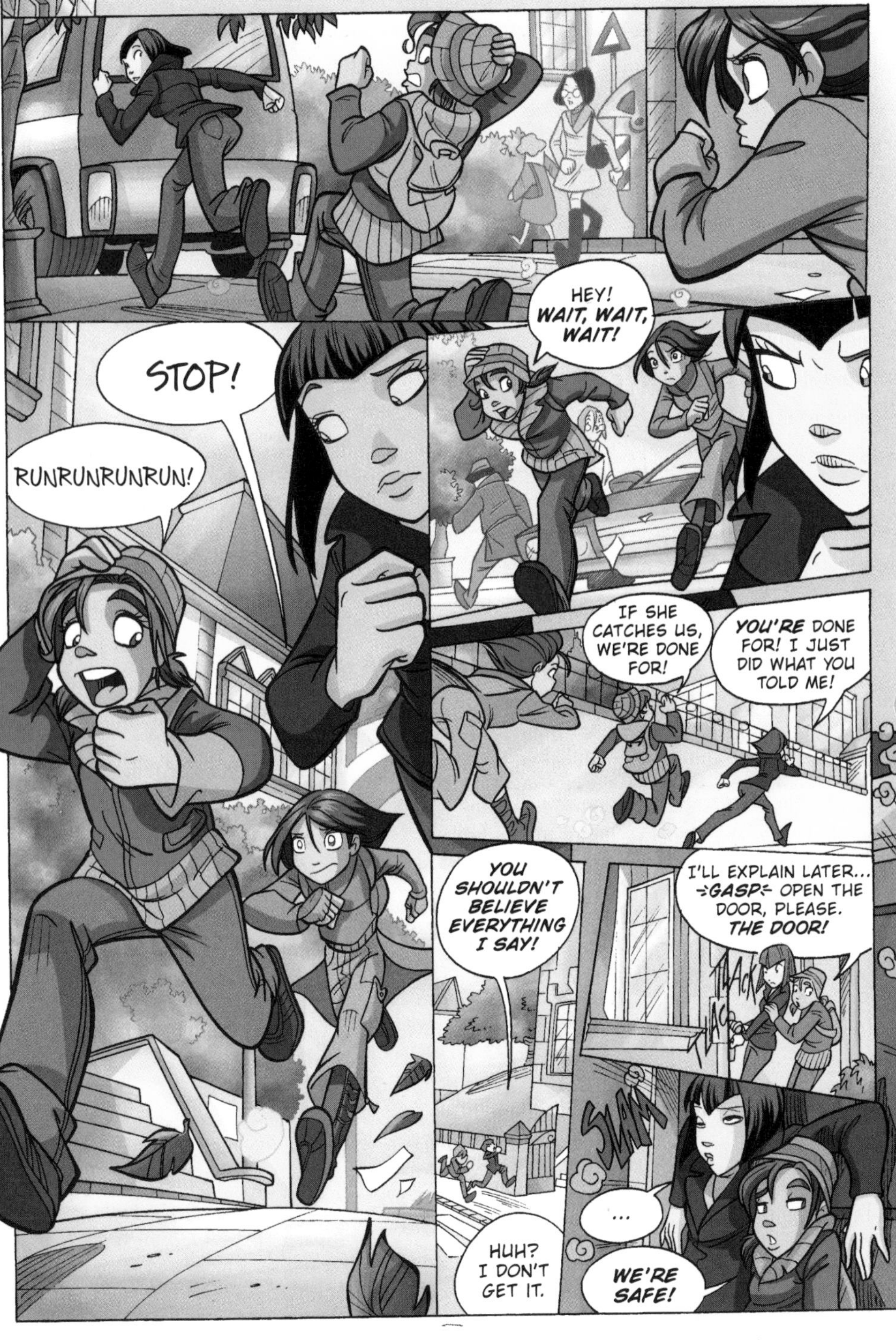
STOP!
RUNRUNRUNRUN!
HEY! WAIT, WAIT, WAIT!
IF SHE CATCHES US, WE'RE DONE FOR!
YOU'RE DONE FOR! I JUST DID WHAT YOU TOLD ME!
YOU SHOULDN'T BELIEVE EVERYTHING I SAY!
HUH? I DON'T GET IT.
I'LL EXPLAIN LATER... GASP OPEN THE DOOR, PLEASE. THE DOOR!
TRACK
TRACK
SLAM
...
WE'RE SAFE!

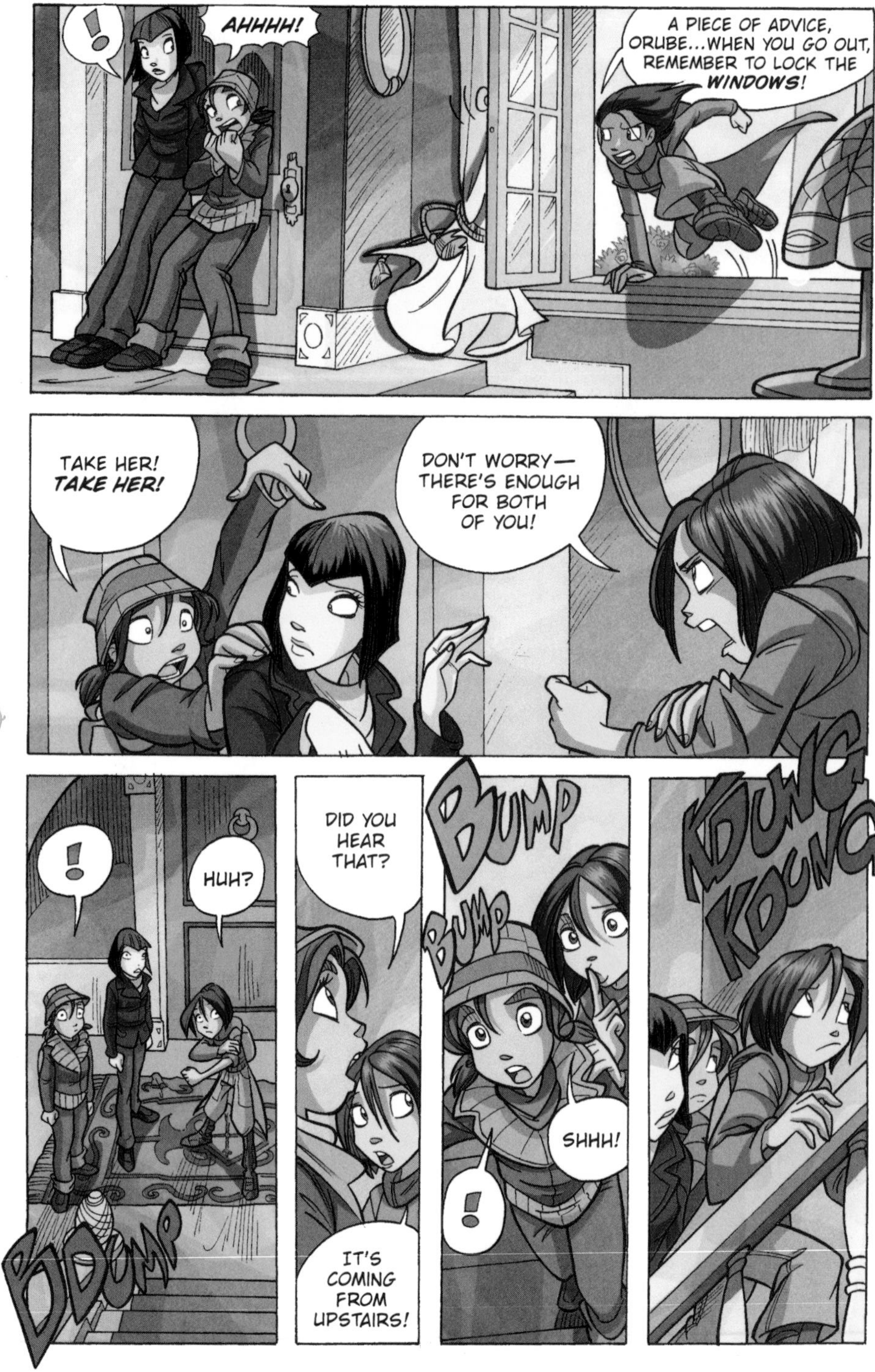
!
AHHHH!
A PIECE OF ADVICE, ORUBE...WHEN YOU GO OUT, REMEMBER TO LOCK THE WINDOWS!
TAKE HER! TAKE HER!
DON'T WORRY— THERE'S ENOUGH FOR BOTH OF YOU!
!
HUH?
BDUMP
DID YOU HEAR THAT?
IT'S COMING FROM UPSTAIRS!
BUMP
BUMP
!
SHHH!
KDUNG
KDUNG

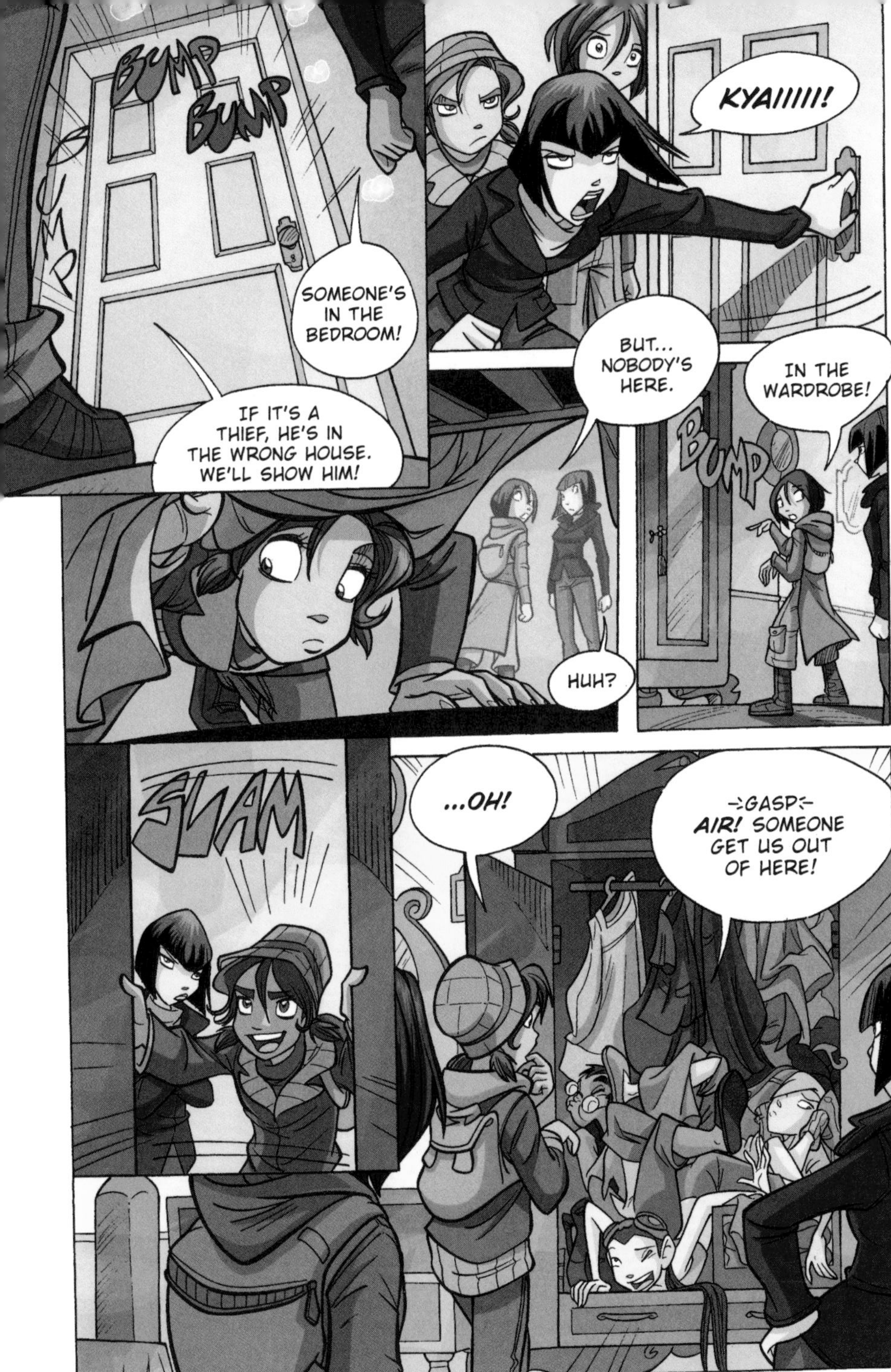
BUMP BUMP
BUMP
SOMEONE'S IN THE BEDROOM!
IF IT'S A THIEF, HE'S IN THE WRONG HOUSE. WE'LL SHOW HIM!
KYAIIIII!
BUT... NOBODY'S HERE.
HUH?
IN THE WARDROBE!
BUMP
SLAM
...OH!
GASP AIR! SOMEONE GET US OUT OF HERE!

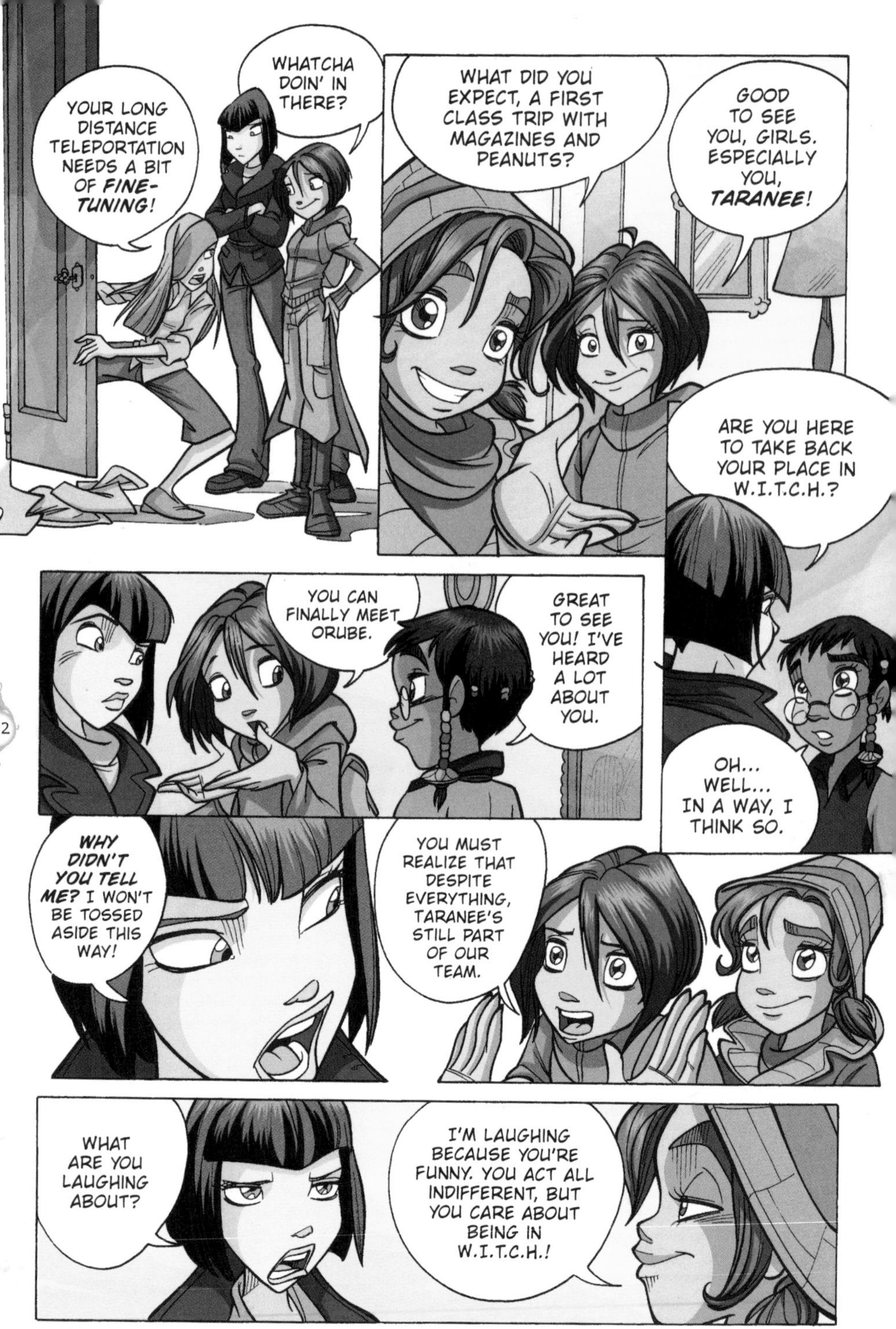
YOUR LONG DISTANCE TELEPORTATION NEEDS A BIT OF **FINE-TUNING**!
WHATCHA DOIN' IN THERE?
WHAT DID YOU EXPECT, A FIRST CLASS TRIP WITH MAGAZINES AND PEANUTS?
GOOD TO SEE YOU, GIRLS. ESPECIALLY YOU, ***TARANEE***!
ARE YOU HERE TO TAKE BACK YOUR PLACE IN W.I.T.C.H.?
YOU CAN FINALLY MEET ORUBE.
GREAT TO SEE YOU! I'VE HEARD A LOT ABOUT YOU.
OH... WELL... IN A WAY, I THINK SO.
WHY DIDN'T YOU TELL ME? I WON'T BE TOSSED ASIDE THIS WAY!
YOU MUST REALIZE THAT DESPITE EVERYTHING, TARANEE'S STILL PART OF OUR TEAM.
WHAT ARE YOU LAUGHING ABOUT?
I'M LAUGHING BECAUSE YOU'RE FUNNY. YOU ACT ALL INDIFFERENT, BUT YOU CARE ABOUT BEING IN W.I.T.C.H.!

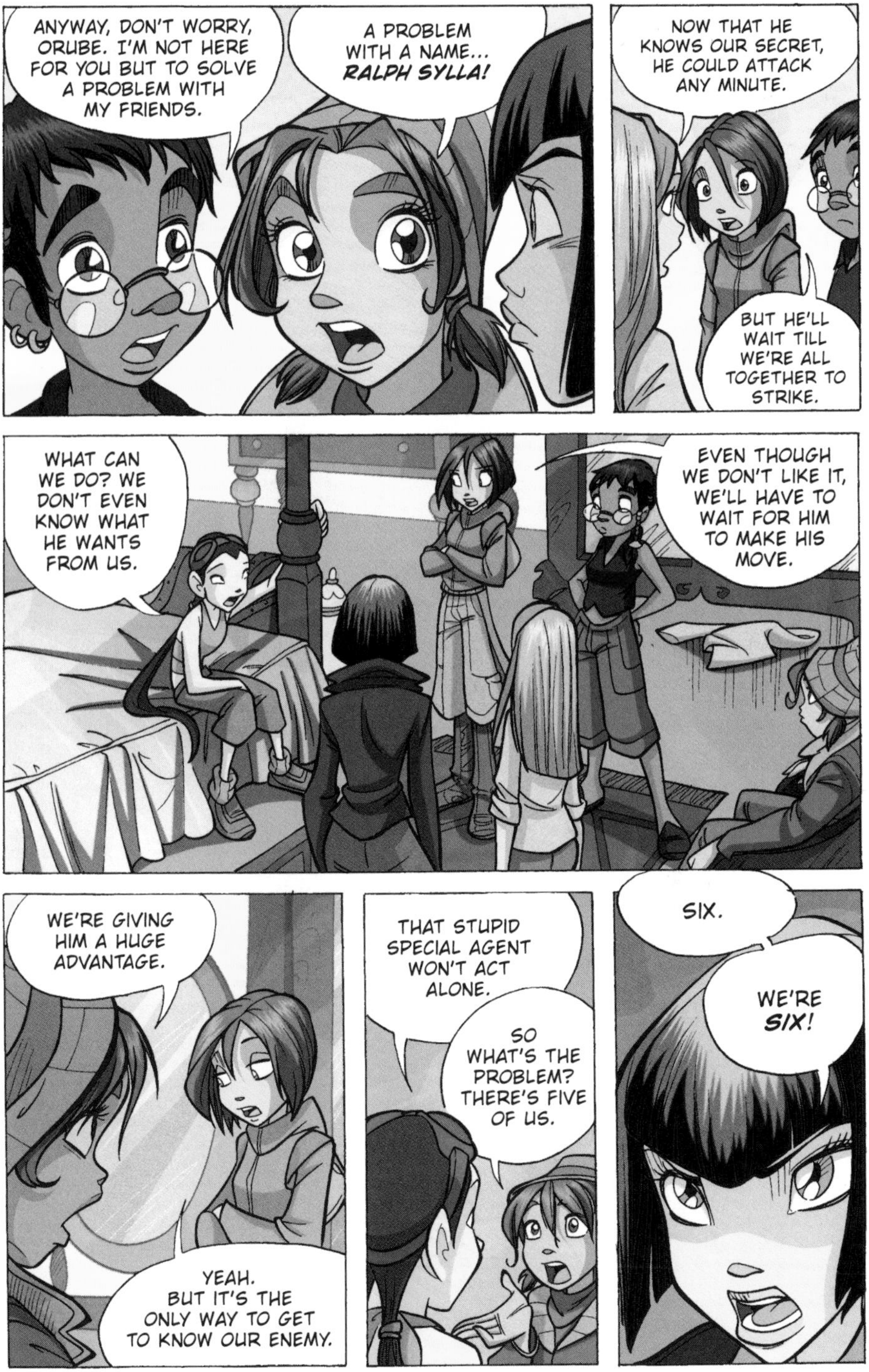
ANYWAY, DON'T WORRY, ORUBE. I'M NOT HERE FOR YOU BUT TO SOLVE A PROBLEM WITH MY FRIENDS.
A PROBLEM WITH A NAME... *RALPH SYLLA!*
NOW THAT HE KNOWS OUR SECRET, HE COULD ATTACK ANY MINUTE.
BUT HE'LL WAIT TILL WE'RE ALL TOGETHER TO STRIKE.
WHAT CAN WE DO? WE DON'T EVEN KNOW WHAT HE WANTS FROM US.
EVEN THOUGH WE DON'T LIKE IT, WE'LL HAVE TO WAIT FOR HIM TO MAKE HIS MOVE.
WE'RE GIVING HIM A HUGE ADVANTAGE.
YEAH. BUT IT'S THE ONLY WAY TO GET TO KNOW OUR ENEMY.
THAT STUPID SPECIAL AGENT WON'T ACT ALONE.
SO WHAT'S THE PROBLEM? THERE'S FIVE OF US.
SIX.
WE'RE *SIX!*

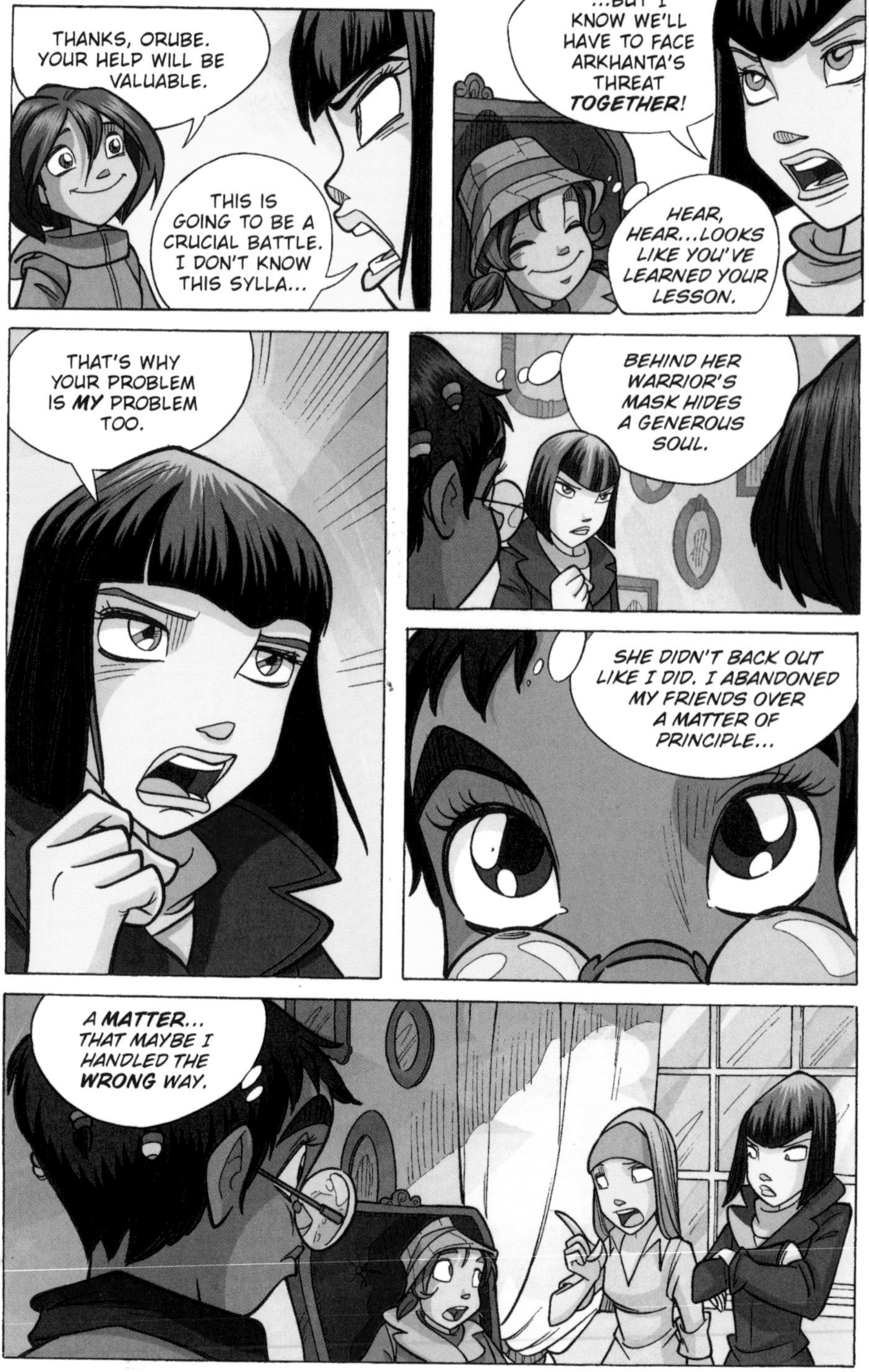
THANKS, ORUBE. YOUR HELP WILL BE VALUABLE.
THIS IS GOING TO BE A CRUCIAL BATTLE. I DON'T KNOW THIS SYLLA...
...BUT I KNOW WE'LL HAVE TO FACE ARKHANTA'S THREAT TOGETHER!
HEAR, HEAR...LOOKS LIKE YOU'VE LEARNED YOUR LESSON.
THAT'S WHY YOUR PROBLEM IS MY PROBLEM TOO.
BEHIND HER WARRIOR'S MASK HIDES A GENEROUS SOUL.
SHE DIDN'T BACK OUT LIKE I DID. I ABANDONED MY FRIENDS OVER A MATTER OF PRINCIPLE...
A MATTER... THAT MAYBE I HANDLED THE WRONG WAY.

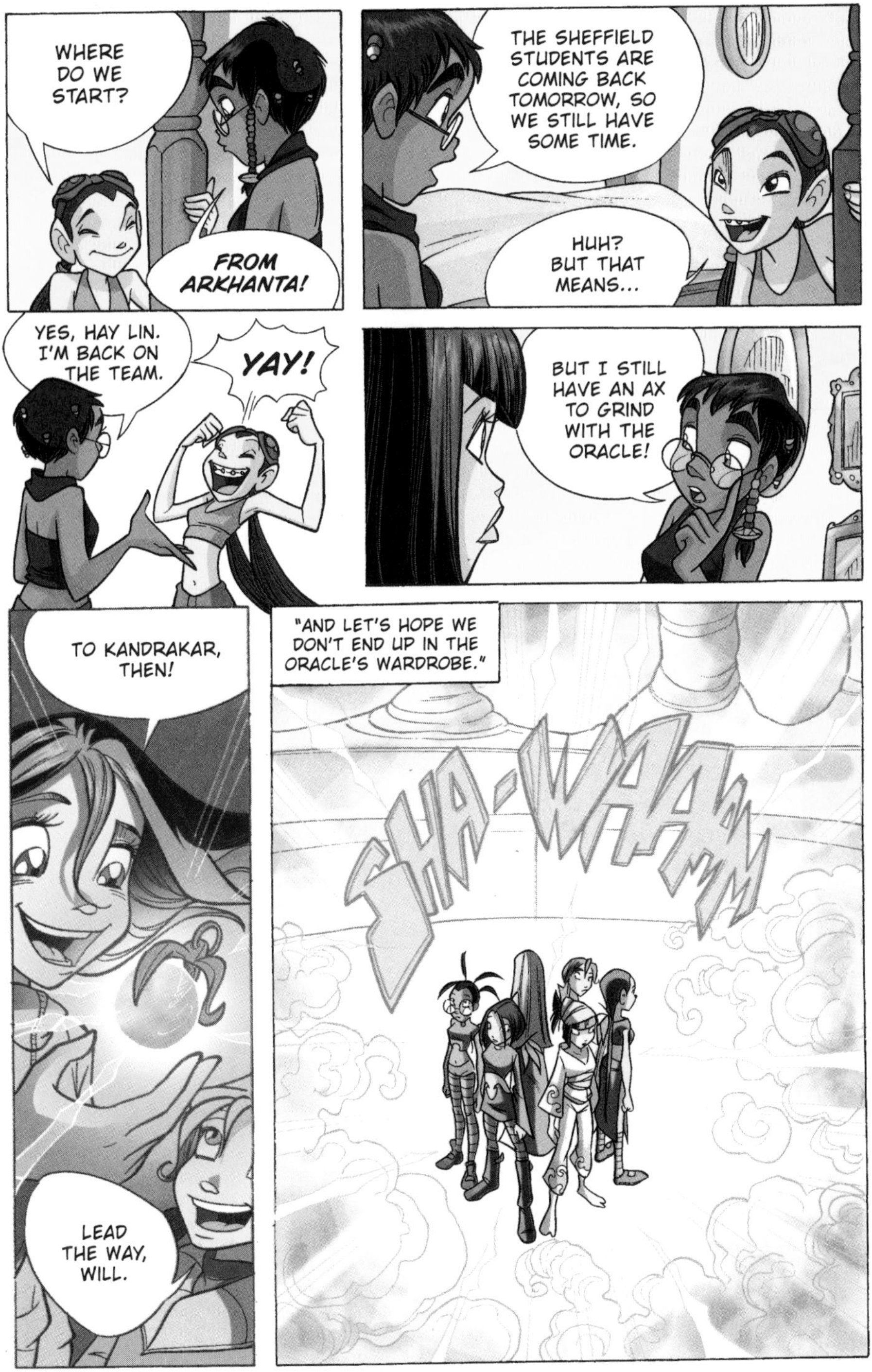
WHERE DO WE START?
FROM ARKHANTA!
THE SHEFFIELD STUDENTS ARE COMING BACK TOMORROW, SO WE STILL HAVE SOME TIME.
HUH? BUT THAT MEANS...
YES, HAY LIN. I'M BACK ON THE TEAM.
YAY!
BUT I STILL HAVE AN AX TO GRIND WITH THE ORACLE!
TO KANDRAKAR, THEN!
LEAD THE WAY, WILL.
"AND LET'S HOPE WE DON'T END UP IN THE ORACLE'S WARDROBE."
SHA-WAAAMM

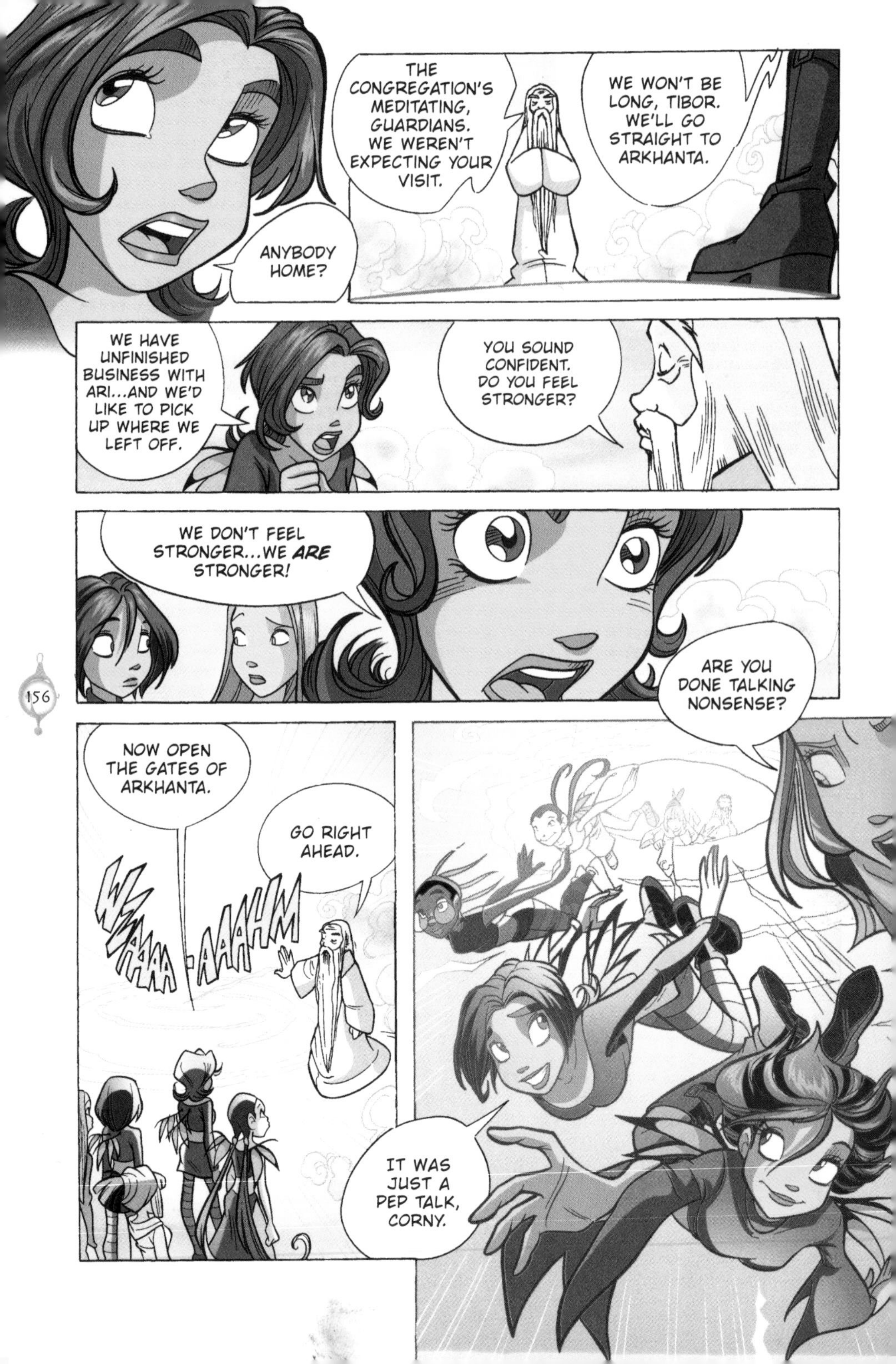
ANYBODY HOME?
THE CONGREGATION'S MEDITATING, GUARDIANS. WE WEREN'T EXPECTING YOUR VISIT.
WE WON'T BE LONG, TIBOR. WE'LL GO STRAIGHT TO ARKHANTA.
WE HAVE UNFINISHED BUSINESS WITH ARI...AND WE'D LIKE TO PICK UP WHERE WE LEFT OFF.
YOU SOUND CONFIDENT. DO YOU FEEL STRONGER?
WE DON'T FEEL STRONGER...WE *ARE* STRONGER!
NOW OPEN THE GATES OF ARKHANTA.
GO RIGHT AHEAD.
WHAAAA-AAAHM
ARE YOU DONE TALKING NONSENSE?
IT WAS JUST A PEP TALK, CORNY.

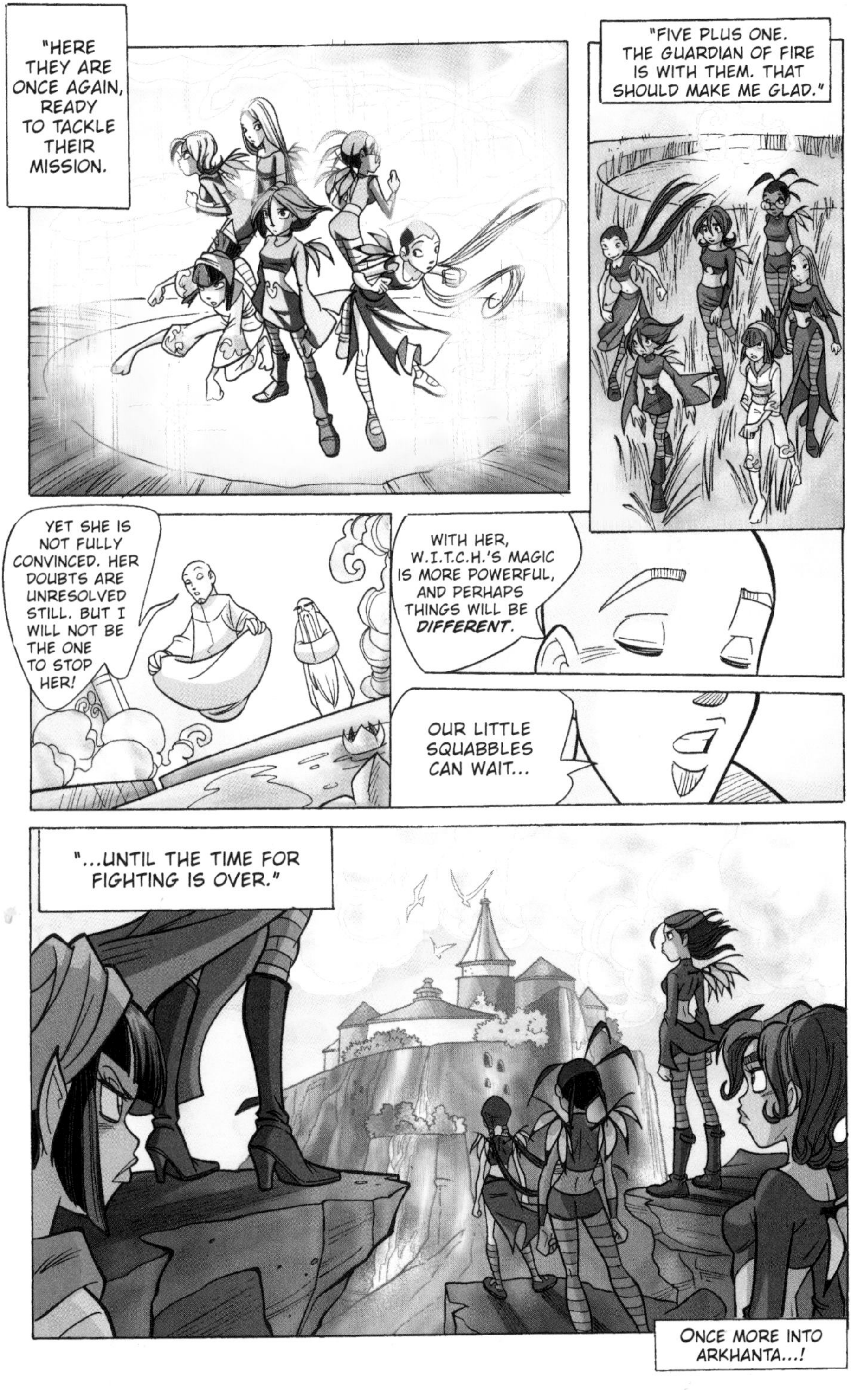
"HERE THEY ARE ONCE AGAIN, READY TO TACKLE THEIR MISSION.
"FIVE PLUS ONE. THE GUARDIAN OF FIRE IS WITH THEM. THAT SHOULD MAKE ME GLAD."
YET SHE IS NOT FULLY CONVINCED. HER DOUBTS ARE UNRESOLVED STILL. BUT I WILL NOT BE THE ONE TO STOP HER!
WITH HER, W.I.T.C.H.'S MAGIC IS MORE POWERFUL, AND PERHAPS THINGS WILL BE *DIFFERENT*.
OUR LITTLE SQUABBLES CAN WAIT...
"...UNTIL THE TIME FOR FIGHTING IS OVER."
ONCE MORE INTO ARKHANTA...!

W.i.t.c.h.

Will Irma Taranee Cornelia Hay Lin

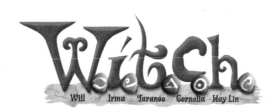

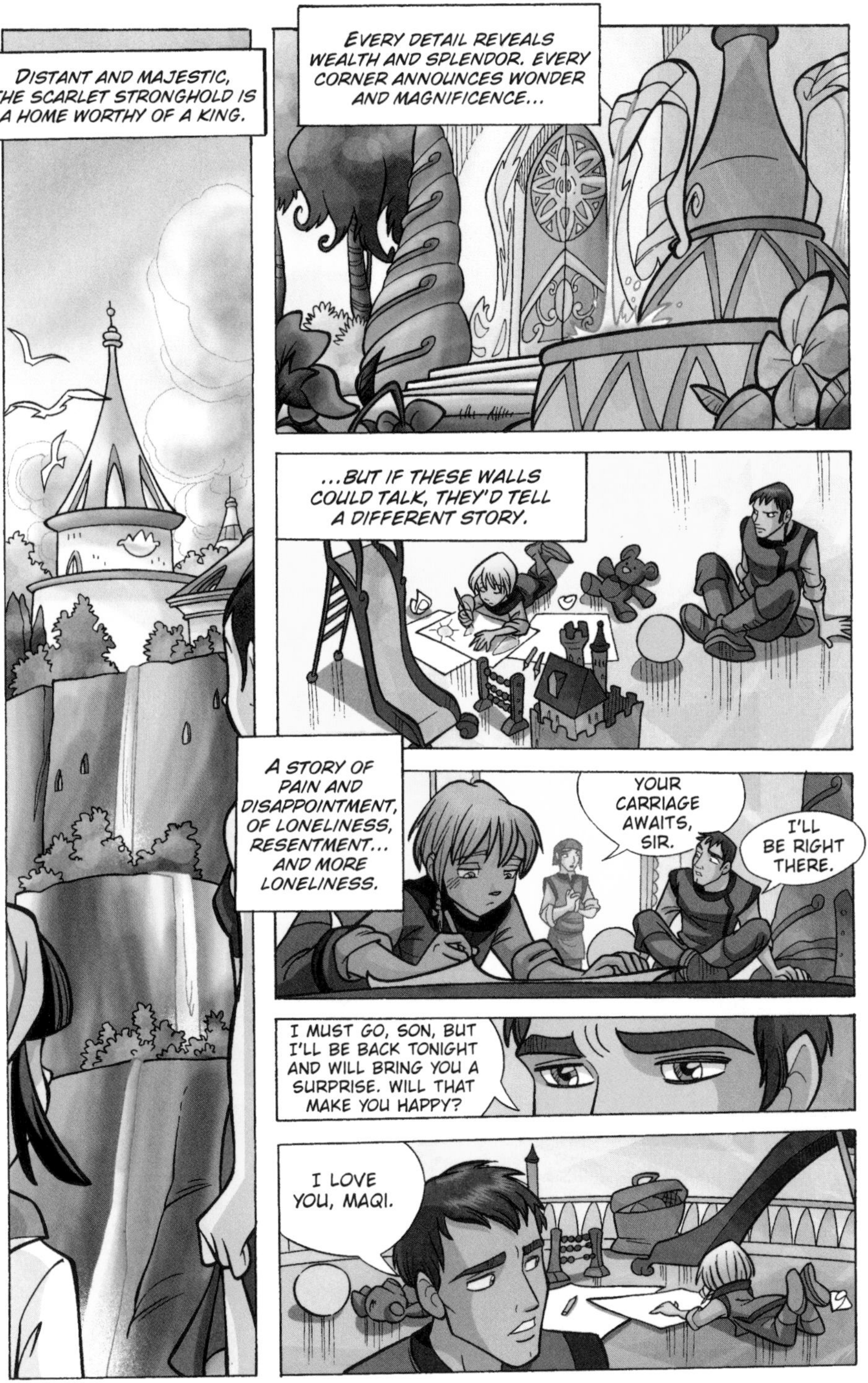

DISTANT AND MAJESTIC, THE SCARLET STRONGHOLD IS A HOME WORTHY OF A KING.
EVERY DETAIL REVEALS WEALTH AND SPLENDOR. EVERY CORNER ANNOUNCES WONDER AND MAGNIFICENCE...
...BUT IF THESE WALLS COULD TALK, THEY'D TELL A DIFFERENT STORY.
A STORY OF PAIN AND DISAPPOINTMENT, OF LONELINESS, RESENTMENT... AND MORE LONELINESS.
YOUR CARRIAGE AWAITS, SIR.
I'LL BE RIGHT THERE.
I MUST GO, SON, BUT I'LL BE BACK TONIGHT AND WILL BRING YOU A SURPRISE. WILL THAT MAKE YOU HAPPY?
I LOVE YOU, MAQI.

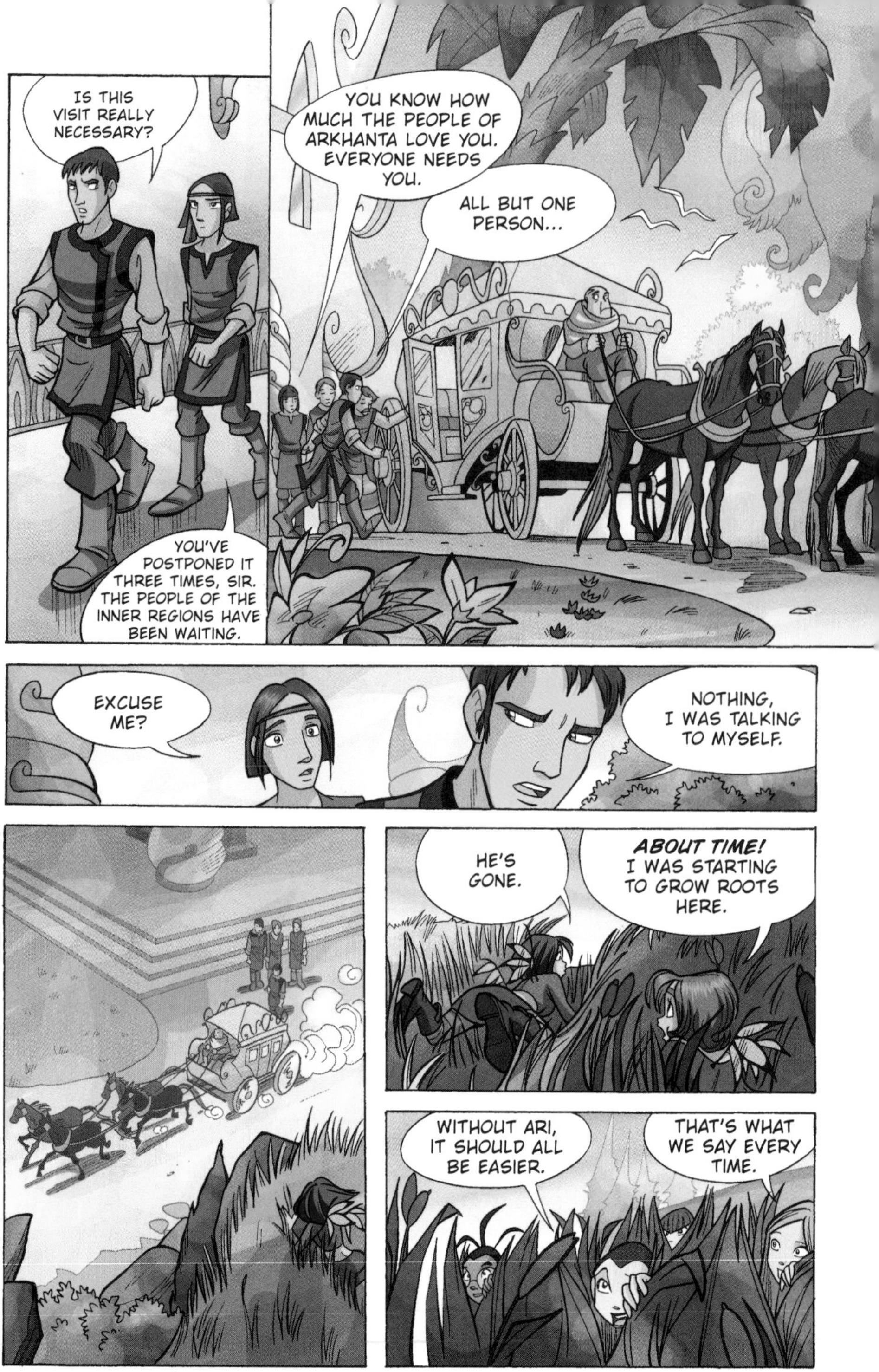
IS THIS VISIT REALLY NECESSARY?
YOU'VE POSTPONED IT THREE TIMES, SIR. THE PEOPLE OF THE INNER REGIONS HAVE BEEN WAITING.
YOU KNOW HOW MUCH THE PEOPLE OF ARKHANTA LOVE YOU. EVERYONE NEEDS YOU.
ALL BUT ONE PERSON...
EXCUSE ME?
NOTHING, I WAS TALKING TO MYSELF.
HE'S GONE.
ABOUT TIME! I WAS STARTING TO GROW ROOTS HERE.
WITHOUT ARI, IT SHOULD ALL BE EASIER.
THAT'S WHAT WE SAY EVERY TIME.

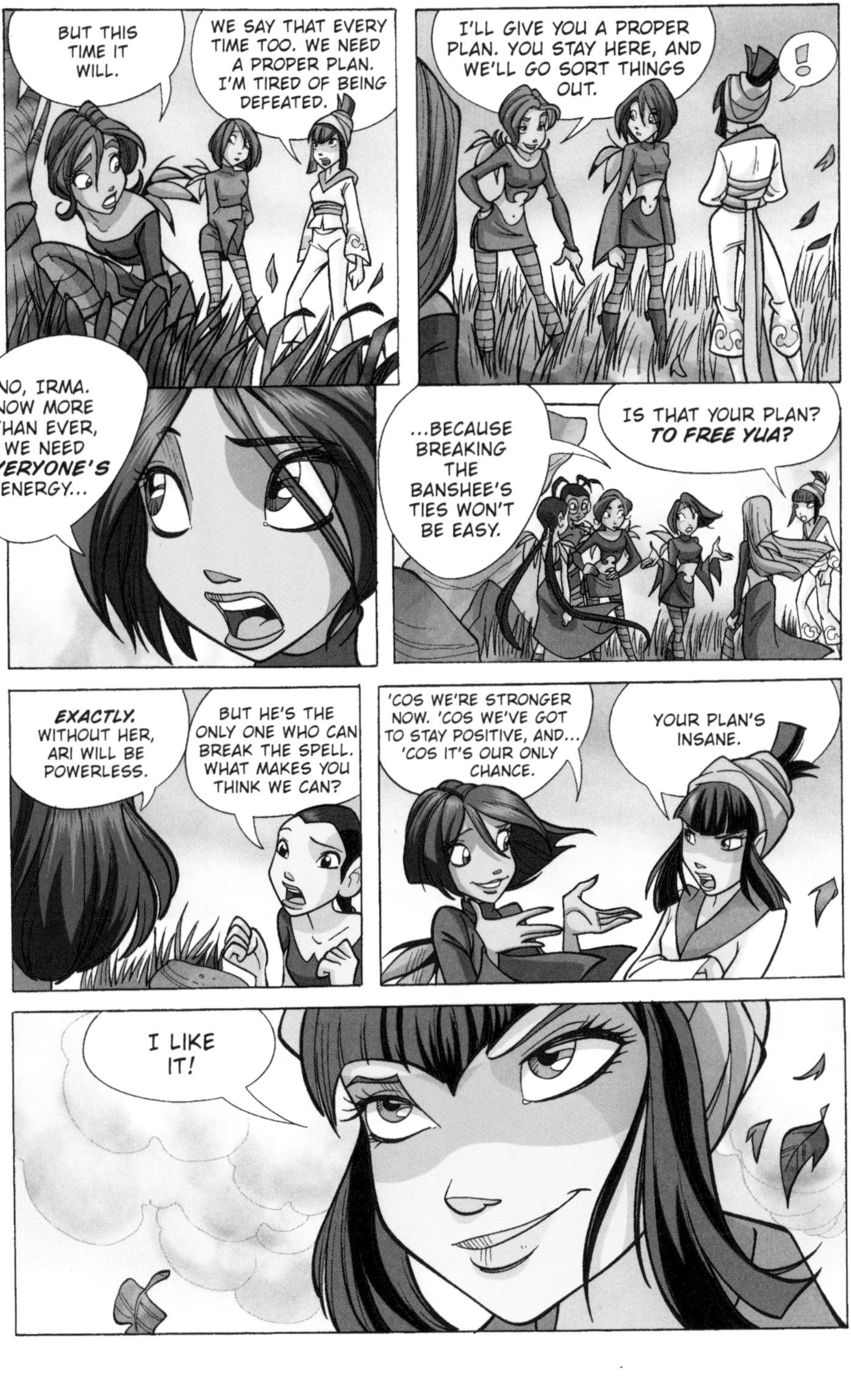
BUT THIS TIME IT WILL.
WE SAY THAT EVERY TIME TOO. WE NEED A PROPER PLAN. I'M TIRED OF BEING DEFEATED.
I'LL GIVE YOU A PROPER PLAN. YOU STAY HERE, AND WE'LL GO SORT THINGS OUT.
!
NO, IRMA. NOW MORE THAN EVER, WE NEED *EVERYONE'S* ENERGY...
IS THAT YOUR PLAN? *TO FREE YUA?*
...BECAUSE BREAKING THE BANSHEE'S TIES WON'T BE EASY.
EXACTLY. WITHOUT HER, ARI WILL BE POWERLESS.
BUT HE'S THE ONLY ONE WHO CAN BREAK THE SPELL. WHAT MAKES YOU THINK WE CAN?
YOUR PLAN'S INSANE.
'COS WE'RE STRONGER NOW. 'COS WE'VE GOT TO STAY POSITIVE, AND... 'COS IT'S OUR ONLY CHANCE.
I LIKE IT!

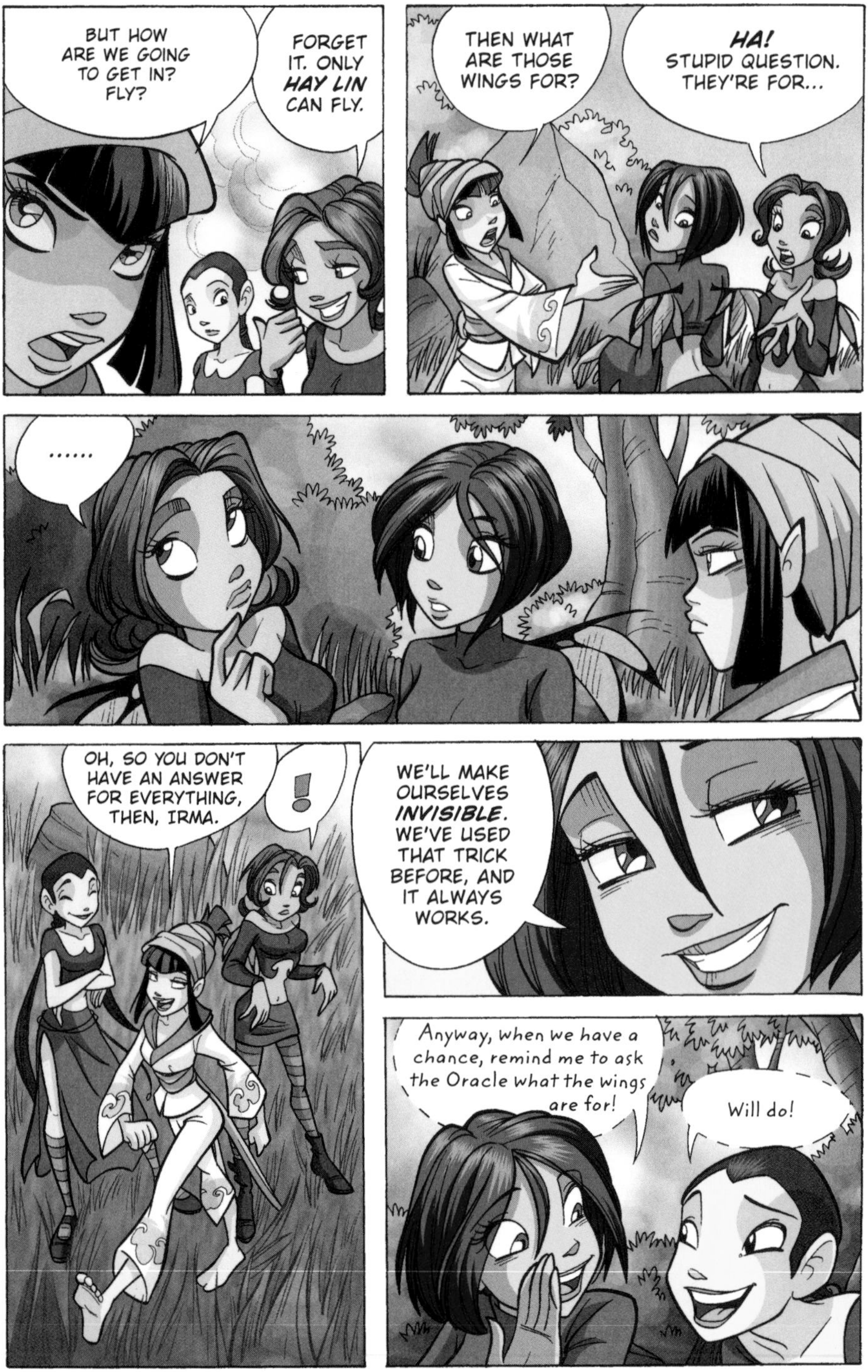
BUT HOW ARE WE GOING TO GET IN? FLY?
FORGET IT. ONLY HAY LIN CAN FLY.
THEN WHAT ARE THOSE WINGS FOR?
HA! STUPID QUESTION. THEY'RE FOR...
......
OH, SO YOU DON'T HAVE AN ANSWER FOR EVERYTHING, THEN, IRMA.
!
WE'LL MAKE OURSELVES INVISIBLE. WE'VE USED THAT TRICK BEFORE, AND IT ALWAYS WORKS.
Anyway, when we have a chance, remind me to ask the Oracle what the wings are for!
Will do!

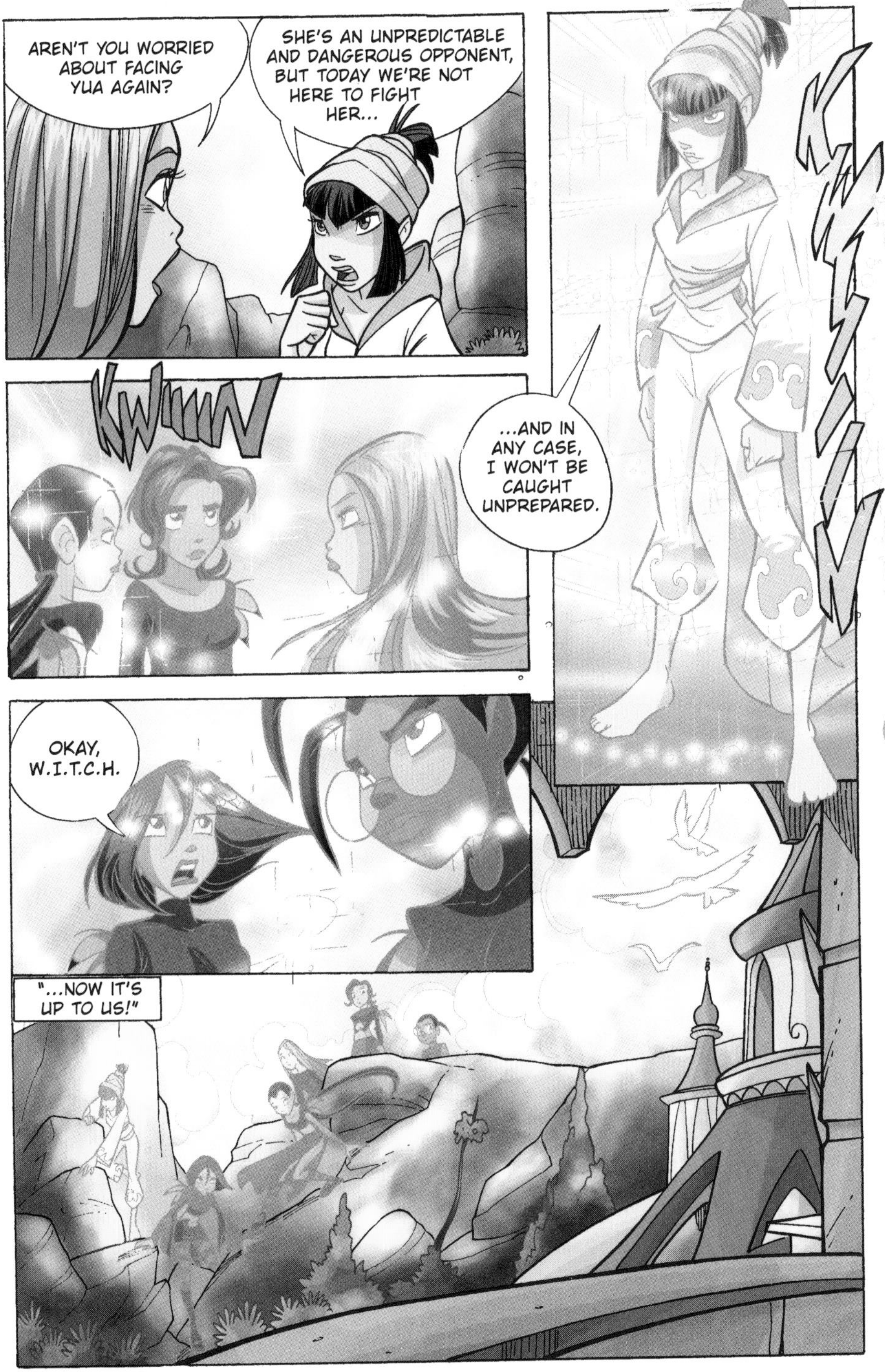
AREN'T YOU WORRIED ABOUT FACING YUA AGAIN?
SHE'S AN UNPREDICTABLE AND DANGEROUS OPPONENT, BUT TODAY WE'RE NOT HERE TO FIGHT HER...
...AND IN ANY CASE, I WON'T BE CAUGHT UNPREPARED.
KWIIIN
OKAY, W.I.T.C.H.
"...NOW IT'S UP TO US!"

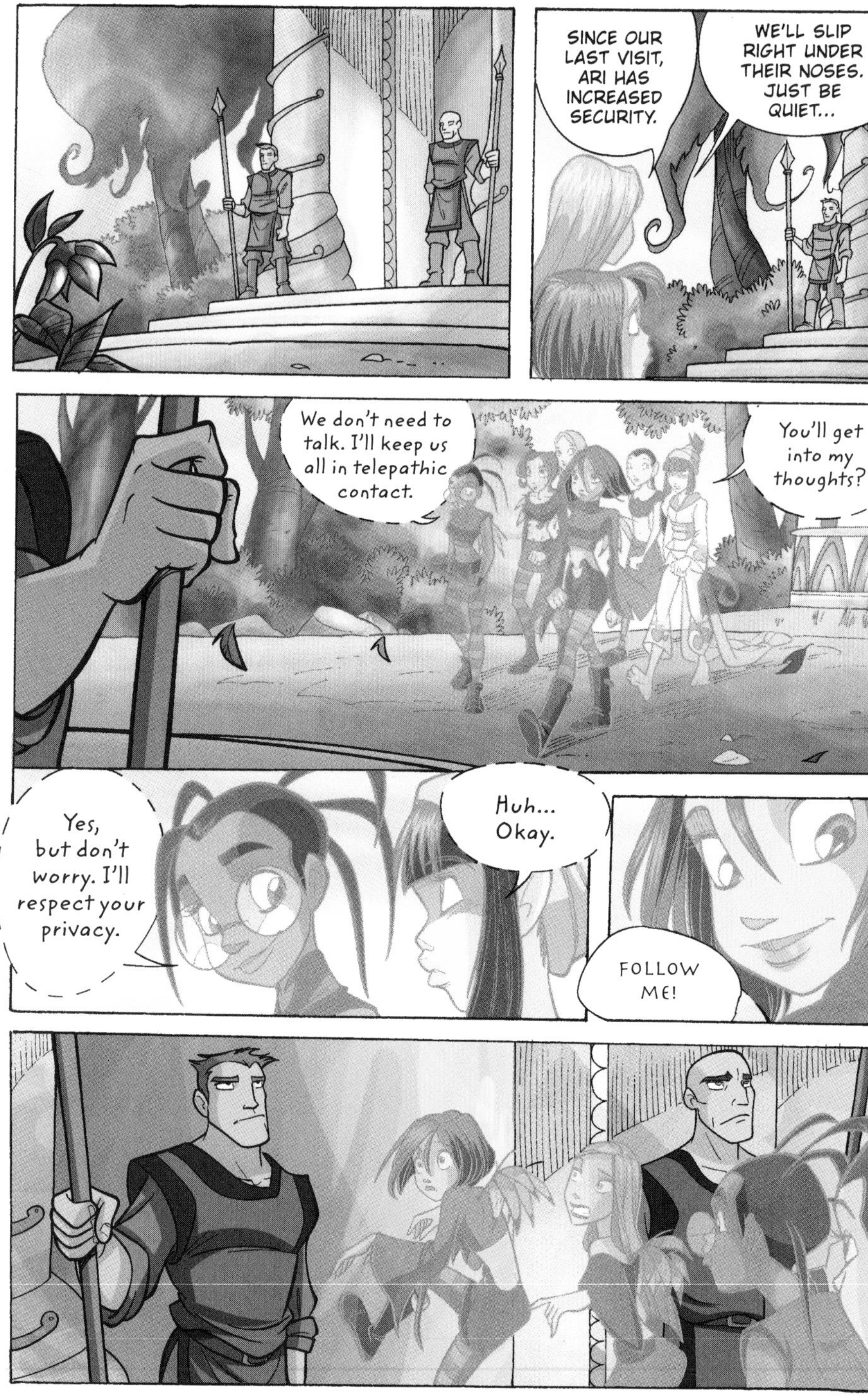
SINCE OUR LAST VISIT, ARI HAS INCREASED SECURITY.
WE'LL SLIP RIGHT UNDER THEIR NOSES. JUST BE QUIET...
We don't need to talk. I'll keep us all in telepathic contact.
You'll get into my thoughts?
Yes, but don't worry. I'll respect your privacy.
Huh... Okay.
FOLLOW ME!

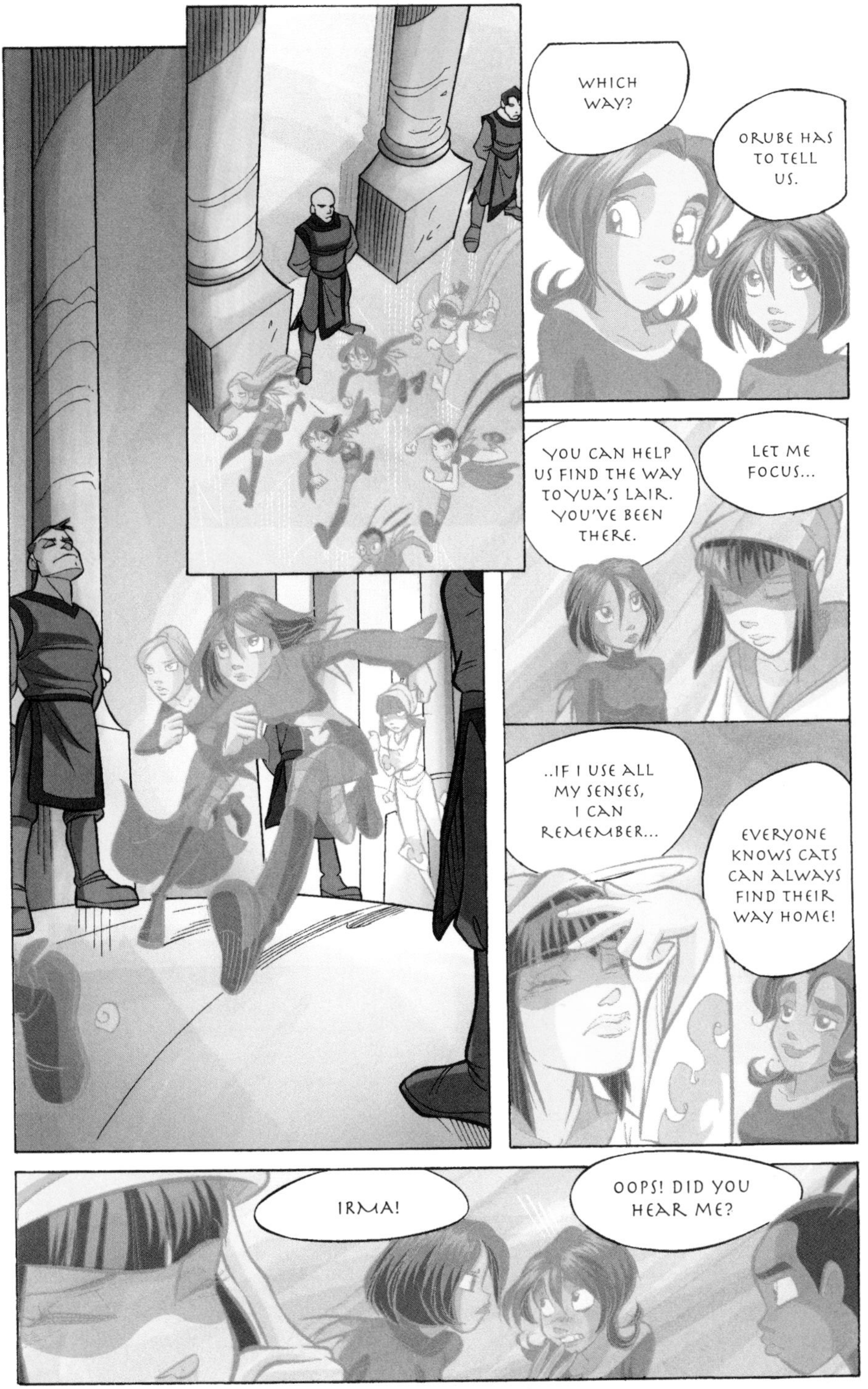
WHICH WAY?
ORUBE HAS TO TELL US.
YOU CAN HELP US FIND THE WAY TO YUA'S LAIR. YOU'VE BEEN THERE.
LET ME FOCUS...
..IF I USE ALL MY SENSES, I CAN REMEMBER...
EVERYONE KNOWS CATS CAN ALWAYS FIND THEIR WAY HOME!
IRMA!
OOPS! DID YOU HEAR ME?

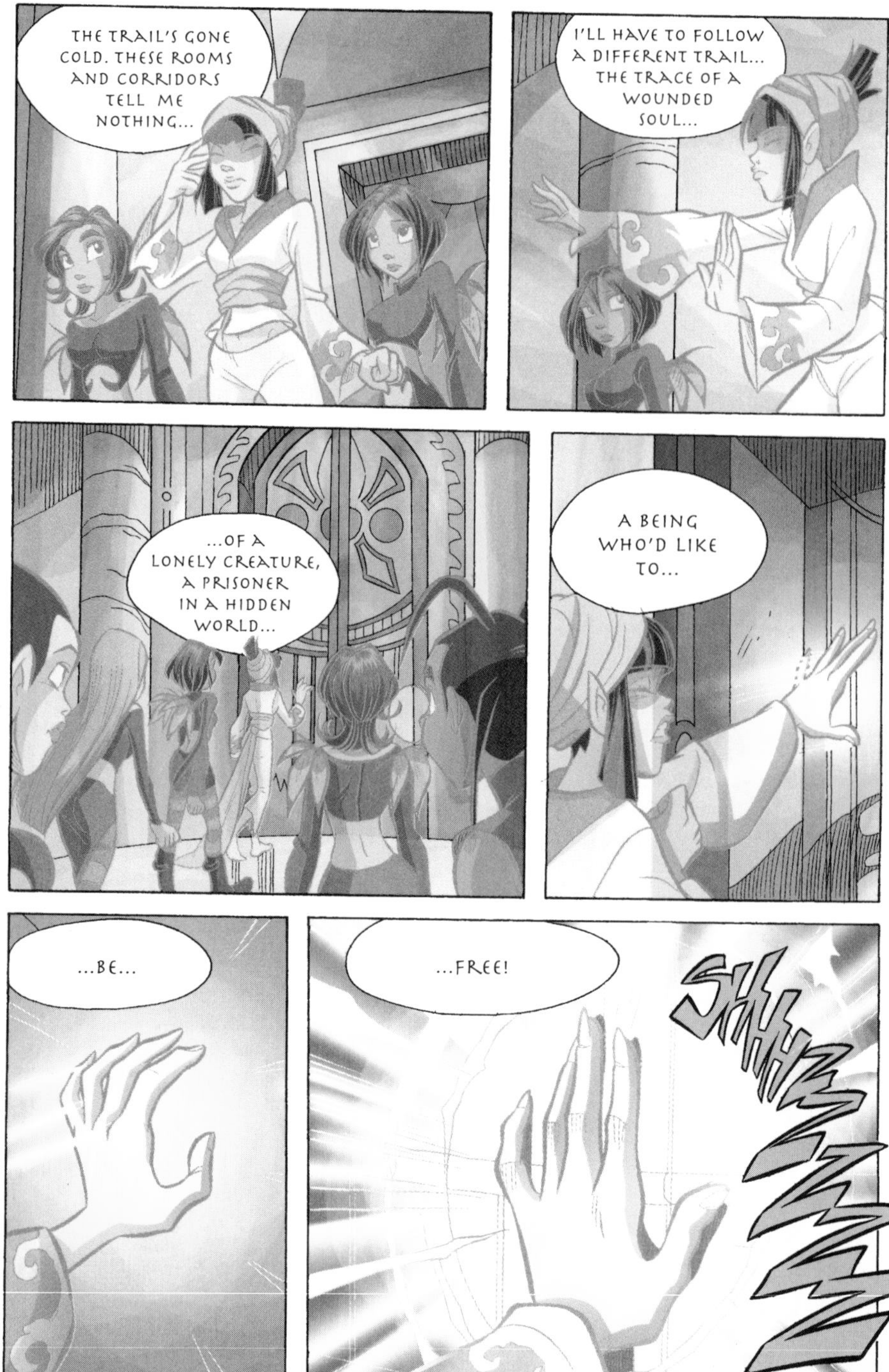
THE TRAIL'S GONE COLD. THESE ROOMS AND CORRIDORS TELL ME NOTHING...
I'LL HAVE TO FOLLOW A DIFFERENT TRAIL... THE TRACE OF A WOUNDED SOUL...
...OF A LONELY CREATURE, A PRISONER IN A HIDDEN WORLD...
A BEING WHO'D LIKE TO...
...BE...
...FREE!
SHHHZMMMMM

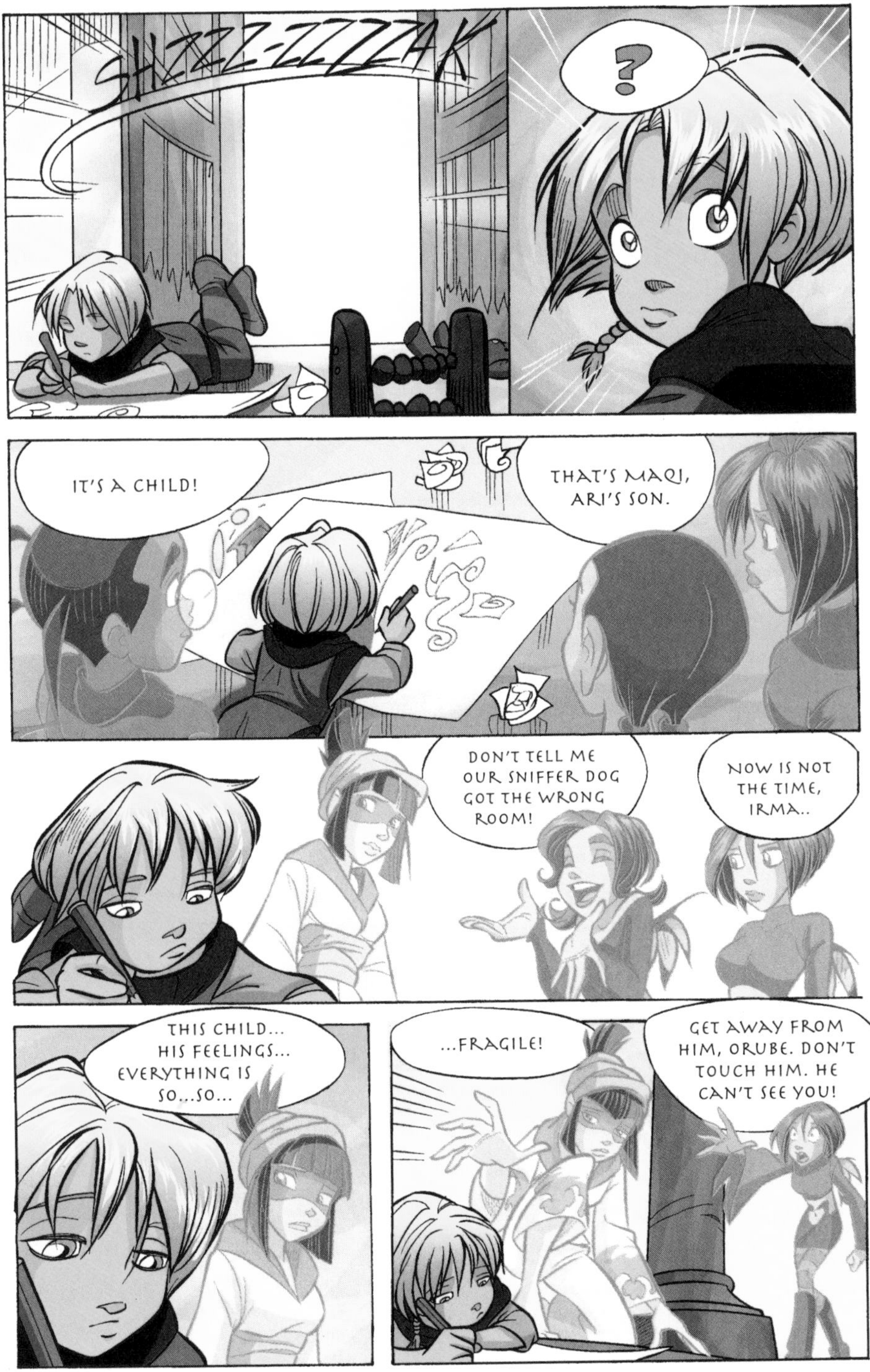
SHZZZ-ZZZZAK
?
IT'S A CHILD!
THAT'S MAQI, ARI'S SON.
DON'T TELL ME OUR SNIFFER DOG GOT THE WRONG ROOM!
NOW IS NOT THE TIME, IRMA..
THIS CHILD... HIS FEELINGS... EVERYTHING IS SO...SO...
...FRAGILE!
GET AWAY FROM HIM, ORUBE. DON'T TOUCH HIM. HE CAN'T SEE YOU!

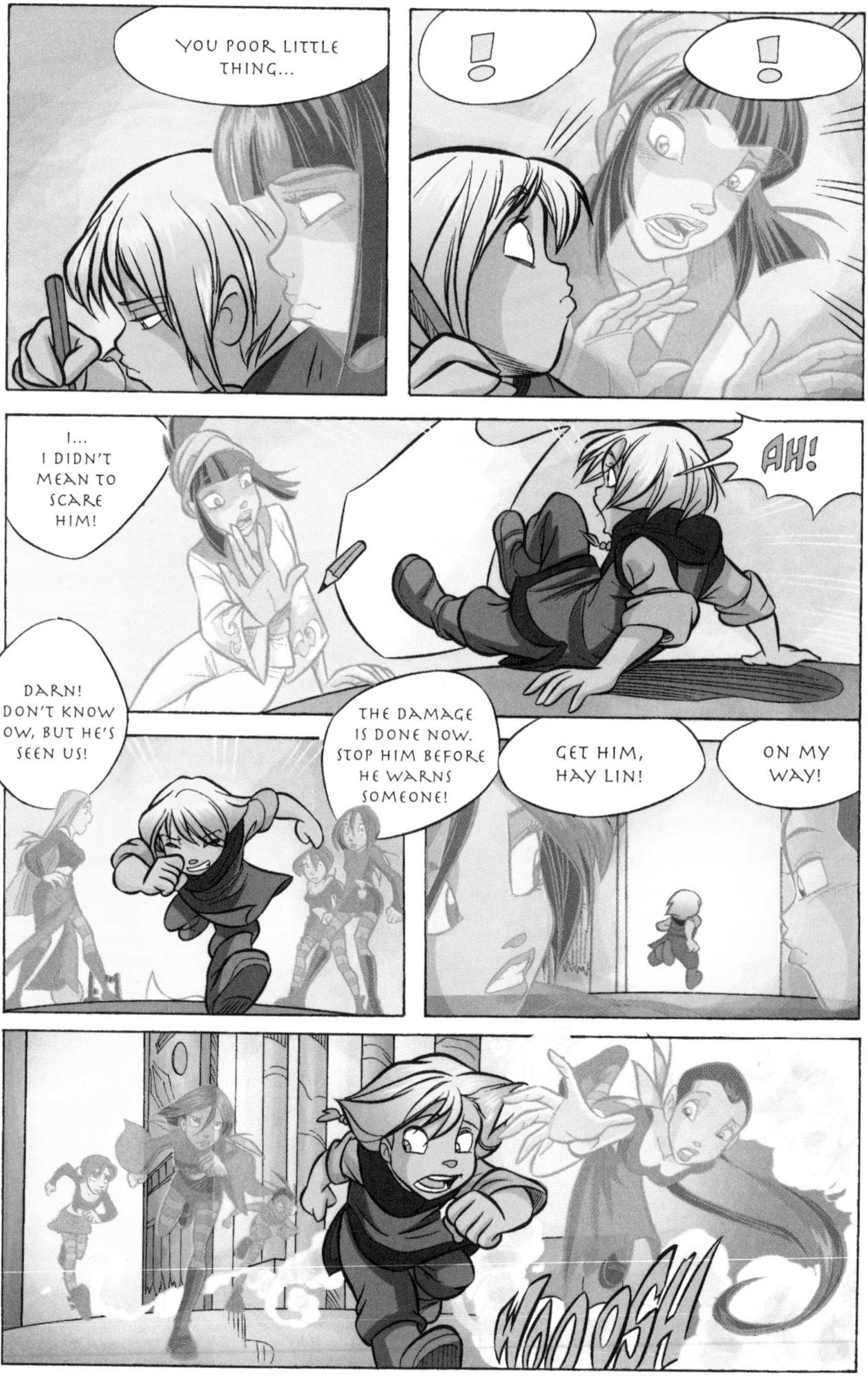

YOU POOR LITTLE THING...
!
!
I... I DIDN'T MEAN TO SCARE HIM!
AH!
DARN! I DON'T KNOW HOW, BUT HE'S SEEN US!
THE DAMAGE IS DONE NOW. STOP HIM BEFORE HE WARNS SOMEONE!
GET HIM, HAY LIN!
ON MY WAY!
WOOOSH

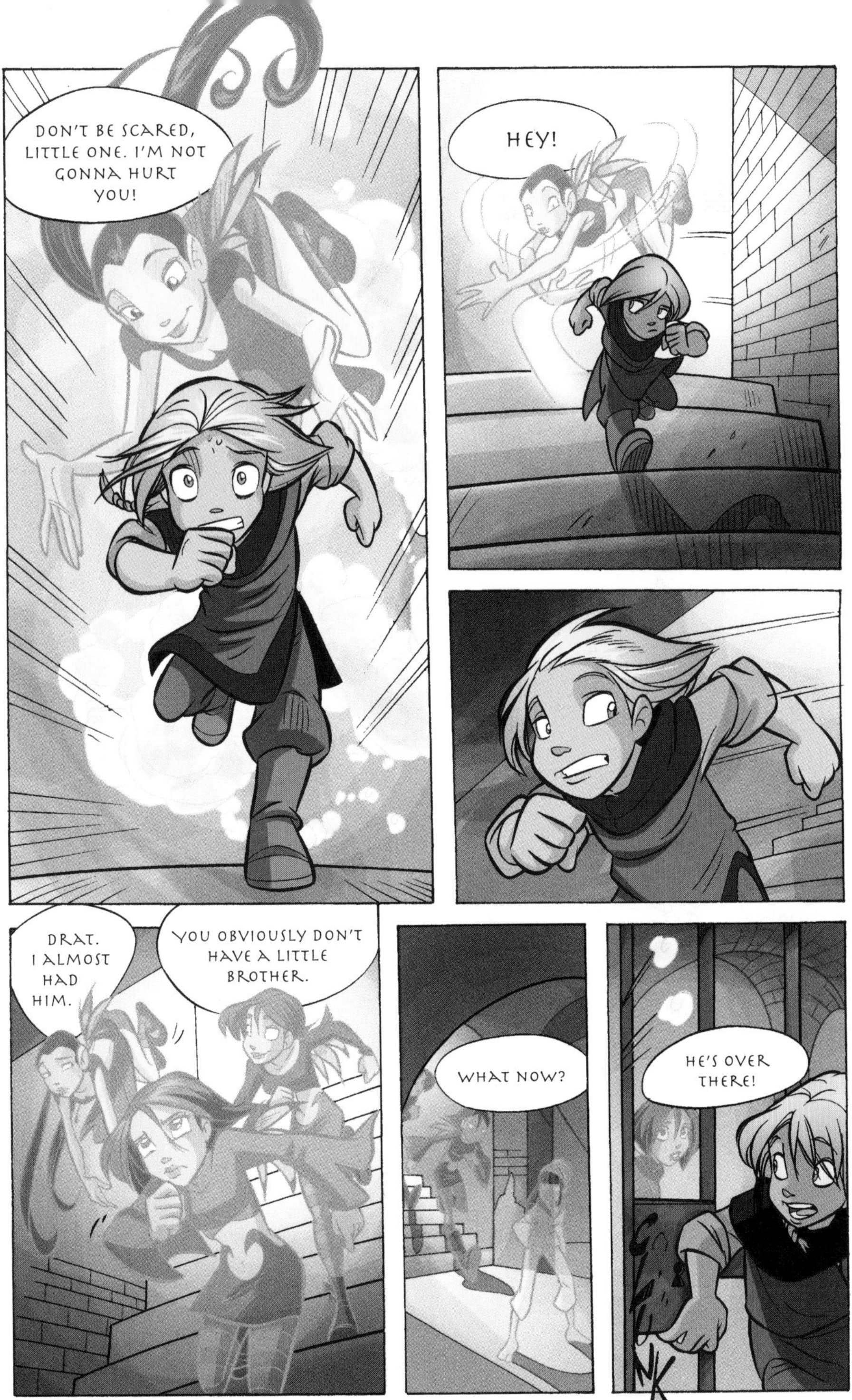
DON'T BE SCARED, LITTLE ONE. I'M NOT GONNA HURT YOU!
HEY!
DRAT. I ALMOST HAD HIM.
YOU OBVIOUSLY DON'T HAVE A LITTLE BROTHER.
WHAT NOW?
HE'S OVER THERE!

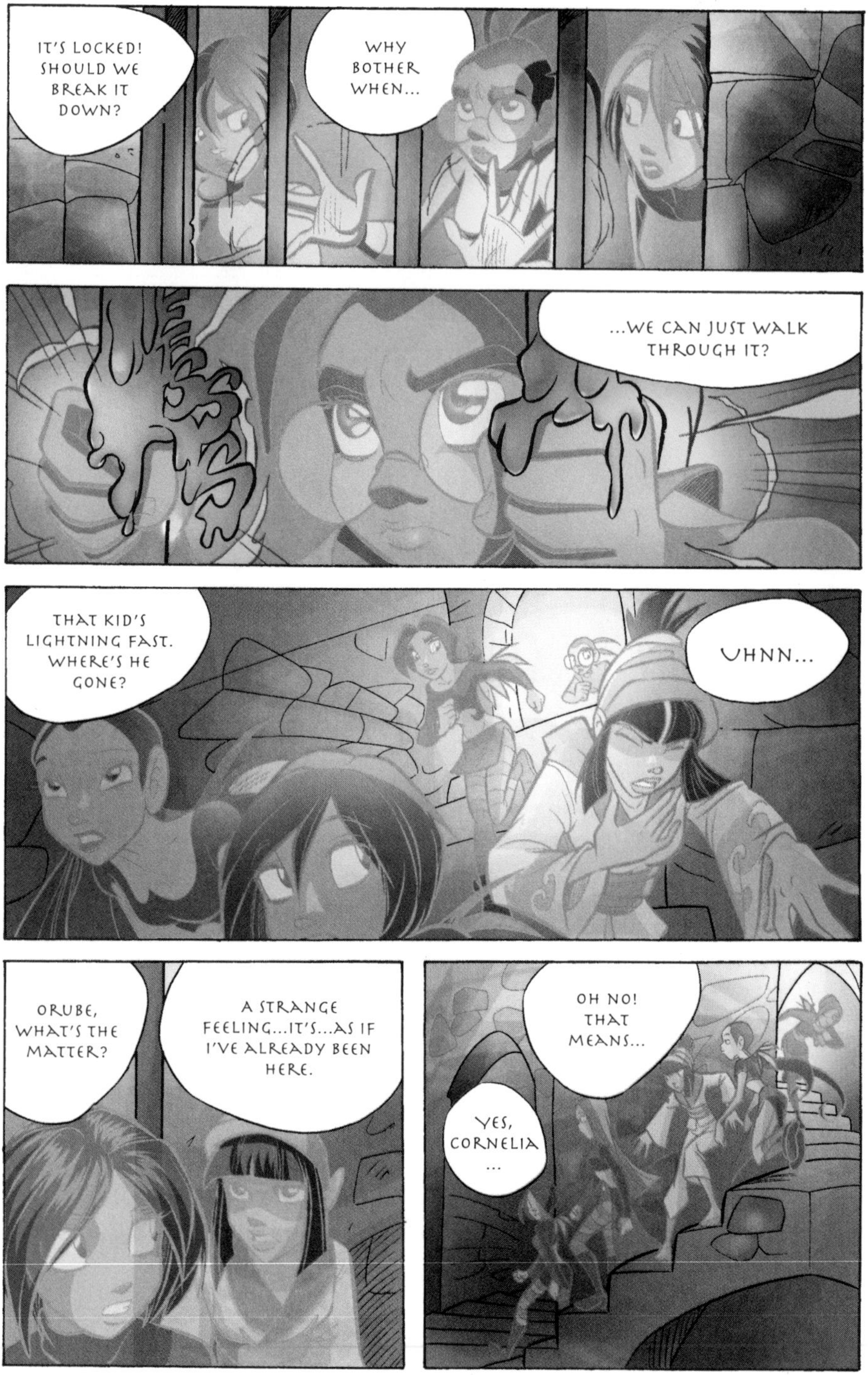

IT'S LOCKED! SHOULD WE BREAK IT DOWN?
WHY BOTHER WHEN...
...WE CAN JUST WALK THROUGH IT?
THAT KID'S LIGHTNING FAST. WHERE'S HE GONE?
UHNN...
ORUBE, WHAT'S THE MATTER?
A STRANGE FEELING...IT'S...AS IF I'VE ALREADY BEEN HERE.
OH NO! THAT MEANS...
YES, CORNELIA...

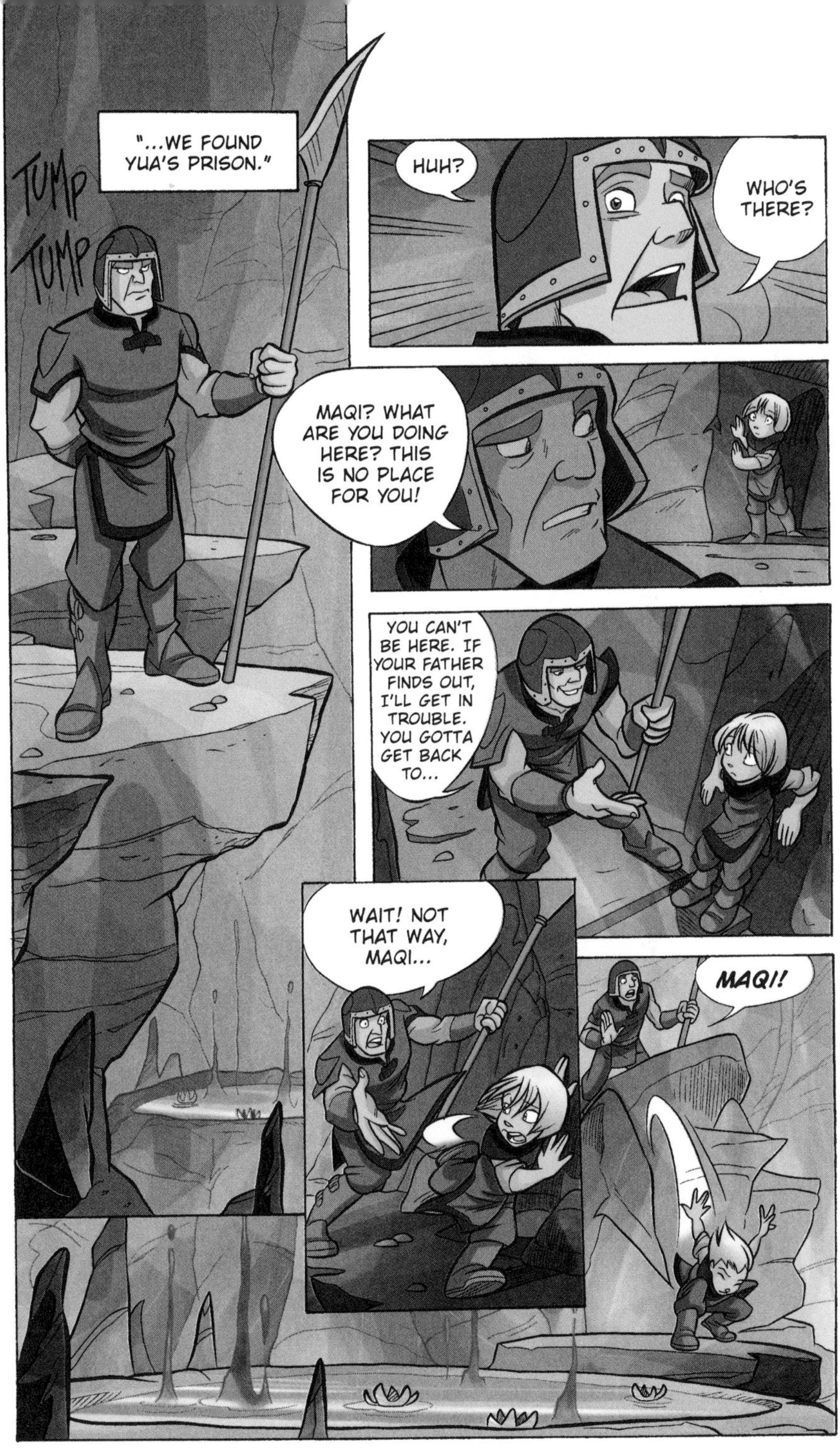
"...WE FOUND YUA'S PRISON."
TUMP TUMP
HUH?
WHO'S THERE?
MAQI? WHAT ARE YOU DOING HERE? THIS IS NO PLACE FOR YOU!
YOU CAN'T BE HERE. IF YOUR FATHER FINDS OUT, I'LL GET IN TROUBLE. YOU GOTTA GET BACK TO...
WAIT! NOT THAT WAY, MAQI...
MAQI!

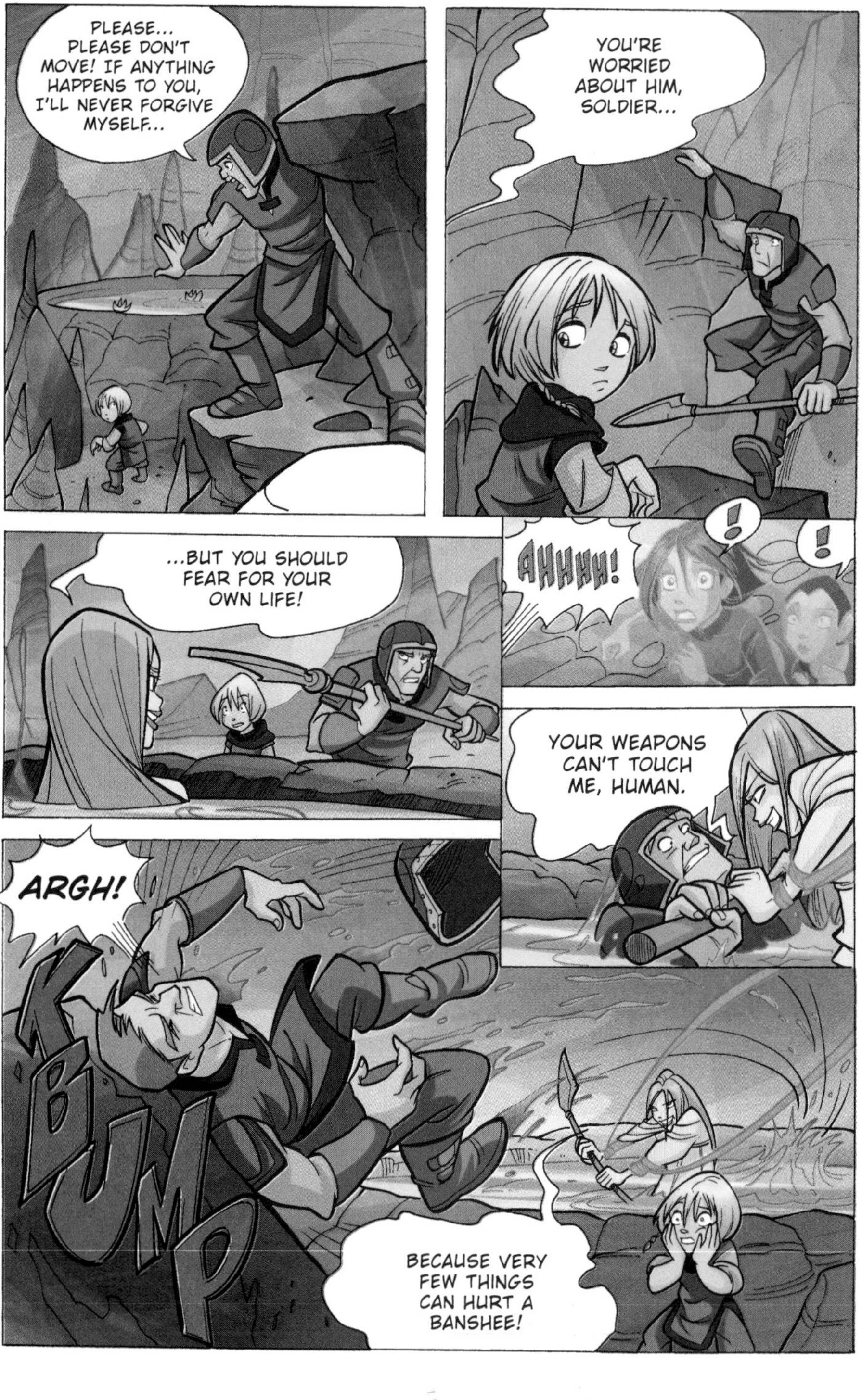
PLEASE... PLEASE DON'T MOVE! IF ANYTHING HAPPENS TO YOU, I'LL NEVER FORGIVE MYSELF...
YOU'RE WORRIED ABOUT HIM, SOLDIER...
...BUT YOU SHOULD FEAR FOR YOUR OWN LIFE!
AHHHH!
!
!
YOUR WEAPONS CAN'T TOUCH ME, HUMAN.
ARGH!
KBUMP
BECAUSE VERY FEW THINGS CAN HURT A BANSHEE!

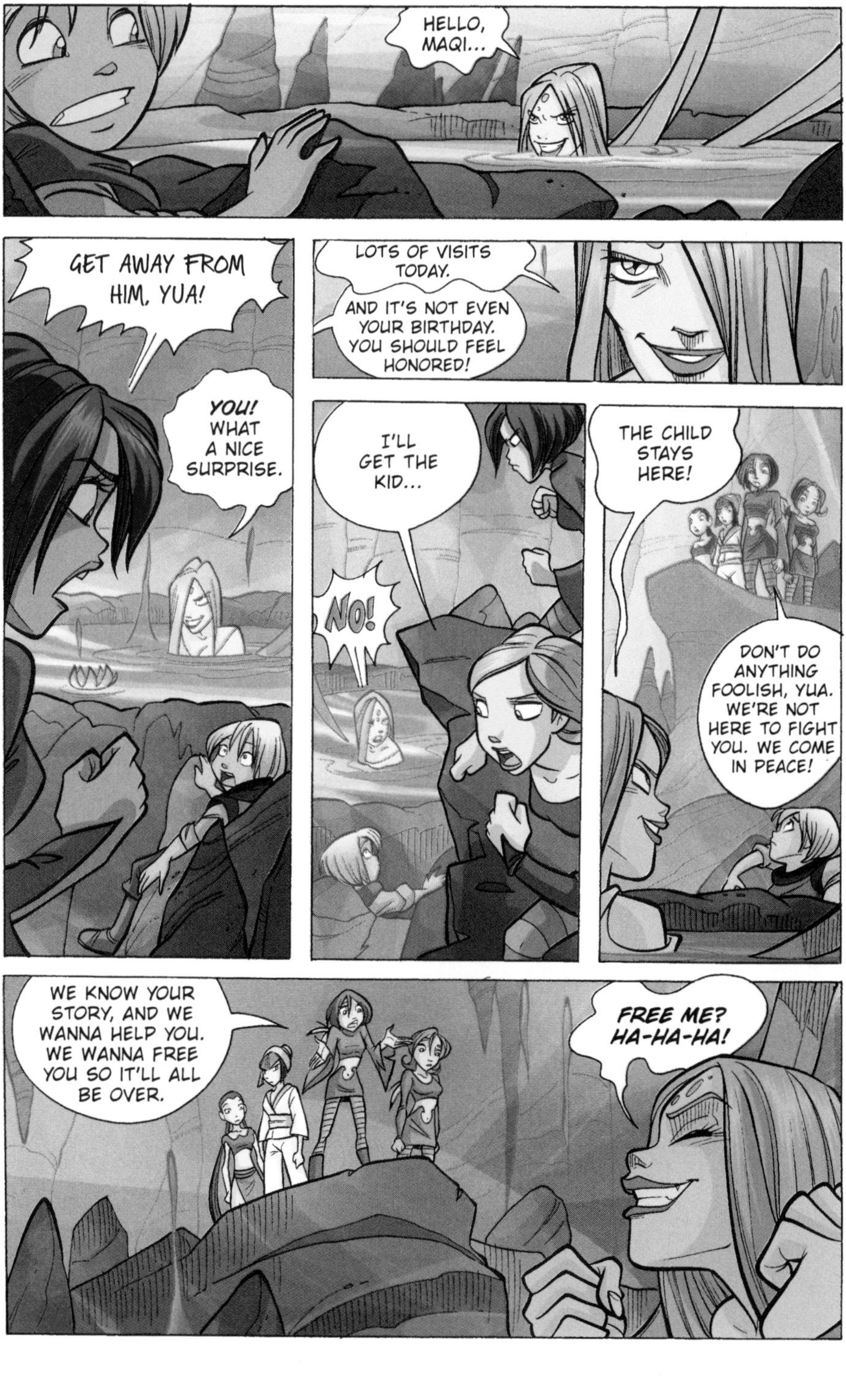
HELLO, MAQI...
GET AWAY FROM HIM, YUA!
YOU! WHAT A NICE SURPRISE.
LOTS OF VISITS TODAY.
AND IT'S NOT EVEN YOUR BIRTHDAY. YOU SHOULD FEEL HONORED!
I'LL GET THE KID...
NO!
THE CHILD STAYS HERE!
DON'T DO ANYTHING FOOLISH, YUA. WE'RE NOT HERE TO FIGHT YOU. WE COME IN PEACE!
WE KNOW YOUR STORY, AND WE WANNA HELP YOU. WE WANNA FREE YOU SO IT'LL ALL BE OVER.
FREE ME? HA-HA-HA!

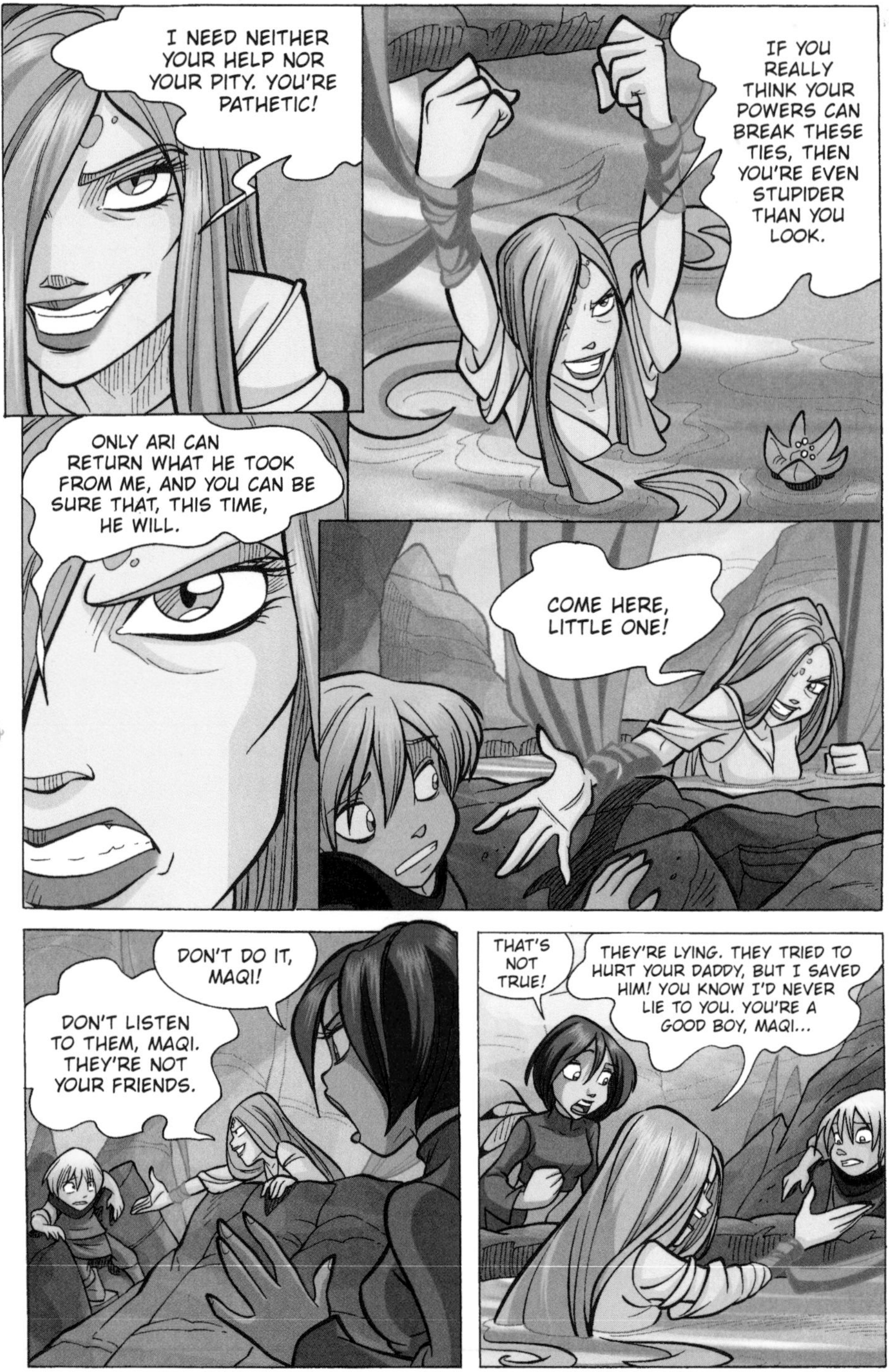
I NEED NEITHER YOUR HELP NOR YOUR PITY. YOU'RE PATHETIC!
IF YOU REALLY THINK YOUR POWERS CAN BREAK THESE TIES, THEN YOU'RE EVEN STUPIDER THAN YOU LOOK.
ONLY ARI CAN RETURN WHAT HE TOOK FROM ME, AND YOU CAN BE SURE THAT, THIS TIME, HE WILL.
COME HERE, LITTLE ONE!
DON'T DO IT, MAQI!
DON'T LISTEN TO THEM, MAQI. THEY'RE NOT YOUR FRIENDS.
THAT'S NOT TRUE!
THEY'RE LYING. THEY TRIED TO HURT YOUR DADDY, BUT I SAVED HIM! YOU KNOW I'D NEVER LIE TO YOU. YOU'RE A GOOD BOY, MAQI...

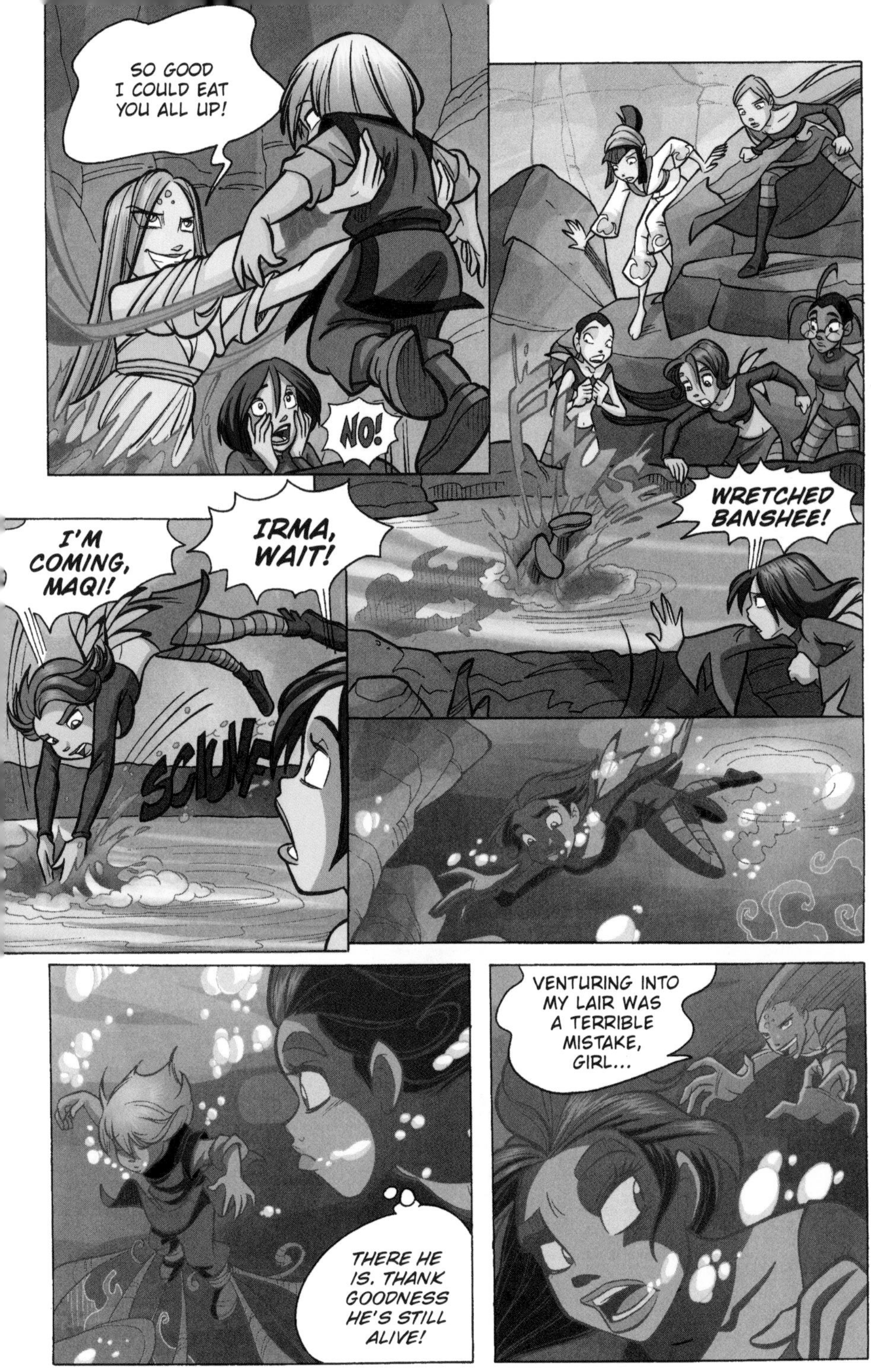
SO GOOD I COULD EAT YOU ALL UP!
NO!
WRETCHED BANSHEE!
IRMA, WAIT!
I'M COMING, MAQI!
SCIUNF
THERE HE IS. THANK GOODNESS HE'S STILL ALIVE!
VENTURING INTO MY LAIR WAS A TERRIBLE MISTAKE, GIRL...

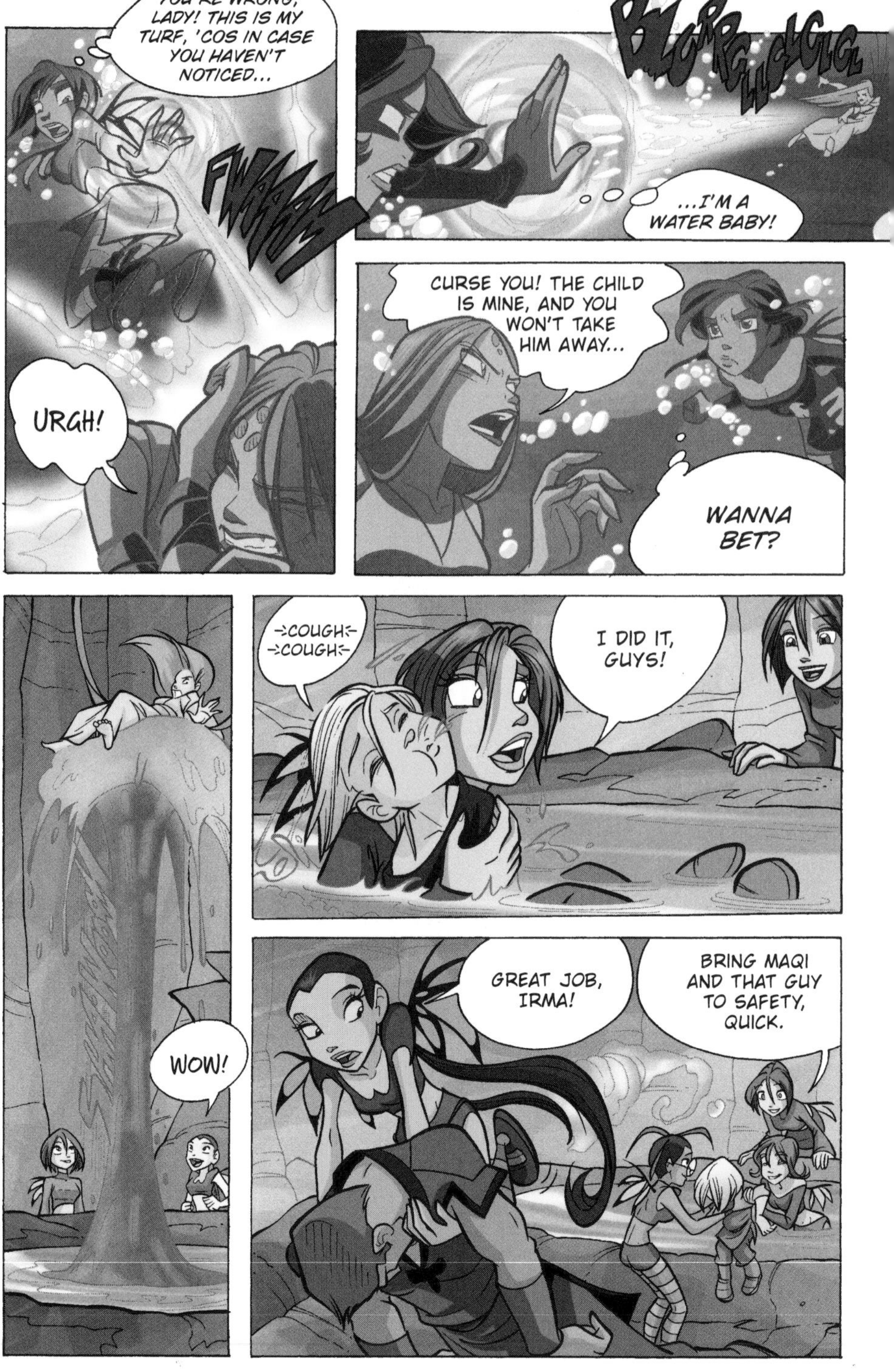
YOU'RE WRONG, LADY! THIS IS MY TURF, 'COS IN CASE YOU HAVEN'T NOTICED...
FWAAAM
BLURBGLGLGL
...I'M A WATER BABY!
URGH!
CURSE YOU! THE CHILD IS MINE, AND YOU WON'T TAKE HIM AWAY...
WANNA BET?
COUGH COUGH
I DID IT, GUYS!
WOW!
GREAT JOB, IRMA!
BRING MAQI AND THAT GUY TO SAFETY, QUICK.

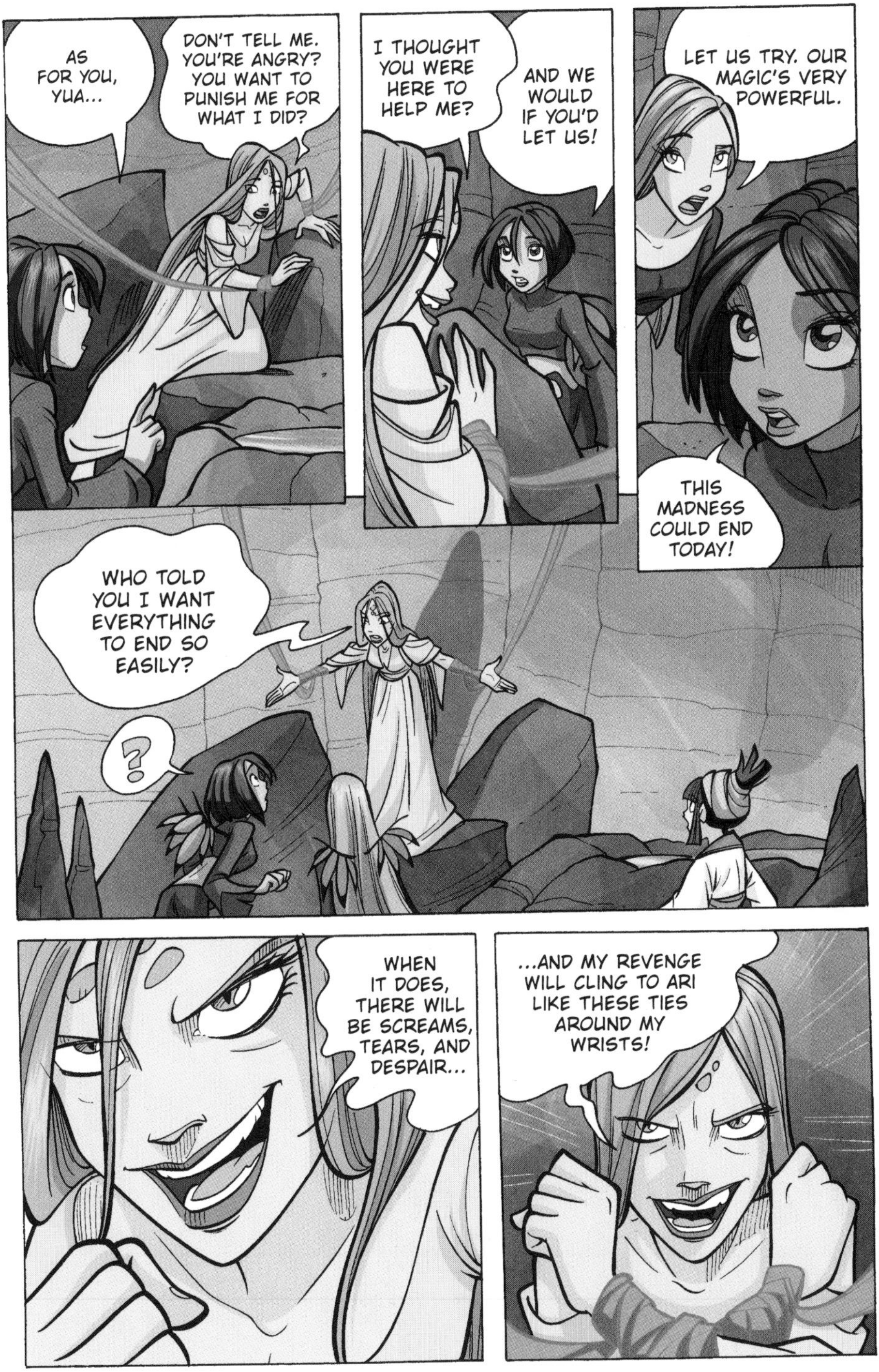
AS FOR YOU, YUA...
DON'T TELL ME. YOU'RE ANGRY? YOU WANT TO PUNISH ME FOR WHAT I DID?
I THOUGHT YOU WERE HERE TO HELP ME?
AND WE WOULD IF YOU'D LET US!
LET US TRY. OUR MAGIC'S VERY POWERFUL.
THIS MADNESS COULD END TODAY!
WHO TOLD YOU I WANT EVERYTHING TO END SO EASILY?
?
WHEN IT DOES, THERE WILL BE SCREAMS, TEARS, AND DESPAIR...
...AND MY REVENGE WILL CLING TO ARI LIKE THESE TIES AROUND MY WRISTS!

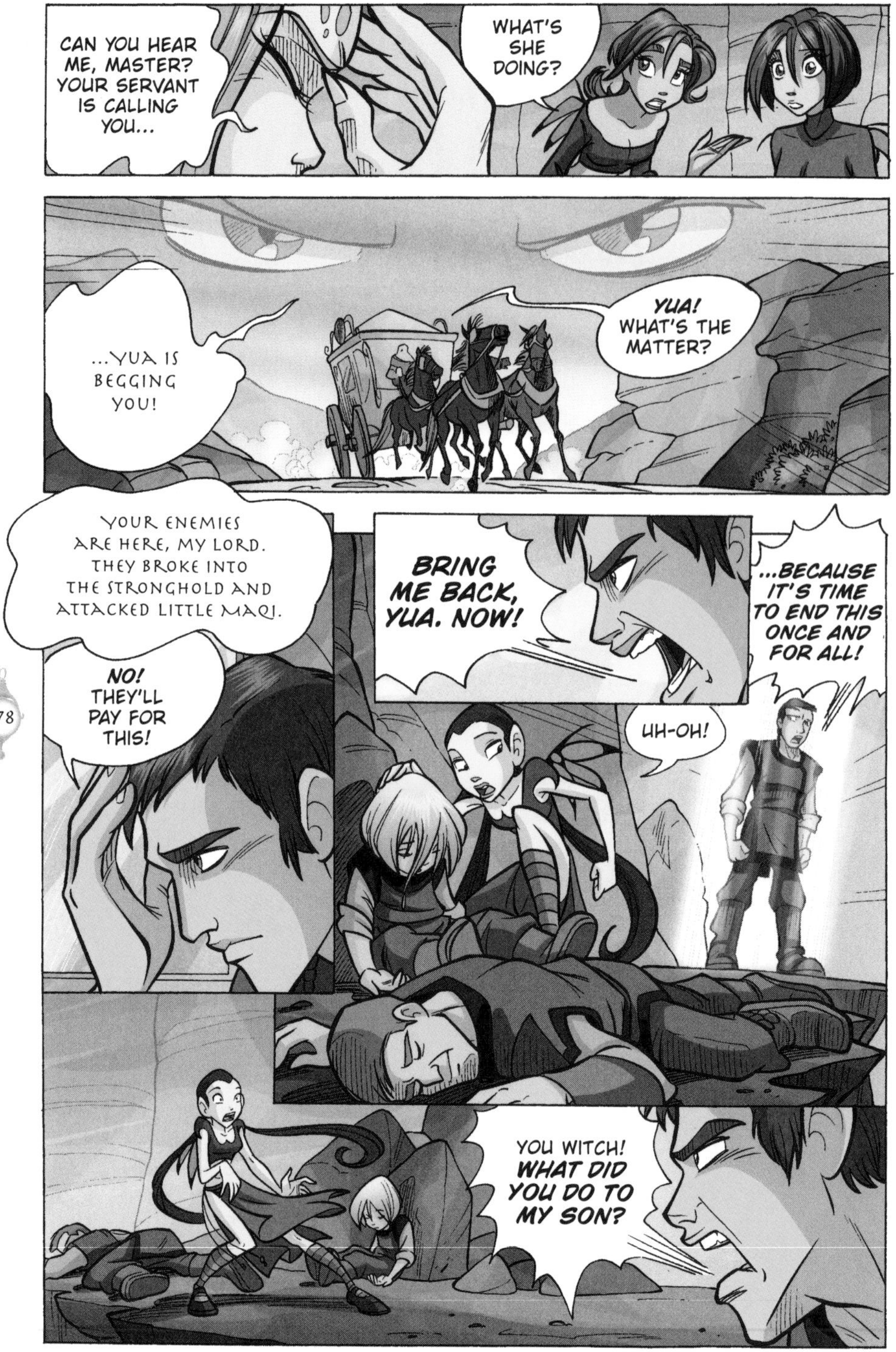
CAN YOU HEAR ME, MASTER? YOUR SERVANT IS CALLING YOU...
WHAT'S SHE DOING?
...YUA IS BEGGING YOU!
YUA! WHAT'S THE MATTER?
YOUR ENEMIES ARE HERE, MY LORD. THEY BROKE INTO THE STRONGHOLD AND ATTACKED LITTLE MAQI.
NO! THEY'LL PAY FOR THIS!
BRING ME BACK, YUA. NOW!
...BECAUSE IT'S TIME TO END THIS ONCE AND FOR ALL!
UH-OH!
YOU WITCH! WHAT DID YOU DO TO MY SON?

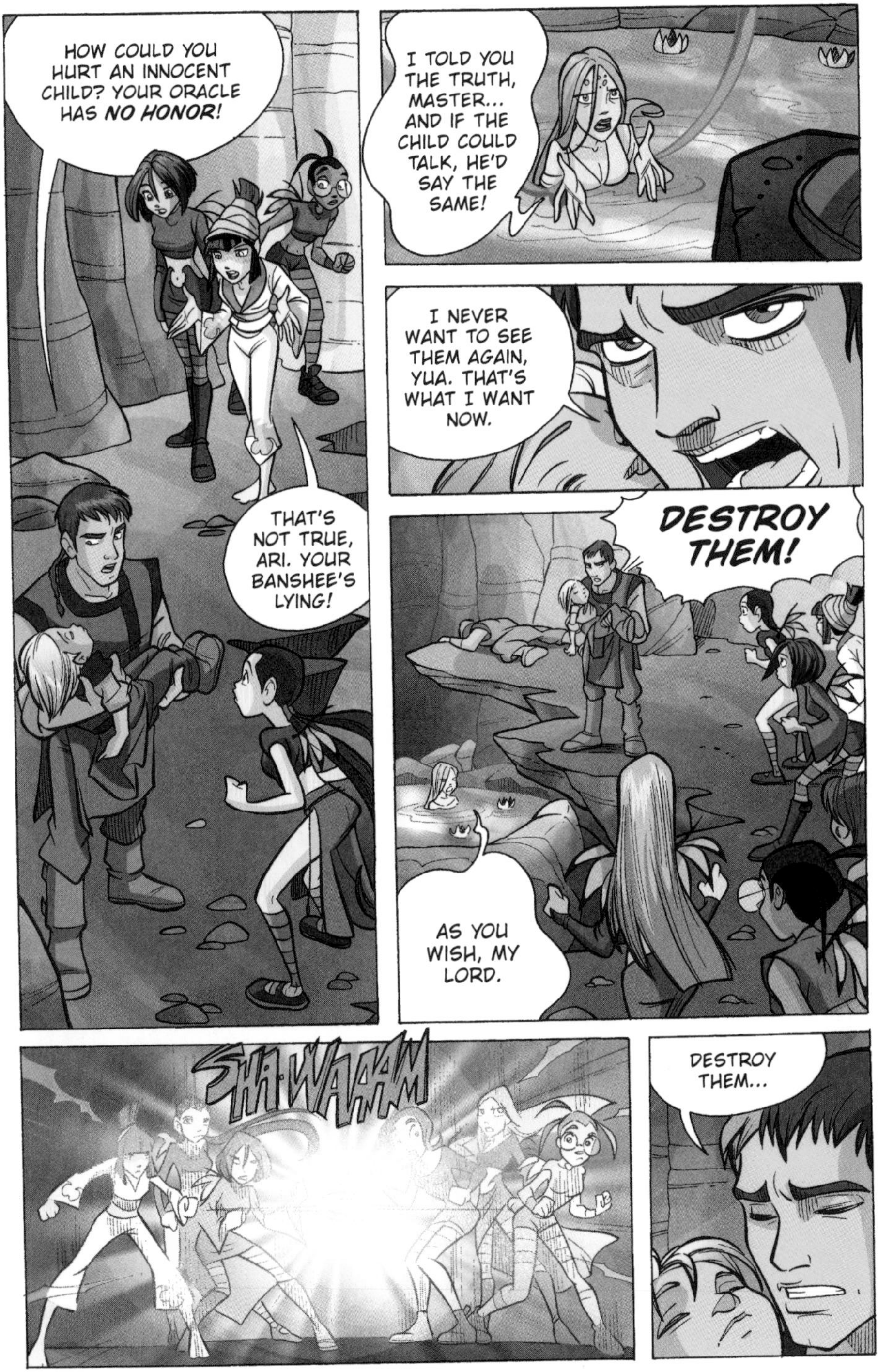
HOW COULD YOU HURT AN INNOCENT CHILD? YOUR ORACLE HAS **NO HONOR**!
I TOLD YOU THE TRUTH, MASTER... AND IF THE CHILD COULD TALK, HE'D SAY THE SAME!
THAT'S NOT TRUE, ARI. YOUR BANSHEE'S LYING!
I NEVER WANT TO SEE THEM AGAIN, YUA. THAT'S WHAT I WANT NOW.
DESTROY THEM!
AS YOU WISH, MY LORD.
SHA-WAAAM
DESTROY THEM...

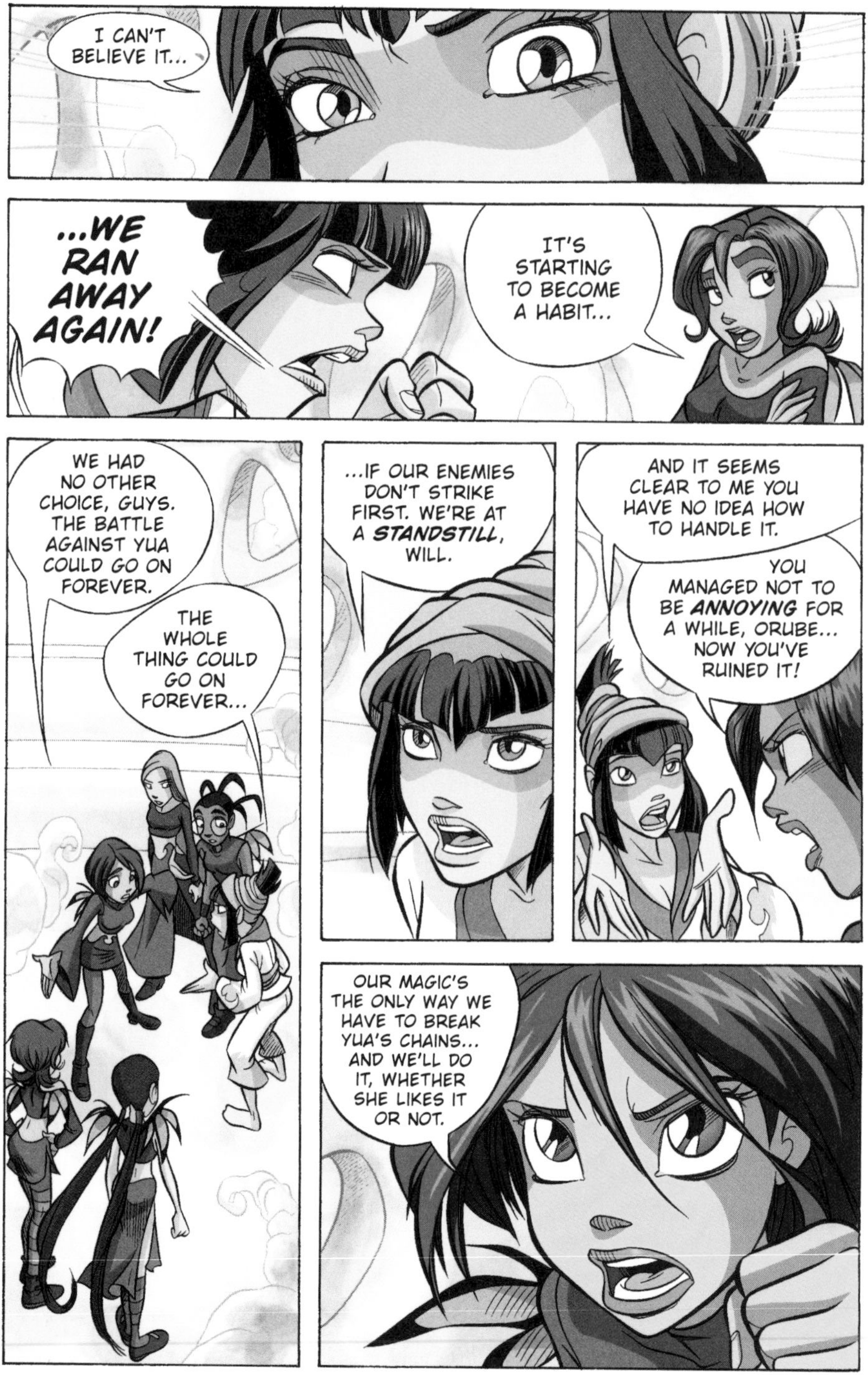
I CAN'T BELIEVE IT...
...WE RAN AWAY AGAIN!
IT'S STARTING TO BECOME A HABIT...
WE HAD NO OTHER CHOICE, GUYS. THE BATTLE AGAINST YUA COULD GO ON FOREVER.
THE WHOLE THING COULD GO ON FOREVER...
...IF OUR ENEMIES DON'T STRIKE FIRST. WE'RE AT A *STANDSTILL*, WILL.
AND IT SEEMS CLEAR TO ME YOU HAVE NO IDEA HOW TO HANDLE IT.
YOU MANAGED NOT TO BE *ANNOYING* FOR A WHILE, ORUBE... NOW YOU'VE RUINED IT!
OUR MAGIC'S THE ONLY WAY WE HAVE TO BREAK YUA'S CHAINS... AND WE'LL DO IT, WHETHER SHE LIKES IT OR NOT.

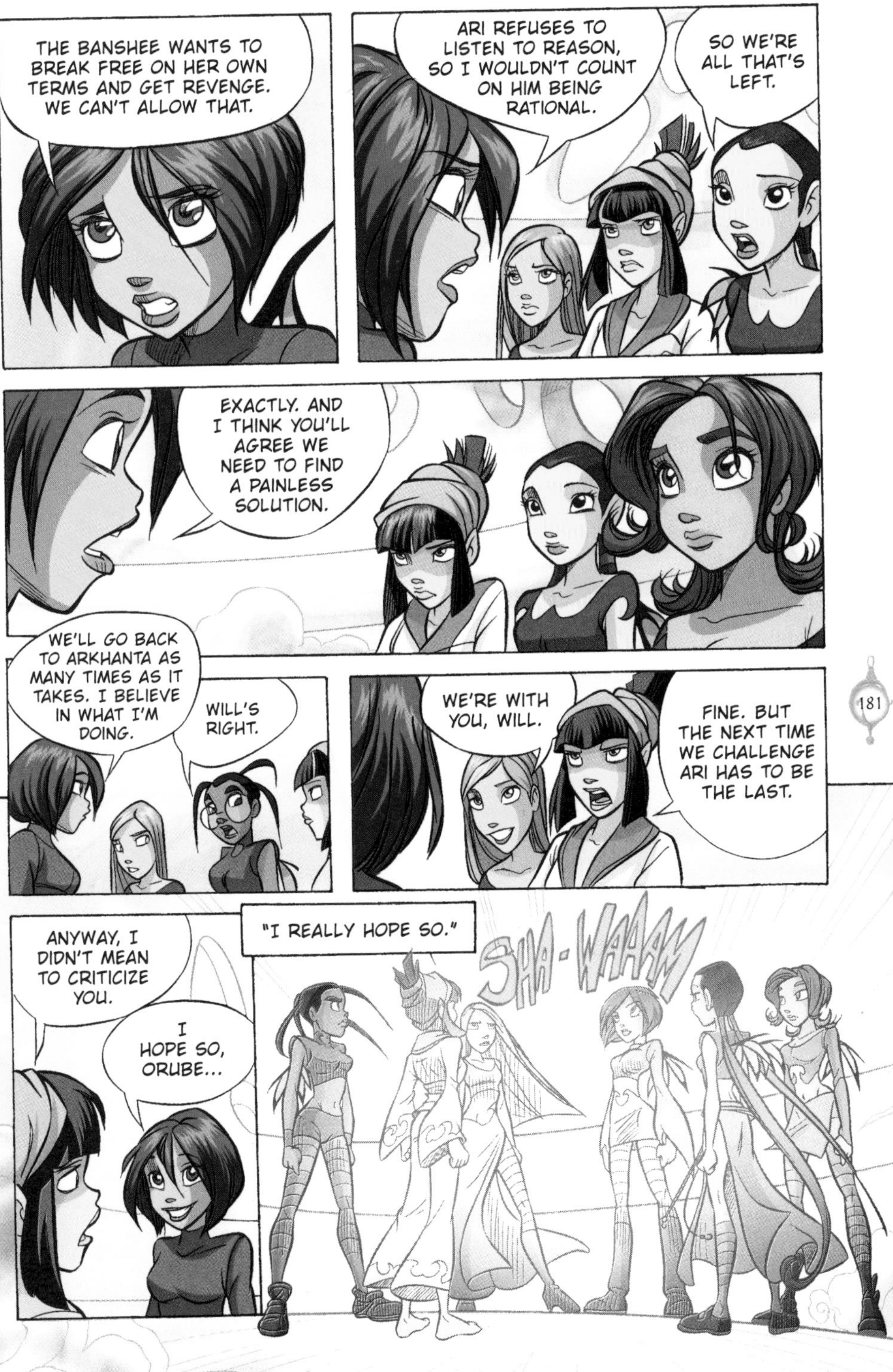
THE BANSHEE WANTS TO BREAK FREE ON HER OWN TERMS AND GET REVENGE. WE CAN'T ALLOW THAT.
ARI REFUSES TO LISTEN TO REASON, SO I WOULDN'T COUNT ON HIM BEING RATIONAL.
SO WE'RE ALL THAT'S LEFT.
EXACTLY. AND I THINK YOU'LL AGREE WE NEED TO FIND A PAINLESS SOLUTION.
WE'LL GO BACK TO ARKHANTA AS MANY TIMES AS IT TAKES. I BELIEVE IN WHAT I'M DOING.
WILL'S RIGHT.
WE'RE WITH YOU, WILL.
FINE. BUT THE NEXT TIME WE CHALLENGE ARI HAS TO BE THE LAST.
ANYWAY, I DIDN'T MEAN TO CRITICIZE YOU.
I HOPE SO, ORUBE...
"I REALLY HOPE SO."
SHA-WAAAM

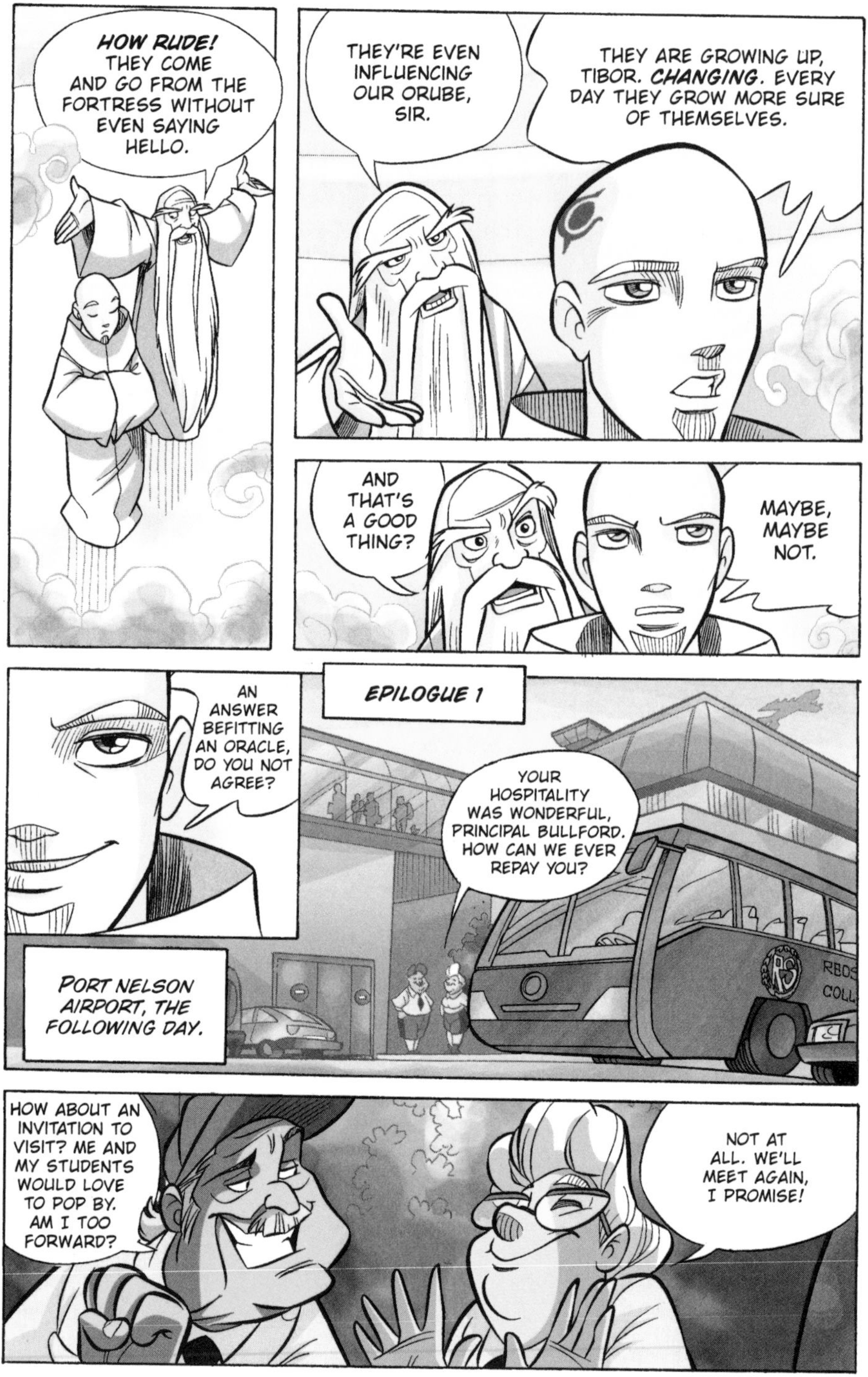
HOW RUDE! THEY COME AND GO FROM THE FORTRESS WITHOUT EVEN SAYING HELLO.
THEY'RE EVEN INFLUENCING OUR ORUBE, SIR.
THEY ARE GROWING UP, TIBOR. CHANGING. EVERY DAY THEY GROW MORE SURE OF THEMSELVES.
AND THAT'S A GOOD THING?
MAYBE, MAYBE NOT.
AN ANSWER BEFITTING AN ORACLE, DO YOU NOT AGREE?
EPILOGUE 1
YOUR HOSPITALITY WAS WONDERFUL, PRINCIPAL BULLFORD. HOW CAN WE EVER REPAY YOU?
PORT NELSON AIRPORT, THE FOLLOWING DAY.
HOW ABOUT AN INVITATION TO VISIT? ME AND MY STUDENTS WOULD LOVE TO POP BY. AM I TOO FORWARD?
NOT AT ALL. WE'LL MEET AGAIN, I PROMISE!

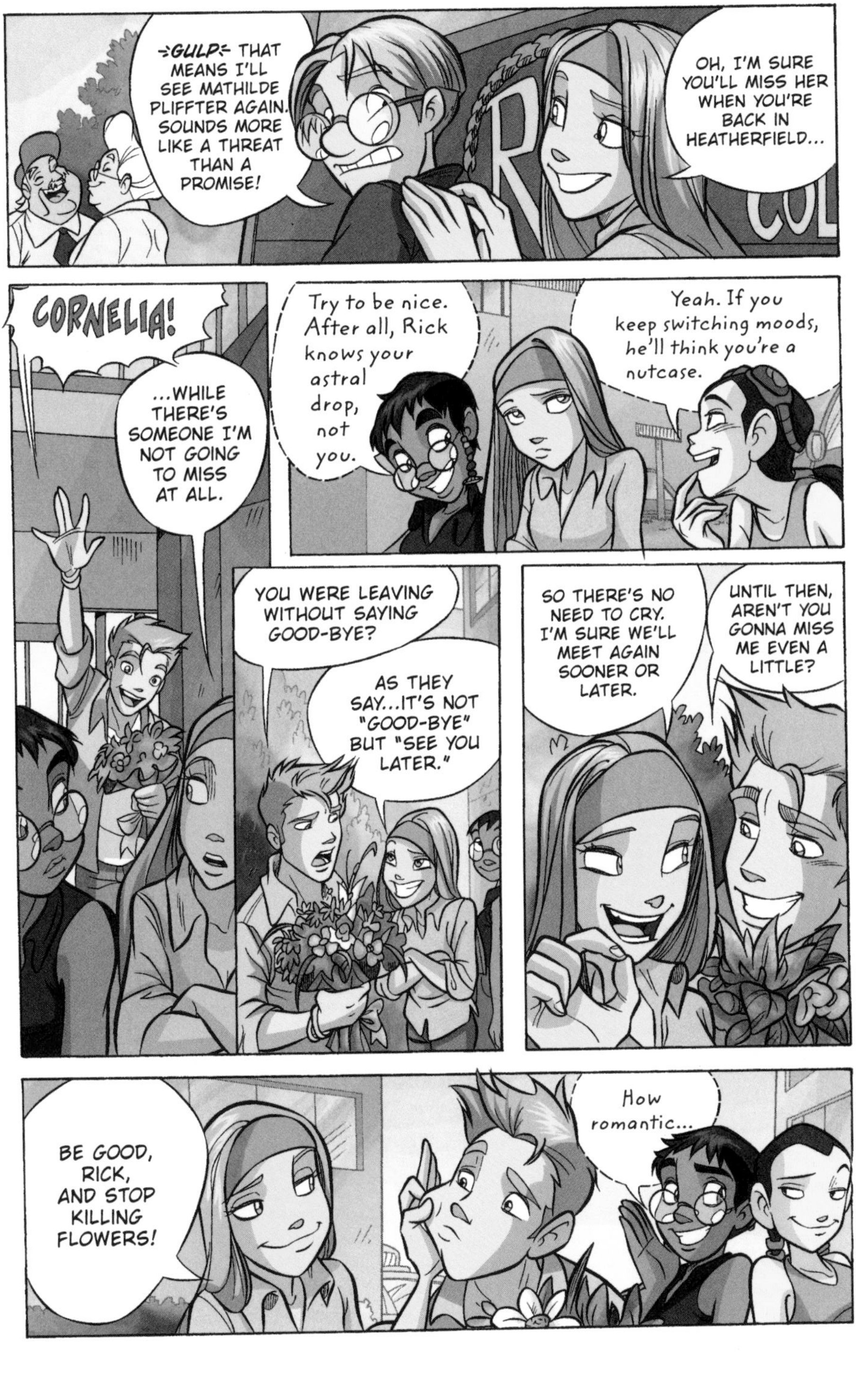

-GULP- THAT MEANS I'LL SEE MATHILDE PLIFFTER AGAIN. SOUNDS MORE LIKE A THREAT THAN A PROMISE!
OH, I'M SURE YOU'LL MISS HER WHEN YOU'RE BACK IN HEATHERFIELD...
CORNELIA!
...WHILE THERE'S SOMEONE I'M NOT GOING TO MISS AT ALL.
Try to be nice. After all, Rick knows your astral drop, not you.
Yeah. If you keep switching moods, he'll think you're a nutcase.
YOU WERE LEAVING WITHOUT SAYING GOOD-BYE?
AS THEY SAY...IT'S NOT "GOOD-BYE" BUT "SEE YOU LATER."
SO THERE'S NO NEED TO CRY. I'M SURE WE'LL MEET AGAIN SOONER OR LATER.
UNTIL THEN, AREN'T YOU GONNA MISS ME EVEN A LITTLE?
BE GOOD, RICK, AND STOP KILLING FLOWERS!
How romantic...

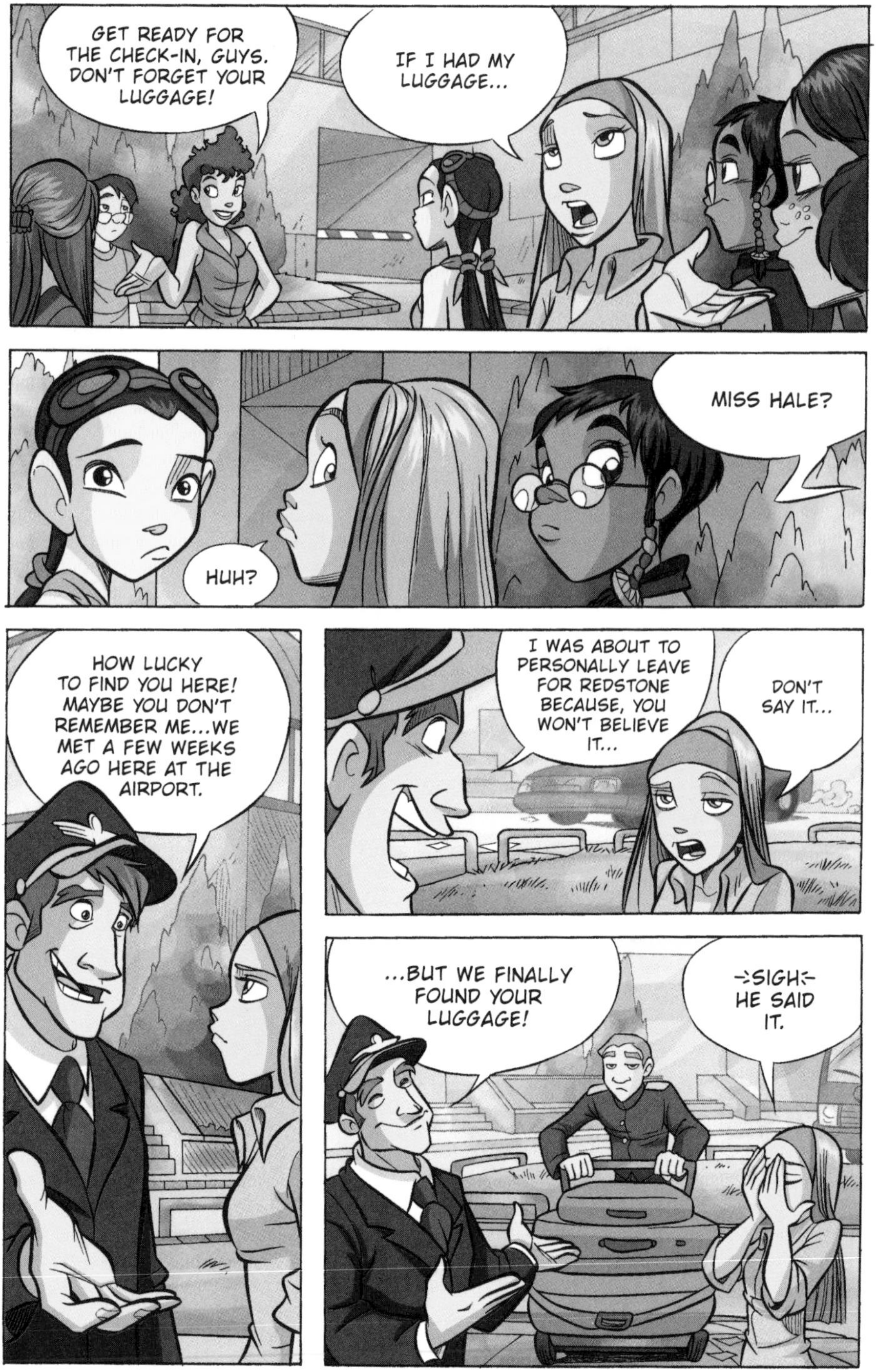
GET READY FOR THE CHECK-IN, GUYS. DON'T FORGET YOUR LUGGAGE!
IF I HAD MY LUGGAGE...
MISS HALE?
HUH?
HOW LUCKY TO FIND YOU HERE! MAYBE YOU DON'T REMEMBER ME...WE MET A FEW WEEKS AGO HERE AT THE AIRPORT.
I WAS ABOUT TO PERSONALLY LEAVE FOR REDSTONE BECAUSE, YOU WON'T BELIEVE IT...
DON'T SAY IT...
...BUT WE FINALLY FOUND YOUR LUGGAGE!
SIGH HE SAID IT.

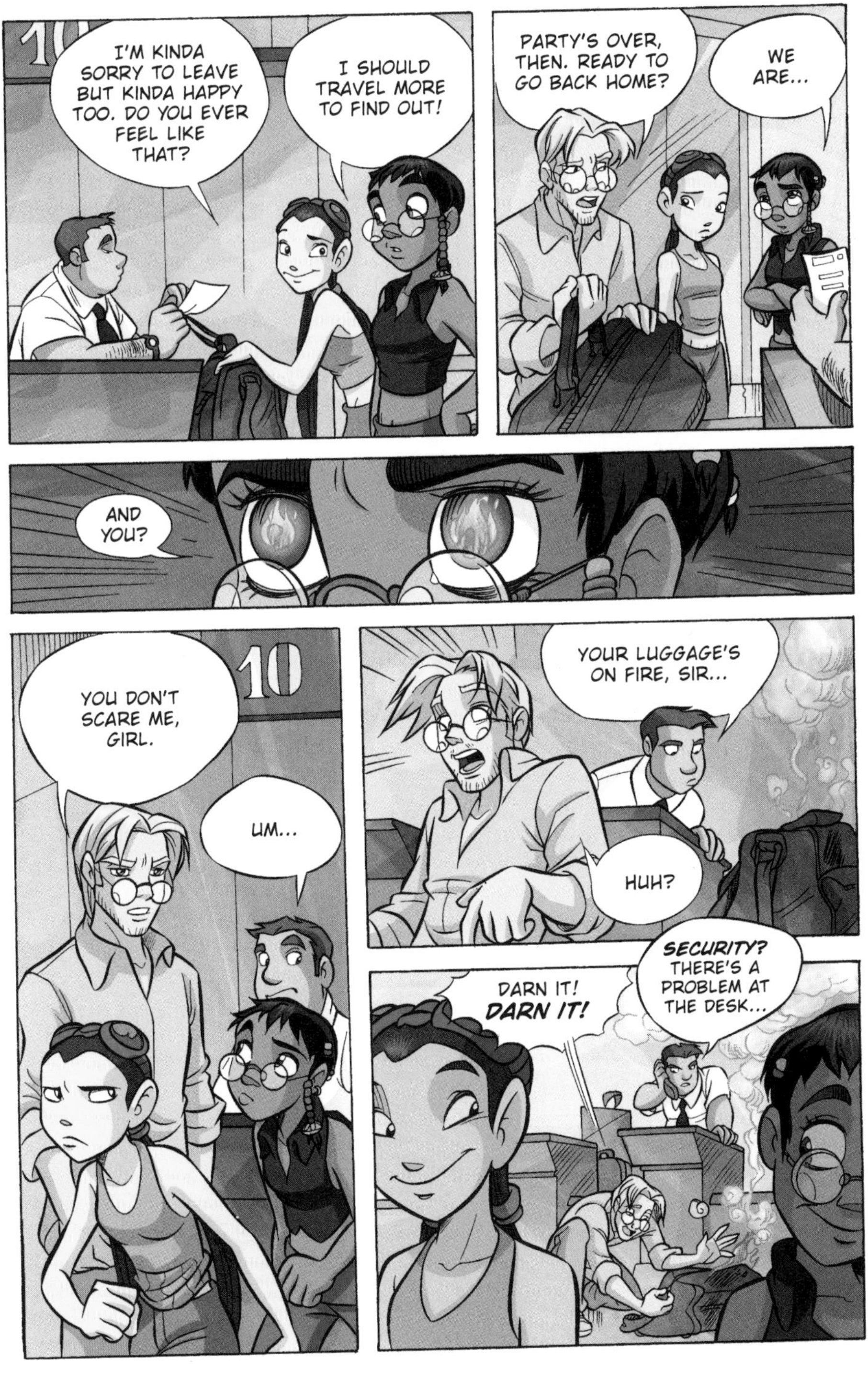

10
I'M KINDA SORRY TO LEAVE BUT KINDA HAPPY TOO. DO YOU EVER FEEL LIKE THAT?
I SHOULD TRAVEL MORE TO FIND OUT!
PARTY'S OVER, THEN. READY TO GO BACK HOME?
WE ARE...
AND YOU?
10
YOU DON'T SCARE ME, GIRL.
UM...
YOUR LUGGAGE'S ON FIRE, SIR...
HUH?
DARN IT! **DARN IT!**
SECURITY? THERE'S A PROBLEM AT THE DESK...

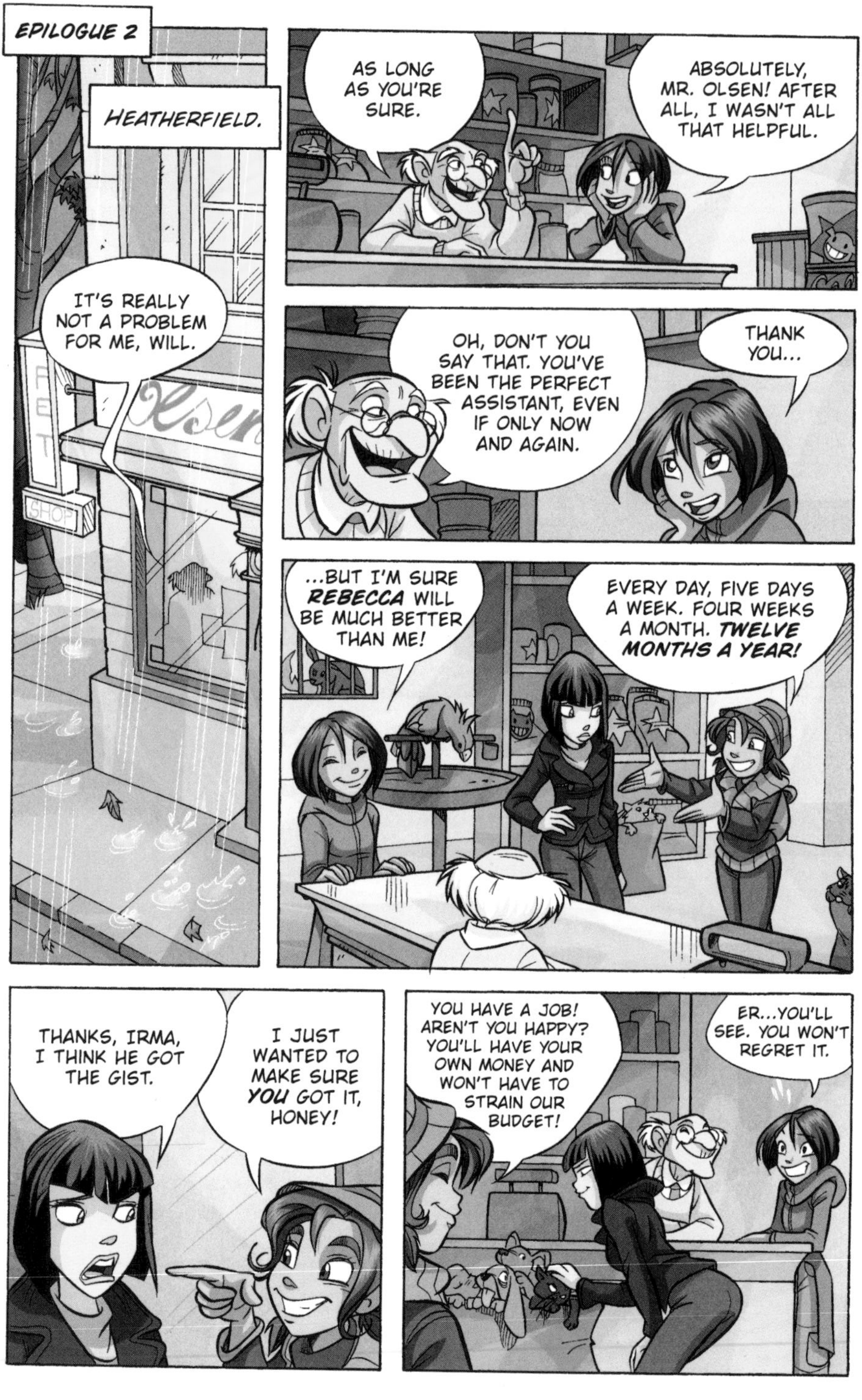
EPILOGUE 2
HEATHERFIELD.
IT'S REALLY NOT A PROBLEM FOR ME, WILL.
OLSEN
SHOP
AS LONG AS YOU'RE SURE.
ABSOLUTELY, MR. OLSEN! AFTER ALL, I WASN'T ALL THAT HELPFUL.
OH, DON'T YOU SAY THAT. YOU'VE BEEN THE PERFECT ASSISTANT, EVEN IF ONLY NOW AND AGAIN.
THANK YOU...
...BUT I'M SURE **REBECCA** WILL BE MUCH BETTER THAN ME!
EVERY DAY, FIVE DAYS A WEEK. FOUR WEEKS A MONTH. ***TWELVE MONTHS A YEAR!***
THANKS, IRMA, I THINK HE GOT THE GIST.
I JUST WANTED TO MAKE SURE ***YOU*** GOT IT, HONEY!
YOU HAVE A JOB! AREN'T YOU HAPPY? YOU'LL HAVE YOUR OWN MONEY AND WON'T HAVE TO STRAIN OUR BUDGET!
ER...YOU'LL SEE. YOU WON'T REGRET IT.

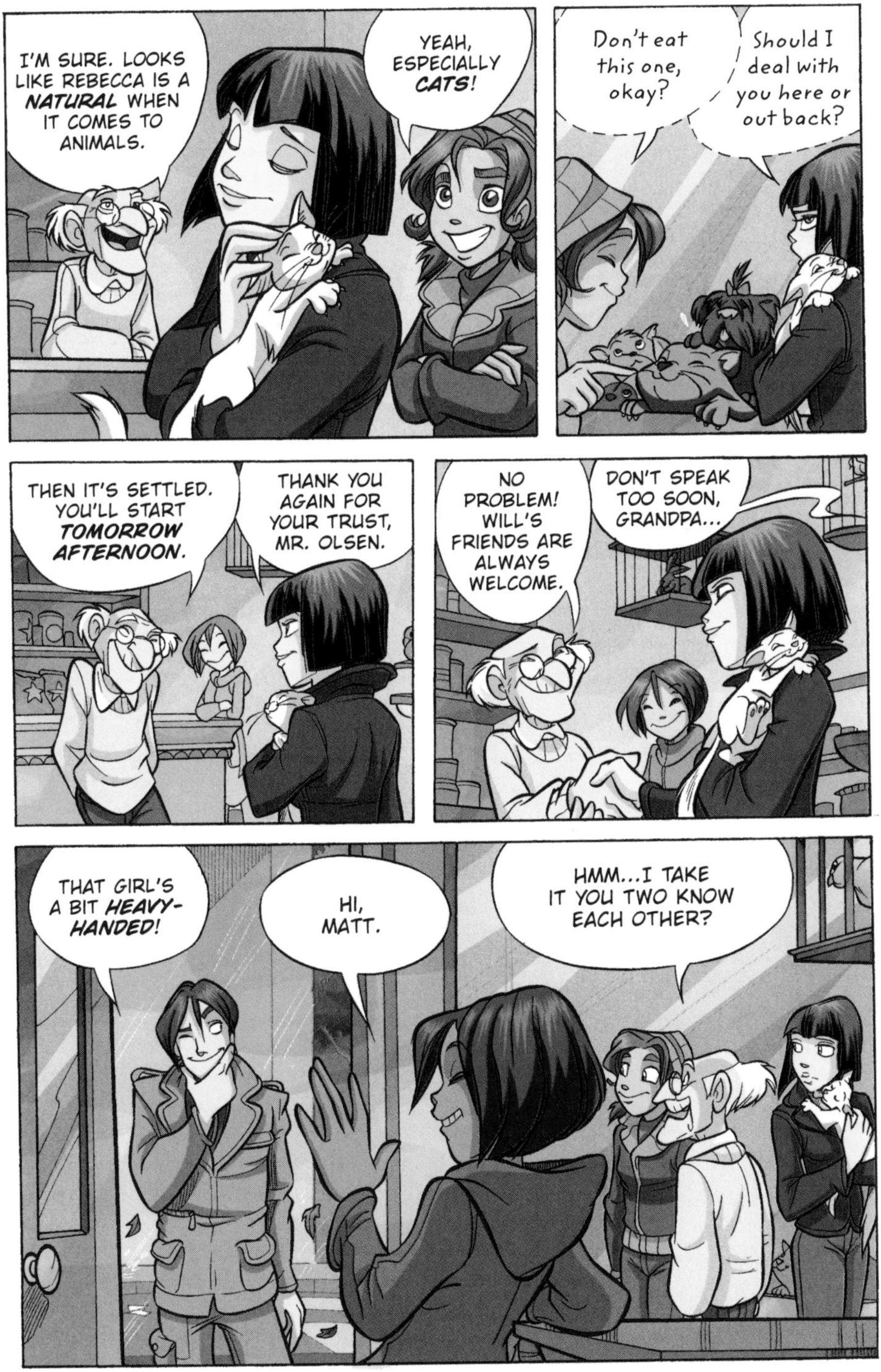
I'M SURE. LOOKS LIKE REBECCA IS A NATURAL WHEN IT COMES TO ANIMALS.
YEAH, ESPECIALLY CATS!
Don't eat this one, okay?
Should I deal with you here or out back?
THEN IT'S SETTLED. YOU'LL START TOMORROW AFTERNOON.
THANK YOU AGAIN FOR YOUR TRUST, MR. OLSEN.
NO PROBLEM! WILL'S FRIENDS ARE ALWAYS WELCOME.
DON'T SPEAK TOO SOON, GRANDPA...
THAT GIRL'S A BIT HEAVY-HANDED!
HI, MATT.
HMM...I TAKE IT YOU TWO KNOW EACH OTHER?

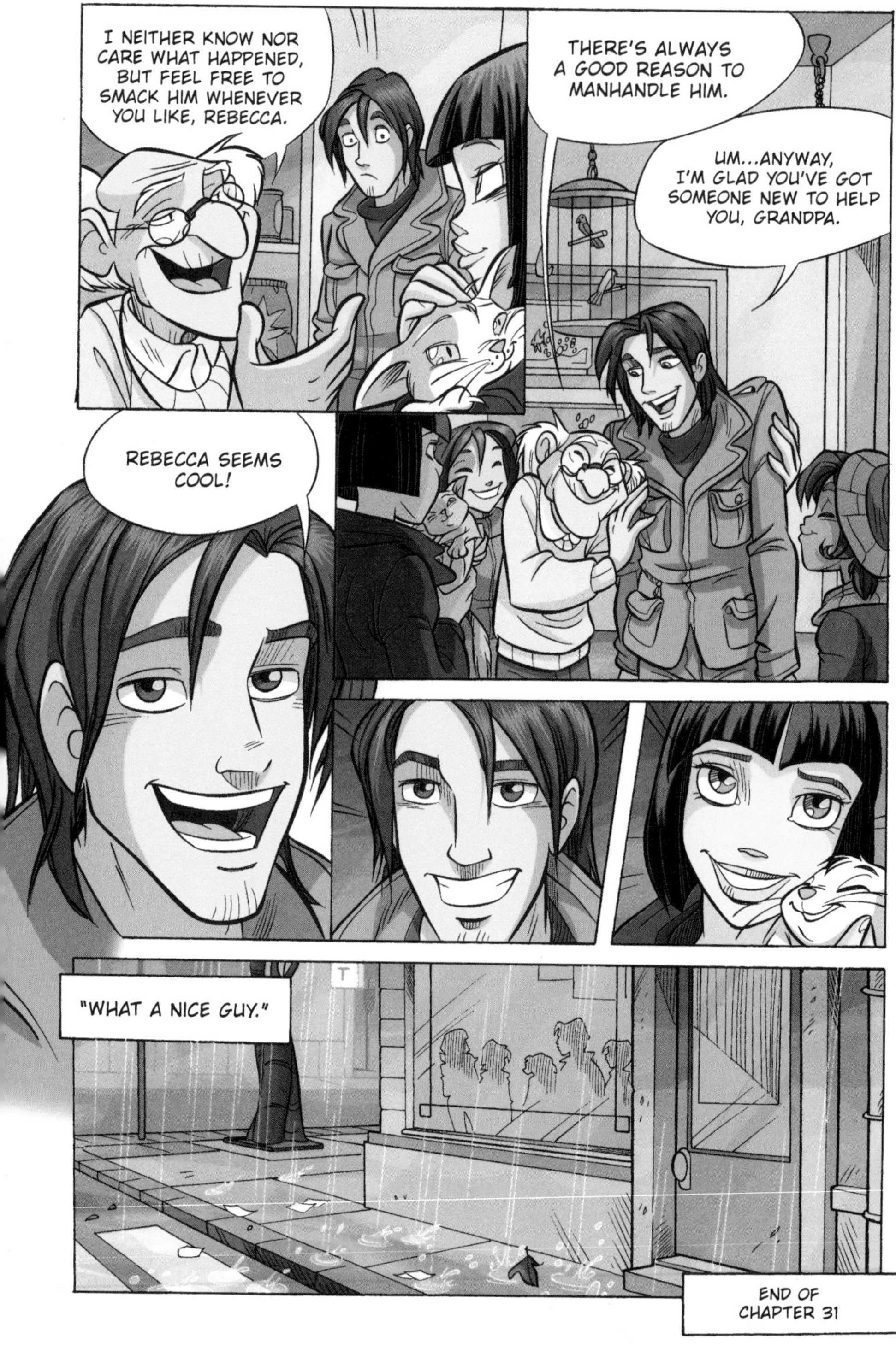
I NEITHER KNOW NOR CARE WHAT HAPPENED, BUT FEEL FREE TO SMACK HIM WHENEVER YOU LIKE, REBECCA.
THERE'S ALWAYS A GOOD REASON TO MANHANDLE HIM.
UM...ANYWAY, I'M GLAD YOU'VE GOT SOMEONE NEW TO HELP YOU, GRANDPA.
REBECCA SEEMS COOL!
"WHAT A NICE GUY."
END OF CHAPTER 31

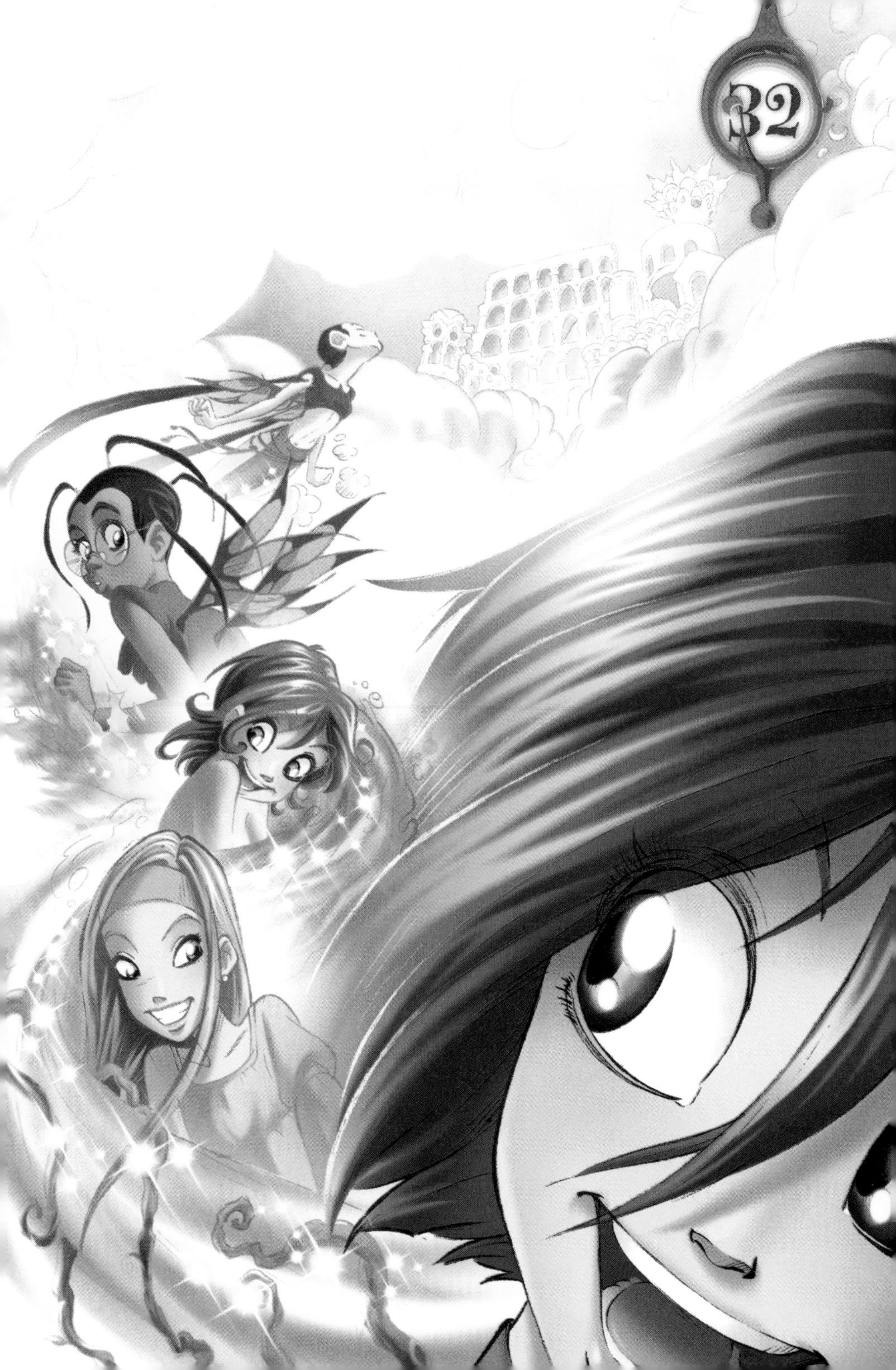
32

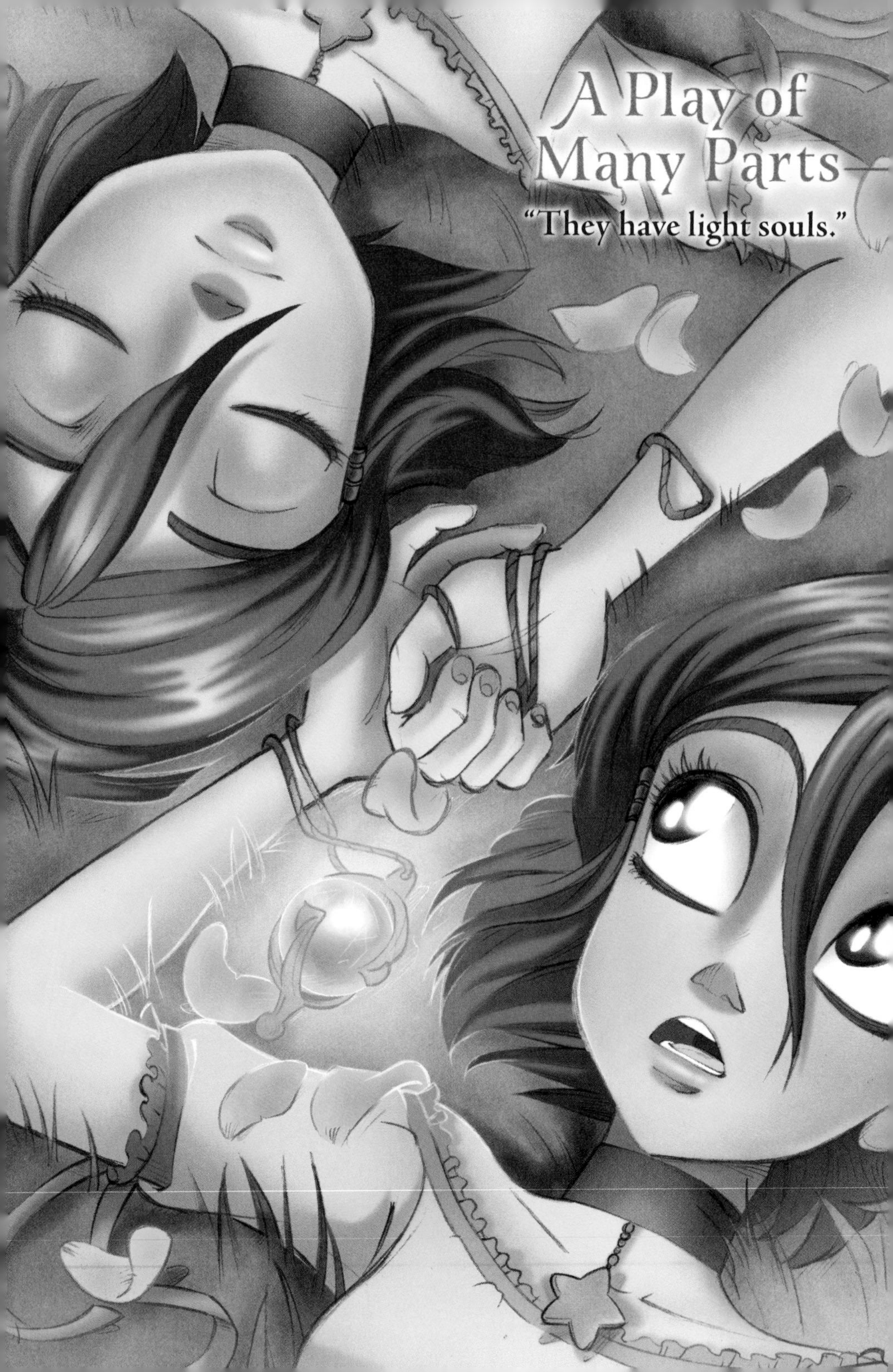
A Play of
Many Parts
"They have light souls."

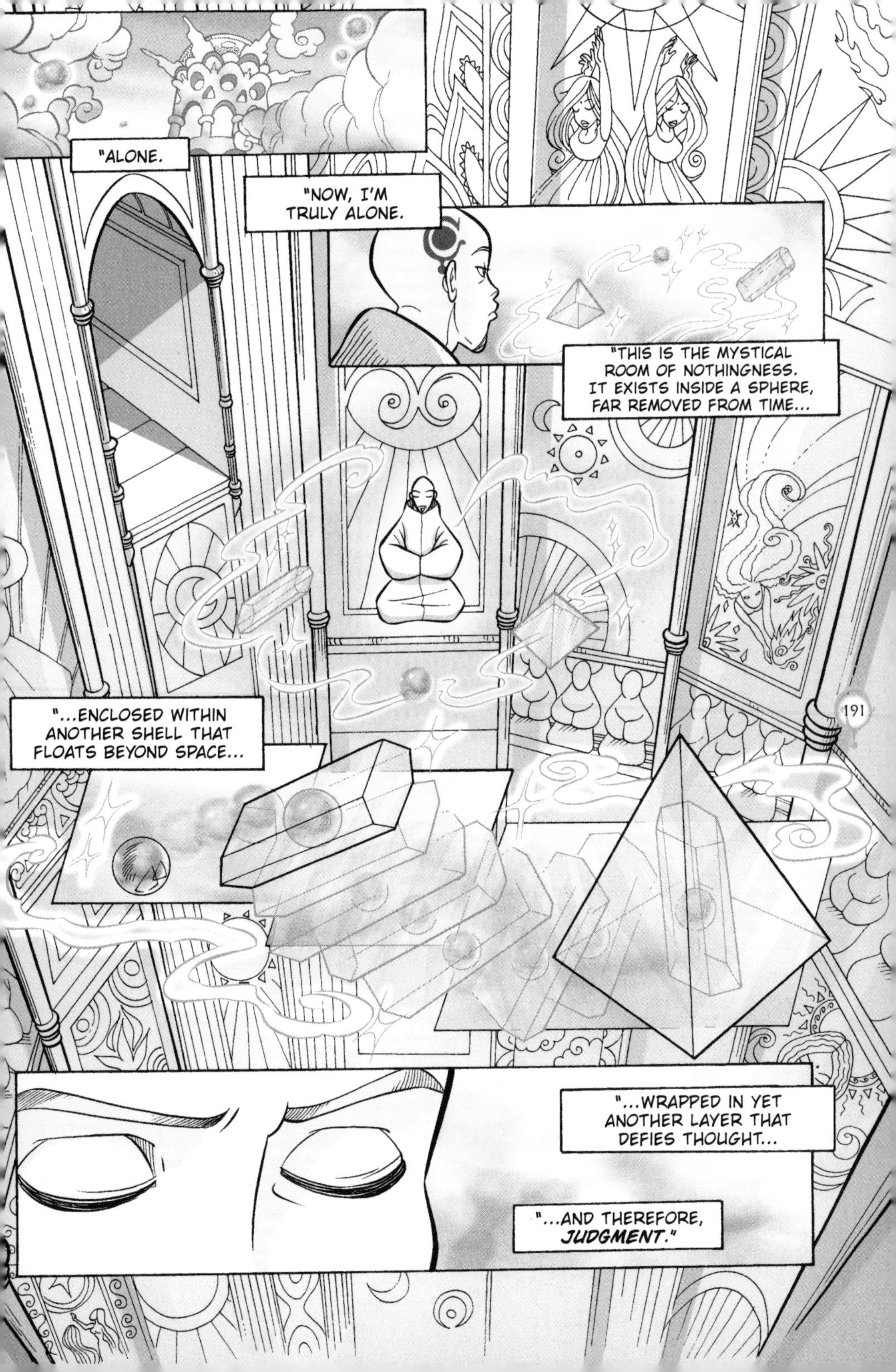

"ALONE.
"NOW, I'M TRULY ALONE.
"THIS IS THE MYSTICAL ROOM OF NOTHINGNESS. IT EXISTS INSIDE A SPHERE, FAR REMOVED FROM TIME...
"...ENCLOSED WITHIN ANOTHER SHELL THAT FLOATS BEYOND SPACE...
"...WRAPPED IN YET ANOTHER LAYER THAT DEFIES THOUGHT...
"...AND THEREFORE, ***JUDGMENT***."

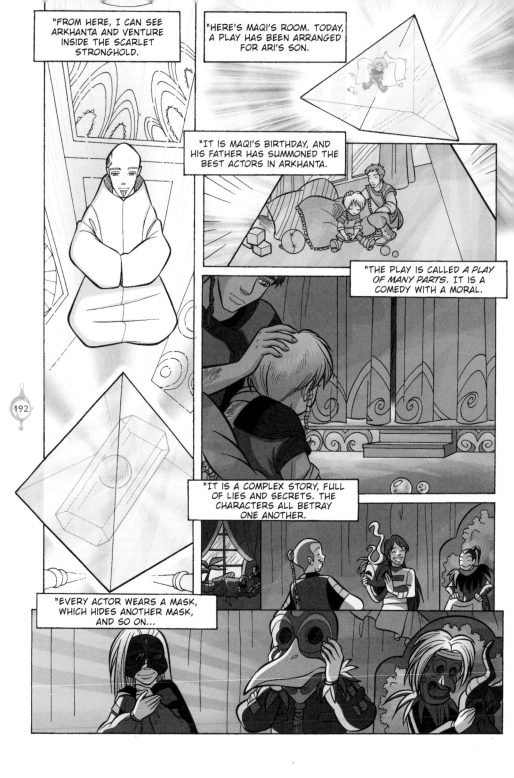

"FROM HERE, I CAN SEE ARKHANTA AND VENTURE INSIDE THE SCARLET STRONGHOLD.

"HERE'S MAQI'S ROOM. TODAY, A PLAY HAS BEEN ARRANGED FOR ARI'S SON.

"IT IS MAQI'S BIRTHDAY, AND HIS FATHER HAS SUMMONED THE BEST ACTORS IN ARKHANTA.

"THE PLAY IS CALLED A PLAY OF MANY PARTS. IT IS A COMEDY WITH A MORAL.

"IT IS A COMPLEX STORY, FULL OF LIES AND SECRETS. THE CHARACTERS ALL BETRAY ONE ANOTHER.

"EVERY ACTOR WEARS A MASK, WHICH HIDES ANOTHER MASK, AND SO ON...

192

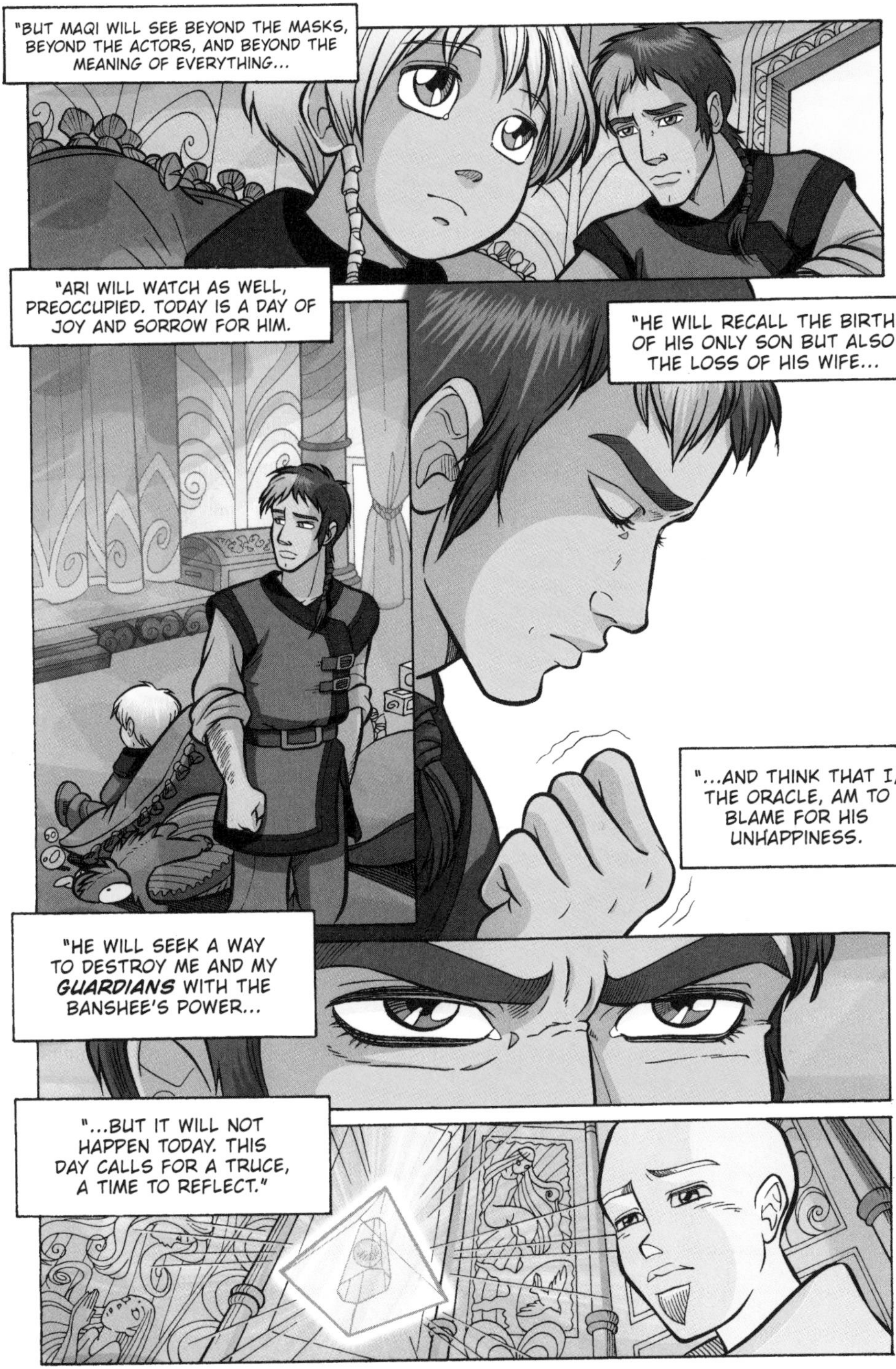
"BUT MAQI WILL SEE BEYOND THE MASKS, BEYOND THE ACTORS, AND BEYOND THE MEANING OF EVERYTHING...
"ARI WILL WATCH AS WELL, PREOCCUPIED. TODAY IS A DAY OF JOY AND SORROW FOR HIM.
"HE WILL RECALL THE BIRTH OF HIS ONLY SON BUT ALSO THE LOSS OF HIS WIFE...
"...AND THINK THAT I, THE ORACLE, AM TO BLAME FOR HIS UNHAPPINESS.
"HE WILL SEEK A WAY TO DESTROY ME AND MY *GUARDIANS* WITH THE BANSHEE'S POWER...
"...BUT IT WILL NOT HAPPEN TODAY. THIS DAY CALLS FOR A TRUCE, A TIME TO REFLECT."

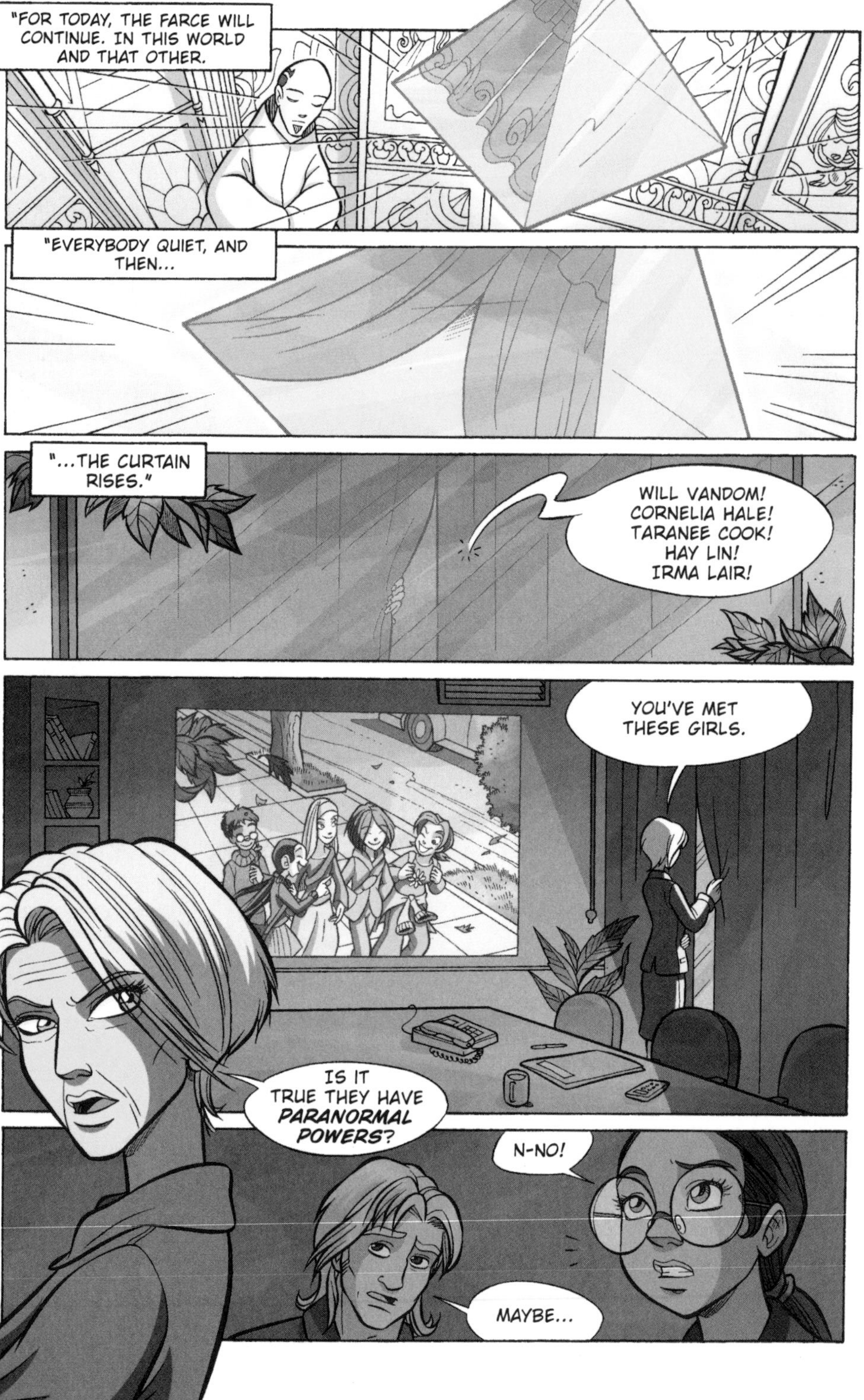
"FOR TODAY, THE FARCE WILL CONTINUE. IN THIS WORLD AND THAT OTHER.
"EVERYBODY QUIET, AND THEN...
"...THE CURTAIN RISES."
WILL VANDOM! CORNELIA HALE! TARANEE COOK! HAY LIN! IRMA LAIR!
YOU'VE MET THESE GIRLS.
IS IT TRUE THEY HAVE *PARANORMAL POWERS*?
N-NO!
MAYBE...

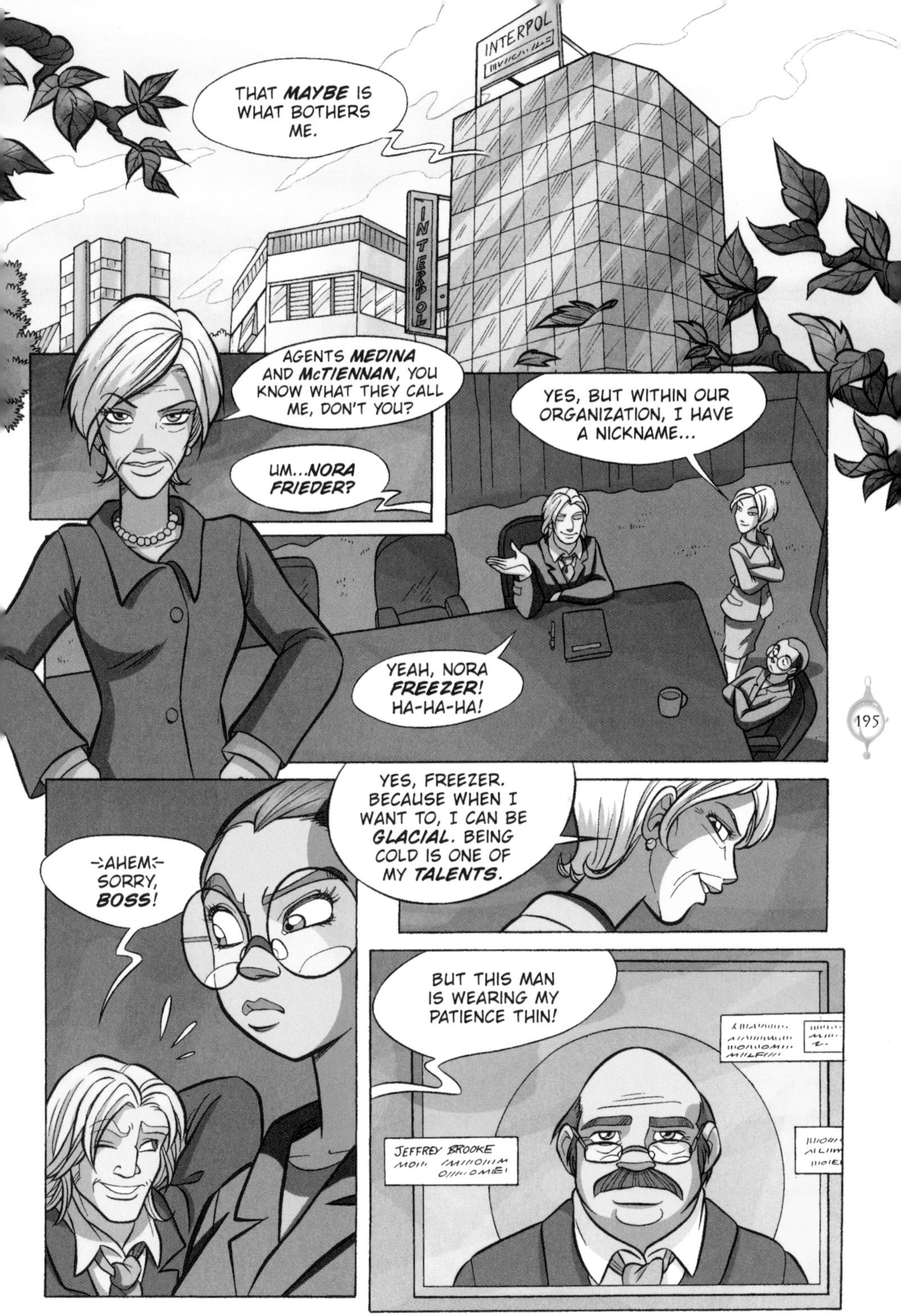
THAT MAYBE IS WHAT BOTHERS ME.
INTERPOL
INTERPOL
AGENTS MEDINA AND McTIENNAN, YOU KNOW WHAT THEY CALL ME, DON'T YOU?
UM...NORA FRIEDER?
YES, BUT WITHIN OUR ORGANIZATION, I HAVE A NICKNAME...
YEAH, NORA FREEZER! HA-HA-HA!
YES, FREEZER. BECAUSE WHEN I WANT TO, I CAN BE GLACIAL. BEING COLD IS ONE OF MY TALENTS.
AHEM SORRY, BOSS!
BUT THIS MAN IS WEARING MY PATIENCE THIN!
JEFFREY BROOKE

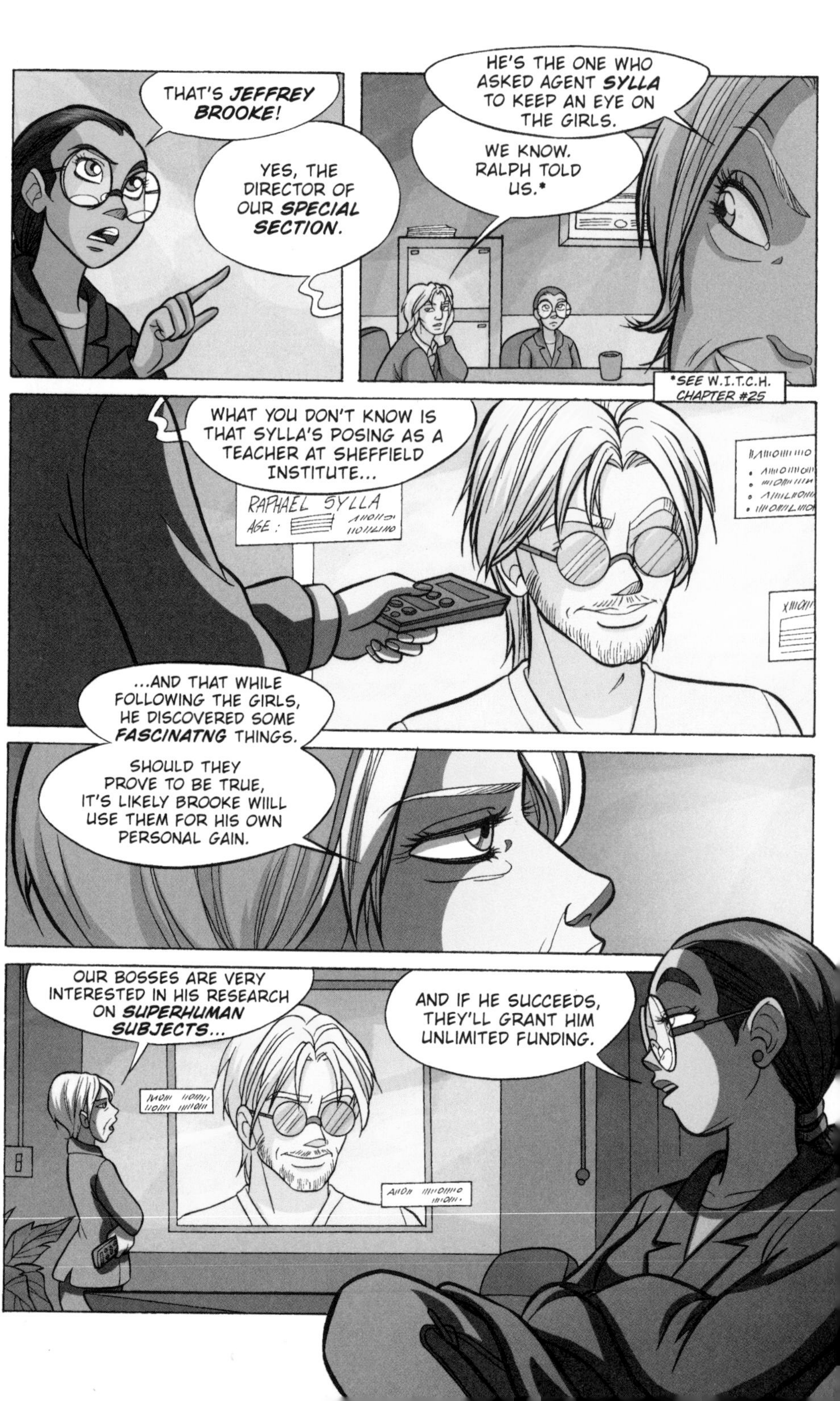
THAT'S JEFFREY BROOKE!
YES, THE DIRECTOR OF OUR SPECIAL SECTION.
HE'S THE ONE WHO ASKED AGENT SYLLA TO KEEP AN EYE ON THE GIRLS.
WE KNOW. RALPH TOLD US.*
*SEE W.I.T.C.H. CHAPTER #25
WHAT YOU DON'T KNOW IS THAT SYLLA'S POSING AS A TEACHER AT SHEFFIELD INSTITUTE...
RAPHAEL SYLLA
AGE :
...AND THAT WHILE FOLLOWING THE GIRLS, HE DISCOVERED SOME FASCINATNG THINGS.
SHOULD THEY PROVE TO BE TRUE, IT'S LIKELY BROOKE WIILL USE THEM FOR HIS OWN PERSONAL GAIN.
OUR BOSSES ARE VERY INTERESTED IN HIS RESEARCH ON SUPERHUMAN SUBJECTS...
AND IF HE SUCCEEDS, THEY'LL GRANT HIM UNLIMITED FUNDING.

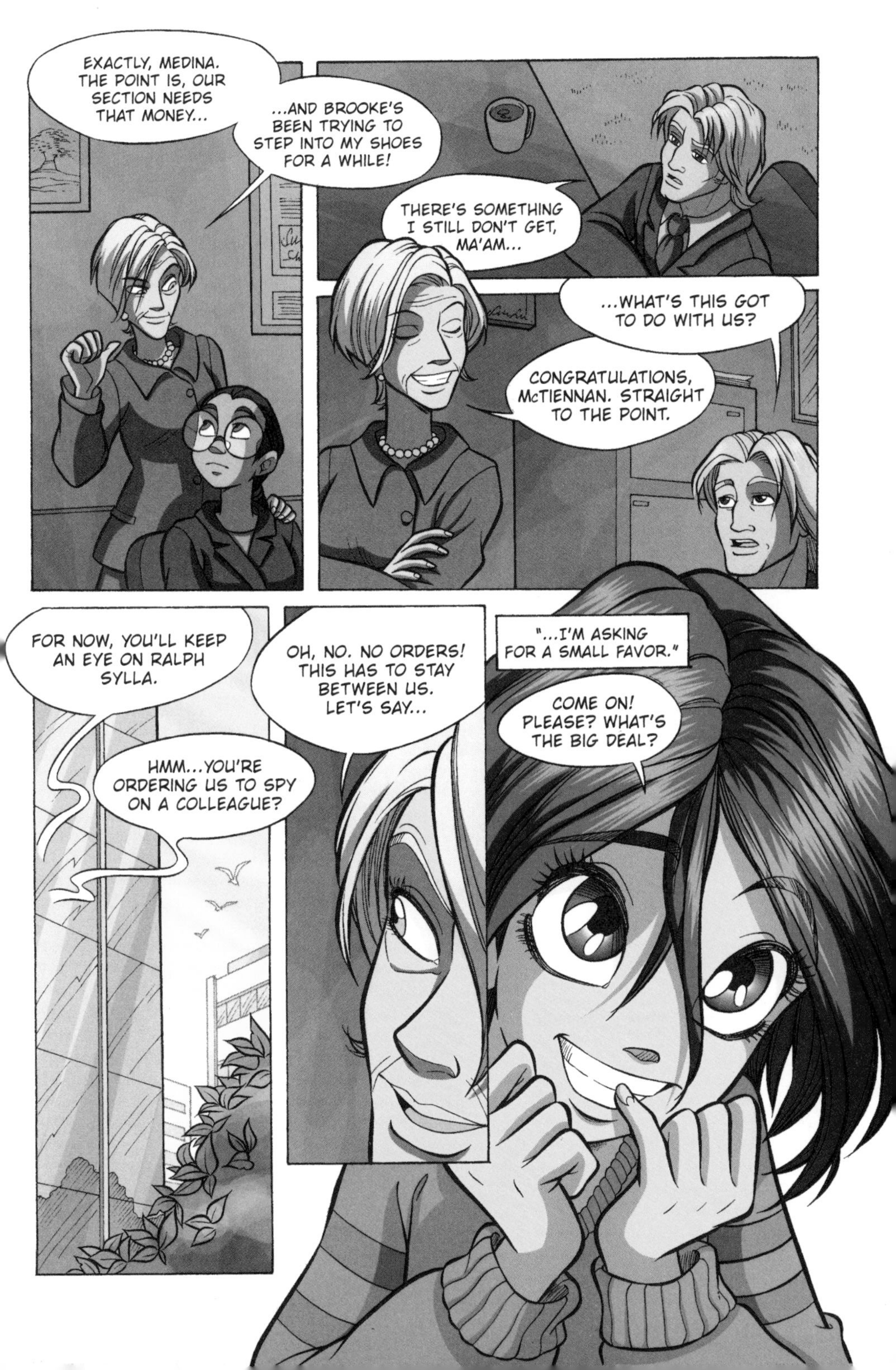
EXACTLY, MEDINA. THE POINT IS, OUR SECTION NEEDS THAT MONEY...
...AND BROOKE'S BEEN TRYING TO STEP INTO MY SHOES FOR A WHILE!
THERE'S SOMETHING I STILL DON'T GET, MA'AM...
...WHAT'S THIS GOT TO DO WITH US?
CONGRATULATIONS, McTIENNAN. STRAIGHT TO THE POINT.
FOR NOW, YOU'LL KEEP AN EYE ON RALPH SYLLA.
HMM...YOU'RE ORDERING US TO SPY ON A COLLEAGUE?
OH, NO. NO ORDERS! THIS HAS TO STAY BETWEEN US. LET'S SAY...
"...I'M ASKING FOR A SMALL FAVOR."
COME ON! PLEASE? WHAT'S THE BIG DEAL?

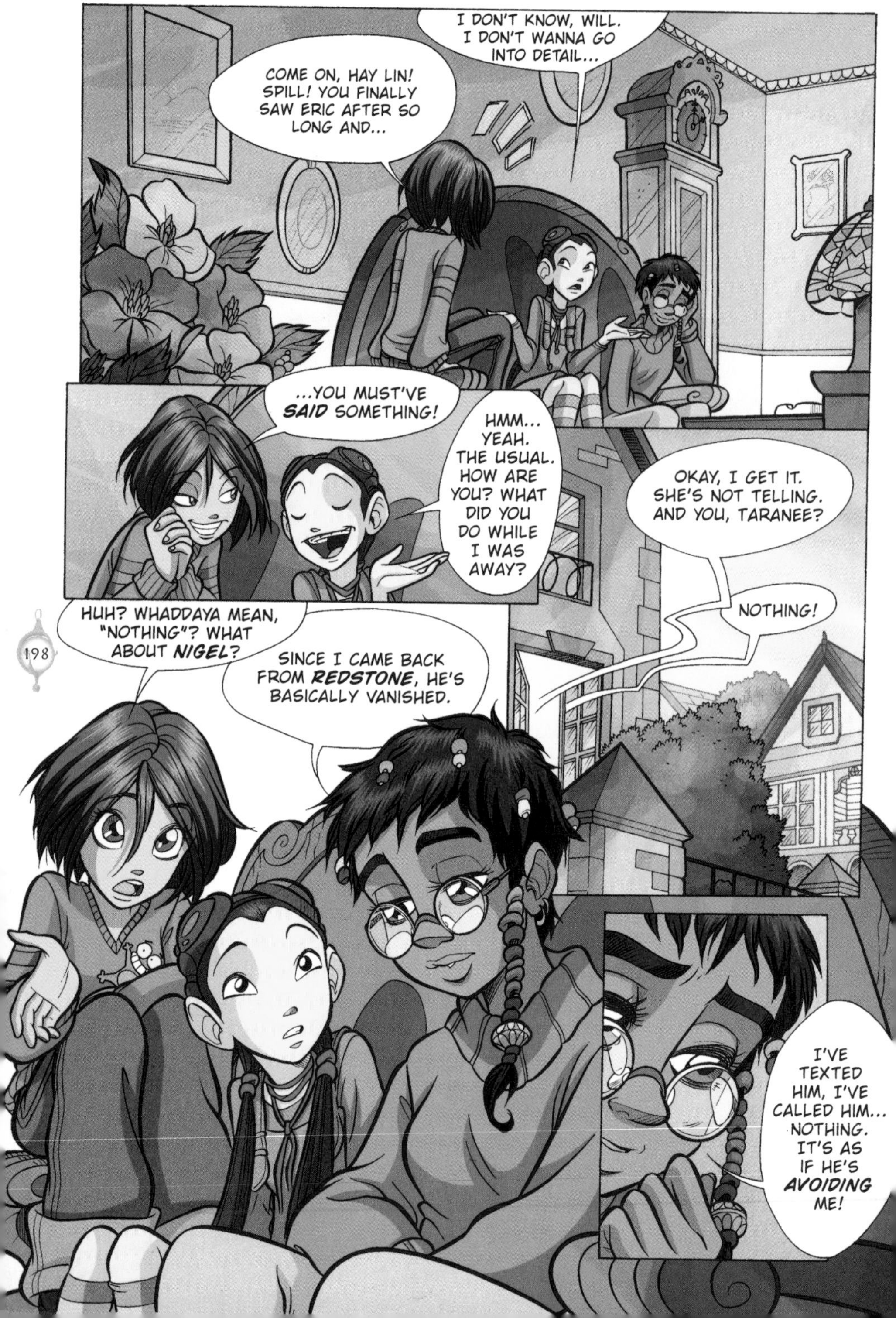
COME ON, HAY LIN! SPILL! YOU FINALLY SAW ERIC AFTER SO LONG AND...
I DON'T KNOW, WILL. I DON'T WANNA GO INTO DETAIL...
...YOU MUST'VE SAID SOMETHING!
HMM... YEAH. THE USUAL. HOW ARE YOU? WHAT DID YOU DO WHILE I WAS AWAY?
OKAY, I GET IT. SHE'S NOT TELLING. AND YOU, TARANEE?
NOTHING!
HUH? WHADDAYA MEAN, "NOTHING"? WHAT ABOUT NIGEL?
SINCE I CAME BACK FROM REDSTONE, HE'S BASICALLY VANISHED.
I'VE TEXTED HIM, I'VE CALLED HIM... NOTHING. IT'S AS IF HE'S AVOIDING ME!

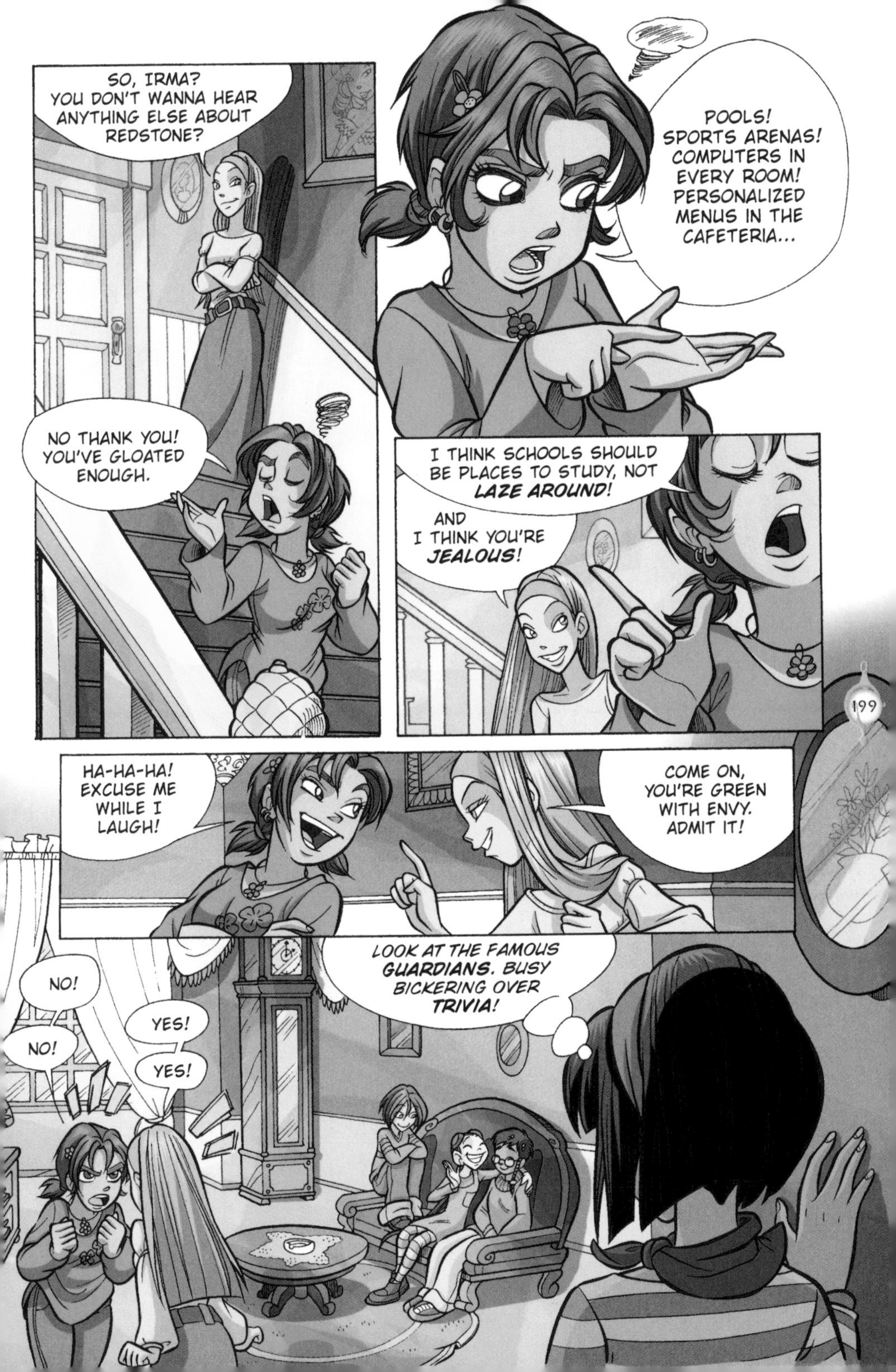
SO, IRMA? YOU DON'T WANNA HEAR ANYTHING ELSE ABOUT REDSTONE?
POOLS! SPORTS ARENAS! COMPUTERS IN EVERY ROOM! PERSONALIZED MENUS IN THE CAFETERIA...
NO THANK YOU! YOU'VE GLOATED ENOUGH.
I THINK SCHOOLS SHOULD BE PLACES TO STUDY, NOT LAZE AROUND!
AND I THINK YOU'RE JEALOUS!
HA-HA-HA! EXCUSE ME WHILE I LAUGH!
COME ON, YOU'RE GREEN WITH ENVY. ADMIT IT!
LOOK AT THE FAMOUS GUARDIANS. BUSY BICKERING OVER TRIVIA!
NO!
NO!
YES!
YES!

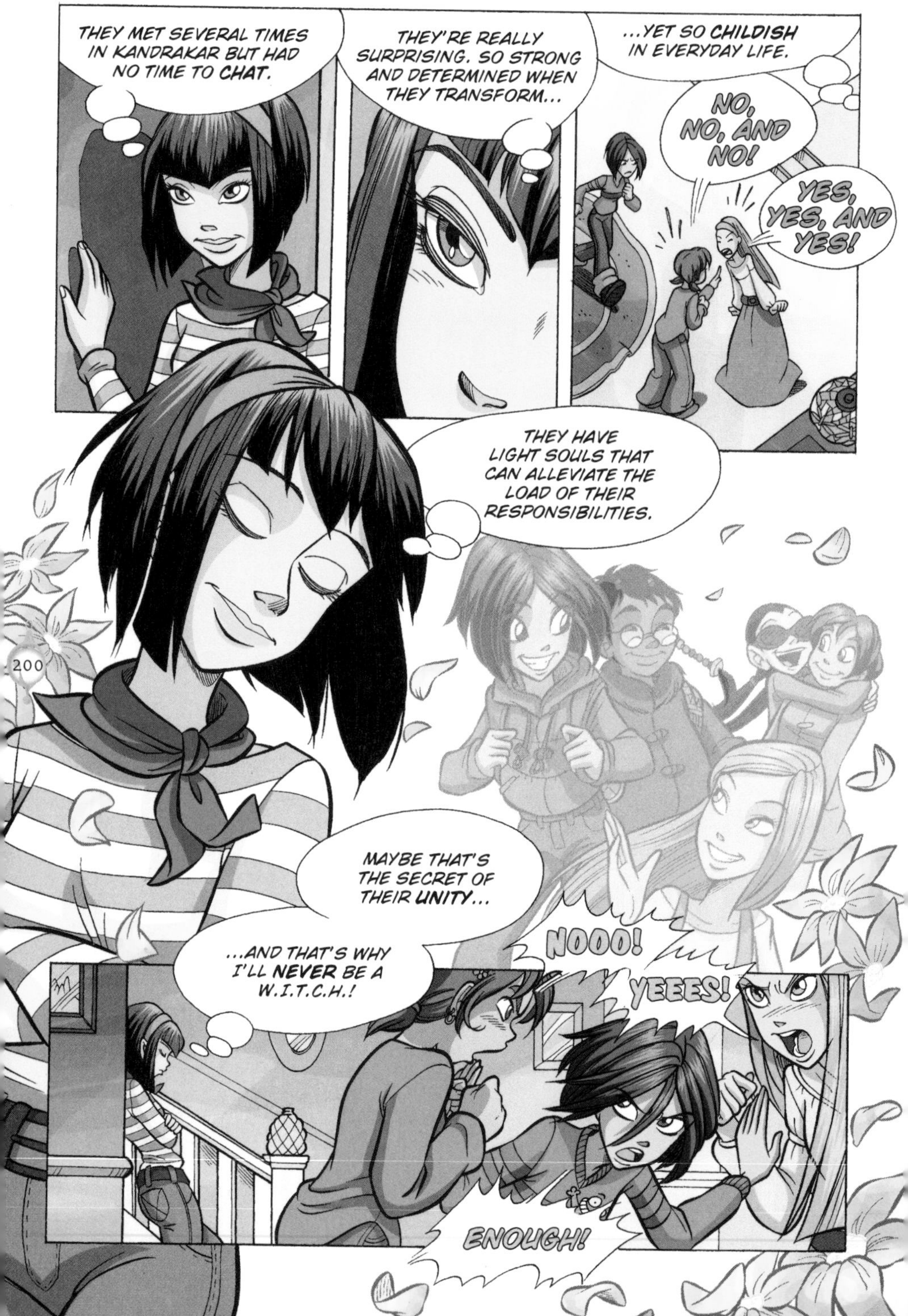
THEY MET SEVERAL TIMES IN KANDRAKAR BUT HAD NO TIME TO CHAT.
THEY'RE REALLY SURPRISING. SO STRONG AND DETERMINED WHEN THEY TRANSFORM...
...YET SO CHILDISH IN EVERYDAY LIFE.
NO, NO, AND NO!
YES, YES, AND YES!
THEY HAVE LIGHT SOULS THAT CAN ALLEVIATE THE LOAD OF THEIR RESPONSIBILITIES.
MAYBE THAT'S THE SECRET OF THEIR UNITY...
...AND THAT'S WHY I'LL NEVER BE A W.I.T.C.H.!
NOOO!
YEEES!
ENOUGH!

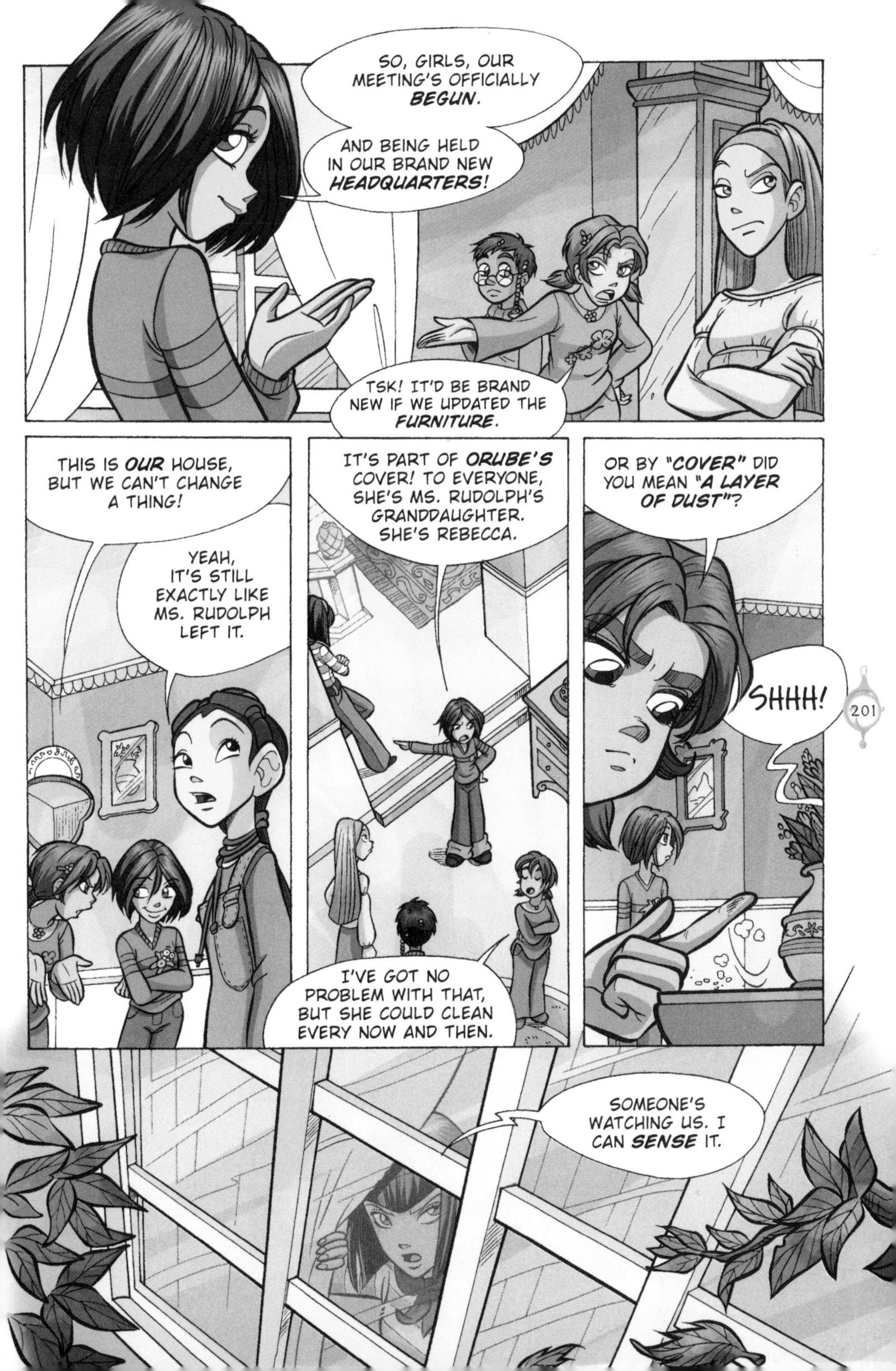

SO, GIRLS, OUR MEETING'S OFFICIALLY BEGUN.
AND BEING HELD IN OUR BRAND NEW HEADQUARTERS!
TSK! IT'D BE BRAND NEW IF WE UPDATED THE FURNITURE.
THIS IS OUR HOUSE, BUT WE CAN'T CHANGE A THING!
YEAH, IT'S STILL EXACTLY LIKE MS. RUDOLPH LEFT IT.
IT'S PART OF ORUBE'S COVER! TO EVERYONE, SHE'S MS. RUDOLPH'S GRANDDAUGHTER. SHE'S REBECCA.
I'VE GOT NO PROBLEM WITH THAT, BUT SHE COULD CLEAN EVERY NOW AND THEN.
OR BY "COVER" DID YOU MEAN "A LAYER OF DUST"?
SHHH!
SOMEONE'S WATCHING US. I CAN SENSE IT.

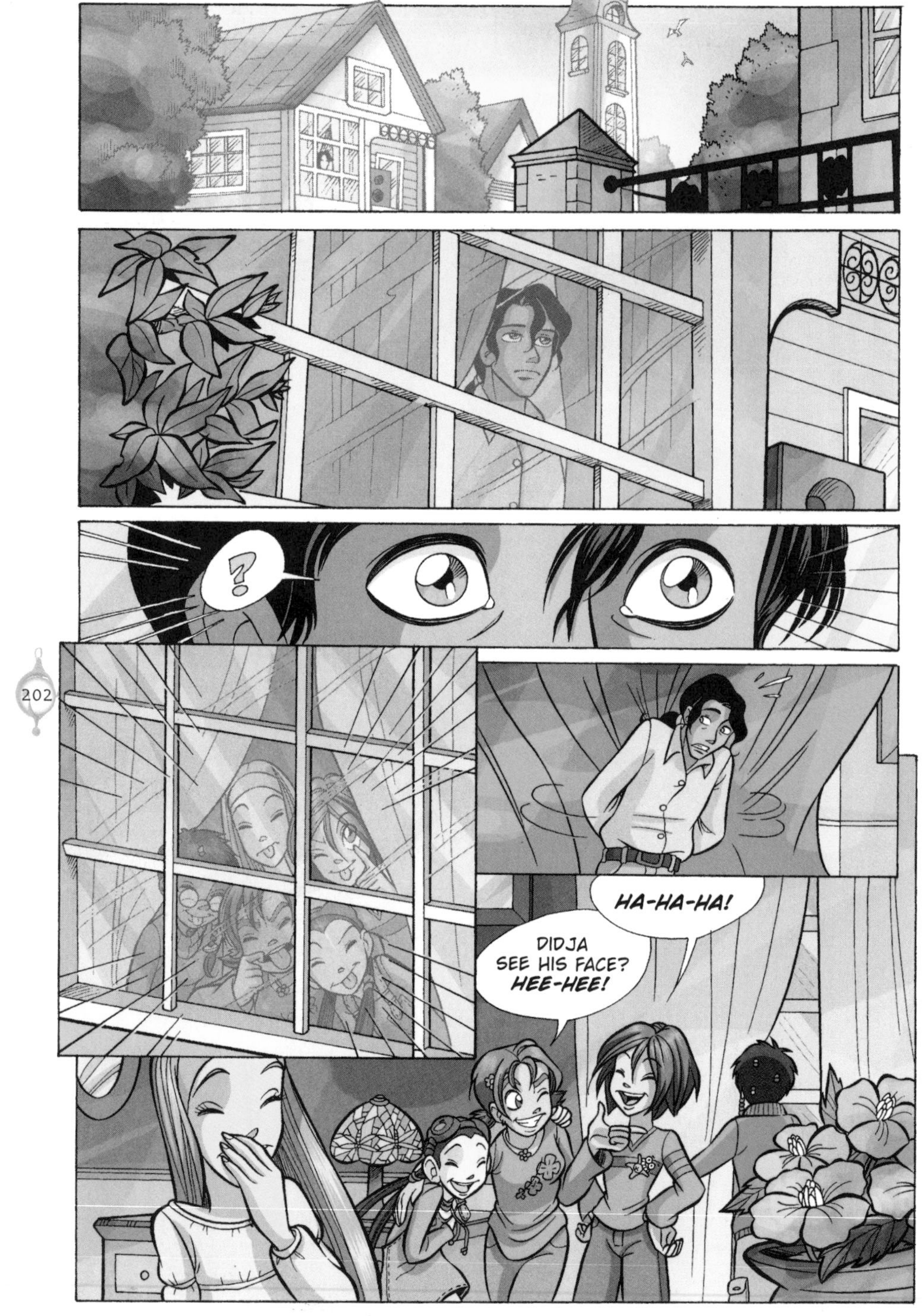
?
HA-HA-HA!
DIDJA SEE HIS FACE? HEE-HEE!

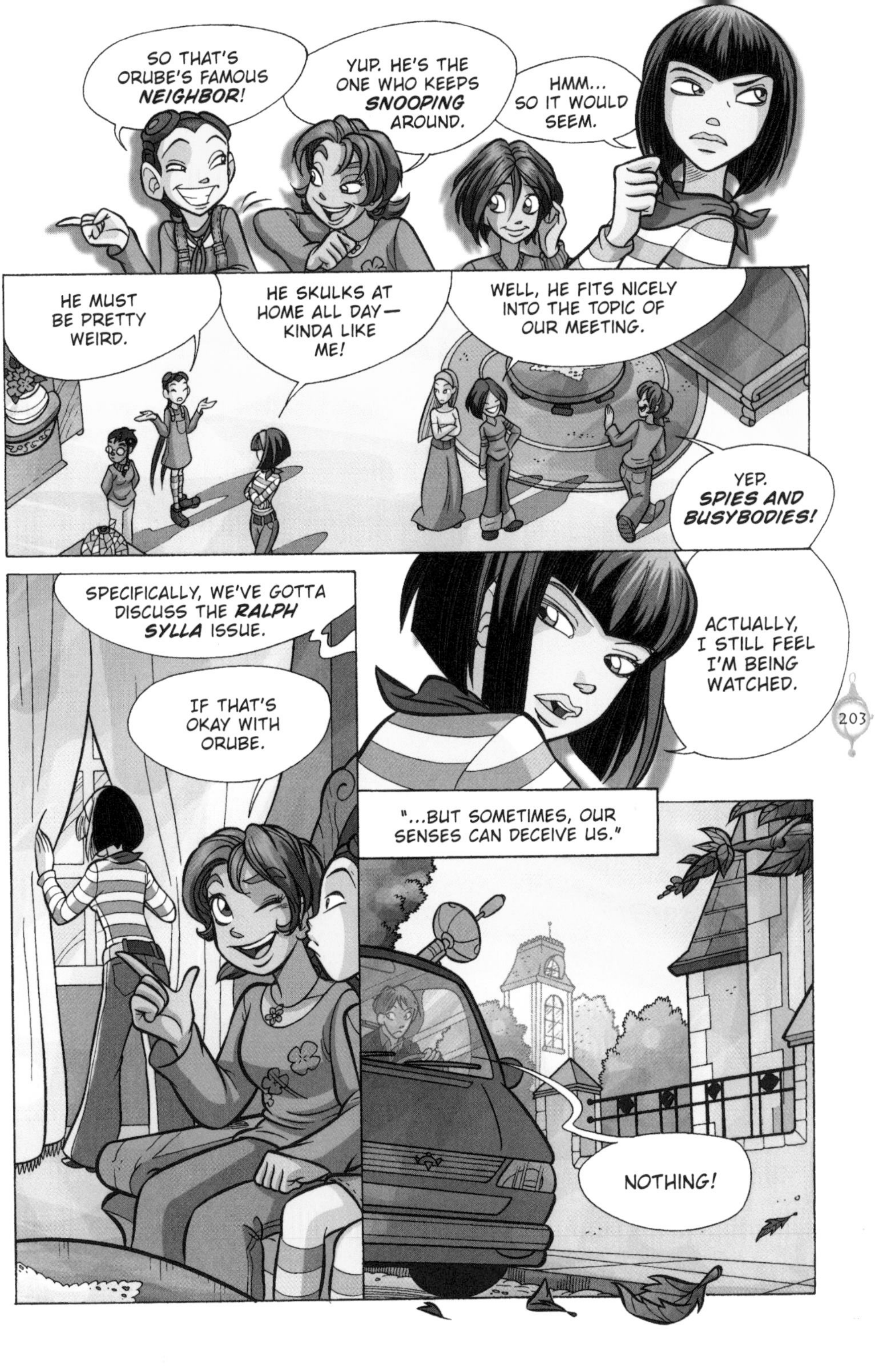
SO THAT'S ORUBE'S FAMOUS **NEIGHBOR**!
YUP. HE'S THE ONE WHO KEEPS **SNOOPING** AROUND.
HMM... SO IT WOULD SEEM.
HE MUST BE PRETTY WEIRD.
HE SKULKS AT HOME ALL DAY— KINDA LIKE ME!
WELL, HE FITS NICELY INTO THE TOPIC OF OUR MEETING.
YEP. **SPIES AND BUSYBODIES!**
SPECIFICALLY, WE'VE GOTTA DISCUSS THE **RALPH SYLLA** ISSUE.
IF THAT'S OKAY WITH ORUBE.
ACTUALLY, I STILL FEEL I'M BEING WATCHED.
"...BUT SOMETIMES, OUR SENSES CAN DECEIVE US."
NOTHING!

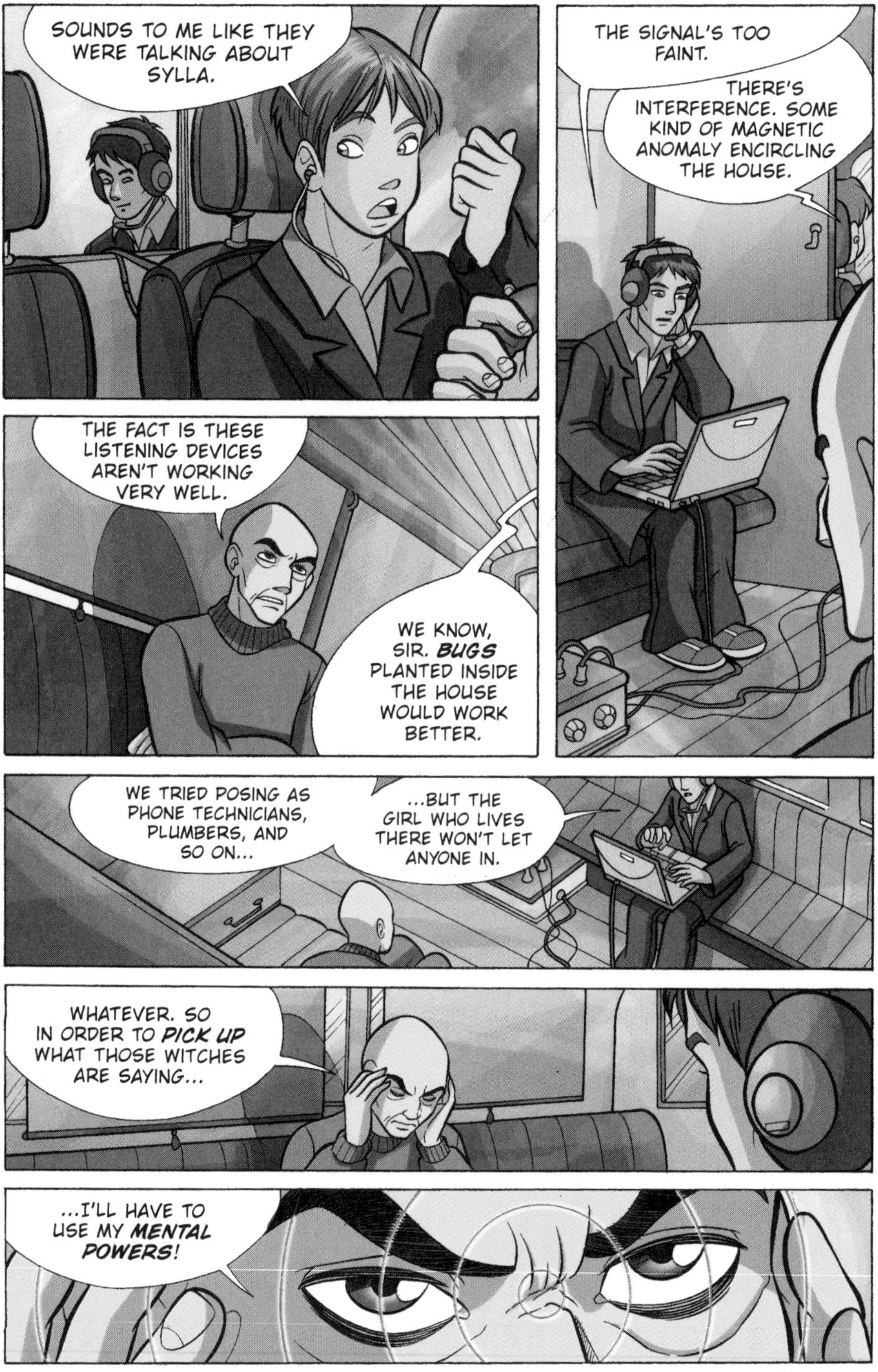
SOUNDS TO ME LIKE THEY WERE TALKING ABOUT SYLLA.
THE SIGNAL'S TOO FAINT.
THERE'S INTERFERENCE. SOME KIND OF MAGNETIC ANOMALY ENCIRCLING THE HOUSE.
THE FACT IS THESE LISTENING DEVICES AREN'T WORKING VERY WELL.
WE KNOW, SIR. BUGS PLANTED INSIDE THE HOUSE WOULD WORK BETTER.
WE TRIED POSING AS PHONE TECHNICIANS, PLUMBERS, AND SO ON...
...BUT THE GIRL WHO LIVES THERE WON'T LET ANYONE IN.
WHATEVER. SO IN ORDER TO PICK UP WHAT THOSE WITCHES ARE SAYING...
...I'LL HAVE TO USE MY MENTAL POWERS!

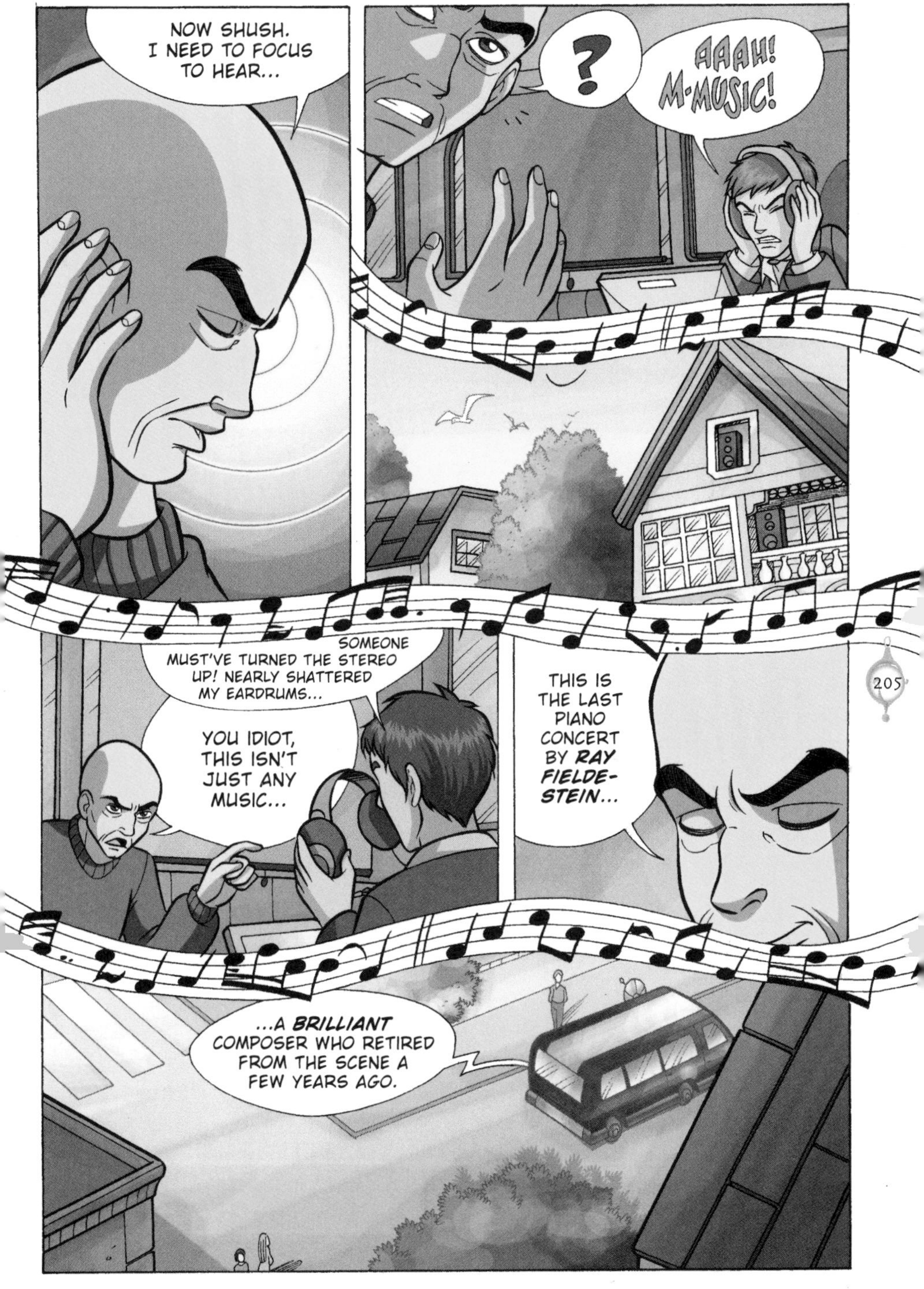
NOW SHUSH. I NEED TO FOCUS TO HEAR...
?
AAAH! M-MUSIC!
SOMEONE MUST'VE TURNED THE STEREO UP! NEARLY SHATTERED MY EARDRUMS...
YOU IDIOT, THIS ISN'T JUST ANY MUSIC...
THIS IS THE LAST PIANO CONCERT BY RAY FIELDE-STEIN...
...A BRILLIANT COMPOSER WHO RETIRED FROM THE SCENE A FEW YEARS AGO.

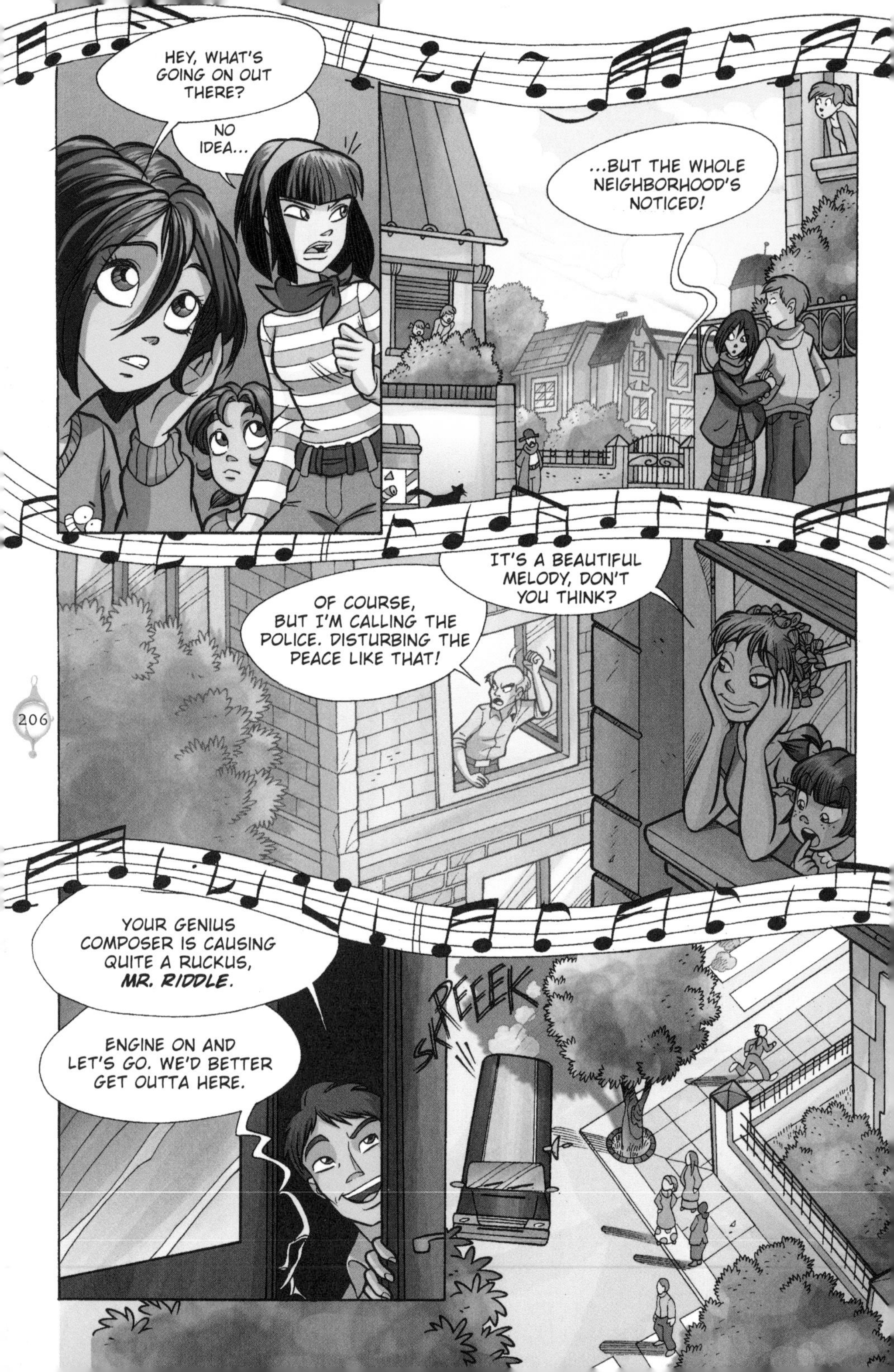
HEY, WHAT'S GOING ON OUT THERE?
NO IDEA...
...BUT THE WHOLE NEIGHBORHOOD'S NOTICED!
IT'S A BEAUTIFUL MELODY, DON'T YOU THINK?
OF COURSE, BUT I'M CALLING THE POLICE. DISTURBING THE PEACE LIKE THAT!
YOUR GENIUS COMPOSER IS CAUSING QUITE A RUCKUS, MR. RIDDLE.
ENGINE ON AND LET'S GO. WE'D BETTER GET OUTTA HERE.
SKREEEK

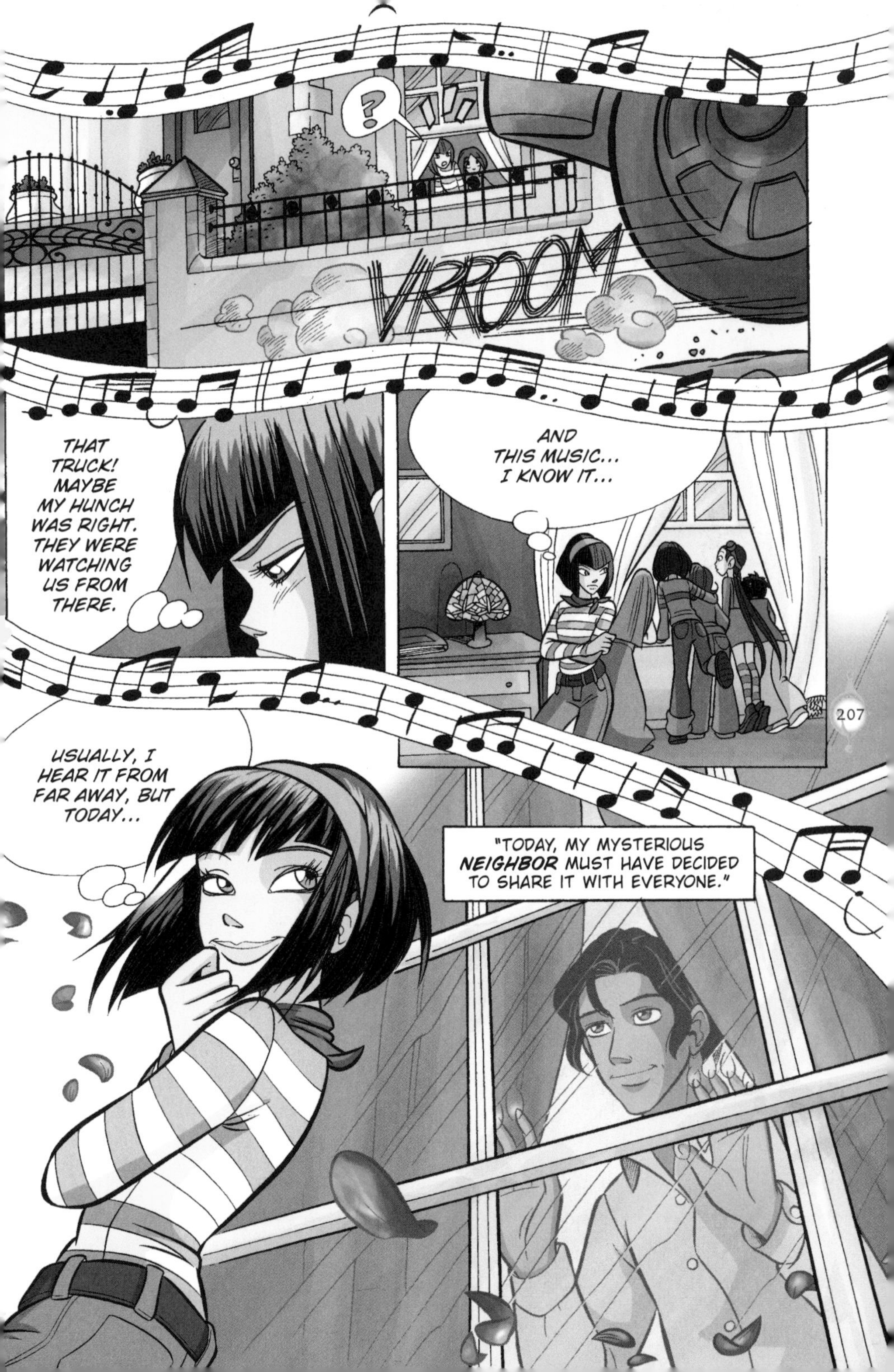
?
VRROOM
THAT TRUCK! MAYBE MY HUNCH WAS RIGHT. THEY WERE WATCHING US FROM THERE.
AND THIS MUSIC... I KNOW IT...
USUALLY, I HEAR IT FROM FAR AWAY, BUT TODAY...
"TODAY, MY MYSTERIOUS NEIGHBOR MUST HAVE DECIDED TO SHARE IT WITH EVERYONE."

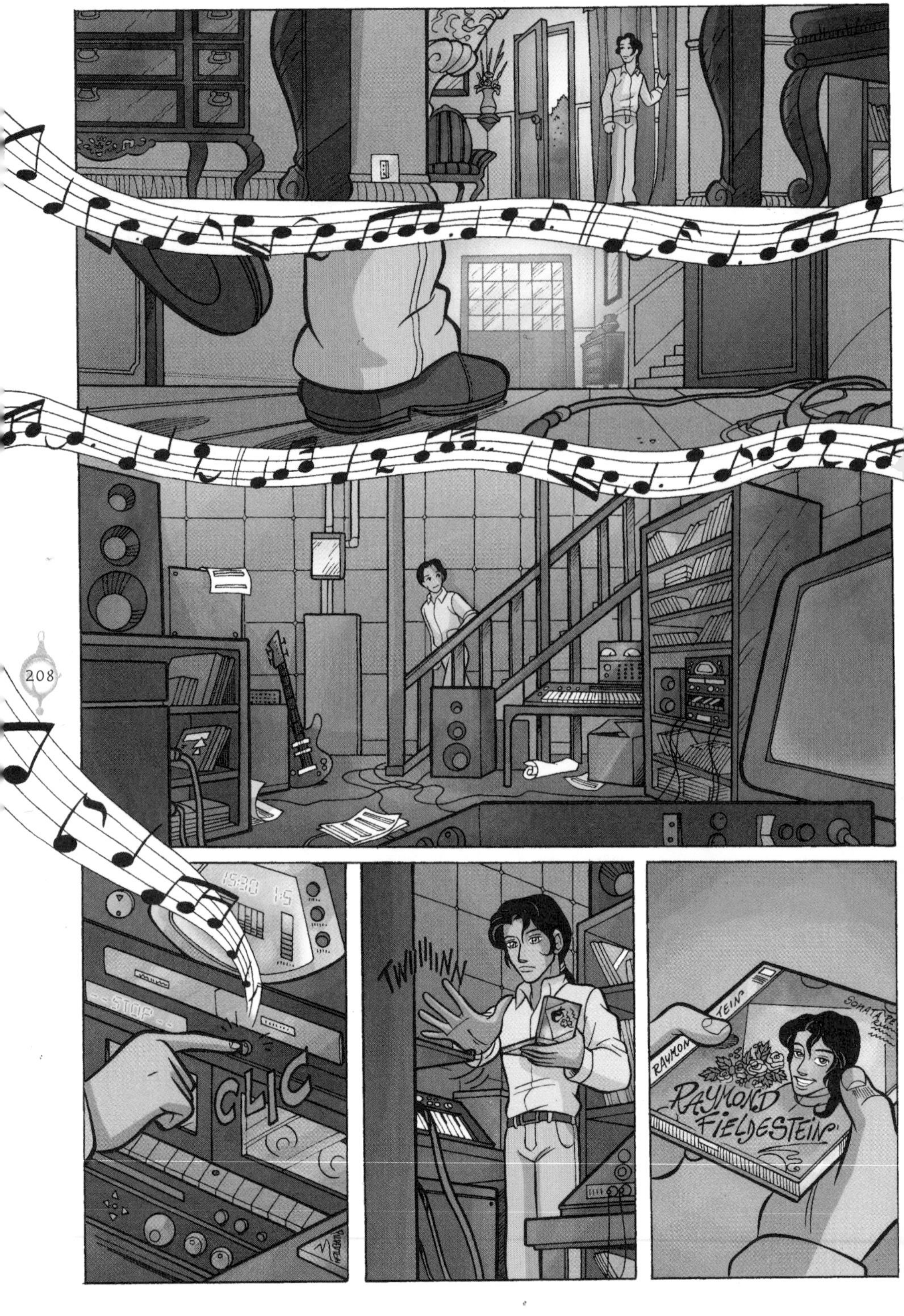
15:30 1:5
--STOP--
CLIC
TWIIIIINN
RAYMON
TEIN
SONATA
RAYMOND FIELDESTEIN

208

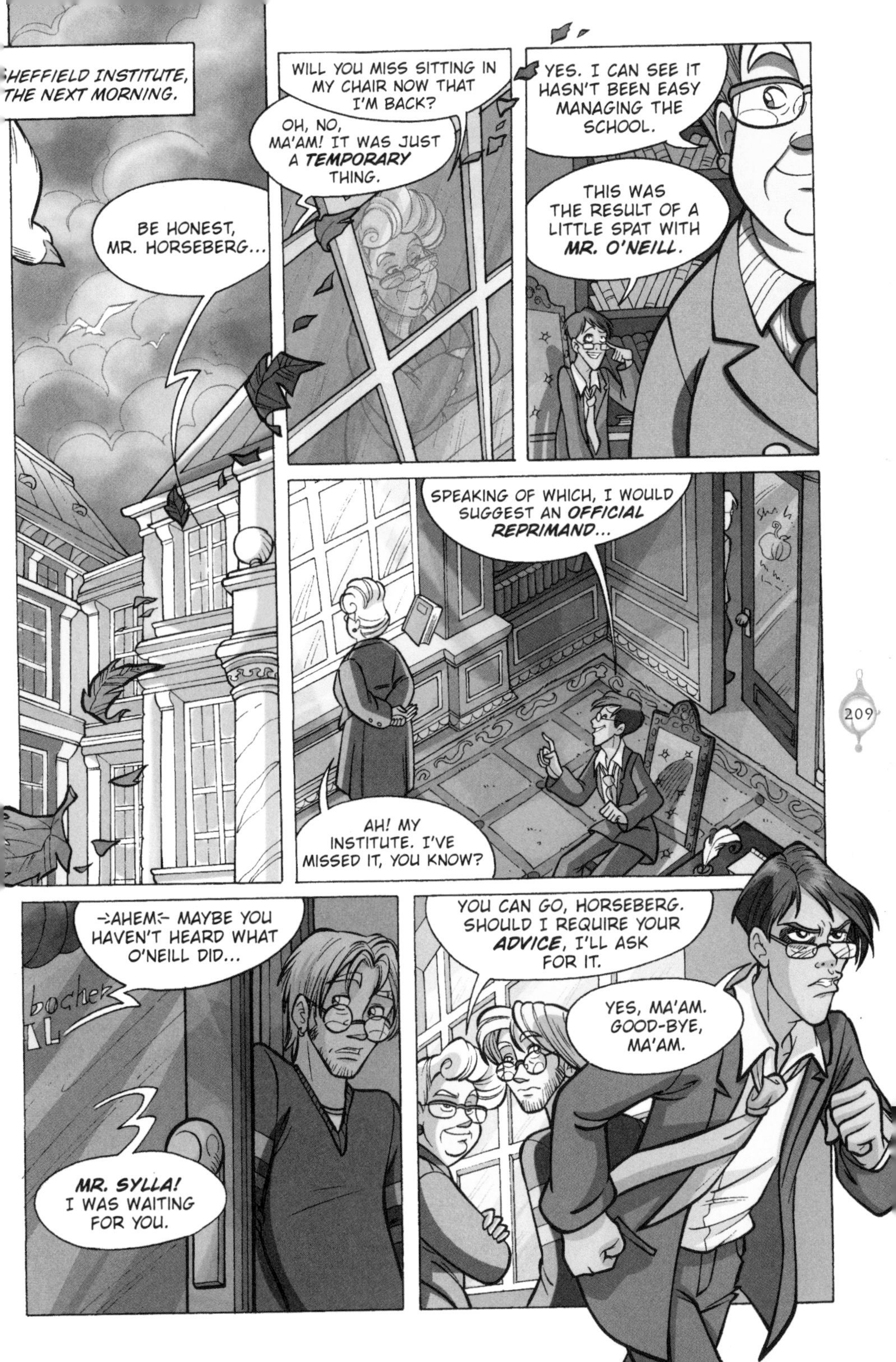
SHEFFIELD INSTITUTE, THE NEXT MORNING.
BE HONEST, MR. HORSEBERG...
WILL YOU MISS SITTING IN MY CHAIR NOW THAT I'M BACK?
OH, NO, MA'AM! IT WAS JUST A *TEMPORARY* THING.
YES. I CAN SEE IT HASN'T BEEN EASY MANAGING THE SCHOOL.
THIS WAS THE RESULT OF A LITTLE SPAT WITH *MR. O'NEILL*.
AH! MY INSTITUTE. I'VE MISSED IT, YOU KNOW?
SPEAKING OF WHICH, I WOULD SUGGEST AN *OFFICIAL REPRIMAND*...
-AHEM- MAYBE YOU HAVEN'T HEARD WHAT O'NEILL DID...
MR. SYLLA! I WAS WAITING FOR YOU.
YOU CAN GO, HORSEBERG. SHOULD I REQUIRE YOUR *ADVICE*, I'LL ASK FOR IT.
YES, MA'AM. GOOD-BYE, MA'AM.

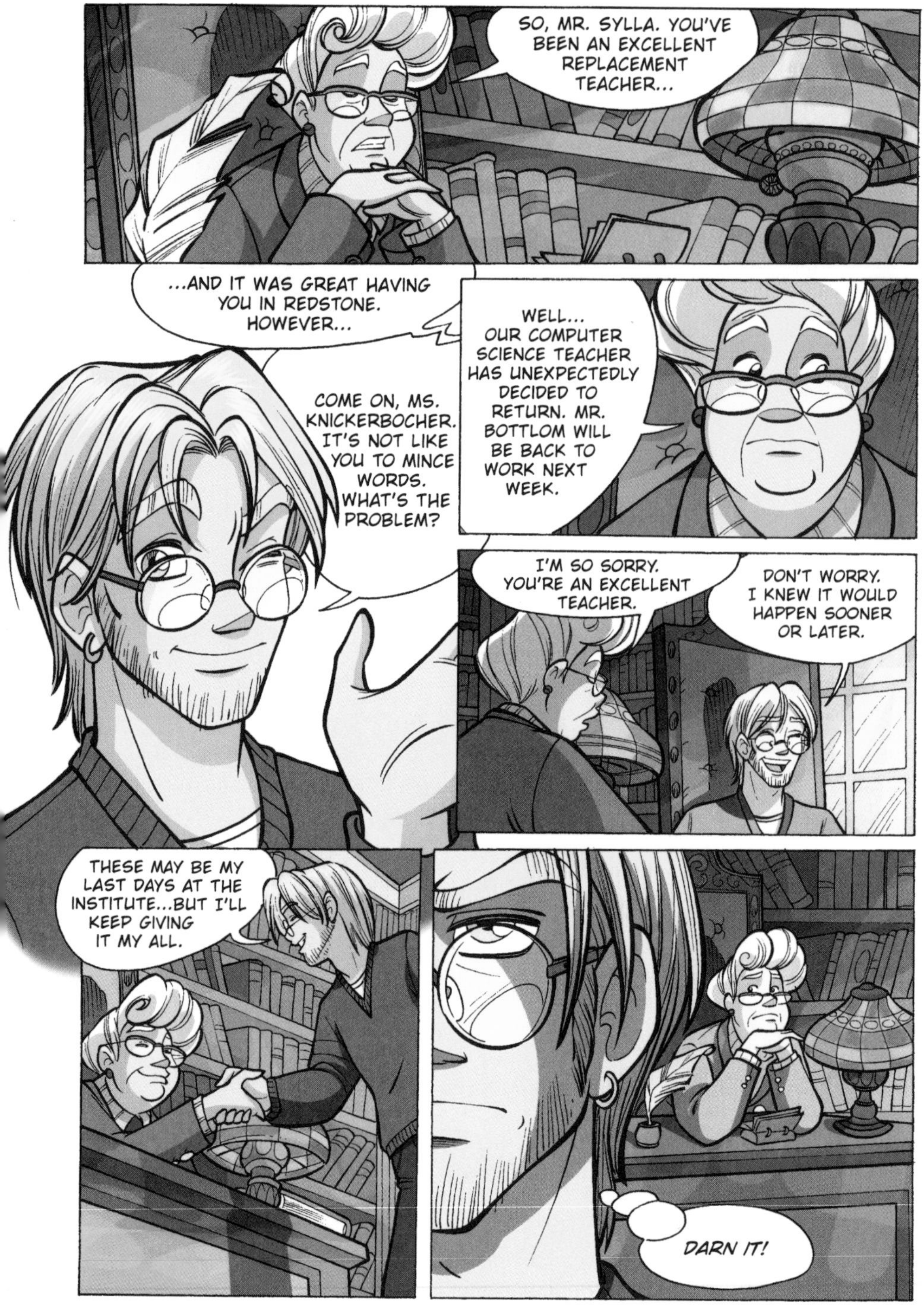
SO, MR. SYLLA. YOU'VE BEEN AN EXCELLENT REPLACEMENT TEACHER...
...AND IT WAS GREAT HAVING YOU IN REDSTONE. HOWEVER...
COME ON, MS. KNICKERBOCHER. IT'S NOT LIKE YOU TO MINCE WORDS. WHAT'S THE PROBLEM?
WELL... OUR COMPUTER SCIENCE TEACHER HAS UNEXPECTEDLY DECIDED TO RETURN. MR. BOTTLOM WILL BE BACK TO WORK NEXT WEEK.
I'M SO SORRY. YOU'RE AN EXCELLENT TEACHER.
DON'T WORRY. I KNEW IT WOULD HAPPEN SOONER OR LATER.
THESE MAY BE MY LAST DAYS AT THE INSTITUTE...BUT I'LL KEEP GIVING IT MY ALL.
DARN IT!

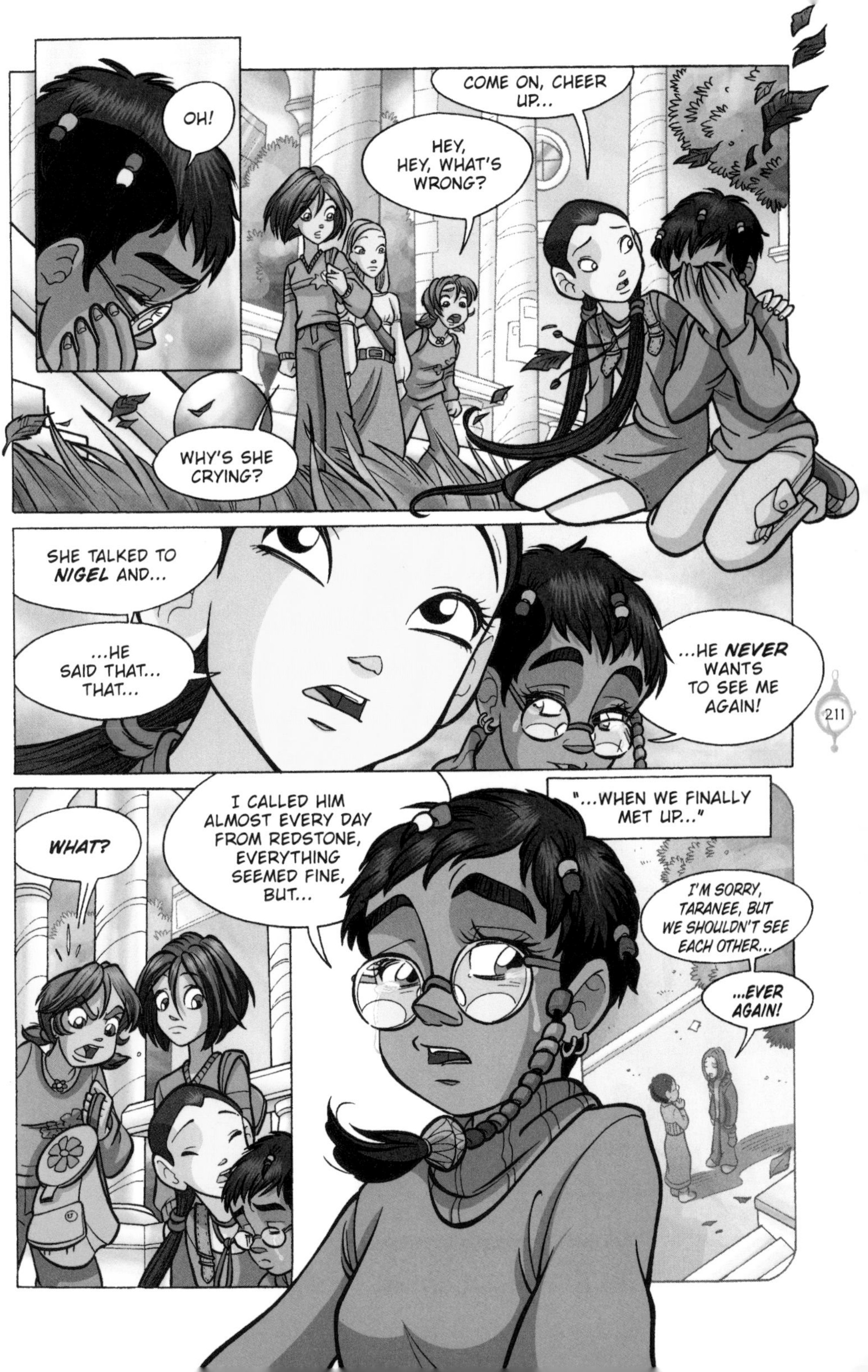
OH!
COME ON, CHEER UP...
HEY, HEY, WHAT'S WRONG?
WHY'S SHE CRYING?
SHE TALKED TO NIGEL AND...
...HE SAID THAT... THAT...
...HE NEVER WANTS TO SEE ME AGAIN!
WHAT?
I CALLED HIM ALMOST EVERY DAY FROM REDSTONE, EVERYTHING SEEMED FINE, BUT...
"...WHEN WE FINALLY MET UP..."
I'M SORRY, TARANEE, BUT WE SHOULDN'T SEE EACH OTHER...
...EVER AGAIN!

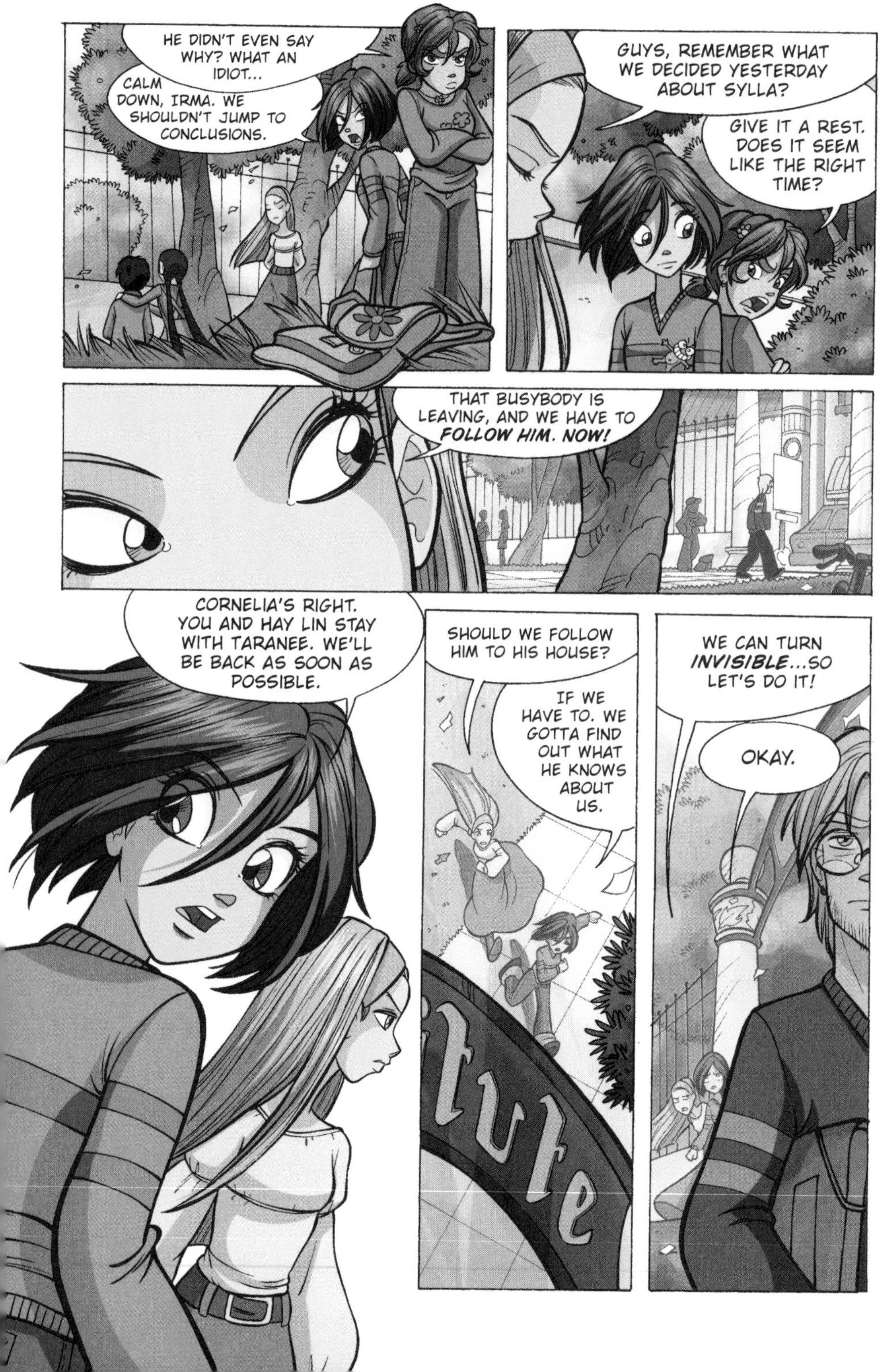
HE DIDN'T EVEN SAY WHY? WHAT AN IDIOT...
CALM DOWN, IRMA. WE SHOULDN'T JUMP TO CONCLUSIONS.
GUYS, REMEMBER WHAT WE DECIDED YESTERDAY ABOUT SYLLA?
GIVE IT A REST. DOES IT SEEM LIKE THE RIGHT TIME?
THAT BUSYBODY IS LEAVING, AND WE HAVE TO ***FOLLOW HIM. NOW!***
CORNELIA'S RIGHT. YOU AND HAY LIN STAY WITH TARANEE. WE'LL BE BACK AS SOON AS POSSIBLE.
SHOULD WE FOLLOW HIM TO HIS HOUSE?
IF WE HAVE TO. WE GOTTA FIND OUT WHAT HE KNOWS ABOUT US.
WE CAN TURN ***INVISIBLE***...SO LET'S DO IT!
OKAY.

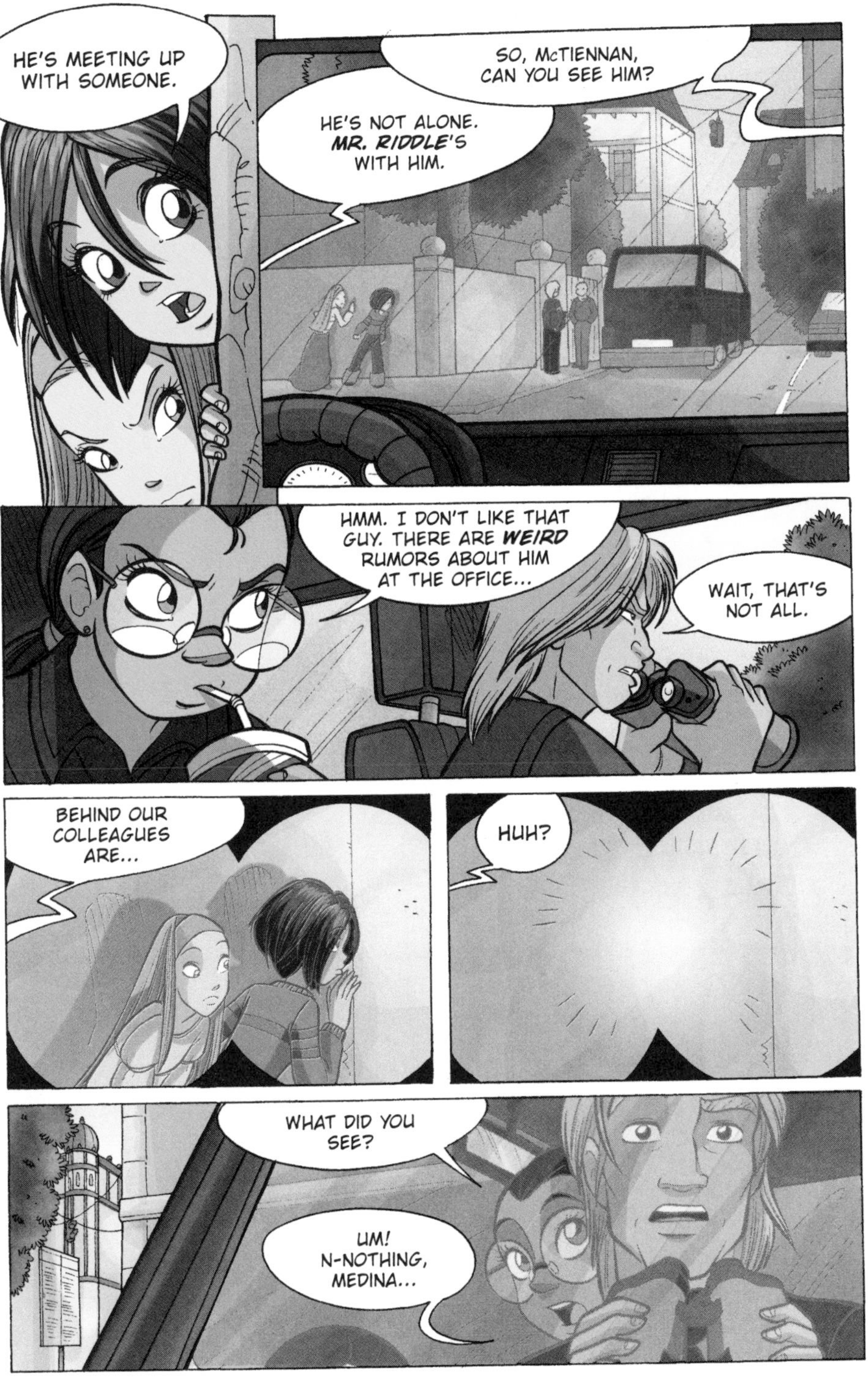
HE'S MEETING UP WITH SOMEONE.
SO, McTIENNAN, CAN YOU SEE HIM?
HE'S NOT ALONE. MR. RIDDLE'S WITH HIM.
HMM. I DON'T LIKE THAT GUY. THERE ARE WEIRD RUMORS ABOUT HIM AT THE OFFICE...
WAIT, THAT'S NOT ALL.
BEHIND OUR COLLEAGUES ARE...
HUH?
WHAT DID YOU SEE?
UM! N-NOTHING, MEDINA...

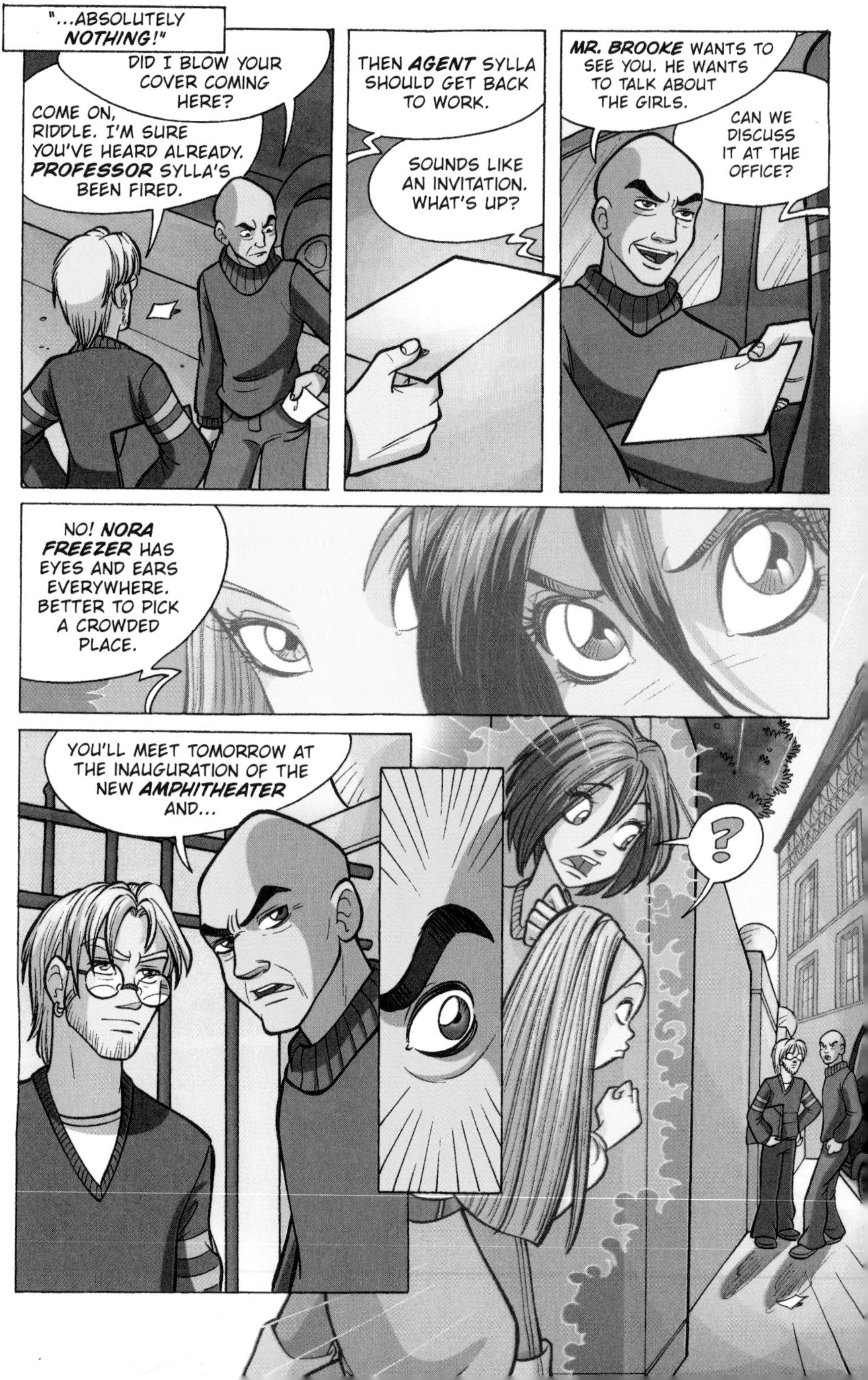
"...ABSOLUTELY NOTHING!"
DID I BLOW YOUR COVER COMING HERE?
COME ON, RIDDLE. I'M SURE YOU'VE HEARD ALREADY. PROFESSOR SYLLA'S BEEN FIRED.
THEN AGENT SYLLA SHOULD GET BACK TO WORK.
SOUNDS LIKE AN INVITATION. WHAT'S UP?
MR. BROOKE WANTS TO SEE YOU. HE WANTS TO TALK ABOUT THE GIRLS.
CAN WE DISCUSS IT AT THE OFFICE?
NO! NORA FREEZER HAS EYES AND EARS EVERYWHERE. BETTER TO PICK A CROWDED PLACE.
YOU'LL MEET TOMORROW AT THE INAUGURATION OF THE NEW AMPHITHEATER AND...
?

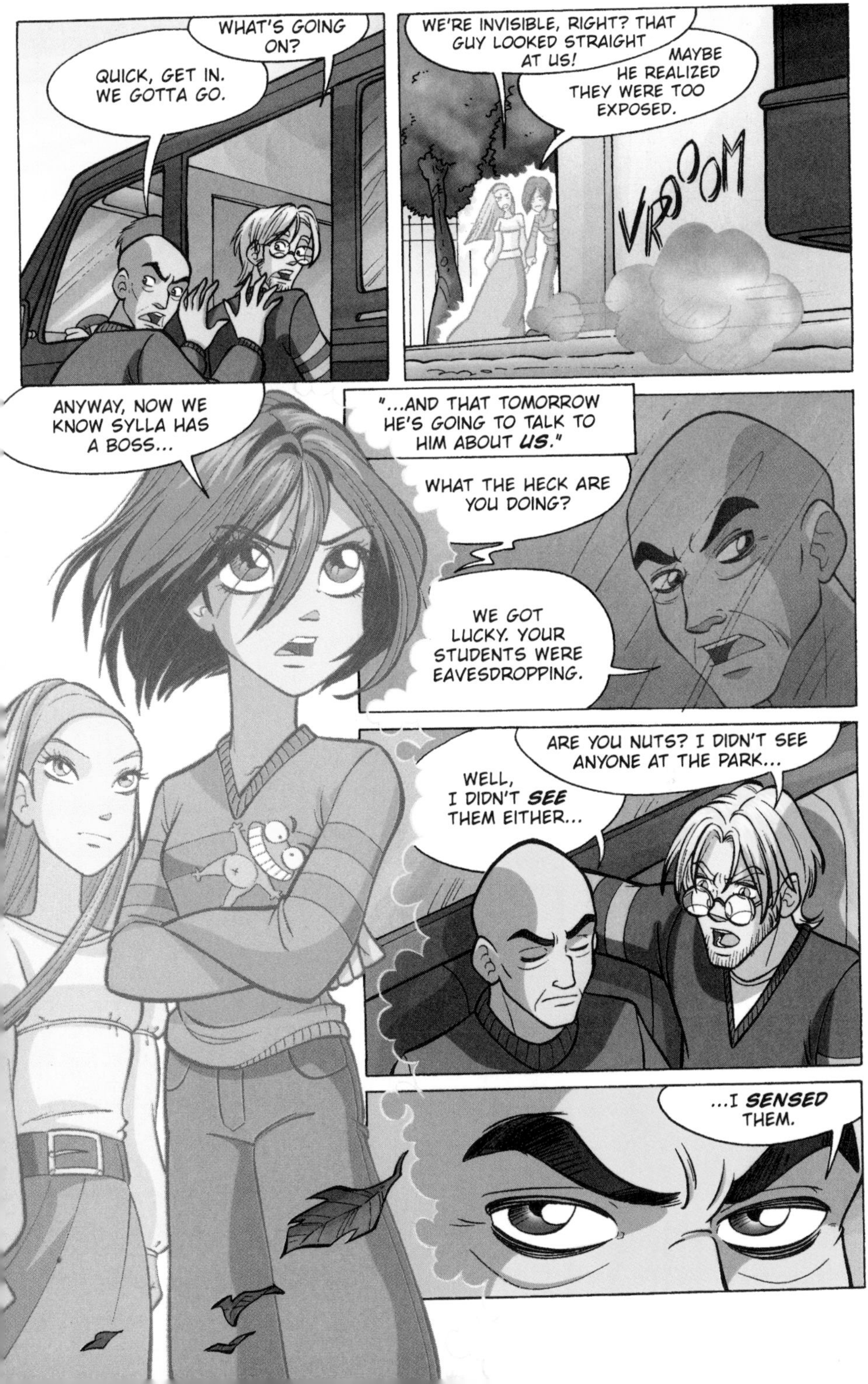
WHAT'S GOING ON?
QUICK, GET IN. WE GOTTA GO.
WE'RE INVISIBLE, RIGHT? THAT GUY LOOKED STRAIGHT AT US!
MAYBE HE REALIZED THEY WERE TOO EXPOSED.
VROOOM
ANYWAY, NOW WE KNOW SYLLA HAS A BOSS...
"...AND THAT TOMORROW HE'S GOING TO TALK TO HIM ABOUT **US**."
WHAT THE HECK ARE YOU DOING?
WE GOT LUCKY. YOUR STUDENTS WERE EAVESDROPPING.
ARE YOU NUTS? I DIDN'T SEE ANYONE AT THE PARK...
WELL, I DIDN'T **SEE** THEM EITHER...
...I **SENSED** THEM.

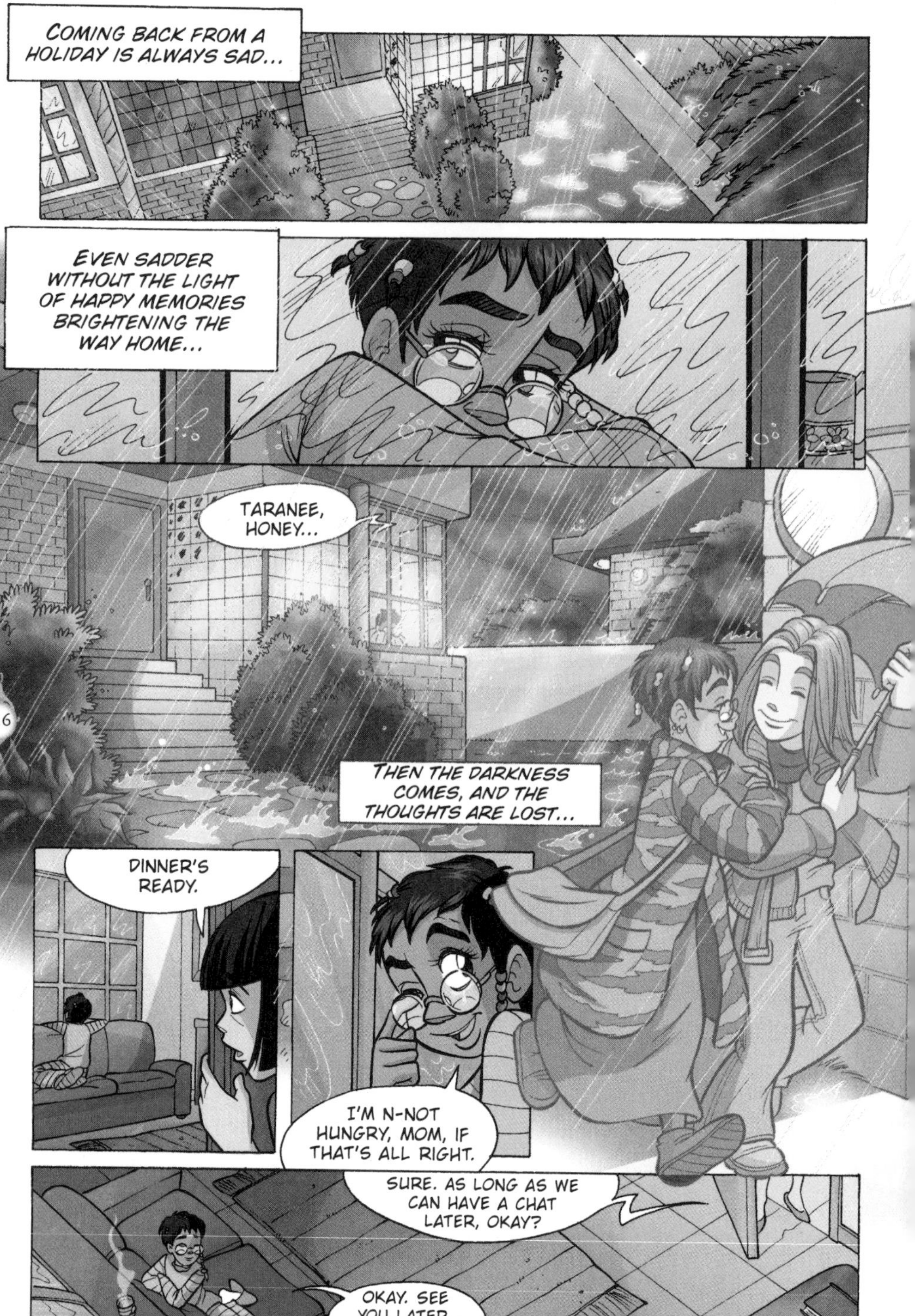

COMING BACK FROM A HOLIDAY IS ALWAYS SAD...
EVEN SADDER WITHOUT THE LIGHT OF HAPPY MEMORIES BRIGHTENING THE WAY HOME...
TARANEE, HONEY...
THEN THE DARKNESS COMES, AND THE THOUGHTS ARE LOST...
DINNER'S READY.
I'M N-NOT HUNGRY, MOM, IF THAT'S ALL RIGHT.
SURE. AS LONG AS WE CAN HAVE A CHAT LATER, OKAY?
OKAY. SEE YOU LATER.

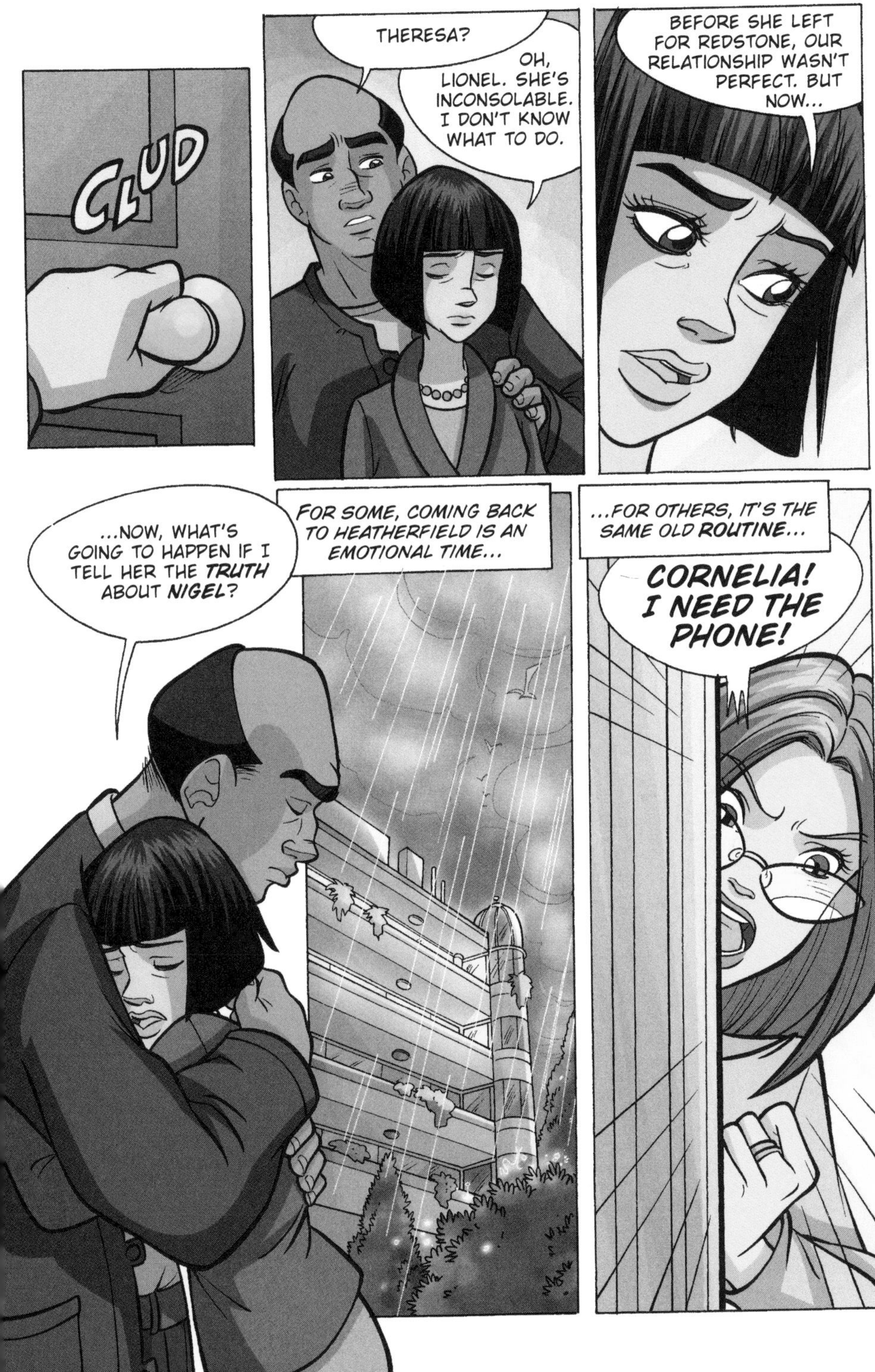
CLUD
THERESA?
OH, LIONEL. SHE'S INCONSOLABLE. I DON'T KNOW WHAT TO DO.
BEFORE SHE LEFT FOR REDSTONE, OUR RELATIONSHIP WASN'T PERFECT. BUT NOW...
...NOW, WHAT'S GOING TO HAPPEN IF I TELL HER THE TRUTH ABOUT NIGEL?
FOR SOME, COMING BACK TO HEATHERFIELD IS AN EMOTIONAL TIME...
...FOR OTHERS, IT'S THE SAME OLD ROUTINE...
CORNELIA! I NEED THE PHONE!

OKAY, I'M HANGING UP NOW!

AND BY "NOW," YOU MEAN *NOW* NOW OR NOW *TOMORROW*?

WITH NOT SO SUBTLE WORDPLAY, MY MOM'S LETTING ME KNOW I NEED TO GO.

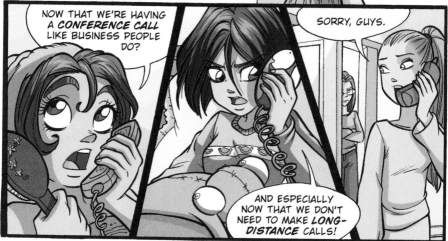

NOW THAT WE'RE HAVING A *CONFERENCE CALL* LIKE BUSINESS PEOPLE DO?

SORRY, GUYS.

AND ESPECIALLY NOW THAT WE DON'T NEED TO MAKE *LONG-DISTANCE* CALLS!

NEVER MIND. AT LEAST WE DECIDED WHAT TO DO ABOUT *SYLLA AND HIS GANG.*

If the others agree, of course.

WHEN HE MEETS HIS BOSS TOMORROW, *WE'LL BE THERE!*

I VOTE FOR ANOTHER MEETING AT MS. RUDOLPH'S HOUSE. WHADDAYA SAY?

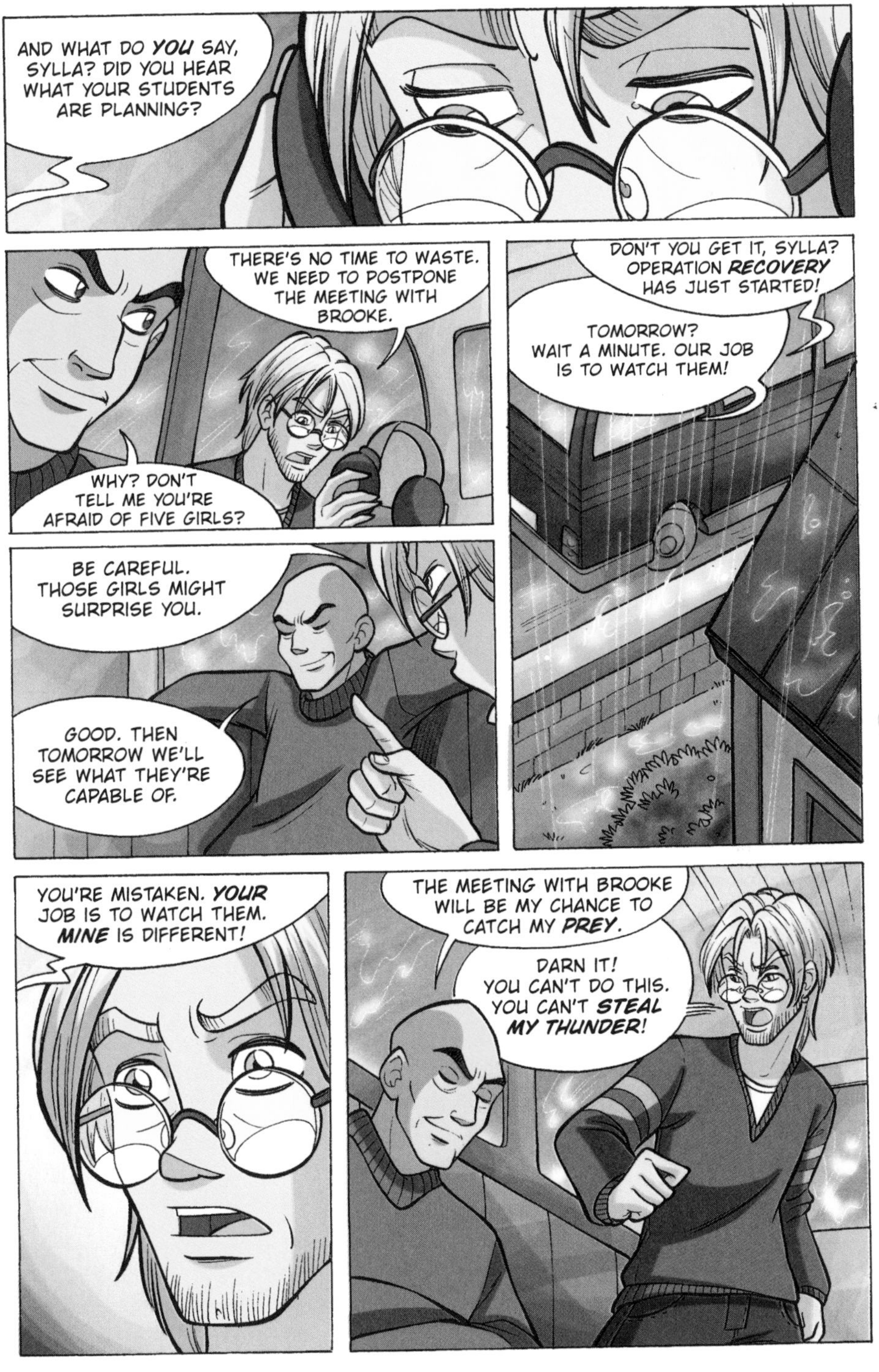
AND WHAT DO *YOU* SAY, SYLLA? DID YOU HEAR WHAT YOUR STUDENTS ARE PLANNING?
THERE'S NO TIME TO WASTE. WE NEED TO POSTPONE THE MEETING WITH BROOKE.
WHY? DON'T TELL ME YOU'RE AFRAID OF FIVE GIRLS?
DON'T YOU GET IT, SYLLA? OPERATION *RECOVERY* HAS JUST STARTED!
TOMORROW? WAIT A MINUTE. OUR JOB IS TO WATCH THEM!
BE CAREFUL. THOSE GIRLS MIGHT SURPRISE YOU.
GOOD. THEN TOMORROW WE'LL SEE WHAT THEY'RE CAPABLE OF.
YOU'RE MISTAKEN. *YOUR* JOB IS TO WATCH THEM. *MINE* IS DIFFERENT!
THE MEETING WITH BROOKE WILL BE MY CHANCE TO CATCH MY *PREY*.
DARN IT! YOU CAN'T DO THIS. YOU CAN'T *STEAL MY THUNDER*!

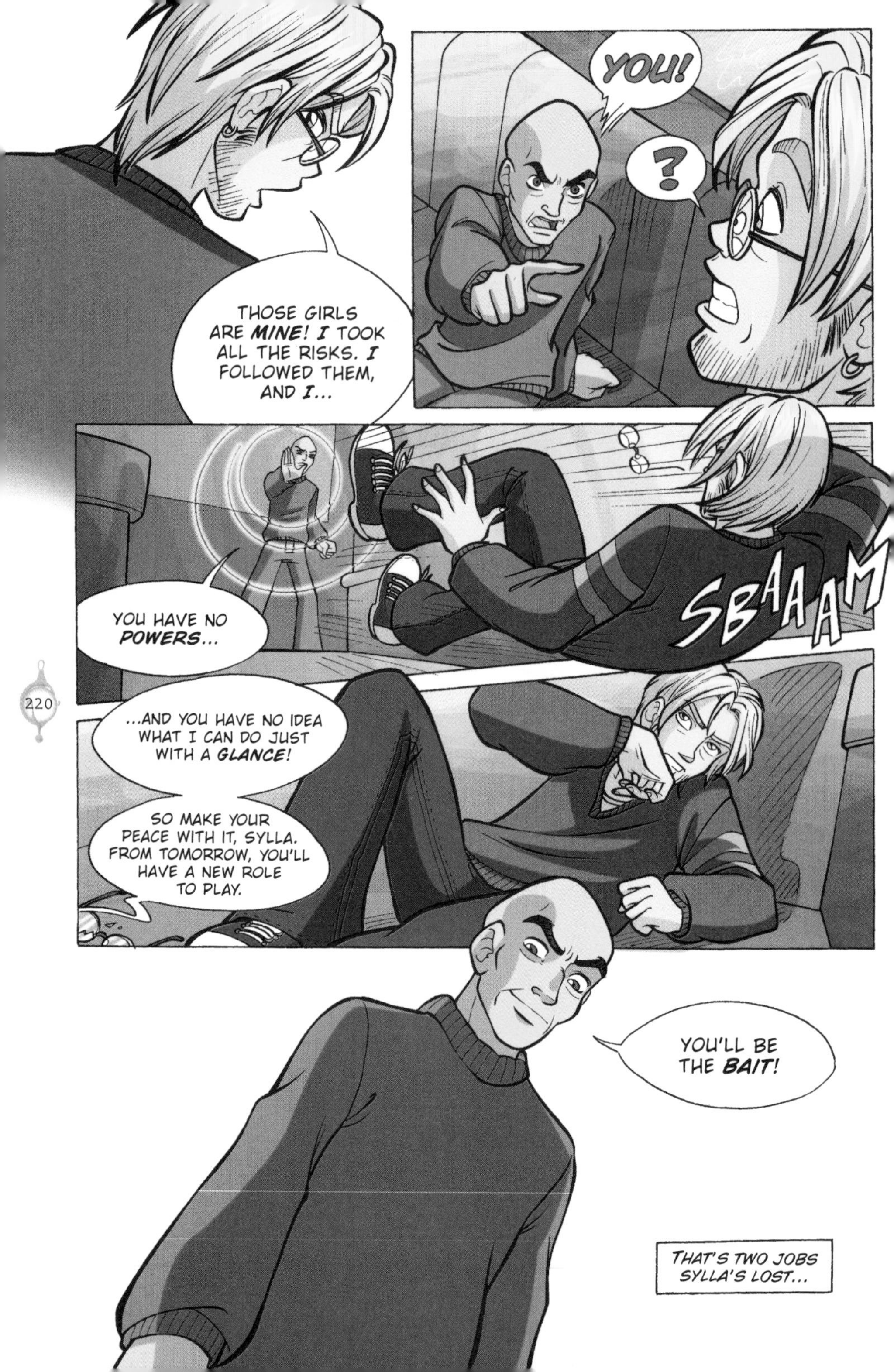
YOU!
?
THOSE GIRLS ARE MINE! I TOOK ALL THE RISKS. I FOLLOWED THEM, AND I...
YOU HAVE NO POWERS...
SBAAAAM
...AND YOU HAVE NO IDEA WHAT I CAN DO JUST WITH A GLANCE!
SO MAKE YOUR PEACE WITH IT, SYLLA. FROM TOMORROW, YOU'LL HAVE A NEW ROLE TO PLAY.
YOU'LL BE THE BAIT!
THAT'S TWO JOBS SYLLA'S LOST...

W.i.t.c.h.

Will Irma Taranee Cornelia Hay Lin

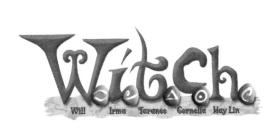

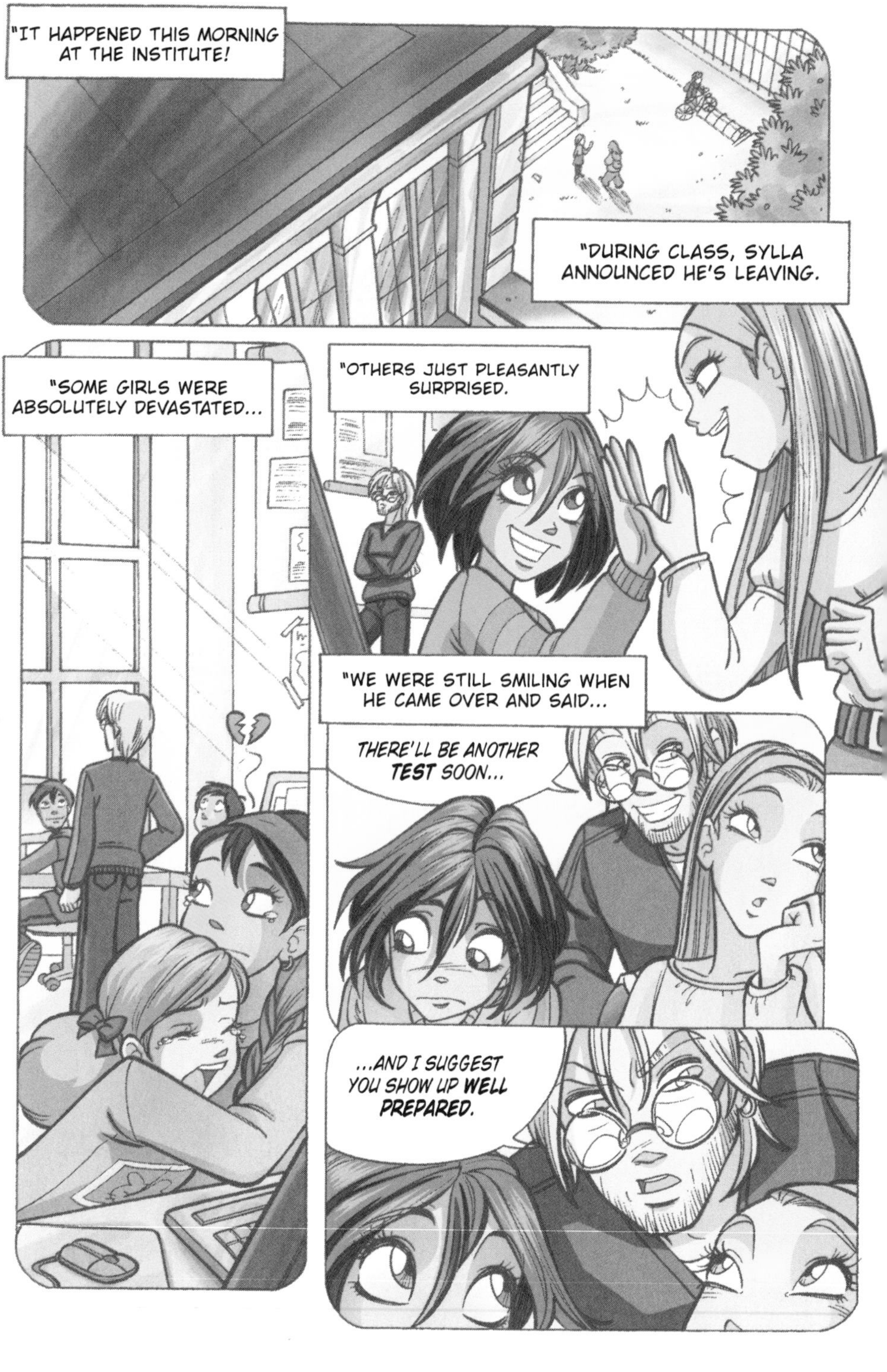
"IT HAPPENED THIS MORNING AT THE INSTITUTE!
"DURING CLASS, SYLLA ANNOUNCED HE'S LEAVING.
"SOME GIRLS WERE ABSOLUTELY DEVASTATED...
"OTHERS JUST PLEASANTLY SURPRISED.
"WE WERE STILL SMILING WHEN HE CAME OVER AND SAID...
THERE'LL BE ANOTHER TEST SOON...
...AND I SUGGEST YOU SHOW UP WELL PREPARED.

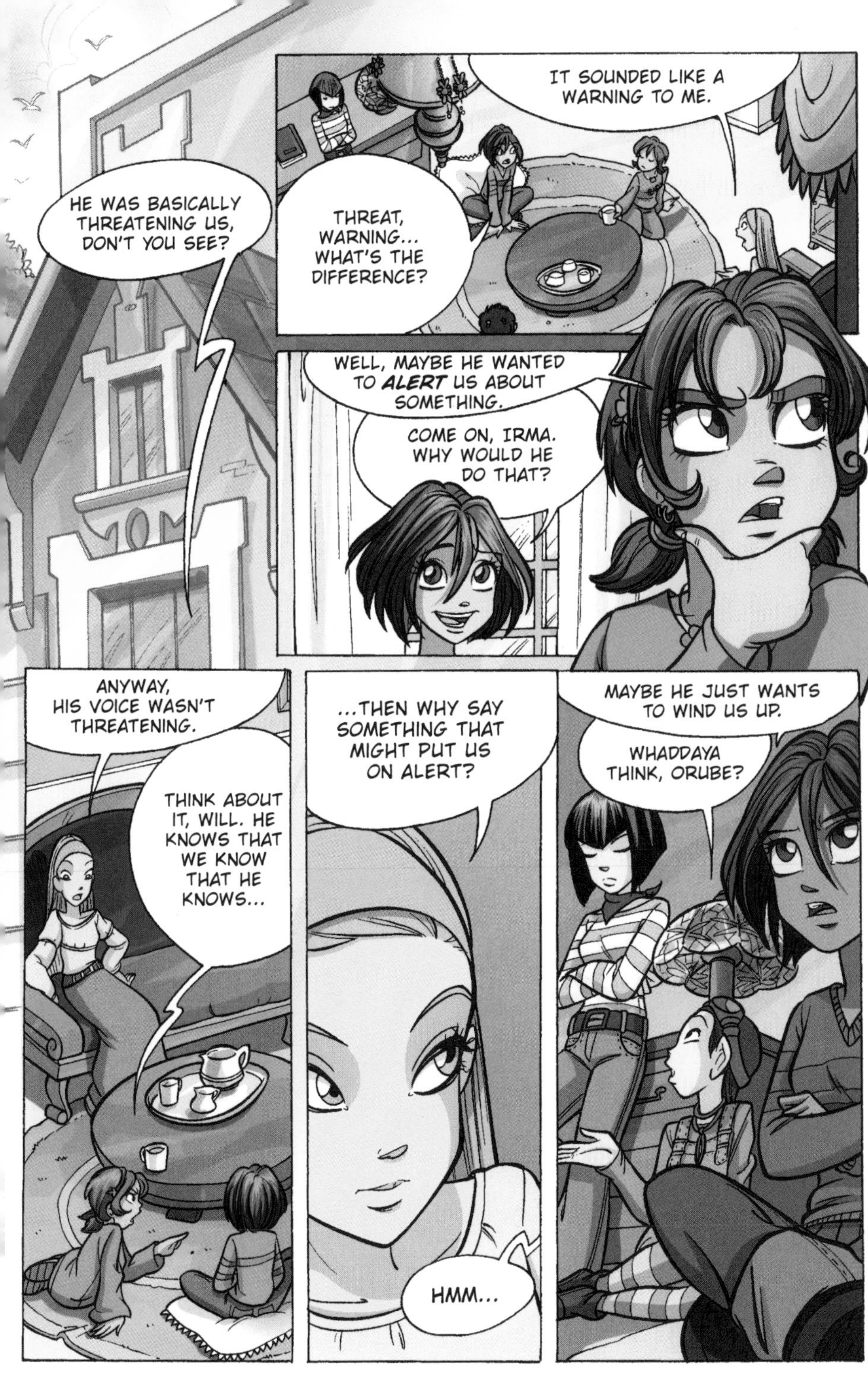

HE WAS BASICALLY THREATENING US, DON'T YOU SEE?
IT SOUNDED LIKE A WARNING TO ME.
THREAT, WARNING... WHAT'S THE DIFFERENCE?
WELL, MAYBE HE WANTED TO ALERT US ABOUT SOMETHING.
COME ON, IRMA. WHY WOULD HE DO THAT?
ANYWAY, HIS VOICE WASN'T THREATENING.
THINK ABOUT IT, WILL. HE KNOWS THAT WE KNOW THAT HE KNOWS...
...THEN WHY SAY SOMETHING THAT MIGHT PUT US ON ALERT?
HMM...
MAYBE HE JUST WANTS TO WIND US UP.
WHADDAYA THINK, ORUBE?

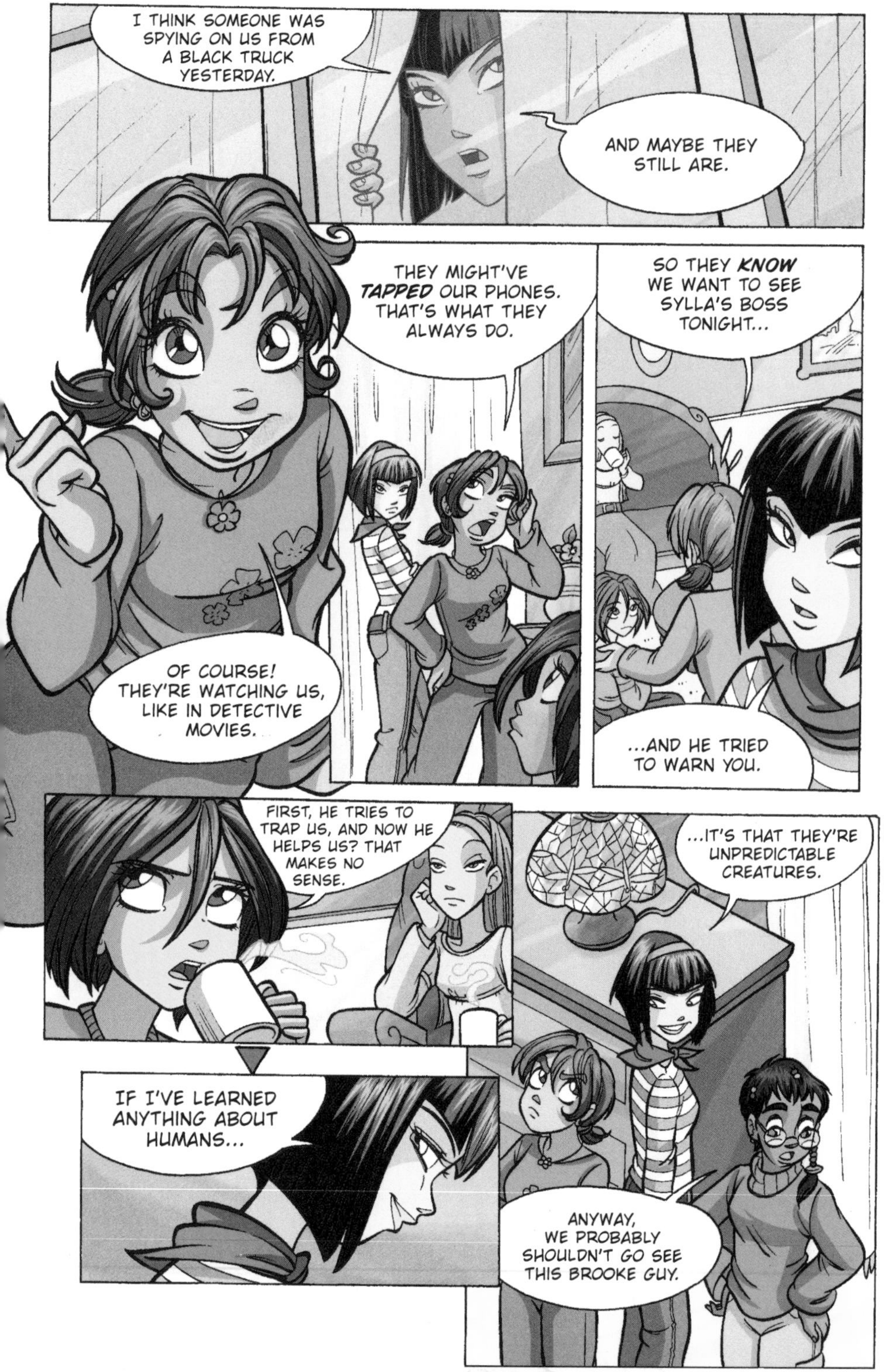
I THINK SOMEONE WAS SPYING ON US FROM A BLACK TRUCK YESTERDAY.
AND MAYBE THEY STILL ARE.
OF COURSE! THEY'RE WATCHING US, LIKE IN DETECTIVE MOVIES.
THEY MIGHT'VE *TAPPED* OUR PHONES. THAT'S WHAT THEY ALWAYS DO.
SO THEY ***KNOW*** WE WANT TO SEE SYLLA'S BOSS TONIGHT...
...AND HE TRIED TO WARN YOU.
FIRST, HE TRIES TO TRAP US, AND NOW HE HELPS US? THAT MAKES NO SENSE.
IF I'VE LEARNED ANYTHING ABOUT HUMANS...
...IT'S THAT THEY'RE UNPREDICTABLE CREATURES.
ANYWAY, WE PROBABLY SHOULDN'T GO SEE THIS BROOKE GUY.

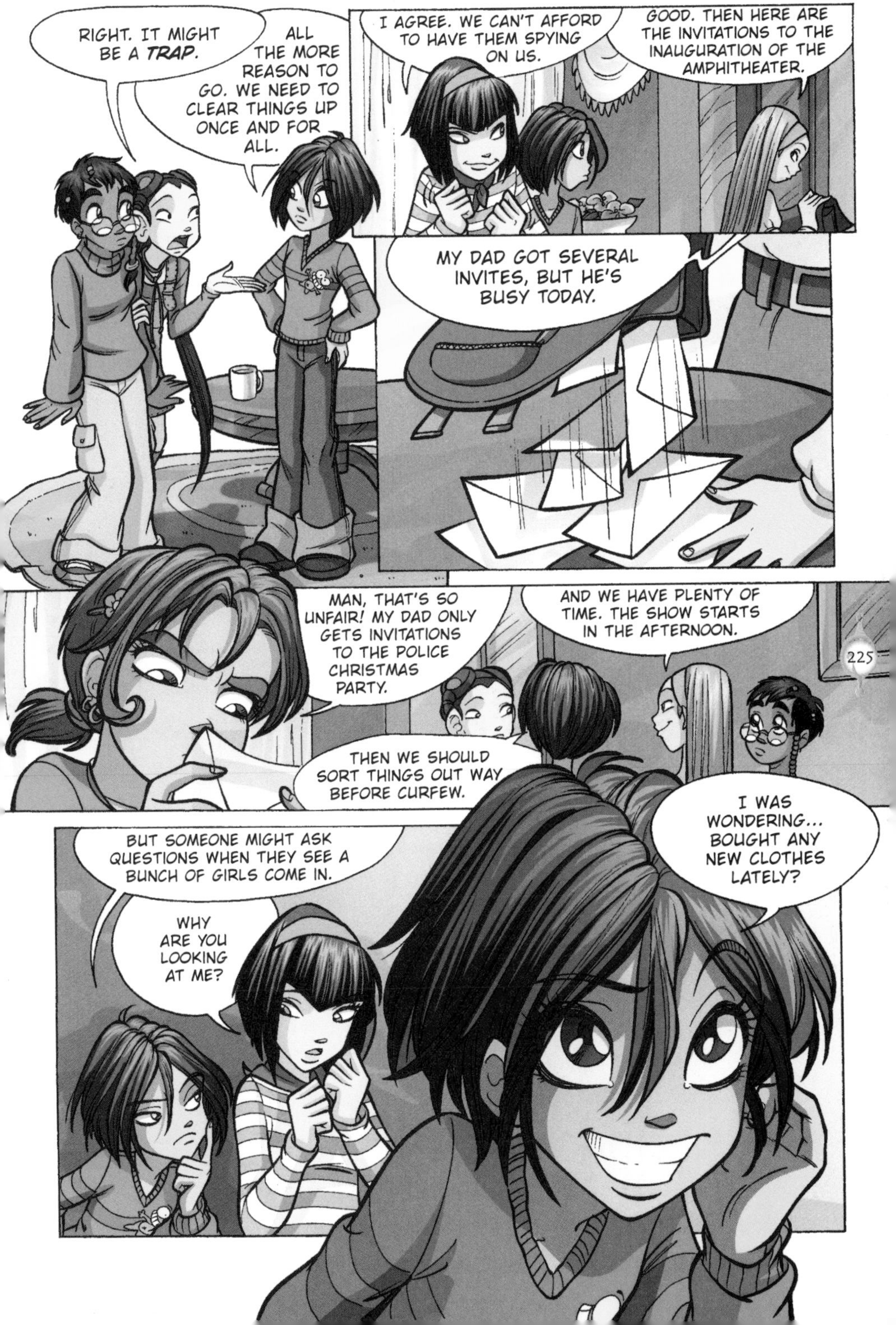
RIGHT. IT MIGHT BE A TRAP.
ALL THE MORE REASON TO GO. WE NEED TO CLEAR THINGS UP ONCE AND FOR ALL.
I AGREE. WE CAN'T AFFORD TO HAVE THEM SPYING ON US.
GOOD. THEN HERE ARE THE INVITATIONS TO THE INAUGURATION OF THE AMPHITHEATER.
MY DAD GOT SEVERAL INVITES, BUT HE'S BUSY TODAY.
MAN, THAT'S SO UNFAIR! MY DAD ONLY GETS INVITATIONS TO THE POLICE CHRISTMAS PARTY.
AND WE HAVE PLENTY OF TIME. THE SHOW STARTS IN THE AFTERNOON.
THEN WE SHOULD SORT THINGS OUT WAY BEFORE CURFEW.
BUT SOMEONE MIGHT ASK QUESTIONS WHEN THEY SEE A BUNCH OF GIRLS COME IN.
WHY ARE YOU LOOKING AT ME?
I WAS WONDERING... BOUGHT ANY NEW CLOTHES LATELY?

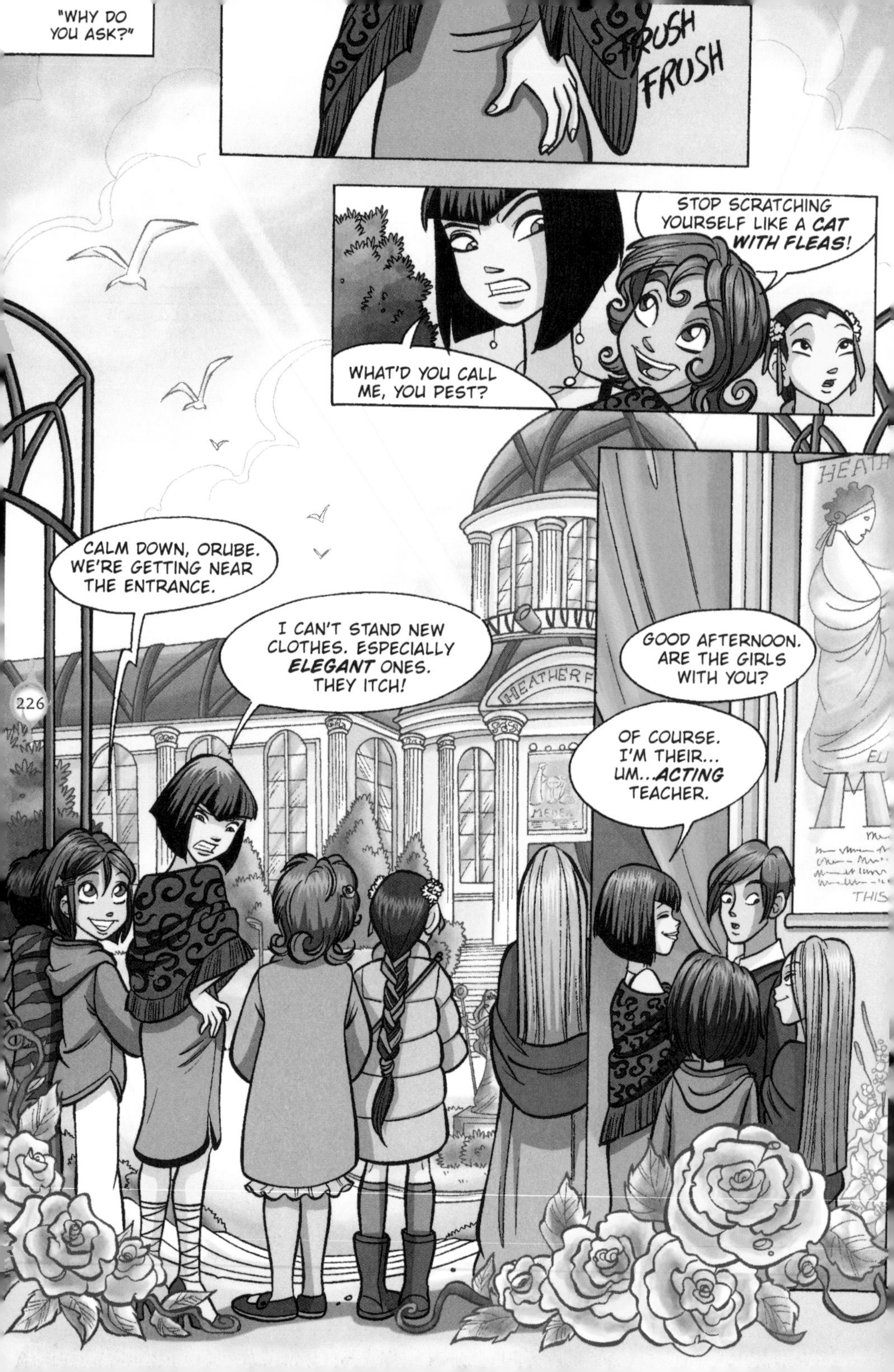
"WHY DO YOU ASK?"
FRUSH FRUSH
STOP SCRATCHING YOURSELF LIKE A CAT WITH FLEAS!
WHAT'D YOU CALL ME, YOU PEST?
CALM DOWN, ORUBE. WE'RE GETTING NEAR THE ENTRANCE.
I CAN'T STAND NEW CLOTHES. ESPECIALLY ELEGANT ONES. THEY ITCH!
GOOD AFTERNOON. ARE THE GIRLS WITH YOU?
OF COURSE. I'M THEIR... UM...ACTING TEACHER.

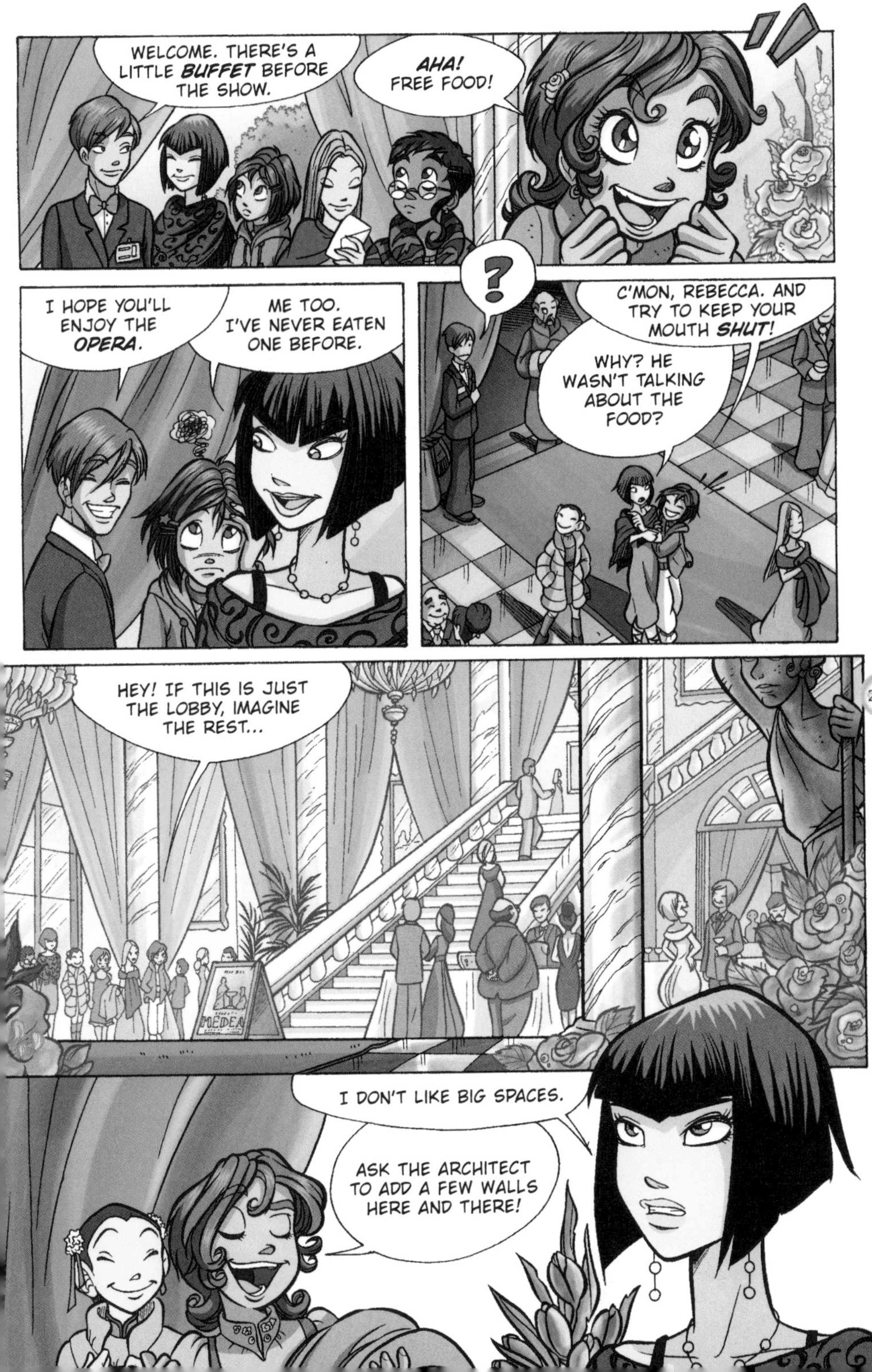
WELCOME. THERE'S A LITTLE BUFFET BEFORE THE SHOW.
AHA! FREE FOOD!
I HOPE YOU'LL ENJOY THE OPERA.
ME TOO. I'VE NEVER EATEN ONE BEFORE.
?
C'MON, REBECCA. AND TRY TO KEEP YOUR MOUTH SHUT!
WHY? HE WASN'T TALKING ABOUT THE FOOD?
HEY! IF THIS IS JUST THE LOBBY, IMAGINE THE REST...
MEDEA
I DON'T LIKE BIG SPACES.
ASK THE ARCHITECT TO ADD A FEW WALLS HERE AND THERE!

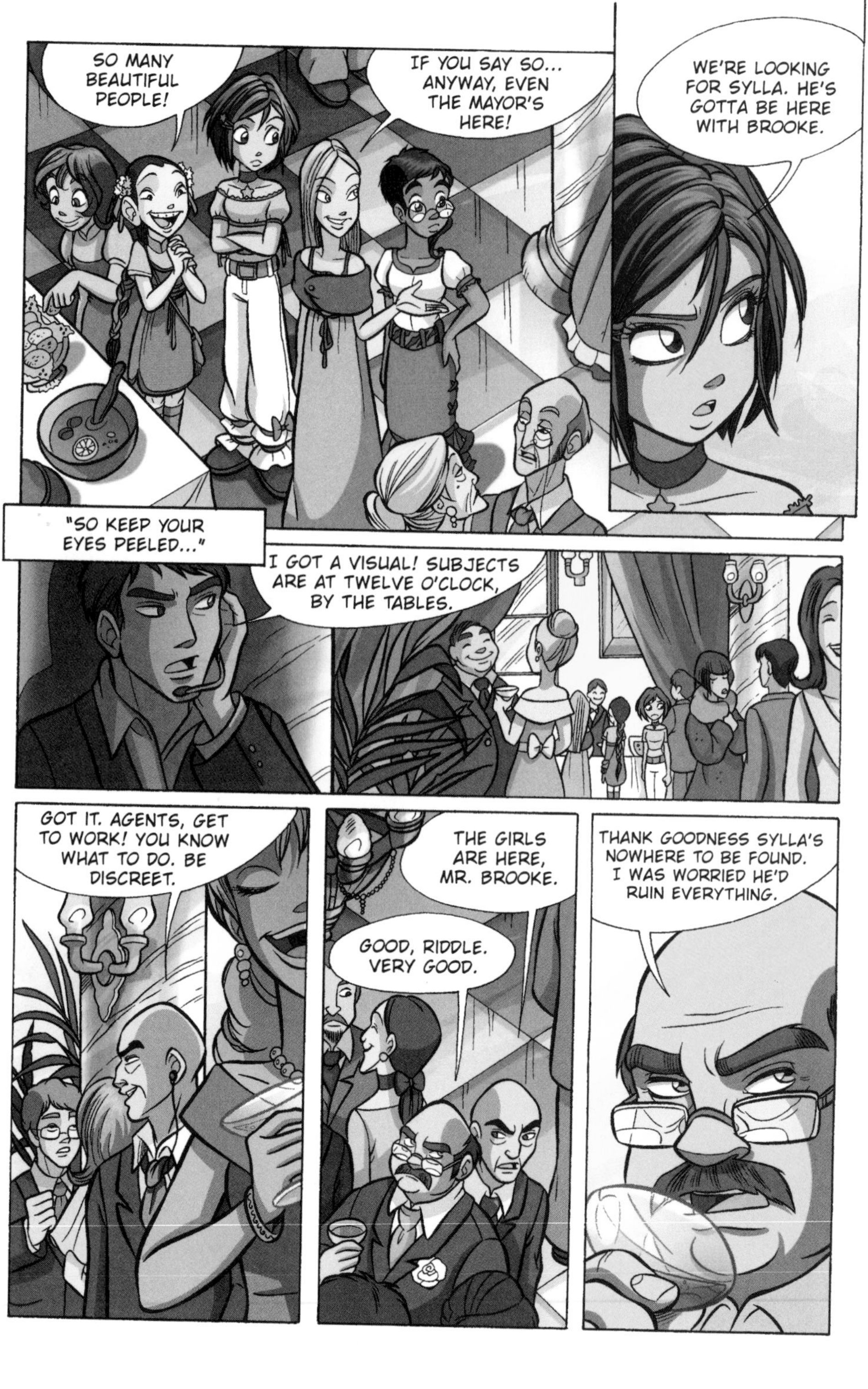

SO MANY BEAUTIFUL PEOPLE!
IF YOU SAY SO... ANYWAY, EVEN THE MAYOR'S HERE!
WE'RE LOOKING FOR SYLLA. HE'S GOTTA BE HERE WITH BROOKE.
"SO KEEP YOUR EYES PEELED..."
I GOT A VISUAL! SUBJECTS ARE AT TWELVE O'CLOCK, BY THE TABLES.
GOT IT. AGENTS, GET TO WORK! YOU KNOW WHAT TO DO. BE DISCREET.
THE GIRLS ARE HERE, MR. BROOKE.
GOOD, RIDDLE. VERY GOOD.
THANK GOODNESS SYLLA'S NOWHERE TO BE FOUND. I WAS WORRIED HE'D RUIN EVERYTHING.

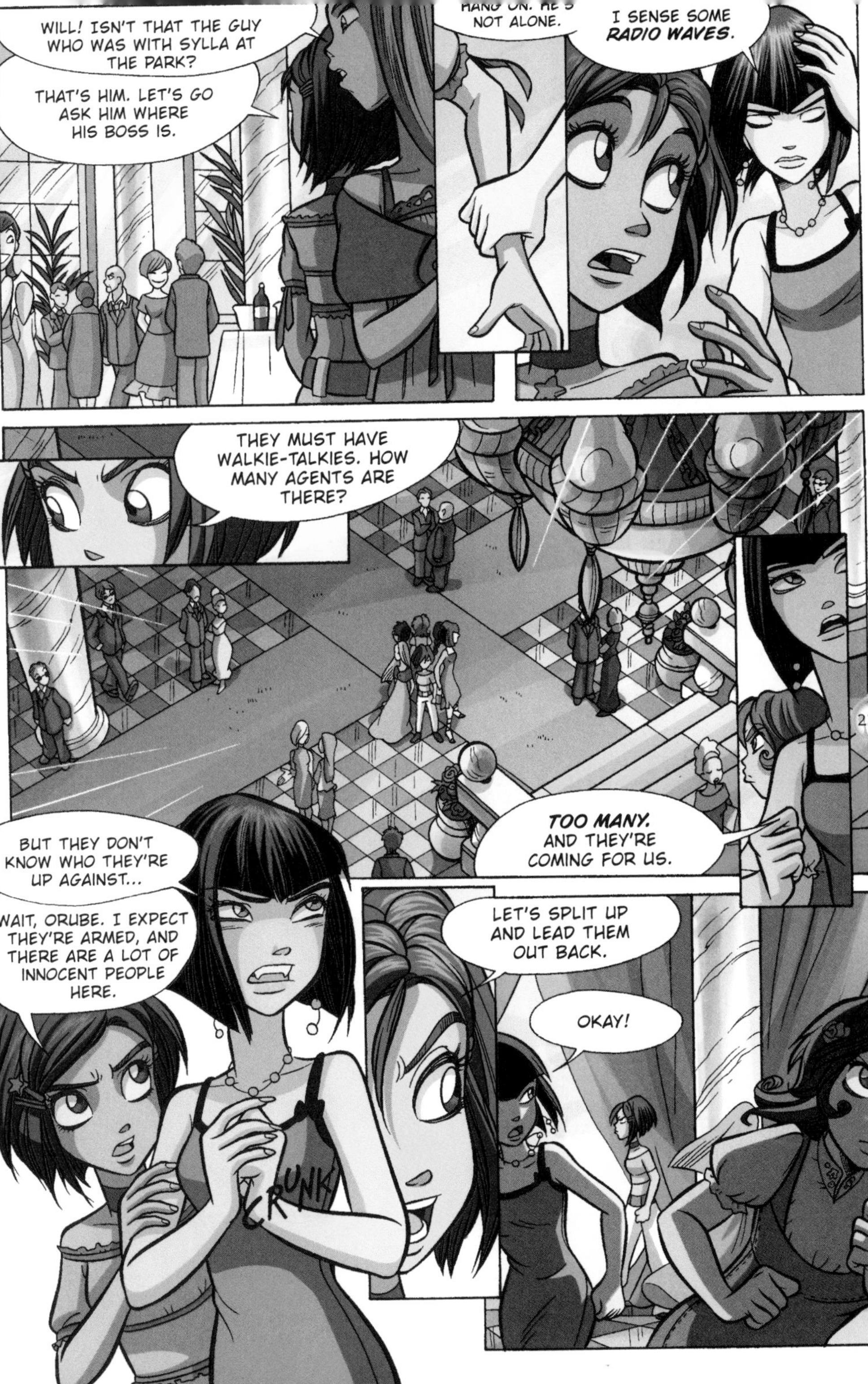
WILL! ISN'T THAT THE GUY WHO WAS WITH SYLLA AT THE PARK?
THAT'S HIM. LET'S GO ASK HIM WHERE HIS BOSS IS.
NOT ALONE.
I SENSE SOME *RADIO WAVES*.
THEY MUST HAVE WALKIE-TALKIES. HOW MANY AGENTS ARE THERE?
TOO MANY. AND THEY'RE COMING FOR US.
BUT THEY DON'T KNOW WHO THEY'RE UP AGAINST...
WAIT, ORUBE. I EXPECT THEY'RE ARMED, AND THERE ARE A LOT OF INNOCENT PEOPLE HERE.
CRUNK
LET'S SPLIT UP AND LEAD THEM OUT BACK.
OKAY!

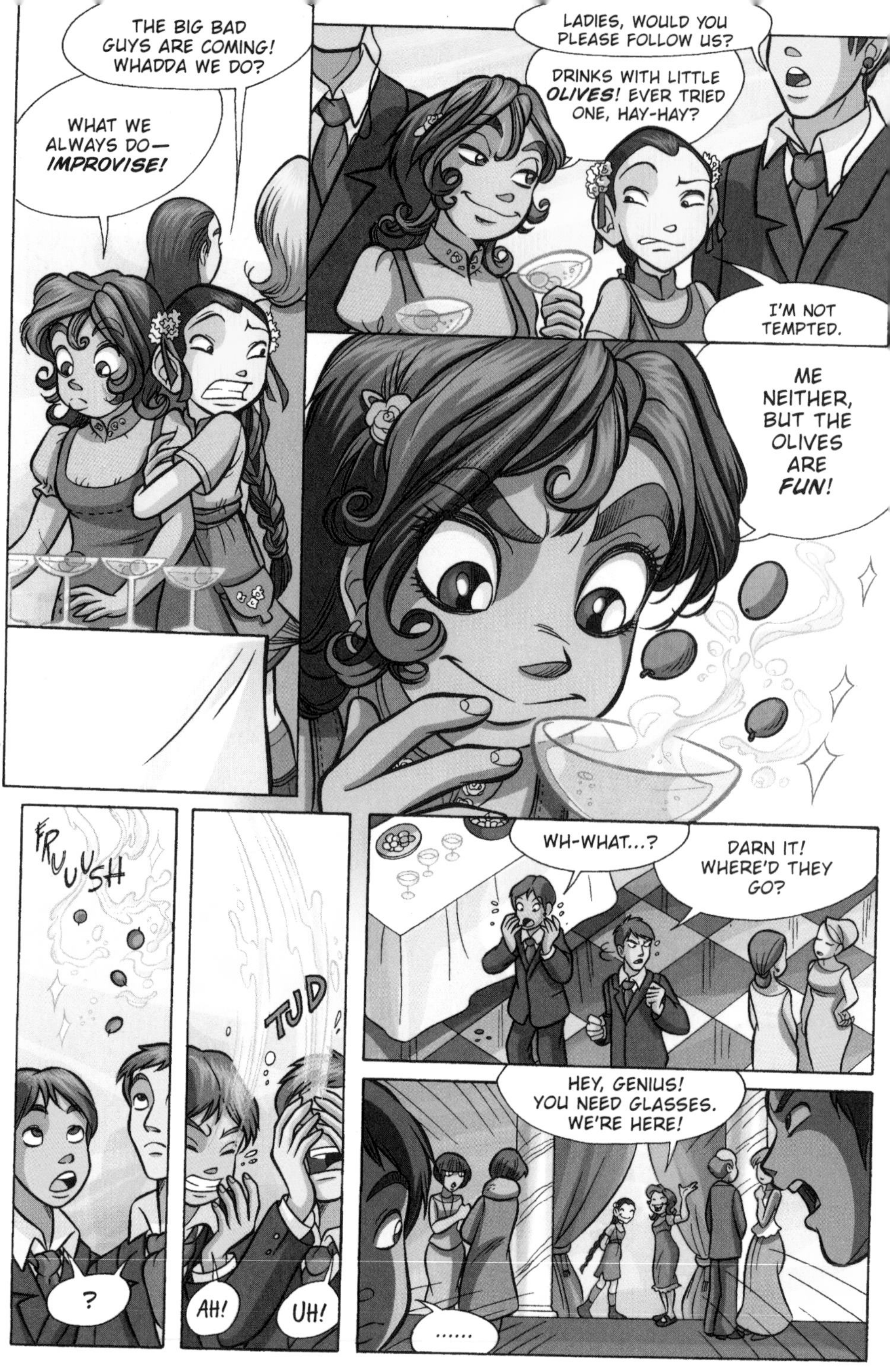
THE BIG BAD GUYS ARE COMING! WHADDA WE DO?
WHAT WE ALWAYS DO— *IMPROVISE!*
LADIES, WOULD YOU PLEASE FOLLOW US?
DRINKS WITH LITTLE *OLIVES!* EVER TRIED ONE, HAY-HAY?
I'M NOT TEMPTED.
ME NEITHER, BUT THE OLIVES ARE *FUN!*
FRUUUSH
TUD
?
AH!
UH!
WH-WHAT...?
DARN IT! WHERE'D THEY GO?
HEY, GENIUS! YOU NEED GLASSES. WE'RE HERE!
......

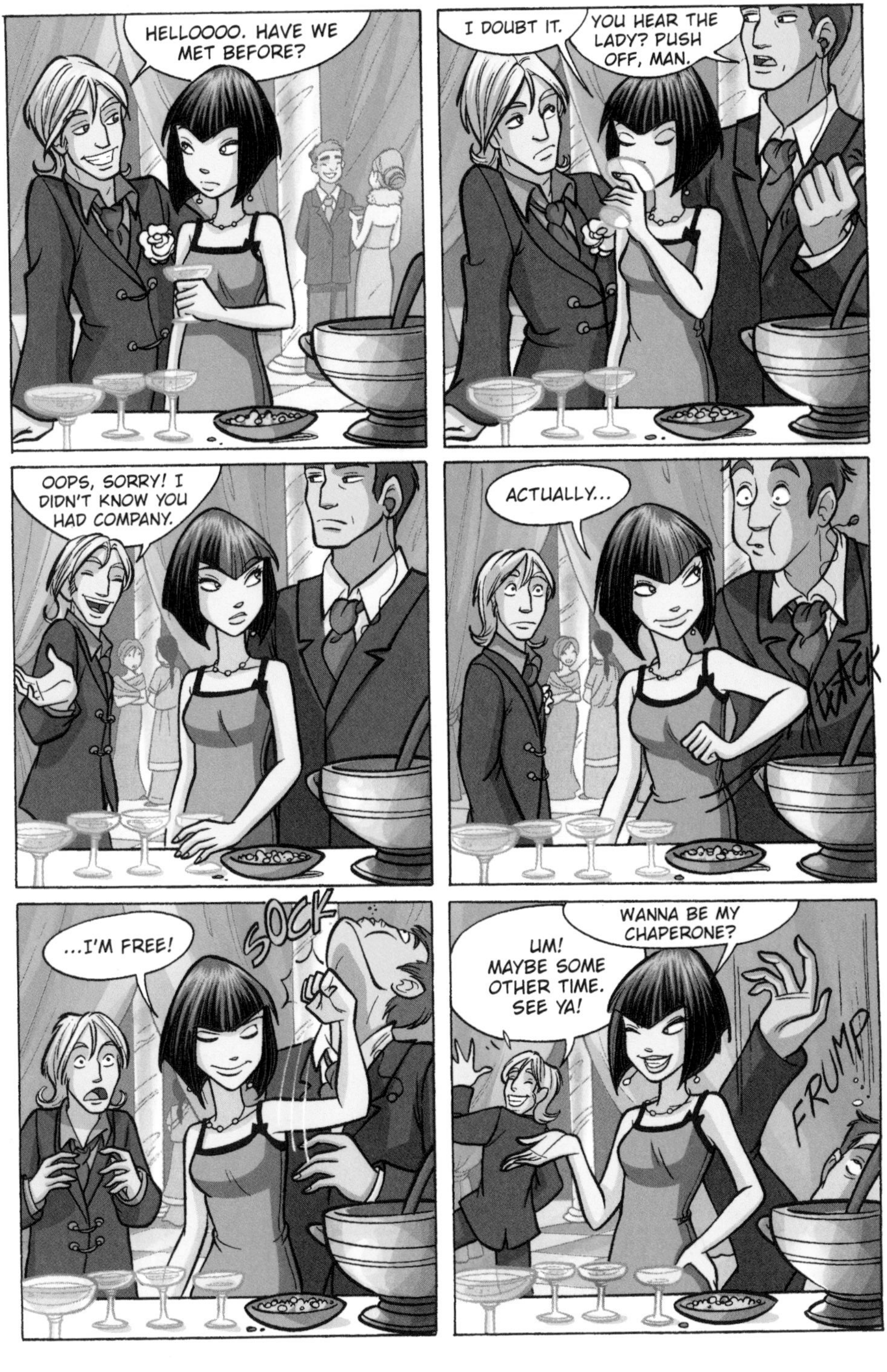
HELLOOOO. HAVE WE MET BEFORE?
I DOUBT IT.
YOU HEAR THE LADY? PUSH OFF, MAN.
OOPS, SORRY! I DIDN'T KNOW YOU HAD COMPANY.
ACTUALLY...
WHACK
...I'M FREE!
SOCK
WANNA BE MY CHAPERONE?
UM! MAYBE SOME OTHER TIME. SEE YA!
FRUMP

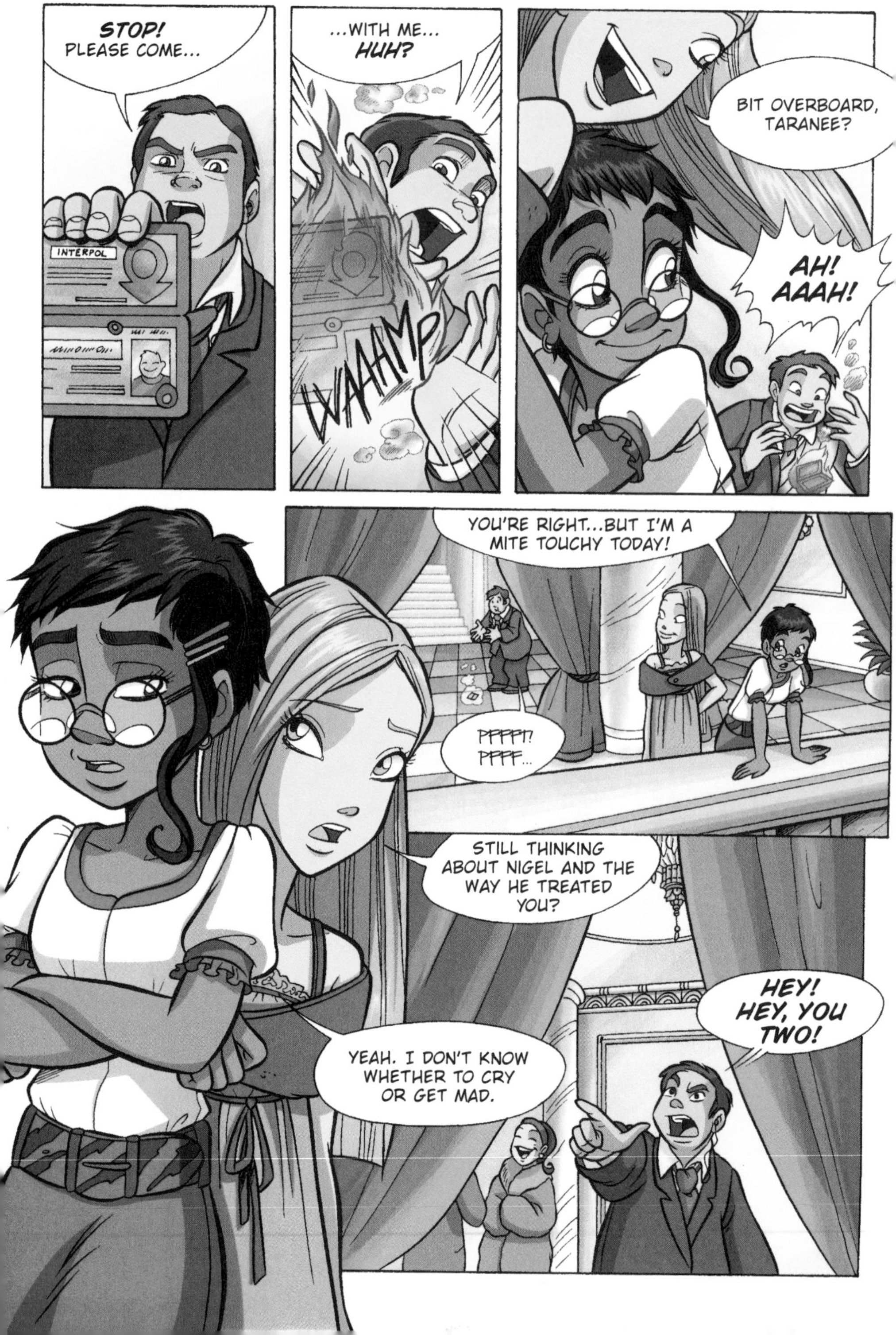
STOP! PLEASE COME...
...WITH ME... HUH?
WAAAMP
BIT OVERBOARD, TARANEE?
AH! AAAH!
YOU'RE RIGHT...BUT I'M A MITE TOUCHY TODAY!
PFFFT! PFFF...
STILL THINKING ABOUT NIGEL AND THE WAY HE TREATED YOU?
YEAH. I DON'T KNOW WHETHER TO CRY OR GET MAD.
HEY! HEY, YOU TWO!

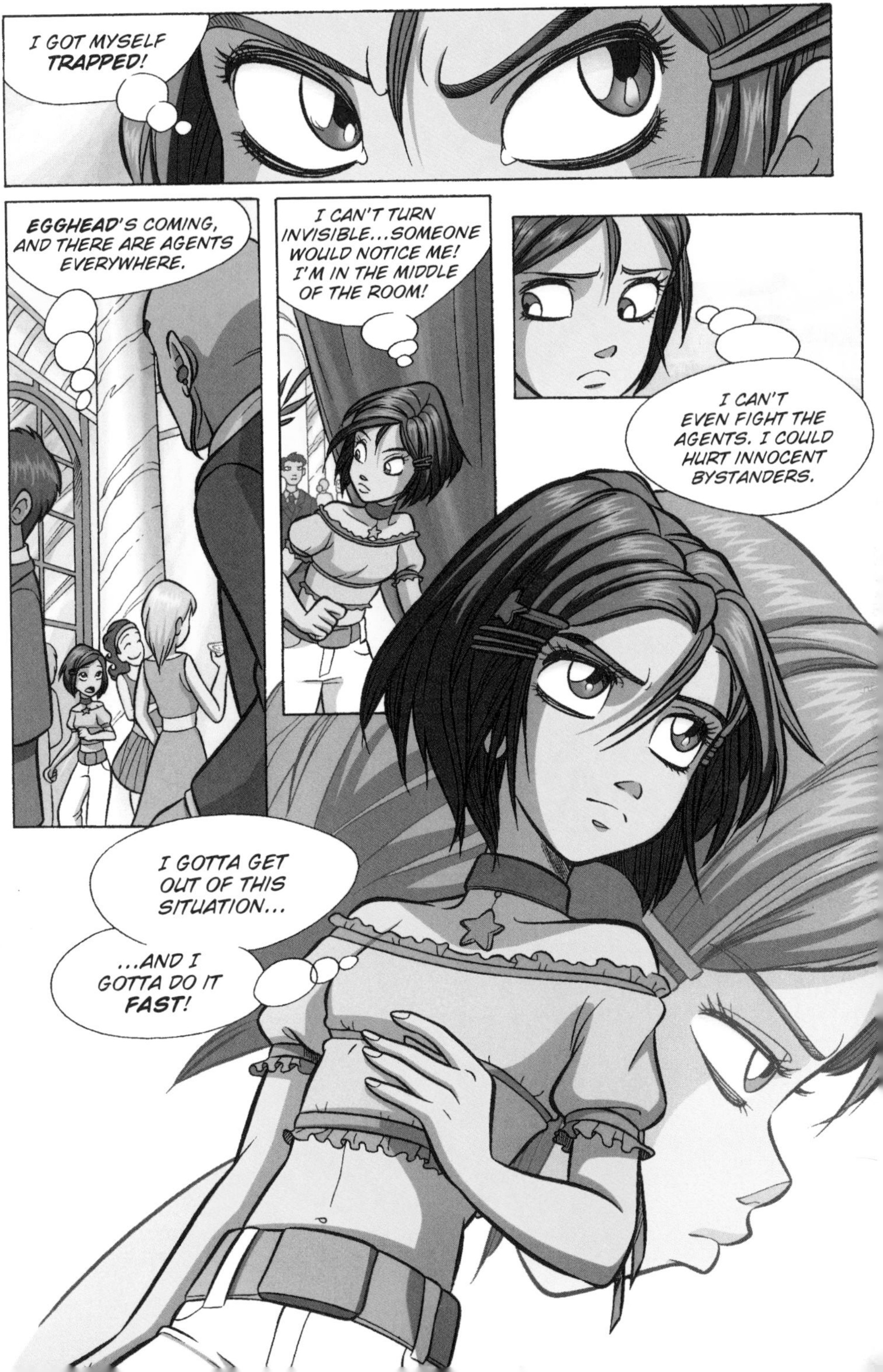
I GOT MYSELF TRAPPED!
EGGHEAD'S COMING, AND THERE ARE AGENTS EVERYWHERE.
I CAN'T TURN INVISIBLE...SOMEONE WOULD NOTICE ME! I'M IN THE MIDDLE OF THE ROOM!
I CAN'T EVEN FIGHT THE AGENTS. I COULD HURT INNOCENT BYSTANDERS.
I GOTTA GET OUT OF THIS SITUATION...
...AND I GOTTA DO IT FAST!

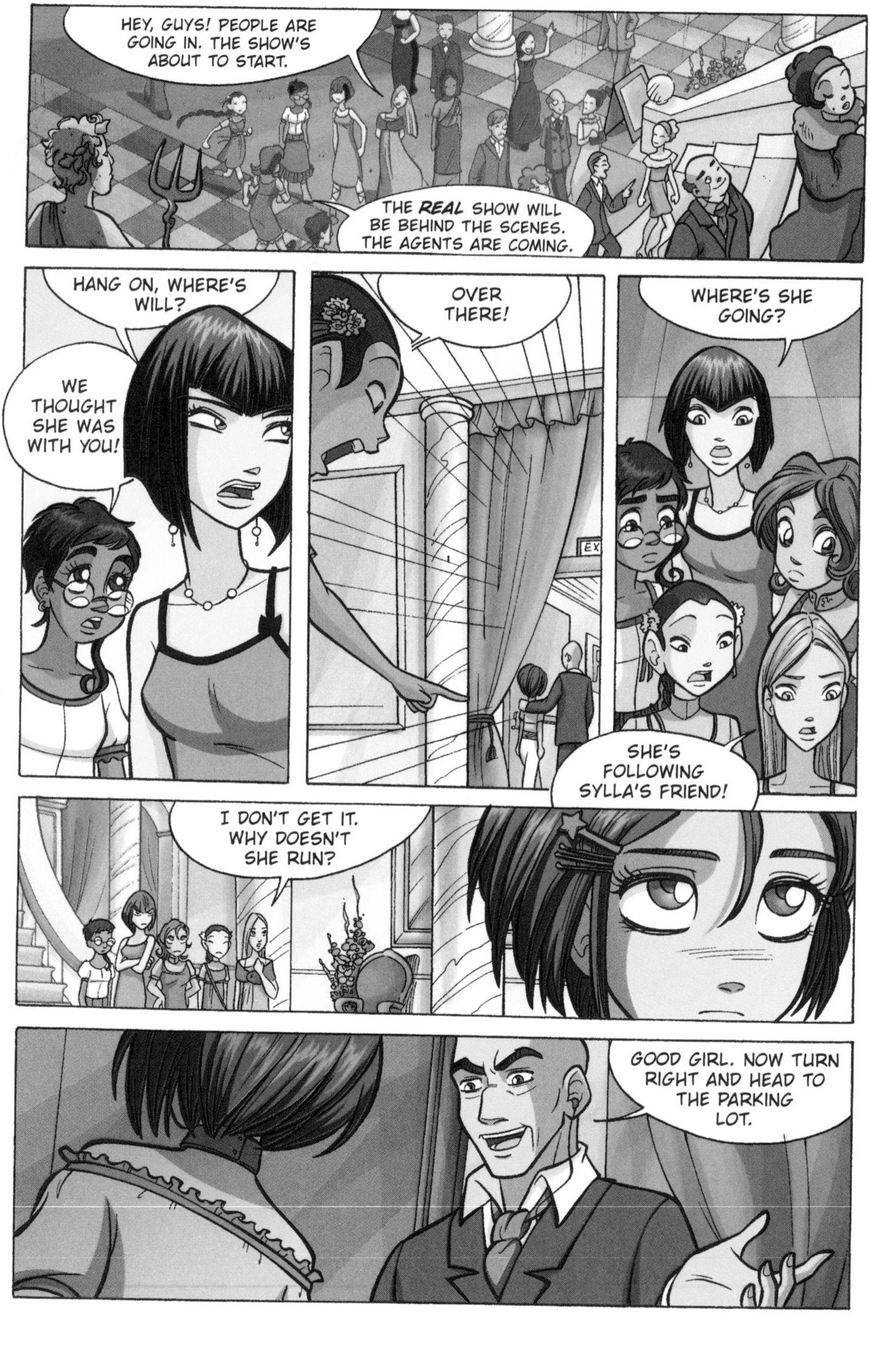

HEY, GUYS! PEOPLE ARE GOING IN. THE SHOW'S ABOUT TO START.
THE *REAL* SHOW WILL BE BEHIND THE SCENES. THE AGENTS ARE COMING.
HANG ON, WHERE'S WILL?
WE THOUGHT SHE WAS WITH YOU!
OVER THERE!
WHERE'S SHE GOING?
SHE'S FOLLOWING SYLLA'S FRIEND!
I DON'T GET IT. WHY DOESN'T SHE RUN?
GOOD GIRL. NOW TURN RIGHT AND HEAD TO THE PARKING LOT.

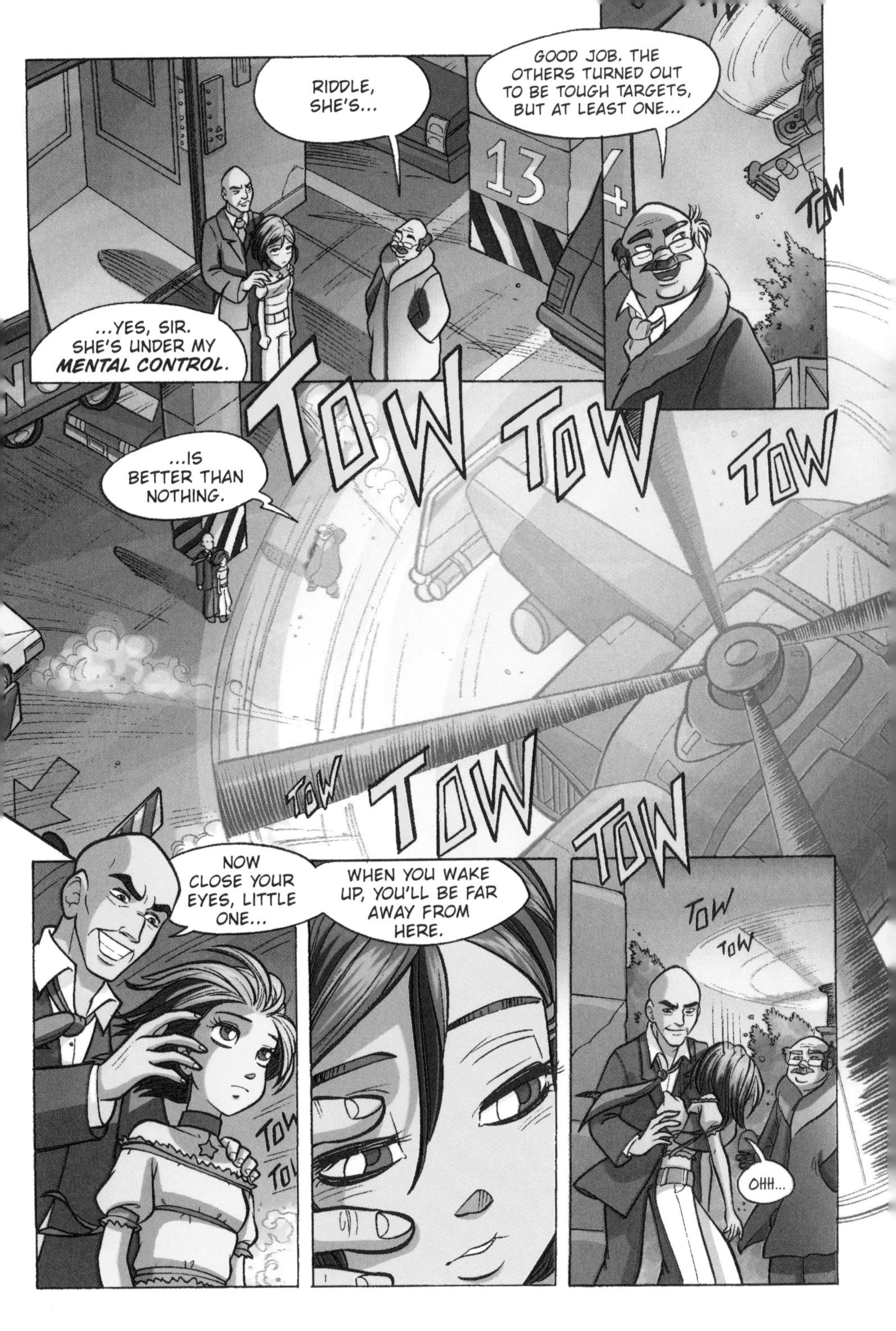
RIDDLE, SHE'S...
...YES, SIR. SHE'S UNDER MY MENTAL CONTROL.
GOOD JOB. THE OTHERS TURNED OUT TO BE TOUGH TARGETS, BUT AT LEAST ONE...
13
TOW
...IS BETTER THAN NOTHING.
TOW TOW TOW
TOW TOW TOW
NOW CLOSE YOUR EYES, LITTLE ONE...
WHEN YOU WAKE UP, YOU'LL BE FAR AWAY FROM HERE.
TOW TOW
TOW TOW
OHH...

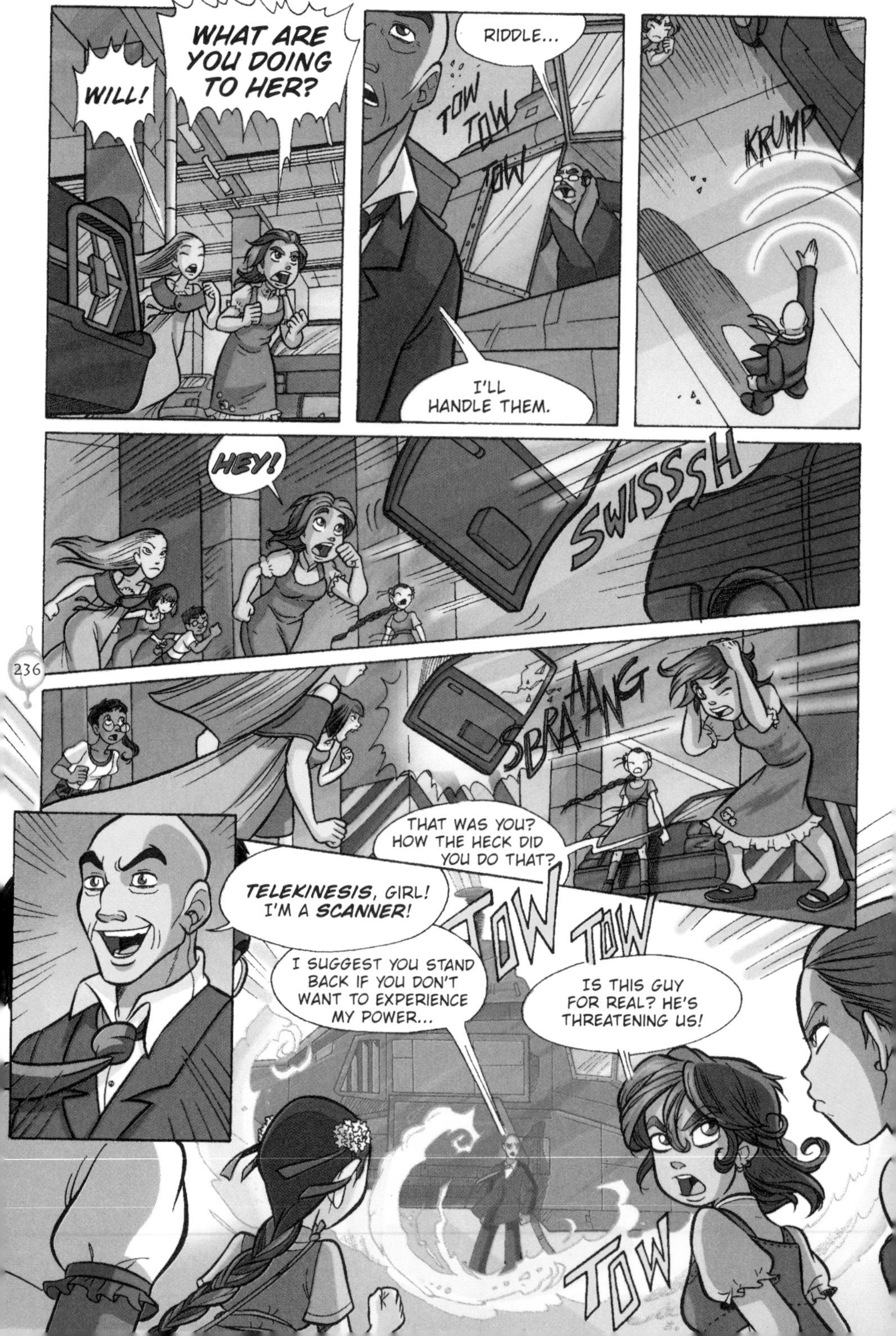
WILL!
WHAT ARE YOU DOING TO HER?
RIDDLE...
TOW TOW TOW
I'LL HANDLE THEM.
KRUMP
HEY!
SWISSSH
SBRAAANG
THAT WAS YOU? HOW THE HECK DID YOU DO THAT?
TELEKINESIS, GIRL! I'M A SCANNER!
I SUGGEST YOU STAND BACK IF YOU DON'T WANT TO EXPERIENCE MY POWER...
TOW TOW
IS THIS GUY FOR REAL? HE'S THREATENING US!
TOW

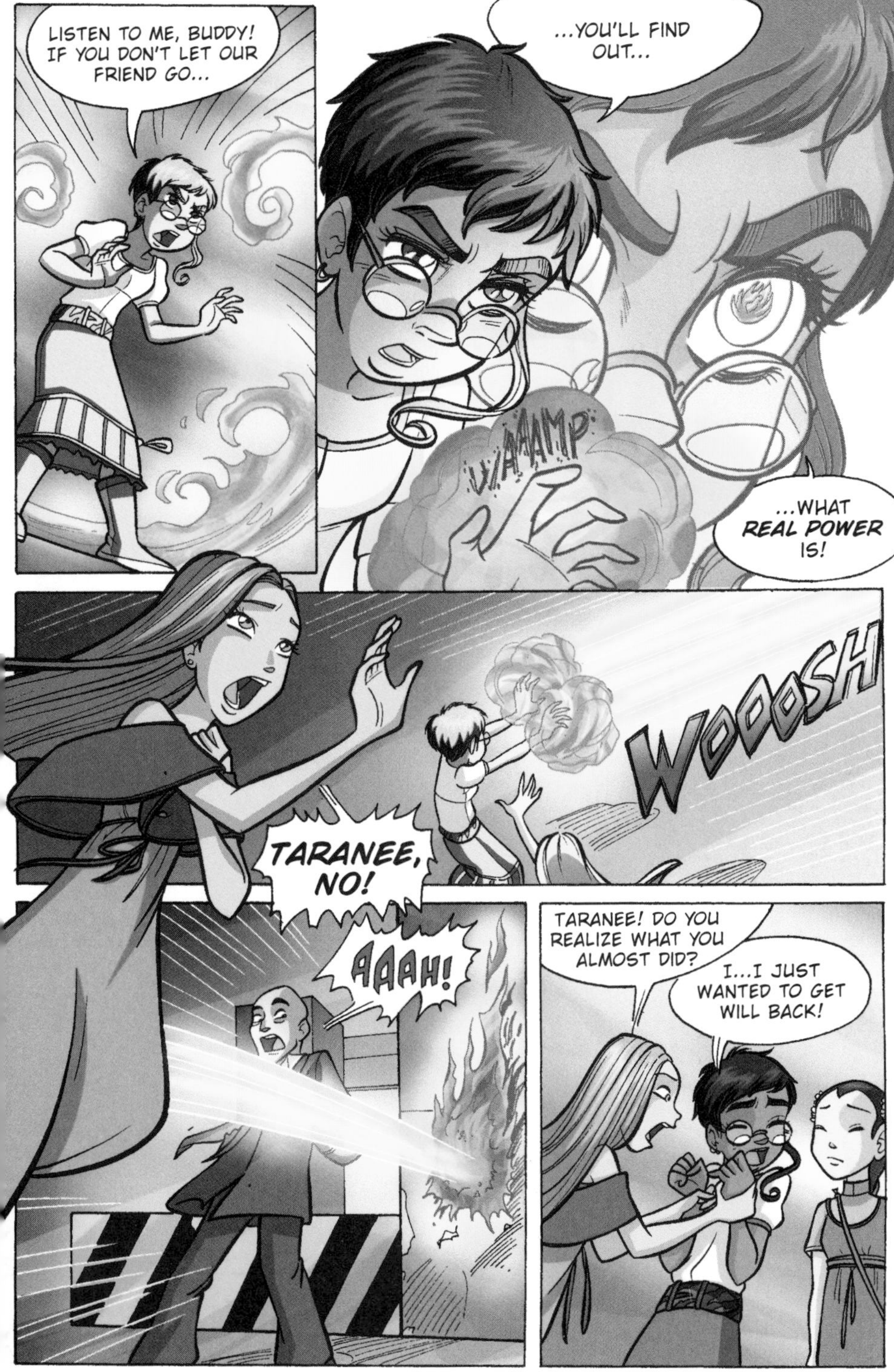
LISTEN TO ME, BUDDY! IF YOU DON'T LET OUR FRIEND GO...
...YOU'LL FIND OUT...
VAAAMP
...WHAT **REAL POWER** IS!
WOOOSH
TARANEE, NO!
AAAH!
TARANEE! DO YOU REALIZE WHAT YOU ALMOST DID?
I...I JUST WANTED TO GET WILL BACK!

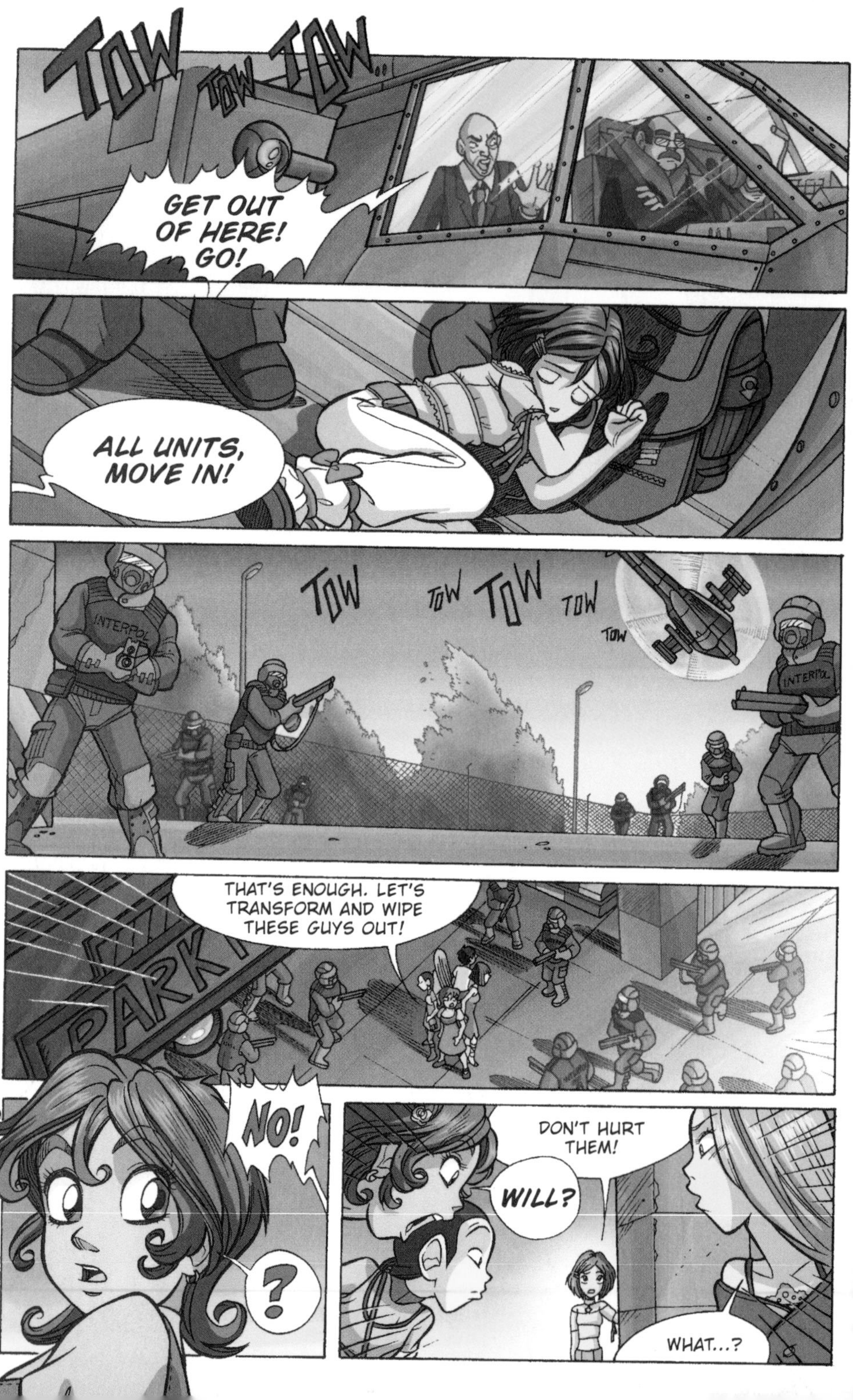
TOW TOW TOW...
GET OUT OF HERE! GO!
ALL UNITS, MOVE IN!
TOW TOW TOW TOW TOW
INTERPOL
INTERPOL
THAT'S ENOUGH. LET'S TRANSFORM AND WIPE THESE GUYS OUT!
PARK
NO!
?
DON'T HURT THEM!
WILL?
WHAT...?

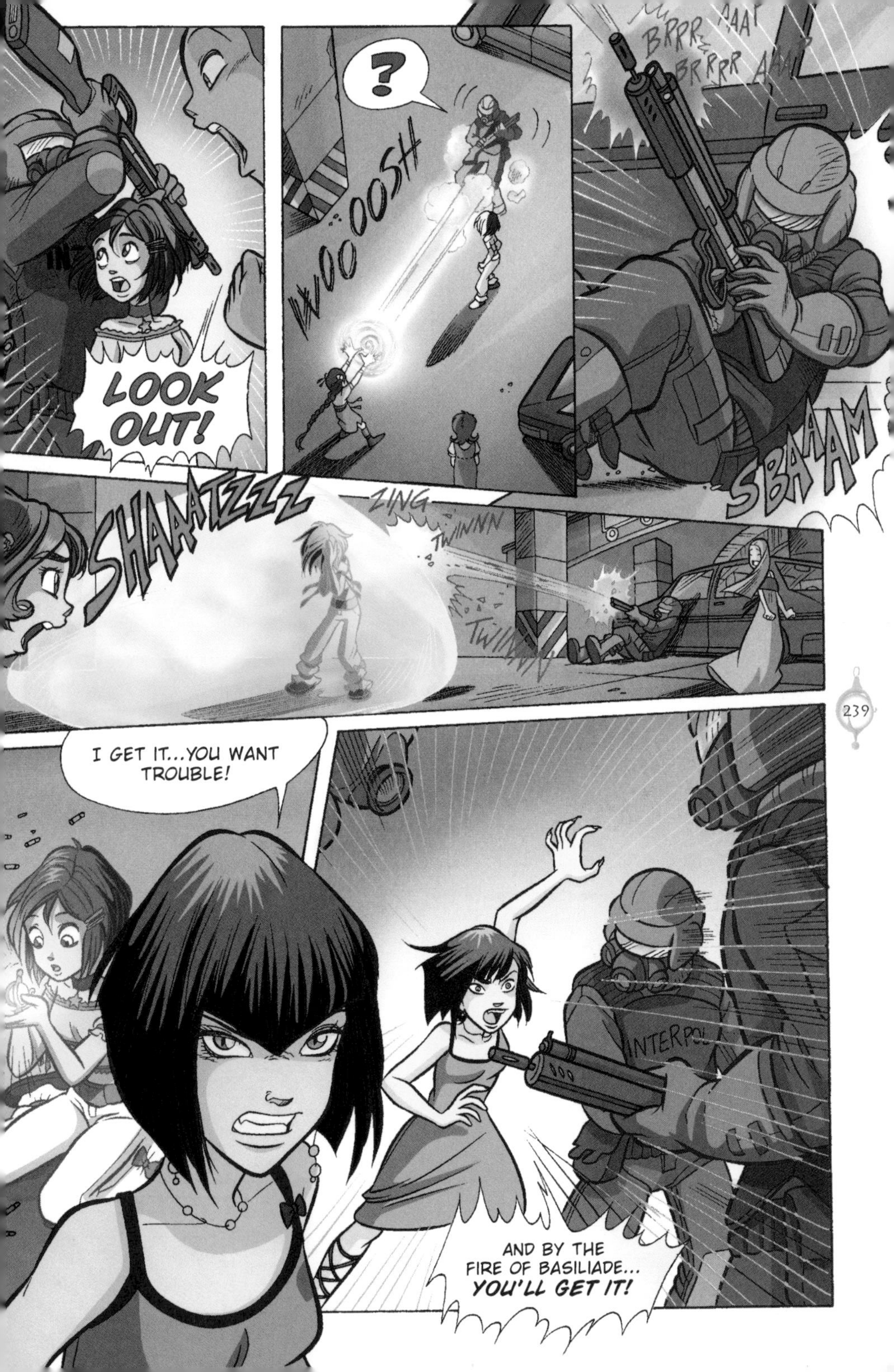

LOOK OUT!
?
WOOOOSH
BRRRR BRRRR
SBAAAM
SHAAATZZZ
ZING
TWINNN
I GET IT...YOU WANT TROUBLE!
INTERPOL
AND BY THE FIRE OF BASILIADE... ***YOU'LL GET IT!***

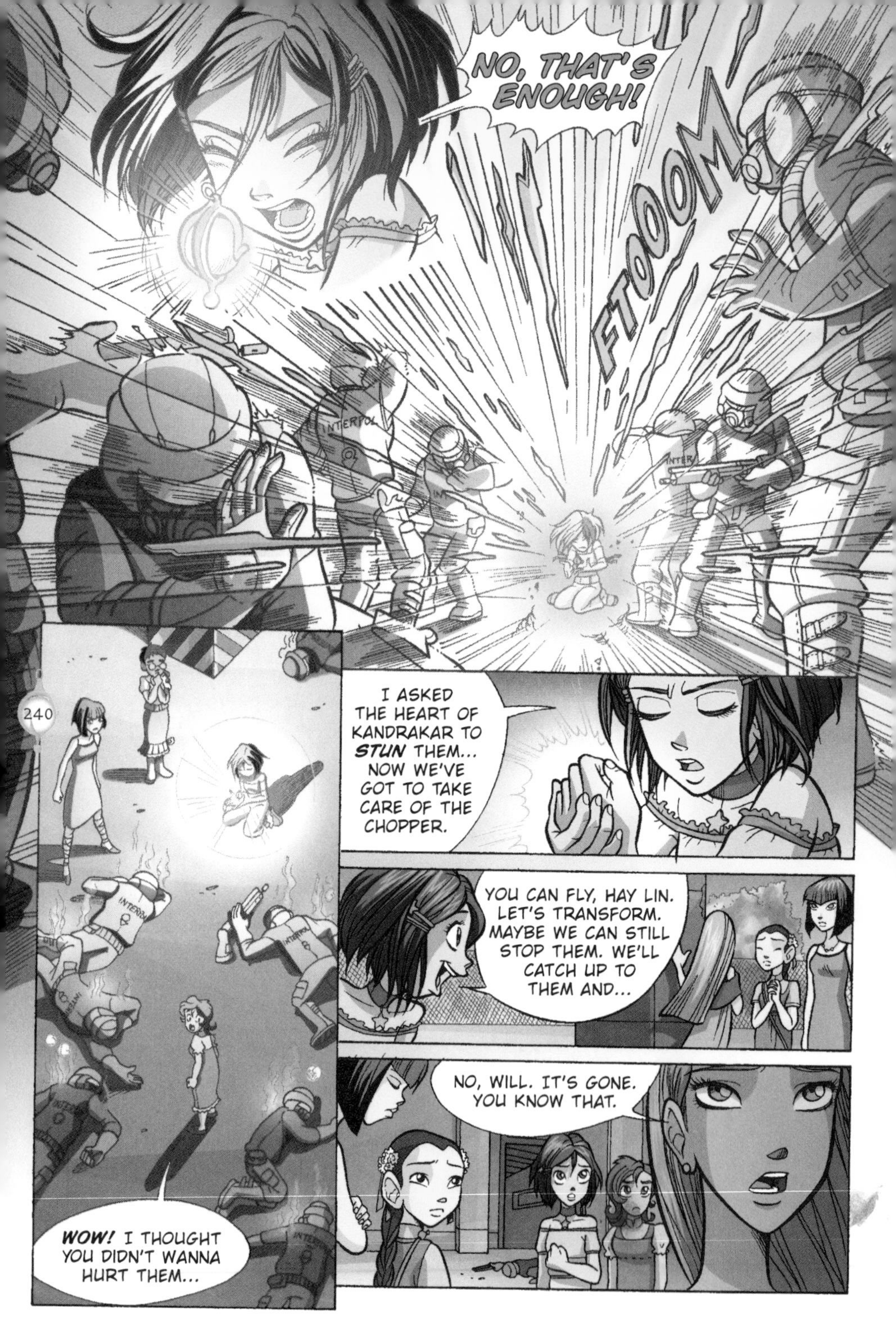
NO, THAT'S ENOUGH!
FTOOOM
INTERPOL
WOW! I THOUGHT YOU DIDN'T WANNA HURT THEM...
I ASKED THE HEART OF KANDRAKAR TO STUN THEM... NOW WE'VE GOT TO TAKE CARE OF THE CHOPPER.
YOU CAN FLY, HAY LIN. LET'S TRANSFORM. MAYBE WE CAN STILL STOP THEM. WE'LL CATCH UP TO THEM AND...
NO, WILL. IT'S GONE. YOU KNOW THAT.

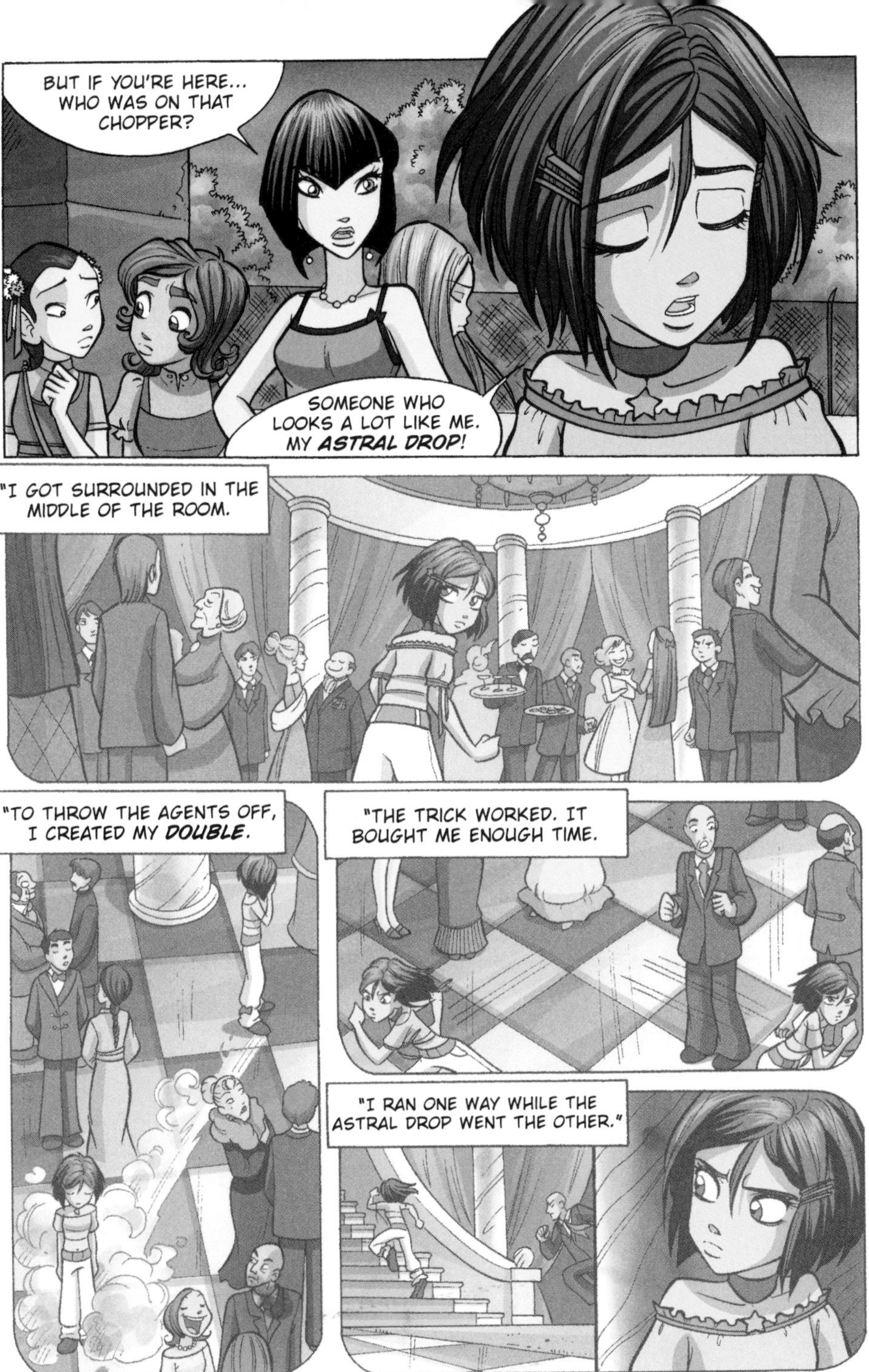
BUT IF YOU'RE HERE... WHO WAS ON THAT CHOPPER?
SOMEONE WHO LOOKS A LOT LIKE ME. MY ASTRAL DROP!
"I GOT SURROUNDED IN THE MIDDLE OF THE ROOM.
"TO THROW THE AGENTS OFF, I CREATED MY DOUBLE.
"THE TRICK WORKED. IT BOUGHT ME ENOUGH TIME.
"I RAN ONE WAY WHILE THE ASTRAL DROP WENT THE OTHER."

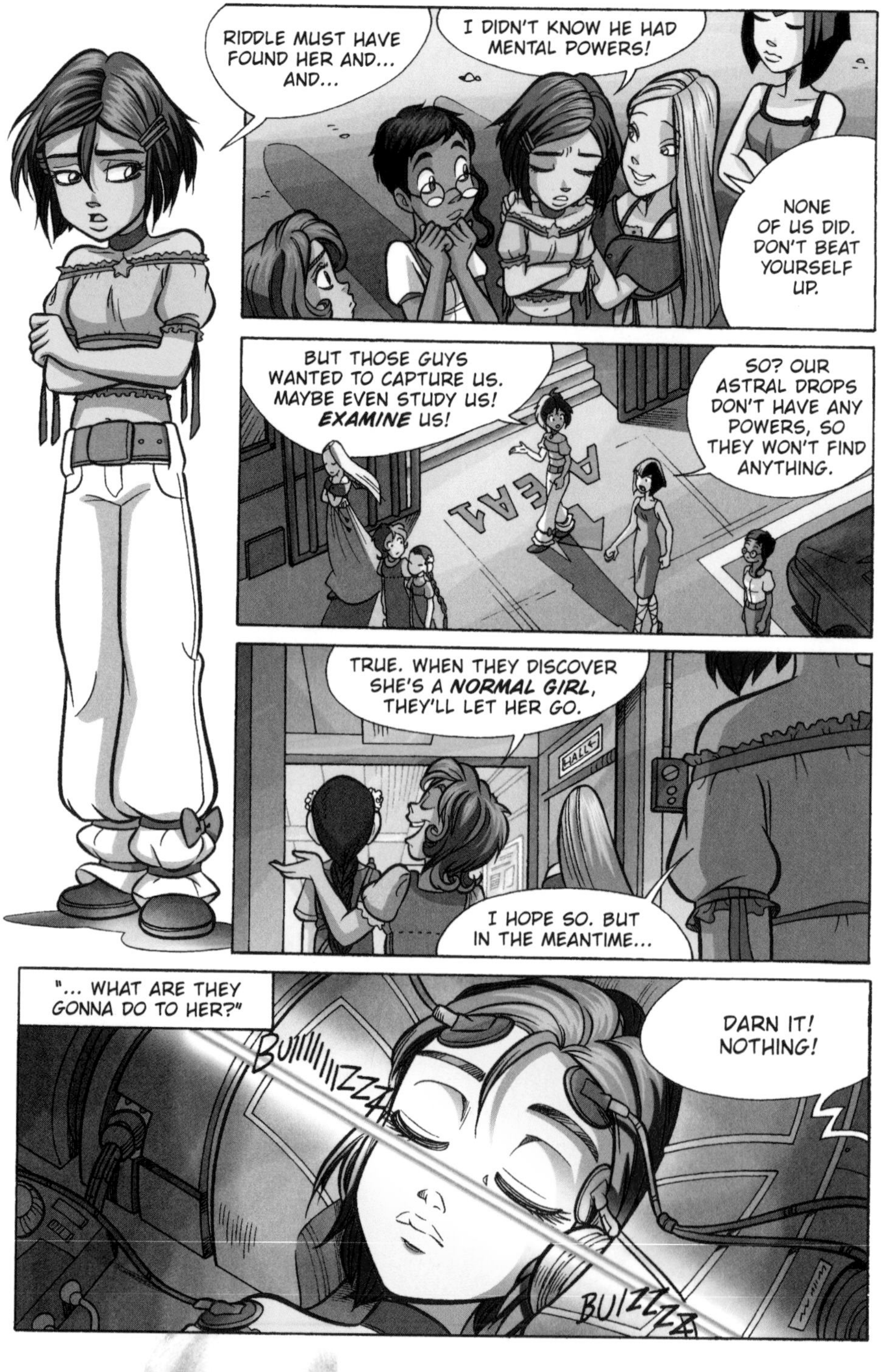
RIDDLE MUST HAVE FOUND HER AND... AND...
I DIDN'T KNOW HE HAD MENTAL POWERS!
NONE OF US DID. DON'T BEAT YOURSELF UP.
BUT THOSE GUYS WANTED TO CAPTURE US. MAYBE EVEN STUDY US! EXAMINE US!
SO? OUR ASTRAL DROPS DON'T HAVE ANY POWERS, SO THEY WON'T FIND ANYTHING.
TRUE. WHEN THEY DISCOVER SHE'S A NORMAL GIRL, THEY'LL LET HER GO.
HALL
I HOPE SO. BUT IN THE MEANTIME...
"... WHAT ARE THEY GONNA DO TO HER?"
BUIIIIIIZZZZ
DARN IT! NOTHING!
BUIZZZZ

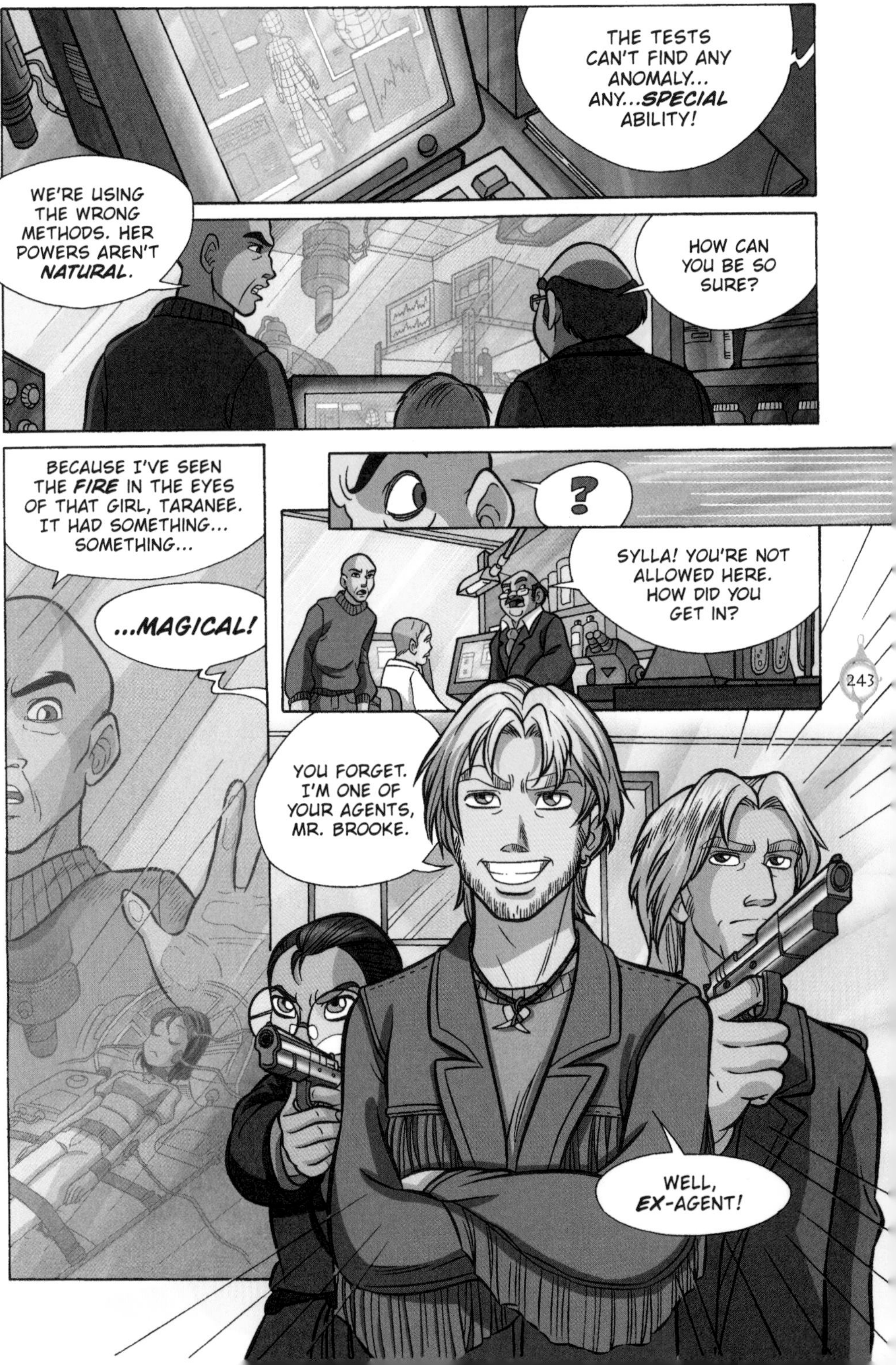

THE TESTS CAN'T FIND ANY ANOMALY... ANY...SPECIAL ABILITY!
WE'RE USING THE WRONG METHODS. HER POWERS AREN'T NATURAL.
HOW CAN YOU BE SO SURE?
BECAUSE I'VE SEEN THE FIRE IN THE EYES OF THAT GIRL, TARANEE. IT HAD SOMETHING... SOMETHING...
...MAGICAL!
?
SYLLA! YOU'RE NOT ALLOWED HERE. HOW DID YOU GET IN?
YOU FORGET. I'M ONE OF YOUR AGENTS, MR. BROOKE.
WELL, EX-AGENT!

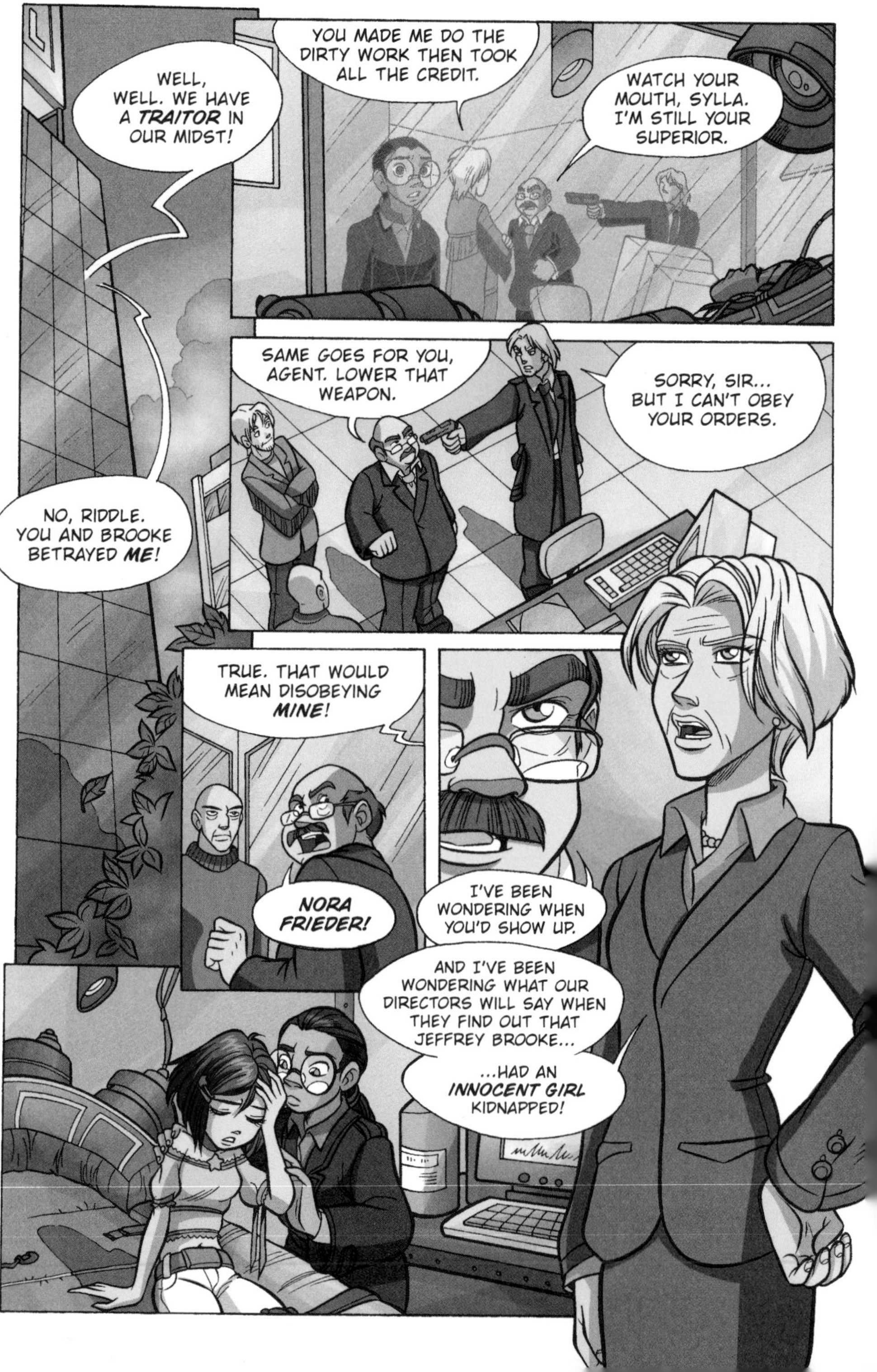
WELL, WELL. WE HAVE A TRAITOR IN OUR MIDST!
YOU MADE ME DO THE DIRTY WORK THEN TOOK ALL THE CREDIT.
WATCH YOUR MOUTH, SYLLA. I'M STILL YOUR SUPERIOR.
SAME GOES FOR YOU, AGENT. LOWER THAT WEAPON.
SORRY, SIR... BUT I CAN'T OBEY YOUR ORDERS.
NO, RIDDLE. YOU AND BROOKE BETRAYED ME!
TRUE. THAT WOULD MEAN DISOBEYING MINE!
NORA FRIEDER!
I'VE BEEN WONDERING WHEN YOU'D SHOW UP.
AND I'VE BEEN WONDERING WHAT OUR DIRECTORS WILL SAY WHEN THEY FIND OUT THAT JEFFREY BROOKE...
...HAD AN INNOCENT GIRL KIDNAPPED!

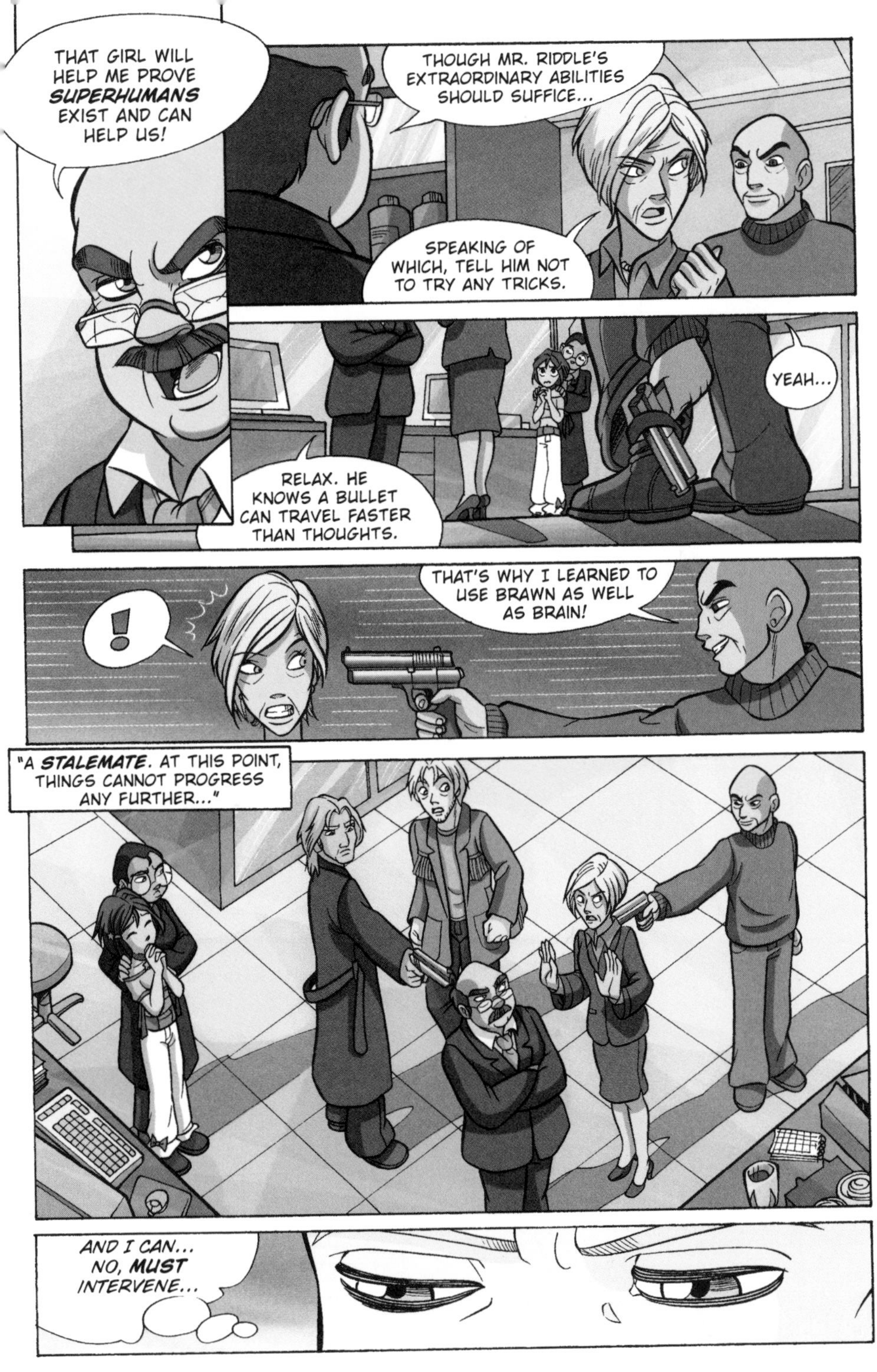
THAT GIRL WILL HELP ME PROVE ***SUPERHUMANS*** EXIST AND CAN HELP US!
THOUGH MR. RIDDLE'S EXTRAORDINARY ABILITIES SHOULD SUFFICE...
SPEAKING OF WHICH, TELL HIM NOT TO TRY ANY TRICKS.
YEAH...
RELAX. HE KNOWS A BULLET CAN TRAVEL FASTER THAN THOUGHTS.
!
THAT'S WHY I LEARNED TO USE BRAWN AS WELL AS BRAIN!
"A ***STALEMATE***. AT THIS POINT, THINGS CANNOT PROGRESS ANY FURTHER..."
AND I CAN... NO, ***MUST*** *INTERVENE...*

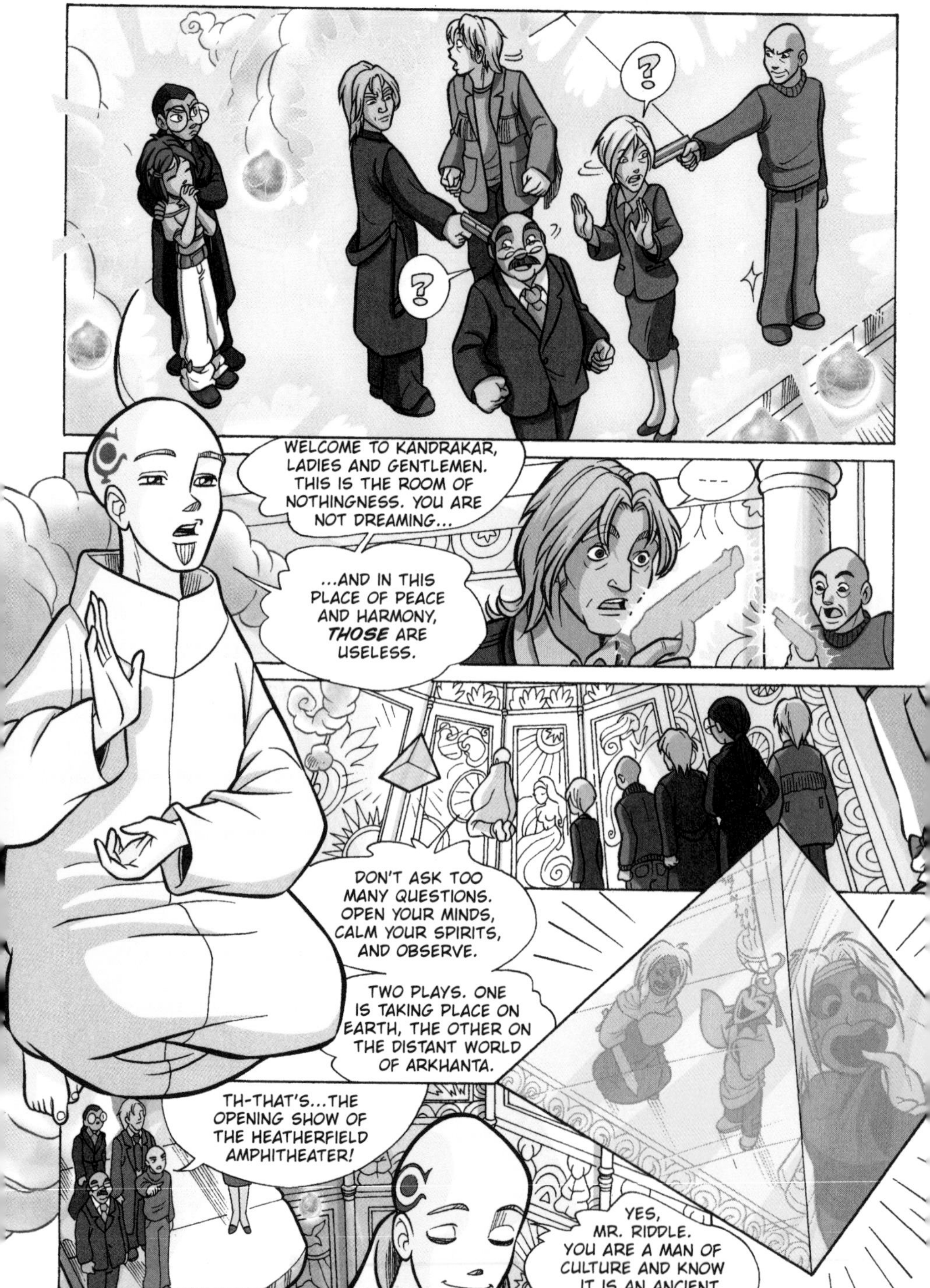
?
?
WELCOME TO KANDRAKAR, LADIES AND GENTLEMEN. THIS IS THE ROOM OF NOTHINGNESS. YOU ARE NOT DREAMING...
...AND IN THIS PLACE OF PEACE AND HARMONY, **THOSE** ARE USELESS.

DON'T ASK TOO MANY QUESTIONS. OPEN YOUR MINDS, CALM YOUR SPIRITS, AND OBSERVE.
TWO PLAYS. ONE IS TAKING PLACE ON EARTH, THE OTHER ON THE DISTANT WORLD OF ARKHANTA.
TH-THAT'S...THE OPENING SHOW OF THE HEATHERFIELD AMPHITHEATER!
YES, MR. RIDDLE. YOU ARE A MAN OF CULTURE AND KNOW IT IS AN ANCIENT **GREEK TRAGEDY**.

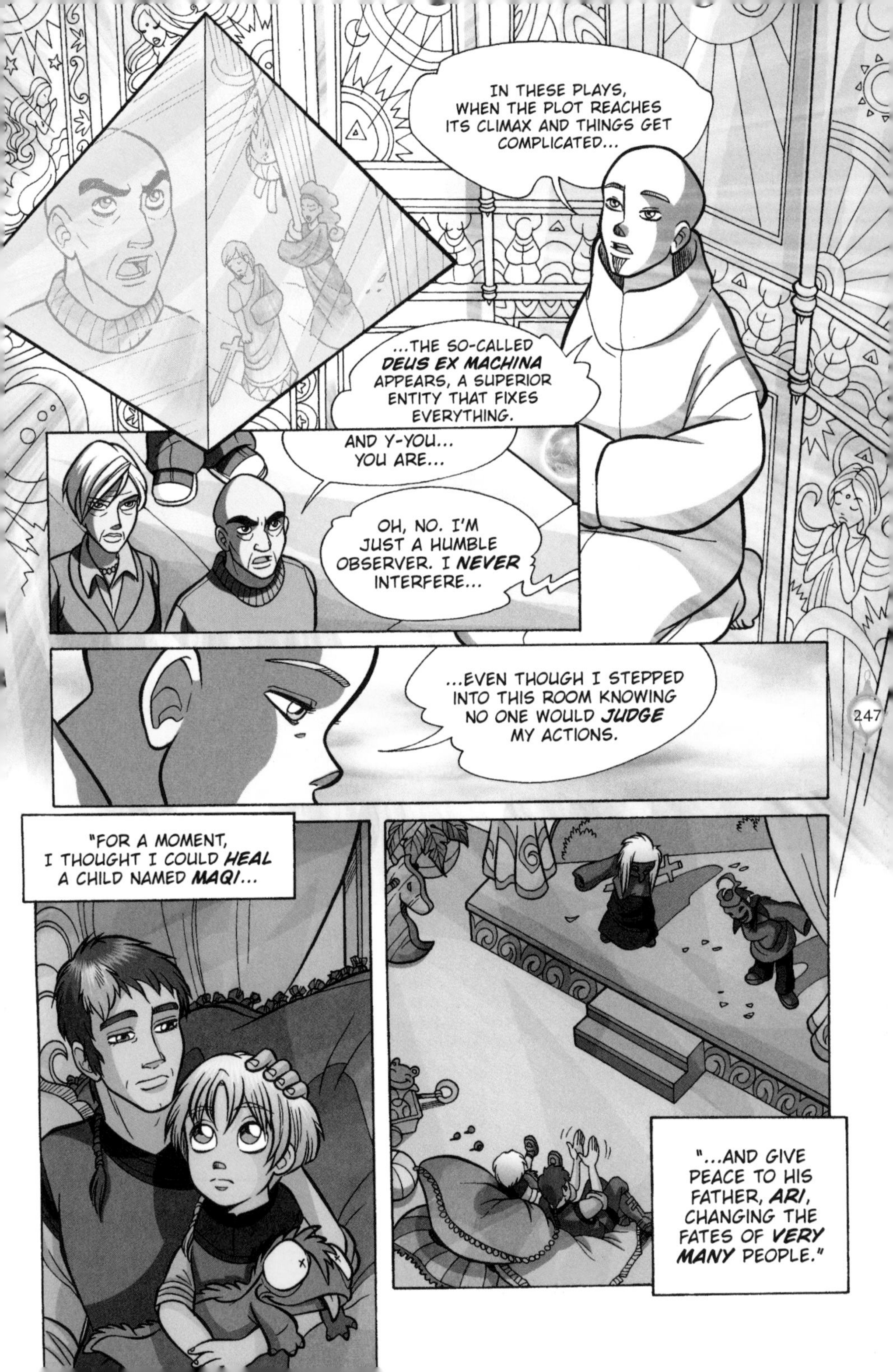
IN THESE PLAYS, WHEN THE PLOT REACHES ITS CLIMAX AND THINGS GET COMPLICATED...
...THE SO-CALLED DEUS EX MACHINA APPEARS, A SUPERIOR ENTITY THAT FIXES EVERYTHING.
AND Y-YOU... YOU ARE...
OH, NO. I'M JUST A HUMBLE OBSERVER. I NEVER INTERFERE...
...EVEN THOUGH I STEPPED INTO THIS ROOM KNOWING NO ONE WOULD JUDGE MY ACTIONS.
"FOR A MOMENT, I THOUGHT I COULD HEAL A CHILD NAMED MAQI...
"...AND GIVE PEACE TO HIS FATHER, ARI, CHANGING THE FATES OF VERY MANY PEOPLE."

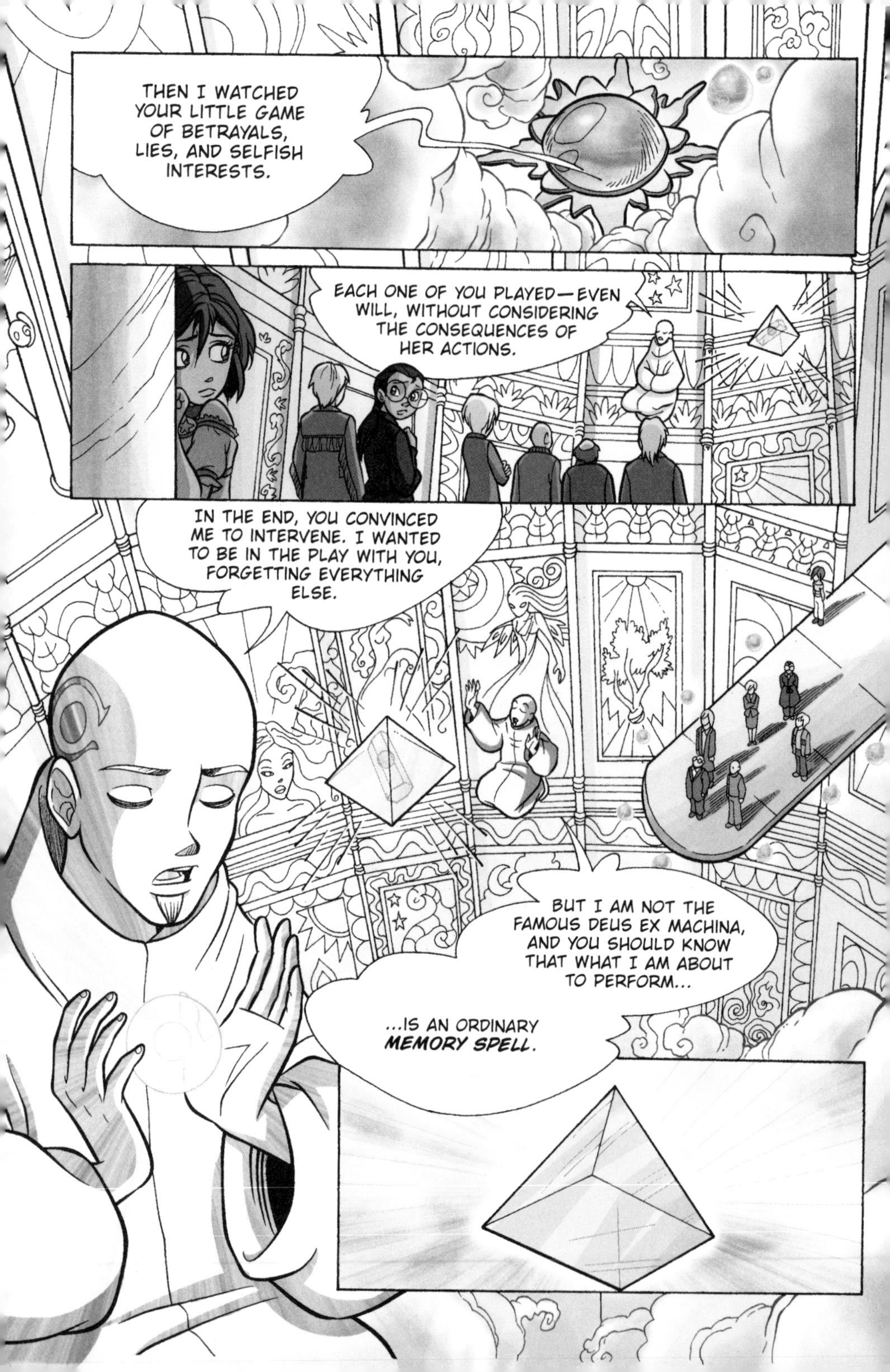
THEN I WATCHED YOUR LITTLE GAME OF BETRAYALS, LIES, AND SELFISH INTERESTS.
EACH ONE OF YOU PLAYED—EVEN WILL, WITHOUT CONSIDERING THE CONSEQUENCES OF HER ACTIONS.
IN THE END, YOU CONVINCED ME TO INTERVENE. I WANTED TO BE IN THE PLAY WITH YOU, FORGETTING EVERYTHING ELSE.
BUT I AM NOT THE FAMOUS DEUS EX MACHINA, AND YOU SHOULD KNOW THAT WHAT I AM ABOUT TO PERFORM...
...IS AN ORDINARY ***MEMORY SPELL***.

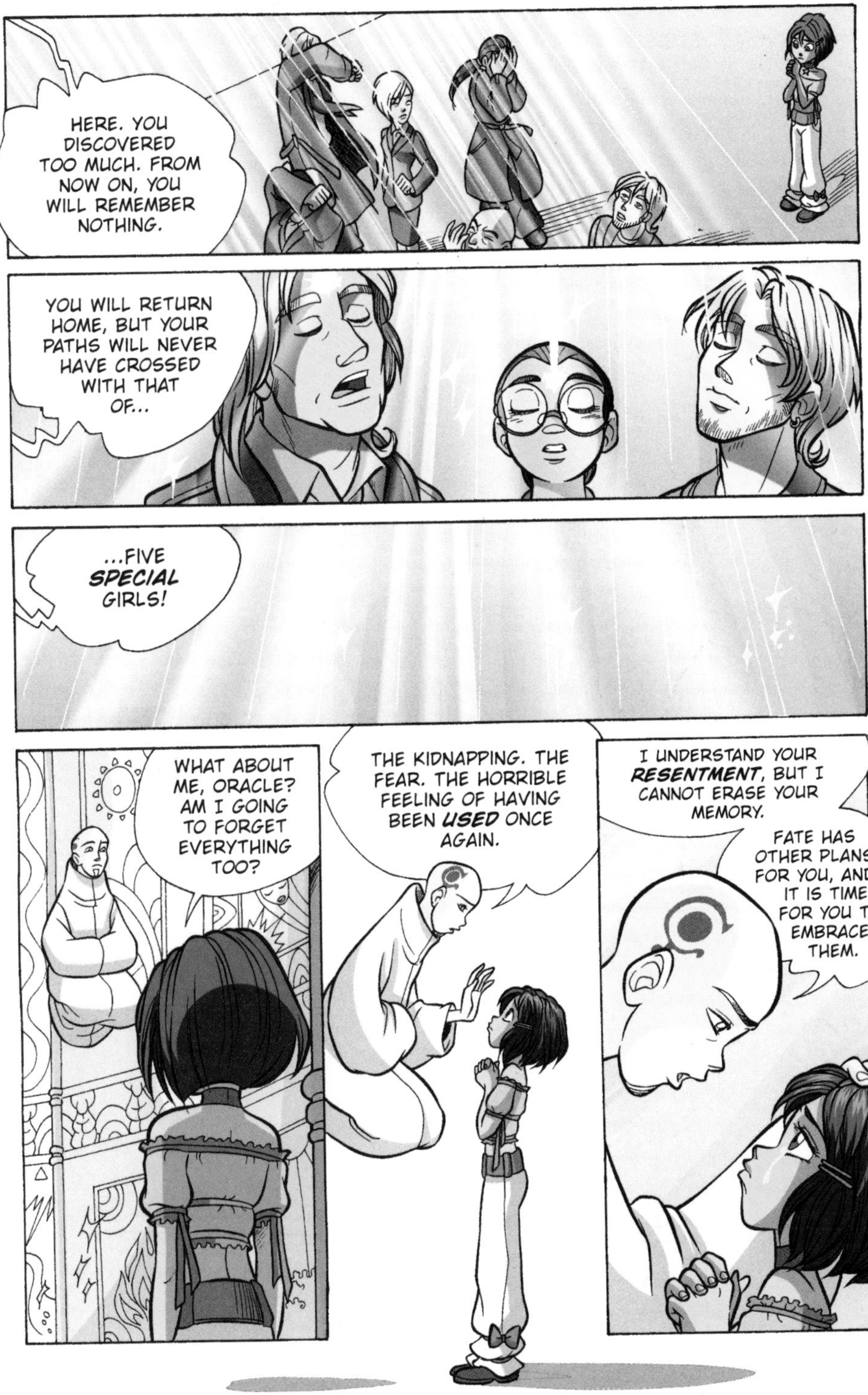
HERE. YOU DISCOVERED TOO MUCH. FROM NOW ON, YOU WILL REMEMBER NOTHING.
YOU WILL RETURN HOME, BUT YOUR PATHS WILL NEVER HAVE CROSSED WITH THAT OF...
...FIVE ***SPECIAL*** GIRLS!
WHAT ABOUT ME, ORACLE? AM I GOING TO FORGET EVERYTHING TOO?
THE KIDNAPPING. THE FEAR. THE HORRIBLE FEELING OF HAVING BEEN ***USED*** ONCE AGAIN.
I UNDERSTAND YOUR ***RESENTMENT***, BUT I CANNOT ERASE YOUR MEMORY.
FATE HAS OTHER PLANS FOR YOU, AND IT IS TIME FOR YOU TO EMBRACE THEM.

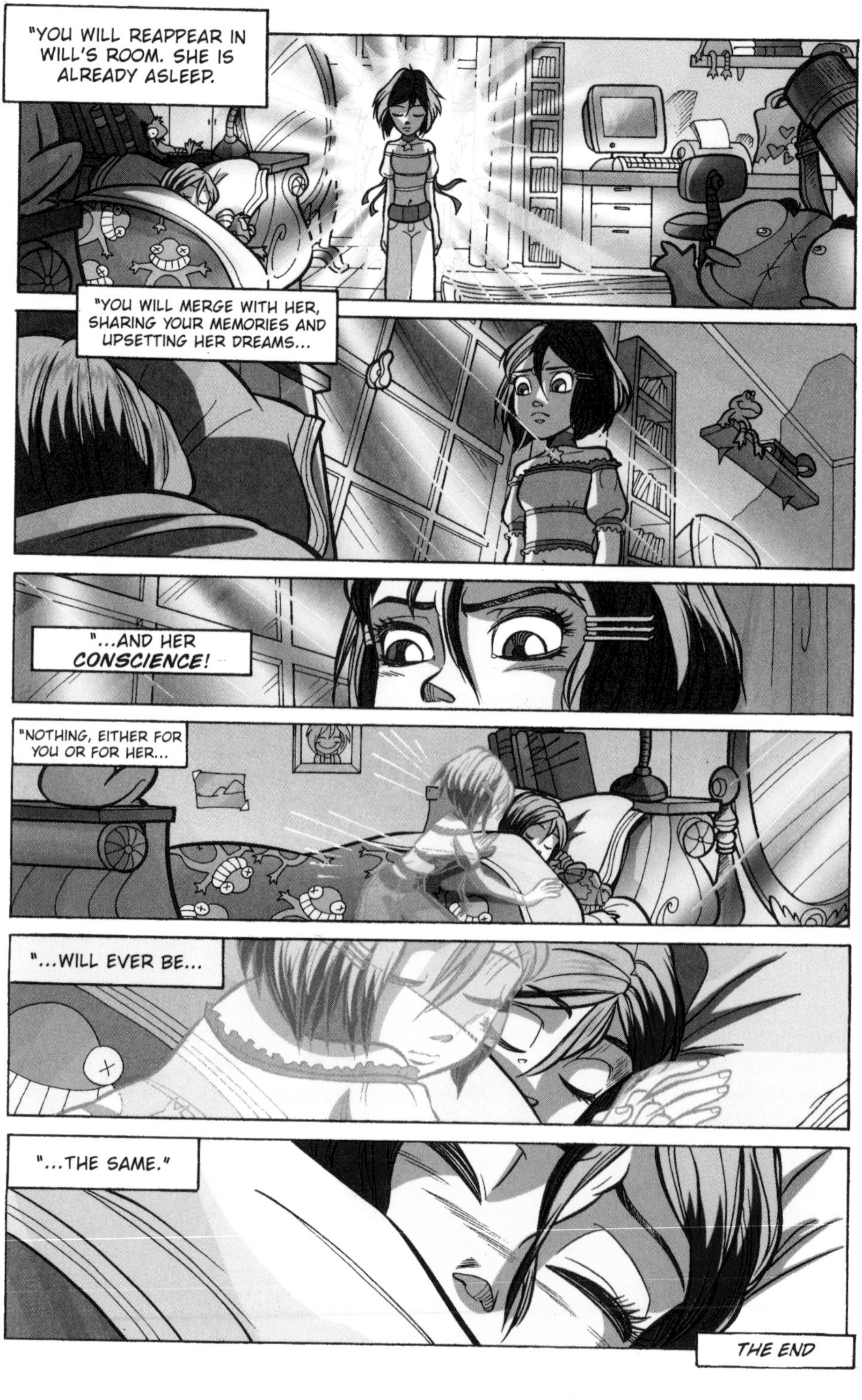
"YOU WILL REAPPEAR IN WILL'S ROOM. SHE IS ALREADY ASLEEP.
"YOU WILL MERGE WITH HER, SHARING YOUR MEMORIES AND UPSETTING HER DREAMS...
"...AND HER CONSCIENCE!
"NOTHING, EITHER FOR YOU OR FOR HER...
"...WILL EVER BE...
"...THE SAME."
THE END

W.I.T.C.H.

Will Irma Taranee Cornelia Hay Lin

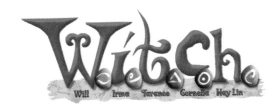

Read on in Volume 9!

Maqi

Ari's Son

Ten years old, Maqi is the only child of Ari, Lord of Arkhanta, and his wife, Jamayeda, who passed away during childbirth. Quiet and distant, Maqi is a special boy who keeps to himself and lives in his own little world, detached from everything else.

Drawing

Maqi loves to draw. In his pictures, he shows his private universe and reveals his feelings. Maqi doesn't laugh or cry, but he's not absent. He pays a lot of attention to details and can spot things other people don't notice.

The Dream

The bond between Maqi and his father is strong, made of silence and a lot of love. His child's happiness is the Lord of Arkhanta's sole purpose in life — a dream that, thus far, has yet to become a reality.

W.I.T.C.H. Planet

Yua

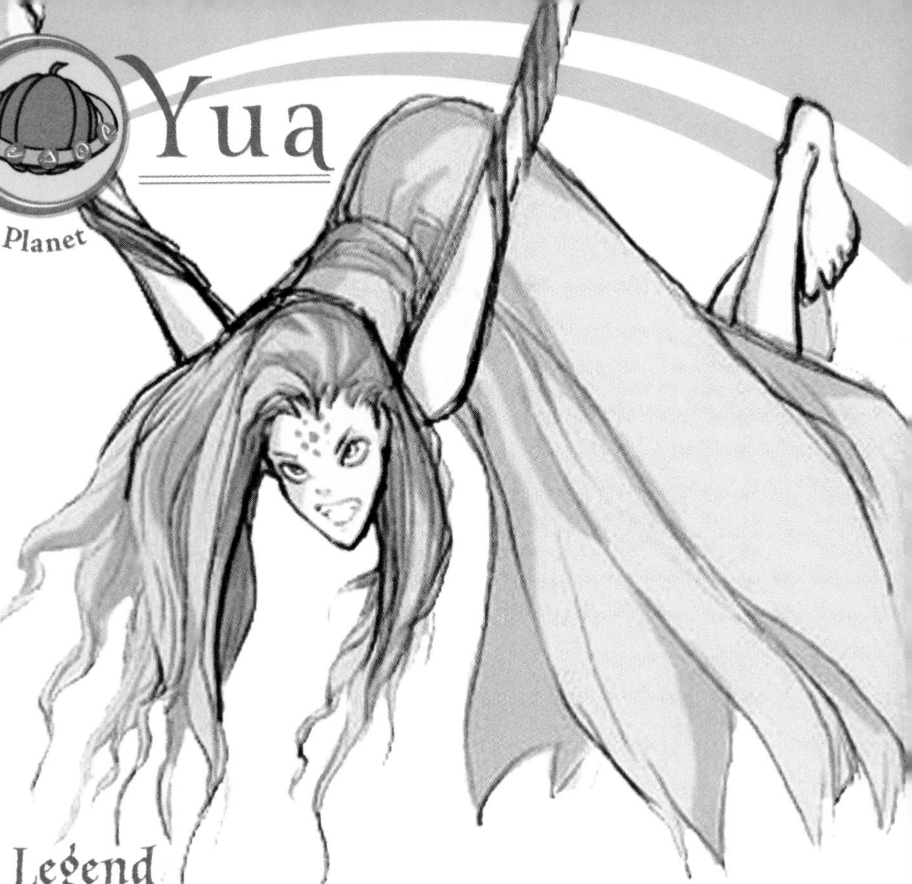

The Legend

They say legends always have a kernel of truth, and Yua is living proof of that. The banshee embodies the myth of the evil spirit chained and forced to make wishes come true. Feared and hated, her origins are lost in the mists of Arkhanta's history. Before being imprisoned by Ari, Yua lived in the swamps, a desolate place that might swallow anyone who dares venture there forever.

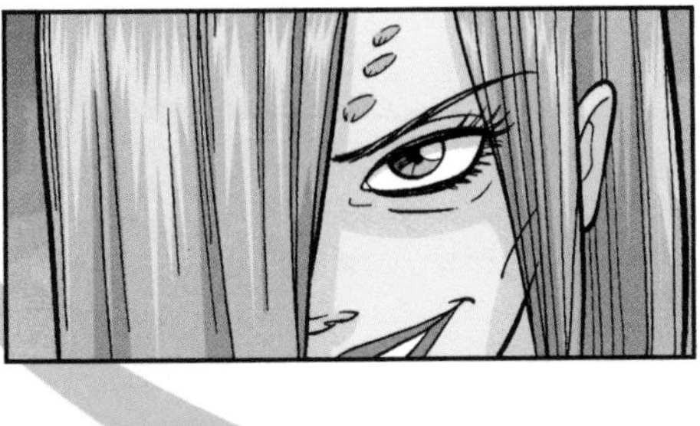

The Banshees

The banshees are evil creatures who enjoy playing with men and use their charm to lure their prey into deadly traps. Looks can be deceiving, and behind their almost elegant appearance, the banshees hide claws and terrible powers. The bond between an imprisoned banshee and her master can be broken only by the latter. That's why no one but Ari can ever set Yua free.

In the wardrobe of...

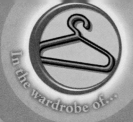

Will's Secret World

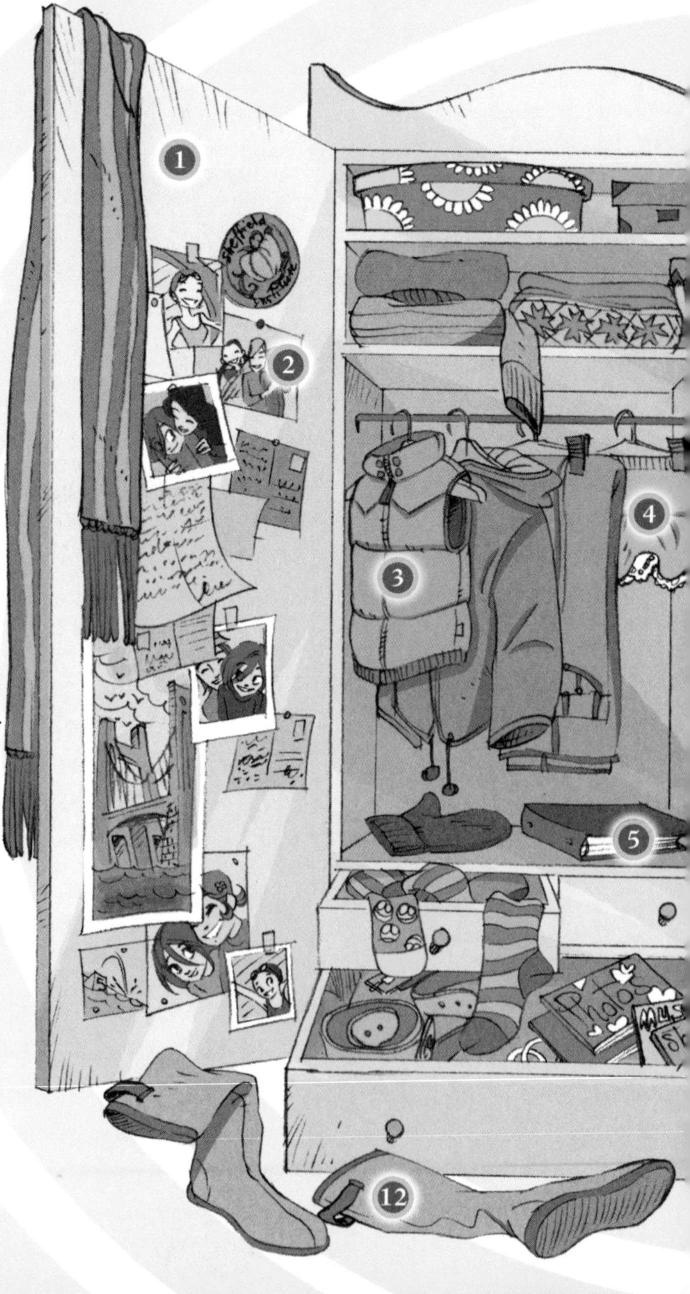

1
2
3
4
5
Photos
12

1. The wardrobe door tells us about Will. There are photos from the past year.

2. A photo she nicked from Corny: blackmail ammunition. Better not to mention who she's hugging (aside from Hay Lin)!

3. Padded vest. A present from Mr. Collins, who's also her mom's boyfriend! Go figure!

4. The only skirt she bought in the last three years. She made her mom happy—and hopefully Matt too!

5. Photo album. It contains the photos she took off the door (see #1).

6. That's where Auntie Rina's frog ended up! It smells of mothballs, just like her, and Will hates it. (The smell, of course!)

7. A souvenir from Camp Cormoran. What a nightmare of a vacation!

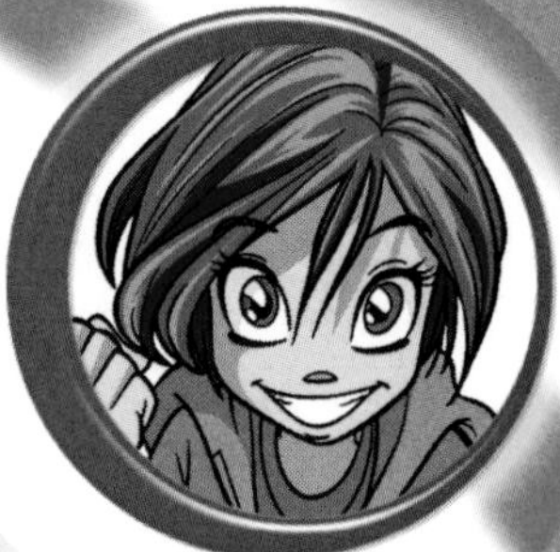

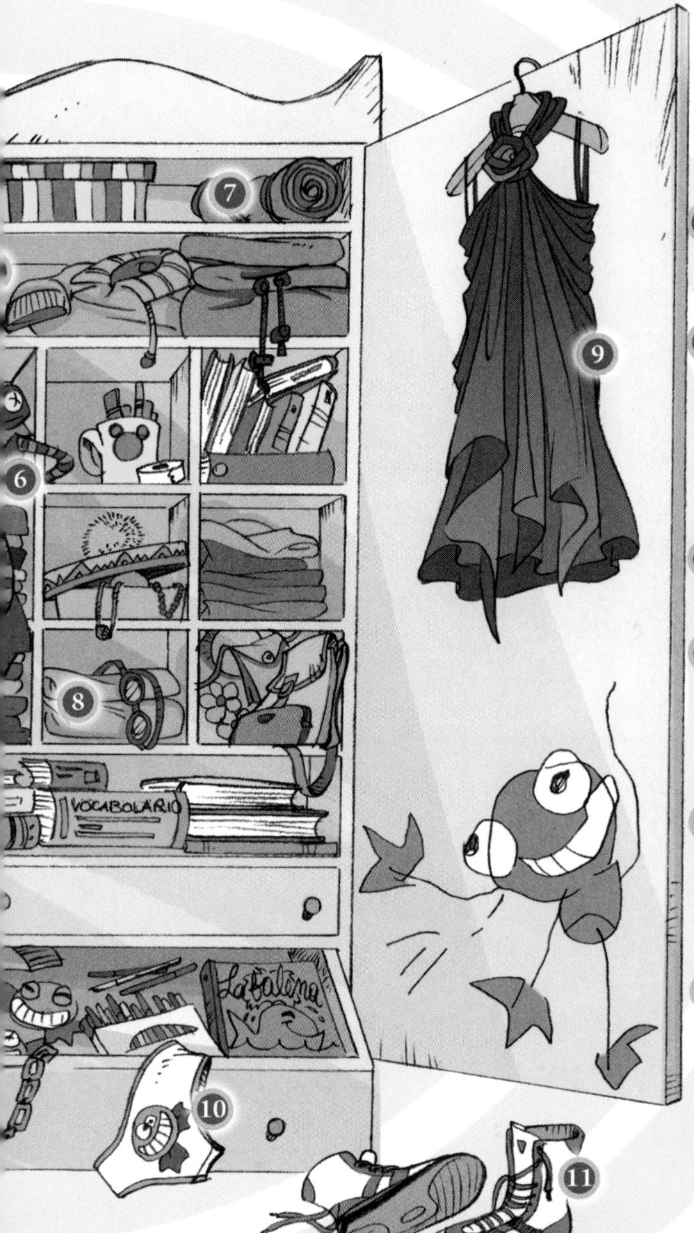

7
6
9
8
VOCABOLARIO
10
11

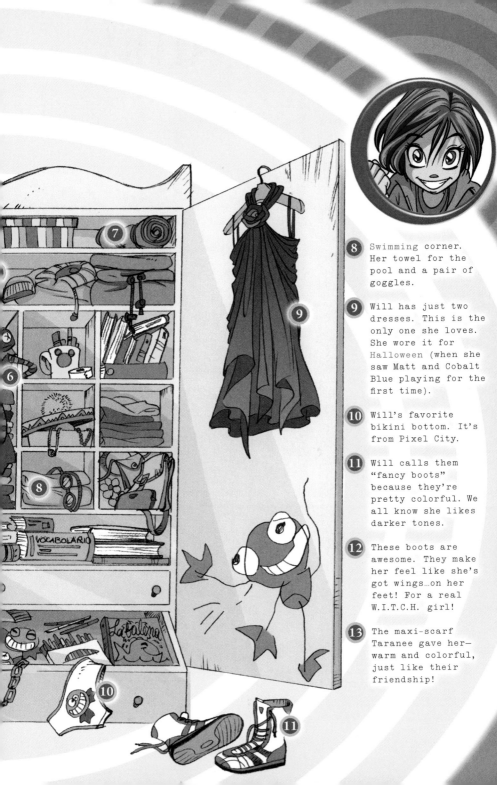

8 Swimming corner. Her towel for the pool and a pair of goggles.

9 Will has just two dresses. This is the only one she loves. She wore it for Halloween (when she saw Matt and Cobalt Blue playing for the first time).

10 Will's favorite bikini bottom. It's from Pixel City.

11 Will calls them "fancy boots" because they're pretty colorful. We all know she likes darker tones.

12 These boots are awesome. They make her feel like she's got wings…on her feet! For a real W.I.T.C.H. girl!

13 The maxi-scarf Taranee gave her—warm and colorful, just like their friendship!

Part III. A Crisis on Both Worlds • Volume 2

8

Series Created by Elisabetta Gnone
Comic Art Direction: Alessandro Barbucci, Barbara Canepa

W.I.T.C.H.: The Graphic Novel, Part III: A Crisis on Both Worlds © Disney Enterprises, Inc.

English translation © 2018 by Disney Enterprises, Inc.

JY
1290 Avenue of the Americas
New York, NY 10104

Visit us at yenpress.com
facebook.com/yenpress
twitter.com/yenpress
yenpress.tumblr.com
instagram.com/yenpress

First JY Edition: May 2018

JY is an imprint of Yen Press, LLC.
The JY name and logo are trademarks of Yen Press, LLC.

The publisher is not responsible for websites (or their content) that are not owned by the publisher.

Library of Congress Control Number: 2017950917

ISBNs:
978-0-316-47709-3 (paperback)
978-1-9753-2658-6 (ebook)

10 9 8 7 6 5 4 3

LSC-C

Printed in the United States of America

Cover Art by Gianluca Panniello
Colors by Andrea Cagol

Translation by Linda Ghio and
Stephanie Dagg at Editing Zone
Lettering by Katie Blakeslee

THE LESSER EVIL

Concept and Script by Bruno Enna
Layout by Gianluca Panniello
Pencils by Giada Perissinotto
Inks by Marina Baggio and Roberta Zanotta
Color and Light Direction by Francesco Legramandi
Title Page Art by Giada Perissinotto
with Colors by Francesco Legramandi

THE PATH OF THE WIND

Concept and Script by Paola Mulazzi
Layout and Pencils by Paolo Campinoti
Inks by Santa Zangari
Color and Light Direction by Francesco Legramandi
Title Page Art by Paolo Campinoti
with Colors by Andrea Cagol and Francesco Legramandi

THE VOICE OF SILENCE

Concept and Script by Francesco Artibani
Layout and Pencils by Manuela Razzi
Inks by Marina Baggio and Roberta Zanotta
Color and Light Direction by Francesco Legramandi
Title Page Art by Manuela Razzi and Paolo Campinoti
with Colors by Andrea Cagol and Francesco Legramandi

A PLAY OF MANY PARTS

Concept and Script by Bruno Enna
Layout and Pencils by Giada Perissinotto
Inks by Marina Baggio and Roberta Zanotta
Color and Light Direction by Francesco Legramandi
Title Page Art by Giada Perissinotto
with Colors by Andrea Cagol and Francesco Legramandi